I0660720

Revealing the Arca Prime

The Rune Fire Cycle, Volume 4

Lance VanGundy

Published by Lance VanGundy, 2026.

REVEALING THE ARCA PRIME

First edition. February 6, 2026.

Copyright © 2026 Lance VanGundy.

ISBN: 979-8988996033

Written by Lance VanGundy.

Table of Contents

The world is divisive. If you've come this far looking for a temporary escape my friend, then I bid the Giver smile on you all your days. Eyes to the horizon.

Preface: Synopsis of Rise of the Abrogators
Book three of The Rune Fire Cycle

At the beginning of Rise of the Abrogators, Kaellor, Laryn, and their nephews have reunited with Reddevek, and a group of Outriders led by the Prime, Karragin Lefledge. This party grapples with the betrayal of Savnah and Dexxin, who are revealed as agents of the Lacuna. After significant discussion, Kaellor confers with his wife, consults his gifts of balance and judgement, and begrudgingly agrees to include the Lacuna sympathizers in their quest to thwart Tarkannen.

The royals believe they might stop Tarkannen if they can discover the origin of his tether to the world of the living. Despite his banishment to the Drift, the abrogator retains a connection to life. Intending to avoid any delays, they travel in relative secrecy across Aarindorn, seeking answers at the Sanitorium in Callinora.

On their journey, they encounter a group of rebels led by Lacuna agents. Ranika and Reddevek also battle a creature from the Drift, a greater feign. The ensuing fight reveals something of Ranika's power as an abrogator. She and Reddevek plan to divulge her secret to Kaellor and the others, but the opportunity never presents itself.

The party divides, with most of them entering Callinora. In the Sanitorium, they stumble across a Lacuna coup and free Docent Venlith. While delving the lower levels, a trio of umbral appear through a portal and attempt to recover "the vessel", a living person sustaining Tarkannen's tether. In the conflict, Lluthean unwittingly becomes the anchor to Tarkannen's tether in the world of the living, though none in the party are wise to this development.

Outside Callinora, Bryndor and Reddevek encounter Ksenia Balladuren. The young sympath rides to investigate Lacuna interests in land holdings adjacent to the Balladuren ranch. Ksenia's activities have drawn the attention of the closed council of the Lacuna, who engage the services of an assassin named the Leech. Together, Reddevek, Bryndor, Ranika, the wolvryn and Ksenia defeat the Leech and his assassins.

While navigating the wilds, a rift between the living world and the Drift opens. The event causes a panicked stampede of animals, both wild and domestic, to flee across the plains. Bryndor and Ksenia barely

1

escape the avalanche of wildlife and finally, the large party regroups at the Balladuren ranch.

They realize they missed their chance to stop Tarkannen and remain ignorant of Lluthean's predicament as the anchor to the abrogator's tether. In addition, the strength of the Lacuna's grip in the capital seems clear. They draft a plan in which Reddevek and the Outriders will act as a decoy, posing as the returning Baellentrells. Meanwhile, the royals travel anonymously with a group of nomadic gypsies called Moonies, or the Luna Rova.

Reddevek divides his team and sends Karragin's quint of Outriders to recover a high-value target of opportunity, Savnah's brother. The warden takes it upon himself to pose as Kaellor. His good fortune is that after killing a group of Lacuna hunters, he meets up with his brother, Overwarden Kaldera. Bolstered by Outriders, Reddevek enters Stone's Grasp.

The royals gain access to Stone's Grasp through a secret passage known only to Kaellor. They arrive during the celebrations of Spring Assembly and are welcomed by the regent, Therek Lefledge. During the festivities, Therek announces their return, but the Lacuna attack. The circle breakers begin to assassinate nobles indiscriminately, then attempt to kill Kaellor and the brothers. Under these dire circumstances, the mantle fractures, allowing Bryndor and Lluthean to access their gift. Both employ rune fire and decimate the Lacuna uprising.

Reddevek encounters Lacuna resistance just inside the front gates to Stone's Grasp, and is slain by the traitor, the Aspect of the Lacuna, Chancle Lellendule. Throughout the book, the inner council of the Lacuna manipulate politics, financial markets, and people. Chancle is a man motivated by personal loss and with a dream of lifting the yoke of nobility from the kingdom. In the end, his own people discover his identity and attempt to kill him as they view his station as antithesis to the Lacuna mandate.

Volencia Lellendule, an abrogator in her own right, toils in the caverns of the Torgrend Mountains, working with grotvonen shamans and umbral to subdue a thousand human sacrifices and complete the Rite of Sundering. Her efforts are successful, and she frees Tarkannen.

His emergence provokes the breaking of the mantle, allowing Bryndor and Lluthean to channel zenith.

Karragin's quad rescues Savnah's brother, Kovesk. The munitions used by the Lacuna damage her hearing, and it's not clear by the end of the book if she will recover. Ranika has evolved into a capable abrogator, but without Reddevek's unconditional support, what will she become in the future?

The book ends with Tarkannen attempting to portal into Stone's Grasp, but the castle defenses bar his access. Some of Tarkannen's motivations are revealed as he retreats to plan a traditional assault on Aarindorn.

The Baellentrell brothers inherit their gifts but also a kingdom divided by political strife. Elements of the Lacuna still operate within Stone's Grasp, and otherworldly beings invade the world of Karsk.

The Giver smiles, the Taker plots . . .and the entire world holds its breath.

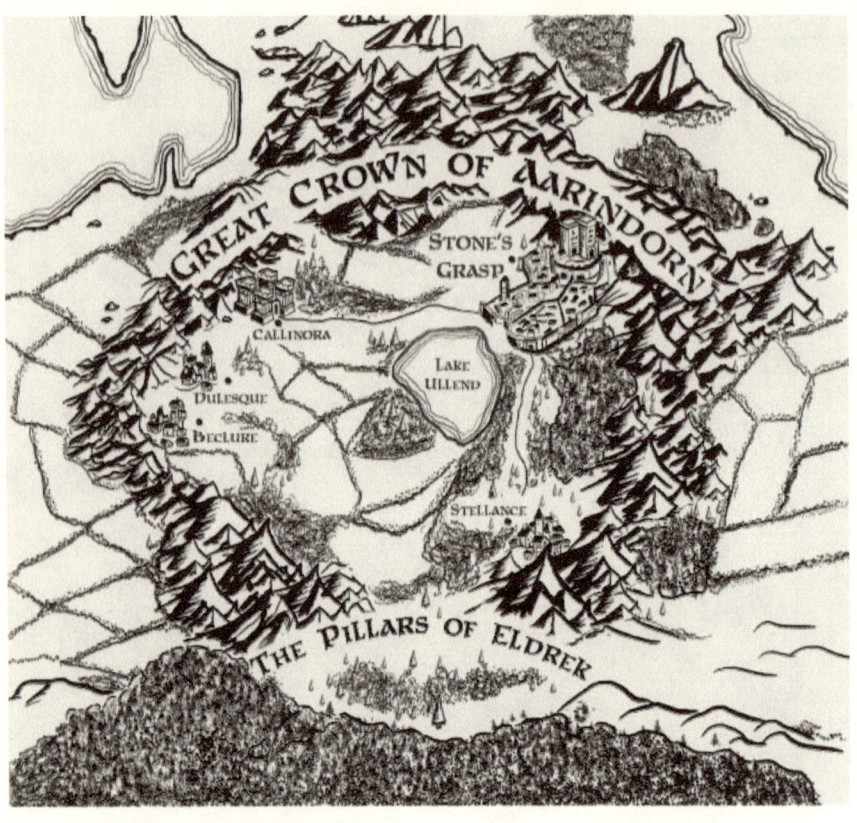

Prologue: The Path to Absolution

AN EASTERLY WIND SKIMMED the ocean, scalloping the surface with whitecaps before cresting over the mountains off the northeast coast of Karsk. The erratic current gusted down the cliffs, turbulent and chaotic, and eventually skirted over the sprawling tree cities of Vellendar and Leandur, buffeting the leaves where the canopy blended with the clouds. An aged ursulu leaf, purple and waxy, broke loose and spiraled hundreds of feet past the myriad of branches and the towering, resolute trunks to land in the shadows beside the feet of a lone wanderer.

He stood on ground made spongy by a carpet of desiccated leaves and strained his senses to hear something of the wind whispering through the trees. But without his mane of flowing hair, he could not capture the voice of the forest, not anymore.

Long, slender fingers of one hand gripped the haft of one of his twin kesaks, the short, spear-like weapons crafted of heartwood, reinforced with metal veining, and tipped with metal points. The other hand ran across his bald head, the outward manifestation of his shame. He snapped the hood of his cloak into place, ugly words forming in his mind. Betrayer, traitor, and worse, for such were the stains anchored to his name, all because his sister had collaborated with the human Tarkannen.

A breeze flapped the fabric across his chest, teasing him with the memory of what could be, reminding him that the song of the forest was still present, but beyond his perception. A memory surfaced from a time when the red moon dominated the night sky. He indulged the sensation, remembering the comforting song of the forest as it filtered through his hair, enriching his soul with a sense of belonging.

A haunted voice displaced the memory. From the Drift, his sister called out, "Seldora, brother, why do you do this to yourself? You know it only compounds your pain."

He cocked his head to the side as if to better capture the mournful, songlike communication from his sister. "I cannot escape what I am, Sephora. You of all the Ilovesh should know this."

Her delicate silhouette formed in the shadows under the ursulu trees. "You have wandered far from the trunks of Leandur, brother. Do you still seek our redemption?"

Seldora stretched his long, corded arms overhead. Sunlight broke through the leaves, and dappled blotches of light highlighted the rune marks under his skin. "What choice do I have? I am the last in our line, and the only one who can make Tarkannen pay for his treachery." *And I'm the only one who can absolve our family name.*

The shade of Sephora swayed back and forth, retreating into the shadows. "Don't do that, brother. Don't diminish my sacrifice. You know that I taught him the secrets of the tether for a reason. The elders might not understand it. They are as the ursulu trunk, stiff and unyielding. But you know that it was my choice."

Her words caused an involuntary snarl to mar his placid face. Yes, he knew that she had entwined her essence with Tarkannen's. But he doubted either of them understood the implications of the bond they had created.

Emotion lifted his voice into a two-toned, melodic speech that flowed out with incongruous anger. "Humans," he spat, but recovered and dropped back to his flat, linear speech. "I will never understand why you felt the need to become tethered to one of them. Wasn't your connection to the Ilovesh enough? Why would you seek to bind yourself to one so fragmented and broken?"

Sephora watched him from the shadows without responding for so long that he began to wonder if she'd retreated fully back to the Drift. More and more, her connection to him slipped as she merged on, becoming more than she ever was in this world. At last, she responded, her voice a softer chorus of soothing tones. "Curiosity, brother. Why should the Ilovesh preserve the secrets of the tether when other people could benefit from the strength and connection it imbues?"

His knuckles paled from gripping the wood haft of his kesak. He mastered his frustration, speaking again in a calm, singular tone, one betraying his exhaustion for the old argument. "Again with this? Others cannot survive it. They are not capable of withstanding the soul-rending effects when the bond is broken. They are not Ilovesh."

The shade of Sephora bowed its head, the chorus of her voice muting to a soft resonance. "Some of what you say is true. I made mistakes. I did not understand how breaking the tether would affect him. And if we had not bound his ability to channel zenith, he might have found the balance. There was a chance for him to become the Eidolon. That seemed like enough justification for the risks."

Her words leeched the anger from his heart. He knew she spoke her truth. Ilovesh lived long lives compared to the other races. And more than that, they lived connected to one another. Even death was understood as just another transition. As such, the sundering of a tether between two Ilovesh was insufficient to rend the soul.

Humans, however, did not connect to one another in such ways. Most of them walked through their time on Karsk fragmented and isolated from one another. Tarkannen had loved Sephora in his limited way. The man had shed his connection to zenith as a demonstration of his virtue, and so she had trusted that he could withstand the effects and entered into a tether with him. But when the tether broke, so too did the man.

She had misjudged his tolerance for the assault. Not even his love was enough to prevent his soul from tearing apart when she died. Despite his convictions and the purity of his intent, Tarkannen could not remain whole when the intimacy of his connection to Sephora sheared away. He became everything the Ilovesh abhorred. Instead of connected, he became isolated. Where Ilovesh naturally progressed through the stages of life, he became a blunt instrument of reduction and destruction.

When the Council of Elders realized how the sundered tether had affected the man, they hunted the abrogator to the edge of the vast ursulu forest. Several Ilovesh warriors died in the struggle, and they failed to capture him. The cost in life alone was deemed too prohibitive, and Tarkannen was left to unleash his destructive nature on the lesser races of the world.

Except for the prophet Somaya, the Council of Elders had ruled unanimously that Seldora, as the lone surviving member of his line, would bear the mark of shame that all would know the consequences of his sister's folly, her betrayal of the sanctity of the tether. With head clean-shaven, a hooded cloak served as the only means by which he could obscure the emotive rune marks on his scalp. In addition, he lost the ability to hear the forest, to become saturated within the belonging.

"All I have is the search. Somaya said I would never find the means to defeat Tarkannen without the sacrifice of another, and not within the ursulu forest. Instead, I must wait and play the part of emissary, whatever that means."

A rustling of leaves caused him to turn, half expecting to see the shade of his sister kicking at the leaves. But she had faded back to the Drift, as was her way. In her place, a bull druska lumbered around one of the ursulu trunks, supported by split cloven hooves. It lowered its head against a tree trunk, attempting to rub the remnant strips of bloody velvet from its broad, flat antlers.

Seldora's songlike voice resonated once again in two tones, now a harmonious reflection of his pleasure. "Come, Kadra, let me help you."

The druska trumpeted with a low pitch that echoed through the timber, then lumbered forward. Seldora patted the creature's leathery black nose as a greeting. He considered using the cutting tip of the kesak to clear off the velvet, but knew it would be easy to tangle in Kadra's antlers. Instead, he kindled zenith into his fingers, elongating the nails on one hand into sharp talons, and neatly trimmed the bloody scraps.

With the grisly task completed, he allowed the nails to recede and suspended his channeling. "Am I to wander toward the Stillness alone today?"

In answer, Kadra stepped forward, tipping his head enough to allow the broad antlers to pass by Seldora's head. The druska halted, waiting for his friend to mount. Seldora trained his gaze back to the east, searching the shadows of the ursulu forest to see if his sister would reappear. He inhaled, breathing in the rich, mossy aroma of decaying leaves, then sighed and turned to the west. Behind him there was peace, the shade of the ursulu, and the comfort of the familiar. But there was also shame and unspoken loathing.

Ahead of him, sunlight revealed a land without the whisper of the wind through the ursulu, without the creaking of the resolute trunks.

And yet, if Somaya the prophet was correct, out there, he would find the path to absolution.

Chapter One: The Regent Lifts His Eyes to the Horizon

Aarindorn, in its first years, was an amalgam of people. Survivors from the armies that battled the abrogator horde gathered to recover and rebuild a life from all that we had lost. Beyond my brothers and sisters of the fo', my childhood friends descended from the lines of all the zeniphiles present in that dire time.

The children of Kal'Malldra struggled more than most, bearing the shame of their mother's failure, or hubris, or both. I think it's strange that so many were willing to believe she would become the Eidolon reborn. What we now know is that only one who commands the ability to wield both zenith and nadir in balance can hope to become the prophesied savior. And yet, if she had not led the armies of the zeniphiles together, even under her false promise, my father, Eldrek, might never have had the chance to use his gift and bring about the end to Mogdurian and his forces.

At any rate, Kal'Malldra's descendants have done well enough, inheriting something of their mother's gift for prophecy and premonition. Others found their calling in the healing arts and have started a school far to the west to further those efforts. Named after a friend of mine, Callin, the place offers respite from the political games developing in the capital city.

Maedraness, the Shaman Queen, left four children and several nieces and nephews with us here in Aarindorn. They were an unusual lot, to be sure, with their sympath abilities. Most of them prefer the company of animals to people. While some scoff at the notion, I can't say that I've ever met an unhappy sympath. My daughter, Naveel, married a sympath, and several of my grandchildren carry the gift. Of all my progeny, they do seem the most well-adjusted.

The folk of the sea who arrived with Barl Fodensk decided to remain, much to my surprise. Some tamed the waters of Lake Ullend, but others seemed content to remain within our city in the mountains. Their abilities to command the elements, water and wind mainly, have been passed down to others in the kingdom as they have married and borne children. And like just the right amount of salt and seasoning to a stew, Stone's Grasp has been all the better for it.

With the aid of my siblings and the three sons of Kelledar Lellendule, a formal arrangement to share power between the high families was entered, as was always Father's intent. My sister, Brekka, wears the title of queen of Aarindorn. Our family's reign has been peaceful and prosperous during the last cycle of the moons. But as the blue moon wanes in the sky, and the red assumes dominance, the Lellendule families bicker over rights of succession.

After the Great War, there was so much cooperation. Looking back, I suspect this was fostered by shared struggle and a mutual desire to see to the defense of the kingdom. Looking forward, the pathway seems less clear.

I realize that my aging mind wanders, and all too often, I'm drawn to focus on the shadows of our past and present circumstances—strange how the maladies of our time seem greater than the miracles. And there is much that the Giver illuminates these days. I will try to focus on those blessings in equal measure.

—The Tome of Nivosh, 75 PC, translated by Ksenia Balladuren

DAWN'S FIRST LIGHT flared behind the craggy peaks of the Great Crown, melting shadows to reveal patches of wild crownberry nestled among the cliffs. The purple-flowered bushes spiced the air with a light, fruity tang and the promise of better days, or so Therek Lefledge, regent of Aarindorn, always thought.

It certainly beats the lingering scent of ash from all the funeral pyres erected since the Reckoning.

Alone in his library, he poured a cup of tea, clasping it in both hands. The heat eased the aches in the small joints of his right hand, the result of hours of handwritten missives and emergency proclamations. He had considered allowing a royal scribe to carry out the work but found that the practice of writing afforded a unique opportunity to slow down. While the events of the last few weeks demanded that he act swiftly, he knew well that utilizing time in all its precious moments made the difference between drafting a law on reflex versus a well-constructed regulation shaped by all the variables.

Some days, that's really all that good governing is: a recognition and accounting of all the variables. Giver, grant me the peace to remember that in the days ahead.

He savored first the rich aroma and then the sharp cut of the tea on the back of his tongue and allowed his thoughts to drift. The distant clatter of boots on stone announced a morning patrol of the sentinels. With his guidance, Hestian Lellendule, Aarindorn's new field marshal, had recruited talented soldiers loyal to the crown to form the castle guard. Recognizable by their crisp, black tabards, the group now maintained security inside the curtain wall.

Despite establishing the new security detail, remnants of the Lacuna still threatened to break the fragile peace. Therek oversaw the criminal proceedings and prosecuted the leadership of any breakers left in the city. Several rounders and even a few Outriders who confessed affiliation with the Lacuna approached, seeking clemency in the days following the Reckoning. Their information allowed the regent to dismantle many of the businesses and holdings of the insurrectionists.

But one piece of information above all fueled his zeal. A breaker familiar with the Leech revealed how the man had been tasked on more than one occasion to assassinate scouts sent into the field over the years. Further investigation exposed the plot to murder at least one of Therek's children while ranging with the Outriders. The Endule families claimed ignorance of the matter and, to mitigate their embarrassment, drove any remnants of the Lacuna out of the duchies, delivering the guilty parties shackled in wagons for the regent's consideration.

Unfortunately, none of the traitors knew the specifics of Warden Reddevek's death. The night of the royal family's return, a fire broke out in the merchant district. The regent had dispatched aquamancers to subdue the flames. In the aftermath, they discovered the mangled bodies of Lacuna and Outriders. Warden Reddevek's broken body lay among the rubble. Only one Outrider, the prime named Baccal, had survived the conflict. Laryn had supervised the healing of the young woman, restoring her to full health. Despite her ministrations, Baccal held only fragmented memories of the events surrounding Reddevek's death.

Several days later, Ksenia Balladuren, of all people, learned of Chancle's final treachery when the sympath engaged Reddevek's mount, the Aarindin he called Zippy. The mount revealed how Chancle had killed the warden and an Outrider medic before abusing his gift and hurtling Baccal into the blast zone of a munitions pack.

The whereabouts of the grand conspirator, the Aspect, Chancle Lellendule, seemed a mystery. In a mixture of shame and rage, Chancle's brother, Hestian, directed Therek's own son, Nolan, into service. Savnah led the mission, and the quad ranged without Karragin, who was still recovering from the wounds she had incurred in the rescue of the dream auger, Kovesk.

For his part, Nolan had followed Chancle's trail into the high places on the eastern edge of the Great Crown. On the ridge of a tall peak that overlooked both horizons, the trail simply vanished. Nolan's quad scoured the area, and at last he determined that if Chancle lived, his trail left the confines of Aarindorn.

The quad had returned with the news only days ago and, when pieced together with rumors from the captured Lacuna, everyone surmised Chancle had used his gift as a guster to escape into the Great Crown or beyond. A vacant, heavy sensation settled in Therek's chest when he thought of all those lost in the last month. Perhaps if he had acted once he became suspicious of Chancle's treachery, things might have been different.

And how am I to deal with you now, old friend?

15

Therek took another sip, retracing past conversations with Chancle. He wondered if his gifts of sapience and discernment began to wither. That happened to elderly gifted sometimes. How had Chancle worked for years under his nose without triggering suspicion? *And how, by the Giver, did a man with so much promise engage in so much treachery? I can't imagine anything that would cause me to carry out similar atrocious acts in defense of the kingdom.*

He sat so long revisiting old memories that his leg began to fall asleep, and he shifted his bony frame on the chair. It suddenly occurred to him that the last time he had employed his gift to understand Chancle's motivations was when they were young men playing games of chance in a local tavern. Not once in all the years since had he chosen to filter any of their conversations.

He groaned with disgust. "I trusted you because I wanted to."

His forehead sagged into the palm of his hand at the realization, and a new emptiness left him unsettled. He was reminded of the moment a condemned man hung in the air, right after the trapdoor opened, but before the noose snapped. But instead of the snap of the noose, he drifted in midair, uncertain and . . . deflated by the betrayal of his friend.

"Old man, you're a fool and a monk twice over. You'll have to deal with Chancle another day."

He stared at the tea leaves in the bottom of his cup and considered pouring a second, but knew it would do little to dissipate the hollow sensation lingering in his core in the wake of self-recrimination.

"Enough. The Taker can have his due later. Keep your eyes to the horizon, Therek," he growled. Years of serving as the regent of Aarindorn had placed him in the position of making the hard choices. In those moments, objectivity, not emotional sentiment, had allowed him to govern with a fair hand. He fell back on that strength now and pushed aside his awareness of the wound left by Chancle's betrayal. Many people in the kingdom had suffered hardships more grievous than his in the past weeks.

Hestian without Chancle, Kaldera without Reddevek . . . how will either man carry on in their brother's absence?

Reddevek's death had unified the Outriders like never before. As a group, the Outriders were ever loyal to Aarindorn, but in the last year, the Lacuna had found its converts among the ranks. The warden's death had done more to turn the tide of public opinion against the circle breakers than anything else. Kaldera had rebuffed any suggestion to take a leave of absence and resumed his duties without delay, returning to the forward base camp. Perhaps Warden Elbiona could shed some light on the man's state of mind.

Therek's thoughts shifted to his daughter. Karragin's welfare and the hard decisions that would confront her in the future threatened to anchor him once again in a dark place, but those concerns were just as easily displaced by the joy he felt in considering Nolan's maturation as the only gifted scout in the Outriders.

An odd thing, that. One would think the Giver would bestow that gift on more of our youth as sort of a logical, divine intervention.

He scoffed at his own thoughts. *And so begins the round and round debate about prophecy and fate versus individual agency and free will. And since your wife is not here to speak common sense truths, tread lightly around that particular rabbit hole, old man.*

A lone, distant chime pulsed from the Church of the Giver, announcing the turn of the hour. "Best be on with it."

He set down his cup, eased back into his chair, then set his mind to the familiar task of activating his arca prime and the gift of premonition. With eyes closed, he inhaled through his nose, the cool feel as much as the scent of the spring air settling in his awareness. He grounded himself in the moment, noticing the floorboards under his left foot warmed by the sun, the sounds of birds chattering on the green outside his window, the sturdy feel of carved wood where his long fingers curled around the chair arms, and the palpable caress of the flows of ambient zenith.

Therek beckoned the currents into his core and directed them to his various runes, awakening them but not triggering their effect. Like a slow tide, he ushered the zenith into his arms, kindling awareness of his gifts of sapience and discernment, then withdrew the force, directing the current into his arca prime. Images flickered in the periphery of his mind, accompanied by voices, some recognizable and others not. Karragin's face flashed forward, illuminated by dim firelight, then obscured in shadow. Shouts and cries of alarm bled into the image, which became distorted by blurred motions and more shadows.

He redirected a trickle of zenith into his forearms, hoping to learn more, but the scene before him fell apart into a maelstrom of shifting colors and sounds. The faces of the royal family tumbled in and out of his awareness, followed by a myriad of petitioners in random succession. A chorus of unrecognizable voices, like idle chatter at a social gathering, muddled into his channeling.

The familiar sound of rune fire echoed, booming shockwaves that shook the foundations of the Great Crown. Boulders tumbled down cliffsides, dragging timber and triggering avalanches. He staggered to remain on his feet as the ground trembled.

Something sucked the very air from his lungs, and for a moment he imagined that even the currents of zenith drained away. Then hot air, as if a furnace door had been opened, blasted into his awareness. Gouts of rune fire swarmed across the night sky, then splashed to the ground, an unbridled deluge of destruction, igniting and incinerating everything in their path. Thick smoke burned the back of his throat and obscured his vision. Embers peppered his face. Therek pushed past the painful heat, seeking clarity in the storm of images.

The firestorm subsided, displaced by a swarm of shadows that swept across his awareness. The abrupt change threatened to overwhelm his orientation. He swam through the confusing array of sights and sounds until at last, one face and one voice rose above all the others. Kaellor Baellentrell stood before him, his voice strong and resonant, reassuring. "I'm here, my friend."

"I'm here, Therek. Therek, are you alright?" Kaellor's confident cadence wavered with uncertainty and Therek deflated, realizing that any clear messages from his arca prime had eluded him once again. He opened his eyes to see his friend standing before him.

He stifled the flow of zenith, allowing his runes to fall dormant, and sighed, then glanced out the window, the bright light of midmorning and Kaellor's arrival confirming that he had lost nearly two hours in worthless meditation. "Sometimes the Giver gives, but not today."

"How long were you at it?" asked Kaellor.

"A few hours, I suspect."

Kaellor took a seat in an adjacent chair. "That sounds like an exercise in frustration. Any luck today?"

He smiled ruefully. "The Giver hasn't seen fit to allow me the privilege of self-governance when it pertains to that portion of my gift. So . . . no, nothing that we could act on, and I learned long ago not to base decisions on fleeting images."

"Still, two hours of channeling and no draft?" Kaellor pulled at the silver tuft of beard in the center of his chin. "I haven't gotten used to that yet. Accessing that much zenith outside of Aarindorn would marinade me so far into the draft, I would need a sickbed for days."

Therek arched a wispy eyebrow. "After the Reckoning, you were in a sickbed for days."

"That had more to do with inhaling veramanth powder and the injuries I sustained. If Laryn and the other healers hadn't been so busy with so many wounded in the aftermath of the Lacuna coup attempt, they would have had me on my feet within hours," said Kaellor.

Therek nodded with understanding. "I know it well. Speaking of veramanth powder, we tracked down the black-market alchemist hired by the Lacuna to refine the product. His stores were confiscated, along with a few journals detailing the process to create the substance."

"And the man himself?"

"His corpse was discovered in the back of his own shop. He met a rather grisly end. Initial reports describe blackened holes burned into his torso. I suspect that remnants of the breakers were tying up a loose end."

Kaellor grunted. "That makes sense, I suppose. I still don't understand how the Lacuna subdued my ability to channel without affecting the boys."

"I suspect it was a combination of blessings: that sword and the Giver's good timing," said Therek. "The veramanth should have completely disrupted your ability to channel, but your sword allowed you some access. Quite remarkable, really. Might I see it once more?"

Kaellor leaned to the side and withdrew the blade, holding it in both hands, flat side up, for Therek's inspection. Therek ran his fingers over the gemstones set into the pommel: one purple and the other polished onyx. Light danced in the depths of the stones, swirling with some exotic property.

Acting on impulse, he channeled into his sapience rune and sensed the gentle tug of zenith flowing into the gemstones. Eventually, he studied the complex array of delicate runes etched into the dark metal. "And the other side?"

Kaellor flipped the sword over, and Therek ran the pad of his finger over the engraving. He sat back, and Kaellor sheathed the weapon. "When you channel, does the weapon magnify your gift?"

Kaellor's eyes became distant. "Yes. It's as if my ability to anticipate danger is heightened. But more than that, the weapon pushes me, driving me to commit everything to the dance."

The two considered one another for a time. "What?" asked Kaellor.

"The sword is . . . in itself, intriguing. I can understand how it allowed you to channel when veramanth should have stifled your ability to do so. Even now it siphons zenith, storing it in the purple gemstone, which acts as a repository, I think. That fact is not so rare. Other mundane items can store zenith—moonstones, wolvryn eyes, and the like. But moons, Kae, where did you find a zeniphile, a master gilder no less, capable of imbuing the weapon specifically for you?"

Kaellor chuckled and scratched at his bearded cheek. "The sword was a gift from the niece of the king of Hammond in the Southlands. As for its make, I cannot say. Apparently, it was a family heirloom; they called it a Logrend blade. But after the boys engraved it, it became my guardian sword."

Therek played the words over in his mind for a moment, then his wispy eyebrows flared. "Giver's truth?"

"Giver's righteous truth, my friend. Before the boys touched it, it was just another sword, of exquisite make to be sure, but nothing more."

"Kae, forgive me for sounding doubtful but . . . are you aware that successful rune-scribing, with actual runes of power, requires a commitment of unconditional—"

Kaellor held up a hand and lifted his gaze to Therek's. The muscles around his eyes softened and the tips of his ears flushed. A genuine smile blossomed on his face. "I'm quite aware, Therek."

Therek slumped back, considering the revelation. "That's . . . quite possibly one of the greatest miracles, and from such a pure and simple thing."

They sat in companionable silence for a bit longer, and eventually Kaellor brushed his knuckles against the streak of silver in the center of his beard. "We were speaking of why that cloud of veramanth affected me but not the boys, and you mentioned something about timing?"

"It was the mantle, I suspect. When the boys were exposed to the veramanth, their mantle was still raised. Veramanth is inert to the ungifted, it doesn't . . . saturate. In the fight, the wolvryn disrupted the gusters. You three engaged the breakers in combat and left the cloud of veramanth behind before their mantle fractured."

"And with their mantle fractured, Tarkannen has no doubt made his return to the world in some form."

Therek's head bobbed from side to side. "In some form, I imagine."

Kaellor's eyes narrowed. "That's some Taker-cursed timing indeed. How long did it take you to sort that out?"

"I didn't. Fagle Hoff did."

"The royal gardener?"

Therek nodded. "He wears that title and more: confidant, ungifted, Dedicant, and speaker for the runeless. Remarkable man."

"Sounds like someone we need to get to know better."

"You should. I think we should consider inviting him to our closed council."

A knock on the door preceded Laryn's face. Her Radiance, the prime healer of Callinora, high lady of house Lellendule, and princess consort, beamed a smile into the room. She entered with a plate of crownberry muffins and set them down at a small table beside Therek, the aroma cinching the strings of hunger around his stomach. She poured herself a cup of tea and sat down in a chair beside them.

Therek resisted the urge to retrieve and devour one of the muffins. Only after Laryn picked one from the plate did he lift it, offering one to Kaellor, who declined. "You know we have servants who can deliver these," Therek said.

"I am aware, but it seemed wasteful when I was already coming this way," said Laryn. She sipped at her tea. "The boys were checking on the wolvryn but should be along momentarily. What have I missed?"

"Therek was just telling me about his proposal for members of the closed council, starting with Fagle Hoff," said Kaellor.

"How is that working out, housing the wolvryn in that alcove on the back side of the castle?" asked Therek.

"It's not ideal, but neither is keeping wolvryn as large as draft horses inside the royal suites," said Kaellor. "I refined the definition to the castle wards, maintaining the restriction against Tarkannen and his minions, and anything from the Drift, umbral and the like. Neska and Boru can come and go at will, but only those who have already passed through the secret entrance can cross the threshold without triggering the wards. Other than Laryn, the boys, and me, that makes just Ksenia Balladuren and Ranika."

"Well, I appreciate that you shared its existence with me," said Therek. "I notice that you didn't bar the members of the Lacuna in the defenses erected across the entirety of Stone's Grasp."

Kaellor sighed and shared a look with Laryn before grumbling his response, "Actually, I did, at first. But Laryn convinced me to practice restraint. We had no clear idea what kind of response might be unleashed by the wards, or whether those who had left the Lacuna with genuine remorse would be spared. So, it felt safer to withhold any reference to the Lacuna from the barrier . . . for now."

Therek tipped his head in agreement. "A wise decision, I think. Now then, back to the closed council. In addition to the Princes Bryndor and Lluthean, and yourselves, I suggest the inclusion of Overwarden Kaldera, Hestian Lellendule, Salveen the leader of the Spicers, the Docent Venlith and . . . with myself and Fagle, that brings the group to ten. Not a bad number."

Kaellor considered his proposal, shared a look with Laryn, then nodded agreement. "All those you mention have proved their loyalty to the crown in the last few weeks. I appreciate elevating Hestian to field marshal. But as Chancle's brother, Hestian's inclusion might raise a few eyebrows."

"I agree," said Therek. "But he's been relentless in his attempts to bring Chancle to justice and efficient in reorganizing the city watch and the sentinels. He and his wife maintain strong social ties to the western duchies, and those are relationships we will need to lean on in the months ahead."

"We don't know much about Salveen, but after the way the Spicers supported us against the Lacuna, her inclusion seems reasonable, if controversial. What can you tell us about her?" asked Laryn.

"Salveen is definitely . . . more than just a leader of the Spicers. Her full name is Salveen fo'Veskari," said Therek.

"Why does that name sound like one of the Luna Rova clans?" asked Laryn

"Because it is. Salveen's clan are lowlanders, and she is singularly one of the most accurate seers I've ever met. She puts my gift to shame," said Therek.

"I wonder what kind of prophecy a Moonie has to experience to convince them to abandon their nomadic life," said Kaellor.

"Indeed. I've posed the same question myself, but she's never provided a solid response," said Therek.

Another knock on the door preceded the entrance of Bryndor and Lluthean. Therek found no small joy in their resemblance to their parents, the late king and queen. Other than the styling of his hair and beard, Bryndor looked every bit the image of his father: strong jawline, piercing gaze with a touch of his mother about the eyes and his father's broad shoulders. *Let's just hope they are sturdy enough to bear the burdens the kingdom will thrust upon them in the days ahead.*

Lluthean walked beside his brother, unmistakably his mother's son. Where Bryndor walked with purpose and an observant eye to the details of the room, Lluthean stepped with an agile grace and seemed more preoccupied with rolling a coin over his knuckles. The younger brother's sharp features, especially the glint in his eye when he smiled, reminded Therek so much of Lluthean's late mother, Nebrine.

"Morning all, sorry we're late," said Bryndor.

"Is everything alright with Boru and Neska?" asked Laryn.

"As far as we can tell, though I might recruit one of the sympaths to be certain," said Bryndor. "I think they actually prefer the solitude of the tunnel to all the noise in the city."

"I know Neska seems more at ease there," echoed Lluthean. "She was aloof when we first arrived. But in the last week, she seems to be more like her old self."

Therek sat forward. "It might seem unusual for me to suggest this, but you should allow them to be seen inside the city and even the castle from time to time. Their reappearance has captivated everyone. I've already passed a ban on hunting wolvryn and decreed a stiff penalty for any members of the kingdom seeking to cause them deliberate harm, though I think a foolish poacher would meet an unkind end were they to attempt such a feat."

Bryndor dipped his head. "That's a kindness, Your Grace. We weren't certain how they would be received, given everything that happened at the spring assembly. Their . . . physicality was displayed for all to see."

Therek nodded with understanding. "True, but you made more friends that day than you realize, and the return of the wolvryn was not an insignificant part of that."

"How so?" asked Lluthean.

"To begin with, your family single-handedly prevented the Lacuna from carrying out the abject slaughter of an entire segment of this city's citizens," said Therek. "But in the hours after, you continued to garner even more respect. Bryndor, you demonstrated both a merciful allowance for the peaceful departure of any who wished to remain loyal to the breakers, and yet an unmistakable purpose-driven intent to distribute justice for any who chose to remain. Beyond that, the surviving nobles witnessed Laryn's work tending to the wounded, all while Kaellor remained incapacitated from the injuries he sustained in the fight. Add to that the majesty of the wolvryn and, well . . . let's just say that I like our odds when it comes to winning the hearts and minds of the citizens of Aarindorn."

Therek studied each of them as he recited his assessment. Kaellor and Laryn shared a look of resolution tempered with mutual admiration.

Bryndor allowed his head to tip forward such that the young man considered the regent's words through a curtain of dark hair that fell before his eyes. Lluthean continued to roll the coin across his knuckles, but Therek sensed that the young man listened intently and absorbed every word.

The regent released a sigh. "And yet, despite all of that, we still have a lot to do to prepare for Bryndor's coronation at the Harvestmoon assembly. I suggest that we begin with these."

Therek retrieved a small box from the table holding the teakettle and produced eleven stickpins. Venlith's brother, Sheklith, was an infuser, a master fabricator. Taking inspiration from the Lacuna's zenith seeds, he had created the matching set. A thin rod of gold the length of Therek's tiny finger and topped with a polished white orb stabbed through two gemstones of red and blue. Delicate silver runes had been scrawled around the white orb.

He handed each of the nobles one of the stickpins. Lluthean stabbed the stickpin into the breast of his tunic. "If I'm not mistaken, Ksenia wears something similar to this, as do other distinguished members in the offices of the regent."

"You are correct, Prince Lluthean. I had those earlier versions commissioned as simple marks of identification, though I must confess that they also allowed me to eavesdrop on their communications. I was trying to determine who among my staff held loyalties to the Lacuna. These, however, serve a different purpose. For a zeniphile, they enable two-way communication."

Kaellor rolled the jewelry between his thumb and forefinger. "I'm intrigued. How does it work?"

"If you would indulge me." Therek rose and walked to the opposite side of the room. He cleared his throat and said, "Now, channel but a trickle of zenith into the white stone."

He waited for a few seconds, then turned and whispered, "The wise man never scorns the gifts of the Giver."

Gasps from the other side of the room indicated the successful deployment of the devices. "I heard it!" said Lluthean.

"So did I," said Bryndor.

25

Therek returned to his chair. Kaellor rattled the box with the remaining stickpins. "I assume you intend the other members of the closed council to wear these?"

"It seems fitting," said Therek.

"Is there a range on these? How close do we have to be for the words to carry?" asked Lluthean.

"I'm not certain. Venlith and I were able to carry out a conversation while she was in Callinora. She has one of the devices. I presumed that you would agree to her selection into our inner circle. It falls to us to dispense the rest of them."

"How many are there in total?" asked Kaellor.

"Twelve in the set, and anyone with a stickpin from this set, when primed with zenith, can listen in on another shek that is also primed with zenith. I asked Venlith's brother to craft a separate set for you four, but to date he has been unable to find more of the necessary reagents. The polished white stone is not stone at all, but some sort of fossilized egg. Sheklith believes that, similar to the zenith seeds, the communication resonates specifically between unique substances of similar property. We know that the zenith seeds only interacted with seeds from the exact same tree. The Lacuna controlled who had access to the seeds, and they did not have to fear their message being discovered by someone attempting to channel into seeds from a different tree."

Lluthean paced to the far side of the room, and his voice buzzed from the stickpins with a question. "So, if we find another petrified egg, Sheklith might be able to craft similar devices?"

Laryn giggled and placed her hand over her breast, covering the stickpin she had placed into the front panel of her dress. "Let me try?"

"That is our hope," Therek murmured into the device. "Be my guest, Laryn."

Laryn's voice, amplified by the duplication through the other four stickpins, carried nearly as loud as if she had spoken to address a large gathering. "Blessings and honor to your house, Therek Lefledge, Regent of Aarindorn."

Her statement made even Kaellor chuckle with a mixture of wonder and disbelief. They spent the next half hour whispering through the stickpins. Bells from the local Church of the Giver rang out, announcing the top of the hour, but Therek had to wait for a break in the conversations to address them all through the devices.

"I asked Venlith to join us at the turn of the hour. Ven, are you there? Can you hear us?" asked Therek. No response came forth, and Therek winced. "I told her to chime in on the hour, she must have—"

"I've been here since the top of the hour. Don't mind me, I'm no stranger to the business of waiting," said the docent as clearly as if she were standing in the room. Her response garnered chuckles, which echoed through the stickpins and gave rise to a wave of laughter as each of them realized their error at transmitting the mirth through the stickpins.

Even Therek failed to contain his enthusiasm, laughing to the point of tears. As he regained his composure, he realized he had not had cause to laugh so hard for what seemed like years.

The docent's voice broke in as the last round of laughs dwindled. "Well, I think we can see, or hear, that these things work. If you all don't mind, I've got to see to a few patients, then prepare a lecture for healers of the first order."

Laryn wiped tears from her eyes. "Oh, Giver's sweet blessings, Ven. We do apologize. Thanks for joins us."

"It's no bother. I will rekindle my shek at this time in four days," said the docent.

"Did you say shek?" asked Therek.

Venlith's voice resonated once more. "If you can think of a better name, tell me at our next meeting. My brother won't claim any credit for the innovation, but I think we can all see how this might change things for Aarindorian society."

"Shek seems perfectly appropriate," said Kaellor. "We'll speak again in four days, Docent."

Kaellor turned to address everyone present in the room, his voice taking on a different timbre than the one they'd each employed when speaking through the sheks. "Four days should give us time to formalize our invitations to the closed council. Let's review the possibilities again."

Over the next hour, Therek reviewed the strengths of each member: Kaldera for his oversight of the Outriders and strategic location at the fortifications between the Pillars of Eldrek, Hestian for his obvious role as field marshal and connections to the high families in the western duchies, Salveen for her position among the Spicers, and Fagle Hoff as the representative of the runeless.

Therek eased back in his chair. "If that's settled, I suggest we break for a bit before this afternoon's meeting with the open council. As I understand it, Endera Endule, the duchess of Beclure, plans to make an appearance."

"Will she be an obstacle to our plans for the future?" asked Kaellor.

"I'm not sure. Maybe? No, probably," said Therek. "My sources informed me long ago that the western duchies maintain a passageway through the Great Crown to the plains bordering Faltusch to the west. After spring assembly, I had hoped that Chancle would be the agent who could get them to officially recognize the existence of the trade route. It's clear to me that Endera and Chancle, even Phelond, the duchess of Dulesque, all tried to keep knowledge of the trade route secret. Despite my subtle overtures, she has been reluctant to reveal its existence."

Kaellor frowned and nodded. "I take it you've already sent others to find this trade route?"

Therek rubbed thumb and middle finger across his eyebrows. "Indeed, and to no avail. I even tasked Rugen Balladuren to coordinate the efforts from Dulesque. The young man is more capable than most understand, but even with his involvement, the expeditions all report getting lost among the endless winding ravines and valleys before returning."

"Why not send Nolan with his scouting capabilities? For that matter, you could send Bryndor or myself. With a wolvryn, I'd wager one of us could find the route if it exists," said Lluthean.

Laryn's voice of reason cooled the embers heating the young prince's offer. "You will soon find that your responsibilities as a prince in the kingdom come with certain privileges, but many more responsibilities, Llu. Your days of seeking adventure for the sake of adventure place too much at risk."

Lluthean pocketed the coin that had previously occupied his attention and shrugged an apologetic expression at his brother. "Can't blame me for trying."

Therek hid his amusement behind another bite of crownberry muffin. "And since those responsibilities include entertaining the nobles of the open council, I suggest we take advantage of the brief time we have and break for an hour. But I look forward to seeing all of you on the royal plaza this afternoon."

As they stood to depart, Therek gave voice to a thought he had earlier in the morning. "Laryn, a moment, please. I wonder if I could speak to you?"

Laryn turned and nodded with a smile. "Not idly does the regent of Aarindorn solicit my time. What is it, my friend?"

"It's Karragin. The healers could not restore her hearing deficit."

Laryn lifted her chin, and her face flushed. "Oh Therek, I'm so sorry. I should have seen to her myself. Of course, I'll go see her right now."

"No. I've spoken with the mother at the House of the Moons here in the castle. I'm quite certain that the damage is permanent. She is . . . ever her mother's daughter, and as such, very hard to read, even for me. I can't seem to pull her out of her shell. I wonder if she might appreciate the perspective of someone like you, who persevered in the face of adversity. Though Karra isn't separated from her gift as you once were, she sees herself as less than she was. I thought perhaps you could offer her some advice."

"Yes, anything. I will check in on her tomorrow morning."

"My thanks. I'm sure that anything you say will be more meaningful to her than you know," said Therek.

He began to exit the room when another thought rose to his awareness. "Laryn, in times past, the royal family always recruited a queen's guard. Hestian has the defenses of Stone's Grasp organized, but still, I think that something like that would be prudent."

Laryn tilted her head to the side, considering his suggestion. "I'm not the queen, but I understand what you mean. Perhaps a small elite group responsible for the safety of the royal family is in order. Have you any suggestions?"

Chapter Two: Vengeance and Discovery

The scent of spiced apples hung thick and fragrant in the air as it wafted out of a bakery in the Delve. The proprietor of the Golden Crust set out several pies, an assortment of muffins, pastries, and rows of bread. Ranika navigated through the stream of people and pressed close to the store window. Her gaze passed over the array of baked goods.

Steam rose from the crust of a loaf of black bread like the kind Ms. Della used to bake back in the Bend. She and Reddevek used to haggle over who got the crusted heel. His gruff voice echoed from her memories. "You see, Nika, the ends are where all the butter settles."

For her part, Ranika liked how the thick heels held more preserves or honey, and there was something satisfying about working one's teeth through the stiff crust to settle into the soft center. "Sort of like you, Red," she mumbled against the glass, then blinked away the salty sting before tears brimmed.

A delicate bell jingled, announcing the entry of a patron into the bakery. The middle-aged man wore tailored clothes with a traveling cloak folded over his arm. The embroidery on his tunic looked much like the uniform of a clerk in the offices of the regent. Ranika walked along the storefront, making a pretense of counting coins in her palm and allowing her eyes to drift back and forth across the mix of baked goods. The clerk exchanged words with the baker but made no purchase.

Another patron, a woman with an empty basket, entered, selected several breads, paid the baker, and left. Once the small lobby cleared, the clerk, who still had made no purchase, flashed the symbol of the circle breakers: thumb to thumb, finger to finger, then he sprang the fingers apart. The shop owner placed one hand over the clerk's, disrupting the gesture, patted the clerk on his shoulder, then welcomed the man behind the counter and into a back room.

That makes three of you waiting. Three plus the baker. Should I go now or wait to see if more of you arrive?

Ranika wavered in indecision. The last time she followed breakers into a back room, she ended up channeling enough nadir that the buzzing kept her awake for a day. That she'd managed to find more members of the Lacuna felt like a lucky roll of Lutney's dice. The Golden Crust had supplied an array of baked goods at one of the other clandestine meetings of the circle breakers. It seemed like a stretch, but she had played longer odds before and come out ahead. Then again, she had also lost track of how many times a "sure thing" on the streets of Callish was really a simple bait-and-switch setup.

She exhaled through her nose. All she needed was information on the identity of the elusive Tixon B'gin. Before she could even start to think about her life in Stone's Grasp, the last leader of the Lacuna had to be brought to justice.

Over the last two weeks, Ranika had placed herself in enough situations to overhear much of the dialogue between the Baellentrells. One could learn all manner of things while combing out an errant burr from Neska's tail. That they treated her as a trusted member of the family didn't hurt either.

And so, she learned about efforts from the Outriders as Nolan Lefledge led a mission to track the grand traitor, Chancle Lellendule, Aspect of the Lacuna. She listened to briefings from the regent as he dismantled the breakers. After two weeks, the vice regent remained unaccounted for and the last member of the Lacuna's inner circle, Tixon B'gin, remained at large.

But not for much longer; not if I can help it. So, get in, listen, get out. Don't let anything they say bring out the stingers. Nobody else needs to die, except Tixon.

"The stingers" were what she called the angry extensions of her will. The first time they erupted, she had lost herself to the channeling, sending all of her pain into their construction, piercing through the bodies of the Lacuna with shards of nadir. The second time had gone much the same, but the third time, she slowed her thoughts and gave definitive purpose to the channeling, creating small darts. She dispatched a room full of breakers with far less effort and didn't experience any of the buzzing restlessness that had plagued her after the first two encounters.

Ranika pushed the door open, the light jingle of the bell announcing her entry. She stepped behind the door and ducked into the shadow at the end of the counter, obscuring herself in a thin veneer of nadir.

"Welcome to the Golden Crust, I'll be right there!" shouted a man, she assumed the baker. The stomping of feet up steps followed his greeting. A moment later, the man rounded the corner, appearing winded from the ascent. He cast his eyes across the small lobby, and, finding it empty, scratched at his belly in confusion.

The baker walked right up to Ranika, but she remained still, secure in the shroud of nadir. She had long ago become accustomed to lurking so close to people that she could smell their breath. The baker was no exception; the sweet aroma of bread dough lifted from his apron.

She pressed back into the corner as the man reached a hand forward to throw a deadbolt, locking the door. He flipped a sign over, indicating that the establishment was closed, then turned and made for the steps. Ranika waited until the sound of footsteps faded, then gave pursuit.

Behind the counter, a back room lined with shelves held ovens and two large tables. She crept down the steps to find a large room used for storage. Barrels of molasses, sacks of flour, and more shelves crammed with spices lined the room. Lamplight spilled from a hallway at the far end.

She proceeded down the hall, finding that it sloped down for thirty paces. The ambient temperature dropped, and she expanded the shroud of nadir to accommodate for the vapor of her breath. As she approached the end of the hall, voices lifted to her awareness.

"Apologies for the intrusion. I should have locked up after you arrived," said the baker.

Ranika hovered at the threshold and peered into the room. Two men sat on sacks of grain. One had the look of a laborer, shirtsleeves rolled up to reveal burly forearms, thick hands, and clothes worn thin at the knees. The other wore the boots and breeches of the disbanded city watch and picked at a callous on his palm using a rusty paring knife. The clerk looked over the baker's shoulder, peering through Ranika into the darkness.

"Are you sure we're safe here? The only reason I'm still alive is because I missed the last meeting of the breakers," said the clerk.

"I understand, Falk," said the baker. "We're safe enough down here. I checked the lobby myself, and there's only the one way down to the cellars. Now, why don't you tell me what a humble baker can do for two of Tixon's toughs and a member of the regent's staff?"

The man with the burly arms shifted his weight. "Tixon's getting scratchy, thinks that the regent might be getting wise as to his identity. Everyone knows the man's a sucker for crownberry muffins. There's no way anything poisoned is going to reach the royal family, but the regent is another matter."

The baker placed his hands behind his back and leaned against a barrel. "Alright, I can whip something up. Should it incapacitate him, or does Tixon desire something more permanent?"

Falk cleared his throat, reached into a pocket, and produced a silver flask with copper filigree. "Make the muffins with your usual expertise, but paint the outside with this."

The baker took the vial and inspected it between thumb and forefinger. "What is it?"

"Widow's tears. An odorless, tasteless poison. It isn't absorbed through the skin, has to be ingested. All the same, be certain to wash your hands. We wouldn't want you contaminating any of your goods," said Falk.

"I can have them ready in the morning, if that's soon enough," said the baker.

Falk turned to the man whittling away at the callous on his palm and nodded. "Half now and half tomorrow, per our usual," said Falk.

The tough retrieved a small pouch and tossed it to the baker. The familiar rattle of coins jingled as the man assessed its weight.

Ranika thought it strange that the men spoke in such casual tones while plotting the murder of the regent. But then she released a self-deprecating huff, knowing that she had already, several times over, embraced the full measure of her gift to kill agents of the Lacuna. *At the end of the day, maybe we're not all that different.*

"Is the meeting still on for next week?" asked the baker.

"Yes, five nights from now at the old, abandoned Church of the Giver in the Sprawl," said Falk. "We've taken great precautions, invitation only, so you'll need this to gain entry."

The clerk reached into a pocket in his doublet and retrieved a small envelope, passing it over to the baker. "Show this at the door, but mind that you come alone. That invitation is for one. There will be a heavy security presence. If you arrive with company, they will be turned away."

Ranika considered her options. If she dispatched these four, she could prevent harm from coming to Therek, and from what she had seen, she liked the old lynx. But if she snuck away now, perhaps she could find this abandoned church. *Best to leave a few rats alive, then follow them to the nest later.*

Before she could retreat, the baker placed the invitation inside his apron and folded his hands over his belly. "Will Tixon be there then?"

At the mention of Tixon, Ranika leaned forward, her interest in the conversation renewed.

The tough with the burly forearms guffawed. "Unlikely. He's not one for takin' risks."

"No, I suppose he isn't," said the baker. "Why doesn't he distribute a fresh supply of zenith seeds? We could resume our meetings without the risk of exposure."

"You ask a lot of questions for a dough boy," said the tough.

The baker glared at the ruffian, and to his credit, seemed to keep his nerve. "Look here, if you want to question my loyalty, you're welcome to take back your coin and find another to take my place. But good luck with that, since the breakers are . . . broken. See right now, you need me more than I need you. My daughters and I can continue to manage the Golden Crust, a respectable, proper business. What have you got if the Lacuna movement fails?"

The tough made a show of cracking his knuckles. "I don't think I like your tone, dough boy."

The baker sighed, but Ranika saw him retrieve a cleaver from somewhere under his apron. "You ought to know better than to insult a man in his own place of business."

"Enough!" Falk raised his arms, the telltale flickers of zenith visible at his wrist as he summoned a whirlwind. Flour and dust from the floor rose in a spinning cloud and caused each of the men to retreat a step. The guster maintained his command of the swirling cloud for several seconds, but stopped when his gaze fell across the threshold where Ranika stood.

The muscles around Falk's eyes tightened. "I can see you. You might as well step forward and be part of the conversation."

Ranika turned to be certain that nobody else stood behind her, and she saw how the cloud of flour had settled all about her, vaguely marking her outline. She considered adjusting the veil of nadir, but realized it was too late, so removed her oversized hat and stepped from the shadows.

Falk inspected her. "I assume this is one of your daughters?"

The baker frowned. "No. And I don't take kindly to rats in my cellar." The rotund man cocked his arm, cleaver raised and clearly prepared to deliver a chop, but before he could so much as take a step, Ranika summoned and released four stingers. The concentrated shards of nadir erupted from her chest and flew forward.

The first caught the baker in the face. Two others speared into the chest and belly of Tixon's toughs. All three men collapsed to the floor. The last stinger seared into the wall above Falk's head. The errant strike allowed the clerk to funnel a dense column of air, and a constant stream of flour and dust and debris struck her in the face, momentarily blinding her. She wiped at her eyes and gave herself over to the full measure of her gift, sensing the flows of nadir coalesce into palpable manifestations of her will.

Before she brought the tentacles forward, a large sack of flour smashed into her chest. The blow launched her backwards. Stunned and gasping for breath, Ranika struggled to see through the haze of sparkly stars in the periphery of her vision. Something sharp, the tip of a knife she suspected, pressed under her chin and Falk straddled her, pinning her in place.

"Are you the one that's been giving the breakers all the trouble of late? You're just a girl, but that trick with the shadows and the knives? That was impressive. It's a shame to end such a talent. Did the regent send you? How much does he know of our plans? Does he know about me? Speak up; this can go slow or easy."

Even if Ranika wanted to speak, the muscles in her belly had seized up the moment she landed, and the added weight of the man astride her made it nearly impossible to draw breath. Falk seemed to guess as much and lifted his weight enough for her to breathe. After allowing her only a few gasps, he increased the pressure of the dagger at her neck.

"You and I are going to have a little fun tonight. First, you'll tell me what I want to know, then we'll see if you can persuade me to let you live."

A warm hand palmed the side of her face, ran along her shoulder, and settled on her breast. The subtle violation was all Ranika needed to regain her focus. She yanked on the flows of nadir, saturating herself in the power. Stingers launched out in each direction, exploding into the lanterns and casting the cellar into darkness. Without pause, Ranika pulled the currents like a veil across her eyes, and the shadowed world erupted as clear as day in her augmented sight.

"Taker's breath, what are you?"

Falk's words cut off as two tentacles of nadir erupted from Ranika's torso, each lashing around the man's arms, holding them out wide. With slow and deliberate effort, she lifted the clerk, suspending him in midair while she rose to her feet.

Falk began to churn another current of air, more dust and debris rising from the floor. She pulled hard on the tethers, and he moaned in pain. Before he could cry out, she drafted the currents of nadir into a volley of onyx shards, launching them forward in a scream of rage. She directed the stingers into his face, his neck, his torso, and all four of his limbs, sundering the man under a continuous barrage of spikes of nadir. In seconds, the overwhelming onslaught of her power obscured his body.

When Ranika drew breath, the remnants of Falk, a garish netting of muscle and tissue, splattered to the floor in a formless heap. She turned in circles as the dust settled, expecting one of the other men to rise and whipping a defensive lash of nadir about the room. When none of them did, she stumbled back against one of the walls and slid down to the ground, pulling knees to her chest to consider the wreckage before her. With an effort, she released the flow of nadir.

Part of her wanted to cry, part of her wished Reddevek could have been with her to carry out this mission of vengeance and discovery, and part of her wished she had never left the streets of Callish. She lost track of how long she stayed there, but eventually her butt cheeks fell asleep.

She began to retreat up the sloping tunnel when a spiral of hair tickled her cheek. With a sigh, Ranika returned to the cellar and searched the room until she found her hat. It lay beside the corpse of the baker. She gathered her hair back in her hands and swept the hat on, trapping the errant curls under the brim, then searched under the baker's apron, retrieving the silver flask of poison and the invitation to next week's gathering.

She trudged up the steps and waited behind the counter for night to arrive. Only when she became convinced that the streets of the Delve were empty did she emerge. Standing before the store window, she faltered, catching a glimpse of her reflection. A ghost, painted in white flour, stared back.

She thought about the number of breakers she had killed in the last two weeks. None of this was what Reddevek wanted for her. It wasn't what she wanted for herself, but then, she wasn't really sure what she wanted. All she knew was how she felt, hollowed out, empty and, by the grumbling of her stomach, hungry.

She turned and placed a coin on the counter, grabbed a loaf of black bread, and sunk her teeth into the heel. The familiar savory taste evoked memories of sitting around Della's table in the common room of the Bashing Ram, peppering Reddevek with questions until he agreed to take her into the Moorlok.

She wiped her nose and swallowed. "One more mission, Red, then I'll be done with it, whether I find Tixon or not."

Chapter Three: Fire and Ash

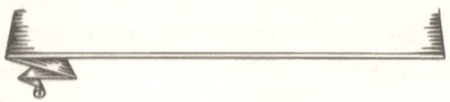

A scout returned earlier this week reporting several discoveries. The summer sun melted enough snow and ice to reveal a pass over the western reaches of the Great Crown. In addition, they discovered a valley with vast herds of wild black horses and other creatures, some docile and others dangerous. One of my granddaughters, Vendara, is a sympath and ranged with the group. She returned with the strangest of companions, a wild wolvryn pup. The beast followed her down from their camp in the high places and never leaves her side. Her mother tried to banish the creature, but, as I write this, both Vendara and her wolvryn-shadow lounge before my zendil. There is uncommon intelligence behind its crystal-blue eyes, but time will tell if this is another gift from the Giver.

—The Tome of Nivosh, 75 PC, translated by Ksenia Balladuren

WISPY CURRENTS OF CLOUD and vapor eddied across the rugged terrain of the Great Crown. The feathery currents swirled under the kindling warmth of the rising sun. Neska ascended a steep trail, relishing the sensation of cool, smooth stones under her paws. As she climbed, a gentle breeze whispered through the trees, carrying with it the aroma of moss and pine needles. She rubbed her neck and shoulder against the rough bark of a tree, both to satisfy an itch and mark their territory. It was a silent and deafening warning to any potential predators that the Great Crown was theirs; hers, Boru's, and their pack's.

She walked out onto a ledge and cast her awareness across the cliffs, assessing, sifting, and synthesizing the information. Far below, in Stone's Grasp, the smell of funeral pyres and taste of ash lingered as a scent memory of the Reckoning and the justice that followed. As they climbed trails into the high places, a sense of ease relaxed her shoulders.

Water vapor hung in the air, caressing her nose. It would rain later today, a welcome cleansing. To the west, a fox ambushed a rodent. To the east, a group of mountain goats foraged, unaware of the panther prowling in their midst. The predator's aura beckoned her to join the hunt, but she chose not to disrupt the cat's mission.

Boru returned from his perimeter patrol and loped forward to sit beside her. In seconds, she surmised by his peaceful bearing that he had encountered no danger. His gait was easy and carefree, no blood stained his maw, and his scent remained singularly his with none of the telltale signs of conflict.

With his belly to the ground and nose to the air, they waited for the brothers to make the climb. In the stillness, she read his thoughts. *"Sister, we should move the den up here. I can breathe."*

"It is the same with me." By all the life that the Giver bestowed, she loved her Lluthean, but when so many humans gathered in one place, the air felt heavy and laden with the oily residue of their scent.

"I don't have to . . . mute everything." He swiveled his head, looking down on the ramparts of Stone's Grasp. *"Down there in the den it's busy . . . the smells, the sounds. I like the air up here. It's not crowded."*

"I know, brother. But then we would have to divide the pack. What did you find on your patrol?"

Boru yawned, his purple tongue lolling out. *"Nothing that you can't already sense from here. I think we will have to follow the sun. Whatever came through down by the ranch has yet to come this way."*

Neska turned her nose to the west. She knew the truth of his observation. A steady westerly had blown across the mountains for several days now, and when the conditions were right, something fouler than moldering flesh tainted the wind. Underneath the mountain sage and pine, behind the scent of the Aarindin herd and all the creatures of the wild, she tasted the corruption on the back of her tongue.

They had encountered the foul smell a few times in the past. The first time was with Ghetti's pack. When the matriarch taught them how to fold into the clouds, they had ascended the summit in moments, emerging from a dense cloud bank onto rocky ground. Ghetti explained that a discharge of zenith colliding with nadir had recently detonated. The shiny black stones, blasted free of snow, had held trace remnants of the decay.

The second time was after the stampede on the plains, down by the Aarindin herd. The oppressive, cloying miasma of rot clung to the blackened patch they had discovered. But neither of those experiences tightened her senses like being around him . . . her Lluthean.

Something parasitic had attached to him, living underneath the surface of his zenith but polluting its purity. Ever since the night he had unleashed rune fire, the strength of the corruption had dwindled, but she could sense it still. The low rumble of a throaty growl bubbled in her throat as she imagined tracking and killing the source of the filth.

Boru huffed once. *"You seem like your Lluthean. We will have to be like my Bryndor if we are to find the source of the taint."*

Neska turned Boru's words over in her mind. Images of her Lluthean, memories from their adventures, bled through her awareness. *"How do you mean?"*

"We have time, but you are restless. We might find it today or we might find it tomorrow, but nothing can challenge our pack."

Instinctively, Neska understood that she and Boru were young, and that something in their bond with the brothers altered their awareness of the passage of time. They would live well beyond any of their kind, become more than any of their kind. And so Boru's observation was right. They had time.

But Boru did not feel the corruption like she did. It was always there, a dark ripple in the center of her Lluthean's shadow, a subtle rasping sound underneath the thrill of his zenith, a parasite leeching tiny but significant parts of his vitality into the ether.

Her constant awareness of the taint made her feel restless. She wanted to collect their entire pack and pursue the threat. Better to find the creature now before it had time to gather its strength. If they cornered it weakened in its lair, they could rid the Great Crown of its presence. Then maybe her Lluthean would be free.

She drew her attention back to their surroundings and realized that she stood on all fours, pushing her focus to the west. With an effort, she sat back down. *This thing, whatever it is, does indeed make me feel a bit like my Lluthean. When did my brother become the patient one?*

"Thank the Giver. There you are!" yelled Lluthean. Sunlight glinted off the delicate runes that adorned his neck and jaw. The gold and silver threadlike marks had always been there, buried underneath a suppressing mantle of zenith. But that day in Stone's Grasp when they fought together, the current of zenith had swelled and fractured the smothering barrier. Ever since, the flows ran freely inside him, flickering in his eyes, permeating his aura.

Yet even so, like walking through a lone strand of spider silk, the corruption tickled her nose, making its presence known. Saliva dripped from her jaw, the precursor to a wave of nausea. A violent shiver started at her back haunches and propagated into her belly, where the muscles seized up. She retched once before mastering the wave of revulsion.

Her Lluthean trudged up the steep path to join them, cupped hands to his face, and shouted back down the valley, "Bryn! I found them! Up here!"

He dropped to his knees beside her, panting, and leaned against her flank. Without words, he caressed the fur under her chin and finally, at that moment, the simple intimacy of their physical connection overshadowed her awareness of the corruption, and she knew contentment. They lingered in silent companionship, communing with one another. The ambiance of his zenith sang with fascination and joy. *How does he look out on the world and see only that?*

After a moment, Lluthean signed, *"Any danger up here?"*

In response, she dipped her nose and licked concentrated beads of sweat from his forehead. *He needs less meat and more water.*

She considered leading him to a nearby stream while the scuffle of loose rock below announced Bryndor's arrival. At the sight of him, Boru rose to his full height, the swish of his tail buffeting Neska in the jaw. Her brother bound down the trail, scattering more loose rock, and only just managed to avoid a collision. The young man shouldered a pack and stepped to the side as Boru slid to a stop.

They greeted one another, Boru acting as if they had just reunited after a long journey. Eventually, Bryndor's words and touch mollified her brother's excitement, and the two of them reached the rocky ledge.

Bryndor removed a worn waterskin, moisture beading along the seam. He drank his fill, then cupped a hand, offering a drink to her and Boru before handing it to Lluthean. She liked how the two of them looked out for one another, how they shared the work as much as the water. Bryndor guarded her Lluthean when she could not, and for that she would always call him pack.

The older brother must have sensed something in her assessment because he exuded affection and knuckled at her ear, the one place that gave her a pleasurable ache all the way down to her hip. She rolled onto her side as he continued the massage and listened to their banter.

"Moons Llu, I thought to complain about the hike this morning, but the view. I could pitch a tent right here and find the Giver's peace the rest of my days."

"I know what you mean. No smoke or ash to greet you first thing in the morning. But I might miss the soft bed and fresh pastries. Do you think we could move the royal kitchen up here, or maybe create some kind of delivery service? I would gladly abdicate any royal status for hot crownberry muffins and this view first thing in the morning," said Lluthean.

"That's the Giver's truth."

Bryndor rummaged through his pack and retrieved a bundle wrapped in layers of cloth. As he unwrapped the parcel, a fragrant floral aroma lifted into the air. He handed a muffin to his brother. "Life in Stone's Grasp comes with a mixture of perks and obligations. The last thing I want is more of the latter. But good company and a quiet breakfast make it bearable."

Lluthean nibbled at the crust. "I don't disagree. I see your quiet breakfast and raise you one breathtaking view." He took a larger bite, then offered some to Neska, but she didn't care for the way the tangy bits stung her tongue, so she turned her nose back into the wind.

"I don't know how you get through it all, Bryn; all the meet and greets, the diplomacy meetings, the council sessions. At least I can blend in. You and Kae are at the center of it all."

Bryndor's shoulders swelled a moment, then fell, dragged down by something heavy that she couldn't see. Boru noticed it too, for her brother tried to make himself small, a ridiculous task these days. His dense mass flopped onto Bryndor's lap in an attempt to distract him. Bryndor grunted and giggled. She enjoyed it when they made that sound. Their auras flared like sunlight and tasted refreshing, like morning dew.

Bryndor struggled with both hands to lift Boru's head and wiggled his hips back. "I haven't had to do much, really. It's mostly Therek and Kae, which is a kindness. But it has been a long week."

"I did see that Ms. Balladuren attends most of the meetings. If I'm right, that takes the sting out at least a little bit?"

Bryndor dropped his head forward, dark hair spilling across his face, but the corners of his mouth lifted.

"I'm right, then? About you and Kess?" asked Lluthean.

Bryndor took his time chewing on the inside of his lower lip. He tipped up the waterskin for another drink. Finally, he squinted against the rising sun. "She does have a way of making me actually look forward to the council sessions."

"After the month we've had, it's a small kindness, I suppose. Do you think she knows that you've taken a shine to her?"

"There's a question for the Giver. I don't know. Maybe?" His eyes scanned side to side, making him appear unusually indecisive.

Eventually, he puffed out a breath of air. "And how about you? Have you been able to steal any time with Karra?"

Now Lluthean looked forlorn, his aura emanating a strong sense of longing. "No. She's secluded herself in her private suite to recover from her injuries. I asked Laryn about her, but all she says is give her time, so I haven't knocked on her door."

"How many times have you passed by her door in the last week?" asked Bryndor.

Lluthean rattled a handful of pebbles in his palm and threw one at his brother, but Bryndor, expecting the playful attack, batted it away. "Only twice."

"Just twice? That doesn't seem like you."

"Well, twice a day, and maybe almost every day," said Lluthean.

At that, they shared a laugh as they watched the sun climb above the eastern tree line. Bryndor stared down at the sprawling city that dwarfed any of the kingdoms they had visited in the past. "In all our travels, none of the Southlands kingdoms hosted so many people. And maybe it's just me, but I can't shake the feeling that they all want something from me, from us."

Lluthean tossed pebbles over the cliff's edge and nodded in agreement. "We're not in Journey's Bend anymore, and I think it's too late to go back, so you may as well get used to it. I think . . . that you should look on every conversation as an opportunity, brother."

"Kae says the same. But that session yesterday with the royals from Beclure made my teeth ache. That Endule duchess . . ." Bryndor shook his head side to side.

"What was her name again?" asked Lluthean.

"Duchess Phelond was from Dulesque, and her cousin was Endera, I think?"

Lluthean snapped his fingers. "That's right. There's something of the Taker inside that woman. I couldn't tell whether she was paying us a compliment or blaming us for all the trouble in the last year. That was a rough introduction."

"Kae says we need the help of the Beclurians to find a pass through the Great Crown, so he practiced 'passive neutrality.' But it wasn't until Karragin arrived that the Endule delegation warmed a bit, or rather, Endera clammed up and left room for the rest of them to speak. There's got to be a story there."

Something inside Lluthean warmed once again at Karragin's name, and Neska sensed his thoughts drift. "I am sure there is. Maybe I'll have to find out; that might be just the excuse I need. What time are we expected today?"

"We have until midday, but after that I think the day is full, so we should probably begin," said Bryndor. "Have you been able to work out how any of the other runes function yet?"

Neska felt the subtle vacuum as currents of zenith flowed into Lluthean. "Beyond rune fire, I don't have a clue. I can direct the flow into the different runes. They tingle when they light up, but I'm not sure what's supposed to happen. It's all I can do to stifle the release of rune fire before I turn my bedchamber into fire and ash."

"It's the same with me. I can feel the vibration of zenith when I touch a placard and open a restricted door inside the castle, but that's about it. I thought it would be safer to practice up here, where we're unlikely to hurt anyone." Bryndor stood and dusted off his leggings. He signed to her, *"Go hunt. We will stay here."*

Boru swiveled his head to the side in response. *"I could eat. Let's run, sister."*

Neska extended her front legs forward and leaned back, stretching her hip muscles. She considered leading Boru to the west, but instead loped along a circuit that would eventually place them upwind of the mountain goats. She grounded herself in the thrill of the hunt, in the rich and complex vapors of life that swirled in the air.

More than an hour later, after they had gorged themselves on the organ meat of an elderly buck, Neska groomed the tangy remnants of blood from her muzzle. Since their awakening, she understood that much of their sustenance came from their absorption of the currents of zenith. They still required the supplementation of meat, though the meal would last them several days.

She tried to better understand the natural currents of zenith. She could always feel when her Lluthean summoned the flow. It had no sound, no taste or smell like so much of the world around them. Even so, she drew in a deep breath of air through her nose, expecting to sense something of the elusive force. Instead, the unmistakable odor of corruption confronted her senses. Instead of just a tickle on the wind, the scent overpowered even that of the dead buck.

Boru simultaneously sensed the taint, startling to his feet and spitting out a bone. Without waiting for her command, he bolted back to the west, toward the ledge where they had left the brothers. Trees and rocky cliffs sped by them in a blur. The friction of the hard ground made the base of her claws ache and gave rise to a burning heat in her paws. They sprinted on, heedless of the pain.

She tried to fold into the clouds as they did in the Valley of the Cloud Walkers, but the flows of zenith were too thin and could not usher her into the vapors. She banked at a natural bend of the rocky path and faltered when the familiar peel of thunder vibrated in her stomach. One of the brothers had cast rune fire.

Boru galloped several strides ahead of her and she struggled to keep pace. *"Boru, wait for me, brother! Attack together, as a pack!"*

The echo of rune fire erupted again in a repetitive cascade, and if her brother heard her bidding, he gave no sign as he charged over the last rise that led to the cliff. As Neska covered the last forty strides, she struggled not to give in to instinct like her brother. The bond with her Lluthean made her more than a simple wolvryn.

A sense of resolve blossomed in her mind, removing all fear and doubt, replacing it with savage clarity. She relaxed her ears and flared her eyes, focusing all of her senses. Something ahead, the source of the corruption, disrupted the flows of zenith. It appeared first at the cliffside, then farther back up the mountainside. It moved with a speed beyond anything in her experience, but as she approached, the entity returned to the ledge.

Neska veered to the side. The deviation would cost precious seconds before she reached her Lluthean, but she knew Boru would attack any danger head-on, so she chose to flank the enemy. As she burst from the sage and scrub brush, what she discovered defied anything from the natural world.

Chapter Four: The Desecration of Dernegia

A sentry walking the western ramparts cast long shadows through the amber light of the gemstones protecting Dernegia. From a shadowed cliff, Tarkannen looked down on the mountain kingdom, studying its defenses. Dernegians, more than any others on Karsk, excelled at infusing gems with zenith. Their artisans fabricated all manner of devices to alter their environment. Some of their creations could heat a stove for a year or more; others chilled an icebox or dampened the noise in a room used for sleeping.

The moon of Baellen hung as a pale crescent in the night sky. Though only a sliver of its mass remained visible this night, it drew an ache from his core. He hungered for what he had lost and what he strived to reclaim: zenith, Aarindorn's deepening well, a pathway to become the Eidolon. He lifted a hand, spying the moon between thumb and forefinger, and imagined crushing it to dust, snuffing out the reflection of Baellentrell power.

"Dernegians are clever artificers," said Volencia interrupting his machinations. "I take it the amber gems along the ramparts serve as some kind of warning or offer a protective barrier."

"Yes, though I can sense that they will only trigger at the approach of the grotvonen. Nothing in their aura indicates a familiarity with nadir or us," said Tarkannen. "You and I should be able to advance close enough to disable the defenses on the western walls."

"You can tell that from here, from this distance?" she asked.

Curiosity more than desire flavored the tone of her question. "It stretches my perception, but yes. You and I will have to descend to the plateau and approach on foot. We need to be within range to affect the outer walls in an hour. I'll have the umbral hold the horde back to give us time."

"What happens if the grot approach before we take down the amber gemstones?" she asked.

"I'm not entirely sure. Something rather unpleasant to do with fire. The good news is that we only have to remove five of the beacons from the western approach. I suspect the Dernegians have never had to defend themselves from anything in the mountains. Most of their strength is placed along their southern and eastern walls. Come then, let's complete our task so our horde can assail the walls under cover of night. I want to see Grasdok's clan in action."

He turned and retrieved the three rods of nadrean, the crystallized remnants salvaged from the Rite of Sundering. The jagged shafts looked like thin slags of shale but for the slow swirl of refined nadir trapped under the surface. To anyone else, even Volencia, he suspected, direct contact with the rods would prove fatal, as they neutralized zenith, snuffing out the vital life force like fingers pinched to candle flame. But dense sigils of abrogation covered Tarkannen's hands and insulated him from the draining effects.

A scattering of loose rock pattered against the stones below, and the remnant of Mallic approached. The four-legged umbral was the last of Tarkannen's creations, and he would probably not have the time or materials to craft more. If they were fortunate, he would not have to, though the issue gave him little concern. If Volencia or Verrador failed in their duty or fell to their enemies, the sigils would enslave them to his purpose, just as with so many others.

Tarkannen drafted a web of nadir and draped it over the umbral, allowing him to communicate in their raspy song. Volencia craned her neck in irritation as the shearing sounds cut through the stillness of the night. *Bring the horde down to the plateau, but do not approach until the amber lights of the west wall disappear. Once the west wall falls to shadow, unleash our forces."*

He dismissed the web without waiting for a response. The umbral required nothing more than the directive and would offer no conversation. Beyond fulfilling his orders, they possessed little agency and proved themselves reliable tools to his intent.

"Let's begin," he said.

He sensed ripples in the ambient nadir as Volencia siphoned the currents. She sprouted several black tentacles and lashed two to the craggy edge. She stepped out into space, turning in a controlled descent to face the cliffside, and dropped like a nimble spider.

You have more to learn than I remembered.

Tarkannen searched his memories, frustrated by the gaps in his knowledge. He had used his incarceration in the Drift to learn much about the secrets of the world, but he sensed that a significant portion of that knowledge remained trapped in the ethereal currents. He had assumed he would arrive back on Karsk with the full measure of his wisdom, and that such revelations would make him godlike.

To his frustration, the deficits, the gaps in knowledge, were clear to his awareness. Maybe he had anticipated his release for too long, building up expectations in his mind. Now that he had stepped back into the living world, he felt less than he assumed he would be. Even as the master abrogator, he experienced the pangs of hunger, the bite of chill wind on his face. Certainly, the ease with which the Baellentrell wards surrounding Stone's Grasp had barred his entry had disabused him of any notion that he was all-powerful.

The power of the Giver and the Taker, held in my hands, would certainly make all of this much easier.

The abrogator pulled his awareness to the ribbons of nadir all around them. He inhaled and drew hard on the currents, infusing his sigils. His skin tingled as they vibrated with the full charge of nadir. He exhaled once and leaped out into the night. A rush of exhilaration surged from his core as the thrill of the plummet overtook him.

He passed Volencia within a few seconds, and still he dropped, savoring the wild sensation. Instantaneously, he drafted a shaft of nadir, connecting himself to the plateau below. His descent slowed, and he dropped to the ground in a rapid but controlled fashion.

Minutes later, Volencia joined him, her tentacles of nadir retracting. He gave her a curt nod, and they set out at a brisk walk. The rocky plateau offered him little resistance, but Volencia stumbled over the uneven terrain.

"Did I not teach you how to see into the ethereal? How to pull nadir like a filter into your eyes?" he snapped.

"No. That sounds like a skill I could have used in the grotvonen caves."

No wonder she did not initially realize how Mallic's soul empowers the umbral. All she sees is what the living world presents her with, not what lies beneath.

"Mind your step. It's a skill that requires practice and time. Once we conquer Dernegia, we can discuss the finer points of augmenting your perception."

Behind them, the hooting, clicky speech of an army of grotvonen echoed, accompanied by the unmistakable rumble of grondle hooves as the last of the horde descended out of the Torgrend Range. In the distance, soldiers gathered on the western ramparts, clearly aware of the commotion.

Tarkannen studied the five amber defense beacons as they advanced. Nothing in the number or intensity of the wards changed, so they pushed on. He drew to a stop several hundred paces away, close enough to hear the note of fear in the muffled voices.

The five warding crystals were housed in giant polished stone saucers mounted on rotating pillars. Slow currents of yellow light swirled up the base to the gemstones, and flickers of orange and red flame popped and sputtered as the flow suffused the crystals above. It was a shame he had no time to study the mechanics of the Dernegian invention. Converting zenith into the raw power of fire was something only a highborn Baellentrell had ever accomplished.

Guards stood at the base of each pillar, swiveling the amber lights back and forth in search of any sign of the approaching horde. Tarkannen and Volencia remained beyond the area swept by the beacons, hidden in the shadows of night.

"We have no idea how far those gems can project their . . . influence, and they might have a trigger effect. Condense nadir into a tight sphere and detonate the two on the left. I'll manage the other three. Release on my command in ten, nine, eight . . ."

As he continued the countdown, Tarkannen coalesced two separate globes of nadir in one fist, the other still occupied with holding the nadrean. When the countdown finished, he released the black orbs. They sped forth as extensions of his will to detonate against the pedestals holding up the gemstone ward. Several seconds later, the condensed nadir exploded with an eruption of onyx shards. Inky shadow flared, momentarily blotting out the amber light.

The two pedestals on the right collapsed, their gemstones toppling back inside the walls. Volencia brought down one of the pillars to the far left, but she had targeted her other sphere directly at the amber light. While the blast clearly damaged the stone saucer holding the ward, a scatter of light still emitted from the damaged implement.

A low-pitched hum, an alarm he assumed, erupted from within Dernegia, and even isolated on the west side of the curtain wall, he could see a nimbus of light cover the city as the Dernegian ward powered up. All across the ramparts, spirals of light climbed up the pillars, igniting the gemstones.

"Again, focus on the pillars." He spoke the words with reassured tones, confident in their progress.

Tarkannen was preparing another set of orbs when a shaft of brilliant amber light burst from the undamaged central pillar. Any ground, whether covered in stone or scrub brush, erupted in flames wherever the light passed. Thick, acrid smoke carried across the plateau.

Before he could launch the globes of nadir, the light shaft swept across the ground toward them, threatening to cross directly over their position. He dismissed the spheres, absorbing the nadir and reshaping it into a wall of shadow. The inky barrier fell into place just before the arrival of the intense ray.

"Get behind me, Volencia, and focus on that pillar in the middle. I'll maintain our defense."

The guards manning the central ward must have realized that they were the source of the disturbance because only seconds after the burning shaft moved away, it returned and focused on their position. A full-throated roar, like that of a great waterfall, tore through the night where the gemstone beam and his wall of shadow collided.

To his surprise, the wall of nadir thinned. A latticework of the onyx streams immediately began weaving back and forth, trying to repair the barrier while the Dernegian beam attempted to burn it away. He siphoned more nadir, fueling his power with his rage at being thwarted. With the shield reinforced, he held the burning shaft at bay.

The currents of nadir wavered as Volencia gathered her strength and launched her projectiles at the ramparts. Moments later, another black eruption detonated against the middle stone pillar. The flash of shadow and crack of stone echoed across the plateau as the beam of light lifted from his barrier, searing a brilliant line into the night sky, then winked out.

Tarkannen maintained his shield, aware of the last gemstone far to the left, the one Volencia had damaged but not destroyed. The yellow and orange currents climbing the pillars flared, and he assumed the guards intended to bring the focused intensity of the array back to their location. Instead, the damaged implement emitted a harsh shearing noise like metal twisting under pressure.

Disorganized flashes of fire pulsed and spewed out into the sky. The gemstone wobbled in its saucer, emitting a strobe effect and spraying gouts of fire across the ramparts. The sound and light magnified in pitch and intensity until, all at once, it exploded. A brilliant flash preceded a wave of heat and the acrid smell of things burned by the zenith-fueled gemstones.

The flare left his eyes recovering, so he pulled nadir across his face, returning his vision to the ethereal. Light flickered on the sides of a gaping rent in the wall where the last warding stone had stood.

Tarkannen released his wall of nadir. "Well done, Vol. And here I thought we might have to knock to gain entry. I'll wager that's more than enough room for even the grondle to enter the city."

The ground beneath their feet trembled, sending vibrations through Tarkannen's body as the stampede of grondle approached. The deafening wails and cries of the Brognaus tribe echoed across the vast plateau. He contemplated constructing an additional barrier to safeguard their position from being overrun. However, his horde surged directly at the breach in the wall, opting for the path of least resistance.

Dernegian soldiers gathered in the breach, each emanating a faint, ethereal glow that encircled them like a protective halo. A formidable shield wall took shape, formed by a block of soldiers twenty warriors wide and three rows deep. They stood resolute in the gap, prepared for the onslaught.

Grotvonen, agile and nimble, sprinted on all fours, their movements resembling a frenetic stream of insects or a flock of birds. Their approach was swift, deceptively chaotic, and relentless as a raging river swollen beyond the confines of its banks.

With a sudden burst of energy, the shield wall flared, repelling the invading grotvonen. Bestial squeals, a mix of surprise and pain, erupted as they hurled themselves at the defenders. All about the sounds of war erupted as the clang of metal weapons and cries of battle filled the air. The impact of the horde reverberated through the soldiers, their bodies and shields absorbing the force. Yet they held their ground, unwavering in their defense.

More grotvonen arrived, throwing their crude spears and surging to the side of the breach, attempting to gain entry. Many leaped over the shield wall, and several were successful, sliding down the back of the defenders' barrier only to be cut down by soldiers waiting for such an attack.

Tarkannen felt Volencia pull on the currents of nadir. Sensing her intention, he said, "Wait, Vol. Give the grondle their due. We need to assess their capabilities."

The abrogator lifted his gaze from the ethereal to observe the raging grondle herd. Where the grotvonen flowed up and around the shield wall, a solid column of grondle charged directly at the breach, their advance announced by the deafening thunder of hooves and snorts of battle rage.

A massive alpha grondle tossed an oversized battle axe over the defenders' shield wall. The weapon clanged harmlessly to the ground. With uncanny grace, the alpha bent low and retrieved a thick stone slab from the ground. After galloping three more strides, the beast swiveled its torso and hurled the boulder at the shield wall. The center of the barrier buckled, and the alpha charged forward, the spear tip of a colossal living ram of grondle.

The Dernegians collapsed from the sheer volume and strength of the assault. Grotvonen hooted and shrieked with glee, and the horde poured into the city. He felt Volencia suspend her grip on nadir, the flows of the dark currents caressing against his sigils like a gust of wind.

Tarkannen nodded. "This will do. Come."

They strode forward, picking their way over the uneven ground, churned and pitted by the passage of the grondle. As they arrived at the breach, he surveyed the damage with tactile awareness, sending forth tiny probing filaments of nadir. The rent in the curtain wall was a gruesome tunnel, its walls coated in a sickly blend of crushed flesh and shattered bones, creating a grotesque painting upon the rubble.

The metallic tang of blood hung heavy in the air, the scent intermingling with the putrid stench of offal. The very essence of violence and death permeated the atmosphere.

In the distance, a pack of grotvonen overwhelmed a small group of defenders. The sheer force of their numbers surrounded and smothered the soldiers, leaving them defenseless against the merciless onslaught.

A grondle charged by them, its hooves pounding against the ground, churning up wet clods of mud. The beast banked at the corner and shot down an alley. Despite a spear shaft and several arrows lodged in its flank, the beast pressed on, swinging its axe with reckless abandon, oblivious to whether its strikes fell upon friend or foe.

An umbral sprang down from the ramparts, chattering commands to the raging grondle. It directed the frenzied attacks toward a small group of soldiers, diverting the unbridled rage away from their forces.

The deafening clash of swords, the agonized cries of fear and suffering, and the pungent stench of death assaulted his senses. The side of Volencia's face not covered by her veil revealed a smile. A sense of accomplishment and even admiration settled in Tarkannen's mind. The ruination of Dernegia would serve as a trial, the initial stride toward comprehending the overwhelming power of the horde.

And so it begins.

Chapter Five: The Long Hunt

Valdesta lifted a guttering torch high overhead, straining to see through the flickering shadows of the catacombs. For more than an hour, she had crept through the abandoned tunnels. Her breath steamed in the stale air that clung to her, cold and damp. Countless stone pallets were carved into the walls like utilitarian bunk beds five plots high. Within each alcove rested the bones of the dead.

Some of the shallow recesses held only one skeleton; others were crammed so tight that random arm or leg bones draped out of their confines. Every so often, the pathway arced in a broad curve, allowing space for tall mosaics of bones. Stacked by body parts, leg bones here, ribs there — she had to admit the meticulously organized displays almost looked like works of art.

Her torchlight passed over a wall covered entirely by skulls arranged in horizontal rows and separated by what appeared to be the rounded end of thigh bones. The mosaic inspired a moment of reflection despite the countless empty eye sockets staring back.

She tapped on one of the skulls, finding it cemented in place. For a moment, she wondered who had spent so much time layering the display. But by all the dead in the Drift, she wasn't going to linger before the tower of bone and try to figure it out.

The winding tunnel opened up into a cavernous room, and dancing shadows played on the ceiling overhead. Her toe stubbed on an irregularity in the stone floor, and she reached out to brace herself against the wall on instinct. A sharp pain flared from her splinted wrist, and she sucked air between her teeth.

"Taker's bite!" she cursed and turned to the right. The Duchess Endera's message had said to follow the winding path until it opened up into a large cave, then turn right twice and then left, cross an underground stream, and continue. She had half a mind to turn around and ignore the invitation, but the duchess of Beclure was no woman to trifle with, and Valdesta had to admit that she was more than a little curious.

Following the directions, she approached the edge of the cave to find another crude tunnel but stopped at the entrance. Strange hoots and clicking sounds cut through the darkness and echoed all about her, undermining her resolve once again. She struggled to determine whether the noises came from ahead or behind. Her hand patted at the hilt of her dagger, and she repositioned a handheld crossbow on her back hip. *That's not a sound man or woman would make. Best to move along, Val.*

Valdesta gathered her cloak around herself and craned her head, half expecting some malevolent spirit of the dead to charge her from the far side of the cavern. When no danger sprang forth, she ignored the cold sensation of dread gathering between her shoulder blades and continued down the path.

Over the next few minutes of the descent, the sound of rushing water set her mind to ease. Eventually, she approached an underground river. Boulders placed every three feet allowed for reasonable egress across the churning dark water, but Valdesta cursed to the Taker that she had ever agreed to meet Endera as her footing slipped on the slick, irregular stones.

Once on the other side, the familiar pine scent of survivor's essence lifted to her awareness. A few steps later, the flickering of lamplight allowed her to extinguish her torch. A man's pained moans echoed from ahead amidst rhythmic mumbling or chanting.

Valdesta pressed on to find a large, circular, domed chamber supported by a central stone pillar. More of the stone pallets ringed the walls, creating a latticework of shadowed alcoves. On the far side, a set of stone steps led up into darkness. Two men wearing dark leather jerkins stood as menacing sentinels by the stairs, lamplight glinting off their steel weapons. More than a few scars marred their knuckles, and

Valdesta surmised they had experience breaking bones for pay. She had used similar men numerous times as muscle for her own clandestine dealings, and their presence actually settled her nerves a little.

From an alcove to her right, blue flares of zenith cast sharp shadows into the chamber. A person lay on one of the stone pallets where the rhythmic moaning and ranting was coming from. Hunched over the tortured soul was a squat, broad-shouldered beast standing on two bowed legs. Coarse black and brown fur sprouted from the collar and sleeves of the crude tunic it wore. The creature swiveled its head like an owl, its oversized ears and wrinkled snout twitching, sniffing the air. Then it turned its dark eyes back to the moaning victim.

The brothel owner was making to turn when another figure stepped forward from the shadows, face obscured by a dark, hooded robe. "Don't mind the grot. He's a shaman here at my request. You made better time than I expected, and you came alone, as instructed. That's good, Valdesta. Step closer. It's long overdue that you and I met."

Her first instinct might have been to resist any such invitation and instead make better surveillance of her surroundings, but the sound of a human voice, a confident woman's voice no less, put her at ease, and she stepped forward. Endera Endule, easily recognizable by her imperious height, turned and pulled back her hood to reveal a high forehead, penetrating dark brown eyes, and square shoulders.

"Is that really a grotvonen? I've never seen one before," said Valdesta.

"Yes. He's an elder member of a tribe that lives beneath the catacombs. You likely heard their sentries above, the strange hoots and clicks? They don't often come so close to the surface, but I had need of this one's healing art, and they agreed to meet me here."

"I see," said Valdesta, but she really didn't. "So . . . you're Duchess Endera Endule then?"

The woman tilted her head. "I am that and more."

"It's pretty strange, a noble asking for a meeting with the likes of me; stranger still down here in this place. If I didn't know you were the duchess, I would assume this whole thing was some kind of ambush orchestrated by one of my rivals."

The woman lifted her chin, then nodded. "I can understand your reluctance, and you are right to be cautious. It's easier for me to accomplish certain negotiations down here and away from prying eyes. Secrecy is one of our most valuable assets. I am sure you, of all people, can understand that, Tixon, is it? Tixon B'gin? The infamous member of the Lacuna hunted by the regent ever since the kingdom's Reckoning?"

The admonition caused Valdesta to falter more than any part of the trek down through the catacombs. She fingered the dagger in the pocket of her cloak and tapped at the stock of the crossbow hidden on the back of her hip. *I could likely take out one of them, maybe two, but not all three.*

Endera held a hand up. "Peace, woman. If I cared to divulge your involvement with the Lacuna, I could have done so weeks ago. Believe me or don't, but at least have the common sense to learn why I asked to meet you."

Valdesta heard the scuffle of boots and looked over her shoulder to discover another set of rough-looking guards covering the tunnel from which she had arrived. "It doesn't seem like I have much of a choice."

"They are only here to make certain that we are not disturbed. You can leave any time that you like," said Endera.

The duchess turned and spoke in a language of hoots and clicks to the beast. One of the creature's ears twitched, and it seemed to bow before reaching thick fingers into a pouch. It retrieved a fistful of glittering dust and sprinkled the powder over the moaning person. A strobe-like scatter of blue light flashed from the alcove for several seconds before Endera turned back. Valdesta considered the woman for a long moment, then finally asked, "Taker's twisted bits, how did you learn to speak grot?"

Endera dipped her head. "That's a long story. Suffice it to say, clans of grot live in caverns underneath most of the Great Crown. My family encountered them generations ago. We felt it advantageous to maintain civil relations with their shamans. Ours is a mutually beneficial relationship. We provide safe access to certain surface materials, medicinal herbs mostly. The grot provide the occasional rare gemstone and offer other unique services."

Valdesta relaxed her stance and scrubbed at an itch on the side of her scalp. "In times past, Stellancian mines provided the only source of rare gemstones. But they were sealed up after the Abrogator's War. Now I understand why Beclurian merchants offer the only ready supply of deep terrain gems for the black market."

Endera's expression softened, and she repositioned the cloak about her shoulders. "My informants said that you were clever."

"Well, not clever enough. I never saw the regent making inroads with the runeless. I certainly never thought the Spicers would toss in with the old lynx. I lost more than half of my holdings in the Reckoning. Then I lost my nephew and too many others to count."

"There is a darkness loose in the kingdom. You will continue to lose breakers and those closest to you if you don't take action. That's why I asked you to meet me."

"You know an awful lot about my situation for someone who is supposed to live on the other side of the kingdom," said Valdesta.

"Most of what I know about you has only been revealed in the last several days," said Endera. She stood and gestured to the stone alcove where the man lay softly moaning. "This is, was, my half-brother, Kevka."

"What happened to him?"

"He was one of my assets within your Lacuna and operated in the city watch. To maintain his cover, he joined the attack on the royal plaza. Kevka was caught up in rune fire, but the blast didn't incinerate him like so many others. Instead, it did this."

Endera motioned for Valdesta to approach. She stepped close enough to smell a sour, rank odor coming from the grotvonen shaman and peered over the beast's hairy shoulder.

Her eyes studied the man lying on the pallet, or rather, the remains of what was once a man. A torso writhed on the crude bed, with four shortened limbs ending in tapered stumps with bandages marred by something dark—dried blood or ash, or both. It was difficult to tell in the lighting of the cave.

The man's face looked like a melted wax taper left too long in the flame. Any features that marked the man as Kevka had been burned away, revealing a warped, rounded head covered with fresh burn scars and a confusing array of runic strands. The silver symbols coalesced like thick spider webbing and fused in such a way that their previous form seemed irrevocably altered. A random flicker of zenith ignited on his temple and streaked down the veining to his chest before scattering light into the cavern.

The man's torso was exposed to the air, allowing the shaman to periodically sprinkle more glittering dust onto bare flesh. Words tumbled from Valdesta's mouth before she had time to reel them in.

"Is that really a man under all that? Where's his face? All I see are . . . holes and—"

More streaks of blue light flared from under the man's glistening flesh, scattering into the cavern like cerulean filaments, only to dissipate into the shadows. Kevka panted with shallow labored gasps and began to mumble, his voice rising into a raspy, rhythmic chant.

"The wild wolvryn, beware the wild wolvryn, for it scars the highborn . . . and then abrogators will come! The tethers . . . they bind, leech, and sustain. Must seek con . . . confluence and balance. The bindings sundered . . . unleash the great abrogator." Kevka's chant broke apart in a raspy fit of coughing. He heaved a ragged breath, and the mumbling continued.

"The Eidolon will be revealed, but only after the sibling passes to the Drift. The time is now, zenith and nadir . . . in opposition. Channel zenith to save the world or nadir to destroy it. Con . . . confluence. Channel confluence to become the Eidolon reborn."

"Grind it, that one again," hissed Endera. The woman spoke a question to the shaman, who upended the pouch, emptying the last of the glitter onto Kevka.

She turned to Valdesta. "Kevka was gifted with runes that allowed him to foretell the seasons and sense when rains might come. He was an invaluable adviser when it came to organizing expeditions or travel across Aarindorn. The rune fire melted his runes, fusing them into something else. He's been mumbling about things from the past, but also things from the future. That's how I learned all about your identity as Tixon."

Valdesta blinked once, considering Endera's words. Disbelief gave way to acceptance as she recalled how carefully she had cultivated the

Tixon B'gin identity. "Let's say for now that I believe you. What was that last bit there?"

"It's old prophecy, called the Abrogator Derivation from *The Book of Seven Prophets*. He keeps coming back to that one."

"Can he be saved?" asked Valdesta.

"Not likely, and not without the concerted efforts of the healers from Callinora. I think he only has a few hours left. But even if he survived the trip, the questions raised might compromise my interests. And if they managed to save him, who knows what the scholars would do to study him. To . . . use him."

Valdesta nodded with understanding as she recalled the Lacuna's reliance on Barl's son, the dream augur, the past few years. "Why did you bring me down here?"

"To show you this, him, so you would believe my warning. In one of Kevka's visions, he spoke about a darkness tied to one of the royals. In another, he referred to 'a channeler of nadir.' My sources believe that there is an abrogator in Stone's Grasp."

Valdesta chewed on her lip, resisting the urge to deny any notion that the breakers still gathered in meaningful numbers. She sighed and dipped her head. "Have you got more Endules embedded in the Lacuna?"

The duchess lifted her chin, speaking down the length of her delicate nose. "I can tell you that the abrogator is hunting your people. More Lacuna will die if you don't take action."

Valdesta thought it strange that Endera refused to answer her question. *Which sort of answers it for me, doesn't it?*

She sighed and dipped her head. "That explains what I saw. It's a girl. I caught a glimpse of her once after she killed a good number of us. Do you know what she wants with me and mine?"

"I can't say. But now that you know, you can prepare. I understand that the Outriders provision their quads with Eldrenol's solution. Figure out how to use it, and maybe the breakers can defeat her."

Valdesta had heard of Eldrenol's solution but always thought it a charlatan's elixir, overpriced and worthless. She made a mental note to pay a call to a black-market alchemist in the Sprawl when she returned.

"You still have questions," said Endera.

"If my people can kill this abrogator, do you think the darkness tied to the royals will be lifted?"

"I really don't know," said Endera. "But I imagine that the Baellentrells would be grateful for such a service performed for the greater good of Aarindorn. And I could vouch for your efforts if you are successful."

The idea that she might carry out a service that would benefit the royals caused Valdesta to snarl her lip involuntarily. Endera must have sensed her conflicted thoughts. "Sometimes the Giver gives."

Valdesta shook her head with disgust. "And sometimes the Taker takes." She stared at the duchess, trying to determine if anything about the woman seemed false. "Tell me one last thing. Why tell me any of this? You could let this abrogator continue to run amok through the breakers and have one less competitor for power in Stone's Grasp."

"That's a quickling. I'm in for the long hunt," said Endera.

Valdesta squinted, puzzled by the odd phrasing. "That must be a western duchy thing?"

Endera tilted her head in agreement. "In the high places, my people gather to hunt the gelspar. It's a four-legged beast with massive knobby antlers that look like driftwood, fur that shimmers in the moonlight, and enough eyes on its broad snout to track eight hunters at once. Anyway, the gelspar is a creature of zenith, elusive, and very shy. Once it realizes it's being pursued, it sheds a miniature copy of itself to mislead hunters, the quickling. The copy only lasts a day before withering and can't be used for any of the restorative properties."

"The long hunt means waiting to kill the real gelspar?"

Endera drew her head back. "Kill the gelspar? Giver no, never. The beast sheds its antlers, and that's all we're after. But the long hunt means tracking the creature through the worst parts of the winter until it casts them off."

Valdesta mulled her words over. The conversation had ventured to places well beyond anything she had imagined in her descent. Eventually, she nodded, pretending to understand the other woman's meaning. She jabbed a thumb over her shoulder at the guards. "Am I free to go? I appreciate everything you've shown me, but if what you say about an abrogator is true, I've got to return before she has a chance to strike again."

"I said before, you were free to go. If you like, my men can escort you back the way you came. From what I've learned from Kevka's rantings, you need to set her on a different path, and soon."

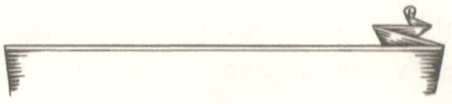

Chapter Six: Silent Contracts

Not a day passes when I'm not surprised by the creative deployment of the Giver's blessings. Word arrived from Callinora of the discovery of a natural botanical that stifles the ability of an abrogator to channel nadir. We've known about veramanth for years, but this latest discovery required the cooperation of alchemists, botanists, and healers utilizing their gifts in ways, I suspect, the Giver never intended. One wonders how much any of us might accomplish if we allow ourselves the imagination to become more than the limitations of our own expectations.

—The Tome of Nivosh, 75 PC, translated by Ksenia Balladuren

THE RHYTHMIC CLATTER of bootheels echoed down the corridors of Stone's Grasp as a patrol of royal guards strode past Laryn in the early morning hours. Vetted by Therek and appointed by Hestian, the first named field martial of Aarindorn in over a decade, each sentinel wore chainmail vests over boiled leather. If the sound of their footfalls didn't announce their presence, the aroma of freshly oiled metal certainly did. Black tabards trimmed with blue stitching and cut with a generous V-neck tapered at the hip of each soldier to reveal short swords in scabbards decorated with silver filigree.

Laryn ticked off the cost to provision the group. *The total allotment for the uniform, equipment, training, and lodging required to support this regiment alone would more than cover Venlith's expenses for a year.*

The hall fell silent as the group of six snapped to attention and bowed their heads in respect when Laryn walked by. Though the breadth of the corridor allowed more than twice their number to pass, protocol and courtly etiquette dictated that they show deference to Her Radiance. She tilted her head and offered a friendly salutation to the group. "Blessings of the Giver, as you were."

Once she passed, the rhythmic staccato of their boots returned as the patrol continued to their destination. Laryn made her way through the hallways and out to the royal plaza. A summer breeze, thick with moisture but made lighter by the fragrance of wild crownberry, gusted off the Great Crown. The wind billowed through the folds of her summer dress, the light material brushing softly against her skin. She secured an empty folio of paper under one arm and tapped a front pocket, finding two zeniscrawls secured in place.

In the center of the plaza, several members of the castle staff labored to erect a Giver's Stone. The pedestal stood perhaps five feet high, and a gifted woman was levitating the heavy bowl as her partners guided the basin into place. Laryn crossed the plaza in silence, contemplating the ceremony that would take place later in the week.

When the mantle fractured, allowing her nephews access to their gifts, so too did the preservation of their parents. Ever since the Abrogator's War, the bodies of Japheth and Nebrine had remained preserved in stasis. A shimmering patina of zenith had prevented their degradation. The night after the Reckoning, Lluthean, of all people, posed the question. He had asked, "If the mantle broke apart and Tarkannen is loose upon the world, what does that mean for our parents?"

Kaellor and the boys had run to the inner sanctum, arriving in time to bear witness as the statues lost their color, fading to muted shades of tan and grey. Over the next several hours, their structures crumbled. What remained of the royal couple disintegrated into ash. Together, the Baellentrells had collected the remains into an urn, which now sat awaiting their release in the ceremony on the Giver's Stone.

Laryn left the staff members to their work and crossed the plaza. She stepped onto the wide stairs that swept out in a gentle curve but stopped a moment to consider the upper tier and green. Time was a thief, but time could also diminish pains from the past. Only a few days ago, the blackened, scorched stones where Bryndor and Lluthean had unleashed rune fire had continued to mark the evidence of their retribution on the Lacuna. Somehow, diligent castle staff had already removed the stains.

Fagle Hoff, the royal gardener, had also covered every trace of damage to the green. Fresh flowering shrubs and healthy patches of blooming lavender flourished under the man's diligent care, and the fragrances lifted her spirits.

Over the next half hour, Laryn made steady progress, nodding politely and offering salutations of the Giver to those members of the staff she passed. Finally, she reached her destination, the suite of Karragin Lefledge. She stood for a moment, rehearsing her proposal. *Giver, this would have been better if I had not lost more than a week since speaking to Therek.*

She lifted a knuckle, prepared to knock, then considered the gesture. *She won't hear that. Best not to start on the wrong foot.*

Instead, she tore loose a leaf of paper, scribbled a greeting, folded the parchment, and slid it under the door. Moments later, Karragin appeared at the threshold. The crease of a pillow across her placid face and tousled slate hair undermined the young woman's characteristic military appearance.

The slightest wrinkle between her eyebrows betrayed her confusion, and Karragin stuck her head into the hall. Finding no one else, the prime snapped to attention. "Your Radiance, forgive my appearance. I didn't expect to receive guests. Would you like to come inside, or can I accompany you somewhere?"

Laryn pointed over Karragin's shoulder, indicating her desire to enter.

"Please, come in," said Karragin. She scurried around the room, collecting a travel pack, two coils of rope, a worn pair of boots, two Outrider uniforms, and several weapons, including at least one spear and curved sword, depositing them all in a corner. The prime retrieved the only chair in the room from a simple desk and offered it to Laryn.

She took the seat and gestured for Karragin to do the same on her bed. Laryn asked a question while Karragin had her head turned. "How bad is your hearing loss, Karra?"

Once Karragin straightened her sheets, she sat facing forward. The two women considered one another in a silence that spoke volumes of the prime's deafness. After a time, Laryn tapped her chin and said with exaggerated enunciation, "If I speak slow enough, can you read my lips?"

Karragin's eye muscle betrayed the slightest hint of focus. "Most of it, Your Radiance."

Laryn nodded with understanding. "Drop the Radiance talk for now. I know Tovnik and a few other healers have tried. Do you mind if I assess your injury?"

Karragin stared intently at Laryn's lips. "I'm sorry, Your . . . Laryn. I missed the last part of that."

Laryn pointed to her own chest. "I want to use my gift to see if I can heal you."

Karragin tipped her chin, granting her consent. Laryn stood and placed one hand on Karragin's shoulder, and another clasped the back of the young woman's neck. She ushered in the flows of zenith, sending some of the currents into the runes on her forearms, where she hoped to gain insight into Karragin's malady. The rest of the force, she filtered through her arca prime.

The resonance of the healer song filled the small suite with a droning murmur. Laryn drafted tiny probing tendrils of zenith, sending them throughout all parts of Karragin's body. She layered the filaments with intimate connection, assessing all of Karragin's senses: touch, smell and taste, sight, and lastly, her ability to hear.

The gift revealed that most of Karragin's senses functioned normally. The young woman could feel Laryn's touch on her neck, and though muted, Karragin could smell Laryn's perfume. When the filaments penetrated Karragin's eyes, Laryn had the odd experience of looking in a mirror, only her eyes were closed. She smiled and stifled a giggle as she realized she was viewing the room through Karragin's eyes.

She withdrew the filaments and focused on Karragin's ability to process sound. Laryn lingered for several minutes, separating out her own awareness of the healer song and investing all her attention in perceiving the world through Karragin's broken sense. Faintly, as if from a great distance, Laryn could sense a vibration, like a remote crack of thunder high in the Great Crown. It happened again in two successive rumbles.

Laryn drew intense focus into the delicate structures of the inner ear. Where the vibration of sound should ripple and convey information to Karragin's senses, the stimulus met strange resistance. Try as she might, her gift found nothing to heal, no broken parts, no swollen tissues to diminish, or clot of blood to drain away—just a dense barrier preventing the woman from capturing the ambient noises about her.

Laryn suspended her assessment and opened her eyes to find Karragin's placid expression staring back. Out of curiosity, Laryn walked to the window to stare at the skyline, searching for storm clouds. Another faint vibration boomed from somewhere deep in the Great Crown and she assumed a spring storm front must be approaching. She turned to face the prime. "I think I understand what happened, but I can't fix it. It's as if something tiny ruptured inside your ears, and the zenith you channel caused it to mend before anyone could figure out how to heal it."

Karragin watched her lips and shook her head from side to side. A rare blush of color warmed her cheeks. "Not catching quite all of that, so I know it didn't work, but thank you for trying all the same."

Laryn retrieved her folio and zeniscrawl and jotted down her conclusions. Once she explained her thoughts on the trauma to Karragin's hearing, she set about offering solutions.

"With your sympath gift, has there ever been a time when your connection allowed you to hear or see what the animal senses?"

Karragin's focus drifted away as she considered the question. "Yes. Once, long ago, I tried to communicate with a moonwing. In the highlands, they call them riftwings. It's a hawk found in the high places of the Great Crown."

Laryn nodded with understanding and rolled her fingers forward, directing Karragin to continue.

"I was able to maintain the link for only a short time, and I could see and hear everything the creature did. But I think my touch was intrusive, and it fled over the peaks. I've never seen another one since."

Laryn considered the revelation, and the gear stowed away in the corner of the room. *"How many nights have you spent searching the Great Crown for another moonwing?"*

The edge of Karragin's mouth lifted in a smile. "Not enough, it seems. I've exhausted myself, neglected most of my duties, all for naught."

"And other birds don't allow you the same connection?"

"Riftwings are the only mute birds I've ever discovered. I think that's why they communicate differently; why they let me see and hear what they do."

"Since the chance of finding a rare moonwing is small, let's get you up to speed with a form of communication you can use now. You've seen the boys, Kae, and me use the hand language of the Cloud Walkers. If Nika could learn it during our travels, so can you."

Using a mixture of lip reading and writing, she began in earnest teaching the young woman the basics of the Damadibo hand language. After more than an hour, Karragin managed to string together salutations and greetings, but the woman was clearly becoming frustrated that her grasp of the signing required mundane repetition.

Sensing her frustration, Laryn held up her hands with a smile, then resumed writing on the folio. *"You are doing fine, and we can easily teach the other members of your quad. Kaellor has plans to train elite members of the Outriders to use it as a secret language."*

A fresh flush of color warmed Karragin's cheeks, and the woman lifted her eyes from the floor to stare at Laryn. "Why are you spending all this time with me, Laryn? I mean, I appreciate it, but surely you've got more important things to attend to now that we are all home."

Laryn continued her written communication. *"Because it's what friends do for one another, for the people they care about."*

They sat in companionable silence for a long time, and eventually, Karragin's eyes misted. The woman flared her nostrils wide and inhaled, then shook her head. "I don't know if I'll ever be what I was. So much of what we do happens in the moment, and my inability to coordinate and communicate will be a liability. I'll not place others at risk."

Laryn watched the prime consider her options, and was reminded—not for the first time—of the steely resolve of Karragin's mother. Though the young woman hid her emotions under a stony mask, in the privacy of her personal chamber, it was evident that the conversation had renewed internal arguments she had already waged with herself. Karragin's lips drew to a thin line, and she stood, indicating her desire to end the conversation.

Alright. I didn't want it to be this way, but strict direction seems to be the only way to get through to you.

Laryn scribbled big, angry letters. *"Sit down, Karra."*

To her credit, the prime hesitated for only a moment and sat back down, a more contemplative expression settling across her face.

"You are singularly the best Outrider I've ever had the privilege of working with. But you are right. You are not the prime that you once were. Do you intend to resign your commission?"

Without pause, Karragin's eyebrows lifted, and she nodded. "Yes. It must be so. I'll not put people I care about in danger."

Her words made Laryn scoff, but she pressed on. *"What's next for you, then?"*

"I might enlist with the builders' guild. My strength can be an asset. It's also possible that I could enlist in the new city watch. The sentinels need a combat trainer."

"Have you discussed this with your father?"

"No . . . not yet." She drew the words out, flavored by the suspicion that Laryn planned to bring Therek into the conversation.

"Relax. That's for you and you alone. When will you resign from the Outriders?"

Laryn turned the paper around for Karragin to read, tapping the bottom line for emphasis. The question, written with blunt disregard for her feelings and pushed to the front of the conversation, caused the young woman's porcelain veneer to crack. A ripple of muscle creased her forehead, and for the second time that morning, her eyes misted over.

Karragin broke from the stare they had shared up to that moment and searched the beams of the ceiling. She swallowed once and grunted to clear phlegm from the back of her throat. "Today. I can do it today."

Laryn penned a crisp response on a fresh piece of paper. *"Good. Since you have no other obligations, I choose you to lead my Mirrare, a force of personal security for myself and the royal family."*

Karragin wiped at a lone tear that streaked down her cheek. "You don't need me, Laryn, and I can't abide charity. You have Kaellor, after all, and there's no better guardian."

Laryn continued writing, more emotion and purpose slanting her lines. *"Kaellor is obligated to the kingdom, and you know from Therek's service how little time he will have to protect me. I need someone I can trust in this city filled with Lacuna rebels. I choose you."*

She underlined the last three words three times with thick lines.

More silence settled between them as the young woman considered Laryn's offer. She flipped to another clean sheet of paper. *"I could make you do this, draft you into my service, but it's not my way. I need you by my side, embedded with my family. It is a position worthy of only the best. Whether you believe it or not, that's you. You are the best, and so I choose you."*

Laryn studied the young woman. Her head tilted ever so slightly to the side, and the healer knew that her words had created a crack in the foundation of the walls Karragin had erected around herself.

Eventually, the young woman replied, "If you are sure, I would be honored."

Laryn sat back in her chair, her shoulder muscles threatening to cramp. She realized that some part of her had feared Karragin would refuse, that she might give up on herself. She set the zeniscrawl to paper once again.

"I will handle the details with the regent. These are my demands. First, you will surrender this room and take up residence among the royal suites on the upper level of Stone's Grasp. I want you close. Next, you will recruit others to your team so that you can have a rotating night watch. I trust you to make the selection, and the members are your responsibility. You will carry yourself with the highest ethical standard, uphold the laws of the kingdom, and swear to protect the royal line with your life. Any questions?"

"When do I begin?"

Laryn squinted, considering the woman. *"Every morning, your sign language lessons will continue with me, Nika, or one of the boys. That starts tomorrow. You have three days to secure the new lodgings, and I expect to meet the team you assemble in five."*

"I can do that. Thank you, Your Radiance."

Laryn shook a finger, indicating her disdain for the title.

"I know, but here and now, it's the only title that seems appropriate."

Laryn set down the folio and slapped the zeniscrawl on top, turned, and pulled Karragin into a warm embrace. The woman stood rigid for a moment, then relaxed and returned the affection. When they parted, Laryn scribbled one last line on the paper.

"I should have warned you. Lellendules are huggers. See you tomorrow morning."

She left the papers and zeniscrawl on the desk and moved to the door. As she made her way back to the royal suites, Laryn wondered how she might go about retrieving a moonwing egg. But she had one more task this morning before she could give further consideration to Karragin's situation.

A brisk walk up to the third tier of the castle left her breathing hard, and she stopped on the top landing to survey the city below. Inside the curtain wall, the staff worked to place the finishing touches on the recovery efforts from the Reckoning. In the merchant district, artisans labored to rebuild the buildings lost to the fires set in the wake of Reddevek's ambush. In other sectors, the citizens of Stone's Grasp busied themselves with the normal activities of commerce and . . . life, she suspected. She wasn't sure whether to feel disturbed that so many people moved on as if little had changed, or relieved that parts of the kingdom had already seemed to recover a sense of normalcy.

A puzzle for another time, I suppose.

Laryn made her way inside the castle and to the receiving area where petitioners waited to meet with the regent, Kaellor, and Bryndor. She knew from speaking with her husband that she still had time to reach Ksenia before her scribing responsibilities began, especially if she hurried.

She pushed open the door to the receiving room to discover no less than twenty men and women clustered in small groups engaged in idle conversation. For the first time all morning, a sense of vulnerability crept up her back, finding purchase in the periphery of her awareness. What if this was a room full of Lacuna?

She dismissed the concern with a huff of air and attempted to navigate around the crowd without drawing much attention, but one young man dressed in the garb of a castle servant bent a knee and bowed his head, muttering, "Your Radiance," in astonished tones. His abrupt reverence spread through the chamber like a swift wave, and all petitioners stopped to genuflect in her presence.

Though she didn't necessarily trust the show of deference, her shoulders relaxed and she felt lighter as she reached the other door on the far side of the room. She paused at the threshold and caught the eye of a young woman. "Please, as you were. The morning's session should begin soon."

Without further delay she entered the chamber Therek used to receive the petitioners. Shafts of sunlight beamed through narrow windows, highlighting the grand empty chair set on a small dais in the center of the room. Ksenia Balladuren sat alone at the scribe station organizing a folio and papers. The young woman beamed a genuine smile and pushed back in her chair. "Your Radiance, I—"

Laryn held up a hand and cut her off. "Please, Kess, I'm starting to believe that deference and adoration are tools the Taker uses to prevent honest people from accomplishing anything. I appreciate your attention to courtly decorum, but when it's just us, let's drop all that nonsense."

"Of course, Your . . . Laryn." Ksenia smiled but remained standing, appearing unsure how far to trust Laryn's dismissal of formal behavior. The two stared at one another for an awkward moment.

"What?" asked Laryn.

"Oh, nothing. I was just thinking that you sound like Bryn, Bryndor, I mean Prince Bryndorllean." Ksenia stammered and made a pretense of straightening the loose papers. "He, uh, he doesn't seem to care for all the courtly etiquette either."

Laryn giggled softly at Ksenia's embarrassment as much as the young woman's observation. "That's the Giver's truth. But I would rather honor the genuine nature of our friendship than cheapen it with superficial titles. Please, have a seat. We have little time, and I have a proposal for you."

The young woman returned to her chair and collected herself, finally nodding at Laryn. "Alright, you have my attention."

"I spent several years among the Cloud Walkers and learned too many things to recount this morning, but one of the things we brought back was their use of signing. It's a silent form of communication using gestures and body language. I need help to train my Mirrare, my new security force, in the technique, and possibly a select group yet to be determined here in Stone's Grasp. I thought perhaps, with your linguistic gift, that you could help me. Would you give it a try?"

Ksenia sat back, considering the request. "I've never tried to learn a language of gestures, but I don't see why it couldn't work."

"Good. Would you mind attempting a bit of it now, before your duties begin? I can speak the phrases out loud to give you plenty of context."

"Not at all. I've already primed my gift. Begin when you are ready."

Laryn nodded and pushed her sleeves back to her elbows. "Blessings and honor to your house, my Ksenia. It is a fine day to learn this silent language and embrace another gift of the Giver. The secret language of the Damadibo allows us to conceal truths while carrying out open communication." Laryn stopped signing and tucked silvery-white locks of hair behind her ears. "How was that?"

Ksenia's focus withdrew into her gift. Delicate flickers of zenith sparkled from the depths of her eyes. At last, the young woman stood and signed back. "Blessings and honor to your house, my Laryn."

Laryn rattled her hands in a playful rhythm on her thighs, then continued speaking as she signed, "That was perfect! Can you meet with me later today after your scribe responsibilities have concluded? With your gift, I'll bet you could master the language in a day or two. Then I would like you to coordinate with the boys, Bryn and Llu, to teach the Mirrare in earnest. You would be compensated for your time, of course."

Ksenia studied Laryn's gestures with focused intensity, eyes fixed on her hands and body language. Yet, the young woman made no reply to Laryn's obvious question, so she pushed forward, speaking and signing in tandem. "And if the royal compensation of the crown is an inadequate incentive, consider that Bryn would appreciate any extra help you could provide."

As Ksenia filtered the phrasing through her gift, she lagged behind the full implication of Laryn's innuendo by a few seconds. At last, she lifted smiling eyes and then searched the room to see if anyone else had overheard.

"So, what do you think? Can you find time in your busy routine for a little princely diversion?" Laryn asked.

Ksenia's eyes flared wide over rosy cheeks, and she said and signed back, "I would be honored to help as long as you discuss certain princely . . . things in the silence of the hand language!" Her hands flapped to her side in exasperation.

"Absolutely brilliant!" said Laryn. "You even managed to communicate emotion! But don't place your foot too far forward unless you mean to imply something salacious."

Ksenia sobered and brought her feet to attention in much the same manner as the guards earlier that morning. "Really?"

"Yes, really," said Laryn. "There are subtle nuances in meaning communicated by a tilt of the head, or position of the feet. We can cover that later. Besides, I think Bryn is unlikely to mistake your intent. That boy wouldn't know salacious if it darkened the moons and kissed him on the lips. For now, it will be our silent understanding."

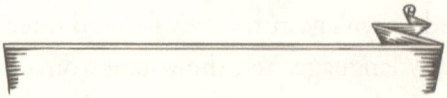

Chapter Seven: Another Blessing from the Giver

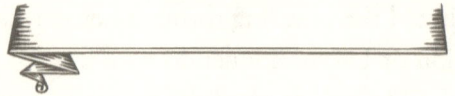

L luthean set his feet and gathered a mass of rune fire, tracking the beast that had appeared behind them on the cliffside. He and Bryndor became aware of the creature at first as a terrible stench, as if the wind had gusted across a dead carcass. As one, they'd turned to discover a headless monster with a girth that rivaled Boru. It swayed over the ground, supported by three thick, snakelike appendages. Muscled arms covered in wet, leathery hide clawed at the air. A myriad of eyes ringed its torso, and a black tongue flicked out from a mouth in the center of a twisted rib cage.

It moved with uncanny speed, spinning side to side, forward and back, dodging Lluthean's release of small bolts of rune fire. When Bryndor called down a thick column of the force, the beast disappeared in a black void that manifested around it, only to reappear thirty paces away from another portal. The molten orbs of rune fire erupted against the mountainside, sending shards of stone into the air. The brief rattle of falling rock accompanied a low rumble of thunder, and then everything fell to stillness.

The putrescence that permeated the air arose from the dark rifts that the beast used. While the swirling, oily slicks only lasted a few seconds, the entire cliffside reeked with the stench of corruption. The beast swiveled and swayed unpredictably, blurring and whirling, the strange cluster of eyes tracking his movements as Lluthean assumed a defensive stance.

He felt Bryndor pull hard on the flows of zenith, then unleash another column of rune fire. The beast winked out of sight, only to reappear between them. A tentacle whipped around from the far side of the creature and struck Lluthean in the chest before he could release more rune fire.

He managed to step back and avoid the full force of the attack. The monster pressed him toward the cliff edge, but he dove to the side, coming up in a roll with one of his swords. He slashed the blade overhead, catching the end of the tentacle, and the beast recoiled.

Lluthean expected to hear a growl of pain, but the susurration of its snakelike appendages rasping over the dirt and rocks was the only sound it made. The alien way it undulated on the ground and pursued them with silent malevolence unnerved him. That and the strange vacuum that he felt right before a rift appeared.

From the far side of the creature, Bryndor lunged with an overhead swing of his sword, but the beast spun once, catching him full in the chest and lifting his feet from the ground. He flew back several feet, landing on his back. The monster surged forward, but then a savage blur of black and silver fur sprang into the melee as Boru attacked. A growl of pure violence announced the massive wolvryn's attack. Boru clamped down onto one of the tentacles and pivoted. The snaky limbs scrabbled at the rocky ground but failed to find purchase, and with a mighty twist of his body, Boru hurled the beast over the cliffside.

Lluthean watched as the thing winked through another rift and reappeared almost at the tree line, more than fifty paces away. He considered attempting another blast of rune fire, but Boru charged again and he feared injuring the wolvryn. Just as Boru leaped for the attack, the thing dropped into another rift.

Lluthean retrieved his second blade from the ground, one held in a defensive posture, the other prepared to lash out. The subtle pulse of a vacuum gave him a split-second warning. He stabbed forward, lunging with one sword extended. The blade found purchase as the beast materialized from another rift. He buried the weapon to the hilt, steel rasping as he wedged it just inside one of the creature's clawed arms, but he overbalanced, and one of his feet slipped over the edge of the oily void of the rift.

He fell back and rolled to the side, avoiding the crash of one of the beast's limbs. Dust and small rocks peppered his face. He hopped up and dove again as another tentacle whipped just over his head. The acrobatics cost him his second blade.

The beast seemed to sense as much. Several of the eyes squinted, keeping him in focus. It swayed to the left, a feint, then spun back to the right. From the backside, a tentacle whipped around, and Lluthean was out of room to dodge away. He crouched low to catch the flailing limb, then Neska burst from the side.

She caught the limb deep in her jaws and thrashed her head side to side, wrenching the monster off-balance. In the distraction, Boru lunged from the opposite side, latching on to another limb, and together the wolvryn held the beast fast. Another vacuum appeared underneath the creature, and its torso began to sink, dragging the wolvryn to its center.

Desperation ignited the flow of zenith through his runes, and the heat of rune fire blazed across Lluthean's shoulders. Roiling cerulean flames coalesced in a cloud overhead, and he strained all his will to constrict the eruption into a thin column. Before the monster dragged the wolvryn any closer, he unleashed the power. A brilliant beam of rune fire seared into the beast's torso, sounding like a deluge of water onto hot coals. The colossal crack of thunder echoed against the mountainside. Foul smoke rose into the air, and Lluthean squinted. Despite the burning in his eyes, he maintained his command of zenith.

The runes across his shoulders burned from the intensity and at last he directed the zenith elsewhere, causing the runes on his flank and hips to tingle. Two of the beast's three snakelike limbs broke away, and the wolvryn toppled back. The otherworldly monster sank into the oily rift, writhing and jerking. Lluthean dropped to his hands and knees, and that's when it happened.

The last tentacle whipped about in the creature's death throes and struck him across the shoulders. For an instant, he felt weightless and windmilled his arms in a frantic attempt to right himself, then he began to fall.

With odd fascination, he looked down. He plummeted toward the distant rocky ground for a few seconds before the runes on his flank and hips took on a palpable quality, pressing against his body. His descent slowed, and the air under his feet gave him slippery purchase.

It reminded him of sliding down a steep snow- and ice-covered hill in the winter at Journey's Bend. He twisted, flailed his arms, and spun about, the uncontrolled currents of wind and zenith taking him in a circular path back to the mountainside. A solid wall of rock halted his descent, and then he slid another ten feet before falling to his back on a shallow ledge of stone.

He lay there dazed and amazed, waiting to feel anything other than mild exhaustion from expending so much zenith. Expecting the sharp pain of a broken rib, he inhaled a cautious, full breath. The air came easy, and he ran hands over his head, torso, and hips.

He lost track of how long he lay there. Eventually, Neska's head appeared high above, looking down. She paced restlessly back and forth on the cliff's edge. Next, Boru's muzzle came into view. The massive wolvryn cocked his head to the side. Finally, Bryndor peered over the edge.

Lluthean lifted a hand and waved at the trio. At his gesture, Bryndor dropped to all fours and shouted down, "Llu? By the moons, how? Why aren't you dead?"

Lluthean heaved a breath, cupped his hands, and shouted back, "I could ask you the same!"

Bryndor stared down at him for several long moments, hair falling in front of his eyes. He coughed once, clearing his throat. "I just got the wind knocked out of me. Are you injured? Anything broken?"

"I don't think so." Lluthean allowed one hand to run along the edge of the cliffside, underscoring how precariously close he was to rolling down the mountainside. "Assuming it's safe up there, I'll need a hand to get back."

His brother shaded his eyes and craned his neck in both directions, searching the mountainside. "I don't know how you did it, but that thing is gone. Boru can't sense it anymore. I'll have to go get some help. I think I can get a rope to you."

Bryndor's face disappeared for a moment, only to return holding the waterskin. He laid it flat against the mountainside. "See if you can catch this. I'll be back as soon as I can."

The waterskin seemed to hang in the air, then dropped with surprising speed. Lluthean braced for the impact, helpless to move out of the way as it plunged onto his midsection. A loud grunt escaped his lips.

"Sorry," said Bryndor. "Be back as soon as I can."

"That sounds good!" he croaked.

After ten minutes, Lluthean's butt cheeks numbed. He shimmied back against the mountainside and sat. Then, slowly, with muscles near to cramping, he lifted one leg, then another, and rose to his feet. Though his back was pressed against the wall of rock, it felt like he could fall forward at any moment.

He chanced a glance down and withdrew his head before any fear had the opportunity to set in. To the right was a sheer cliff. To the left, however, he could see one of the switchbacks that formed the trail they had used earlier in the morning.

The next half hour passed with painful tedium. Out of pure restless curiosity, he channeled zenith, pushing the flow into the runes on his flank and hips, testing the security of his footing. One foot slipped forward and the other to the side, no different than standing on a smooth sheet of ice. Despite how he tried to recover, to press his back to stone, he continued to slip and slide.

Griiiiiiind me!

Without meaning to, Lluthean drifted away from the cliffside, yelling a whoop that was one part fear, one part exhilaration. His stomach flipped and rolled as he struggled to right himself, but eventually he found the balance and slid on a current of air in a lazy circle that brought him down and around to the switchback. He landed on his hands and knees in a cloud of dust and promptly and completely severed the flow of zenith.

Minutes later, Neska appeared from up the trail. Instead of greeting him, she circled in a nervous perimeter, patrolling their immediate surroundings.

Lluthean stood and whistled a greeting to her. "Neska, I'm fine. I think we're safe now. Come here." Only after sweeping another circle in which she investigated their surroundings did she come to his side. She leaned her head into his chest and trapped one of his feet between her paws. When Lluthean fell back, she licked him on the face, then placed a heavy paw on his chest, pinning him to the ground. The gesture caused him to release a hearty laugh.

"Alright Neska, I yield. No more running off, I promise."

Neska cocked her head to the side, blue eyes glaring at him. Eventually, she sat back on her haunches. Lluthean sat up and ruffled the fur under her neck with a mixture of gratitude and affection.

Bryndor's voice interrupted their reunion. "You have got to be some kind of crazy or some kind of stupid. What were you thinking, Llu?"

Lluthean turned his head to the side, considering his brother. "Ahh you know me, Bryn. It was a bit of both, I expect."

His brother shook his head in disbelief. "Kae will never let us out of the castle when he learns about this. I had to argue with him for over an hour to allow us to take the wolvryn without a full patrol of sentries."

"That's the Giver's truth, but only if he actually hears about it. The way I see it, what we learned was just another blessing of the Giver, no?"

"How do you figure?" asked Bryndor.

"Back in Callinora, when the umbral breeched the Sanitorium, their portals carried the same stink of decay. And now that I think about it, Neska sensed the same thing from that black patch of ground we discovered at the Balladuren ranch. Somehow, it's all related."

He searched Bryndor's face, looking for a sign of consensus. "What is it, Bryn?"

"These hikes might be our only escape from . . . everything in there." Bryndor gestured down at Stone's Grasp. He shook his head and chewed on his lower lip. "I can't believe I'm saying this, because he really should know, but for now, let's not tell Kae about any of this. If we do, I have the feeling it will be the last time we set foot outside of the curtain wall. And I need this, you know?"

Lluthean winked. He enjoyed seeing his brother strain against the bonds of expectation once in a while. "Like I said, the whole morning's just been another blessing of the Giver."

Bryndor wrinkled his nose and sniffed. "It smells more like something from the Taker. We should get back. At this rate, we'll barely make it in time to avoid suspicion."

They set off down the switchback, Boru on point and Neska trailing behind. Bryndor turned his head and spoke over his shoulder. "And later tonight, when it's just you and me, you're going to tell me exactly how you managed to drop several hundred feet with only the dust on your back to show for it."

"If I figure it out, you'll be the first to know."

Chapter Eight: Tangled Mysteries

Kaellor walked a tight circle around his nephews, allowing the morning light to reveal the intricacies of the runes that scrolled up their arms and shoulders before weaving unique gold and silver patterns along the jawline. He channeled into his rune of balance and judgment, hoping to discern the full measure of the Giver's gifts.

"Stand closer to the window, side by side here a moment so I can compare," he said.

His nephews turned their bare backs to him and faced the others in the anteroom of the royal suite he shared with Laryn. Therek Lefledge sat in an armchair, leaning forward, elbows on knees, a curious lynx prepared to pounce on any new information. Beside him stood the robust Hestian Lellendule. The man pursed his lips in a thoughtful expression that caused the hairs of his ginger beard to stand on end.

Balancing out the men, Laryn paced an orbit opposite Kaellor, scrutinizing, studying. Her touch and examination were at once both clinical and more compassionate than his. Kaellor looked over Lluthean's shoulder and caught her eye. She winked, pulled a lock of white hair behind her ear, and refocused her attention on studying the runes.

"I recognize something in the make of these," said Kaellor. He ran a finger over the edge of Bryndor's shoulder, tracing a line from his neck across the muscled ridge to the upper arm. "It doesn't seem that the scars the wolvryn left made any difference to the weaving of the runes."

He stepped around to inspect the way the same pattern adorned Lluthean's upper back and arms. The symbols appeared identical except where the runes approached the shadow mark. There, the weave of gold and silver veining silhouetted the crab-like silvery scar, embellishing the mark like a regal symbol and not a reflection of the near-mortal wound.

Lluthean tapped his fingers on the side of his hip. At first glance, the gestures appeared to be the fidgeting of a restless mind. But closer inspection showed that his nephew was signing in the hand language of the Cloud Walkers.

"Hurry, Kae. There's a chill in your rooms this morning."

Kaellor scratched at his beard but gave little thought to his nephew's concern. "We should have done this weeks ago."

"You know as well as I do that time has been a scarce resource since our return," said Laryn.

He considered all that they had accomplished in the past several weeks since their return to Stone's Grasp and the Reckoning. The dismantling of the Lacuna, the restructuring of security both within and beyond the curtain wall. The employment of combined patrols of the runeless and the Spicers. *But how long can that latter arrangement hold out, I wonder?*

He glanced at Therek and Hestian, both men engrossed in studying his nephews' runes. "We have indeed had our days and nights filled with more than we expected. Boys, that night, on the royal plaza, when you unleashed rune fire. Do you recall—did the zenith take shape through these runes on your shoulders?"

The brothers shared a quizzical look, and each nodded. "Yes," said Lluthean. "Right before the mantle broke, I could sense the currents of zenith, but the pain was like nothing I've ever felt, and I couldn't focus the flow, so it sort of scattered all around me, everywhere at once."

Bryndor, who until then had been chewing on the inside of his cheek, spoke up. "It was the same for me until the mantle fractured. After that, I sensed a bit of what we could do, and the currents gathered at my shoulders."

"That's understandable," said Kaellor. "My grandfather, Bierden, wore similar runes, and he was the last in our family to summon rune fire."

"Well, let's learn what we can before the others return," said Laryn. She grabbed Lluthean's wrist and lifted his arm overhead. "It's rare to see runes continue along the torso and flank here. What do you make of these?"

She stepped back, allowing the others in the room a better view.

Therek cleared his throat. "Along Prince Lluthean's ribs, there is a strange amalgam of rather unrelated symbols, but I think the reference is 'sky over land' or 'cloud over water,' something along those lines. It's difficult to be certain; the way they blend, it's nothing I've ever seen before."

Lluthean's face flushed, reminding Kaellor of a time when Rona caught him returning from an evening of games of chance at the Bashing Ram. He glanced at Bryndor, who was studying Lluthean's runes with focused intensity. *Taker's grip, what have you two been up to already?*

Kaellor considered pressing the issue but thought better of embarrassing the boys before their current company. They had more than enough to deal with already.

Hestian stepped closer with arms folded, head cocked to the side. "Have they any sign of your martial talents, Kae? Any guardian runes?"

Kaellor searched Bryndor's arms and torso. "No guardian runes, though they have yet to inherit their arca prime."

The field marshal grunted. "When do you plan to have them sit for their Rite of Revealing? It's customary for novices to practice their skill for years before attempting the trial."

Kaellor searched Hestian's face, then Therek's. "Though the Rite of Revealing is rarely fatal, I would prefer that they waited, as you say, Hes, to become more competent in their gifts."

"I sense a but," said Therek.

"But we have no idea about Tarkannen's plans or how much time we have. I should not like to face the usurper without the full measure of their talent revealed," said Kaellor.

Bryndor interrupted the silence that fell across the room as each person considered Kaellor's words. "The trial sounds dangerous. I would hear your counsel if you have it to give."

Therek cleared his throat. "It's true that in the last five years, we lost one petitioner to the Rite of Revealing. An Endule youth named Zachus."

"What happened to him?" asked Lluthean.

"We don't know," said the regent. "The Rite of Revealing places the petitioner in a zentrist. It's something resembling a dozenth, but much more complex. To initiate the process, five adults in full command of their gifts link before the statue of Eldrek. Somehow, the weaving of the cocoon and the constraints of the Rite of Revealing are shaped by the connection to both Eldrek's statue and the pool in the inner sanctum. We have theories that some gifted are transported on a journey over time and space. Such was likely the fate of Zachus; one moment, he lay within the zentrist, and the next, he simply vanished."

"Are most petitioners endowed with martial talents?" asked Bryndor.

"Not really," said Hestian. "Remember, Your Highness, that those of your bloodline and the Lellendules often inherit gifts designed for the defense of the kingdom. Your Aunt Laryn is a notable exception, although what she lacks in martial prowess, she more than makes up for in other talents."

Bryndor sucked at his teeth. "Well, I defer to your judgment, Kae."

"Fortunately, we don't have to decide right this moment," said Kaellor. He grabbed Bryndor's wrist and returned his focus to studying his runes.

"Bryn, these on your left arm will require time to understand. I believe they hint at discernment and insight, and these on your right have something to do with premonition. They resemble the runes Karragin wears. Do they not?"

Therek stood and stepped closer, nodding in agreement. "Yes, I believe you are correct, but with much more embellishment."

Kaellor lifted Bryndor's arms, following the complex weave of runes traveling down his flank and disappearing beyond the waistline of his breeches. "Mind if we see these as well?"

Bryndor shrugged indifference and lowered his trousers, exposing his naked hip and thigh. Kaellor's initial wonder at the sheer volume of runes withered under his confusion. "Has anyone a notion what these mean?"

The adults took turns inspecting the tapestry on both of them, but all appeared perplexed. At last, Laryn broke the silence. "Bryndor has something akin to judgment and perception on his forearms, but I admit, I've never seen the like of these columns of runes on anyone. It's like the pattern is too dense to tease out the individual symbols."

Kaellor stepped back and motioned for the boys to dress just as someone knocked at the door. "Hestian, would you see to that?"

The rotund field marshal returned with the Lefledge siblings and Savnah Derrigand. The two Outriders had shed their ranging gear for midnight blue uniforms with leather-reinforced joints and silver embroidery along the high neck and shoulders.

Karragin wore similar attire dyed deep purple. Where the front panels of her tunic crossed, silver and gold veining formed a shield, the new standard of the Mirrare. The woman padded in like a silent cat on the prowl, surveying the room's occupants. *Laryn chose wisely, as usual.*

Karragin lifted an eyebrow as she glanced at Lluthean's reflection in a wall mirror. Though the indecent parts of him were covered, much of the rune column on his torso was exposed. She gave Bryndor a similar appraisal as both worked to button up their shirts.

"Is everything ready?" asked Kaellor.

"Yes, Your Highness," said Nolan. "The ashes you collected from the crumbling statues of Japheth and Nebrine have been placed beside the Giver's Stone. A rector from the Church of the Giver is present to oversee the ceremony."

Kaellor resisted his first impulse to wrinkle his nose. Instead, he turned to Therek. "I assume the man passed your scrutiny? Several clergy were in league with the Lacuna or found to owe debts of one kind or another to Tixon B'gin."

Therek nodded. "Rest assured that we've removed those senior members tainted by the breakers. As for Tixon, the search continues. The rector for today's ceremony is a runeless, Heathering Hoff. She is Fagle's second daughter. Though also ungifted, she sees the world with uncommon wisdom and grace. I think we can trust her to offer balanced and truthful counsel."

Laryn made a humming noise of appreciation at Therek's words. "After what we learned in rounding up the others, I shouldn't be surprised that the first reputable rector in the Church of the Giver is a woman."

"Agreed," said Kaellor.

"Your Highness, Field Marshal Lellendule, Your Grace," Nolan spoke last to his father. He spared a glance at his sister before continuing. "We also bring word from Salveen, the leader of the Spicers."

"You're odd messengers for that group. Why didn't she just use the shek?" asked Kaellor.

Nolan shrugged his shoulders. "Sometimes the Giver places peculiar people on the same path, Your Highness. I can't say why she chose not to use the shek."

"I placed Outriders at Salveen's disposal to assist in keeping the peace, but also to help root out any pockets of Lacuna resistance," explained Hestian. A frown creased his forehead. "Come to think of it, I haven't received word of any incursions for several days now, and she has not attended our closed council meetings of late. Surely Salveen's network hasn't identified all those loyal to the Lacuna who remained in Stone's Grasp?"

Nolan shook his head and deferred to his new prime, Savnah. The woman took her cue, hooked thumbs over her belt, and nodded. "No, sir. Together, we've discovered two safe houses and infiltrated three other gatherings in the last week."

Hestian glowered. Deep furrows creased his forehead, silhouetting his eyes with an expression both pained and guilt-ridden. "I've had no word of this. My orders were that any Lacuna discovered were to be processed, brought before the regent for a speedy trial, then handed to my staff for questioning before carrying out any sentence. One of them might provide insights to Chancle's whereabouts."

Savnah's expression remained placid, schooled to professional indifference. *She's learned a few things from Karragin.*

The prime dipped her head. "That's correct, sir. We discovered the locations, but in each instance, it seems we arrived too late."

"Do you think there could be a mole in the Spicers or the Outriders? Did someone warn the breakers before you could take action?" asked Therek.

"I don't think so, Your Grace. In each instance, we arrived to discover the members of the Lacuna slaughtered. Someone else reached them before we could," said Savnah.

Kaellor studied them both. Before Karragin relinquished her position to assume responsibility as Laryn's personal guard, Savnah had struggled to hold her tongue or act with any resemblance of courtly decorum. *Something altered you both on that last mission—one for better and one for worse.*

Therek noticed the change too, for his eyebrows flared in surprise, though whether this was from the new information or Savnah's demeanor, it was hard to tell. The field marshal gripped his fists at his side, frustrated by the open display of his ignorance.

Laryn turned to face Savnah. "Is there a chance someone else, perhaps the runeless, killed the breakers as an act of retribution?"

"It's not likely, Your Highness," said Savnah. "Something impaled every one of the dead we discovered. Something that left a black hole. Whether they were stabbed in the chest, belly, or head, all the victims showed similar wounds."

Kaellor grunted. "It almost sounds like you're describing—"

"Nadir burns," said Laryn. "What have you done with the bodies?"

"On Karragin's advice, we took the liberty of securing the bodies in a restricted vault in the lower levels of the castle," said Savnah. "Three trusted healers from a local chapter of the House of the Moons have agreed to preserve the bodies, but I left instructions to leave the wounds undisturbed."

"A wise decision," said Laryn. "After the ceremony, please escort me there. I should like to see for myself the nature of these wounds."

Savnah tipped her head in deference. "Of course, Your Highness."

Kaellor sighed. "I suggest that, until Laryn has a chance to learn more, we keep the nature of your discovery a state secret. The last thing the people of Stone's Grasp need is the rumor of a vigilante killing our citizens, even if they were loyal to the Lacuna."

"The Outriders are treating the issue with dark moon secrecy. As for the Spicers, we can only rely on Salveen's discretion, but I can't reliably speak to her ability to control her people," said Savnah.

"Leave that to me," said Therek. "Unless there is anything more to report, I suggest we turn our attention to the ceremony?"

"There is one other thing to report," said Savnah. "Four bodies were recovered from the cellar of the Golden Crust, the bakery in the Delve. We only just learned of the business as a possible gathering place for members of the Lacuna. The assassin struck before we got the chance to begin our surveillance. However, there were two witnesses to the attack. Two girls, one age five or six, the other not more than nine. They described seeing a white ghost with spirals of white hair leaving the room after the attack."

"Did they actually see the attack?" asked Therek.

"I don't think so, Your Grace. They hid under the stairwell, and the back cellar, where the bodies were discovered, is down a long and narrow hallway."

"What do you make of their report, Savnah?" asked Kaellor.

The prime lifted her eyebrows, inhaled, then exhaled through her nose. "The back room was covered in flour, so it is possible that they saw someone leave looking . . . ghosty. They both describe a lean person, no taller than myself, with distinctive hair and carrying a hat. By the footprints on the floor, someone, a lone survivor, left the scene."

"It almost sounds like Ranika, but the poor girl has been reluctant to venture out of the family estate in the high district since we arrived," said Laryn.

"We had the same thought, Your Radiance, so I took the liberty of questioning your house staff, and nobody has seen her venture out of the estate until today. She waits in attendance with the others in the royal plaza. But we will keep working the lead, and may the Giver reward the relentless."

"I understand your diligence, Savnah, but Nika has saved my life and defended all of us more than once," said Kaellor. "Report anything you discover to Field Marshal Lellendule, the regent, or me. The Taker weaves a tangled knot. Unraveling it all will take more time than we have this afternoon."

He turned to inspect his nephews. They both had already pulled on black overcoats adorned with blue stitching and stiff collars accented with gold and silver filigree. Kaellor wore similar attire and held his arm forward, demonstrating how to pull the cuff of the dress shirt down to display yet more ornate stitching.

He hooked a finger under a necklace woven of gold and silver veining, craned his neck back, and lifted a pendant previously hidden under his shirt. Twin dragons of silver and gold ringed the pendant, their serpentine bodies creating the shape. One clutched a red gemstone, the other blue. From an interior pocket of his overcoat, he removed two more identical pendants.

"Today's ceremony is mostly about paying respect to your parents, to their sacrifice. But in Stone's Grasp, everything we do is on display." He walked behind Bryndor, adjusting a scabbard and longsword to sit on his left hip, then circled to catch Bryndor's eye. His nephew stared out a window, chewing on his lower lip, eyes fixed on something beyond the curtain wall.

Kaellor leaned forward and pitched his voice low. "Bryn? The loss of your parents, the turmoil in the kingdom . . . I know it's a lot. But you've got all of us to walk with you. Are you ready, son?"

Color flared on his cheeks, and Bryndor nodded. "Yes, sorry, Kae. I was just thinking about Savnah's report. I'm ready. Thanks."

Kaellor considered his nephew. If an abrogator walked the streets of Stone's Grasp, even one aligned against the Lacuna, they would have to deal with the threat soon enough. But not today. He lifted one of the gold chains and placed it over Bryndor's head, adjusting the pendant on his chest.

Recognition dawned on Bryndor's face as he fingered the pendant. "Are these the same ones you showed us that night in the Bend?"

"The very same. I didn't tell you before, but your parents requisitioned them before creating your mantle. It seems appropriate that on the day we lift their ashes to the Giver, we remember their last gift."

He grabbed the back of Bryndor's neck and placed their foreheads together. "As it has always been, all of us together, with eyes to the horizon."

Bryndor withdrew, smiled, and nodded agreement. But the expression failed to reach his eyes, and Kaellor could tell the responsibilities of the kingdom kept him preoccupied.

The Giver lift you up, Bryn. Get through today and we'll turn our attention to any abrogator threat in the days ahead.

Chapter Nine: The Way of Things

Karragin watched as Kaellor gave words of encouragement to his nephews. She positioned herself next to Laryn in the anteroom of the royal couple's suite. Her limited ability to read lips led to significant gaps in the conversation, but Laryn translated, dancing her fingers through various gestures. Karragin's fledgling grasp of the subtleties of the Cloud Walker hand signing would have left frequent holes in the conversation were it not for Savnah and Nolan.

The two of them had sought her opinion of the account made by the baker's daughters. After a tedious review of the story, Karragin thought the description matched Ranika, though couldn't fathom that the young woman had traveled with them across the greater part of Aarindorn as an abrogator in hiding. Still, a lead was a lead, so she suggested Savnah question the house staff at Laryn's manor in the high district regarding Ranika's comings and goings.

Afterward, Karragin thanked them for trusting her with the information, but suggested that they exclude her from future similar conversations. As she had relinquished her commission among the Outriders, their breach of secrecy could serve as grounds for dishonorable discharge. Savnah swore a few oaths to the Taker, and even Nolan seemed reluctant to leave her out of future conversations.

She understood that they still looked to her for guidance, but the title of prime belonged to Savnah now, and Karragin was certain that she was more than up to the task. With her brother, Kovesk, safe at home and dosing himself with veramanth, Savnah had assumed the position with renewed zeal. The woman might be difficult on a long ranging, especially if rations ran low, but Karragin trusted nobody else with

Nolan's safety. And if she couldn't be there to watch his back, she was grateful that Savnah had assumed the responsibility.

She dismissed those thoughts and strained to follow the conversations. Laryn continued to sign, but the entire experience was an exercise in frustration. At least she had a reason to avoid making eye contact with Lluthean. She had understood for weeks now that he fancied her. Savnah recognized the signs long before they returned to Stone's Grasp. Karragin didn't give the notion much concern until Lluthean called on her three nights in a row under the guise of tutoring her in the hand language.

That she stood here, still missing up to half of the conversation, underscored the value of his gesture, but his intentions had concerned her. And so, two nights ago, when he knocked at her door, she told him that she preferred to limit her instruction to Ksenia and Ranika. She could see that the statement confused him, but she chose to offer no further explanation, believing that a clean declaration was best.

To his credit, the young prince had accepted her refusal without argument. Now, as she stood in the same room with the entire royal family, she sensed she had damaged what was a reasonable friendship. Lluthean's position in the room made it easy to avoid making eye contact, which was not in itself unusual. But he seemed more serious, or less carefree, perhaps.

She chanced a glance in his direction. He stood at attention, hands clasped, listening with unusual focus. Perhaps the somber nature of the ceremony weighed heavily on them all. But she couldn't help but think it was something else.

She replayed the conversation in her mind. "Prince Lluthean, the effort that you've made in teaching me the hand signing is unnecessary and I'm quite certain that a prince in line for the throne has better things to waste his time on than me. Besides, I would prefer to limit my sessions to Ksenia and Ranika if it's all the same. And it is, so good night."

She had closed the door as he bowed his head, and that was the end of it. Her father's voice echoed in her mind. "Karra, you are exactly like your mother. Don't be so dismissive of friendship or of love. Both can change your life, but only if you leave room for them."

Grind it, Karra, you can be a real ass. You didn't even tell him thanks. Still, he will find some noblewoman to strike his fancy and forget ever spending time with me. You've got friends, and for now, that's enough.

Everyone turned to watch Kaellor as he addressed his nephews. Bryndor appeared more somber than usual, preoccupied even. *And now you begin to feel the weight of responsibility thrust upon you, young prince. For the sake of the kingdom, let's hope you acquit yourself in this new role as well as you did on the way here.*

Next, Kaellor placed an ornate gold and silver necklace over Lluthean's head. Situated between the crisp black lapels, the jewelry conveyed a distinctive element without appearing ostentatious. And for the first time that she could remember, the younger man actually looked like a prince of the kingdom. *So there is hope for you yet.*

And just as she had the thought, Lluthean flicked the pendant between thumb and finger, twirling it first one way and then another before allowing it to rest on his chest.

Kaellor must have had a similar notion or said something she missed, because Lluthean sobered to attention and allowed his restless hands to rest once again. His uncle adjusted the young man's twin short swords, balancing them on his hips, and together the three of them turned in response to a gesture from Laryn. She stepped forward and the royal family gathered in a tight circle, sharing a private moment.

An uncharacteristic shiver ran across Karragin's shoulders, running down to her forearms, and for a moment, she thought her rune of premonition might be activating. Then she realized that in their travels, she had developed affection for this most unlikely family who had been sundered, scattered across the land, only to reunite at a time when the kingdom needed them most.

A soft "hmm" escaped her throat upon recognizing the emotion, and she considered once again that perhaps she had callously diminished the friendship with Lluthean. She would need to mend fences with him in the future. For now, she had responsibilities, and when the family separated, Laryn turned to face her.

"We depart soon. Where is the rest of the Mirrare?" signed Laryn.

"Amniah and Baccal have secured the royal plaza, Your—"

Laryn held up a palm, then signed, *"We have time. Sign it."*

Karragin tongued the grooved scar of her upper lip and nodded. *"Amniah and Baccal are up top."*

She hoped that was sufficient, because she couldn't manage the signs for at least half of the other words in her head.

Laryn smiled and nodded, signing back. *"Good. You're coming along. Did you understand the meaning of the nadir burns?"* She spelled out the last two words by letter.

"Most of it."

"I want the entire guard with me today. Together, we will inspect the corpses."

Karragin tilted her head, trying to decipher the signing, so Laryn mouthed the words.

"Of course," Karragin replied.

Hestian Lellendule clapped his hands together and led the entourage out of the suite, through the corridors, and to the royal plaza. The royal family followed him, and Karragin fell in immediately behind, joined by her father, with the Outriders bringing up the rear.

As the party stepped out onto the royal plaza, the scent of survivor's essence displaced any lingering smell of the funeral pyres. Karragin shaded her eyes and surveyed the perimeter. A rector stood in purple robes beside the Giver's Stone. An audience of nobles stood to the right, all dressed in the finery of the aristocracy. She searched the faces of the crowd as they approached and, sensing no obvious hostilities, pulled her attention to the left.

Ksenia Balladuren stood between the wolvryn, the late-morning sun silhouetting the edges of their fur in a golden nimbus. Another young woman stood beside Ksenia wearing light blue silks cut in contemporary fashion with a divided skirt for riding. Her hair was elaborately braided in a weave that tapered at the nape of her neck, bound with a blue and silver cord. Karragin faltered a step when she realized it was Ranika.

She couldn't imagine Reddevek's shadow without her oversized hat and leather travel gear stained with trail dust. When their eyes met, Karragin couldn't help the soft smile that crept up her cheeks.

Ranika flushed and signed with a defensive gesture, *"What?"*

Karragin nodded as if to say nothing and signed back, *"You look good."*

At the moment, that was all she could accurately sign, but the girl really did look like an entirely different person with her wild, spun-glass hair tamed in the entwined braids and her dirt-smudged attire exchanged for the refined ensemble.

She crossed the plaza, veering to the left to stand near the wolvryn, then surveyed the faces of the nobles, eventually landing on Baccal, who was posted at the periphery of the gathering. The Mirrare tilted her head ever so slightly in a gesture of recognition. Karragin dipped her head and searched for Amniah, the third member of their newly formed team.

If the guster stood on the royal plaza, Karragin couldn't find her. Searching further, she noticed a figure standing in the shadows behind the door they'd used to gain egress onto the plaza. Karragin shaded her eyes and recognized the unassuming woman in the matching purple uniform. Amniah met her dispassionate gaze with a mirrored, stoic expression of her own, and their eyes locked. After a few seconds, the guster nodded once and shifted her surveillance to the crowd. *You cheeky grinder. Points for diligence, Amniah.*

The rector drew everyone's attention to the Giver's Stone and must have initiated the ceremony by the way the crowd drew their focus to the woman. Karragin stood at attention for several minutes but maintained her observance of the crowd. If ever there were a time for a lone actor to attempt harm to the royals, when they were all gathered in one place seemed like the right opportunity. *Giver knows the Lacuna proved that theory when they slaughtered so many of the nobles gathered on the lower green.*

Laryn's hand reached out to hold Kaellor's. The gesture, both intimate and instinctual, would appear uncouth carried out by anyone else but the pair of them, and yet from Karragin's observations of the couple, she understood the gesture to be one of natural ease and not for the art of the display, as her mother used to say.

Mother, what would you think of all of this now? Your friends reunited. Father in position to set down his burden. Nolan an invaluable part of the Outriders.

97

She pushed the thought aside and studied the princes. Bryndor chewed on the inside of his lower lip, contemplating something the rector had said, and Lluthean stood with professional polite attention, his restless fingers stilled at his sides.

As she watched them, the gravity of the role she agreed to, protecting Laryn and in turn her family, settled on her shoulders. She fought a desire to crane her neck and search for any threats, then had an idea. She chanced using her gift to link to Neska.

She opened herself to the flow of zenith and allowed the force to awaken her sympath rune. Ever so gently, she reached out, holding the line of communication open, but waiting for permission to engage the wolvryn.

Neska sat between the boys, lifting her nose to something on the wind. Eventually, an ear twitched and her broad head made a slow swivel. Eyes of blue crystal considered Karragin a moment, blinked once, then the wolvryn turned back to watch the rector.

"Neska, may I ask you a question?"

"Yes." The simple response was laced with echoes of the sounds and smells around them. Faintly, Karragin became aware of the heady perfume worn by one of the minor nobles. The resonant tones of the rector bled into the conversation and Karragin strained to make out the words, but it sounded like a muffled echo beyond a long hallway and a heavy door.

"Do you sense any danger up here, on the plaza? Can you sense if anyone is hostile?"

After a long pause, Neska responded, *"Some in the crowd smell apprehensive, but Boru and I do not sense any danger."*

"If anyone tries to harm Lluthean—"

"I will not allow any harm to come to my Lluthean, or anyone in our pack."

Her reply flowed across the connection like a strong wind breaking at the leading edge of a storm front and yet, there was no anger or venom in Neska's response. Rather, Karragin was left with an utter feeling of resolute commitment. It was a fact, stated plainly and leaving no room for argument.

"Yes. I know you would protect Lluthean and . . . the pack. I too want to protect them. So, if you sense any danger, would you let me know?"

"Of course. It is our pack. Be ready if you hear one of us growl."

Karragin sighed and dropped her head for a moment.

"What troubles you? You smell of loss and anger."

"I can't hear you growl anymore, Neska. I was damaged in a fight. I can see and smell, feel and sense you through this link, but I won't be able to hear you or Boru. So, if you need to alert me to danger, could you lift your front paw?"

The image of a large game bird stepping in an awkward dance and displaying garish feathers flickered through the link, accompanied by an unmistakable feeling of mirth. *"That's a silly way to get your attention."*

"I know. But others would not notice. It could be our sign for danger, yes?"

After a long pause, Neska exhaled through her nose. *"Yes. Two others here wear the same color as you. They walk like you, like cats on the hunt, but do not indicate any hostile intent."*

"Yes, those two we can trust. They are here to protect Laryn and the pack. Amniah commands the winds and Baccal has sight that rivals yours." Karragin sensed mild apprehension through the link. *"Give them time. Once you know them better you will trust them."*

"Are they to be part of the pack?"

Karragin considered the question, a part or her awareness marveling at the intricacies of the conversation. She had employed her gift to communicate with all manner of creatures from cave rats in the grotvonen warrens to Aarindin, but none of them had ever matched Neska's ability to conceptualize. *"Am I part of the pack, Neska?"*

Neska's head tilted to the side, and Karragin barely stifled a laugh at the decidedly human gesture that seemed to say, "Really?"

Instead, the wolvryn laced her response with an unmistakable emotion of reassurance. *"Of course. All of us who traveled here together are pack."*

"Right. Well, I think that you should get to know Amniah and Baccal. Then you can decide if they are pack. But I trust them."

Motion caught her eye as Bryndor, Lluthean, and Kaellor stepped forward. Together, they lifted a large urn and deposited the ashes from Japheth and Nebrine into the bowl of the Giver's Stone. When he stepped back in line, Lluthean glanced up, then diverted his eyes to the ground.

Their procession reminded Karragin of their loss, and she felt doubly awful for rebuffing Lluthean's attempts to tutor her in the hand language. *He needs his space, and you need yours if you are to do this new job right. Besides, once he gets used to his new role, he'll forget all about you.*

Hestian Lellendule stepped forward with a flourish of his hands and drafted a swirl of air. A palpable flow of zenith funneled into his channeling. Under his will, air currents gathered in a tight spiral, lifting the ashes into the heavens. The field marshal maintained his command of the vortex for several minutes, sending the ashes northward into the Great Crown surrounding Stone's Grasp.

The rector addressed the crowd a final time, and Karragin released her connection to Neska. Groups of nobles approached to pay their respects, and Karragin used the isolation to renew her surveillance of the area, thankful that she had an excuse to avoid the small talk. Castle staff had organized a reception with refreshments on the lower green, and more than two hours later, when the last of the nobles retreated below, a woman dressed in dark robes accentuated by a brightly colored scarf and sash approached while holding a silver urn.

Therek stepped forward, appearing to make introductions, and Karragin considered the woman. She wore the garb of a Moonie, but they rarely ventured into Stone's Grasp. She didn't think much of the interaction until Neska lifted her left paw. Karragin flared her sympath rune. *"What is it?"*

Instead of the rich chorus of senses that announced Neska's thoughts, a woman's voice echoed through her sympath gift. *"Don't be alarmed. It's me, Ksenia. I don't know why we didn't think of this before, but together we can share a conversation through Neska. I asked Laryn, and she thinks it's wise to include you."*

Karragin closed her eyes and shook her head, amazed and the colossal monkery of not thinking of that herself. *"That's brilliant. You have my thanks, Kess."*

Ksenia tipped her chin. *"Thanks. Look, this woman standing before us is Sintra Salveen, the leader of the Spicers. Did you know she was Luna Rova?"*

"Father might have mentioned it."

"That urn she holds—it contains Reddevek's ashes."

Ksenia's presence in their connection faded, or maybe Karragin became less aware of the link as Reddevek's name, echoed so intimately in her mind, triggered a wave of sadness. Ranika stepped forward to retrieve the urn when Salveen held it forward. The young woman clutched the vessel to her chest, then stepped back, casting a suspicious eye to Kaellor. For his part, the prince nodded and placed a reassuring hand on Ranika's shoulder.

"Therek is making introductions," said Ksenia. *"It seems that Salveen was preoccupied these last days preparing Reddevek's body for cremation. The Luna Rova are very particular about not allowing someone's ashes to mingle with those from outside their clan. That's apparently why she missed the closed council meetings. Anyway, custom dictates that Reddevek's ashes be returned to his people. The Dev'advari clan are currently roaming the Great Crown somewhere north of Callinora."*

"Is Salveen from Reddevek's clan?"

"No, she's from a different family."

The conversation carried on a few minutes, Salveen appearing to convey information with an apologetic demeanor, hands clasped together, a soft expression evident in her eyes. Whatever she said, it triggered responses from both Bryndor and Lluthean, and caused Kaellor to assume a defensive posture.

Karragin became aware of the scent of survivor's essence once again. A gentle vibration tickled her heel, and she turned to see a servant pulling a wheeled table weighed down with tubs of ice and freshwater crab legs from Lake Ullend. Sensing no danger, she checked Neska's posture, then made eye contact with Baccal and Amniah. Both women gave her a reassuring nod.

Ksenia's voice resonated through the link once again. *"The sintra indicates that the clan would consider it a great honor if at least one of the wolvryn attended the expedition, but she is not making a demand."* There was a pause and Karragin watched Salveen bow low, then depart for the lower green.

"Taker's breath, she's good," said Ksenia.

"What do you mean?"

"She basically guilted at least one of the royals into making the trip. Salveen is a member of the fo'Veskari, a lowland clan, and cannot make the journey herself. Regardless, the Luna Rova custom dictates that a family member return his ashes, but his brother, Overwarden Kaldera, is committed to organizing forces between the Pillars of Eldrek. The sintra agreed that Ranika is the next closest thing Reddevek had to family, but appropriate honor would only be established if at least one of the royals attended the expedition."

Kaellor paced a slow circle, staring at the northern skyline. Karragin sensed him channel zenith, and he fell into a trance, then turned and had words with Therek.

"Your father says Salveen spoke only words of truth, and that her words have merit," said Ksenia.

Kaellor turned, appearing exasperated, then mollified by Laryn's touch on his shoulder. Bryndor and Lluthean contributed once again to the conversation. Kaellor brushed his knuckles along the streak of silver in his beard, then appeared resigned to some solution.

"We should not divide the pack. We are stronger together," said Neska.

"I know, but it will only be for a short time, Neska," said Ksenia.

"What are you talking about?" asked Karragin.

"You and the Mirrare are to accompany Laryn, Nika, Lluthean, and Neska I imagine, on a rather extended funeral procession. Ranika is taking Reddevek's ashes back to his people. Kaellor and Bryn will remain here. Both of the princes offered to make the trip. Bryn seems eager to go. But Kaellor wants him to remain here and continue to learn about the role he will assume when he takes the crown. Kaellor, it seems, can't leave. The defenses around Stone's Grasp rely on his presence. If he leaves and a

Baellentrell without their arca prime isn't within the capital city, he thinks the wards will fail."

"And that would leave us vulnerable to Tarkannen," said Karragin

She studied the faces of the small group. Apprehension tightened Kaellor's posture, and he kept gripping the pommel of his guardian sword. Even her father, a man who had seen the kingdom through some of the worst turmoil in generations, seemed weighed down, his wispy eyebrows drooping more than normal.

"Kess, let them know that we should recruit Nolan, maybe even his quint, for the journey. His ability to track could prove invaluable when it comes to locating the Dev'advari clan," said Karragin.

As Ksenia relayed the suggestion, nearly everyone in the group turned questioning eyes to Karragin, at which point, Ksenia must have explained their ability to communicate through the shared sympath link. More discussion followed and the group seemed to come to a consensus.

"They agree. You will leave in three days' time. Hestian argued for a large escort of sentinels, but the logistics of organizing and provisioning such a group would delay departure and add days, if not weeks, to the journey. Laryn herself said she would prefer to travel unencumbered. It will likely be Savnah's quint, with Nolan along, and Dexxin to relay your progress. The Mirrare, Ranika, Her Radiance, Lluthean, and you, Neska," said Ksenia.

"Why is Laryn going? That seems like an unnecessary risk," said Karragin.

"It's a concession of sorts. Until the official coronation over the Harvestmoon festivities, neither Bryndor nor Lluthean are considered true members of the nobility. But Laryn, with her dual role as Her Radiance, will convey the appropriate respect and honor the procession demands. I do wonder, though. Why not leave Lluthean here and send Neska along?" asked Ksenia.

In response, Neska pushed an array of experiences through the link: the smell of damp soil as rain fell in steady cadence from thick storm clouds, the mist that gathered at the base of a waterfall with a full-throated roar that drowned out all other sounds, the fragrance of a wildflower, petals stretched open to greet the sun.

Karragin studied the imagery, understanding rippling through her sympath rune. *"It's the way of things, isn't it Neska? It's natural that where one of you goes, the other follows. And you can't think of . . . being any other way."*

Neska's voice, a maternal resonance that conveyed at once an awareness of self, of being grounded, and a feeling of wisdom well beyond her physical age, flowed through the link. *"Splitting the pack is unnatural, but I cannot separate myself from who I am, from my Lluthean."*

Karragin allowed her sympath rune to fall dormant. Not for the first time that morning, she wondered at the nature of the wolvryn, of their connection to the princes, and in particular, the way Neska made her feel like she was the naïve one in the conversation. *Giver's tears, Neska, let's hope you never have to.*

Chapter Ten: To the Bone

Spring assembly just concluded, and there is so much division in Aarindorn. The Taker weaves silent threads in the hearts of men and women seeking power over their neighbors. I trust the musings of a resco-marinated youth over these high-minded lesser nobles intoxicated with notions of their own importance. How they have already forgotten the lessons of the Great War is a mystery, but it's clear to me now that even some of the best consciences have been bought and sold with the vacant promise of supremacy.

—The Tome of Nivosh, 75 PC, translated by Ksenia Balladuren

LARYN SWEPT HER GAZE across her friends and family. The group of nearly a dozen loitered about the Giver's Stone. No one wanted to be the first to descend to the green full of nobles. A formal ceremony honoring the dead was one thing, but the mingling afterward could be exhausting. Still, she understood that person-to-person conversation was one of the best ways to dispel all the misinformation planted by Lacuna sympathizers over the years.

Ranika stood alone, balancing the urn of Reddevek's ashes on the top of the balustrade. Laryn wandered over to stand beside her. On the green below, nobles sat gathered in friendly conversation as they proceeded through a small buffet.

"I haven't had the chance to talk to you these past few weeks, Nika. I'm sorry for that. Kae and I wanted to invite you to dinner, but the affairs of the kingdom leave little time for pleasantries."

"I understand," said Ranika in a flat tone bereft of her normal sass.

"How do you like the manor house? Are the staff treating you well? You really should come live inside Stone's Grasp with us." Laryn asked.

"They're fine. It's all fine. It's more than a girl like me should expect."

The response made Laryn's heart ache more than any portion of the morning's ceremony. *You need more than room and board. You need friends, a purpose, and people to make you believe you're worthy. Reddevek ignited that spark, and we've allowed it to fade to a pale ember.*

"I like your hair. The braids are distinctive. Did you do that yourself?"

Ranika leaned forward, hugging the urn. "Yes."

Not giving me a lot to work with then. What would Reddevek say to awaken you from this lethargy?

"Nika, could you help me with something?" asked Laryn.

"I suppose."

"Good. Kae, the boys, and I will have to make nice for the next few hours with the nobles down there. Do you think you could blend in? Eavesdrop on any conversations?"

Ranika looked askance out of the corner of her eye, then smiled. "I can do that. What am I listening for?"

"Well, anything about the Lacuna for a start. And if you overhear any conversations in which people sound hostile to our return, that would be helpful."

Ranika straightened, stretching her back, and gave a perfunctory nod, then walked back toward the stairs.

"Where are you going?" Laryn asked.

The young woman turned and shrugged her shoulders. "It's hard to blend in if people assume I'm one of you. I can do more on my own."

"I see. Would you like me to have one of the staff hold the urn for you?"

Ranika's head pulled back, and she adjusted her arms across the urn. "No, it's no bother. Red stays with me. I'll manage fine. See you on the green."

With that, the young woman turned and made for the steps. A moment later, Kaellor's firm hands began to massage the tension from Laryn's shoulders. "How did that go?"

She kissed the top of his hand as she watched Ranika descend to the green. "Oh, love, I'm not sure. I'm glad we're going on this trip to find the Dev'advari. We've been neglecting her, and I think she feels alone. No family, no friends to return to. She just called that urn Red."

Kaellor stepped beside her, thick hands gripping the rail of the balustrade. "We're her family, or we could be if she allows it."

"I know. I've suggested that she take up residence in one of the suites in the west wing, but she's evasive. I can't put my finger on it. It will be good to spend more time with her out there and away from all of this."

"I wish I were coming with you. It's bound to be better than managing these kinds of affairs," he said, tilting his head to the green.

"I know you don't enjoy the art of the display, but you're better at it than you think," she said.

He sighed and offered her his elbow. "The sooner begun, the sooner done?"

She linked her arm through his and leaned against his shoulder for a moment, then joined him in step, descending to the green.

He pitched his voice low. "Just promise me one thing."

"Name it, love."

He pressed the knuckle of his index finger against his eye as if rubbing at an irritation. "If you see me doing this, it's my personal sign for 'if I stuck my finger through my eye and twirled it in my brain, it would still be less painful than talking to this person any longer.' So, come rescue me, and I shall do the same."

"You could actually sign that to me, you know."

"I know, but my gesture is less conspicuous," he said.

"I will do my best."

They descended with synchronized grace, and five steps from the green, Kaellor sighed. "Once more into the fray."

In answer to his grumble, an Endule noblewoman from Beclure approached them directly. "Your Highness, Your Radiance, the ceremony was moving. I wonder if I might get your opinion on the stability of investing in properties throughout the lower commons, or even the Sprawl? Though the Lacuna worked to undermine the crown, they did maintain a certain order in those quarters of Stone's Grasp.

I understand that most of their holdings will be auctioned off with proceeds to benefit the kingdom, but also wondered what steps you will take to guarantee the current state of law and order?"

Kaellor's grip tightened, and Laryn stifled a giggle. "I would be only too happy to offer you my opinion, though I think my husband is more qualified to speak to those particular questions."

Kaellor's lips momentarily parted, and he looked about to argue Laryn's point. Instead, he inhaled a deep breath before clearing his throat to offer a response. She moved to step away, intending to migrate through the buffet, when another noble materialized from behind the Endule woman. The man solicited her opinion on the future of textile and other exports, noting that while the regent had opened up trade routes, the defensive palisade hardly instilled a sense of certainty in any future investments. And so, the next few hours dragged on with what many would consider mind-numbing drudgery.

Yet, in every conversation, Laryn managed to instill a sense of empathy tempered by honest engagement. More than once, she had to remind herself that these moments, though trivial to her, were the start of dispelling any misinformation the Lacuna had disseminated over the years.

When a break in the conversations arrived, she caught Karragin's attention and signed, *"In ten minutes, round up the Mirrare. I need a reason to depart, and we need to inspect the bodies of the dead Lacuna."*

"Did you get something on your hand, Your Radiance?" Endera, the duchess of Beclure held forth a black silk. The woman wore a smartly tailored black dress cut in the latest fashion and a hat with a jewel-encrusted veil. The elegance of her ensemble seemed more appropriate for a formal ball than Reddevek's funeral. She sniffed once. "I'm not surprised when one considers the mixed company."

Laryn turned to regard the woman, but had difficulty seeing her eyes behind the pattern of gemstones on her veil. "No, but thank you all the same. The Giver's smile to you, Endera."

"Oh, well I just thought, with the way you were flicking your hand and all." The woman replaced her silk with a sigh. "I appreciate the blessing, especially since the Giver seems to withhold her favor from time to time."

"The Endules have suffered much in the past year," said Laryn.

Endera glared across the crowd. "No more or less than others. I'm sorry to learn of Chancle's treachery. Another smear on the Lellendule legacy, I'm afraid."

Laryn considered rubbing at her eye with a knuckle, but Kaellor was currently attempting to extract himself from a conversation with three merchants from Stellance.

"Your husband seems to be holding his own, which is more than I can say for your nephews," said Endera.

"Prince Bryndorllean and Prince Llutheandellen are no strangers to life at court, Endera. Beyond Kaellor, they have more experience than anyone on the green when it comes to dealing with foreign nobility."

"Why would you believe that, exactly?"

"They grew up in the Southlands, as I'm sure your informants have indicated. While there, Kaellor was not idle. Together, they cultivated numerous meaningful relationships."

"The Southlands?" Endera looked like she had bitten into a cookie and, finding the batter poorly mixed, was now working over an unpleasant lump of salt. "Unless the Giver herself has blessed you with a secret trade route to Callish, I don't know what good that will amount to. Still, Kaellor shows more maturity than that brutish display of force Prince Bryndor unleashed on the Reckoning."

Laryn's jaw muscles ached. She rubbed at her eye, but Kaellor had his back turned. She stifled a number of curt retorts and inhaled a deep breath. "Endera, were you on the second green with most of the other royal families that night?"

"Me? No, I had retired to the manor house to nurse a headache. Besides, I've heard enough of the regent's speeches over the years."

"I see, so . . ." Laryn inhaled another deep breath and only slowly released the air, using the time to pick softer words. "Help me understand why you think Bryndor's use of force to save the lives of countless innocents was a brutish display?"

"Well, those are not my words!" Endera feigned exasperation. "No, that's just what many of the senior members of the high houses are whispering these days. And who could blame them, I mean, those wolvryn alone make my point."

"Anyone well versed in Aarindorian history would know that many gifted, noble and otherwise, held sacred relationships with the wolvryn. They were a normal part of courtly life during the last Lellendule rule," said Laryn.

She stepped to the side to retrieve two glasses of wine from a passing servant and handed one to Endera. The noblewoman inclined her head and raised the glass. "Thank you, Your Radiance, for the wine and the history lesson. Some people might resist an unknown entity assuming control of the throne."

Laryn allowed her head to nod with agreement. "They are new to Aarindorn. That's the Giver's truth. But with time, I'm certain the people will come to see all the things they have done and will continue to do, for the safety and prosperity of the kingdom."

"For the sake of the kingdom, I hope you are correct. The high families need assurances of stability after everything that has transpired since their arrival."

"There's a saying in Callinora, among the healers, 'to the bone.' It means a medic or healer must always investigate an infection or injury down to the bone. Sometimes the surface of a wound would appear to heal, but deep underneath, there could be infection or other injury, and if those things are missed, the tissue could fall to rot. The lesson to young healers is that one shouldn't make assumptions based on superficial appearances."

The tone in Endera's voice lifted as if humoring the assumptions of a child. "Oh, I understand that all too well, as do the high families. Just because someone can cast a ball of fire into the sky and warm their feet at night with an oversized lap dog does not mean that they are fit to rule the kingdom."

Laryn sipped once, swallowed hard, and then took a larger gulp of the spring wine. She waved and smiled at a young girl walking by, holding her father's hand. "Equalitus diplomatica, Endera,"

The noblewoman frowned but offered no response.

"Surely, you are familiar with Aarindorian due process. Equalitus diplomatica serves as one of the founding principles of judicial law. It means one shouldn't make judgments without hearing all of the facts from both parties. For example, you wouldn't want anyone making assumptions about your convenient absence from the green on the night the Lacuna rounded up every other noble in an assassination attempt, not without them understanding that you were suffering a malady. I mean, some people might jump to the wrong conclusion and assume that you had foreknowledge of the attack and conveniently failed to warn everyone else. But that mistake would only occur if they made a decision without weighing all of the evidence."

The veil obscured Endera's cheeks, but her lips puckered ever so slightly. Endera lifted her glass and took several long sips. "You make a fair point, Your Radiance. I'm glad a refined Lellendule can offer wise counsel to our young princes. They will surely need it in the days ahead."

Now I know what Kae means when he says people make his teeth ache.

She considered probing Endera's last statement for clarity when Karragin approached with Amniah and Baccal. "Apologies Your Radiance. Your expertise is urgently required by fellow healers. I was asked to escort you with all haste," said Karragin.

Laryn anticipated some difficulty extricating herself from the conversation, but the duchess, a normally self-absorbed woman, seemed mollified by Karragin's timely interruption. "I should like to continue our conversation another time, Endera."

Endera bowed. "Of course, I appreciate the time we've shared this morning. Eyes to the horizon, Your Radiance."

"Eyes to the horizon, Duchess of Beclure," said Laryn. She turned to follow Karragin and stopped, signaling to Amniah. The woman strode forward.

"Your Radiance?" asked Amniah.

"In a moment, we are going inside to inspect the corpses Savnah recovered. See if Ksenia Balladuren can accompany us. That way, Karragin misses nothing. We'll need to recruit one of the wolvryn as well, I suspect."

She watched the guster melt into the crowd, only to appear at the periphery to engage Ksenia in conversation. Laryn began the ascent back to the royal plaza and stopped on the fifth step to gaze across the green. The brothers stood together, holding their own in conversation with a group of Callinoran scholars intrigued by the wolvryn. A group of enthusiastic merchants surrounded Kaellor, peppering him with flattery. He turned in her direction, and when their eyes met, he pressed a knuckle firmly against his eye, rubbing vigorously. She smiled and shook her head, waved him on, then turned to climb the steps.

Chapter Eleven: Nadir Burns on Display

"I don't know how she does it, but it's a kindness that she leaves me out of it," said Elbend Balladuren.

Ksenia stood beside her father at the periphery of the green, watching the nobles mingle after the ceremony of the ashes at the Giver's Stone. Her mother made the rounds, gifted as she was in the art of politicking, a blessing for which she and her father were eternally grateful. She nibbled at the edge of a pastry, frowning when her teeth worked over a piece of gristle. She'd meant to grab a crownberry puff, and now, as she sniffed at the spiced meat, she realized her error.

She held out the morsel to her father, who declined, patting his belly, showing he had consumed his fill. Instead, she kindled her sympath rune and linked to Boru, just enough of a connection to tickle his curiosity. The wolvryn rolled his head in her direction. She shook the pastry between thumb and finger, and he trotted over. Ksenia offered up the treat on an open palm. Boru sniffed once, retrieved the food, then licked her hand for good measure before settling on his haunches beside her.

Even sitting, the wolvryn's silhouette blocked the glare of the sun. She leaned a shoulder against him and let her fingers scrub along the side of his jaw. She began to wonder how long they would need to remain after the ceremony. Her mother would, no doubt, linger as one of the last in friendly conversation. Elbend would weather it all without complaint, waiting to accompany her to their manor house in the high district.

One of the Mirrare, the guster Amniah, wound her way through the crowds and approached them. Dark hair framed the flat mask of the woman's expression. Ksenia had already begun training them in the hand language, and Amniah excelled beyond her peers. The way the language conveyed complex thought and emotion without facial expression played to the woman's strengths.

"*Hello, Ksenia,*" signed Amniah.

"*Hello Amniah,*" she signed back. "*This is my father, Elbend Balladuren.*"

Amniah bobbed her chin once. "*I know Kervin. Neither of you look much like your father. You favor your mother. Kervin is a good man to have when you need an Aarindin to grip. We ranged in the same flank into the Great Crown.*"

"*That sounds like my brother.*"

They stood in awkward silence, Amniah looking past them all, appearing to survey everything except the nobles. Eventually, she cleared her throat. "Ksenia, does the regent require your services this afternoon?"

"No. I have the day off," said Ksenia.

"Then I am to make a request of your time. Her Radiance bid me invite you to accompany us into the castle. Karragin still struggles with the hand language. Her Radiance hopes you can link to Neska and use your gift to translate."

"That's quite alright. If Laryn, Her Radiance, has need of me, then I am all too happy to accompany you." She turned to Elbend. "Father, it seems my services are needed. If I have time, I promised Winter a ride. Don't hold supper for me. I'll be back after sunset."

Elbend winked once and began a slow saunter toward his wife. Ksenia turned to Amniah. "Lead on."

The guster signed to Karragin and Baccal. In moments, she followed a strange procession with Laryn, the Mirrare, and Neska. Ksenia thought that the wolvryn's attendance without Lluthean seemed strange. Neska must have had the same thought, for she hesitated a moment and scanned back across the throng of people milling about the green. Lluthean stood with Bryndor, both appearing to hold their own in conversation with a crowd of lesser nobles and merchants.

The wolvryn turned, focusing crystalline blue eyes on her, blinked once, then began the ascent. Ksenia humphed once. *I get it; any chance to leave the crowd behind is welcome.* They climbed the steps to the royal plaza and withdrew inside the castle.

Laryn gathered the small group inside, then signed to Karragin and the others, *"Secure the room, then we can speak."*

A gentle vacuum tugged on the flows of zenith, and iridescent blue light flared from Baccal's eyes. The woman rotated as if taking in the panorama of an expansive view, stopping when she completed a full turn. Karragin and Amniah took up positions at the hallways leading out of the chamber.

"All clear, Your Radiance," said Baccal.

"Good. Kess, thanks for joining us. I could use your help this afternoon."

"Certainly."

Laryn held up a hand. "Don't be too eager. I'll need your promise of confidentiality first. Very few people have knowledge of what we are going to see today, and, for the security of the kingdom, it will need to remain that way. We are going to view the bodies of Lacuna slain after the Reckoning. There is a good chance that we will bear witness to things that should be considered a matter of royal secrecy."

Ksenia received the news with a mixture of morbid curiosity and trepidation. "I understand. It's not anything I don't already manage on behalf of the regent every week."

"That's only one of the reasons I asked you to join us," said Laryn. "I would like you to act once again as a medium, so that Karragin can both understand and contribute to the conversation. She and Baccal still have only a rudimentary command of the sign language."

"The Giver affords each of us unique opportunities in service to Aarindorn," said Ksenia.

"Just so. Let's be off then," said Laryn.

Baccal took the lead, winding through the upper corridors of Stone's Grasp, eventually to a tower of stairs that dropped all the way to the lower levels of the castle. She had not set foot on the steps since they entered the castle on the Day of Reckoning. Within minutes, they left behind anything resembling the familiar passages Ksenia used on a daily basis.

At the end of a corridor, a pair of sentries stood guard. As Laryn approached, they saluted and stepped to the side. By the way Neska followed along, Ksenia assumed Karragin must have already communicated everything to the wolvryn.

"Mind your footing. The stones are smooth but damp, and the way drops." The voice, Amniah's if Ksenia guessed right, spoke with little inflection and echoed from the front of the strange entourage.

Neska's tail swished in front of Ksenia's face, a welcome distraction from the stagnant air. Even with the responsibilities as a scribe for the regent, she had no cause to regularly travel so deep into the backside of the castle. The cool, damp air felt oppressive, and still they continued.

Fortunately, crystal fabrications harnessed zenith and emitted a sterile blue light. While better than bumbling around in darkness, the pallid color added a somber quality to the journey, which began to feel not unlike another funeral procession.

Neska padded along in pensive silence, ears perked forward, nose searching the air. Ksenia awakened her sympath rune and reached out.

"What troubles you, Neska?"

The wolvryn responded with phrasing laced with the scent of things rotting and decayed. Instead of a chorus of intermingled senses, an unsettling silence permeated the response, devoid of ambient sounds, and by the Giver, somehow, she conveyed the palpable quality of oppressive weight. For the briefest moment, Ksenia staggered against the wall, compelled by an overwhelming need to inhale an exaggerated breath and expand her rib cage against the suffocating feeling. The weight subsided and Neska's thoughts rippled through the link. *"There is death in the air; death and the residue of something from the Drift."*

When am I going to stop being astonished by this creature's mind? Ksenia pushed aside her sense of wonder. *"Are we in danger?"*

Neska walked several paces without response. The scent of oiled metal and an uplifting feeling of strength layered over an image of Karragin.

Right. I suppose nothing down here could rival Karra's martial skill. Ksenia's initial assumption of the wolvryn's communication withered as a feeling of reprimand echoed through her sympath rune, and then she understood. *"You want me to invite Karra to our conversation?"*

A feeling of affirmation resonated back.

Ksenia quickstepped around the wolvryn and touched Karragin on the forearm, tapping on the woman's sympath rune. Karragin glanced once to Neska, then nodded in understanding. In moments, she joined the conversation. Neska shared her assessment of the corridor, and to her credit, Karragin didn't miss a step, but her posture stiffened, and her hand gripped the hilt of her sword.

Karragin exhaled through pursed lips. *"Thank you, Neska. A little warning next time, Kess?"*

"Sorry. I asked Neska what she thought of this place and if we were in danger. She bid me invite you to the conversation."

"I see," said Karragin. *"Well, beyond the door is a room with several bodies. They have been preserved by healers from Callinora. Neska must sense them. Savnah and her quad delivered the bodies here under secrecy and there has been a continuous guard, so I don't think we will encounter any danger."*

Ksenia felt reassured, but an undertone of vigilance still rippled out from Neska and through their collective link. Laryn stopped at the door, turned to see that everyone was prepared, then ushered them inside. More of the sterile blue light fell on bodies shrouded with burial robes lined with sashes of survivor's essence. Laryn's healers had also preserved the bodies against rot, allowing the gentle fragrance of pine needles to permeate the room.

Two rows of long tables held over five bodies. Laryn stepped forward and removed a slip of paper placed into the folds of the death shroud, then unwrapped the covering about the face of the first body. Her delicate fingers folded the shroud back with meticulous care and reverence. Ksenia had seen dead animals before, but had never had cause to linger so close to a corpse. A mixture of morbid curiosity and anxiety swelled in her mind, but something in the composed professionalism of Laryn's motions put Ksenia's mind at ease.

The first body Laryn uncovered revealed the face of a middle-aged woman. She then exposed the corpse completely, and Ksenia stood, riveted. She must have been someone of influence, as her hair was styled in the latest fashion with spiraled braids swept up into an artful pattern. While a waxy pallor had settled across the woman's body, rouge still accented high cheekbones, and expensive paints adorned the eyelids and lips.

Ksenia's gaze traveled across the dead woman's features: strong but delicate shoulders, sagging breasts that did little to hide an unnatural black burn scar over the woman's lower right rib cage, a proud mound of pubic hair, and bruises that mottled the knees. She wasn't sure what she had expected, but seeing the woman stripped bare and reduced at the end to this . . . she began to understand why Laryn handled the corpse with so much dignity.

Laryn cleared her throat to gather everyone's attention. "Are you two linked? So Karragin can understand everything?"

Through their shared connection to Neska, Ksenia translated Laryn's words verbatim.

"Yes, Your Radiance," said Karragin.

Laryn flipped open the folded paper she had retrieved and recited. "Middle-aged woman, body recovered from the back room of a tavern in the Sprawl. Limited information supports affiliation with the Lacuna. No witnesses available to corroborate cause of death."

Laryn set down the paper and looked up. "What do you make of the wound on her chest?"

After a few seconds of silence, Baccal spoke up. "Does it pierce through to the back? Was she impaled by, I don't know, a hot fire poker?"

"Not a bad thought. All of you, step close and help me turn her. You too, Kess," said Laryn.

Ksenia grasped an arm and shoulder, surprised by how cold and stiff the corpse felt. Any apprehension she felt withered under simple curiosity as they rolled the body to its side, where a matching burn wound appeared just inside the shoulder blade. Ksenia leaned down to better inspect the injury and could see flickers of motion as Laryn's hands probed the front of the corpse.

"It bores all the way; not a clean track, but I can definitely see through," said Ksenia.

"Come, turn her completely over," Laryn directed.

In unison, they rolled the corpse to a prone position, and Laryn stooped to more closely inspect the wound. The soft, whirring murmur of the healer song betrayed her probing. After only a few seconds, Laryn released her gift and then set both palms on the table as if grounding herself.

"Baccal's idea is sound. Any other theories?" asked Laryn.

Ksenia had no other ideas and looked at the other women in the room. Amniah stared at the wounds and Karragin nibbled at the scar on her upper lip.

At last, Amniah probed the edge of the blackened hole with a finger. Her voice broke the silence, even more hollow and devoid of emotion than usual. "She could have been caught by shrapnel from a munition. That might explain the projectile nature, but the tissue isn't so much burned as melted."

The guster held up her fingers, showing them free of any stain or ash. "See, no soot. Unless there is something special in how the healers preserved the body, a munition burn this severe should leave soot behind. The flesh here is melted, like the ends of my feet. Is there an umbral loose in Stone's Grasp?"

"It's not likely with the ward that Kaellor erected, but your observations are correct, nonetheless. This is a nadir burn," said Laryn.

"Abrogator then? Or someone wanting us to think it's an abrogator?" asked Karragin.

"Taker's grip," mumbled Baccal. Ksenia thought her own expression must match the surprise on Baccal's face.

"Come, let's unwrap these other three. Savnah brought these here because she recognized a pattern. Let's see what we can learn. Kess and Karra, you two manage one. Baccal and Niah, another. I'll take the third."

Without further prodding, they unwrapped the bodies in silence. After a few minutes, they stepped back, surveying the corpses of three men. The soft shuffle of paper created the only sound in the room as Laryn read through the reports attached to each body.

The obvious appearance of matching wounds overshadowed any shock Ksenia might have had at seeing three grown men lay so exposed. Her eyes flicked past their curious bits, settling on the clear causes of their death. One man had a nadir burn in the center of his chest, the

119

other in the abdomen, and a garish blackened hole had obliterated the face of the one she and Karragin unwrapped.

Ksenia stared with confusion at the faceless man. A ridge of forehead and bushy eyebrows crowned the upper rim of the crater, and the remnants of a chin marked the lower edge. The rest of the man's face appeared to melt into a blackened void.

"Taker's breath. I don't understand what I'm looking at here," said Ksenia through the link.

"It's . . . more than I expected as well," echoed Karragin.

"Neska, you said this room smelled of death and something from the Drift. What did you mean exactly?" asked Ksenia.

The wolvryn lay casually in a corner of the room, belly against the cold stone floor. She flared her nostrils and lifted her head from her paws. Violent images of a black tentacled beast laced with an overwhelming scent of decay and corrupted flesh flared through the link. *"Something from the Drift found us in the mountains, but we killed it, sent it back. The wounds remind me of that beast."*

"Do you think the beast killed these people, Neska?" asked Karragin.

Blessedly, the cacophony of sounds and smells Neska used to convey her thoughts muted to stillness. *"No,"* the wolvryn responded.

Ksenia drew her gaze to one of the other men, then back, trying to make sense of the faceless corpse. At least with the others, they still looked like people. She could conceive something about their past, who they might have been. But the faceless corpse left her bereft of any ability to imagine what he might have been.

Laryn's voice pulled her from the shock of the moment. "These last three, it seems, were recovered from the basement of a bakery where Lacuna sympathizers were meeting. It's no doubt how they met their end."

"What about the final bundle there? Is it a child?" asked Karragin. She pointed to the last shrouded corpse. The size indicated an adolescent.

"I've seen enough for one day, if it's all the same," said Ksenia.

"As have we all," said Laryn. "Savnah's report states that the last one holds the remnants of a corpse also removed from the bakery, but that it is so damaged that the remains were formless. They identified him by the papers he carried in a coat. He was a clerk named Falk."

Recognition washed over Ksenia. "Falk? I know him—know of him, anyway. He worked in the regent's administration."

"What did you know of the man?" asked Karragin.

"Not much, really. Quiet, punctual, even polite," said Ksenia.

"It's not a surprise that Lacuna sympathizers worked in the offices of the regent," said Laryn. "What is a surprise, and is the reason I brought you down here to see this firsthand, is so that you understand what we could be up against. Kaellor's wards prevent anything from the Drift from crossing the boundary into Stones' Grasp. But Amniah has it right, these are nadir burns. So, it's likely that an abrogator walks the streets. News of that would cause panic among the citizens."

Amniah's voice chimed in with her odd monotone quality, devoid of angst or surprise, as if the discovery were made years ago and they were only now discussing the potential ramifications. "Have nadir burns been discovered on anyone not associated with the breakers?"

Laryn tipped her head, acknowledging the question. "Not that we know of. What do you think of that?"

The guster shrugged. "It's all the more reason to keep the discovery secret."

Karragin shook her head in disbelief. "If people learned an abrogator hunted Lacuna sympathizers, they might think to blame the crown as the source of the violence. And while the Giver is said to bless the luck of monks and simpletons alike, it wouldn't take her blessing for some folks to knit those things together."

"Exactly," said Laryn.

Karragin walked around the table, assessing the wounded bodies one last time. She stopped by the remnants of Falk and chanced a look inside the folds of his burial shroud. Her voice carried unmistakable exasperation through their link. *"Moons . . . I can't even tell this was a man."*

She replaced the cloth over Falk's remains and rested a single palm on the parcel. A steely professionalism strengthened Karragin's posture. "Tarkannen was the first abrogator since the Cataclysm. We'll need to research how to stop them with more than Eldrenol's solution, but I'll see to provisioning us each with a ready supply. Amniah, you might be our best defense inside closed quarters. The solution is volatile, but with practice, you could disperse it into a room or down a hall."

"Does it work like veramanth? Does an abrogator need to ingest it, or is skin contact enough?" asked Baccal.

"I was taught that the solution is inhaled, but whether a simple breath will do or a heavy inoculation is required is beyond me," said Laryn.

"With a little time, I can likely find the answers," said Ksenia. "I've been translating an ancient tome from the time of the founding of Aarindorn. It might contain some clues, and I have a friend in the archives who can help."

"Good," said Laryn. "But keep your inquiries vague so as not to raise suspicion. The ceremony today was but one step on a long road we have yet to pave as we guide the kingdom on a path of reconciliation. The last thing we need is an agent of the Taker dividing us once again."

Chapter Twelve: The Chill of the Storm

The steady patter of rain on the slate rooftops muted the throaty growl of the wolvryn. Bryndor hugged the shadows of the curtain wall at the western edge of the Sprawl. He leaned forward and whispered to his companion, "Easy, Boru. I don't like the smell any more than you do, but we've got to find her tonight before she goes too far."

He rubbed errantly at the scar on his right shoulder and thought briefly of Boru's mother. That he'd survived the attack of a feral wolvryn was no small blessing of the Giver. On nights like tonight, when the clouds ushered in thunder and lightning, the old injury ached. Tonight, it throbbed more than usual and sent tingling lances of pain down to his elbow.

His fingers combed through the wolvryn's neck to pacify their collective unease. A group of four Spicers on patrol walked by, keeping to the dry boardwalk on the opposite side of the road. They meandered past and turned into an alley, disappearing into the warren of crowded buildings. A random fork of lightning scattered overhead, followed by the soft rumble of thunder a few seconds later.

Bryndor ran his hand along Boru's shoulder, the wet fur clumping between his fingers. He settled his palm against corded muscles and synchronized their breathing, all his focus given to seeking the peace that the intimacy of their connection offered. In an instant, the world assaulted his awareness, and he nearly severed the link.

The chatter of human voices near and far cut through the clatter of rain. Vermin of various sizes scampered about in the darkness. A feral cat darted out from under the boardwalk, then retreated with a rat twitching in its jaws. None of that alarmed him so much as the utter reek of human excrement fermented and magnified by the rain.

Bryndor felt his mouth water in anticipation of retching. "Taker's bitter breath, how do you stand it?"

He thought to bury his nose in his sleeve but knew it would change nothing, and he had to remain connected to Boru if he had any chance of finding Ranika. After several minutes, he sifted through the commingled senses, pushing aside the sounds and smells of the gutter. Dimly, he found the trail of Ranika's essence, like a weak scent memory on top of the polluted environment.

A quick scan of the area showed the auras of more than a dozen people. They meandered inside a rundown pub, the scent of stale beer, piss, and lust wafting out the doors. Raucous laughter and the clamor of conversation gave him pause, but after a few minutes of observation, it became clear that none of them were likely to brave the rain.

He signaled to Boru. *"Find Nika, keep to the shadows."*

The great wolvryn padded down the road, keeping close to the curtain wall, and Bryndor maintained their bond. They passed by several more alleys and small streets, all lined with ramshackle homes crowded together like so many barnacles seeking purchase on the underside of a great frigate. Even without Boru's enhanced senses, Bryndor could tell they were approaching a portion of the derelict neighborhood bereft of foot traffic. No lanterns or candles glowed in the windows, and the oppressive stink of too many humans faded.

Ranika's scent trail became easier to follow, and Boru turned onto a dark street. Fifty paces in, he stopped and turned again into an alley that took an odd serpentine course. Another skitter of lightning slashed across the sky, and Bryndor froze, expecting the brief illumination to betray their position.

He strained through Boru's senses. After what felt like several long moments, he sensed no cry of alarm, no scent of fear . . . no signs that any other human walked the narrow alley. But something in the vicinity rose to his awareness. Boru noticed it as well, for a low rumble rose in his throat once again. The smell of man sweat and anticipation lifted faintly on the wind. And something else—oil.

Bryndor searched his memory. The last time he encountered the smell was over a month ago at the spring assembly, the day his mantle fractured, when he unleashed rune fire on the members of the Lacuna embedded in the city watch. Oil had protected their chainmail and lubricated the gears of their crossbows.

The realization made him suck at his teeth in concern. *Nika, by all the dead in the Drift, what are you walking into?*

Bryndor signed to Boru, "*They are close now. Stay in the shadows and move forward.*"

Together, they approached the end of the alley, where it spilled into an open courtyard before what appeared to be an abandoned two-story building. It had the look of an old church. A lightning strike had damaged the steeple, where he guessed a bell had once rested. Rain dripped through holes in the roof of the front entrance to fall on a weathered front porch. The scent of wet hay and moldering wood lingered in the air. Flickering light spilled out through cracks in the walls and the sundered rooftop.

Bryndor searched the surrounding houses and rooftops, but nobody prowled about the vicinity. They crossed the edge of the courtyard, keeping to the shadows, and stopped near a boarded-up window. He rubbed again at the throbbing in his right shoulder and cast an angry glare at the sky, as if nature itself could sense his unease and dissipate the storm front that was causing his old wound to ache.

Voices from inside the building interrupted his thoughts. He urged Boru to walk toward one of the few remaining windows. Though the position left them exposed to the rain, the wolvryn's enhanced perception gave him a clear understanding of the interior.

The room inside was larger than he expected and lit with several lanterns. Nine men and women stood in a circle on the main floor. But hidden on a second-floor balcony, more than twenty others hovered out of sight. Where those on the main floor smelled of nervous anticipation, the others reminded him of the predatory confidence of the nadir cats from the Korjinth Mountains.

Standing on the main floor at the far side of the room, her head covered by that ridiculous broad-brimmed hat, was Ranika. She held herself with uncommon hypervigilance, weight resting on the balls of her feet, head frequently checking the exits. Even without Boru's vision, he would recognize her lean frame and posture. Where others might see a reedy girl, fidgety and restless, he saw a svelte hunter capable of uncommon agility and lethal purpose.

One of the men paced the room, speaking in a voice that felt loud to Bryndor's senses. He wore a rain-soaked cloak over what appeared to be the chainmail of the now-dismantled city watch. A dark purple stain, like the cloud of an unfortunate birthmark, painted his nose and mouth.

"Let us begin, friends. My name is Woodruk. I was a member of the city watch and the last surviving member of the group that dispatched Warden Reddevek. Tixon B'gin sends his greetings, and you have my apologies for the strange precautions. As you are well aware, three of our last five meetings were infiltrated by an agent of the crown. More than thirty of our members have fallen to their treachery."

"I was told Tixon would be here tonight," said a man wearing a cape over the clothes of a merchant. He gestured at his face, where a similar purple mark stained his nose and mouth. "First, you make us brave the worst storm in a month, then you paint us in this strange substance."

"I agree," said a woman in a rain-soaked dress. "I would never have assumed such a risk for anything less. What guarantees can you give any of us that we aren't in peril right now?"

Woodruk nodded with understanding. "I understand your misgivings. You have all taken great personal risks not just in coming here, but in furthering our plans to overthrow the royals. It's only by the Taker's ill timing that our plans to assassinate the regent and the Baellentrells have failed in these past weeks. You ask for guarantees, so I'll tell you this. When you arrived, we barred entrance until each of you inhaled a puff of Eldrenol's solution."

The merchant rubbed at the staining covering his nose. "That's no guarantee at all. Eldrenol's solution is a useless, albeit expensive tincture carried by the Outriders."

"And why do our esteemed border guards provision themselves with such a costly item?" asked Woodruk.

The merchant folded his arms together and tilted his head in disbelief. "Preposterous. You think an abrogator wanders the streets?"

The woman lifted her chin. "Woodruk, are you suggesting that the person responsible for killing all our friends is an abrogator?"

Bryndor wasn't sure what to make of the conversation, but something in Ranika's bearing shifted. She staggered a few steps, then dropped to her knees. Woodruk walked over and flipped off her hat, then grabbed a fistful of her hair, blond spirals clenched between his fingers. He lifted her face for all to see. A purple stain of Eldrenol's solution covered her nose and mouth. Thin rivulets of nadir streamed about her cheeks, the oily black currents playing over her skin. In seconds, the nadir receded, vanishing without a trace.

Grind it, Nika. Why would you take such a risk? You could have obscured yourself in the shadows and none would be the wiser. Bryndor had no direct experience with Eldrenol's solution, but the Outriders had mentioned it alongside campfire conversations about veramanth. And if only a part of that misery was imparted by the purple staining, he guessed she was in for a rough night.

More than one person cried out with shock and alarm. "Taker's breath!" a man cursed.

"She may not look like much, but this girl is an abrogator," said Woodruk.

Ranika panted, then lurched forward and vomited between his boots. Woodruk slapped her across the cheek and withdrew a sword. "What I want to know, girl, is who sent you and why?"

Bryndor gathered zenith, collecting it in his core, but hesitated, unsure how to release rune fire without causing harm to his friend. As he held the power primed for release, some of the flow leeched across the runes on his forearm, and the strangest feeling of calm detachment settled across his mind. Something made him believe he should wait.

Ranika's shoulders shuddered, and at first, he thought she might be weeping, but he realized she was laughing. She leaned back on her knees and wiped blood-streaked drool from her mouth before another wave of retching overtook her.

"By the Giver. She's mad. Put her to the sword, Woodruk," said the merchant.

Woodruk nodded grimly and stepped forward. In the same moment, the convulsions caused Ranika to topple forward. But instead of spilling more vomit onto the floor, she lashed out faster than a striking snake and plunged her dagger through the man's boot. There was a moment of stunned surprise as the man stared at the ruby hilt protruding from his foot. He bellowed in pain, the shock of the attack—and the dagger—rooting him in place.

Ranika withdrew her blade, punched a hole through the tendon of the man's opposite heel, and then rolled back into the shadows. A staccato of crossbow bolts pincushioned the floor where she had crouched. More than one struck Woodruk's backside, and he collapsed to the ground.

Everyone in the room scattered, shouting cries of alarm and rushing for the door. Through Boru's vision, he saw a swirl of zenith gather on the balcony. Somewhere overhead, a zeniphile channeled, and layers of ice coalesced over the windows and front door. On the far side of the room, Ranika hammered the butt of her dagger against the iced barrier.

Bryndor signed to Boru, *Retrieve Ranika from the far side.*

The wolvryn loped off, and Bryndor focused the last seconds of his enhanced vision on Ranika. When she dropped below the window, he flared zenith across the runes on his shoulders. The intensity of the flow gathered into a dense globe of rune fire, and he hurtled it through the window. The blue flame streaked through the room to smash through the far window, decimating the icy barrier. He could just make out Ranika's astonished face before she dropped to the floor, recovered her hat, then scampered over the smoking window frame.

The twang of crossbows announced another volley, and Bryndor stepped to the side. Several bolts flew through the window, splashing into the mud, and more battered the interior walls. Someone from inside hollered, "Breakers up top, don't let her get away!"

Bryndor chewed on his lower lip. Another cascade of lightning scattered across the night sky, followed by booming thunder. *There's no help for it, and you'll not likely have better cover.*

He siphoned zenith across his runes once again and prepared to detonate rune fire from directly above the building. Before he could release the explosion, a figure dropped from an overhead window. Something clubbed the side of Bryndor's head, and he staggered back, flickering lights dancing in the periphery of his vision. Zenith dispersed across his runes in a chaotic fashion and the rune fire lost all cohesion, scattering as harmless streamers into the night sky.

His assailant's deep voice cut through the fog of pain. "If I had known a Baellentrell was going to crash our party, I would have brought friends."

Bryndor shook his head and reached up to his collar, removing a cold shard of ice. "You hit me with ice? You're a chiller?"

The man shrugged, and the delicate glow of zenith flared at his neckline. "We each have to use what gifts the Giver gives. Besides, if I never carry a weapon stained with blood, no tracker can ever find me after my task is complete."

Shards of ice formed in the man's grip, and he twirled them with casual dexterity.

"So, you've done this before? How many times?" asked Bryndor.

He sensed the man's feet change position. Bryndor shifted his shoulders, then stepped back and out of range as the chiller stabbed once high, a clear feint, before swiping low. Bryndor flowed out of the way and pushed at the man's wrist, deflecting the second strike. The scar on his shoulder and arm flared again, but he ignored the sensation and focused on the combatant. Even without Kaellor's endless training, he sensed the man's moves before he made them.

"It doesn't have to be this way. You can't win here. But you can leave now before it's too late," said Bryndor.

The chiller grunted and bared his teeth. "The breakers will sing songs about me. Mikkum the chiller, who iced the prince."

Mikkum flared a sheet of ice across the mud, but Bryndor leaped to the side, finding stable footing. The man flowed over the ice with a controlled slide, slashing again and lunging. Bryndor feinted a backstep but shouldered into the chiller, causing him to fall to his side.

As the breaker slid to a stop, he flung out shards of ice. Sensing the attack, Bryndor spun, avoiding the first three, but the last grazed his ear, leaving a burning pain.

Mikkum rose to his feet and produced two crystalline daggers. "I claim first blood!"

Bryndor shook his head and stepped to the middle of the alley. He glanced overhead, sensing the clatter of men on the rooftop. He growled in frustration and unsheathed his longsword.

"Were you in Stone's Grasp during the spring assembly?" asked Bryndor.

"Yeah, what of it!" Mikkum swirled his hands in an arc, and tiny crystals of ice gusted out, obscuring Bryndor's vision. Bryndor turned away, dropped to a knee, and pivoted, slicing forward for the attack he knew would follow. His blade rasped across a leather jerkin, but at the last second, he extended his wrists, feeling the metal bite into muscled flesh. Mikkum grunted as Bryndor cleared the sleet from his eyes.

He turned to face the man. The chiller held one hand to a gash along his flank. Even in the darkness, Bryndor could see blood staining the man's trousers. He watched as Mikkum attempted to stanch the wound with a plug of ice. The distraction allowed Bryndor to siphon zenith, gathering the familiar power of rune fire, preparing to give it shape and purpose.

"That's clever," said Bryndor. "You had a chance to leave the city in peace or join the fight against Tarkannen. But I told you all if you stayed, I would bring rune fire down on every last breaker."

Mikkum straightened, appearing to have recovered somewhat from his wound. "You know what I think? I think you royals talk too much."

Bryndor sheathed his weapon and looked over the chiller's shoulder in time to see Boru leap from the shadows. The wolvryn savaged a bite across Mikkum's head and chest, crushing the man's skull, then tossed the floppy corpse against the dilapidated building.

"And you should have brought more friends."

Without hesitation, Bryndor released a furious detonation of rune fire. He centered the eruption on the rooftop of the ruined church. In the flash of light, countless flaming bodies could be seen arcing up into the night sky. A deafening crack of thunder preceded the collapse of the structure.

The ensuing demolition lasted longer than he expected as massive burning timbers sagged, swayed, and finally collapsed into the building. Bryndor followed the initial detonation with a column of rune fire designed to both incinerate and deflect any debris. Despite the rain, roaring flames rose into the night sky.

Ranika's head appeared over Boru's shoulder. "I think you got them all, Bryn. We should probably go before anyone sees us."

He nodded once and signaled Boru to lead the way. They retreated through the shadows along the curtain wall. Bells rang out, summoning aquamancers to fight the flames. The wolvryn paused on a few occasions to allow people to run toward the disturbance. None of them bothered to search the shadows for Bryndor or his companions. Eventually, they reached the royal stables. Instead of approaching the castle entrance, Boru led them through the Timber Gate and deep into the Crown's Timber.

"Where are you taking us?" asked Ranika.

"Unless I miss my guess, you can't make yourself invisible, not yet anyway. I can't sneak Boru past the entry gates, and I would prefer the locals to think that lightning caused that fire. We could likely rest in an empty pen in the royal stables, but I'm not sure how safe even that is after tonight. There's a cluster of pine that can offer us a place to dry out. Then you and I are going to have a talk. And for Reddevek's sake, you're gonna listen."

Chapter Thirteen: In the Crown's Timber

The scent of woodsmoke lingered on the fur between Boru's shoulders. Nika huddled forward, absorbing the wolvryn's warmth as Bryndor led them deeper into the Crown's Timber. They left the sounds and smells of the Sprawl behind, retreating through the vast wood, the steady patter of rainfall drowning out all other sounds. Boru's agile gait rocked with a rhythmic motion, lulling her nearly to sleep. Yet the insidious effects of the toxin continued to grip her insides with involuntary cramping.

Her clothes, soaked by rain, clung to the small of her back, and cold rivulets trickled down her hips and thighs. She gave a brief thought to shifting her weight to the side—perhaps some of the water would run off—but her fatigue left her bereft of initiative. The circle breaker had called it Eldrenol's solution. Nika thought if she ever met Eldrenol, she would introduce him to the pointy side of her ruby-hilted dagger.

The notion made her reach a hand down to her hip, patting the dagger's hilt in reassurance. Memories of the day she swiped the weapon from Reddevek played in her mind. The images gave rise to a swell of emotions, like a bellows on hot embers, and her anguish flared. A flame of vengeance rose in her chest and caused her eyes to sting. She decided that once she recovered, she would sneak off and search through the wreckage of the old church where the breakers had gathered.

A timid echo in the back of her conscience reminded her she intended to stop after tonight's adventure. But Tixon remained as the last leader of the Lacuna. Just that last one, and then she might feel a sense of peace. Then, perhaps, she could rest.

Boru stopped and must have dropped his belly to the ground. The cessation of the swaying motion from the wolvryn's mind-numbing gait allowed her awareness to lift from that place between sleep and wakefulness. Bryndor had led them to a dense stand of pine, and the crisp aroma lightened her mood.

"We're here, Nika. You can slide down. It's not the suite at Laryn's mansion, but I'll get a fire going, and we can dry out," said Bryndor.

Ranika slid one leg around Boru's back and, with as much grace as a poorly balanced sack of potatoes, she flopped to the ground. Her muscles felt sluggish, but the nausea and abdominal cramps were fading.

She stood and pressed her cheek against Boru's jaw, massaging her fingers through the fur under his chin. "Thanks, Boru."

The wolvryn paced to the opposite side of the tree, then shivered, whipped, and rolled his fur back and forth, scattering rain from his coat. He returned, appearing fluffy and rejuvenated, settled on the ground, and rested his broad head on his front legs.

Like a distant thunderstrike, a silent, lone pulse vibrated across her core. Bryndor cupped his hands together and collected a tiny globe of rune fire. Intense cerulean swirls coalesced into a bright marble that illuminated his face. He dropped the glowing orb into a hole in the ground. A moment later, hearty flames licked up the sticks he must have placed within.

Ranika sensed the flows of nadir all around her, and thought to shift her vision to the shadows, but couldn't seem to grip the force or shape it to her purpose. She removed her moonstone and placed it on the ground. The crystal emitted a gentle light, and she studied their surroundings.

Under the canopy of massive pine trees, the patter of rain echoed all around them, but Bryndor's camp remained dry. He set three flat rocks like a small chimney over the fire hole, then grabbed a kettle hanging from a branch overhead.

"There's a stream nearby. I'll be right back," he said.

He returned and placed the kettle over the flame. A second hole in the ground, only two or three feet away, vented the smoke, making it almost undetectable to her senses.

"Red used to make that same fire hole. Did he teach you that trick?" she asked.

Bryndor peeled off his outer coat, hanging it over a branch that seemed positioned for the chore. He hung his sword and scabbard over a peg, the broken remnant of another branch. "I learned it in the Southlands. We were traveling the coastal plains and encountered a tribe of nomads. The winds make traditional campfires dangerous, and you get more direct heat with less wood. But I've seen the Outriders use the same trick."

"How long have you been coming here?" she asked.

Bryndor finger-combed wet bangs from his face and stared at the flames. Tendrils of zenith swam behind his eyes, and delicate gold runes flowed up his neck to the edge of his jaw, both affectations a reflection of his unshackled gift. Their appearance still surprised her. "A few weeks now, ever since the Reckoning. Lluthean and I have a separate camp up in the Great Crown too. We take the wolvryn out. They hunt, and we . . ." He lifted his gaze and shrugged.

"Escape," she finished.

A smile brightened his eyes, and he huffed a laugh. "I suppose that's true. I can only take so many introductions to esteemed members of the kingdom before my teeth ache."

An involuntary shiver rippled from her core, tightening her shoulder muscles. The fire hole made for an efficient means to heat the kettle but did little to take the chill out of the air. Rain continued to fall beyond their camp, and lightning streaked in random flashes across the sky. She removed her broad-brimmed hat and pulled her outercoat off, placing both on the branch next to Bryndor's jacket. She collapsed back against Boru and tucked her knees to her chest. Despite the wolvryn's warmth, her skin quickly became prickled and bumpy.

Bryndor stood and reached overhead to retrieve two large metal cups and a set of square tins. The first tin popped open to reveal fragrant tea leaves. He set that one on the ground. The other held strips of jerky. He tore off a hunk and handed her the rest.

"Th-th-thanks," said Ranika, the cold causing her jaw to vibrate involuntarily.

Bryndor turned with a frown. "You don't look so good. That purple stain around your nose . . . I heard the breaker say it prevents you from using nadir. And that weakens you, makes you feel sick?"

She tucked her lips under the neckline of her shirt to capture the heat from her breath. "It's getting better. I just need to dry out."

He nodded once, then lifted his chin. "Maybe we should have returned to the stables or back to your room at Laryn's estate. She could probably figure out a way to help you recover."

Her chin popped above her collar. "No. Please, n-no. I'm not ready yet. And you promised to keep my secret."

His head fell for a moment, but when he looked up, a softness flavored his expression. "That I did, but that was before I knew everything."

A sour feeling hollowed out Ranika's stomach at his words. Bryndor smiled and held up a hand gesturing for peace. "Easy, Nika. It's no matter. I am in no mood to have anyone discover that Boru and I were wandering the streets on a night when more breakers fell to rune fire. Kaellor might say that the appearance of such an act would undermine our attempts to unify the kingdom."

"I'm sorry I never told you before. About being . . . being an abrogator." The words left her mouth, but she couldn't believe she was saying them out loud. Abrogator. Just the mention of her dark power made her feel uneasy. She couldn't imagine what he must think of her now.

An oppressive weight settled over her chest, displacing any perception of the cold and damp. She felt like the little girl cowering under a merchant's cart in the dark streets of Callish as Lord Drassle approached.

The thrumming of her heartbeat drowned out the sound of the pattering rain and the grip of dread twisted her stomach, rekindling the residual effects of the toxin. Ranika swallowed the water gathered in her mouth and pursed her lips to slow her breathing. Time crystallized as the phantom of Lord Drassle staggered closer, each step an agonizing, inevitable amplification of her terror.

The ambient scent of pine vanished, replaced by the briny kiss of the port, the dampness of cobblestones and the metallic tang of fear on her tongue. Lord Drassle carried a bloodied stein in one hand. He held her moonstone high in the other, revealing her hiding place under the cart. She clutched at the shadows once again, willing the flows of nadir to envelop her in a cocoon of safety. But the dark currents continued to slip through her grasp.

Firm hands clutched her shoulders, lifting her from the depths of the dark memory. "Nika? Nika!"

Her gaze sharpened to their camp under the pine boughs, dispersing the memories. "I'm fine. Everything is fine."

She sensed his eyes on her and tried to slow the pace of her breathing. But the episode left her fingers and toes tingling, the prickly remnant of fear slow to vacate her mind.

Bryndor leaned forward on his knees, brow knitted with concern. "Taker's grip, your face. For a moment, you were covered in black veining. That's what nadir looks like?"

She bobbed her head up and down.

"Huh. Well, it's gone now."

Her gaze lingered on the pine needles matting the ground. The rain continued a gentle patter in the woods and Bryndor sat back, content to remain with her in companionable silence. Eventually, curiosity wore down her reluctance, and she lifted her eyes, expecting condemnation. His only response was a half-smile and shrug of the shoulders, and she nearly burst into tears at his silent acceptance of it all.

"I get the feeling you're not too sure what everyone will think if they know you can use nadir," said Bryndor.

Ranika blew warmth into cupped hands and spoke through the shivering. "Remember on the journey here, when I told you that being a monk was more Lluthean's thing?"

The smile receded from his eyes, replaced by a look of empathy. "I'm not the one afraid to reveal my gifts to the people who care about me. That sort of seems like something a monk might do."

A strange defensiveness welled up inside her. "It's not that easy and you know it," she snapped.

Bryndor bobbed his head from side to side. "I know. Sometimes confronting the truth, even about ourselves, can feel like the hardest thing to do. But what you're trying to do? Hiding who you really are from us? That's got to be some serious weight to drag around every day."

"Not all of us had a father or uncle to teach us about life's important lessons."

"That's fair," he said. "But it wasn't Kaellor who taught me that lesson. It was Rona."

She looked back to the ground, a wave of guilt replacing her anger. In the silence of their simple camp, the weight of his words seeped into her, soothing her apprehension. Yet still, like some long-imagined monster hiding under the bed in the darkness, her fear clawed at her, constricting her throat and preventing her from speaking.

In the periphery of her vision, she sensed motion and looked up to find him holding out a cup of hot tea. When their eyes touched, he winked. The gesture and his uncanny patience finally broke through. Ranika sighed. "I'm sorry, that was . . . I don't know why I said that, Bryn."

She sipped at the tea, warmed by the combination of sweet herbs and spices. "It's good," she said.

Bryndor nodded and sipped at his cup. "It reminds me of the Bend. It's not Rona's blend, but it's close." He took another sip, then nibbled on the inside of his lower lip.

"Ask away or tell me whatever . . . horrible thing you're thinking," said Ranika.

He blew air through pursed lips. "If you don't mind, how did it happen? How did you become an abrogator, exactly?"

"Exactly? I'm not sure. I was raised by my mother, never knew my father, but I think he was one of Tarkannen's abrogators."

Bryndor trilled a short whistle of astonishment. "That's a solid kick in each berry." He sipped at his tea but eyed her over the top of the cup, and the corners of his mouth turned up into a smile.

He held her gaze, waiting, and eventually she returned a soft smile. He cleared his throat. "It might surprise you to learn that I've known others who used nadir before. When we were with the Cloud Walkers, they could perform rituals to purify water or remove disease from inside a person. Laryn once said her greatest regret in leaving them was that she never had the chance to study how they accomplished what even the healers at Callinora could not."

"Hmm. Reddevek didn't teach me any of that. I don't suppose he could, though."

He tossed back most of his tea and set his cup down, rubbing at his arms. "Tell you what. If I can get us warmed up, would you consider telling me what you can do with your gift?"

Another involuntary shiver rolled across her shoulders. "Sounds like a fair trade."

Bryndor squeezed a fistful of his coat, water dripping from his fingers, and his eyes took on a distant expression. "This feels more like something Llu would try. If this doesn't work, I'll buy you a new coat."

He stood and chewed on his lower lip, then shook out his hands. Another lone pulse vibrated through her core, his power at once resonant and silent. A ball of zenith, bright and roiling, grew between his palms. Between outstretched hands, he shaped the orb into a saucer. Heat waves warped the light from her moonstone and radiated before him.

He ran the saucer up and down, even under the edges of his jacket. In moments, steam rose from the garment. He repeated the maneuver with her coat and hat before turning to face her, eyes fixed on the rune fire collected between his hands.

"I think I've got the hang of it. Stand up," he said.

Ranika held out a hand to assess how much heat emitted from the glowing blue disc. Currents of blue light swirled on its surface. It wasn't as hot as a raging bonfire, and it emitted a strange galvanic scent, but a significant amount of heat rippled forth. She struggled to her feet and turned in slow circles, lifting her knees high and even leaning forward to ruffle the spirals of her hair made kinky by the rain.

Eventually, she retrieved her hat and coat, now dry and, by the Seven, warm. With a sigh, she sat down.

"Better?" he asked.

"Much. It doesn't burn your hands?"

"No. It's strange. I can control the direction of the heat, but I can't feel it, not like I can feel an actual flame." Bryndor focused on his channeling, flickers of zenith reflected in his gaze. He ran the saucer of zenith up and down his pant legs, causing more steam to rise, then tried to palm the disc with one hand and pass it behind his back. Blue light flared, sputtered, and winked out. He chuckled. "It's just as well, I suppose. Might cause more harm than good passing that behind my backside."

Her eyes readjusted to the dim illumination from the moonstone and fire hole. Snuggled in a now-dry coat and hat, she relaxed against Boru's flank, the tension in her shoulders and back muscles finally easing.

"Alright, I'm impressed. What do you want to know?" she asked.

He nibbled at the corner of his mouth. "What kind of things can you do? I mean, that breaker tonight, Woodruk? He said you sent thirty of them to the Drift."

Ranika hesitated for a moment, uncertain where to begin. She searched his eyes, looking for any hint of anger, but found only genuine curiosity. "For the longest time, I never knew I was an abrogator. It wasn't until Red saw me pull my shadow that I began to understand it."

She continued to explain how, back in the Bend, she bet Reddevek that she could evade his tracking skills. That story led to others and brought up memories of her mother and using the ability to hide to survive life on the streets of Callish.

She recounted the attack by the greater feign and how, in a moment of desperation, her gift had unleashed coils of nadir that sprang forth to save Reddevek's life. "I didn't plan to use that much power again. I couldn't sleep for two days after that night on account of my head buzzing. That's what happens if I pull too much nadir.

"So, I try to smother it, keep it buried. At least I did until that day on the royal plaza, when that breaker announced that Red was dead. Then I think I sort of didn't care anymore what anybody thought. I used everything Red taught me: how to hide in the shadows, use my skill in the dark. One time, I found a group of breakers boasting about 'killing the warden,' and I got so angry. Before I knew it, I sent stingers at every last one of them. And I'm gonna keep hunting them until I find the last leader of the Lacuna, Tixon."

"What are stingers exactly?" he asked.

Visions from that night and others flickered through her mind. With an effort, she drew her focus to the ground. "See that pine cone?"

Without stopping to explain, she reached out to the nadir, pleasantly surprised that she could command the flows once again. A thin barb of condensed nadir materialized in her hand, and she flung it at the pine cone. A faint hissing announced the release of her skill as the pine cone shuddered and crumpled inward.

A lithe tendril of nadir rose from her forearm. She used the extension to retrieve the pine cone and dropped it into Bryndor's lap, then released her command of nadir. He sniffed hesitantly at the deformed cone. Finding nothing nefarious, he pulled at the edges, and the bits crumbled in his hands.

"So, stingers, then?" he asked.

"I don't know what anyone else calls them."

"Stingers seems about right." He shook his head in disbelief. "And 'pull your shadow?' Is that how you got the upper hand on Captain Oren?"

She channeled nadir once again, pulling her shadow and drafting the currents around her in a cocoon of obscurement. Bryndor's jaw fell slack only a moment, then he whistled again. He reached out a finger and poked her in the ribs, eyebrows lifting when his finger probed solid flesh. She giggled and allowed the currents to dissipate.

"So, what do you think?" she asked.

"Nika, that's . . . I don't have words to describe it."

Words popped into her head. Words like dark and cursed. Before she could add to the list, he continued, "But amazing is a good place to start. All the same, tonight they almost had you. You've got to promise me you'll stop."

She drew a breath and exhaled through her nose, shaking her head. "I told myself tonight was going to be the last time, but . . . I am so angry. Ever since Red died, I'm angry all the time. And I don't know how to feel anything else."

Bryndor stared off into the flickering flames. "There's nothing short of a touch from the Giver that will take away that pain, not right away. It does get better. I still get an ache in my gut when I think about Rona, about how she died. But in the last month, I've been able to tell some of her stories and remember the good times."

She grabbed a few pine needles and tossed them into the fire hole, watching as they ignited in flares of orange. Bryndor offered no further words, choosing instead to refill the teakettle from the stream. When the water boiled, he prepared two more cups of tea.

She cradled the fresh cup in her hands for more warmth, and they sat in silence for a time. Her shoulders wriggled once again into Boru's flank and the great wolvryn groaned a sound of pleasure, shifted onto his side, and surrounded her with his legs. "So, I figured out how you found me, with Boru and all. What I can't figure out is why you came looking."

Bryndor settled his coat over his shoulders and fed a few sticks into the fire. "Someone saw you, Nika."

The revelation might have caused her hands to shake earlier, but both her mind and body felt numb with fatigue now. She lifted the cup of tea, pouring her focus into savoring the taste and the aroma. Her lower lip ran over the metal rim, and she blew at the surface, then sipped.

"I didn't leave any survivors." She forced out the words, feeling far less certain than she sounded.

Bryndor sighed. "I sit in on all the regent's security briefings. Kae, Therek, and the others are well aware of a vigilante killing off remnants of the breakers. I think they intended to let you continue for a little while. But you left clues and a few witnesses a couple of nights ago back at the bakery in the Delve. Two young girls hid under a staircase. One of them said the attacker appeared out of nowhere, like she was invisible. Another got a glimpse of dandelion hair. I had a hunch that meant you."

"Those must have been the baker's daughters. Your uncle always says the Taker never makes it easy, but grind me. I never wanted them to see any of that. Did the girls think the attacker was a woman, or is that just you piecing it all together?"

He nibbled on the inside of his lip. "I think that was me, actually. But your hair is distinctive. Sooner or later, others are going to figure it out if you continue."

She knew the truth of his words. Though she had only been in Stone's Grasp a short time, she had never seen another with hair similar to hers. "What clues did I leave behind?"

"Nadir burns," said Bryndor.

Ranika thought she misunderstood him. The words made little sense. He must have read the confusion on her face.

"That's the word Laryn used. The bodies of most of the slain Lacuna, the ones you . . . dispatched, were recovered. Laryn studied their wounds, like that pine cone there. Your gift, the stingers, they leave a telltale hole. Kae and Laryn know it for a nadir burn."

The revelation might have shocked her, but something else Bryndor said offset her anxiety. He called her power a gift. Not a curse or a taint, as she so often thought of it.

"I get why you're doing what you're doing, Nika. I know the anger you're feeling. But you've got to know Red would swear oaths to the Taker if he saw how much danger you've placed yourself in." Instead of speaking with the voice of authority, Bryndor waited for her to look into his eyes, and he smiled. "You know I'm right. You . . . mattered to him, like no other."

Ranika resisted the urge to smile back and looked down at her lap, picking at a hangnail. "It's not just for Red."

"Alright, I'm listening. Tell me why."

"You and Llu are easy marks with the wolvryn. A few of them, a group of men from the watch mostly, planned to follow you on an outing. Some others had a plan to get jobs as servants in the castle and spoke of capturing Laryn for a ransom. In the bakery, I stopped that man from making poison muffins for the regent. There's still loads of people that mean you harm, just . . . not those folks, not anymore."

The crackling embers in the fire hole popped, shooting sparks into the night. The rhythmic pitter-patter of rain magnified to a droning chorus as the storm intensified. Somehow, their camp remained a dry oasis against the downpour. Compared to Lluthean, Bryndor kept his own council, and her words must have stirred a whirlwind of thoughts within him. Her restless fingers picked at a cluster of tiny seeds clinging to the side of Boru's ankle while she waited for him to return to the conversation.

Eventually, he jammed a few stout sticks into the fire hole, re-summoned rune fire, and set them to blaze. "Grind it. Life was easier in the Southlands. How many breakers have you killed, Nika?"

She shrugged. She never really bothered to keep count.

"North of twenty? North of thirty?" he asked.

"Maybe north of twenty, but all breakers, every one of them."

She studied his face as he considered her words. Nobody understood her like Red, but Bryndor's way of listening without making her feel judged? That was a kindness she could gamble with, and she had sworn oaths to Lutney's dice for less.

"Well, it's less than Llu and me, but significantly more than I expected."

He stared at another streak of lightning, then turned back. "I will probably never know everything you've done for me and my family. From saving Kae in the Bend, protecting us on the way here, what you did for Therek on the Reckoning . . . but Nika, you have to stop."

"There's just the one more, Tixon and then—"

"No more. It's already too much. Look, I know what it is to wake up and the first thing you think about is how you're going to kill your enemy. I still wrestle with the grip of that anger, and the man who killed Rona has wandered the Drift for a year now. I've got to believe that's not the life Red would want for you."

Ranika stared at the swirls of indigo and cerulean beneath her friend's eyes, and tears stung her own. "I want to hurt all of them, so bad."

Bryndor's head fell forward with a soft chuckle. "I know. Some days, I do too. But it never makes you feel better, not in the way you hope. And I think there are far better uses for your gift."

His words, so reminiscent of something Reddevek might say, caused the tears to brim over and her nose to flush. She wiped at her eyes with frustration. "It's what I'm good at. What else is an abrogator supposed to do in a kingdom of zeniphiles?"

"I don't know exactly, not yet. But I know someone who does."

"Who?"

"Laryn."

She shook her head from side to side. "You can't tell her, you promised."

"I'm not going to tell her, Nika. Giver knows, I'm . . . keeping my own secrets from them these days." He spoke the words with an air of self-recrimination. "Do you remember the day we swapped secret for secret?"

She did recall how he had earned a measure of her trust that day as they rode across Aarindorn. Anticipation of his proposal caused her to push back into Boru's warmth.

"Come with me and hear what I've got to say to Kae and Laryn. See for yourself how they react, and if it feels right, you should tell them. If anyone can help you use your talent for more than killing, it's them."

Chapter Fourteen: True to One's Nature

The embers of predawn light kindled beyond the mountain range east of Dernegia. Volencia rubbed a chill from her forearms and stilled her sigils of abrogation. After she and Tarkannen had dismantled the city's defenses, their horde of grotvonen and grondle poured through the breach in the walls, overwhelming the defenders with pure brutality. Where pockets of Dernegians had rallied, umbral unleashed whips and globes of nadir, further decimating the citizens.

On more than one occasion, she detonated bursts of her condensed nadir to overwhelm defenders wielding gem-infused shields and weapons. Now, in the strange half-light before dawn, her head slightly buzzing with the frenze, she studied the sigils on her forearms. Within the layering of the symbols, black and silver mercurial slicks swirled throughout the marks of abrogation.

She rolled her forearm palm up and traced a finger along a blue vein that coursed under her pale skin and up to her elbow. Soon enough, Tarkannen would reward her by inscribing another sigil for her to command, embellishing her talents in abrogation and increasing the power she could wield. The pain would be significant, but in the long run, a small sacrifice.

She adjusted her coin purse, made heavy by a mixture of gold and silver plundered from a nobleman. A streamer of smoke spiraled dark against the grey sky, a remnant of the absolute butchery carried out by the grotvonen horde. Even now the screams of the dying echoed down the streets as the Brognaus discovered the last of Dernegia's inhabitants and put them to the sword. The horde scurried about in the early light, some attracted by the screams, others eager to parcel out the spoils of war.

Most retreated into the cellars and halls of Dernegia, avoiding the direct light of the sun until Tarkannen forced a march.

For now, he left the horde to their grisly plunder, and had retired to a bluff to observe the conflict. Volencia considered joining him, but she desired to see the grondle up close in action. The half-man, half-bull creatures organized in crushes of nine or ten and made for impressive shock troops. A strong alpha could keep the crush from surrendering to bloodlust and coordinate their brute force to carry out the most damage. Add an umbral to coordinate and support the attack, and the units were more than formidable. Once the wave of grondle rolled over a defensive position, grotvonen poured in to efficiently butcher the remnants.

The clatter of lone hooves on stone announced the approach of an alpha, double-bladed battle axe bouncing on one muscled shoulder and the bloodied hindquarter of a horse hoisted over the other. Their eyes met, and the creature inhaled through the gill slits on his chest. His tail, once swishing, now stilled as he drew to attention.

Volencia tipped her chin in acknowledgment and the grondle genuflected, tilting its massive head and dipping the point of a curved ebony horn. The alpha adjusted the horse meat on his back, then proceeded down a rubble-laden street.

From the opposite direction, an elite grotvonen wearing fitted armor approached. The creature used a discarded Dernegian longsword as a walking stick to balance its herky-jerky clamber. They always appeared more graceful while prowling on their knuckles, but then the elite would have to relinquish its prize.

The alpha shouldered past the grot, then jolted to a halt, jerking its massive head around. In her time among the grotvonen, Volencia had learned much of their mannerisms. She had not developed the same understanding of the grondle, especially an alpha, but she felt certain that a mixture of surprise and anger laced the alpha's snort.

The smaller grotvonen strode on, intent on leaving the alpha behind. For its part, the alpha snorted again, this time speaking in its guttural tongue. When the grotvonen paid it no mind, the alpha dropped the horse flank to the ground, rolled its shoulders, and hefted its battle axe in both hands.

Volencia leaned forward, curious to see how the alpha might enforce its will on the lesser creature. The grotvonen blinked at her, oblivious to the offense it had given to the superior grondle, and continued its trek down the street. Something in the undaunted approach of the beast and the way the alpha pursued ignited a sense of danger, and she channeled nadir, priming the sigils on her arms.

The alpha trotted the few remaining steps, preparing to take the smaller creature to task, when the grotvonen elite shifted, morphing into a cloud of shadow. The grondle reared back in surprise and swept out in a clumsy swing with the battle axe, but the mass of shadow flowed low to the ground, under the arc of the blade, then reassumed the shape of the smaller grotvonen against a stone wall.

Using the momentum of its swing, the alpha charged, intending to pin the creature with its mass. The thing that was clearly not a grotvonen shifted again, becoming a shapeless mound of jellied shadow. Onyx tentacles slick with the telltale sheen of abrogation erupted to grapple the grondle, wrapping around its arms, neck, and front legs.

The grondle reared back, thrashing and pulling at the ropelike tethers. It tore at the bindings, but the more the beast struggled, the more the shadow creature seemed to gain purchase, creating two lashings for every one that the grondle ripped apart. The alpha threw itself against the stone wall and lurched several paces, clearly intending to shear away its attacker.

Shifting again, the shadow mass found safe purchase between the grondle's muscled forelegs. In moments, the alpha grunted, rasped, then collapsed to the ground. A cloud of dust rose as the beast continued to thrash, grating its curved horns on stone. Volencia leaned forward with fascination as the shapeless substance seeped into the fenestrations on the grondle's chest. A pitiful mewling groan escaped the alpha's throat as it shuddered several seconds and kicked a hind leg in staggered repetition. The death throes lasted more than a minute, but eventually, the massive beast lay still.

Volencia drafted a defensive mesh of nadir between herself and the grondle corpse, then sent a probing tendril forward. Just as she prepared to make contact, the alpha jerked its head, then rose to all fours, appearing bewildered and staggering about with all the grace of a longshoreman thoroughly marinated with resco.

The possessed alpha turned a clumsy circle, studying its surroundings. Steam fumed from its gill slits and the bull snout as it searched the air, inhaling and exhaling with labored, wheezy breaths. Recognition or orientation seemed to settle in, for the grondle lifted its snout to stare directly at her. Where before the alpha's gaze had held cunning and understanding, along with an awareness of its surroundings, now the pitch-black orbs stared ahead with all the expression of a snake. It cocked its head, considering her a moment, then took a step forward.

"That's close enough," she said, then unleashed three lashings of nadir: two cemented the beast's front hooves to the ground and a third coiled around its humanoid torso, wrapping all the way up to its snout. The alpha made no effort to resist her tethers, instead appearing to inspect the lashings and eventually lifting lifeless eyes to meet hers.

When she had contended with grondle before, her lashings abraded against coarse hair and corded muscles, and yet, underneath her bindings now, she sensed the presence of nadir as the thing that had taken up residence inside the grondle probed at her restraints.

"Can you understand me? Produce my speech?" she asked.

"It hasn't had time to assimilate." Tarkannen's voice surprised her, but she maintained her bindings.

"You know what this is? It's inside the grondle."

"I sensed as much. You should release your bindings. Some of the denizens from the Drift can use the . . . intimacy of such tethers against you." Tarkannen tilted his head to the meshwork of her lashings. "Can you feel it? Even now it sends probing tendrils back along your lines of nadir. If they reach you, it will have the ability to overpower your senses. Release the nadir, Volencia."

As he spoke the words, she became aware of a subtle corruption leeching through her connection, like the realization that one has bitten into a morsel of rotten food, affecting the texture but not the taste or smell. The awareness of the intrusion caused her to cleave the restraints. Her lines of force dissipated, but wispy threads of nadir, like invasive filaments of spider silk, billowed out from the creature. The thing inside the grondle had already begun to seek her out through the connection.

The realization left her feeling vulnerable for the first time in years. She allowed herself only a moment of reflection, then squashed the feeling. The curiosity that had caused her to observe the interaction between the grondle and this creature from the Drift withered under the intensity of self-deprecating anger. "How can we kill it if it feeds off nadir?"

Underneath a tangle of sigils, Tarkannen's forehead creased, just for a moment, but enough to betray his concentration. "I . . . used to know. It's one of the things I lost when I crossed back from the Drift." He cocked his head, studying the ataxic movement of the grondle as it staggered in a slow, drunken circle, its tendrils of nadir reaching out.

"Mursk," he muttered, then nodded to himself. "That's what they were called. Something of a distant relative to a feign but with much less agency. They are more like the homeless crabs that wander the ocean floor in search of empty shells to inhabit. Only they consume the host."

His face, a shifting myriad of sigils, seldom betrayed his thoughts or mood, but it seemed evident that he was struggling to sift through memories. After a time, his expression sharpened, focus returning to his eyes. "I think I recall now."

She sensed a flutter in the currents of nadir as he siphoned the force of abrogation, empowering his sigils. A dense sheet of darkness coalesced before them, hanging in midair. She watched as he folded the substance in on itself, then rolled it into a tube, stretching it until it took the shape of a javelin. How he accomplished the task without appearing to have a direct connection, like a tentacle, was a question for another day. For now, she remained silent, observant, learning.

Tarkannen propelled the spear of nadir at the possessed grondle, but instead of searing into its flesh or appearing to cause pain, the weapon seemed to dissolve into the chest of the beast.

"You remember the lessons in pithing the gourd, how nadir can be used to dissolve and burrow through bone? I've folded the nadir back on itself and imbued it with a property of saturation. Even now, my construct unravels and penetrates the mursk, but since it does not destroy or cause anything resembling pain, the creature welcomes the intrusion like a gift of raw power. But the mursk is a parasite and cannot escape the truth of its nature. Part of it sees the gift of nadir as something to be devoured, regardless of the consequences."

In affirmation of his words, the mursk's sensory tendrils curled inward and darted into the flesh of the grondle corpse. Though the beast remained upright, rigid muscles spasmed in tetany. Islands of jellied, black stains appeared on the flank, chest, and neck of the beast, as if the corruption inside was seeping out. The patches wriggled, betraying the activity of the mursk underneath, growing and fusing together. The tissues dissolved into oily black slicks, and all at once, the carcass collapsed to the ground, a mass of partially digested meat barely resembling the proud alpha.

Volencia resisted the urge to kick a boot at the decomposed flesh. "Is it . . . is the mursk gone?"

"Yes. Its hunger to consume exceeds any sense of self-preservation," said Tarkannen.

"How did that thing get here? I was vigilant in guarding against any contamination during the Rite of Sundering," said Volencia.

He stared out across the ruins of Dernegia for a time. "Are you religious, Volencia?"

"Not particularly. I understand that we can control nadir and use it as a tool. I don't think the Giver or the Taker placed designs on what we do or the choices we make. That we do it at all is a reflection of free will. You stripped away my runes and imbued me with sigils. Not the Taker."

"True enough, but there is something out there, beyond the veil that separates our world from the Drift. Something directs the forces of zenith and nadir to . . . struggle for dominance. Sometimes, the currents of nadir cause tiny tears in the barrier. Those defects last only brief moments, sutured up by whatever governs the two forces. Sometimes . . . something slips through."

"Does our use of nadir make these tears more likely? Should we expect more of those things then?"

"Our employment of nadir is no more a factor than spitting into the ocean. But we should expect more creatures from the Drift. We were fortunate that the mursk is a thing of instinct, somewhat mindless. If this were a feign or worse, a greater feign, it would have known to avoid contact with us until it grew in strength. I should not like to contend with a greater feign once it had time to establish itself in our world."

"Is there a way to reinforce the barrier or prevent the tears from occurring?" she asked.

He turned and offered her a rare, soft smile. The gesture was reassuring, but with the way sigils slid around his mouth and lips, it was also a bit intimidating. "Yes. Confluence. During the Cataclysm, when Eldrek Baellentrell unified the zeniphiles of Karsk, he nearly managed it. But he could never become the Eidolon and so instead, he . . . commingled what I can only describe as the most colossal deluge of zenith with an equal measure of nadir to seal up a breach in the veil."

"I sense a but coming in here."

"But, the confluence, the . . . merging of both zenith and nadir . . . it was incomplete, imbalanced. Where Eldrek gave over the full measure of the power he commanded, an abrogator named Mogdurian withheld some of his power. The resulting imbalance nearly destroyed the world, but the breach was patched."

"And now that patch is what, fraying?" she asked.

"Something like that," said Tarkannen. He turned and began to walk deeper into the ruins of Dernegia. "I know you have more questions. But the presence of a mursk means that time is not on our side in this, not anymore. Come, let us gather the umbral. They can be useful in detecting any creatures like the mursk or worse, should anything else slip through the veil."

Volencia stifled her desire to press for more answers, but she understood by his body language that Tarkannen's focus lay elsewhere. His time in the Drift had altered him. His sigils seemed to have developed an autonomy, shifting at times without his conscious thought, or so it appeared to her. Now, at least, she understood a bit more of his motivation and why he always seemed too preoccupied to engage her in long conversations about the specifics of their mission.

If Eldrek Baellentrell couldn't manage confluence, how can you, and what happens to the rest of us if you gamble with the Taker and lose?

The sound of metal rasping against stone drew her attention. Tarkannen stabbed two of the three rods of refined nadir into the ground. The nadrean's cobblestoned surface drank the light. Where her eyes fixed, thin, shimmering wisps unfurled, like smoky vapors of power. Silence pressed in, thick and heavy, a damp shroud muffling her senses. The acrid smoke from the fires razing Dernegia faded, and the dust settled, bereft of any wind.

"Can you feel it?" he asked.

"Yes, they seem to suppress everything."

Tarkannen dipped his chin once, acknowledging the truth of her statement. He retrieved all three nadrean rods, clutching them in a fist. Instantly, a portion of the oppressive weight lifted, and she gasped a full, easy breath. "I placed sigils along the shafts. The full measure of their power activates only when wedged into the ground. Together, two of these rods should be enough to disrupt winds along the coast northeast of Kreeg. Within weeks, the region will fall to drought."

"You mean to weaken any resistance along our trek to Aarindorn?"

"Yes, but it's not the physical resistance I care about. Do you understand?"

Without a gentle breeze, the air became an oppressive wet blanket around them, and her veil clung to her face. She removed the covering, expecting relief, but found none. She knew he expected an answer and turned her mind to the question. "When drought sweeps across the region, people will not starve this year, but it will weaken them and pull all their attention into stockpiling resources and supplies. Faced with scarcity, we can . . . offer them the promise of salvation through the plunder and spoils of war."

"I watched this world from my confinement in the Drift, and while I don't recall everything I learned during my time there, I did learn this: people will justify visiting all manner of atrocities on their neighbors if they become hungry or thirsty enough. And when we convince them that the northern plains of Karsk struggle while the mountain kingdom thrives, they will be all too eager to join our ranks."

Volencia considered the proposition. "A drought will push people to search for salvation, and that is the bait, but it needs something more to set the hook, I think . . . propaganda whispered among the plains people about how the mountain kingdom stole a resource."

"That's why Verrador and others work to prepare the way. By the time we reach Kreeg, the hearts and minds of the common man should be well marinated with stories of the witch-king of Aarindorn and his dark minions," said Tarkannen.

She began to see the scope and breadth of his plan, admiring both the irony and the manipulative cunning involved. Where her games had led the people of Sifter's Valley to their doom, his plans would enslave an entire region to their bidding.

"Can you see it now?" he asked.

"Yes. But unless we intend to wait another year for your plan to unfold, we need the drought to begin as soon as possible."

"That is where you come in," said Tarkannen.

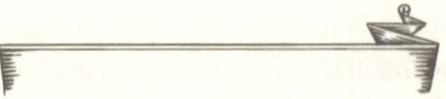

Chapter Fifteen: Shadowbeasts and Abrogators in the Light of Day

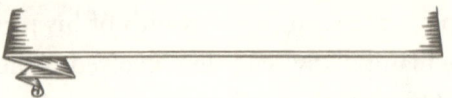

Kaellor rasped calloused hands over the polished stone balustrade and stared up into the night sky. A branching silver vein ran through the stone, emitting a reassuring vibration that the castle ward remained intact. He studied the horizon alone on the private balcony outside the royal suite he and Laryn occupied. From his vantage point, the half-moon of Baellen shimmered over Lake Ullend. A lush breeze gusted off the Great Crown, scalloping the watery reflection and promising rain in the days ahead.

The volatile aroma of resco lifted to his awareness, and he turned to see Laryn holding out a glass of the amber liquid. She leaned a shoulder against the doorframe and swirled the glass, eyebrow arched with a mischievous expression. He stepped close and retrieved the drink, inhaled the smoky vapors, then took a curious sip. "That's smooth, but two fingers love? You've either got some bad news to share or I'm in for some adventure. So, which is it?"

Laryn smiled and retrieved the glass, taking a sip herself. "The return to Aarindorn has wound you up tighter than a first-year acolyte at Callinora. Can't a lady enjoy a cocktail with her love before setting out on high adventure?"

She wrapped an arm around his waist. He tapped his chin on the top of her head. "Hmm, sounds like you're trying to numb the pain of separation, but I'm sure you'll have more fun out there than we will back here. You won't miss me that much."

He felt the rhythm of her soft laugh. She took another sip, pressed the glass into his hand and embraced him with both arms. "Oh my prince, I wish a brief separation was our only concern."

They stood in companionable silence, studying the skyline. Eventually, she leaned back to look him full in the face, one eye glittering blue, the other flecked with shards of red. "What road do your troubled thoughts wander?"

He sighed. "Two roads, actually. The first is a path of memory. Japheth and I stood out here when he told me he planned to propose to Nebrine. It was a night much like this one. He was so . . . full of anticipation. Nervous, to be sure, but unfettered by any sense of trepidation."

"Those were good days. These are too. We just have to work a little harder to see the Giver's blessings. What was the second?"

"I caught myself reaching for the thrum of the castle wards, making sure that they remain whole and intact. I suppose it reminded me of the way you always check my pulse before drifting off to sleep."

"Can't you sense the flows of zenith through your gift?"

His cheeks warmed, either from the resco or his mirth. "I could say the same of you when you check my pulse or listen to my heartbeat. There is something reassuring in the physical, tactile measure of a thing."

"True enough," she said.

He took another sip of resco, savoring the notes of the drink as the volatile liquid left his tongue. He offered her the glass, but she declined, stating, "One sip cures the rot and two makes you brave. I think I've had my due for the night."

The distant thump of a knock on the door interrupted his reply. "Expecting anyone?"

Her brows lifted in an expression of denial. Kaellor walked back through their suite to the door and siphoned zenith, priming his runes, but Bryndor's voice eased his wariness.

"Kae? It's me, Bryn. I'm with Nika. Can we come in?"

With a puzzled expression, he turned to Laryn and signed, *It's Bryn and Nika. What are they doing here at this hour?*

Laryn arched an eyebrow and stifled a smile while signing, *"I don't know, so why don't you let your nephew in and see?"*

"Right." Kaellor opened the door and welcomed them in.

Bryndor stood in the threshold, eyes trained on the floor. "Sorry for the late hour. Ranika and I were talking about the expedition to deliver Reddevek's ashes and things and well . . . before you all set out, we thought there are some things that you should know."

Bryndor was always self-effacing, but something in his bearing seemed even more earnest than usual. "No apologies needed between family. That includes you, Nika. Come, let's sit."

They situated themselves in chairs at the small round table he and Laryn used for private meals. The stiff furniture had seen little use since they began occupying the royal suite. Kaellor tapped the rim of the glass of resco. "Can I offer either of you a drink?"

Ranika shook her head and removed her oversized hat. The braids she wore for the funeral rites of Japheth and Nebrine had lasted only a few days, and now her distinctive hair was kinked with even more spirals than usual. "None for me, thanks."

"Thanks, Kae. I think I'll wait," said Bryndor as he eyed the glass. "On second thought, maybe two sips worth, for bravery and all?"

Kaellor retrieved a glass and the decanter of resco, poured a finger, and slid the glass to his nephew. They sat in silence for a moment while Bryndor took his first sip of the amber spirit. He frowned, blew air through pursed lips, then tried to mask a grimace. "I'll go first, if you don't mind."

Ranika shrugged indifference. However, Bryndor's statement hinted that each of them had something to reveal this night.

"Alright, so Kae, Laryn . . . both of you. There are some things you should probably know about Llu and me. On one of our hikes with the wolvryn this week, we ran into a bit of trouble in the Great Crown."

Kaellor looked to Laryn, prepared to react with an "I told you so," but she lifted fingers from the table and said softly. "Tell us about it, Bryn. We're listening."

And so, he wove a tale that bordered on the fanciful, describing an encounter with a creature from the Drift. Kaellor might have disbelieved parts of his story, except that embellishment was more Lluthean's thing. Bryndor explained how the creature had appeared, how it could portal about and, finally, how they sent it back to the Drift. He offered a theory that the creature had caused the stampede and left behind a swath of scorched prairie on the Balladuren ranch. He then concluded by explaining how Lluthean had discovered something of an ability to slide on currents of wind.

Kaellor studied his nephew. He had so many questions about the creature, how it attacked them, and how they dispatched it. But he set those to the side and focused on Bryndor. The young man had revealed the information with eyes cast into the glass of resco. There was no pride in the revelations; rather he seemed to retreat into the memory of the event, and when he finished, only slowly lifted his gaze.

Kaellor resisted the urge to speak his mind, instead gathering the chin hairs of his beard between thumb and forefinger. He looked to Laryn, who tilted her head toward Bryndor as if to say, "Give him the Giver's peace." At last, he cleared his throat. "Help me understand, Bryn. I'm missing something. Why . . . why didn't you feel you could tell me any of this? It sounds like you both acquitted yourselves quite well, yet you—I don't know. It's like you think you did something wrong."

Bryndor frowned and considered the question. "I think it's this place, Kae. The people, the customs, the expectations . . . there was nothing like any of it in the Southlands, and sometimes it feels like I need to escape into the mountains to get away from it all. When I'm up there, I can look back at it all and, I don't know, breathe easy?"

Bryndor spoke the words with unvarnished honesty, and Kaellor understood the sense of loss carried in the undertone of the statement: loss of the familiar, loss of the comfortable, the simple loss of all their freedoms in Journey's Bend.

He found himself nodding. "You were afraid to tell me because you knew I would resist your treks into the Great Crown. But it's my fault, Bryn. I didn't have enough time to prepare you for all of this. Before your mantle began to fracture, I thought we would live out our days in the Southlands. After our windfall from the king of Hammond, it was a foregone conclusion. One moment we were floating along on easy currents, the next our lives diverted to a different fork in the river, and we've been tumbling down rapids ever since."

Bryndor's shoulders relaxed, and he smiled for the first time since entering the suite. "It led us to the wolvryn and you to Laryn. We never would have met Nika. It's not all bad, but some days, it's a lot."

"I know it is, son. And the sad thing is that I'm going to drag you through more of it. It's the only way we can get you ready for the stresses of the crown. But, from now on, I want you to know you can tell me these things, and I promise to do my best to listen."

Their eyes met, and Bryndor nodded in agreement. "I know, Kae. I will."

Kaellor leaned back in his chair, stretching stiff muscles, and shifted his attention to Ranika. The girl sat with her chin resting on her forearms, which were folded across the table. He splashed a small amount of resco into his glass and pushed it across the table to rest before her. She studied the drink a moment before grabbing it and tapping the base on the table. Kaellor obliged, poured a little more, then stoppered the decanter. Ranika sat back and took a small sip of the spirit. Her expression remained neutral. She pursed her lips, took another sip, then slid the glass back to Kaellor.

"I think you might need this more than me, both of you more likely," said the young woman.

"Hmm, alright," said Kaellor. He reached for the glass, but Laryn grabbed it first. She mimed a toast, winked at Ranika, and took a sip, then passed him the glass. He repeated the gesture.

Ranika sat straight and tried to tuck an unruly spiral of hair behind an ear, but it sprang back out. She shook her head as if to say, "Why do I even bother?" Her eyes searched the table, and she looked to Bryndor, who offered her a reassuring nod and smile. Instead of bolstering her confidence, Ranika seemed to shrink back into herself. She sat on her hands, shrugged her shoulders, and squeezed her eyes tight.

Laryn reached across the table and laid a reassuring hand on Ranika's forearm. "Nika, whatever it is, you don't have to tell us if you're not ready."

Ranika stared into her lap, her inner turmoil obvious. Kaellor resisted the urge to prod her to speak. Instead, he took a cue from his wife, took a breath, and tried to understand the young woman. He had never seen her appear so defeated. Something in her wilted appearance, bereft of the bubbly spirit that had accompanied them all the way from the Bend, pinched at his heart. With all the responsibilities thrust upon them in the last months, he felt now the weight of their neglect of the young woman, and he began to wonder what obstacle the Taker had placed in her life.

Ranika mumbled into the table, "I don't think I can say what I need to say if you're looking at me."

Kaellor tried to lighten the moment by swiveling on his chair in dramatic fashion, turning his back and crossing a leg. He said over his shoulder, "Is this better? If you prefer, I could rustle up a few zenith seeds. You and Bryn could stay here while we retire to the balcony."

"I'm about the last person in the world who could use a zenith seed," said Ranika. "You can turn around, Kae."

Kaellor swiveled back and Ranika set her elbows on the table, then dropped her forehead into her palms. "Alright, here it is. You know all those dead breakers, the ones with the black holes burned in them? It's me. I'm the abrogator."

Her words caused Laryn to lean forward, eyes squinted, dissecting their meaning. Kaellor assumed he'd misunderstood and played her words over in his mind. Nothing in the delivery or inflection hinted at humor. Yet the statement seemed so outrageous that he couldn't hide a smile, still expecting a joke. "What?"

"It's me. Nadir burns, killing the Lacuna, it's all been me," she said.

Kaellor's mind raced to catch up to the reality of the revelation as he searched Bryndor's face for confirmation, but his nephew was focused on Ranika with an empathetic expression. As usual, Laryn found her voice before he did. "Is that how you were able to come to Therek's defense and dispatch Captain Oren?" she asked.

Ranika nodded. "Yes. Red trained me to use it to protect people."

"And that wasn't the first or the last time," said Bryndor.

Bryndor's honest interjection sobered Kaellor's thoughts to the reality of the conversation. In moments, he sorted numerous experiences, reordering his assessment and recollection of Ranika's accomplishments. He'd assumed all this time that she had survived the streets of Callish on nothing more than wit and guile and no small amount of the Giver's blessing. Reddevek had mentioned that he had schooled her in woodcraft, stealth techniques, and the basics of hand-to-hand combat. Kaellor never thought to search for anything more than that in the young woman.

"Well? Say . . . anything?" Ranika pleaded.

Kaellor turned to Laryn, who still had a hand on Ranika's forearm. Again, he resisted the urge to react and instead took a cue from his wife's bearing. She stared in wonder at the young woman. He exhaled through his nose and rested his hand on his wife's. "Nika, we owe you an apology. I know what it feels like to feel isolated and . . . different from everyone else around you. I'm ashamed that I never realized how difficult things might be for you, especially since Red's passing. Thank you for trusting us with your secret."

His words clearly caught her off guard, and she shook her head, befuddled. "What?"

Kaellor couldn't help but release a soft laugh. "Nika, you saved my life in the Bend, Red's too. Then you gave the warden, my dear friend, some of the only moments of joy he's ever known. And in all that time, I'm not sure we ever really saw you. But if you can tell us more, we'll listen. It's how we should treat a member of our family, and it's the least you deserve."

A low-pitched screech broke the silence as she pushed back in her chair, stood up, and paced around the table. Ranika fanned her face, shoulders heaving in sobs, and eventually fell into Kaellor's arms. Her reaction surprised him more than a little, but he recovered quickly and held her close for a time, until she regained her composure. When it felt right, he relaxed the grip of his embrace, coughed to clear the swollen feeling that had gathered in his throat, and rubbed at his nose where a sprig of kinky hair had tickled him.

Ranika giggled and wiped her eyes dry. "Sorry."

She returned to her seat, and Kaellor offered her another sip from the glass of resco. Ranika shook her head and shivered. "No, thank you. That stuff is awful, and it makes my nose burn."

"I couldn't stand it much when I was your age," said Kaellor. He swirled the glass. "Do you think you can tell us more about your abilities?"

"Sure," she said and so began a conversation that carried well into the predawn hours. Once she started, the stories tumbled out like a messy confessional. Laryn redirected the young woman with questions about how she channeled nadir, what it felt like, and its limitations. Kaellor sat back, too engrossed in the details of her experiences to ask his own questions.

Ranika described how Reddevek's death had set her on a path of revenge, and how her gift manifested when she felt threatened. Any feelings of alarm regarding her lethal skill were replaced by the revelation that Lacuna sympathizers still worked to harm his friends and family.

A full-mouthed yawn interrupted his next question, and the contagious reflex spread to everyone in minutes. He labored to control a second yawn and finally held his hands up in submission to the late hour.

"I think we've all had enough for one night," said Kaellor. "We can pick up the conversation tomorrow evening. For now, Nika, I have a few requests."

She bobbed her head once and pushed a knuckle into her mouth to stifle a yawn.

"You've trusted us with the secret of your gift, and we will keep it between us. But Bryndor is right, Red would be distressed if he knew how much danger you placed yourself in, so no more hunting Lacuna, not by yourself anyway. You've done more than enough. The last thing is, we want you to move up here into the royal suites. You can still come and go, and the corner room has window views of both the city and the sunset over the mountains."

Ranika straightened up at his suggestion, but Laryn cut in. "It's not for you, Nika, it's for all of us, together. We don't have as much free time as we had hoped for and can't often get to the manor house. This way, maybe we can start to be the family you deserve."

Either the physical fatigue of the late hour or the emotional stress of the evening eroded any resistance she might have offered. Ranika stood and grabbed her hat. "Lead the way."

"Bryn, would you show her to the corner suite? It's the one next to yours. The locking placard will release under your touch. I'll show you both how to set it to recognize Nika tomorrow," said Kaellor.

He ushered them out and turned to find Laryn standing, hands wedged to support her low back and stretching. "You handled that much better than I expected. And you used my line."

"Starting out with a variation of 'help me understand' does sort of set a different tone for conversations. I suppose you could say that I've learned a thing or two from you about listening."

She stepped in and gave him an embrace. "We need to get to sleep."

"We need to talk about everything. How are we going to safely train her? Is she dangerous?"

"She is obviously quite dangerous, but not to us," said Laryn. "When we returned here and you set the castle wards, were they set to thwart all abrogators?"

"Giver, I hadn't thought of that. When I . . . gave definition to the barrier, I had Tarkannen and his minions in mind, maybe even the umbral, anyone who would bring us or the kingdom harm. What would have happened if I had barred all abrogators? This . . . changes everything."

She stepped away and pulled him by the hand to the bedchamber. "It changes nothing, love. Tomorrow the sun will rise. You and Bryn will work through a slate of petitioners while Llu and I prepare to depart with Reddevek's ashes. I can think of several ways that allow us to leave in relative secrecy."

"Taker's bite. After everything we've learned tonight, not just Ranika but Bryndor's tale about that thing in the Great Crown, you must know that it's not safe to travel."

"I think all of it will make more sense after a good night of sleep. Better that we deal with shadowbeasts and abrogators in the light of day."

He nodded. Once again, she had gently guided him to the truth of things. He set his concerns for Ranika to the side and thought again of Bryndor's struggles. Something in the combination of the late hour, the resco, and the night's revelations settled on him with an oppressive weight.

Laryn sighed, and concern stole across her face. "Kae, what is it?"

He swallowed hard, not for the first time that night. "We've always been stronger together. But I've been so caught up in everything that I failed to see that he was floundering. Promise me you'll always remind me to see them first, before the kingdom, before the politics, before Tarkannen and anyone else in our path. Don't let me ever forget to see our family first, Laryn."

Without words she smiled, nodded, then inclined her head to the bedchamber, where neither of them found sleep.

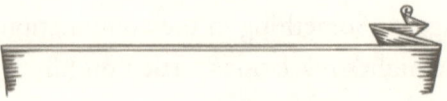

Chapter Sixteen: A Formidable Company

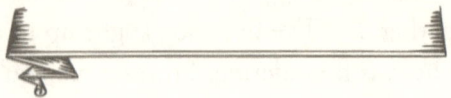

F ather was right—there is something miraculous about Aarindorn, or maybe it's the collective union of all the different zeniphiles, but when one remains within the confines of the kingdom, the ability to channel zenith is replenished at rates that far exceed what we experienced before we settled here. My brother, Neldrek, theorized that we are all connected, and where we gather, we magnify both the gift and the ability to recover.

I don't know that I fully agree, for I have patrolled the Borderlands in my day with more than thirty of our kin and not felt the same strength to channel as when I return home. Perhaps another will solve the mystery after the Giver has swept up my ashes.

At any rate, the last foundation stones of the curtain wall were set this year. This massive undertaking, directed by the artisans in the mason's guild, is supposed to allow the wards triggered by Father's statue to effectively shelter Stone's Grasp. I can't say that I understand it all, but Queen Brekka assures me she can sense that the artisans' creation will advance our collective security. I do wonder, though; what does it say about our world that we must place so much emphasis on our defense?

—The Tome of Nivosh, 75 PC, translated by Ksenia Balladuren

LLUTHEAN LIFTED A GLOWING orb above Neska's shoulder to better search the end of the secret tunnel. The petrified wolvryn eye cast enough light to dissipate the shadows where the passageway resolved to solid stone. Though he and Bryndor had frequented the secret exit several times since first discovering its location, Bryndor was usually the one who led them through the stone corridor, always so eager to escape to the high places in the Great Crown. *I suppose if I were expected to wear that particular pair of boots, I might look to escape a bit more myself.*

A silver seam in the stonework thrummed at his touch and he followed the pulse as it streaked forward to merge with a dense cluster of veins. The latticework flared, revealing a pattern of delicate blue lines not unlike broken glass. Lluthean placed his hand over the cluster. The surface of the stone bumped out in what could be construed as a placard, he supposed, but seemed more like an imperfection to Lluthean's consideration.

"Everyone ready?" asked Lluthean. He turned to search the faces of those he accompanied. Ranika stood behind him in the secret corridor leading out of the castle. She shifted the strap of a pack over her shoulder, adjusting her cargo, the urn holding Reddevek's ashes. After patting the object with a reassuring thump, she nodded her readiness.

Behind Ranika, Kaellor glowered in the shadows. Though his uncle made no open remarks, Lluthean knew by the set of his jaw and the way he fiddled with the silver streak of beard in the center of his chin that their departure was leaving him unsettled. His uncle had gifted Lluthean with the wolvryn eye the day before. Bryndor carried its match. But that gesture of goodwill was as much as Kaellor could manage this morning. Laryn must have sensed it as well. She shook her head at Kaellor's angst, patted the side of his jaw, and stepped in for an embrace.

"There's more danger lurking in the halls of Stone's Grasp than up in the Great Crown. We'll be back before you know it," she said. "Besides, if my Mirrare, Nika, and Llu aren't enough, we have Neska to keep us safe."

At the mention of her name, Neska craned her neck back once, toward where Bryndor and Boru stood waiting. Lluthean pressed his cheek to hers and said in a soft voice, "I know you don't like to break up the pack, Nes. But I have to go, and I need you."

Neska swished her tail and opened her jaw with what he knew to be a gesture of acceptance. Lluthean stood straight. "Right, then. Let's be off. We have a small hike ahead of us before the rendezvous with the Mirrare."

He rested his palm on the placard and siphoned a trickle of zenith, then ushered the flow into the dense collection of veins in the stone. A gentle vibration carried through his boots as currents of zenith flared through the silvery veining that spanned the end of the corridor. Soundlessly, the stone shifted, receding into the walls as if made of hot wax. Light spilled into the passageway, accompanied by a gentle gust of cool air carrying the scent of pine.

He hadn't realized until that moment how the scent of wolvryn lingered in the passageway. Neska and Boru often retired to the chamber, preferring the quiet solitude found deep under the ancient stones to the bustle of the city above. A set of vestek antlers marred by tooth marks lay on the ground, and dust balls of wolvryn fur tumbled across the floor. He sighed and rattled restless fingers against his thigh, hoping that his brother wouldn't notice that he had neglected to clean out the area last week.

Lluthean pocketed the wolvryn orb and stepped forward, searching up into the foothills, then side to side. He gestured to Neska and attuned to her senses. The world exploded with the complex mixture of sight, sound, and smell that he had become accustomed to whenever he merged with her senses. A survey of the area showed only the normal wildlife of the forest, nothing of the taint from the Drift or other people.

He lifted his hand and adjusted his bow and travel pack. "All clear."

Ranika stepped out into the light, followed by Laryn. Kaellor stood at the threshold, shielding his eyes, bookended by Bryndor and Boru. His uncle set his palm to the placard. He and Laryn shared a look for several seconds before she tucked white locks of hair behind her ears.

"We'll see you in ten days, love. Sooner if we find Reddevek's people straight away."

Kaellor nodded, looked to the ground, then back up, a smile dissipating the creased lines about his eyes. "You've made me my father."

"How so?" said Laryn.

"I was just about to say 'don't make me go out there to find you.' But then I realized I meant to say, 'take me with you.'"

Laryn cocked her head to the side. "Stone's Grasp needs your presence here now more than ever, you and Bryn. You won't have time to miss us. But I'll use the shek to stay in touch."

Kaellor nodded agreement and activated the placard. The stone flowed back into place. "Ten days, love!" he shouted before the secret entrance sealed over.

Laryn chuckled. "That man. Bryndor is going to have an interesting week, I think."

"How so?" asked Ranika.

"Kae is more worried than he lets on. He usually makes a point to let me have the last word. Managing the royals stresses him little compared to letting go. Bryn's not just going to have to manage all the responsibilities of learning to be the head of state—he's got Kae's poorly veiled fear to contend with."

Lluthean whistled. "I've never seen that side of Kae up close."

"I get the feeling you were usually the source of his concern," teased Ranika.

"You're not wrong. All the same, let's get moving before he plows through that wall to drag us back."

"Sounds good," said Laryn. "You told Karragin and the Mirrare to meet us where, exactly?"

Lluthean gestured to Neska, and she began a steady ascent up familiar trails into the Great Crown. He spoke over his shoulder. "We're to connect with them at a camp Bryndor and I frequent. It's a good hour hike into the timber. Karragin spoke with Neska to learn the specifics."

"Do you ever worry that those two talk about you?" asked Ranika.

He held back a wayward pine branch to prevent it from swatting Ranika or Laryn in the face, then took up the rear of their column. "Not worried so much as jealous a little, maybe?"

"You and Neska have a unique bond. I've seen it. You understand one another more than most realize," said Laryn through lightly panted breaths.

"That's the Giver's truth," he said. "And who knows what might happen after I sit for the Rite of Revealing?"

"We'll see. The rite is not something to be rushed. You and Bryn need to mature your skill sets and learn the strengths and limitations of your other gifts before sitting for your arca prime. We don't even know what some of your runes can do. To that end, have you been practicing?" asked Laryn.

"Some. I've tried to engage the runes, flood them with zenith. Other than finding different ways to shape rune fire or float down to the ground, I've yet to discover anything new."

Laryn stopped on the trail, holding back another branch and allowing him to pass. She caught his eye and winked, then fell in behind him. "Keep at it, Llu. Everything in the Giver's good time."

"How long did you have to practice to discover what your runes could manage?"

"A long time. Years, but Taker's breath, how much higher is the climb?" she panted.

"The trail flattens out for a bit around this bend, but then we have three more steep climbs before we get there."

"Llu, not that I don't . . . appreciate the need for . . . secrecy," said a nearly breathless Ranika. "But you could have had Karragin meet us . . . oh, I don't know, right behind the castle walls!"

He sensed her exasperation. "Let's play a game, shall we?" he suggested. "We'll keep track of the daily misdemeanors, missteps, and errors in judgment, and call each a monk point. At the end of the day, the one with the most monk points is the monk of the day. For example, you fine ladies might assign me a point for not arranging a closer rendezvous with our escort."

"That might not be the best way to build morale with the group," said Laryn.

"What happens to the person with the most points at the end of the day?" asked Ranika.

"They wear the title of monk of the day and have to make dinner for everyone else," said Lluthean.

"Is your cooking anywhere near as good as your brother's?" asked Ranika.

"I can make a decent trail stew. But you sound pretty confident, and the day is just starting," said Lluthean.

"The way I see it," said Ranika, "you may as well figure out a meal rotation for the week."

Lluthean laughed. "Come on, I'm not that bad, and I've only scored one point for the day."

They climbed in silence, using the pause in conversation to recover their breaths. Eventually, when the trail evened out, Ranika answered his unspoken question. "Two points, Llu, because you pretty much start every day with one point. I mean, can any of your traveling companions even be considered a true monk?"

Lluthean chewed on his response, thinking at first to offer any number of embarrassing observations from the recent past. Then the logic of Ranika's statement struck him. *Right. Man of no knowledge, not woman of no knowledge. Why didn't I think of that?*

Ranika cleared her throat. "It's monk not . . . wonk. I'm not even sure wonk is a word in the Kindred tongue after all—"

"Yes, yes, I got it already. Fair enough, two points for the young man from the Bend!" he announced to the forest. A trio of grouse fluttered up from the underbrush, one of them squawking out a screechy alarm.

Lluthean turned to catch Laryn's expression. She arched an eyebrow and quirked a smile as if to say, "I tried to warn you." Lluthean puffed air through billowed cheeks and shrugged. "My version of campfire stew is going to get pretty old after a few nights. Maybe the monk of the day should be responsible for something else, like pitching a tent or tending to the mounts."

The silence of panting breaths followed his statement until both women burst out laughing. "Oh Giver, Llu, now it's up to three points. Pitch a tent? Honestly," said Ranika.

"How is that a bad thing?" he asked.

The women chuckled a bit longer. "When we return, you'll have to run that particular phrase by your brother, or maybe your uncle can explain it. But Nika has the right of it, you're up to three points. And for the sake of this mission, do not ask the Mirrare why that phrase is so funny," said Laryn.

"Besides, I'm not sure I want to trust the actual construction of my sleeping tent to the fella that earned the most monk points, but don't worry, I'm sure we'll all think of something by the day's end," said Ranika.

The hike continued another hour until, at last, they reached the rocky bluff that overlooked the kingdom below. Eight Aarindin nibbled at the underbrush nearby. Neska loped forward and sniffed at Karragin, who sat sharpening a saber of some type. The two shared a look for several seconds, then the wolvryn trotted off into the forest on a short patrol.

Lluthean adjusted his shoulders and took a knee. A patch of sweat had gathered under his pack, which chilled him as a breeze blew by, but not so much as the realization that he was the only male in a group of very formidable women. *Giver, keep one hand on my mouth and guide me with the other so I don't make a fool of myself in front of her. Moons, not in front of any of them.*

He blinked away a bead of sweat and lifted his gaze to Karragin. The breeze blew a lock of slate-grey hair across her placid face and sharp eyes. When her gaze met his, they locked together for a moment, only breaking when she nodded a subtle greeting. He stood to return her gesture, intending to deliver a witty remark about the Mirrare, but Neska had returned from her patrol and moved to stand directly before him. Something twinkled within the crystalline depths of her blue eyes, and the wolvryn cocked her head to the side.

Lluthean exhaled through his nose. "Right. I get it Nes. They are all on mission, and so are we."

Neska considered him a long moment, then turned to regard the group. The three elites stood at attention. Something in their professional demeanor further sobered him to the moment, and he stepped forward. Karragin waited for them to gather. "Your Highness, Your Radiance, Nika. How was the climb?"

Laryn used the Cloud Walker sign language. *"Let's sign as much as we can. Let me know if you miss anything."*

Karragin's eyes tightened in concentration, and she tilted her head. They formed a circle to better communicate, and Laryn began. *"The hike was one way to start the day, but I'll be glad for the Aarindin all the same. Did anyone notice your departure?"*

"No, and Baccal kept a vigil for the past several hours. We're the only people in the Great Crown this morning," Karragin signed, then seemed to withdraw into herself, her expression even more stoney than usual as if calculating a hand in king's gambit. *"Some of the next words, Your Radiance, escape me. To save time, if you'll indulge me?"*

"It's not a competition. Use the signing when you can," Laryn replied with nimble fingers.

Karragin gave a sharp nod. *"Baccal scanned the horizon to the northwest."*

Karragin eyed Baccal, who replied with signing of her own, *"There are smoke trails far off, campfires, I think. We believe Reddevek's clan has made summer camp in a distant valley."*

Karragin cleared her throat and continued the report, "It's thin gruel, but it's all we have to go on. Salveen had little else to offer, as her clan keeps to the lowlands. Savnah's quint hasn't replaced me. Her quad went ahead to scout. We estimate three days to reach the area. I've conditioned the Aarindin to be receptive to gripping you, so travel should be reasonable."

"That's no small task. Doesn't it usually take weeks for an Aarindin to grip?" signed Laryn.

"Sometimes the Giver gives," signed Karragin.

"What about Nika?" Lluthean signed.

Karragin took a few steps and retrieved a leather satchel full of apples. "Nika will ride Zippy. He didn't take to the saddle until I told him that Ranika herself would give him one of these every day. The extra Aarindin will carry our supplies. We can rotate the mounts through the work to keep them fresh."

Ranika's face beamed. She retrieved an apple and retreated to greet the Aarindin.

Amniah broke her statuesque demeanor to contribute to the signed conversation. *"We should begin when you are ready. If we leave soon, we can climb beyond this ridge and drop into the first valley. The air rises from the south today and is thick with moisture. Rain is likely, but travel will be better north of the ridgeline."*

Neska stood beside Lluthean, and he grounded himself in her silent presence as she shouldered up to him. *"I am ready when you are. Neska found nothing on patrol,"* he signed.

"The sooner begun, the sooner done," signed Laryn.

The soft vacuum of channeled zenith preceded Karragin's deployment of her gift as the entire group of Aarindin walked forward, tails swishing and heads held eager. They perked their ears and seemed to study Neska, but not a one appeared skittish. Lluthean had expected a whinny or restless pawing at the ground, but each Aarindin stood with casual alertness.

Karragin tossed a saddle over Zippy's back and began to cinch the front strap. Without thinking, Lluthean stepped forward and rested a hand on the saddle horn. Once he had her attention, he signed, *"Blanket first, then saddle. May I show you?"*

Karragin stared at him a moment, her expression unreadable. Eventually, she nodded her understanding and removed the saddle. Lluthean retrieved the saddle blanket, a high-quality padding with wool felt layered over fleece. He fingered the material, admiring the selection, then swung it into place. Karragin set the saddle over Zippy's back, and Lluthean situated it to sit behind the mount's shoulder blades.

Ranika walked over as he began adjusting the front and rear cinch straps. "Got time for a fast lesson, Nika?"

The young woman hoisted her pack and walked around Zippy, running a hand along his nose and cheek. "The way I see it, that's at least one monk point for Karra. You're not looking to subtract from your tally, are you?"

Lluthean flushed and glanced to Karragin, who was lifting a canteen to her lips, oblivious to Ranika's jibe. "You care about Zippy, right? Well, outside of Laryn, I might be the only one in this group with any idea about how to adjust the saddle to prevent it causing him injury, and at the same time prevent you from falling off."

Ranika removed her hat, gathered errant spirals of hair in her other hand, and replaced the hat. "Alright. I'm all ears."

He used the next twenty minutes to adjust the saddle, demonstrating how to secure the cinch straps, then adjusted the stirrup length. Then he released the cinches and asked Ranika to repeat the maneuvers, teaching her how to manage most of the work herself and offering subtle points about how to shape the straps and knots to prevent unnecessary chafing against the Aarindin's hide. He began to give her advice on how to signal the Aarindin with the reins, but Ranika waved him off. "Zip and I are old friends, Llu. I've got that part."

Lluthean shook his head and backed up a few paces to give the saddle one last inspection. "Right. Sorry. Just trying to help. If you like, at day's end, I would be happy to groom him."

She flicked the front brim of her oversized hat, and smiled. "Hmm . . . let's say you're back to only one point. I'll think about it. Thanks for setting up the saddle, Llu."

He found the one lone Aarindin without a rider or packed with gear and approached the mount, a muscular gelding. He offered the back of his hand, letting the creature inhale his scent, and when it felt right, stepped forward while speaking in low tones, running a hand along the Aarindin's neck and across muscled shoulders before tracing the tight slope of his back.

He turned and waited for Karragin to look in his direction, then signed, *"Does he have a name?"*

Karragin's face softened with part of a smile. *"That's Tacit. After Tini here, he's my favorite Aarindin. He's one of the best."*

"My thanks." Lluthean wondered if Karragin had saved "one of the best" mounts for him, or if it was mere circumstance. Before he thought to ask, she siphoned zenith, the flows again a palpable, gentle current to his awareness. All the other mounts began to walk toward the tree line. Lluthean pitched his voice low and whispered to Tacit, "Right. Don't go reading signs where none exist."

Lluthean signaled and Tacit lowered to the ground, allowing him to throw a leg over the mount's back. Tacit rose without a grunt and walked forward, trailing the other Aarindin. Lluthean shifted back a few inches, adjusted his bow and pack, then prepared for a long day of travel. He had not taken the opportunity to ride much in the last few weeks and knew by the day's end, the travel would take a toll.

Something rippled through Tacit and Lluthean felt his legs grip without effort onto the Aarindin's back. He found that he could shift about, but as soon as he settled, the Aarindin gripped him, and a subtle force seemed to support his lower back, preventing him from lurching around. Lluthean reached a hand back, expecting to feel the ridge of a saddle.

Instead, his fingers brushed against the sleek hair on the Aarindin's back. Tacit felt warm and alive beneath his touch. The subtle current of zenith thrumming from the creature reminded him of the flows within the walls of Stone's Grasp. When he concentrated, he could sense the gentle vibration of power emanating from the mount.

Secure in Tacit's grip, Lluthean's gaze wandered to the far horizon. To the south, the sun burned behind dense storm clouds, confirmation of Amniah's warning. He signaled Tacit to catch up to the other riders, and the Aarindin cantered, causing the air to strike him anew with the crisp scent of pine.

He inhaled, savoring the intoxicating aroma that filled his senses. A gentle breeze caressed his face, whispering the promise of untamed adventure. He thought of Bryndor's plight and offered a silent prayer of thanks to the Giver that their situations weren't reversed.

As the afternoon wore on, Lluthean's connection with the Aarindin grew stronger, more familiar. He could feel its powerful muscles flexing beneath him, responding to his slightest direction—the nudge of a toe, the lifting of a knee.

Nolan had told him about the Aarindin's grip on their travels to Stone's Grasp, but something in the scout's rendition had diminished the intimacy of the partnership he already felt after only a short time. He began to wonder if Tacit's grip fostered a false sense of trust and understanding. When he dismounted, would he still feel the same way about the creature? Regardless, the sense of security he felt flowed effortlessly between them.

Lost in the enchantment of the moment, Lluthean's hand remained suspended in the air, no longer searching for a saddle but instead reaching out to pull his fingers through the flows of zenith that surrounded them, seeking to better understand the arcane force that governed all life on Karsk.

Finding no obvious answers, he lowered his hand to pat Tacit between the shoulders. "Tacit, this could be the beginning of a beautiful friendship."

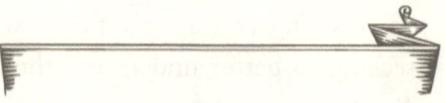

Chapter Seventeen: Opening Bids

The tailored sleeves of Bryndor's jacket pinched into his armpits, and he shifted his shoulders in a feeble attempt to relieve the discomfort. The action caused a beam of sunlight to reflect off his dragon pendant and into Ksenia's eyes as she sat at her desk scribing for the regent. She sat up straight and the light fell across her chest, accentuating her neckline. His eyes locked onto hers for a moment until she arched one eyebrow and flicked her fingers through the Cloud Walker language, signing, *"See anything interesting, my prince?"*

He felt the flare of heat at his neckline and signed an apology, then turned his torso, deflecting the offensive glare. With an effort, he focused his attention on the proceedings as Therek received another petitioner before the court. On more than one occasion, the regent had offered to relinquish the responsibility, but neither he nor Kaellor felt prepared to preside on behalf of the kingdom without a better understanding of all the factors involved. In his short time attending court, Bryndor had become familiar with the formalities of how to receive petitioners and address the various nobles. But he still felt unprepared to assume the responsibilities of the kingdom.

Therek artfully demonstrated the mechanics of running an efficient yet polite interaction. More than that, the regent commanded a unique ability to solicit truthful information and ferret out half-truths. After only a few morning sessions, Bryndor had come to realize that most of the petitioners offered skewed versions of the truth. Many arrived ignorant of the various laws and restrictions in place. Therek had educated the previous petitioner regarding a law that prevented dumping waste into Lake Ullend. Other citizens had run afoul of articles of restriction that governed fair trade practices between guilds.

Years of holding the throne gave Therek a masterful understanding of each and every one of the legalities involved. Bryndor's ignorance of the complexities of Aarindorian law bothered him only half as much as those who arrived with a deliberate intent to circumvent a restriction or mislead the court. Such a petitioner stood before them now, an obsequious merchant from the Delve intent on securing permission to refine and distribute vellevlin, an expensive perfume.

The man produced a decorative glass bottle, its edges scored with facets to resemble a large crystal. He spritzed a fine purple mist into the air and fanned the cloud to distribute the fragrance. In seconds, the strange and rather musty scent of vellevlin wafted across the room. The scribbling of Ksenia's zeniscrawl paused as she recoiled from the heavy fragrance.

Therek remained at ease in the regent's chair, a high-backed, oversized throne set on a raised dais. Kaellor stood to one side and Bryndor the other. He felt the gentle tug of zenith flow through the room as both older men charged their gifts. When neither acted with alarm, Bryndor allowed the tension in his shoulders to ease, only just now aware that something in the merchant's demeanor had set him on guard.

The regent waved a hand before his face. "A bit too cloying for my taste. Regardless, what is it you seek exactly, Lord Choff? To my understanding, your list of reagents passed the requirements of safety administered by the guild of alchemists, the patent you secured is sound, and none of your competitors issued a challenge to the marketing of vellevlin. The samples you provided are an acquired taste, though the crown thanks you for your generous donation to the royal gardener's guild. All that said, again, why are you here this morning?"

The merchant wrapped a silk around the bottle and dipped his head. "Vellevlin has a protective benefit beyond its attractive fragrance, Your Grace. I believe it is restorative, but its key ingredient is the ground larva of crown beetles. I was rather hoping to obtain the crown's permission to harvest certain crops of the larvae as they come into maturity."

Therek strummed his fingers on the arm of one of the chairs. He turned to Bryndor and pitched his voice low. "What do you think, Your Highness?"

Bryndor considered the man before them. Something in the merchant's demeanor tickled a nerve of unease. "I suppose I need to know more about what else crown beetles and their larvae are used for and exactly how much of the population Lord Choff intends to harvest before I could make a decision, Your Grace."

Therek's eyebrows flared up with his smile. He laid one long, bony finger to the side of his nose, then pointed at Bryndor. "That's exactly right. You're learning fast."

Therek turned back to Lord Choff. "Master Choff, can you tell me why there are laws governing the protection and management of crown beetles and their larvae?"

The merchant blinked once, befuddled by the question. "Uhh. No, Your Grace."

"Well, allow me to educate you." Therek sighed. "Crown beetles are necessary for the pollination of crownberry bushes, a crop that no small part of Aarindorn relies upon. In addition, the beetles molt three times before maturity, and the shells left behind are distilled into Eldrenol's solution, the only natural protection bestowed by the Giver against the Taker's long reach. But I suspect you already knew that and sought to circumvent the protections governing the collection, distribution, and utilization of such a critical resource."

Color flared high on the cheeks of Lord Choff. "Your Grace, I assure you I had no such motivations. If I desired to mislead anyone, I would simply harvest the larvae without seeking permission. I only sought approval—"

"Be that as it may," interrupted Therek. "Your petition is denied. We cannot risk disrupting the delicate balance so you can turn a profit from a fragrance that even now tests my ability to keep a straight face. I suggest that you find a way to utilize crown beetle shells in your distillation and then purchase them legally on the open market like everyone else."

Lord Choff pushed out his lips and nodded, appearing to both accept and appreciate Therek's judgment. The man broke his gaze to consider Kaellor and then Bryndor. He even seemed to leer at Ksenia, who diligently recorded the interaction. An awkward, pregnant pause drew out, as if he expected one of them to rescue him from Therek's ruling. Finally, he bowed his head in acceptance. "I see. I appreciate both the advice and your time. As you say, I will find acceptable alternative ways to utilize the . . . kingdom's resources. I shall not take any more of the court's time."

The merchant turned and departed. A moment later, the clerk assigned to the lobby stuck his head through the door. "Your Grace. Are you ready for the last petitioner?"

"Give us five minutes," said Therek. He waited for the clerk to close the door, then continued, "What do you make of Lord Choff's request?"

"Odd man," said Bryndor. "It seemed like he expected your ruling."

"I suspect you are correct, but why do you say that?" asked Therek.

"He cared enough about the proposal to send a soft bribe to the royal gardener's guild but then left without a rebuttal or even the appearance of being disappointed. It seemed like he was waiting for one of us to find the scent so alluring that we would support his petition," said Bryndor.

Therek turned to Kaellor. "Why am I still sitting in this chair?"

Kaellor ran a palm across his bearded jaw and winked. "Bryndor is a quick study, my friend, but neither of us know the laws as you do, and we are both catching up on a decade of political tangles. Besides, you and I both know there was something more insidious in Choff exposing us to nothing more than a volatile concoction of Eldrenol's solution."

"You did remember," said Therek, eyebrows flaring in wispy surprise.

"Not much else smells like a mixture of musk and moldy hay. The real question is why he felt the need to expose any of us to the substance," said Kaellor.

"If I may, what exactly is Eldrenol's solution?" asked Bryndor.

"It is a volatile purple liquid that, when inhaled, prevents an abrogator from channeling nadir," said Kaellor. "It is to an abrogator what veramanth is to a zeniphile."

As Kaellor finished his explanation, Bryndor's mind retreated to the night he helped Ranika escape the trap set by the remnants of the Lacuna. The same stink of wet, moldy hay had permeated the building.

At the time, he assumed it was something to do with the rainstorm and the rotting timbers, but now he suspected otherwise.

Therek sighed. "Tarkannen's attempt to breach the castle wards on the night of the Reckoning has clearly placed people on edge."

"No. It was more than that," said Kaellor. "He deliberately exposed everyone in the room, then waited to see how we would react. I suspect if we were to track the halls he used to arrive and depart, we would find he managed to fumigate more than half of the castle staff, searching for a response."

Confirmation washed over Bryndor, and he thought of Ranika, of how ill she'd appeared, an obvious reaction to the solution staining her face. Before he could edit his thoughts, he blurted out, "He's looking for an abrogator."

From the edge of his vision, he sensed that Ksenia had the common sense not to record the conversation. Her zeniscrawl lay dormant on a pile of papers.

"Again, why am I sitting in this chair?" asked Therek.

Kaellor chuckled. "The official coronation is set to coincide with the Harvestmoon festival. You and I both know we can use the time to allow everyone in Stone's Grasp to acclimate. Besides, the panel of arbiters and tribunes is set to assume most of these appointments next week. Frankly, I'm surprised you never delegated the work before now."

Something in Kaellor's words deflated the regent, his shoulders sagging back into the chair. "The volume of petitioners has risen since your arrival. Many, I suspect, are coming before the court out of curiosity. But even then, I never realized how much Chancle did to organize and mitigate the work. I only wish I had discovered his treachery sooner."

"Before you descend into an afternoon of self-loathing, let's see to the last petitioner," said Kaellor.

Bryndor turned to regard Ksenia, and she flashed a smile while brandishing her zeniscrawl. The turn in conversation seemed to deflect even Therek's sharp mind from dwelling on the possibility that an abrogator walked the halls of Stone's Grasp. Bryndor approached the door before the lobby to welcome in the last petitioner.

A man dressed in the refined, tailored clothing of the nobility walked into the room. He had at least ten years on Bryndor, black hair and beard styled in the manner of a noble from one of the western duchies: locks of hair groomed into curly rivulets and an ostentatious mustache oiled into long tails that swept across the cheeks like a set of horns.

The man drew up short upon realizing who had opened the door. He dipped rather than bowed his head once. "Your Highness, I am honored to meet you. My name is Lord Edlemund Endule."

"Well met, Lord Endule. Please come in. The regent is prepared to hear your petition," said Bryndor.

Edlemund inspected Bryndor from head to toe, then surveyed the room before walking to the center. He waited to begin his address until Bryndor returned to Therek's side. "Your Highness, Your Highness," said Edlemund, tipping his head to Kaellor and then Bryndor. "Your Grace. Thank you for your time. I know it's a precious commodity these days."

"Lord Edlemund is the oldest son of the duchess of Beclure, Endera Endule," said Therek.

Kaellor nodded. "As I recall, we met at the reception after the ceremony to release the royal ashes."

Edlemund bowed his head. "Yes, I'm flattered that you would remember me from the countless people seeking your attention that day."

"I understood that the duchess departed for Beclure only a day ago. Tell me then, what brings you to the regent's court?" asked Therek.

Edlemund stared at the regent a moment, inhaled a breath, then nodded, as if committing to a course of action in his mind. "With the return of the Baellentrells to the kingdom, a fact that will surely lead Aarindorn forward with prosperity and security, the high and noble houses have reinstated a prima dicta to advocate for their interests during and in between the biannual assembly meetings."

But for Ksenia's scribing, another uneasy silence fell across the room. "I assume that they have appointed you as prima dicta?" asked Therek.

"Yes, Your Grace," said Edlemund.

Therek pushed back slightly in the grand chair and seemed to fill the expansive backrest with his simple presence. The regent considered the man, during which time even Bryndor felt a strange desire to squirm. To his credit, Edlemund looked ahead, unflinching.

"I see," said Therek. "Let's hear the terms, for that is surely why you have arrived today."

"Pursuant to a request made by your office, the Beclurian and Dulescan houses have discovered a reasonable passage that may serve as a trade route through a channel of valleys out of the Great Crown and to the plains west of Aarindorn."

Once again, Therek lightly thrummed his fingertips on the top of the armrest. "This discovery seems to be no small blessing of the Giver, since I only recently made the request, and yet no such egress has been possible since the inception of the kingdom. Quite the coincidence really, but don't let me distract you, young man. Your terms."

"As it pertains to the passageway, we propose a three percent tariff on all goods entering the kingdom and a surtax of two percent on all goods leaving as recompense for the labor and forces necessary to both develop and secure the passageway," said Edlemund.

"Your mother must feel certain that the trade route through the Pillars of Eldrek will not offer competitive importation of goods and services, since the proposed tariff on goods passing through there is only point five percent."

Edlemund responded with a flat smile that left Bryndor wondering about the man's motives. Was he frustrated by the discrepancy in the tariff or just mad that Therek suggested Edlemund's mother was behind the decisions?

The prima dicta shifted his predatory gaze to Kaellor and then Bryndor. "Your Grace, in the interest of time, and I mean no offense, let me offer the rest of the terms, which all the high houses have mandated me to deliver. If your scribe is prepared?"

A swift flutter of paper erupted from Ksenia's desk as she retrieved a fresh sheet from her folio. Without words, she lifted her eyes to indicate her readiness.

"Please do continue," said Therek.

"First, we propose that the new passageway be titled the Endulian Pass, since the sons and daughters of the western duchies were the ones who labored to secure a safe means of travel. Next, the prima dicta will require office space here in Stone's Grasp, somewhere on the first tier should suffice. We intend to employ routine staff, and such representatives of the office will require monthly meetings with the regent and eventually the heir, as was customary in times past. Also, commensurate with times past, a stipend from the royal coffers shall be drawn per annum to reimburse the office of the prima dicta and associated staff. And finally, as the first act of the office of prima dicta, we propose a reinstatement of the doctrine of nonus performitae."

Therek sighed, and only when the scrawling noise of Ksenia's zeniscrawl stopped did he speak. "Since you've spoken so plainly young man, I shall do you the courtesy of the same. The offices of the prima dicta were a bloated affair that stagnated any innovation in the kingdom, all while lining the pockets of those who served in its expansive and wasteful wing. Under the Lellendule rule, before the changing of the moons, it became the single most costly branch of government which managed to accomplish precisely nothing, unless you count frustration, obfuscation, and extortion as something to aspire to. Aarindorn will never regress to that again, not while I draw breath, and certainly not while I sit in this chair. However, I am well aware of the concerns of the western duchies."

"The position of prima dicta represents the interests of all the high and noble houses, Your Grace," interrupted Edlemund.

"Ed-le-mund," said Therek, drawing out each syllable to emphasize his disbelief. "For the sake of brevity and even posterity." He glanced over at Ksenia. "I am quite certain that no representative from House Baellentrell, Lellendule, and most likely none of the houses in Stellance have consented to your proposals, which means barely a majority of the high houses hold fast to your terms.

"Regardless, since you brought it up, I expect an official tally of all those voting for and against the creation of your office, as well as a full accounting of the cost for the exploration, creation, and maintenance of the passageway, this Endulian Pass. Once I receive an accurate accounting of the past and ongoing expenses, only then will we negotiate a fair and equitable tariff and taxation system. Next, you and I will meet on a weekly basis—after all, we have so much to discuss on behalf of the kingdom. I will not waste my time with your lackeys. Your offices will be located on the second tier, as the previous space occupied by the prima dicta was long ago repurposed to an accessory House of the Moons, a small but efficient sanitorium that serves the interests of both those who work within and without the castle grounds. What else did he propose?" Therek turned to Ksenia.

She lifted her zeniscrawl and tapped at the parchment. "A royal stipend for the office, Your Grace, and the reinstatement of nonus performitae."

Therek nodded and rolled one bony, long finger in a tight circle. "Right, right. I tell you what, it seems fair to support the interests of the high houses, so how about you and I agree to reimburse the position of prima dicta from the royal coffers at the same rate as the stipend I draw in my role as regent?"

Edlemund's eyebrows lifted. "That seems more than fair, Your Grace. What about ancillary staff?"

"The crown will agree to reimburse your offices for the cost of two scribes and a full-time clerk to coordinate communications, but only at the same rate as those who might seek employment in the offices of the regent."

"And the issue of nonus performitae, Your Grace?" pressed Edlemund.

"We can discuss it, but I suspect it's an issue to be put forth to the entire assembly. The concept is not without merit, Edlemund, but you will have to convince me why I should limit the ability to act nimbly and swiftly to engage any enemies outside the kingdom precisely at a time when so much is in turmoil."

"Your Grace, I look forward to the opportunity to do just so," said Edlemund.

"Yes, well, it will have to wait for our first meeting. Shall we say this time next week? That should give you the chance to organize your staff."

"One week. I look forward to it." He turned to address Kaellor. "Your Highness, Endera the duchess of Beclure asked me to pass along her appreciation to your wife, Her Radiance."

"I'm not sure I follow," said Kaellor.

"Well, apparently it was your wife who inspired the resurrection of the prima dicta."

Kaellor's eyebrows lifted, and he tilted his chin but made no reply, so Edlemund continued, "They spoke of equalitus diplomatica, and so Mother thought that the nobles should ensure that their interests were conveyed with equal opportunity. So, do please pass along the gratitude of the duchess."

Edlemund turned to face Therek. "By your leave, Your Grace," said Edlemund.

At Therek's nod, the man dipped his head to Kaellor and Bryndor, muttering, "Your Highness," as an afterthought. Finally, he departed the chamber.

"Did you get all that, Ms. Balladuren?" asked Therek.

Ksenia smiled. "Of course, Your Grace."

"Would you mind delivering the transcript right away to the records office? I want copies made for the archives, and one for my personal review. Then submit a formal notice that Edlemund, in his role as prima dicta, will occupy a two-room office suite on the second tier, southwest corner," said Therek.

Ksenia shuffled the papers into her folio, tapped it on the desk, and stood. "I can see to it at once, Your Grace."

Bryndor watched the young woman leave through the scribe's door at the back of the room. She bumped the door open with a hip and turned once, catching his eye and offering a half-smile, then disappeared.

Therek pressed knobby fingers against his wispy eyebrows. Kaellor paced a slow circle and tugged at his beard. Bryndor cleared his throat. "Is it that bad?"

The regent sighed. "It could be worse."

"I remember Father fuming over the tedium imposed by the last prima dicta. You did a nice job limiting the scope of his initiative. But why did you agree to meet with him on a weekly basis?" asked Kaellor.

Therek puffed out a breath. "As you said, the tribunes and arbiters will assume most of this work starting next week. If Edlemund and his mother seek to play their games with the fate of all Aarindorn, I think they will find that I am more than capable of burying them in a mountain of archaic rules and regulations. Meeting with him once a week should enable me to keep him on a short leash."

"You conceded a lot to his initial demands. You even validated his claim as prima dicta without seeking the approval of the assembly," said Kaellor.

"I'm quite sure that Edlemund has the support of the western duchies, and Endera likely pressured enough of the high houses to give him an honest, if narrow, majority. Still, he does take liberties. Certainly his claim is far-reaching since he has not the backing of the families from Stellance, not to mention the utter failure to consult with house Baellentrell or Lellendule."

Kaellor grunted agreement. "Can we be so sure that the Stellancians wouldn't support him? More than a few tossed in with the Lacuna."

Therek waved a hand, dismissing Kaellor's concern. "Stellance stands to benefit from trade through the Pillars, and the merchants will never embrace the cost incurred with a longer trade route, let alone the taxes Edlemund proposed."

Kaellor nodded agreement. "True enough. It sort of feels like a deliberate step to limit Bryndor's future rule."

"What do you think about it all, Bryn?" asked Therek.

Bryndor stopped chewing on the inside of his cheek and wet his lips, considering everything that had transpired in the past fifteen minutes. "I would like to believe that the prima dicta could be a person to collaborate with. I would welcome the advice of those who hold high the interests of Aarindorn. But meeting Edlemund makes me want to wash my hands."

"That's the Giver's truth," said Kaellor. He smiled ruefully, then shook his head and uttered a curse. "Taker's grip, nonus performitae?"

"What is . . . nonus performitae?" asked Bryndor.

Therek cleared his throat. "It pertains to foreign policy, Bryn. More specifically, it means that the crown will not commit the kingdom to any offensive initiatives, treaties, or binding agreements with any nation outside of Aarindorn without the ratification of the prima dicta. In short, it is a proposal to limit the ability of me, and eventually you, to govern."

"That sounds like a bold move. Do you think he intends to follow through?" asked Kaellor.

"Not really," said Therek. "A ratification of that type would require submission to the entire assembly. I suspect he knew I would never consent to the concept."

"It was an opening bid meant to be a sacrifice," said Bryndor. "He knew that you would deny nonus performitae, but that made his other requests, even validating his role as prima dicta, seem harmless."

Therek stood and massaged the muscles in his lower back. "You are most likely correct. Don't worry about Edlemund. He's about to find that I have already placed a few obstacles in his path."

A smile spread across Kaellor's face. "How so?"

A twinkle of mischief glittered in Therek's eye. "First of all, the rooms I commissioned for him are absolutely sweltering and have no windows. He will have to employ a chiller just to make the space tolerable. More than that, he will soon find out that there is no monetary reimbursement involved. With my family's holdings and investments, I never had need. Besides, I assumed the regency as an act of service to the kingdom. If I drew a salary, that would undermine the faith people placed in me, which was tested in the years after the Abrogator's War."

Kaellor barked a laugh. "And you got him to commit to the same. Poor lad. Endera will tongue-lash him for the misstep."

"Edlemund is well versed in the game, but he's used to watching the good people of Beclure cower in his presence. It will do him some good to be reminded that he casts a much smaller shadow in Stone's Grasp," said Therek.

"I hope you're right, my friend. Just promise me you'll be careful," said Kaellor. "He seemed confident and driven, like the kind of man who seeks revenge when his goals are thwarted."

"True enough," said Therek.

"Are you going to pass along Endera's remarks to Laryn?" asked Bryndor.

Kaellor puffed out his cheeks. "No, I don't think so. I like to be thought of as the man who makes your aunt smile, and the duchess is a sharp burr stuck under a saddle blanket. Best to just carefully set her to the side before the long ride, you know?"

Chapter Eighteen: The Start of Something

After supervising the duplication of her transcripts from the morning petitioners, Ksenia considered dedicating more time in the archives to continue deciphering *The Tome of Nivosh*. But the morning's scribing session left her hand fatigued and her thoughts scattered. With little conscious thought, her feet made their way into the stables, where the smell of horse and hay unfettered her thoughts and made her long for freedom.

Just steps inside the door, Winter's head protruded out of her stable, one pink-lashed eye blinking at her. Ksenia walked forward without charging her sympath rune and gave the Aarindin a carrot. Winter accepted the treat, and Ksenia ran her palm along the Aarindin's muscled jaw and neck. They shared a moment of silent communion until Winter pawed at the ground, restless to be released.

Ksenia smiled and shook her head, charging her sympath rune. *"Hello, Winter. Would you fancy a—"*

"Are we going for a ride? We could run across the plains or climb into the mountains. It's a good day for a ride!" The Aarindin's voice broke into the conversation.

Ksenia giggled out loud, retrieved a small shoulder pack, and opened the gate. *"Yes please. Get me out of here."*

Within the hour, she and Winter left through the Timber Gate and climbed the wooded trails into the foothills of the Great Crown. Winter trotted along with barely constrained enthusiasm. More than once, Ksenia had to lean forward to avoid a low-hanging branch.

"Easy, Winter. Some of us don't like being smacked by tree branches!"

The Aarindin slowed her pace a little until the trail dropped into an open meadow. *"Alright, girl, show me what you've got today."*

Winter surged ahead into a full gallop. Secured by the Aarindin's grip, the smooth cadence felt like gliding over the grasslands. Winter splashed through a shallow stream, the spray cooling to Ksenia's arms and face in the afternoon sun. After circumnavigating the meadow twice, she slowed to a canter and eventually a walk, breathing with exhilaration more than exertion.

They roamed for more than an hour up into the Great Crown, over game trails, and along streams before heading back. A vine sporting delicate white flowers brushed her shoulder, emitting a sensually sweet fragrance. Ksenia plucked one of the blooms and tucked it behind an ear.

Through her sympath gift, she listened to the buzz of life all around them. Birds chattered at one another, some singing songs to attract a mate, others to defend a territory. One especially persnickety woodchuck charged out of its burrow to chastise them.

"Off my grass, off my grass!" The simple berating was laced with images of a lush carpet of green in front of the burrow.

Out of spite, Winter lowered her head and threatened to nibble at the grasses, at which point the woodchuck rose to its hind legs and chattered with vehemence and anger. The brave display made even Winter nicker with humor. Ksenia directed them away a few strides.

"What has him so hot and bothered? One stomp could end all that noise," said Winter.

Ksenia knew the Aarindin would never act on the threat. *"He's trying to attract a mate and, I suspect, is governed by something other than fear for your size. Come on, let's wander over to the stream."*

Ksenia dismounted and squatted on the bank to splash water on her face and forearms. She shaded her eyes from the late afternoon sun and stared off to the west, thinking about the family ranch, and suddenly realized that she had not considered returning home for over a month now.

"Hmm. When did that happen?" she asked of herself.

"When did what happen?" asked Winter.

"I don't know how to explain it, really. I think maybe I am just getting familiar with Stone's Grasp, the work, the people."

Winter dropped her head and made a pretense of drinking water, but flipped her face to the side, splashing Ksenia with a spray of water. *"It's not the people. It's one person."*

Ksenia shook her head in defensive disbelief. *"We are not so entwined that you would know, my dear. But you . . . might have a point. What is it you think you know?"*

"You are happy when he is about, and your smell changes. And it lingers. You think of him long after he has left. I can sense when you have spent time with him," said Winter. She craned her neck to pluck at tender shoots of sweetvine.

Ksenia sat back, giving Winter's words consideration. *"My smell? What does that even mean?"*

"There was a time when Craxton altered your smell, but with him it is more."

"What do you mean more?" Ksenia pressed.

"More . . . more like you should be. It's the same when we gallop, and when we share a secret, when you give me treats . . . you have a similar smell when we race your brothers, and when we are gripped. It's like all of these, but different . . . more."

Ksenia felt a little heat rise under her chin and couldn't help but smile. *"Suppose that you are right—"*

"I am not wrong."

Ksenia huffed a chuckle. *"If you are right, who do you suppose has this effect on me?"*

Winter chewed her mouthful and seemed about to respond when the chattering birds and the creatures all around stilled. A gentle breeze gusted from the west and Winter lifted her nose high, ears perked forward with alarm.

Ksenia rose to her feet, dusted off her breeches, and was preparing to mount the Aarindin when something massive splashed down into the stream just beyond a hillside. A greater cave lark might make the same noise, but only a predator would cause the wildlife to become so dormant.

"Winter, ease back here."

"No," said the Aarindin. Before she could elaborate, Boru loped around the bend, thick paws plopping through the water. He stopped and lowered his belly into the current, then considered them a moment before stepping from the water, tail wagging, jaw relaxed open in a goofy smile.

"Oh Giver's tits, Boru! You scared me half to death," said Ksenia. She invited Boru to the link she shared with Winter. *"Are you here alone? Where is Bryndor?"*

His response rippled back through her gift, a complex mingling of the image of Bryndor climbing a trail, the sound of his footsteps, and the not-unpleasant smell of oiled leather. *"He is close."*

Boru whipped his fur back and forth, dispersing the water. Winter regarded the wolvryn with casual disregard, then returned to foraging for sweetvine. *"Winter, you could have told me it was Boru."*

"You were going to see for yourself soon enough," said Winter.

Ksenia walked forward and stroked her fingers through the wolvryn's wet beard, the aroma of wet dog strangely absent. Something prickly poked out from a gnarl of fur behind his jaw and he reached a hind paw up to scratch at it.

"Stop, you'll make it worse, silly. Let me see," said Ksenia.

Boru sat back on his haunches still panting, but even so, she had to reach up to tend to the tangle. *"Lower please, belly to the ground if you can,"* said Ksenia.

The wolvryn obliged, adopting a relaxed posture on the ground. She used the tip of a small knife to tease apart the charcoal and silver hairs and uncover a cluster of burrs. Several minutes later, the entire offending thorny clutch released into her palm. She tossed it into the stream just as Bryndor crested the rise from the same hill.

He dropped to his knees, then fell onto his back, panting from the exertion of the climb. Ksenia called out, "Bryn, are you alright?"

He held up a hand and yelled back through gasping breaths, "I just need a moment! I should have guessed what he was up to."

Ksenia retrieved a small water canteen from her shoulder pack, filled it from the stream, and climbed up the hill. Bryndor wore a thin leather vest over a blue linen shirt, sleeves rolled up to his forearms. Sweat matted hair to his forehead and stained the shirt a midnight blue. He sat up and squinted against the glare of the sun. Ksenia sidestepped, allowing her shadow to fall on his face, and held the canteen forward.

"You're the Giver's blessing," he said, and upended the canteen. After he drank his fill, he pushed strands of hair back from his face with one brawny hand and held the other out.

She stepped close, wedging her feet against his, then heaved with both her hands clasped around his. His grip was firm but gentle, his touch warm—unusually warm. He rose to his feet and freed his hand, then gripped his wrist as if in pain. Zenith flared across the runes on his right forearm and flickered in the depths of his eyes. She felt the gentle tug on the ambient current and searched his face. He stared at the interplay of runes, momentarily lost to some internal vision.

When his focus returned, he met her gaze and spoke in awed tones. "Kess, take my hand again, just hold it, you . . . something of my gift triggered."

"Alright." She reached forward and placed one of her hands in his, but the runes on his forearm remained dormant.

"It felt so natural, and now I can't seem to feel how to get the flow to stick," he said. "Use both hands, like you did a moment ago."

She reached forward and clasped his hand within hers. He returned the gentle grip. She studied him as he closed his eyes in concentration. After a long minute, he sighed and eased his hold. "Grind it. Nothing. There was something there, though."

"That's natural. It takes most gifted years of trial and error to fully understand how to channel into their runes. Did you at least get a sense for what these might do?" she asked and tapped a finger on his forearm.

"I . . . maybe? There were flickering images, almost like when you wake from a dream and can remember pieces, but the whole thing seems nonsensical."

"That's good," she said. "Tell me more about the images, and especially what you felt. That can help you understand what the Giver is trying to share with you."

He puffed out his lips and tilted his head, then seemed to see her as if for the first time. "Moons," he muttered and reached forward to grab the sprig of flower that she had tucked behind her ear.

"I think I saw you pluck this from a vine when you were riding, and I remember the fragrance. But then, I also saw you talk to a woodchuck, and later to Winter. I can almost make out the words of the conversation, but it's slipping." He closed his eyes, concentrating, which was just as well, because Ksenia's face flared with heat.

He laughed once. "The woodchuck was angry at you for something, brave little guy. And then—" She grabbed the canteen from his hand and walked over to refill it, using the separation to collect her thoughts.

"Grind it, I can't . . . it's gone, but there was definitely something there. Something about smells or the way you smell. Does any of that make sense?" he asked.

A wave of relief washed over her that he didn't glean anything more meaningful from the recent events, and she splashed cool water on her face and neck. "Well, as it happens, Winter and I were berated by a rather surly woodchuck. I think you are onto something."

His head tilted with surprise, and he rubbed at the runes on his forearm. "A puzzle for another day. I apologize for interrupting your hike. Boru led me on a rather spirited chase. I was afraid that maybe he caught the scent of something from the Drift. I'm glad it was you, even if he did lead me halfway into the Great Crown."

"It was no bother," she said, and then reconsidered his words. "Did you run all the way up here?"

"It beats listening to Lord Choff and his ilk, but I expect I'll have sore muscles for days." He looked at the western horizon. "I've got just enough daylight to make it back. You are welcome to join me, but I know Winter can safely return you with ease."

"Nonsense. Now that your gift has awakened, Winter can grip us both, but you'll have to mount first, then hoist me up. Together, we might be a bit much for her to rise from the prone position."

Bryndor smiled and pulled at his leather vest. "Are you certain? I'm no less soiled than the last time we shared a ride."

"It's fine, and believe me, you were in a much sorrier state that night." She used her sympath gift to relay the plan to Winter, who walked over and lowered belly to the ground. After Bryndor threw a leg over, the Aarindin rose to all fours.

He leaned down to offer her a hand and hoist her up, and Winter's voice rippled through their link as she found her seat in front of him. *"Like I said, your smell changes when you are with him."*

Ksenia sensed Boru's unspoken question, but stifled her gift before either of them could use the link to press her for details. She waited to feel Winter's grip, then turned her head and spoke over her shoulder. "Are you gripped?"

"A moment. Her grip is . . . different from other Aarindin." She sensed him shift his weight behind her. "Uhh Kess, this may sound strange, but I can't feel Winter's grip. Maybe I should hop down."

"Don't be a monk, Bryn. It's at least an hour to walk back to Stone's Grasp. Slide forward and grab my waist like before."

He hesitated, then shifted his hips forward until their legs touched. "Huh. I can feel her grip now. She must center it on you. Is this alright?"

She clicked her tongue, and Winter began a comfortable descent to the castle. "Are you settled then?"

"I think so. Just go easy."

She leaned back into him, testing Winter's grip. "Seems like she has you tight enough. Hold on."

Ksenia signaled Winter into a canter. Bryndor managed to keep his hands on his thighs until the Aarindin galloped down a steep drop then back up, at which point he clasped his hands around her waist. The Aarindin kept up the pace, even galloping across an open meadow, but then slowed to a walk when they returned to the forested trails.

Bryndor cleared his throat and said into her ear, "I don't recall you being so mischievous on our last ride to your family ranch."

"Hmm, well, first, my mother was our chaperone, and second, you were quite badly injured. Something about surviving a stampede of herd animals, as I recall."

He chuckled. "Not my finest hour."

"But the look on Mother's face when she realized the truth of your identity. I could live through that entire day once again just for that moment."

They continued in companionable silence for a time, and he loosened his grip to a polite position on the side of her hips. One of his fingers began to tap with restless fidgeting that reminded her of Lluthean. She had half a mind to signal Winter into another gallop.

"I'll trade a moon for your thoughts?" she asked.

He exhaled a heavy sigh. "Let's hope the Giver favors the bold. I was just thinking about you and . . . me."

She felt her eyebrow cock up and tilted her head, speaking again over her shoulder. "That's more honesty than I anticipated. So . . . what about you and me?"

He dropped his forehead onto her shoulder, and she leaned to the side and craned her neck around to double-check that he was unharmed. His expression appeared wretchedly miserable, cheeks and forehead flared to crimson. His gaze was fixed on the ground, and she waited for him to look up before she asked, "Are you unwell?"

Bryndor shook his head and twirled a finger in a slow circle, directing her to face forward. "No, but you're not making this easy."

She swiveled her head forward and waited, pinching her lips between her teeth to squash the smile that threatened to pucker her cheeks. Winter strode down another descent, breaking briefly into a trot. When they climbed the far rise, he found his courage. "I don't know what the proper protocol is to begin to court someone here in Aarindorn. But if I wanted to begin something like that, I mean, if we wanted to start something . . ."

"If we wanted to start something," she repeated as if considering the novel idea. "Do we . . . want to start something, my prince?"

He groaned. "Would you be favorable to something like that? With me?"

"I suppose it is something I would consider if you would ask me politely and clearly."

She sensed him inhale a deep breath. "Ksenia Balladuren, I would like to . . . court you. Would you honor me with your favor in that regard?"

She directed Winter ahead several paces, then had her stop and release her grip directly under a low-hanging branch. Before he could question the gesture, Ksenia reached overhead, lifted herself from the Aarindin's back and spun to face him, then lowered herself with her legs hitched over his, their faces but inches apart.

The intimacy of their bodies tangled together drove a prickly heat from her core to the nape of her neck, and she felt her breath become full and heady. His scent was intoxicating, but his uncertainty was somehow empowering to her and unbridled her agency.

He chewed on the inside of his lower lip and dipped his head, allowing hair to spill in front of his face. She placed a finger under his chin with one hand, the soft stubble under his jaw shifting as he swallowed hard. With the other hand, she finger-combed the hair from his face, waiting. They sat in silence a moment, he searching her eyes, and she studying his. She became momentarily intoxicated in the acute and sacred awareness of every place where their bodies touched. A soft smile graced her face, and he returned one in kind.

She placed a hand over his breast. "There are some moments in life that I should like to face directly. That way I can remember them all the better. So, Bryndorllean Baellentrell. Ask me again, but not like any other man might. You ask me the way a man who traveled all the way from the Southlands might, the way a man who crossed the Korjinth and faced grondle might. I want to be asked by that man."

The muscles around his eyes tightened, and he tilted his head, considering her suggestion. Eventually, he nodded once and leaned back from her, creating enough space to sign, his fingers flowing through the dialogue with an artistry she thought beyond him. *"Ksenia Balladuren. Blessings and honor to your house. I want you ask you politely."* He paused and kissed the top of her hand. *"And clearly."* He paused again, but this time kissed her on the side of the neck. *"If you would honor me, and start not just something,"* he signed, and waggled a finger at her playfully, *"but this thing, here and now, with me and only me. If so, I would sprint to the horizon that you set your eyes upon, that even the Giver—"*

Ksenia gripped the front of his leather vest and pressed her lips to his, reveling in the way his body responded with a wave of surprise, overtaken immediately by desire as he pressed forward, engaging the kiss. Her breath quickened, and she withdrew, then sought him again with a soft flick of the tongue. He responded, his tongue caressing the edge of her lower lip. His hand found the small of her back and migrated up to her neck, where the simple heat of his gentle grip stole her breath. They lingered a moment longer, then separated.

She found herself panting and did not have to wonder if he felt the same. When he spoke, his voice started low and gravelly. "So, that's a yes, then."

She searched his face, the angle of his jaw, the crystalline pigments in his eyes, marking the moment as an indelible memory. She signed back to him, *"Yes, Bryndor."*

He clasped her hands and shook his head side to side, then spoke out loud as he signed, *"From now on, you hook your little finger against your thumb when you sign my name, for that means 'my Bryndor.' Just as this means, 'my Ksenia.'"*

A twig snapped up ahead and Boru loped forward, made a visual inspection, then turned back to his patrol. Winter nickered with an unmistakable sound of discontent, and both of them giggled. "Well, my Bryndor," she said with mild emphasis, listening to the sound of the claim. "We should probably continue our journey back."

He leaned back and made a deliberate show of resting his hands on his own hips. "I'm not the one sitting backward."

She gripped his vest again and pecked him hard and fast on the lips, then reached overhead to grasp the branch, hoisted herself up, and returned to face forward. Winter re-gripped them, and Ksenia lounged back into Bryndor's chest. She draped his arms over her abdomen, and they continued in that fashion for the better part of the next hour.

As the walls of Stone's Grasp came into view, Bryndor signed to Boru, and the wolvryn stretched, then bounded off into the woods.

"Where does he go? I rarely see him inside the castle grounds," said Ksenia.

"It's a lot for him to endure. To the wolvryn, the smells and the sounds of the city are like clanging pots and pans in a fetid sea of human waste. So, I sent him out to hunt. I made sure that he has access to the secret chamber at the back of the castle."

"Your uncle isn't concerned about anyone discovering the passageway?"

"Not really. Even if someone managed to track him to the entrance, Kae altered the ward, defining who can or can't pass through."

The sun lingered low on the horizon, a brilliant orange ember casting long shadows as they returned through the Timber Gate. The guards nodded a greeting to them both, and Ksenia couldn't decide if she felt relieved for their relative anonymity. Part of her thought it might be fun to have everyone in the city wonder at the young woman riding double with a prince of Aarindorn. But the more she thought about it, the more she appreciated the value of their secret.

He accompanied her to Winter's stall, where they made quick work of the grooming. Without being asked, he retrieved a curry brush and saw to fresh water and hay for the Aarindin, who nickered a soft approval. As they finished, her stomach gurgled loud enough that even Winter turned her head.

"Mine's been doing that for the better part of the last hour. Care to grab a quick bite?" he asked.

Her eyes flared with relief. "Yes. Kitchens or the Sprawl? Everything in the Delve is closed."

He stuffed hands into pockets and shrugged. "Either sounds good, but can you really get food from the kitchens this late?"

She couldn't decide if he was joking, then realized he was serious and looped an arm through his. They beat a path directly to the kitchens, where her familiarity with the staff would be enough to garner a plate of leftovers. She stopped him just outside the kitchen doors, the smell of savory meats and baked bread sending her stomach roiling anew.

"How do you want this, fast and easy or slow and formal?" she asked.

Bryndor folded his arms and leaned back, a lone eyebrow arched in mischief. "I'm not sure I understand your intent, Ms. Balladuren."

She punched him hard on the arm and he chuckled, then held his hands up in surrender. "I get it. If they see me, we won't leave here for two hours. Fast and easy is fine."

"Good. Wait here. I'll be right back." She entered the kitchens alone and navigated to a familiar face, a young woman stirring a large kettle of stew. In just minutes, she departed with a large bowl of stew balanced on a plate with cheese and bread, and a mug of ale trapped under her elbow.

Bryndor rescued her as she exited the kitchens, retrieving the ale just before it slipped from her grip. They made their way outside and climbed up the outer steps to the second-tier green. Bryndor sat down on the edge of a fountain, panting from the labor of the hike. "This seems like as good a place as any?"

She stared out across the city. A faint nimbus of blue light hovered low where zenith-powered sconces illuminated the castle and high districts. In the distance, amber lanterns and torches cast flickering light, and above it all, the moon of Baellen waxed as a thin crescent while the red moon of Lellen flickered as a distant ember.

She sat down beside him, tore the bread in two, and they took turns dipping it into the stew. He spoke of times in the Southlands when he and Lluthean would share a similar meal looking at the same moon and stars. His story reminded her of family meals under the stars at the ranch. And so they took turns sharing stories, engaged in the adventures that had shaped their pasts.

Hours later, the night wind brought a chill to her shoulders. She rubbed her arms and spoke through shivers. "So, you will be tied up with the regent, your uncle, and petitioners for the next two days, and I will be scribing, then working on *The Tome of Nivosh*."

He nodded and held his arms open for a hug. She eyed him dubiously. "I've never met a highborn given to . . . hugs."

"Suit yourself, but I'm the one kept warm by rune fire and you're the one shivering."

She stepped in, enjoying the warmth of his embrace and the sweet scent of leather mixed with an oddly familiar fragrance. She sniffed out loud, her nose searching across his neckline to a pocket on his vest, where he removed the flower he had plucked from her hair earlier in the day. "Neat trick, my prince."

He replaced the flower behind her ear and hugged her tight one last time. "Thanks for today, Kess. It's been perfect."

She squeezed him tight, locking her hands around his lower back, and they held the embrace until it felt natural to release. Afterward, they walked together up to the royal plaza. She was reaching for the door when he placed a hand on her forearm, then was about to exclaim that a woman capable of wrangling Aarindin could open her own doors when he held a finger to her lips.

She drew back, and he signed in the dim light, *"There should be a pair of guards stationed here. Where are the guards?"*

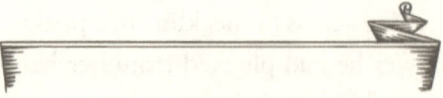

Chapter Nineteen: Steps on a Very Long Journey

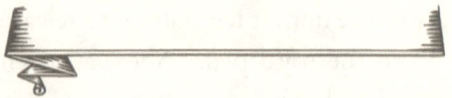

Seagulls screeched in annoyance and lifted into the sky as Volencia approached the rugged coast of the Rodendian Sea. Their haunting cries heralded the exhaustion of her mount, a dapple-grey gelding. She had employed streamers of nadir to remove the beast's awareness of its own fatigue, pushing it for days beyond any normal physical tolerance. The horse lurched to the side, groaning a pitiful sound. Through the haze of the frenze, Volencia lashed out with a whip of nadir, fixing it to a boulder to tug herself free of the saddle before the horse collapsed.

Her feet found purchase among the emerald grasses lining the craggy cliffs and she stood at the precipice of the world, gazing out across the vast expanse of the sea, its rhythmic waves crashing far below. She ran her tongue over the rough scar on the side of her face. Her brine-crusted skin felt unnaturally thick, but the crisp sea air, fragrant with seaweed, at least dissipated the lingering stink of horse from her nose.

Shafts of pale sunlight pierced the scuttling clouds, casting an ethereal glow across the whitecaps. She sensed that on a different day, she might appreciate the natural beauty all around her, but the wonder of it all failed to penetrate the mind-numbing sensation of the frenze. Two days ago, she had drunk the last of her stilben root tea, the relaxing tincture that allowed her to function and critically think during the few times the restless malady had overwhelmed her.

The clacking staccato of Mallic's remnant, the four-legged umbral, rose in the periphery of her awareness and drew her focus back. She turned to see the gangly creature holding the rods of refined nadir cradled in its withered arms. She could not physically handle the artifacts as her master had, but something in the umbral's make allowed it to ferry the rods without ill effect.

Her mount lifted its head once, feet scrabbling at the ground as the remnant approached, but the animal failed to rise, and she suspected it never would. Panting on its side, the horse laid its head back in the grass and searched the sky, wide-eyed.

Days of continuous channeling had left her eager to sever any connection to nadir, but something in the animal's pathetic whinny cut through her scattered thoughts. Without further consideration, she channeled a spike-tipped whip and plunged the barb into the base of the gelding's skull. A single grunt escaped, and it was over. The horse deflated, exhaling its last breath.

The umbral swiveled its head, appearing to consider her act of charity. Volencia swallowed back a sour feeling in her stomach and suspended her connection to nadir, then shrugged her shoulders. "A girl's gotta eat."

She searched the eyeless head for anything resembling a response, and, finding none, studied the sigils etched across the top of its head. A ragged scar that she assumed represented a reflection of the mortal wound Mallic endured before becoming enslaved was furrowed deep into the strange chitinous surface. She reached out with a finger to trace the wound, but resisted the impulse at the last moment.

I never fancied your touch when you were alive. I don't imagine it's any better between us now.

She shifted her inspection to the nadrean rods. Sigils of power, some she recognized but others she did not, seemed to rise to the surface on them. The longer she studied the work, the more she became convinced that the sigils did not rise to the surface so much as absorb any light into the center of the rod. The effect was mildly hypnotic, and she lost track of how long she stood there, the coastal winds at her back and the sun tracking over her right shoulder.

How had Tarkannen accumulated the knowledge to craft such a thing? And how much of that knowledge would he share with her? Eventually, her veil tore loose, fluttering to the ground. She shook herself free of the strange trance and retrieved the garment.

"If you can understand me, this is the place. Set one of the rods into the rock here, and I'll do the rest."

She stepped back a moment and watched. Mallic's remnant tilted its head once, then shifted its weight back, looking even more like a giant spider reclining on its bulbous thorax. A hooked claw from one of its four legs wrapped around one rod and drove it into the stone. Its task complete, the umbral retreated several paces.

The unwelcome but familiar power of the nadrean rod settled as a weight on her shoulder and made her breath feel short. Volencia inhaled and siphoned nadir once again, folding the force, shaping it into a stout shaft tipped with a condensed ball. The buzzing sensation of the frenze soured her stomach and churned her guts to water, but she clenched her jaw and swung the mallet of nadir on top of the rod.

A wrenching sound, as of metal snapping and stone fracturing, echoed across the cliffside, and with it, the sigils along the rod darkened with inky intensity. All the energy and sound of life on the coast stilled. She struck again, and the nadrean sank but a finger's width farther. The sigils along the shaft flared shadows that intensified the already gloomy afternoon. After three more strikes, the grasses underfoot wilted, all their color leeching from vibrant green to brown and eventually black, as if scorched by flame.

Again and again, she struck until her head felt marinated in nadir. When she reached her limit, she cut off her connection to the current and staggered to the side, the edge of the cliff careening in her vision. Her foot lost purchase, and she windmilled an arm, oddly euphorically relieved for it all to end. Her body felt heavy and exhausted, sick even, but her mind, so steeped in the frenze, swirled with indecision. If she fell now, she wouldn't have to find her way out of the paranoia and agitation that would surely follow.

Something cold and abrasive lashed around her torso, retracting her from the escape of death. The world upended as the umbral hoisted her onto its back, and she felt her weight rock back and forth as Mallic's remnant migrated east along the coast. She allowed herself to be ferried with all the sophistication of a sack of grain.

The umbral made a poor mount, but she grabbed a ridge along its back to right herself and straddled the creature. Tiny spines embedded into her flesh, and blood welled from her palm. She sucked in a breath. *Grind it!*

She considered using nadir to dissipate the offending barbs but settled on picking at them with her teeth. The tough bits released only after significant effort. Any pain she experienced seemed dull compared to the rancid taste and smell of the umbral's flesh.

Her mind wandered, jumping randomly from thoughts of failing Tarkannen and becoming enslaved to the form of an umbral, to dreaming of her role in his new world and the power she might stand to inherit. Time and again, panic and anxiety infiltrated her train of thought. She knew the sensations were a result of the frenze, but just when she talked herself out of tumbling down one dark rabbit hole of self-loathing and paranoia, she would immediately discover the slippery descent into another.

Sobs overwhelmed her more than once as she lamented her broken relationship with her mother and the pity she witnessed the last time she encountered her brother, Veldrek, in the halls of Callinora. Color edged into the periphery of her awareness, and as Mallic's remnant clambered along the cliffs, the grasses went from black and dead to tan clumps, and eventually, anemic, yellow-green vegetation appeared.

She turned to look back in the direction from which they had traveled and found herself alarmed at the distance the umbral had covered, and at the utter devastation of the landscape. Tracking back across the western horizon, it looked as if a blanket of nadir had stilled all life. The plants and grasses stood in a lifeless panorama of black and grey, looking more like a charcoal sketch of the coastline than anything real.

Even more bizarre was the utter stillness and silence. No wind gusted up from the sea, and even the eternal rhythm of the Rodendian tides came to a stop. The surface of the sea looked more like a smooth, mercurial slick from the Drift than anything that belonged in the world of the living. For a moment, Volencia thrashed about, turning first one way and then another, convinced that the umbral had ferried her directly into the Drift without her awareness.

She even considered that the cataclysm Tarkannen claimed to want to stop might have already occurred. What if, while she was in her addled state, the barrier keeping the Drift separate from the world of the living had fractured? Her head swiveled fast one way and then another, expecting a mursk or some other formless creature to leap out at her.

From the east, a weak gust of sea air carrying the fresh fragrance of the ocean lifted her from her latest spiral of panic. She searched the ground, forcing her gaze to find further signs of life. The umbral passed over a patch of ground cover, remarkable for the short, twisty shoots with yellow-green leaves. Before her mind could migrate into another swell of nonsense, Volencia flopped off the umbral, landing on hands and knees.

She clawed eagerly at the plants, gathering up clumps of wild stilben root. Her jaw worked feverishly, chewing with ravenous desire, and she sucked hard at the juices of the crushed stems. She panted, waiting expectantly, and finally the faint taste of licorice graced the back of her tongue.

In her mind, the discovery served as a dim beacon of light in a swirling storm of confusion and darkness. The sensation made her eyes well with tears and her nose congest and sting as she nearly burst out into sobs of joy. She choked once and giggled while working on the oversized cud of stilben root. "Sometimes the Giver gives."

The irony of the thought made her stomach muscles seize with the need to laugh, but she feared choking on the barely macerated herb, and so she sat on the withered coast, chewing and swallowing with deliberate intent. Gradually, over the next few hours, the racing and unbridled nature of her jumbled thoughts stilled, the wild stilben quieting the worst parts of the frenze.

As a test, she forced her mind to consider the next steps of her mission and how her task fit into the greater plan. Her shoulders sagged with relief upon realizing that she remained capable of unfettered, linear thought. She imagined completing the task and understood how placing the second nadrean rod with its sigils of power would plunge the entire region into drought.

"So fast," she mumbled to herself. The umbral, perched not more than ten feet away, clacked its feet on the ground as it rotated to consider her words. The beast made no other attempt to communicate, remaining as still as the dead western horizon. "I didn't think the drought could happen so fast, but I see it now."

With a fresh supply of stilben, they could push on. She and the umbral could meet Tarkannen in Kreeg, marshal their forces for the final push, and conquer Aarindorn. *And then what, exactly? What do you want, Volencia?*

The thought hovered unanswered, but instead of giving the notion any weight, she dismissed it as a latent affectation of the frenze. With her pockets crammed full of stilben root, Volencia stood.

"Come on . . . Mallic." She wondered if the remnant of the former abrogator registered anything from the use of his name, but calling the umbral anything else seemed just as strange. She watched the creature for any recognition, any sign of discomfort. But the construct remained inert.

"We probably shouldn't linger here after I evoked the Giver's blessing." *That will either sour the divine lady or piss off the Taker, and neither is a consequence I care to endure.*

She marched farther east. But for the clattering of its chitinous legs, the umbral remained her silent companion. They pushed on well past sunset, climbing a gentle rise. In the last hour, she became aware of the rhythmic sound of the Rodendian Sea crashing against the cliffs, a reassuring return of the familiar. The odor of livestock and hay announced a small farm in the distance. In minutes, the light of the blue moon outlined a modest home and barn.

She was not sure if the combination of a long hike and the stilben root had settled her nerves, or if the discovery of something so provincial as a lone farmstead eased her mind, but she stood there feeling more at peace than at any other part of the journey that week.

"Meet me on the far side. I'm grabbing a mount."

She watched as Mallic's remnant retreated inland, skirting the farmstead. Volencia withdrew her crumpled veil from a pocket, fixed it in place to hide the ruined half of her face, then began the descent toward the farmstead. Her approach brought her to the back side of the barn, which stood twice as broad as the house not fifty paces away.

Inside, a wide central aisle ran the length of the building, dividing three stalls on each side. Volencia stepped forward, peering into each stall. The first stood empty save for two saddles and tack, a few barrels, and a small pile of hay. The next housed a few goats, while another penned in several sheep. A cage holding two geese sat in one of the middle stalls, and one of them squawked at her in annoyance. Finally, the last two pens held a single horse each, some kind of draft horse and a brown mare with patches of white.

Volencia walked back to the first stall and grabbed a fistful of hay. She returned to find the mare's head leaning out of the stall and held forth the hay by way of greeting.

After allowing the horse to nibble, she offered the back of her hand, and the mare sniffed, then nickered softly. "Good girl. How would you like to come out of that pen and see me through the last of my journey?"

A shadow fell across the doorway, obscuring the light of Baellen. "You'll step away from my horse if you know what's good for ya."

Volencia stopped stroking the mare's forehead and turned to consider the man silhouetted in the moonlight. She primed the sigils on her forearms but kept the power at bay. In the last few hours of travel, her mind had worked free from the worst parts of the frenze, and she had no desire to return.

The farmer held a pitchfork in both hands and took a confident step forward. "I said step away from my horse. You've got no business in our barn."

The sigils on her forearm thrummed, and the familiar shape of a shard of nadir coalesced in her mind, prepared for release. Just before she launched the projectile, a child stepped into the barn, his small, round head peering out from behind the farmer. "Who is that, Pa?"

Without thinking, Volencia drafted a second shard of nadir and prepared to launch both with deadly intent. Something in the man's bearing shifted, and he allowed the butt end of the pitchfork to rest on the ground. His other hand wrapped around the boy, holding him close.

"Aldrik, I told you to stay inside. Get back to your mother, boy. This lady and I were just having a talk."

"But I don't wanna," whined the boy.

"Aldrik, mind me now." The lad lingered only a moment, then withdrew, scampering out of the barn.

Volencia stifled her sigils, allowing the shards to dissipate. "I . . . had a brother named Aldrik. Not a common name."

"It's common enough in these parts." The farmer leaned the pitchfork against the wall, reached into a pocket, and retrieved something small. Without explanation, he knelt down and expertly struck flint to steel, igniting a small torch on the dirt floor. He set the torch in a sconce on a beam, dragged a short stool out of the stall used for storage, then sat down and used the tip of a small folding knife to clean the dirt from under his nails.

In the torchlight, she inspected his face. Sun weathered his cheeks. The man shaved his upper lip while a curly, black beard tufted out from his jaw and chin. He looked up and studied her for the first time, taking in her appearance with casual regard.

"You don't look like the average beggar," said the man.

"No, I suppose I don't at that. Do you get many this far out?" she asked.

"Every now and again one stumbles in here, usually to escape a storm or searching for a break from the Taker's wrath."

"I see," said Volencia.

The man finished cleaning his nails and replaced the knife in a pocket. He stood with a sigh and grabbed the pitchfork. But instead of brandishing it as a weapon, he reached above a rafter and stabbed into something, then lowered a set of blankets.

"I can't let you take the mare, but you can sleep in the stall here one night. You'll need to be gone by first light."

"Why?" asked Volencia.

"My kids start chores at first light, and we have a full day tomorrow. I'm sorry, but my wife is with child, and your presence is a distraction we don't need."

"No. I mean, why would you allow a complete stranger to sleep here, especially when it's clear that I arrived with rather dubious motives?"

"How can we expect the Giver to bless us if we aren't willing to do the same for others? Besides, that mare is more nag than mount."

Volencia used the torchlight to better assess the horse's conformation. "She looks sound: strong lines, full coat, young even."

"She's got something of the Taker's spirit in her; been stolen no less than three times and each time she managed to unhorse the rider only to return here within a few days. Last year she tossed a fella right off the cliffs into the Rodendian. That's why I can't let you take her."

"I see. Have you tried to sell her then?"

"Yes, but it's no use. Everyone in these parts knows her history."

"What about the markets in Faltusch? Surely you could offload her there."

"Wife and I considered it. But the journey takes more than a week, and it don't seem right to burden anyone else with Mag's temperament. There's nothing gained by pushing our misfortune onto another. Life, whether by the Giver's scarcity or the Taker's gaze, always has a way of tipping the scales back into balance."

"Mag? Her name is Mag?" asked Volencia.

"Mag the nag. Short for Maggie." The farmer grabbed the small torch and turned to exit the barn.

Before he could leave, Volencia removed a bag of coins, residual salvage from the sacking of Dernegia. She took out several silver pieces, cinched the small bag closed, and tossed it at his feet. The clinking sound drew him to a stop, and he turned, then retrieved the purse.

He considered the sum with a passive expression for a moment, eyebrows lifting in question. "These carry the Dernegian seal. What drives a woman through the dead of night all the way from the mountain kingdom?"

"Let's just say that I'm only a few steps in on a very long journey." She nodded at the purse. "That enough for the mare and the saddle?"

"Lady, it's enough to buy the farm twice over."

"Good. You're going to need it for what's coming."

The man hefted the coin purse in his palm, considering its weight. Volencia made to walk past him into the storage stall to retrieve the saddle, but the farmer waved her off. "You're leaving now? In the middle of the night?"

"We all answer to masters, and mine is no more patient than any other."

"Here then, let me. This way, maybe Mag will see you're the rightful owner."

He saddled the mare and adjusted the stirrups, shortening them to her height. In minutes, she walked Mag out of the barn, lifted a leg into the stirrup, and found her balance in the saddle. "Is she bit or leg trained?"

"Mag? Give her the bit and she'll go where you need."

"Good." She clicked her tongue on the back of her teeth, and the mare began to saunter across the farm. Volencia called back. "Do you have a wagon for that draft horse?"

"Yes, ma'am."

"I meant what I said. Gather your things, Aldrik, and that pregnant wife of yours, and get to Faltusch as soon as you can. You had best be away in one or two days. You don't want to see what's coming."

Taker's bite, I'm not sure I want to see what's coming anymore.

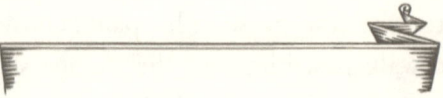

Chapter Twenty: Underestimating Abilities

Neldrek returned from a ranging into the Great Crown with only half of his original party. They ran afoul of a creature born of abrogation. To this day we struggle to comprehend and catalog the number of beasts that leached into the world during the Great War. The Giver smile on the monks foolish enough to venture into the mountains alone.

—The Tome of Nivosh, 75 PC, translated by Ksenia Balladuren

A PLUME OF DUST PRECEDED the emergence of a lone rider cresting the rocky ridgeline to the northwest. Karragin recognized the graceful silhouette of an Aarindin mount in the fading light. She tracked the approach of the rider until Baccal rode close enough to recognize her hand signals.

"All clear that way. No sign of the Moonies," signed Baccal.

"Any sign of their passage? Tracks? Anything?" Karragin signed back.

Baccal shook her head in the negative.

"Where is the prince? Did he stay close?" asked Karragin.

Baccal exhaled through pursed lips and shook her head again. Karragin considered tasking her to find and watch the young man but trusted that Neska was more than able to keep him safe. Besides, if Baccal's enhanced vision failed to discover any danger, it was unlikely Lluthean would.

"Range southeast and hook up with Amniah. Let me know if either of you find anything," signed Karragin. She shaded her eyes and considered

the sun's low position. *"Be back within the hour and we'll hand patrol over to Savnah's quad."*

Baccal tipped her head, then wheeled her Aarindin to the southeast.

A savory aroma drew Karragin's attention to the cookfire, where Savnah Derrigand sprinkled a pinch of salt over a skewered vestek flank. Karragin walked over to her friend. They'd had little chance to reconnect in the last weeks. Her duties leading the Mirrare and Savnah's managing a quad had pulled them in different directions.

"It smells good, like something Bryndor would cook up." Karragin's voice vibrated in her neck, but her inability to hear the resonance of her own words created a still-unfamiliar sensation after all the weeks since rescuing Kovesk. The act of feeling the speech without hearing it created an alien sense of being disconnected from her body. She squeezed the grips of the twin sabers strapped to each hip, trying to disperse the detached feeling.

Savnah carved away a small strip and handed the sample to Karragin. Without speaking, she wiped her hands on her trousers, then signed, *"Use the hand language."*

Karragin popped the meat into her mouth, exhaling to dissipate the heat as she chewed. Though still a bit tough, she couldn't complain about the flavor. Savnah's response, however, caught her off guard, and she aspirated a glob of spit, then spent the next few moments coughing and wiping away tears.

"Giver's . . . smile. Does it taste that bad?" asked Savnah.

Karragin recovered enough to croak a response. "Giver's smile?"

A mischievous smile sprouted on Savnah's face. *"I don't have all my swearing worked out yet. It was either Giver's smile or Giver's feet. I don't know the sign for any of the good parts, so I went with smile."*

"You sign better than me. How is that?"

The prime inhaled and wrinkled her nose. *"You can't be the best at everything, Lefledge."*

Karragin folded her arms and waited. Savnah made a pretense of turning the homemade spit for a moment and eventually stepped back. *"Fine. Lluthean's been teaching me . . . us. He teaches the quad lessons at night."*

"He gave me lessons some nights. He and Laryn, sometimes Ksenia, but I'm still not . . . you are better. You take the lessons more seriously than I do," signed Karragin.

Savnah tucked her thumbs over her belt, and the two shared a look. Karragin searched her friend's face for answers. Eventually, a furrow creased Savnah's forehead and her eyes glistened. She drew her lips to a tight line but seemed unable to offer a response. A wave of empathy settled in the pit of Karragin's stomach, and she considered retreating behind her own professional mask, but Savnah deserved better. It took a moment for her to find the words, but eventually Karragin broke the silence, mindful to speak the words with a soft feel since she couldn't hear them. "It's not your fault, Savnah."

Savnah responded with sharp, angry gestures. *"It is. It's my fault, Karra. I walk in your boots, lead your quad, listen to your brother when we range. All of it . . . my fault."*

The intensity of Savnah's gestures left no doubt about the weight of guilt she carried. Under normal circumstances, Karragin might have stepped back and allowed more space for her friend to vent. Instead, she moved closer and waited for Savnah to lift her eyes.

"Sister, bury it. I know you, and I understand it. My decisions nearly cost Amniah her life. But I need you to be the prime I know you to be, for me, for my brother, all of us. And you can't do that unless you bury it. Otherwise, everything that happened, even rescuing your brother, becomes meaningless."

Savnah dropped her gaze back to the ground for a long moment, seemed to consider the words, then lifted her chin, nodding in agreement.

"Bury it. Can you do that for me?" asked Karragin.

Savnah signed back, *"Aye, Karra. I can do that."*

They stood together, Karragin sensing that her words were enough. Savnah returned to turning the spit, and Karragin watched the others in the camp. Ranika brushed her Aarindin, Zippy, all the while speaking to him in a one-sided conversation. Laryn sat not ten feet away rereading *The Book of Seven Prophets*, while Nolan, Dexxin, and Tovnik crouched in a circle tossing dice.

A thought struck Karragin, and she signed to Savnah, *"Why did Lluthean teach you the signing?"*

"Outriders are going to use it in the field," signed Savnah.

"Are other quads using it?"

Savnah smiled and continued signing with a flourish of motions that left no doubt that she enjoyed the moment, *"Not yet."*

"But why Lluthean and not another suited to the task, like Ksenia?" Karragin asked aloud.

Savnah rolled one index finger in a circular motion. *"Keep going, you might get there."*

Karragin narrowed her eyes, trying to suss out Savnah's meaning. "He's taken a strange interest in the Outriders."

Savnah's eyes rolled to the sky, and she huffed a laugh. *"He's taken an interest in someone, but I don't think it's us."*

Karragin searched her face, expecting the punchline of a bawdy joke to fall. Savnah just shook her head and removed the meat from the fire, then signed, *"You're a monk, Lefledge. He taught us so you wouldn't be alone."*

Karragin felt an odd flush under her jawline and resumed signing. *"Why would he care about that?"*

Savnah dropped her head to the side, appearing defeated, then shook it in what appeared to be disbelief. *"Dumb as a monk and twice as stubborn."*

Before Karragin could argue, Neska trotted into camp. The wolvryn wove around the Aarindin, past Laryn, and stopped in front of Karragin, then lifted a paw. It took a moment for her to realize the significance of the strange gesture before she charged her sympath rune and opened herself to Neska.

"I'm listening. What is it? Where is Lluthean?"

"My Lluthean is fine. He watches. We found a camp. Reddevek's people were there, and something else." The tapestry of Neska's maternal voice, enriched by the sights and sounds of the mountains, rooted Karragin in place, and for a moment she forgot herself. Involuntarily, her hands lifted to her ears, and she struggled to prevent her eyes from brimming with

tears. The immersion into all the wolvryn's senses, but especially sound, threatened to overwhelm her.

She swallowed hard and focused on the link to Neska. *"Something else?"*

"Something foul."

A rancid stench rose to Karragin's awareness, spoiling everything else in the connection. She labored to swallow a wave of nausea and pulled a face. Despite hocking a glob of spit, the sensation painted the back of her tongue with a greasy musk. The contamination reminded her of the grotvonen, but worse, more revolting and somehow more pungent.

"Do you know what gives rise to that scent?"

"Not yet. My Lluthean sent me to bring you. Together we will find it. Find it and kill it."

She considered pushing for more details, but the imagery of Neska's response conveyed a clear expectation that everyone would travel together. *"I understand. I will gather everyone immediately."*

"I must go keep my Lluthean safe. Your brother can follow me." Neska turned to lope back to the north just as Amniah and Baccal rode back into camp.

She turned to Savnah. "I need you to gather everyone here."

The prime placed her thumb and finger between her teeth and whistled with what Karragin knew would be a spine-arching trill. Savnah waved everyone forward. Karragin waited to be certain that they could also see her signing.

"Neska and Lluthean found Reddevek's people. Their camp is north, and there's something else."

Karragin struggled to find the words to describe the sensation conveyed through her sympath rune. She glanced once at Amniah and considered how to pick the right phrasing. She didn't trust her signing, so tightened the muscles in her neck and spoke. "The wolvryn picked up the scent of something foul. Something that left a heavy residue."

"Worse than grot-soiled leathers?" signed Savnah.

Karragin smiled at the memory of crawling from the grotvonen warrens with leather gear so befouled by grot blood that a bonfire was the only answer for the soiled uniforms. "Maybe it's the way Neska senses the threat, but yes, much worse. We should ride out in groups. Savnah's quad should take the lead. Nolan can guide us to Lluthean's position."

Amniah maintained a stony expression but squeezed a small bag of metallic beads in her fist. Karragin had no doubt of the woman's courage, but wondered now about the wisdom of deploying her in the field when they might encounter something akin to umbral. *How will she react if we encounter another one of the Taker's minions? Giver, how would I?*

Savnah stepped forward, signing, *"Did Neska tell you anything else? Did she give numbers? What of the Moonies? Did they seem hostile?"*

"Not in words, but . . ." Karragin reviewed the images Neska had revealed. Numerous conical tents of hide ringed a central larger structure. A pelt serving as a door flap snapped in the wind. The coal and ash of dormant campfires blackened the ground, but no smoke rose into the sky. "I think the camp is empty. Empty or abandoned."

"There is less than an hour of light. How far away is the camp?" pressed the prime.

The question was reasonable. Giver, Karragin would want to know about all of the variables if she were in Savnah's boots, but Neska's concept of time didn't translate well. "If we ride out now, it will still be dark when we arrive."

Savnah listened with hands resting on the haft of her crescent moon axes. After a moment of consideration, she took action, dancing her fingers through the signing for Karragin's benefit. *"Three minutes to eat, then we skin out. We'll ride close, approach under cover of the dark. Nolan, you have point. Quad ranging formation. Karra, give us a ten-minute lead."*

Karragin nodded agreement, still more than a little impressed at Savnah's command of the signing. The admiration she felt warred with a hollow sense of loss. Watching her friend take charge was both a blessing and a reminder of her own sense of inadequacy.

Savnah butchered chunks of the cooked vestek, doling out portions in rapid succession. The Outriders gathered their Aarindin, and Nolan caught her eye, offering her a wink and a smile. The muscles at the side of her mouth tightened in a soft smile. *"Mind your prime, little brother,"* she signed.

217

Bright eyes considered her through errant curls of ginger hair. *"Eyes to the horizon, sister,"* he signed back.

She watched them ride out, then turned to find Laryn working in concert with Ranika to get Zippy saddled. Amniah and Baccal mounted their Aarindin, and together they waited. Karragin situated herself astride Trini's back and waited for the familiar comfort of the mount's grip.

She sensed a conversation unfold between Laryn and Ranika and turned to see Her Radiance gesturing with motherly concern. For her part, Ranika received the advice, whatever it was, without resistance. When Laryn finished speaking, the young woman inclined her head in a gesture of agreement, then removed the oversized hat she was never without, holding the brim between her teeth. She shook her head, letting the wind tousle spirals of hair before gathering it all back in a tight knot at the nape of her neck, only to slide the hat on before the entire untidy mess sprang loose from her fingers.

She wondered briefly what would become of Ranika when all of this was over. Perhaps she could attempt to join the Outriders. But then again, if Zippy couldn't grip her, it was unlikely any of the Aarindin would, and membership in the elite ranks required that the person be gifted. Beyond some ability in close-quarters combat, Karragin doubted that the young woman possessed the requisite skills.

She withdrew into her sympath gift and opened a connection to her Aarindin. Before sending any form of communication, Karragin strained her senses through the link, hoping for some resemblance of the rich experience she enjoyed when communicating with Neska. After sitting in silence for nearly a minute, the Aarindin craned her head in question.

"Trini, in a few minutes, we will ride out. Keep pace with Baccal. Let me know if you sense any danger. A threat lurks in the place we go to."

Trini's anxious thoughts broke into the conversation. *"Why do you always ride toward danger?"*

Karragin placed hands on her thighs and stretched her back. *"I only do what must be done. This is our mission today. As long as we are together, we will be safe."*

Trini stepped lightly, shifting her weight from one front hoof to the other, eventually settling to stillness. *"I know. We are always safe together. I will make sure the others know of the danger."*

Karragin released her grip on zenith and checked the security of her sabers, more as an unconscious habit than out of any genuine concern. When it felt like ten minutes had passed, she cleared her throat and spoke. "Baccal, you take lead. I'll follow. Your Radiance and Nika, ride behind me. Amniah, you are the rear guard."

They rode out in formation. Within a half an hour, the sun dipped below the summit of the Great Crown and a chill swept across the mountainside. Karragin retreated to the warmth Trini provided but kept the vest of her riding gear open. *If we're in for a muddle, better to have the freedom of movement.*

Over the next hour, the stars began to decorate the night sky, and the half-moon of Baellen afforded enough light to make out Baccal's silhouette. More sure-footed than common horses, the Aarindin trotted and cantered along without missing a step. Karragin considered rekindling her sympath run to communicate with Trini, but the filly's talkative nature was more of a distraction than she cared to manage at the moment. Eventually, Trini's steps slowed, and Tovnik came into view, sitting alone on his mount.

Ranika brought Zippy to a halt beside Karragin. The young woman grabbed her wrist, then dropped a rock with faceted gems into Karragin's open palm. Ripples of pale light wove back and forth through the crystals, building in enough intensity that Karragin could easily make out everyone's facial expressions, and, more importantly, their gestures.

"It's a moonstone. You can use it for now," signed Ranika. *"You need it more than I do."*

Karragin studied the young woman's face. Her first instinct was to resist the gift. It felt like admitting something vulnerable about her disability. But everyone present knew of her situation, so she swallowed back her pride and tilted her head in acceptance. *"My thanks,"* she signed.

Tovnik stepped into the nimbus of light created by the moonstone and signed, *"Lluthean and the others are perched up there."* He pointed

219

where the blanket of stars appeared above the ridgeline some two hundred paces away. *"Savnah ordered the Aarindin here."*

The faint reek of decay carried on the wind, the same odor from Neska's communication but far less pungent. Karragin dismounted and made eye contact with Laryn. She was about to request that Her Radiance remain behind for her own safety.

"Stop. Better together. Always better together," signed Laryn. *"We're coming. Lead on."*

Karragin nodded once, signaled the Aarindin to stay, and led the group up the rocky incline. Halfway up, she pocketed the moonstone, allowing her eyes to adjust. Before her head rose above the summit, she crouched down, and everyone followed her example. The cliffside dropped away into a sweeping valley. Moonlight glinted off a burbling stream, and she could just make out the outlines of conical tents, but no embers glowed from the dormant cookfires.

Someone touched her elbow, and she turned to find Tovnik. He gestured to a cluster of brambles and trees a short distance to the east. Karragin retreated down the slope, then led the company on a brisk walk to the trees. Lluthean dropped from a perch high in the branches, then buried a hand in Neska's fur and stared down into the valley. Savnah, Dexxin, and Nolan remained vigilant, surveying the horizon in different directions.

Karragin signaled Amniah and Baccal to assume defensive positions, and together they waited. Eventually, Lluthean turned and joined them while Neska loped down into the valley. He upended a small pouch, and the petrified wolvryn eye fell into his hands, emitting more light than the moonstone. He set the glowing orb on the ground and waved everyone close.

"The Moonies are here. Their scent is strong, but Neska can't see them," signed Lluthean.

Nolan nodded agreement. *"I agree. There are signals of humans everywhere, but they are two days old at best."*

"Something stinks down there. Are they all dead?" signed Savnah.

"No. There are bodies, dead horses and more. But the smell is not death; it's something else," Lluthean signed.

"Are there skip trails, like with the umbral?" Karragin pressed.

"Giver's good fortune, no," signed Nolan.

"What made that stink, then?" Savnah asked.

Before anyone could answer, a vibration rippled through the ground, emanating from somewhere down in the valley. Karragin felt it simultaneously in her core as much as rising through her legs. The intensity and persistence of the tremor caused an annoying burning sensation in her feet. She watched as everyone clutched their ears and fell to the ground in pain.

Even Savnah seemed overwhelmed. Karragin grabbed the wolvryn eye and sprinted to the ridgeline, toward the source of the disturbance. She skidded to a stop, barely keeping her footing along the loose rock, and scanned the abandoned camp. From beyond one of the distant tents, close to the stream, Neska's figure appeared in the moonlight. The wolvryn had hunched her shoulders and was shaking her head from side to side in pain. She gathered her feet to charge when another intense rippling vibration rose from the valley floor, and Neska cringed, even dropping her chin to the ground.

Giver help us, what kind of threat causes you to cower?

Karragin hurled the wolvryn eye, tracking the streaking beacon as it landed far below, rolling to a stop twenty paces in front of the wolvryn. At the edge of the pale blue light prowled an otherworldly creature. It rivaled Boru for size, but lumbered forward with less grace on four muscled legs that ended in thick claws. It gripped the ground, preparing to charge, and so did Karragin.

Zenith thrummed through her arca prime, and she gave over to the full, unbridled fury of her gift. A single leap brought her skidding among loose stones more than halfway down the cliffside. She sprinted to intercept the beast, dropping low to the ground to retrieve a boulder the size of one of her atlas stones.

Neska retreated to the edge of the darkness as the strange beast plodded forward. Uncertain of the creature's capabilities, Karragin decided to hurl the boulder before getting any closer. The rock smashed into its shoulder, causing it to spin and careen away into the darkness. For a moment, the strange vibrations stopped.

With her sympath rune charged, she opened a link to Neska, and spoke in the commanding tone of a prime and made it clear she would tolerate no dissent. *"Neska. This is a fight you can't win. Get to Lluthean. Protect the pack. Now!"*

The wolvryn lifted her head and considered the threat. Karragin sensed the vibrations return, and Neska's head rolled to the side in pain. The wolvryn wheeled about and sprinted back up to the cluster of trees, where Karragin hoped the others were recovering.

She withdrew the moonstone and tossed it to the edge of the light cast by the wolvryn eye. Something shifted in the shadows, and the beast prowled forward. The friction of steel against leather sheaths grounded her in the moment as she withdrew twin sabers and set her feet, studying the make of the thing.

A crown of ridged horns curled around a bony face that housed lidless eyes. Something of the horn material spread across broad front shoulders like plated armor. When it crept forward, light reflected off a myriad of similar smaller eyes lining the shoulders and running along its flank.

Gonna be hard to surprise you from the side.

The beast tilted back onto its hind legs and exposed thick ridges similar to a dense rib cage. Karragin thought the creature was about to pounce, but instead, it remained in place, and its entire torso quaked, causing the ridges to undulate back and forth along the central line of what she could only think of as its breastbone. A cascade of painful vibrations flowed from the beast.

So that's how you do it.

This close to the beast, the intensity of the vibrations it created caused her stomach to cramp, and a dull headache blossomed in the back of her head. But Karragin had dealt with worse, much worse.

But you don't know that, do you?

Instinct told her she could likely outmaneuver the thing, but it would clearly see her approach from the side. She dropped to a knee, feigning pain as if she was affected like Neska, but kept a wary eye on the thing. It continued to shudder and rumble, taking half steps and sending wave after wave of the vibrations out before it. Though the beast made slow progress, it never faltered and never limped.

That thought unnerved Karragin. The boulder she'd hurled was heavy enough to crush a horse, but this thing didn't appear marred in the least. In fact, as it approached, the light shined off an oily, muscled hide, but there was no sign of any bleeding.

She continued to crouch, waiting, baiting the thing closer and gathering her strength. The beast gnashed its teeth together and continued the endless barrage of its vibratory attack. Up close, the rancid reek of the creature became a palpable quality in the air and on the back of her tongue.

She didn't have to fake being in pain anymore and clutched an arm across her abdomen. After a few panting breaths, she inhaled once and set her weight on her back foot. With a lunge fueled by zenith, she surged directly at the beast's chest. With flawless precision, she swiped a saber forward, intending to wedge it deep between the vibrating ridges. Right before the blade landed, something throttled into her left side.

The blow threw her well beyond the halo of light and brought to mind memories of the strength of the alpha grondle. She managed to roll to her feet but lost one of her sabers in the assault. A sharp stab of pain flared from her left rib cage with every breath.

Now that she stood to the side of the beast, she could see a set of thick tails waving back and forth. Instead of tapering to a point, a blunt mass of something that looked more like a mace and less like a tail whipped in and out of the light. Another vibration rumbled across the valley, and the nimbus of rune fire flared into the night sky from beyond the ridgeline.

Sneaky grinder, you were baiting me the whole time, and there's at least one more of you up there. My turn then.

Five swift paces placed her toward the front of the beast, then she leaped off a boulder and lashed out, striking the creature along its flank. Instead of pulling the blade for a deep cut, she lifted the tip, raking across a row of the beast's eyes. The saber rattled against bone and chitin, but the incessant vibration attack stopped, and she sensed the beast shudder in pain.

Karragin sprinted behind it, hopping over a swipe of one tail, then dashed to the beast's other side. She intended to repeat the slashing maneuver, but the creature rolled its body, and the other thick tail came in for a backswing. She grunted through the pain in her side and brought her blade down in an overhead arc with both hands. The force of the blow nearly wrenched the weapon from her grasp and she skidded back several feet, but the back half of the tail lopped off, hot ichor steaming on the ground.

A series of uncontrolled vibrations from the ridged chest cage echoed in the night as the beast bucked and thrashed about. It turned to sniff at the amputated appendage on the ground. Karragin retreated to the edge of the light, her breaths coming fast and labored, the pain in her ribs flaring with more intensity.

Several sets of eyes blinked as the thing panted and trained its focus on her. It clawed into the stone in preparation to charge, but instead, it lurched back onto its hind legs, ripped away a slab of stone, and heaved it at Karragin. The surprise attack froze her in place long enough that all she could manage was to collapse to the ground, letting the stony mass fly overhead. But now the beast had her.

In one fluid motion, it returned to all fours and charged her. She grunted to rise despite the pain in her ribs, but could see it now, the ruse, the creature's intelligence. She had underestimated its ability to strategize, and now she was too slow. The beast must have sensed it too, as it placed all its fury into the charge.

She had enough time to set herself, barely aware of the sharp rocks grinding into her knee, and raised her saber for one more strike. The beast lunged, and a wave of light from the moonstone glistened along its chest. Then something cold and ropelike lashed around her waist, jerking her to the side. The strange tether appeared one moment, then disappeared, leaving her bewildered. Her mind struggled to process the oddity, for as she landed, pain erupted with a brilliant and piercing intensity radiating from her ribs.

A tingly, lightheaded sensation overwhelmed her, causing her to take labored, splinted breaths. She rolled onto her left side, using the ground to brace against any unnecessary movement. Through tear-blurred

224

vision, two silhouettes stalked forward. Savnah prowled before the creature, clanging her moonblade axes in repeated challenge. The halo of zenith from her arca prime illuminated the grim determination of her expression.

The other, though, a lithe figure with the unmistakable frenzied spirals of hair bouncing with every step, was Ranika. While Savnah made a show of gathering the beast's attention, Ranika stopped just inside the circle of light cast by the moonstone and wolvryn eye, cocked her head, and considered the beast.

The two women shared a look and a nod before Ranika set her feet. Oily shadow coalesced at Ranika's feet, weaving up her legs and dimming the light for several feet around her. Black veining flowed up her neck and obscured her face. The beast jerked its head away from Savnah, the myriad of eyes blinking and squinting, considering the new threat manifesting in the young woman swirled in shadow.

For the first time, the creature retreated a step. It fell back on its original attack, resuming the vibrations from the repetitive clacking of its ridged chest cage. Ranika cupped hands to her ears, but a volley of black shards still launched from her shoulders. Some glanced harmlessly off its armored carapace, but others found purchase, blinding the beast. A dense tentacle sprouted from Ranika's torso and wedged itself between the beast's ridged chest. A snarl appeared on the young woman's face, and finally, the painful vibrations ceased.

A similar set of tentacles erupted from Ranika's arms and lashed around the beast's forelegs. Savnah wasted no time and charged at the creature's blind side. Her moonblades glinted in the light as she cleaved once into a muscled hip joint, burying the axe between ridges of chitinous armor. The creature listed as its useless hind leg splayed out. She spun, bringing both hands around in an overhand swing that looked wild and desperate, and the remaining tail flew off into the darkness.

Ichor sprayed Savnah's face, and she hocked a glob of spit before turning to lock eyes with Karragin. They shared a look, and Savnah nodded grimly, then marched to the front of the beast where Ranika labored to hold the thing at bay.

Karragin willed the women on. *Kill the grinder!*

Savnah swung with reckless abandon, heaving everything into her strikes. Her blade rose and fell, chopping deeper and deeper into the muscled neck behind the thick armored carapace covering its head and shoulders. The beast thrashed with frantic intensity but remained held fast by Ranika's black tethers, and the air curdled with a sour odor.

After a while, Ranika staggered, and she looked about to lose her footing when Savnah's axe lifted and fell one last time. The creature shuddered, then collapsed to the ground. Savnah dropped to her knees, panting, but Ranika turned and emptied her stomach into the darkness. Karragin lay on her side, attempting to control her breathing.

The damp cold of the ground under her ribs eased the pain only a little. Minutes passed before Ranika stepped back into the light, bereft of any sign of the oily shadow that had coalesced at her feet.

Savnah's shoulder spasmed with the rhythm of a chuckle, and she turned to face Karragin, a severe bruise marring the side of her face. She spoke slowly and mouthed words for Karragin's benefit. "Giver's shiny bum, Lefledge. When you muddle, you don't grind around!"

A soft smile was all Karragin could manage, too afraid to laugh for the pain it might cause. Savnah rose to her feet, a look of concern darkening her expression. She retrieved both the moonstone and wolvryn eye and dropped them together on the ground, then knelt down.

"How bad is it?" signed the prime.

"My ribs, maybe the lung. I'm not sure," grunted Karragin. "Is Her Radiance, the prince, are they—"

"They are safe. Rest here. I will get Laryn," signed Savnah.

"I will go," signed Ranika. Before Savnah could rise to her feet, the young woman bounded off on light feet into the darkness. Savnah waved a weary hand, hitched her butt cheeks to the ground, rested her hands over her knees, and dipped her head forward. They remained there, Karragin focused on the cadence of her breathing despite the pain, and Savnah panting from the labor of her exertions.

"I'm glad you were here. I made mistakes, assuming there was only one. I sensed rune fire. Did another one attack on the ridge?"

"The other was smaller. Your prince, Amniah and Ranika made quick work of the one up there," signed Savnah.

"He's our prince," said Karragin.

"Tell him that. Laryn ordered him to stay behind, but I could see he was biting at the bit to join you."

"Well, you two saved me. Again, I find myself in your debt, sister. That thing . . . nearly had me," said Karragin.

Eventually, Savnah turned her head. She wiped a sleeve across her face and neck to remove splatters of ichor, then winked. Her fingers danced in the pale light. *"You almost had it."*

"No. I was—I don't know. I reacted without thinking. I'm still adjusting. I think I was trying to prove something to myself."

They sat in silence while Savnah considered the statement. At last, she signed, *"Did you get hit on the head? You never talk this much."*

An easy smile swelled on Karragin's face. "Maybe," she answered.

"Well, before the others return, there's something we should settle," Savnah signed.

Karragin sensed another jibe coming from her friend. Whether it be about the prince or the mistakes she made this night, she was too weary to deflect the barb. "What's that?"

Savnah leaned closer and mouthed the words with deliberate intent. "Even though she pulled you from certain death, what are we going to do about that abrogator?"

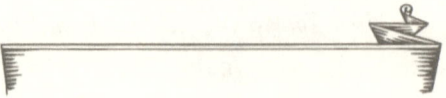

Chapter Twenty-One: Blunt Revelations

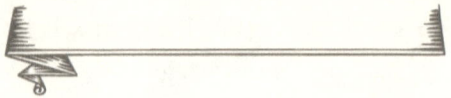

Kaellor folded his arms against the evening chill and stared at the starry sky. He paced back and forth across the balcony to the private suite he shared with Laryn, brooding. Despite kindling a continuous connection into the shek, the pendant remained dormant. He flicked a finger at the base of the stickpin, waiting to see if her voice would respond. Laryn had either forgotten their predetermined meeting, or, more likely, was prevented from using the shek. That latter possibility fed a disquietude that he struggled to master.

He had half a mind to ask Bryndor to test the device and ensure that it still worked, but he had it on good authority that his nephew had ventured outside of Stone's Grasp with Boru, and he wasn't sure that they had returned yet.

Therek could engage the pendant, but Kaellor couldn't bring himself to bother the regent at the late hour, and such action would only validate the restless feeling in the pit of his stomach. He stopped at the far end of the balcony and turned, placed his hips against the balustrade, and craned his neck back to find the half-moon of Baellen. The muscles in his shoulders cramped, and he sighed with self-recrimination.

Giver's last word, Laryn. Where are you?

He turned to place his hands on the stone rail and attempted to ground his thoughts. After a deep inhalation, he sorted through the smells of the city. Kitchens had extinguished hearths hours ago, and the overripe aroma of the Sprawl steeped the air with the rank odor of too many humans until a breeze gusted off the Great Crown laced with the fragrance of conifer and wildflower, and finally, he relaxed, opening his eyes.

Across the city, lanterns and torchlight flickered amber and yellow, casting dancing shadows in the lower commons and the Sprawl. The effect made the streets and alleyways appear alive with activity compared to the high district. In the affluent neighborhoods, zenith-powered artifacts cast steady pale blue light from windows in manors. Set just beyond the inner curtain wall, these residences created a tranquil, blue aura around the castle.

An annoying, persistent buzzing sensation rose to his awareness, reminiscent of late summer locusts from the Southlands. Kaellor swept his gaze across the city, even into the night sky, in search of the source of the oddity. Upon withdrawing his hands from the balustrade, the sound dissipated.

"Giver, mark me as a monk."

He replaced a hand on the stone railing and the intensity of the buzzing returned, an amplified expression of the castle defenses becoming active. The realization gave urgency to his step as he returned to the sitting room and found his guardian sword. The weapon lay sheathed, resting against a chair. As his hands gripped the hilt, zenith surged into his runes unbidden.

A brilliant guardian ward flared out, toppling the table and chairs before he reduced the intensity of the construct, bringing the sword's amplification under control. He held the flat of the blade up for closer inspection, watching the flickers of zenith play across the scrolling runes engraved into the metal.

Words of reprimand came to mind, and he almost chided the weapon as one would a warhorse eager for the charge. The absurdity of speaking to an inanimate object felt like something a child might do, and he set the notion to the side, focusing on the way the sword was interacting with his gift. While he intuitively understood that the weapon primed his defenses, something in the way it rose unbidden felt like losing control. With deliberate effort, he dissipated the guardian ward and released his hold on the flows of zenith.

That was when he noticed the gentle tug on the ambient flows around him. Someone else very close had also channeled zenith. Kaellor allowed a slow trickle of the force to flow back into his runes of judgment and perception. A cold ripple of foreboding rose to his awareness.

Gently, so as not to alert any hostile zeniphiles—though the sword's earlier display may have already done that—he eased the flow into his arca prime, manifesting a guardian ward as an aura. When he turned to the door, he caught sight of his silhouette in the window. A translucent nimbus of zenith outlined his body, making him appear almost wraithlike. In the future, he would need to work on bringing the shielding to bear as an invisible barrier.

"No help for it now."

He placed a palm flat on the door and listened, straining for any sign of the danger beyond. After thirty heartbeats, he pulled the door open a few inches. No shadows disturbed the light, so he stepped into the corridor. To the right, the doors to Bryndor and Lluthean's individual suites remained closed. Beyond that, the hall turned, ending in the door to rooms Ranika now occupied.

He exhaled through his nose. *And it's the Giver's good fortune that none of you are home.*

To the left, ten paces away, the door granting entrance to the wing of rooms stood cracked open. Either the guards had been derelict in their duties, or someone unauthorized had gained access. Kaellor raised his sword in a defensive position and prowled forward.

Before he had time to form a plan, the clamor of battle and crashing swords echoed from the room beyond. He pressed a shoulder against the heavy timbers and heaved, but something barred the door's motion. Kaellor looked down and saw a piece of leather or material wedged there.

The clang of swords paused, then resumed, accompanied by a cry of pain. Kaellor unleashed a focused column of force, blasting the door open and stepping into the large room. Chaos greeted him, but his focused mind quickly took in the scene, calculating the threats in moments.

The corpse of a dead sentinel lay at his feet, tangled with the smoldering wreckage of an invader rendered lifeless by either rune fire or the castle wards. Together, the corpses had obstructed the door. Across the room, two other guards engaged a masked assailant dressed in tight-fitted black garb. The invader wielded two stout metal rods and in the space of only a few seconds disarmed then incapacitated both sentinels.

Bryndor held his ground on the far corner of the room against another masked assailant wielding similar rods. To the left, another assailant held a guard hostage with a knife blade under the chin. Bryndor parried and backstepped into the corner, keeping himself between the assassins and Ksenia Balladuren.

Something flickered from the shadows to his right, and a thwack preceded the flight of a crossbow bolt. The missile streaked from down the hallway, clanging to the floor when it struck his guardian ward. *Why aren't the castle wards preventing this attack?*

He slapped a hand against the wall, searching for the familiar thrum of the warding. With a thought, the wards activated and three bell-like warning tolls rumbled through the walls, alerting the guards of intruders.

Another crossbow bolt flew directly at his head, again deflected by his warding. With a slash of his sword, Kaellor sent a crescent of force down the hallway to his right, then lunged into the melee. The closest assailant turned to face him, spinning one metal rod high and the other low in a defensive stance.

The guardian blade flicked out with unnatural speed for a longsword, but the assassin parried Kaellor's probing attack with one rod and brought the other around in a tight circle designed to disarm. He sensed the danger and withdrew just in time to deflect the blow without losing his grip on the hilt, but a throbbing burn vibrated into his forearm from the force of the attack.

The realization of his opponent's expertise broke through the tight shackle Kaellor kept on his gift, and he gave in to the battle lust. He set his feet and executed a flurry of deadly blows against his attacker, but the assassin deftly avoided and blocked him, only to spin back with a surprising string of attacks designed to incapacitate or disarm.

Kaellor sidestepped and deflected a vicious swing meant for his knee. He pulsed a wave of force directly at the assassin, but the invader twisted with the surge of energy, landing safely ten feet away only to charge and renew the attack. That's when he felt it again: a distinct tug on the ambient flows of zenith. This enemy, at least, was a zeniphile.

Kaellor barely managed to bring the guardian sword around to deflect a string of attacks that seemed to appear from the least logical place based on his recognition of the other's footwork and stance. Finally, the assassin gambled too close, and Kaellor struck the top of his hand with the cross guard, causing him to drop one of the strange rods.

His assailant switched stances and gripped the rod with two hands, but Kaellor charged to prevent his foe from recovering. He jabbed, arced, feinted, parried, swung, feinted again, and flowed through stances. More than once, Kaellor assumed he would land a blow that would bring the fight to an end, but each time the assassin met his attack.

They danced back and forth with neither gaining the upper hand, but the assassin's eyes widened when Kaellor absorbed a brutal swing for his head. Kaellor had anticipated the attack and reinforced his shielding, deflecting the blow, then swept the guardian blade about with a strike meant to decapitate.

Somehow, the assassin pulled back, and the sword tip slashed through the black mask, scoring a thin cut along the jawline. The space created, finally allowed Kaellor to turn, and he pulsed a column of force at Bryndor's foe. The current throttled the other assassin against the far wall with bone-jarring force, and he crumpled to the floor, lifeless.

Kaellor quickstepped beside his nephew, then flared his guardian ward to include Ksenia and Bryndor under its protective shielding. He studied the room. One assassin still held a knife under the chin of a sentinel, who whimpered in pain. The other retrieved the discarded metal rod and glared back. Despite the defiant posture, the invader's shoulders heaved with labored breaths. Blood darkened her mask and dripped onto the front panel of her shirt from the wound he had scored across her jaw, but she seemed oblivious to the injury.

"How did you get this far without activating the castle wards?" growled Kaellor through his own panted breaths.

The assassin shrugged once, then delicately poked a metal rod at the edge of the blue ward that stood between them all. The resonant alto voice of a woman answered his question in a thick, foreign accent. "It was never about you, or your family, Your . . . Highness. Some might say our intent is to free your family from a dark shadow."

Understanding displaced his initial surprise, and realization washed over Kaellor. He had laced the definitions of the castle defenses with a layer of intent. He would have to refine the barriers later. "If you're not my enemy, then why are you here? You would do well to tell me what this is about before anyone else gets hurt."

"I'm afraid that I must decline." The woman spoke with what sounded like genuine regret, but then gestured down the hall as footsteps approached, signaling the arrival of more invaders.

"Let my guard go, and I promise not to end all of you. Try to run, and I'll find you," said Kaellor.

The woman stood with her rods crossed, weight balanced on the balls of her feet. "Your only tracker is on a mission in the Great Crown and your nephew's wolvryn is hunting in the timber. There is no person you can deploy who will pick up our trail in time. Not everything is as it seems, Your Highness. Once I am done here, I'm quite certain that you will never see me again. The deaths of your guard and my men are a shame and were never our intention. Leave us to our business, and no other guards need to be harmed."

"What is your business?" Kaellor pressed.

The lead invader ignored his question and gestured, directing her party through the door that led to the royal suites. Two more black-clad assailants sprinted on silent feet from the shadows and ducked through the door, followed by the leader. Her partner, still holding the guard hostage at knifepoint, backed slowly through the door.

At the last moment, the sentinel's knees buckled, and he was thrown to the floor, then the door slammed closed. The sound of three hard strikes followed, as if someone had rammed spikes into the door and frame.

Kaellor maintained his ward and turned to Bryndor. "Are either of you injured?"

Bryndor gestured to the corpse of the assassin he had battled. "No. I don't think he or she was trying to kill me. It seemed like all the swings were pulled. Once I realized the attacks were meant to disarm, they became predictable."

"It makes sense. That's why the castle defenses didn't dispatch them outright. I'm going to have to alter the definitions later. Did you burn that invader by the door?" asked Kaellor.

"No, I don't know what happened there," said Bryndor.

"I think that the castle defenses activated when one of their members killed that sentinel. A cascade of blue lightning erupted from the wall," said Ksenia.

"I'm sorry, Kae, I didn't know if I could control my gift in such tight quarters, and I didn't want to hurt the guards," said Bryndor.

Kaellor kept his eyes trained on the door and the shadowed hallway, waiting for any surprise attacks. "You did well, especially against such an unorthodox opponent. How did all of this unfold? What drew you here?"

"When we returned from the plaza, there weren't any guards stationed at the entry. We followed the trail of at least eight incapacitated sentinels here. What are they after?" asked Bryndor.

"That's what we are going to find out," said Kaellor.

Zenith streamed loose and free into his arca prime, but he reduced the size of the ward to conserve his stamina, then anchored it in place. "Ksenia, remain here until we know more. You should be safe behind the ward. You can step through at any time, but none can enter save by my leave. Bryndor, you're with me."

Kaellor stepped through the barrier, a tingle of static stinging his ears and fingertips as he passed through. Bryndor followed, grunting in surprise. They approached the incapacitated sentinel previously held hostage. The man lay prone but still appeared to breathe.

He recalled the crossbow attacks and glanced down the shadowed hallway. "Bryn, give me a controlled burst of rune fire down that corridor."

"You sure?" asked Bryndor.

"Do it. A short burst."

Bryndor inhaled, and the momentary vacuum of zenith made Kaellor shiver. Thirty paces away, a brilliant sphere of rune fire erupted.

The sound of glass windows shattering accompanied a gust of hot air as a back draft roiled toward them. Kaellor pulsed a column of force into the hallway, and the debris swirled in a harmless, cloudy vortex.

Kaellor dropped his chin to chest with a sigh. "I said a short burst."

"I know. The room was smaller than I accounted for. Sorry," said Bryndor.

"That's . . . on me, I suppose." Kaellor breathed a bit easier without the fear of archers from the shadows. He crouched beside the prone sentinel and turned him to the side, expecting to find a bleeding wound. Other than a purple welt on the temple, he discovered no obvious injuries. They pulled him to safety beside the ward, then considered the door to the royal suites.

Bryndor held one of the discarded crossbow bolts in his hand and rubbed a thumb over its blunt tip. "I don't get it."

"If they entered with an intent to kill, the castle wards would have incinerated them. Those bolts are stunners. Take one in the head and you might lose an eye, but you'll live to talk about it the next day," said Kaellor.

"If I may, where are the reinforcements?" Ksenia called from the corner.

Kaellor scratched, then tugged at his chin hairs. "With the four guards here, plus the eight you encountered on the way in, that's a full shift rotation. Others will follow protocol and secure their posts. I suspect it will take several more minutes before they discover the break in communication from this level."

He turned back to the door. "Bryn, I'll set a ward just inside the door, then try to pull it open."

He ushered zenith through his arca prime, shaping it to his will. Crafting the barrier several feet ahead while maintaining the ward around Ksenia strained his focus, but he felt the zenith-infused wall take shape. "It's done. Give it a go."

Bryndor reached for the door handle and pulled at first with one hand and then two, but the door held fast. Eventually, he relaxed and leaned in, inspecting the doorframe. He ran his fingers along the edge and withdrew, hissing in pain. "Grind it. They used daggers to wedge the door closed from the other side. It's not budging."

Bryndor stepped back, a puzzled expression on his face. "Nobody is in there, Kae. Not Lluthean or Laryn or Ranika. Taker's grip, what are they after?"

The same question plagued Kaellor, but he set it aside. "I don't know. Focus on what's in front of us. Can you shape rune fire in a way that lets you burn away enough of the door to get it open without blasting a hole into the entire wing?"

"Maybe. I can try," said Bryndor.

Kaellor looked over his shoulder to ensure that Ksenia remained behind the ward. "Just, less boom and more finesse."

Another vacuum disturbed the ambient flows of zenith as Bryndor manifested a globe of rune fire between his hands. Instead of hurling the flame, he condensed it into a thin column that flowed against the wood while emitting a soft roaring sound, like a distant waterfall. The smell of woodsmoke filled the room as Bryndor's gift surged, burning at first as a blue flame, then magnifying into a blinding white stream. Once he had the intensity of the beam refined, he seared away small sections of the door around the daggers until it swung open to reveal Kaellor's ward just beyond.

"Well done. Get behind me, Bryn," said Kaellor, and he moved the shielding forward as they crept down the hallway. They stopped and looked into Kaellor's rooms, and finding them empty, checked Bryndor's door.

Bryndor was about to place his hand on the locking placard outside the door when he stopped and stepped back. "If the placards lock these doors to all but a Baellentrell, then nobody should be in my rooms or Lluthean's. That just leaves Ranika's suites, and since she can't wield zenith—"

"There's no lock on her door. Alright, Nika's rooms then. Keep alert, and keep your gift primed," said Kaellor. He crept down the hall, inching the guardian ward before them. They turned the corner and saw that the door to Ranika's receiving room was propped open.

"Give me a bit of light. We're going in," said Kaellor.

Kaellor stepped through the door, expanding his shielding out in a circular arc. Bryndor held globes of rune fire high in each hand, dashing away the shadows in the room. The receiving room held several padded chairs to entertain guests. A few small tables with bowls of fruit remained undisturbed. A musty fragrance lingered in the chamber despite a strong breeze that gusted in from an open window.

On the far side of the room, the door to Ranika's private sleeping chamber stood open. *"Forward,"* signed Kaellor. Bryndor nodded and followed. As they crept closer, Kaellor reshaped and enveloped them in his warding. The light from Bryndor's rune fire illuminated an empty bedchamber. The bed remained undisturbed, and the only sound came from curtains that billowed out into the night.

Once he felt certain that none of the invaders remained, Kaellor approached the window. He stared back across the dancing lights of the city, looking for any sign of the assailants. The subtle flicker of motion outside the curtain wall almost escaped his notice. A lithe figure floated down through the hazy nimbus of watery, blue light cast by zendils. She turned to stare back up at him, blood now staining most of the front of her shirt, then dashed away into the darkness.

Kaellor suspended his connection to zenith and let his arca prime fall dormant. A quick search outside the windows revealed no ropes or climbing gear. "Taker's breath, they must have more than one glider in their ranks. They definitely came this way, but they're gone. Let's look around, see if we can find what they were here for."

Kaellor returned to the receiving room while Bryndor searched the bedchamber. None of the furnishings appeared out of place. Minutes later, Ksenia called from down the hallway, "Your Highness, reinforcements have arrived. Is it safe to proceed?"

Kaellor stepped into the doorway to see Ksenia standing beside a wide-eyed guard. "It's safe now. They got whatever they came for and left out the window, of all things. You there, secure this level."

Kaellor considered barking more commands, then remembered the stickpin. He activated the device and chanced a conversation. "This is Kaellor. Is anyone listening?"

The regent's breathy voice rasped through the shek. "Giver's breath, Kae. This is Therek, and Hestian is listening as well. Are you alright? What's going on?"

"Bryndor and I are safe. We foiled some kind of attack in the royal suites. They killed one sentinel, and we dispatched two of their number. There are about a dozen wounded guards who will need the services of the healers, and we need replacement guards on this floor immediately."

"I can see to that, Kae. What else can we do to secure the castle?" asked Hestian.

"I'm not sure. For the moment, it looks like the invaders fled. They had gifted, gliders most likely, and left through a window in one of the suites. I think we are safe enough for now," said Kaellor.

"We should gather for a debriefing as soon as you are able," suggested Hestian.

"Agreed. I propose we meet in my private chambers within the hour," said Kaellor.

"We will see you then," said Therek.

The stickpin fell silent, and Kaellor turned to see Ksenia walking down the hallway, a confused look creasing her brow. "Your Highness, there's something—"

Kaellor held up a hand. "Kess, I appreciate the formal address when others are about, but I think we know each other well enough to drop the titles."

Ksenia dipped her chin. "Of course, sorry I . . ." She squinted her eyes and tilted her head to the side as Bryndor walked back into the receiving room.

"Nothing seems out of place back there. I even tossed the bed, Kae," said Bryndor.

"There is something off," said Ksenia. She turned a slow circle, inspecting the room. "Am I imagining things, or does Ranika's room seem heavily doused in vellevlin?"

"Nika wouldn't use vellevlin," said Bryndor.

Kaellor shot a stiff glance at Bryndor. "Nika wouldn't use any kind of perfume. The cost if not the reek of vellevlin would definitely turn her away."

Ksenia rolled her left wrist inside the fingers of her right hand. "So .
. . why did a group of assassins storm the castle, try very hard not to kill anyone, and then cover their tracks with a fragrance that offends most of us but subdues an abrogator?"

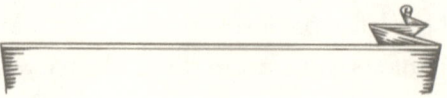

Chapter Twenty-Two: More Than Meets the Eye

Of all the gifted in Aarindorn, perhaps I am most grateful to those who wear the mantle of healer. The descendants of Maedreness, the Shaman Queen, enrich us more perhaps than any others in Aarindorn. These talented men and women mend us from our brokenness, lift us from our darkest moments, and battle the Taker's influence with the Giver's blessings. I could rightly devote an entire book to their work, but such words would still be inadequate to convey the depth of my respect for their art.

—The Tome of Nivosh, 75 PC, translated by Ksenia Balladuren

THE WHIRRING HUM OF the healer song drifted across the camp as Laryn continued her ministrations. She knelt by Karragin and shook her head, alarmed by the discoveries of her probing. Fracture lines crossed six ribs on the woman's left, and one of them had punctured the sack around the lung. More than that, nearly all of her internal organs were swollen and wept fluid as an insidious latent effect of the beast's attack.

It was the Giver's mercy that your deafness allowed you to engage that rumbler thing despite its manipulation of sound, but in the process you endured more trauma than you know.

Tovnik knelt beside them both, donating channeled zenith, lending Laryn his strength while observing her techniques. His support was essential, given the complexity of the weaving required. She drafted individual currents of zenith and placed blocks at the base of the nerve clusters running along the damaged ribs. As the last block slid into place, the beads of sweat rolling off of Karragin's pale face dissipated, and a hint of color returned to her face.

"Thank you, Your Radiance," said Karragin. The young woman tried to sit up despite Laryn's hand on her shoulder.

Laryn signed a curt response. *"You are in shock. Lie still. I will tell you when to rise."*

Laryn considered lifting one of the pain blocks, but something in the commanding nature of her signing broke through the woman's dazed confusion and she nodded in agreement, muttering, "Yes. Of course."

Over the next hour, Laryn labored to seal the rent in the lung's lining and reshape the broken bones, but the integrity of the lower two challenged her skill. Where the upper ribs revealed simple cracks, these were sundered. Reshaping the tiny bits into something resembling the natural curvature of a rib felt like assembling a vase from shards of broken pottery. Fortunately, fresh bone fragments melded together under the influence of her gift, but the effort required an expenditure of far more zenith than she would have imagined.

When the last bit smoothed into place, Laryn paused to check on Tovnik, who was beginning to show signs of fatigue. "That's enough, Tov. Save your strength and watch. I'm nearly done."

The medic puffed out his cheeks, exhaling through pursed lips, and gave a curt nod. Laryn returned her attention to Karragin's other injuries. She rechecked the integrity of the repair of the lung's lining, then coaxed the reabsorption of blood and fluids that had collected around the internal injuries. As a wave of fatigue cramped in her shoulders, she removed the tapestry of healing tendrils penetrating Karragin's body.

Karragin lay still with her eyes closed, waking to full alertness as Laryn spoke. "Tovnik, I'm going to check on the others. Don't let her do more than sit for the next hour. The worst parts are healed, but the delicate parts of the lung need time to expand. If she does too much, the coughing fits will only slow her recovery."

"I understand," said Tovnik.

"In my pack there, you'll find spiritwort tea and dried lammen berries. See that she gets them both down," said Laryn.

She stood and walked closer to a blazing fire tended by Amniah. Fleeting images of the guster wounding the smaller rumbler beast entered Laryn's mind. Amniah was among the first of them to take action after Karragin made to dispatch the larger creature. Somehow, she had deployed a tight funnel of wind to launch small metallic marbles like projectiles. The attack disrupted the smaller beast's concentration and allowed the others enough time to recover and subdue the creature. Now she fed a gentle but steady current of wind over the flames, using the smoke to obscure something of the awful residual taint left by the rumbler's corpse.

"Thanks, Amniah. I don't think I could have focused on Karra's healing if you didn't work to keep us upwind of that odor. Does it tax you much? I would prefer that Karragin remain still for another hour."

The placid-faced guster stared at the corpse of the beast twenty paces away. "No, Your Radiance. It's the Giver's good fortune that a natural current rolls down from the north. I just have to remind it now and again to stay on course."

"Good enough. Keep at it but mind the draft. I'm going to check you for any injuries."

Amniah's face remained flat, a single blink the only indication of her mental awareness. "As you wish, but I feel well enough."

"All the same. I want to make sure that those rumbler things didn't damage your senses. I'll not have any of you follow in Karragin's footsteps now that we understand something of how latent damage can affect your hearing."

Amniah turned at the words, lifting her eyebrows in surprise, and tilting her head, consented to the probing nature of Laryn's assessment. In just minutes, Laryn gave the guster the reassurance that she'd found no signs of any internal injuries.

Over the next hour, she made the rounds, checking on each of them in similar fashion. The sender, Dexxin, remained without injury, one of the blessed few in the group. As she completed her survey, he was focused on something distant, as if transfixed on the horizon, but a moment later, his eyes sharpened on her face. "Your Radiance, my sister, Mullayne, is stationed at the forward base camp. Apparently, your husband has been trying to reach you through something called the shek. He relayed a message to the overwarden, who then passed it on to Mullayne."

"Taker's breath. I completely forgot about the shek." The realization compounded her growing sense of fatigue. "Alright, Dexxin, please relay everything that happened here to Mullayne, with instructions to pass the information to Kaellor. Let him know that once I've completed my work this morning, I will try to reach out. Be certain to describe everything you can about the rumblers. Tell the overwarden if they encounter anything like that, all effort should focus on keeping those things from rattling their chest plates."

Dexxin nodded and his vision drifted off. With that, she continued to triage the other Outriders. The inspection of the last member of the group, Savnah, revealed significant damage to the delicate structures of the ear, but unlike Karragin's trauma, there was time to mend the damage before the tissues fused back together. In addition, the woman showed signs of internal inflammation similar to Karragin's damaged body but with much less progression. *It must be something about standing directly before the rumbler's attack.*

Savnah's injuries required far less expenditure of Laryn's stamina than she anticipated. Something about the way the woman kept all pain at bay by channeling into her arca prime allowed Laryn to focus on the healing without concern for mitigating pain. But more than that, Laryn discovered she could redirect the flow of Savnah's zenith, shaping it to the purpose of healing the inflamed tissues.

It must be related to how she charges her arca prime. I'll have to test that theory later.

As she worked, fatigued muscles in her lower back became taut in response to her continuous channeling. She eventually drew her attention back to Tovnik, thinking to brew a stiff cup of tea, and her gaze swept across the corpse of the rumbler. Images from the night's conflict ran through her mind, and she recalled how Neska had slashed in from the darkness to attack the smaller rumbler on the ridge. Her attack had further disrupted the creature's debilitating onslaught and allowed Lluthean and the others to bring their gifts to bear to subdue the beast.

And where are you now, Nes? You likely sustained as much trauma as any of them. She shaded her eyes and searched for Lluthean, but her nephew had wandered off again.

Giver cool my tongue, but if that young man steps into trouble this early in the day, I'll let Savnah take him to task.

Laryn walked back toward the fire, where Nolan stood in conversation with Amniah. "Nolan, I need to find Neska, but she and Lluthean have wandered off somewhere. Find their trail but wait for me."

She cleared her throat and raised her voice. "Baccal, I need your eyes!"

Nolan fell into his gift and walked a slow perimeter as Baccal trotted closer. "Your Radiance?"

"Can you see where Lluthean or Neska have wandered off to?" asked Laryn.

Zenith flared as an intense cerulean flame behind Baccal's eyes, visible even in the light of day. The woman rotated, searching the far horizon and stopping as her brow creased in concentration.

"What is it?" Laryn pressed.

Baccal lifted a finger and pointed to the northwest. "I don't understand what he's doing, but the prince seems to be scaling a cliff and Neska is . . . I think she is lying on a ledge high in the cliffs, and she's not moving. Very odd."

Laryn inhaled a deep breath and released it slowly through pursed lips, mastering a heavy wave of concern that rippled across her chest. Savnah stepped beside her, thumbing the edge of her crescent moon axes. "Why do I get the feeling Lluthean has need of aid?" asked the prime.

"Because you've got good instincts, I suspect," said Laryn. She turned to find Dexxin leading the Aarindin closer to camp. Ranika had already saddled Zippy and sat waiting with a hand on the saddlebag holding Reddevek's ashes. Even Karragin had risen to her feet to approach. "It seems you've all got good instincts. Karra, are you well enough to ride?"

Karragin squinted her eyes, focusing on Laryn's lips, and Laryn cursed inwardly at her mental error, then signed, *"Can you ride?"*

"I can ride," signed Karragin.

"Stay mounted today. Your body needs time to recover," signed Laryn. She wondered how long that directive would stick with the leader of her Mirrare but pushed the concern to the side. "Savnah, let's see how much of the Taker's trouble Lluthean has stumbled into. Lead on and we'll follow."

"Mount up, quad formation, Nolan on point!" yelled the prime.

Laryn signaled her mount, and the Aarindin lowered belly to the ground, allowing her to toss a leg over and settle on the creature's back. The mount gracefully rose and gripped her without need for command. Laryn looked over her shoulder to cast a disapproving glare at Karragin, who sat on her own Aarindin but looked chagrined at being caught channeling.

"I know he grips me at your urging. It's a kindness. But save your strength and stifle your gift," signed Laryn. Karragin acquiesced with a nod and they rode out.

In minutes, the Aarindin carried them across the rocky hills. Laryn and her elites followed behind the quad to the base of a steep incline. By the time they arrived, Lluthean had already made the ascent. Laryn drew up a safe distance away to allow Savnah's quad time to survey the area for any threats.

"Baccal, what do you see?" asked Laryn.

"He's definitely up there. He's sitting with Neska just beyond the lip of that rocky ledge," replied the elite.

Savnah communicated with her team, then signed that it was safe to approach. Laryn urged her mount forward and cupped her hands around her mouth and shouted, "Lluthean!"

A few seconds later, Lluthean's voice echoed from high above. "Laryn? I'm up here with Neska. She's in trouble. Please climb up if you can."

A fast inspection revealed small trails crisscrossing up the mountainside, around boulders and clusters of scrub brush. Fleeting memories of gathering herbs high in the Korjinth Mountains rose to her awareness. *It doesn't look any worse than the high places, except you can't fold into the clouds.*

Laryn dismounted. "Nolan, find me the best way up there, fast."

None of them argued with her terse command. Nolan fell into his gift a moment, then led them along a narrow trail that switched back and forth up the rocky terrain. Laryn kept pace with the young man, the only sound between them the susurrations of panted breaths and the scuffle of boots over rocky ground. She stumbled once and lurched back, but Savnah was right behind her. The prime placed a hand on her buttock and pushed, allowing Laryn to leap forward and back onto the trail. They continued scrambling up parts of the incline and skirting along the narrow paths until, at last, they reached a ledge that recessed back into the mountain.

It took a moment for Laryn's eyes to adjust and even longer for her to regain her breath. Her sweat-stained shirt clung to the small of her back. She stepped into the shadowed alcove to find Lluthean leaning back against a strange, smooth slab of polished rock. He cradled Neska's broad head in his lap. Pink, frothy foam bubbled from the wolvryn's nose, and she lay still but for labored, panted breathing.

Laryn dropped to her knees. "What happened? Why didn't you come get me?"

"I don't know. Something drew her up here, and I followed when she stopped responding to my call. I tried to use the shek, but Kae is the only one listening."

A tinny echo of Kaellor's voice rang out from Lluthean's shek. "Laryn? Giver's breath, what's going on there?"

Laryn dropped her chin to her chest, a number of curses running through her mind. Not only had she forgotten to check in with Kaellor last night, but she just realized that she could have used the device to communicate with her nephew. "Taker, grind me for a monk. I'm sorry, Kae, Llu, both of you. It's been . . . last night was a lot. I forgot about the shek. Let me see what we've got here."

Laryn sat down, taking a moment to settle into a comfortable position. She ushered zenith into her arca prime and drafted probing tendrils into Neska. The familiar thrum of Neska's innate zenith ran strong, but everywhere Laryn searched, she discovered damaged and swollen tissue. The wolvryn's heartbeat thrummed with an erratic, thready pace, and fluid swelled in the air spaces of her lungs.

Laryn withdrew from her probing and caressed Neska's muzzle. "Oh my girl, why didn't you come to me first?" She lifted her eyes to Savnah. "Get Karra up here, and fast. There's not much time. I'll need her to keep Neska calm."

The prime turned and yelled for Amniah to signal Karragin to make the climb. Laryn considered all she would need to accomplish and internally acknowledged the risk of slipping into the draft, but committed to the healing without hesitation.

"What's wrong with her?" asked Lluthean.

Laryn adjusted her back against the rocky wall to sit beside her nephew. "The things we fought last night, their sound attacks cause much more trauma than meets the eye. Savnah and Karra both sustained deep internal injuries. Neska must have withstood more damage than we realized. But we have time, Llu. She's stronger than any of us. Slide over so that her head can rest on the both of us and listen to me closely. I'm going to need your strength, your ability to channel zenith."

"Laryn, I'm not sure that's a good idea," chimed Kaellor through Lluthean's shek.

Laryn leaned closer, speaking to the stickpin visible at Lluthean's neckline. "Hello, love. I'm sorry to do this to you, but we don't have time, and I promise to explain it all later. Right now, I need Lluthean to suspend communication and focus on my direction. Trust me in this, and all will be well."

She could almost hear him sigh through the device. "I know, and I do. Just promise me you'll be . . . never mind. I know you will. Reach out when you can, and Giver's touch on your work, both of you."

"Let it go, Llu," said Laryn.

He inhaled and nodded once. She rocked her hips closer to him so that their legs touched side by side, and together they heaved Neska's limp body further onto their laps. "Alright, now I want you to channel a bit of zenith into one of your runes. Not rune fire, just to be safe, one of the others. Prime the rune, charge it, but not for release, and then I'm going to send you a tiny portion of zenith just so you can feel what I'm talking about."

Without hesitation, Lluthean siphoned the ambient zenith around them, his command of the force evoking an unmistakable vacuum sensation in the currents. She allowed a tiny current of zenith to flow through the contact of their legs into him, and Lluthean's face brightened.

"You feel that, right? You can sense how my power is adding to yours?"

He stroked the fur under Neska's ear and swallowed hard, then nodded. "Alright. Now is the tricky part, Llu. Your command of zenith is—" She shook her head, trying to explain herself. "It's utterly massive compared to mine. So, you have to restrict how much you send me, portion it out like a tiny current. When you do this, you'll be able to watch me work, but don't ask questions and don't interrupt. Just watch and we'll see her through this. Whatever you do, don't flood me with zenith or I'll choke on it, and I don't think I can recover from that in time to save her. But the most important thing, even more important than lending me your strength, is that you stifle the flow if it begins to make you feel ill. I can't heal Neska and monitor you at the same time. If you give me too much of yourself, it will plunge you past the draft. It could even kill you. Do you understand?"

Lluthean chewed on the inside of his cheek, looking more like his brother than she had ever seen before. "I understand."

"Say it, repeat it back to me, Llu. Your uncle would never admit as much, but Kae nearly died back at the Cloud Walkers when we healed you. He would have given everything to bring you back. I can't have you go that far for Neska."

He blew a puff of air through pursed lips. "I understand. Lend you my strength but control the flow. Shut up and watch. Stop if I start to feel sick."

She stared into his eyes, searching one and then the other, watching as subtle currents of zenith flowed deep under the surface. *Giver, he's got the touch of his mother about him. Be with him today, Nebrine.* She nodded once, feeling like he understood her warnings. She held out a hand, and he grasped it, interlocking their fingers. "Good. Alright then, let's do this."

A grunt announced Karragin's arrival as she leaped up to the ledge. She braced herself against the rock wall, overwhelmed with wracking coughs, but recovered just as fast. Laryn pulled her hand free to sign, mindful to keep the words generic for Karragin's benefit. *"She's barely alive. Link to her as I work and keep her still."*

"She won't like it. She . . . I need permission to enter her mind," said Karragin.

Lluthean's fingers danced in the air. *"Tell her it's for me. She'll listen if you tell her it's for me."*

Karragin took a seat beside them, grimacing as she worked to find a comfortable position. She looked at Neska's limp form, and her normally stoic expression softened. Slowly, her eyes lifted to Lluthean and then to Laryn, and she nodded. "I'm ready. I'll do my best to keep her preoccupied when she wakes."

Laryn grabbed Lluthean's hand once again and set to work.

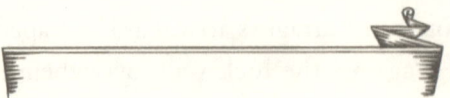

Chapter Twenty-Three: Following Neska's Lead

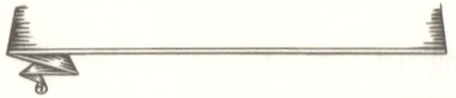

Luthean lingered at the edge of sleep, his mind replaying images from the day. After Laryn had carried out her ministrations, they each surrendered to exhaustion. He propped a travel pack behind his back while Neska recovered, using his thighs like a pillow. He felt more fatigue from fear than from any channeling of zenith: fear that Neska wouldn't survive the night, fear that his spontaneous misadventures had endangered them all once again.

Most of the time, he gave little consideration to planning out his actions. It felt thrilling to leap without knowing where he might land. In the haze of half-sleep, he replayed all the decisions he had made in the last day. The culmination of those decisions, of Neska's injuries and the effort Laryn spent to heal them . . . all of it weighed him down, constricting his chest, pulling him underwater.

He flashed back to the struggle against Bruug Hawklin, when the bully nearly drowned him and his gift had escaped the bindings of the mantle. The man's burly arms had crushed around his ribs, pressing in and preventing him from drawing breath. He recalled the stinging cuts on the bottoms of his feet when he'd scrambled against sharp rocks, trying to lift his head above the murky, cold water. The images shifted, and he remembered standing before the dark portal in the basement of the Sanitorium. An ice-cold stab of pain had flared through his arm and sank into his core when he thrust the dagger through the umbral.

He startled awake, shivering at the chill feeling on his legs where Neska had previously kept him warm. The musty smell of the cave oriented him at once, but his sleepy mind feared that the cold sensation meant she had passed. To his relief, the wolvryn padded across the front of the shallow cave, stretched backward, and groaned, her casual gesture setting his mind at ease.

She walked a deliberate circle around both Laryn and Karragin, who slept only ten paces away. She sniffed at each of them, tail swishing with interest. A full, open-mouthed yawn overtook the wolvryn, then she shook her head. Lluthean held fingers to lips, an unnecessary gesture perhaps, as Neska only growled at threats and never barked. She seemed to understand, padded forward, and licked him once on the forehead before sitting on her haunches and staring out across the mountain valley below.

He reached his hands overhead and brushed against the unusually smooth stone wall, then stood to consider its make. *You came up here for a reason, but I never figured it out.*

Lluthean stepped lightly past the still sleeping forms of Karragin and Laryn. What they had accomplished earlier was miraculous. Through his connection to Laryn, he had watched, mesmerized, as she labored to restore Neska's damaged tissues. That Karragin coaxed Neska to remain still through it all was equally impressive. His connection to Laryn had allowed him to witness the complex tapestry of filaments she employed in her craft, but he wished he could have eavesdropped on the conversation between Neska and Karragin. He would gamble with the Taker for the chance to hear Neska's voice.

Two billow seeds found their way into his palm, and he rattled them together before retrieving his bow and quiver and standing at the edge of the shallow cave to study the group below. Amniah and Baccal were posted at different points along the switchback that led up to the cave. Nolan and Dexxin walked a perimeter patrol, while Tovnik and Savnah sat in conversation around a small cookfire. He tossed a pebble toward Amniah, and the guster turned.

"Is everything alright?" he signed.

"Yes. No threats. How are Karragin and Her Radiance?" signed Amniah.

"Both sleep easy," he signed.

Neska pushed past him and out onto the switchback, but instead of descending, she grunted and hopped higher into the mountainside. Lluthean heaved his shoulders and signed to Amniah, *"I guess I'm going up. Something brought her up here. Come get me if you need me, or have Laryn use the shek."*

Amniah stared at him for so long, he thought she must be considering what to make of his decision to strike out unaccompanied. Eventually, she just nodded once, then turned back, keeping her vigil. *Humph, not the chatty type.*

He labored up the trail, climbing higher up the mountain. Within minutes, his thigh muscles burned with fatigue, and he strained to catch up to Neska. She sat at the bend where it switched back, oblivious to the steep drop to the valley floor. As he approached, she trotted ahead once again until the trail tapered to nothing more than breaks in the scrub brush and rocks. He lost sight of her again and pushed to keep up, finding her sitting at the edge of a cliff. Neska dropped belly to the ground, and he sat down beside her, dangling his feet over the edge.

From their vantage point, the entire world stretched out as craggy peaks of the Great Crown rose above collars of verdant greens. Storm clouds bruised the northern skyline, obscuring the horizon in a hazy mist, but he could follow the arc of the mountain range as it extended in a crescent around Aarindorn.

"Well," he said through panted breaths, "other than this incredible view, what's up here that has you so preoccupied?"

He settled his hand between her shoulders and followed the cadence of her breathing. With tedious effort, he slowed his breathing and stilled his heartbeat, synchronizing to her movements, waiting for the flows of their zenith to commingle. All around them, the world exploded with a complex tapestry of sights and sounds.

The alpine forests created a light, crisp feel to the air, and some quality of the stone carried a subtle tang he had not noticed before, enriched by moisture from the storm clouds to the north. Vines sprouting delicate wildflowers lent a fragrance to the wind, but underneath it all, he could still sense a lingering taint from the corpses of the rumblers.

He sat in silent communion, observing as Neska stretched her awareness beyond the Great Crown to the valley below. Wherever her focus tracked, the songs of birds, the shuffle of leaves on the wind, and the rustle of unseen creatures sang with an immersive vibrance. Through it all, he sensed Neska's profound peace and realized that she was lingering in this moment, waiting for him to understand.

He swallowed at the swollen feeling in his throat and rested his head against her muscled shoulder. "I know, Nes. It's magnificent. You're magnificent for making me see it. If I could, I would stay up here with you forever."

At his words, she exhaled an easy sigh, then directed her surveillance to the individual members of their party, each one of them haloed in an aura of zenith tempered by their mood or intention. From his vantage point, he couldn't bring the full color of Neska's perceptions to bear on Laryn or Karragin, resting as they were inside the cave. The Outriders, however, made easy subjects for his inspection. Each of them disturbed the currents of zenith, holding it primed or engaging their gifts, and every one of them resonated with a state of professional readiness.

Baccal scanned the horizons with her gifted sight, even turning to wave at him as their focus intersected. Lluthean's cheeks flared with heat at the realization that his actions felt a little voyeuristic and intrusive. He waved back, then realized that the woman had signed something.

He maintained his link to Neska and signed back, *"Sorry, I missed that."*

"Are you well, Prince Lluthean. Should I send an escort?" she signed back.

"No danger here. I'm fine, thanks."

The intensity of her gaze lingered on him several long moments, and her aura shifted from professional detachment to curiosity. *"If I might ask, what exactly are you doing up there?"*

"Following Neska's lead." He intended to offer a more thorough explanation, but with one hand maintaining his connection to Neska, a simple response with his off hand was all he could manage. Baccal seemed satisfied with his response and returned to her surveillance of the mountainside.

Probably something I should do as well.

He sifted through Neska's perceptions, searching for any clues to the location of the Moonies who had left their camp abandoned. She understood his intent, and sharpened her attention on the scent trail, where people had walked into the peculiar cave that sheltered Karragin and Laryn. *We'll check that out soon enough.*

Just before he separated from Neska's awareness, she drew her attention back and overhead, where a small beacon of zenith glimmered like a star in the night sky. He waited for her to direct her attention elsewhere, but her focus lingered on the aberration. "Is that what brought you up here? Grind it, Nes, you don't pick easy."

He removed his hand, muting his experience of the world back to normal, and studied the craggy tower of rock that supported whatever gave rise to the beacon of zenith. After giving only brief consideration to the berating he would receive if Laryn found him making the ascent, he set his mind to the task. "Lutney can't reward those who never toss the dice."

He set the Logrend bow and a quiver on the ground, shifted his belt knife to his backside, then began the precarious climb. Almost immediately, his breaths came rapid and labored, but instead of fatigue, a wave of exhilaration propelled him upward. He reached, pulled, stepped, and hopped, clambering up the cliff face without stopping to consider the audacity of his actions.

Finally, he heaved up to the edge, where a nest of sticks and grasses protruded from a defect in the rock. With barely enough room to kneel, he leaned forward, peering into the shadowed alcove. Feathers of varying lengths littered the ground and mounded up inside the nest. Downy white fluff covered their base, but each feather lengthened into silver and black filaments edged with a blue sheen.

He craned his neck forward, letting his eyes adjust, and froze upon recognizing the form of a large hawk sleeping in the nest. The creature curled its head under its wing and remained still. Lluthean eased back and looked down at Neska. Sweat ran down his chin as the weathered rock radiated the sun's warmth. He made to climb back down, but the wolvryn shifted her weight from one leg to the other and huffed a grunt of disapproval.

"Moons, Nes, seriously?" he hissed.

In answer, Neska lurched forward, placing her front paws on the base of the column of rock.

"Join the escort, meet the Dev'advari, have an adventure," he muttered with self-deprecation.

Turning back to the alcove, he ran his fingers over the ledge until he found a bit of loose rock. Thinking to scare the hawk away, he kept the ledge at eye level, then tossed the stone. A hollow *thunk* echoed from the nest, but the hawk remained still. Lluthean pulled himself back up and waited for any sign of motion. *Ahh, so not asleep, then.*

He reached forward, intending to lift the wing of the bird, but the entire carcass shifted back to reveal a palm-sized egg. A patina of dark blue markings speckled the off-white surface. *That might make for a fair breakfast, I suppose.*

Lluthean ran the flat of his hand around and under the egg, expecting to find a jewel like Ranika's moonstone. He probed his fingers under twigs and dug into the packed clay along the floor of the nest, but discovered nothing else.

This can't be it.

He retrieved the egg and held it out for Neska's inspection. The wolvryn pushed back from the column to sit on her haunches and lifted her nose to the air in a gesture of approval.

"How do you propose I get down while holding on to this, Nes?"

A flicker of zenith glinted behind her crystal-blue eyes, and realization settled on him. "I don't know if I can do it. The last time was a complete accident."

Neska considered him a moment, then turned to go back down the trail.

"Wait, Neska. Hold!" he said with more force than intended. "Grind me for a monk, if you bring one of them up here, I'll never hear the end of it! I'll do it. Just . . . give me a moment. I can do it."

Neska paused, considering his words, then returned to her post at the base of the rock column. With the egg held to his chest, he lurched and twisted to sit on the ledge with his legs dangling in open air. Sticks from the nest poked into his back, and he wriggled, trying to find a comfortable position. Once settled, he drew his attention inward.

The flows of zenith curled all about and he welcomed the current, ushering it into the runes on his flank and hip. With one hand clutching the egg and the other held out for balance, he waited. As the wind gusted by, he sensed how his gift created a palpable friction between himself and the currents of air.

With an uncommon focus of will, he directed a continuous flow of zenith into the runes, unshackled any restraint from the current, then allowed the next current of air to lift him from the perch. The sense of weight dissipated from his buttocks, and he hovered a moment, then lost control of the channeling, dropping with a grunt back onto the ledge.

A particularly stout stick from the nest jabbed into the muscle under his shoulder blade like a hot poker. Lluthean reached back with his free hand and fingered the wet, pointy tip of the branch. He puzzled at the sensation until he saw that his fingers were sticky with blood.

With a grunt, he dislodged the offending branch, scattering debris from the nest. Neska sniffed at the twigs and detritus, rubbing a paw across her nose and eyes.

"Sorry! Sort of."

The egg emitted subtle warmth against his chest and he stared down, expecting something to burst forth. Sunlight shimmered over the surface, and he realized the shell possessed more depth than he initially appreciated. The speckled blue marks wove in patterns underneath the white outer shell. He ran a thumb over the smooth edge, expecting to feel an imperfection. Neska huffed with impatience, and he waved at her with the other hand.

"I know, I know. Let me try again."

He inhaled once, thankful that the action provoked little pain despite the clingy press of fabric to his upper back, where the stick had jabbed him. He primed zenith into the runes on his flank once again but held it in a steady state, directing the current with tight control. The action tested his patience, but gradually, the surrounding air coalesced into something palpable.

Another gust of wind carried across the ledge, and with it, his feet found purchase, his gift evoking friction against the very air. He took a breath and leaned forward, all concentration on his channeling. Like sliding over ice-glazed ground, he descended in a spiral. He felt how a depression of his toes created more resistance, slowing and controlling the descent. In only moments, he dropped all the way down to Neska, then continued a controlled and gradual descent down to the shallow cave where Karragin and Laryn recovered.

He hopped forward and released his hold of zenith, relieved to feel stone underfoot. Neska loped down the trail and stopped before him. She sniffed at the egg, then opened her jaw to retrieve the item, holding it like a delicate treasure. The wolvryn turned and walked into the cave with an uncharacteristic bounce in her step, her tail lifting like a banner.

"You're welcome," said Lluthean to nobody in particular. Curiosity drove him forward though, and he followed her into the cave. Karragin and Laryn sat together, nibbling on some kind of medicinal berries. Both women smacked their lips, and even Karragin pulled a bitter face. The wolvryn walked right up to Karragin and placed the egg in her lap.

Karragin raised her eyebrows, appraising the gift, then set it on the ground. "Never too early for breakfast, but I'm afraid we're short one fry pan, Neska."

She reached forward to ruffle the wolvryn's fur, but stopped short when Neska lifted one paw in an awkward gesture. Lluthean watched as Karragin's entire demeanor shifted. Despite the tangled mess of slate-grey hair and her wrinkled clothes, she adopted a posture of professional vigilance . . . for a few seconds. Then, as if the Giver herself were breathing raw emotion into the woman, Karragin's stoic expression shifted to utter bewilderment. She set her palms flat on the ground, her eyebrows rose, and color flared in her cheeks. Slowly, her expression melted, shifting to unvarnished joy as her head dipped forward and eyes brimmed with tears.

With tremulous hands, Karragin retrieved the egg and clutched it to her chest. Only after she cleared her throat could the woman speak, and even then it was with a heady, raspy voice. "Oh moons, Neska, I promise, I will."

Laryn shot a puzzled look at Lluthean and flicked her fingers. *"Is that what I think it is?"*

Lluthean shrugged his shoulders and signed back, *"After what I went through to get it, I'm pretty sure it's not breakfast."*

Karragin stared down at the egg, mystified. "Laryn, it's a moonwing egg. Neska said its mother perished, but the nest and the sun somehow kept it warm. It's alive but unhatched. She . . . brought me a moonwing egg."

Lluthean watched as Karragin swaddled the egg in a blanket. He shifted his gaze to Laryn, who flared her eyes and signed, *"You can tell her the truth, Llu!"*

He waited for Karragin to look up, then signed, *"It's the least we can offer you, for everything you did last night."*

Karragin leaned to the side and gave a one-armed embrace to Laryn, then stood and offered the same to Neska. She turned, flared a full smile, and shook her head in astonishment. "I can't believe it. I mean, it's a chance, Llu. A chance I might be able to hear again. I've got to find something safe to carry it in."

He stepped aside as she exited the shallow cave, then turned to find Laryn holding her hands up. He grabbed them and hoisted her to her feet, the pain from the wound under his shoulder blade now burning for attention. Laryn grabbed Neska by the jaw and stared into the wolvryn's eyes. "That was a wonderful gift."

The wolvryn dipped her nose and pressed her forehead to Laryn's, tail wagging. Laryn held the contact a moment, then turned to consider him. "From both of you, I suspect."

"I didn't lie. I helped, but it was Neska who made me climb up there and retrieve it. When I first saw it, I actually thought it was breakfast. It doesn't matter. I got all the thanks I need," said Lluthean.

Laryn squinted her eyes at him, then accepted his statement. "Is that the first time she called you Llu?"

"You know, I think it might be at that."

He turned and thumbed at the wound on his back. "If you can see to helping me out with this, it was all worth it," he said.

Laryn tsk'd at him. "Shirt off, let me have a look."

He grunted as much from her cold fingers as any pain when she probed at the wound. "Lluthean, honestly. Do I even want to know what happened?"

"Can't we just agree to be happy with Neska's gift and leave it at that?"

She never answered. Instead, the whirring murmur of Laryn's gift filled the cave. In moments, the biting sting of the wound vanished. She patted him on the shoulder as the healer song dissipated. "The wound is sealed and will be fine, which is more than I can say for your shirt."

The scuffle of feet caused them both to turn. Baccal skidded to a stop in front of the cave and caught her breath. "Apologies, Your Radiance, Your Highness."

"Baccal, what is it?" asked Laryn.

Zenith flared behind Baccal's eyes. She stared right through them and waved a hand, beckoning them to exit the cave. "Behind that flat rock, there are scores of people—maybe the Moonies, I can't be certain. I didn't look for them before, but they seem to be trapped behind the rock at the back of the cave."

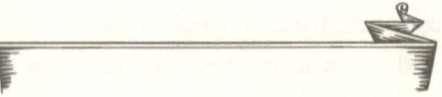

Chapter Twenty-Four: The Great Leveler

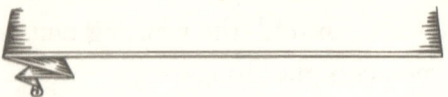

Tarkannen walked his mount to the shore of a vast lake northwest of the city of Kreeg. Ripples fanned out across an otherwise smooth surface when the horse drank. Late-morning clouds and even a faint image of the moon of Baellen reflected on the crystal waters, for no wind disturbed the surface. *A sure sign that Volencia makes good time in her task.*

He fixed the moon's reflection between thumb and forefinger and imagined siphoning zenith once again. Now that he walked the world of living, the longing for that source beckoned to him. With a sigh, he stabbed the rod of crystalized nadir into the earth a few times. The butt of the rod ground into the sandy soil, blackening the delicate plants in an irregular radius.

His horse lifted its neck and whickered at the approach of a cowled man riding a kruga, the robust horse breed revered by the people of Kreeg. Distinguished by its grey and white marbled coat, the mount appeared hewn from the mountains that gave rise to the headwaters of the mighty Rodemar River.

The rider pushed back the hood of his cloak to reveal the familiar, sharp features of a Dulescan noble: high cheekbones, pointy nose and chin. Verrador waved and dismounted, letting his kruga drink its fill.

The abrogator dipped his head in deference. "Master, you made exceptional time."

When Verrador stood to full height, he searched the woods behind Tarkannen, a puzzled expression evident on his face. "I left them behind," said Tarkannen.

"Master?"

"The grotvonen and grondle herd. I took your advice and left them on the north bank of the lake. Grasdok and the host of umbral will keep them confined to the area until we have what we need."

Verrador nodded. "A wise choice given the state of things in Kreeg." The man's eyes narrowed, and he pointed at Tarkannen's walking stick. "Is that what I think it is?"

"Crystalized nadir. It took a consort of umbral months to refine it. I was able to salvage three rods from their labors. I tasked Volencia with placing the other two along the coast near the Rodendian Sea. I have plans for this one."

"Might I know the purpose of the other two? The ones Volencia has?"

"I inscribed them with sigils of disruption and leeching. Already the air grows stagnant; soon a drought will fall across the region. We will arrive in time to warn the Kreeg of the impending doom and offer a solution that will draw them into the conflict with Aarindorn."

"Is there danger being so close to the rod you carry?"

"Only if you attempt to grasp it; even the wood sheath might not protect you from its leeching effects."

"The thirsty man requires little motivation to steal water from his neighbor. If we play it right, that could certainly motivate the Kreeg," said Verrador.

Tarkannen searched his memories, trying to recall what he could of the Kreeg. He recalled that the Kreegorian, the military caste, could prove a mighty weapon or an obstacle to his plans to capture the Pillars of Eldrek. "Let's mount up. You can tell me of your findings."

Verrador recovered his horse and held the reins out. "You should ride the kruga. The breed rivals the Aarindin. Not as intelligent and they can't grip you, of course, but they are fearless, almost eager for the fight."

Tarkannen situated himself in the saddle, slid the crystalized rod of nadir across his back, and adjusted to the muscled girth of the horse. The beast stood alert, awaiting his command, and showed none of the restlessness that he usually encountered among lesser breeds. He grunted with approval, nudged the mount with a heel, and they set out. "Your last message indicated a proposal. Tell me what you've learned of the Kreeg and why we shouldn't simply ride over them as we did Dernegia."

"Kreeg and Dernegia are two different animals, Master. Dernegians were content to remain behind their mountain fortress, and as such were easily overwhelmed when their walls were breached. But we should not underestimate the Kreeg."

They rode on in silence for a time. "They have earned your respect. Tell me, why should they possess mine?"

"Kreeg is a military society unlike anything I've encountered on Karsk," said Verrador. "Every facet of their daily life revolves around military achievement. Their schools educate boys and girls alike in military history and strategy. You'll not find any silk merchants or glass blowers in their markets. Instead, blacksmiths and provisioners supply all manner of goods designed for combat and rough travel. Their highest honor is to contribute to the military ranks, earn a position among the Kreegorian, or win glory in the coliseum."

Tarkannen thought back to the geographical location of Kreeg, straddling the headwaters of the Rodemar River and abutted by miles of fertile plains. He had intended to ride over or around the city and yet, some part of his memory tugged at his awareness from the shadows of the Drift, urging him to caution. So, he had deployed Verrador as a scout.

"It's strange that a kingdom flush with abundant resources would emphasize such a limited view of success."

"That was my thought at first, as well," said Verrador.

"What changed your mind?"

"It's their focus, Master. Their healers, called the medici, have advanced their art to rival that of the docents in Callinora. What better way to support an elite soldier than speed their recovery to return to the ranks? Their artists sculpt busts and statues glorifying military conquest. There is an entire caste of people, the physicars, whose sole purpose is to design and produce drugs that numb pain, enhance stamina, and sharpen focus—and all of it with the intent of supporting the Kreegorian."

A subtle tone of wonder flavored Verrador's report. "Tell me of their zeniphiles," said Tarkannen.

"That's just it, there are none. All of their accomplishments are carried out without even a shred of awareness for zenith, let alone nadir."

"How are they governed?"

"Zsheck rules Kreeg. He is the krug rai'al, a monarch of sorts. He was crowned after vanquishing all his foes in the coliseum more than ten years ago. A council of generals, men and women with distinguished service in the Kreegorian, both advise and implement Zsheck's commands. I set up a meeting later today with General Havka."

Over the next hour, Verrador recounted what he had learned of Kreeg, its people, and the numerous marvels created by a city full of ungifted. By midday, the outskirts of the settlement broke the horizon. Instead of a stone wall, a myriad of buildings crowded around broad roads that accommodated horse traffic in and out of the city.

Southwest of the city, a cloud of dust preceded the approach of a sea of mounted riders. The distant blaring horns and flags signaled the riders to advance, then split and whirl back into formation. The precision of the calvary left no doubt in Tarkannen's mind that his undisciplined horde of grot and grondle would have struggled to overpower such a force were it brought to bear en masse.

A ten-story column rose in the center of Kreeg. The massive circular building towered above the rest of the city. Tarkannen shaded his eyes, studying the structure.

"Master, that spire in the center of the city is the Dalkreeg, the coliseum. What the locals call the great leveler. And it is there that we will find our audience before the krug rai'al."

Tarkannen considered the Dalkreeg, appreciating the craftsmanship, made even more wondrous when he considered no zeniphiles contributed to its construction. "What religion is practiced in Kreeg?"

"They don't worship gods, but pay homage to their ancestors, especially those with notable military contributions," said Verrador.

Tarkannen sighed. "Your advice is sound. Our forces would struggle to overwhelm their defenses. Earlier, you spoke about the state of affairs in Kreeg. What did you mean?"

"Taken together, the forces of Kreeg are a weapon primed for conflict, but they have no enemies to vanquish, no . . . vent for their desire to fight, and the krug rai'al knows it. They control the plains to the east and west and are uncontested all the way to the shores of the Rodendian Sea. How long can a soldier pull on the bowstring without letting loose the arrow he is trained to shoot? This, I think, is the crisis we can exploit."

"What of Faltusch or Millstone?"

Verrador nodded in understanding, anticipating the question. "Both kingdoms have engaged in decades of favorable trade with Kreeg. The only fight there involves merchants haggling over the price of imports. We will need to entice the krug rai'al with the promise of something greater than the slaughter of merchants," said Verrador.

Verrador's words confirmed the assumptions Tarkannen had made despite the gaps left from his unclaimed memories. This was the reason he'd sent Volencia out with the rods of nadir. If her actions could provoke a drought, and if he could blame that on the Baellentrells, an army primed for conflict would be all the more ready to march across Karsk and engage the mountain kingdom. He breathed in a deep breath of confidence upon sensing the pieces click into place.

The abrogator led them onto a well-traveled road, wide enough to accommodate horse traffic in both directions and set with pavers. As they approached a group of wagons exiting the city, Tarkannen adjusted the hood of his cowled robe to obscure his sigils.

"Master, I left out one last thing. The Kreeg record their military service and accomplishments with black tattoos. None here will be put off by your sigils."

Tarkannen folded back his hood, studying the approaching caravan. "How will these people react to abrogation?"

Before Verrador could answer, they passed the wagons and, to a person, each merchant dipped their head in deferential greeting. Once they had passed, Verrador urged his horse into a canter, leading them into the heart of Kreeg. The scent of horse dissipated under a pervasive mixture of oiled metal and boiled leather.

Stone statues and monuments adorned every street corner. One depicted a mighty kruga stallion rearing back; others immortalized warriors posed in combat. True to Verrador's description, markets provided an ample selection of weapons and armor with little space dedicated to anything else. Instead of a single vendor offering an array of weapons, however, each specialized in a specific item. An array of sabers lined the racks of one proprietor's booth, while the next stall held only endless rows of knives and daggers. The next sold only bows of various lengths, and the one after that sold weapons specialized for close-quarters hand-to-hand combat.

After passing several districts and neighborhoods, they rode by a vast training yard surrounded by barracks and bustling with the sounds of clashing swords and the disciplined shouts of soldiers in training. Tarkannen directed his kruga to the side of the yard, inspecting the activities.

Where he expected to see young adults training, instead, rows of children clad in padded leather armor sparred in pairs. A bare-chested man with black tattoos adorning his muscled arms and chest stood on a raised platform shouting commands. In unison, the pupils stepped forward, slashing swords to be blocked and parried by their training partners. With synchronized precision, they retreated two steps to reset, awaiting the next command.

He turned the kruga to rejoin Verrador, who waited patiently. They walked the horses along the broad streets and eventually dismounted at a tavern tucked into the shadow of the massive coliseum. The roaring sound of a cheering crowd echoed from beyond the walls of the Dalkreeg.

Verrador tipped a groom and held the front door open. "They run games most of the day and into the night. Today, two of the elite training schools face off in a staged competition called the Trial of Nines. Come inside. We're due to meet General Havka soon."

Verrador signaled the proprietor, who led them to a secluded corner table at the back of the tavern. Servants poured cups of tea and placed a tray set with grilled vegetables, bread, and strips of spiced meat. After sampling the fare, Tarkannen sat back and folded his arms, surveying the tavern. Unlike the inns of his youth, the establishment was well lit and quiet. Several patrons dined on similar trays of food and glasses of water or tea. The room seemed more spacious than he expected and lacked any of the seedy trappings of a typical alehouse.

"There's no bar. Is Kreeg a dry city?" asked Tarkannen.

"Just so, Master. By decree of the krug rai'al, no alcohol is to be consumed within the city limits," said Verrador. "Nothing that would undermine a warrior's battle prowess. Offenders lose a thumb with no warning given. Excuse me, Master. I see General Havka now."

Verrador stood and waved the general over. Havka entered the establishment accompanied by three soldiers, but dismissed them and joined Verrador at the table. The general stood nearly as tall as Tarkannen. Arms of corded muscle folded over a fitted leather jerkin and delicate black tattoos adorned his sun-leathered skin, accentuating his chest and neck up to the jawline. A hint of salt and pepper flavored a sharply manicured beard. Havka nodded once at Verrador, then scrutinized Tarkannen's face.

Verrador pulled back a chair and spoke in the Kindred tongue. "General Havka, may I introduce my master, Tarkannen, conqueror of Dernegia and high abrogator of Aarind—"

Before Verrador could finish, Havka placed his hands on the table and leaned forward, staring overlong. The man's eyes narrowed as he scrutinized Tarkannen's sigils. Eventually, the general thrust a forearm forward, and Tarkannen grasped it, but instead of a greeting, the general pushed back Tarkannen's sleeve, further inspecting the sigils.

Tarkannen glanced to Verrador, who shrugged once. "Verrador tells me that your people receive tattoos as a reflection of their accomplishments. My sigils reflect that and more."

The general scoffed, then spoke with thickly accented Kindred speech, the words coming from the back of his mouth with a guttural intonation. "A painted man does not a warrior make. What do the markings rendered from a foreign kingdom prove?"

Tarkannen channeled a trickle of nadir, allowing the flow to penetrate his sigils, which shifted over the surface of his skin. A thin onyx tentacle sprouted from his wrist. He intended to pour the man a cup of tea, but the general spat out a curse, stepped back, and with blinding speed, unsheathed a saber, swiping it through the tentacle.

The Kreeg blade slashed through the tentacle, cutting a deep furrow into the tabletop. With little concern, Tarkannen reformed the appendage, then filled the general's cup to the brim.

The general retreated two steps and shouted a command over his shoulder. The sound of quiet chatter stopped as chairs slid across the floor and four soldiers stepped beside the general, each brandishing a saber.

Verrador sighed. "I was afraid of that. It's customary among the Kreeg to issue a challenge before giving a foe, or an ally, any respectful consideration. Just don't kill all of them, Master."

Tarkannen pushed back from the table, holding his hands out to the side, demonstrating that he held no weapons. He replaced his chair under the table, pulled at the edges of his tunic, then rolled his shoulders. He dipped his head in a single nod, and two of the soldiers engaged him in combat.

The currents of nadir bent to his will, materializing as a translucent casing of armor covering his entire body. Nadir blades, the equal of the Kreeg saber, sprouted in his hands. The deployment of nadir for such purposes required his utmost concentration as he folded the force back on itself. If the balance slipped, the force could swirl into an endless loop, siphoning all of his power until he stifled his channeling.

But not all of his lessons learned in the Drift had dissipated, and his mind responded with a nimble clarity. He deflected, parried, and blocked the attacks before slicing his weapons in swift arcs that disarmed each opponent. The men stepped back, shocked expressions on their faces, and stared as Tarkannen drafted two more tentacles, retrieved the sabers, and held them out for the soldiers to recover.

General Havka scratched at his beard, then sliced a hand forward, issuing a single command in the Kreeg tongue. As one, all four soldiers sprang forward, and Tarkannen flared a spherical burst of nadir shielding, catching the Kreeg blades and deflecting them harmlessly. He stood with arms relaxed at his side, but trained his eyes on the general's gaze as each soldier stabbed or hacked repeatedly at the translucent shielding.

The clangs of sabers shearing against the stonelike nadir barrier filled the room for several seconds. Tarkannen raised his voice above the din. "What gesture will garner the general's respect?"

Havka spat to the side, then said in thickly accented Kindred speech, "I granted your man this meeting out of curiosity. His claims were bold, but you would need to slay every soldier in this tavern."

"As you wish," said Tarkannen. He flared a single tentacle and lashed it forward, snaking around the general and forcing the man to his knees. Havka cried out, a sound of outrage more than pain. Two of his soldiers hacked at the appendage, while the other two attempted to penetrate Tarkannen's shielding. All of their strikes glanced off without harm.

Tarkannen wedged a loop of nadir under the general's chin, forcing the man to look up, then turned to Verrador, who remained seated, nibbling at a bit of fruit. A palpable vacuum gathered as Tarkannen siphoned nadir, holding it in his mind, shaping it to his will. With a single pulse, a razor-thin crescent of nadir flared out in all directions across the room, just above the apex of the general's head.

The clatter of dropped weapons, toppled tables, and sundered bodies falling erupted for several seconds, and then the room fell silent but for the sound of body parts sliding in a congealed mess to the floor. Tarkannen released the general, allowing him to stand. The man stood slowly and lifted a hand to his scalp, fingers returning stained with his own bright red blood.

Havka considered the room, blinking a few times, then retrieved and sheathed his saber. He stepped around the tavern, inspecting the beheaded and vivisected bodies still leaking blood and other bodily contents onto the floor. Over twenty citizens of Kreeg littered the tavern. The unmistakable tang of blood and feces permeated the air.

Havka's thin smile revealed white teeth, but failed to reach his eyes. Menace more than fear flavored his tone. "Well met, High . . . Abrogator. I will take you to the Dalkreeg. Any foreigners who wish to treat with the krug rai'al must face the great leveler. If you survive, he might grant you a private audience."

Tarkannen drafted a thin veneer of nadir into a malleable suit of armor. Light absorbed into the surface of the construct, emitting swirls and slicks of color. Satisfied with his control of the defense, he searched Verrador's face.

The abrogator sighed. "The Kreeg are true to their words, and no harm should come to us while in the general's company, but your precautions are understandable."

They followed Havka out of the ruined tavern. The man whistled three sharp chirps, and within twenty paces, two quads of soldiers fell in as an escort of eight. None of the men or women spoke. Each wore leather cuirasses, buckler arm shields, and a short sword belted at the waist. Havka beat a direct path to the Dalkreeg, walking around the backside of the massive circular structure.

The entourage stopped to allow a cart to exit the coliseum from an archway with a set of wood double doors reinforced with metal bands. Two porters with bloodstained tunics towed the cart along, their cargo of bludgeoned and hacked corpses of combatants visible for all to see.

Havka resumed his brisk walk as the cheers and roar of the crowd surged from inside the coliseum. At last, they approached an arched entrance with a metal portcullis. Four guards stood at attention. Havka saluted once, then spoke in hushed tones. Something in his introduction gave the soldiers pause, as they shot Tarkannen suspicious glances.

Eventually, one of the guards stepped forward, his Kindred speech only slightly less guttural than the general's. "General Havka says you wish to challenge the great leveler. Is this so, stranger?"

Tarkannen searched Verrador's face. The abrogator shrugged his shoulders. "It seems to be the only way to secure the krug rai'al's attention." The general tipped his head with a slight nod of consensus.

Tarkannen turned back to the guard. "Yes. I accept the challenge."

The soldier rested a lazy hand on the pommel of his sword and inspected Tarkannen from head to toe. "The Dalkreeg is a sacred arena, and I don't think that you are worthy to tip the scales of the great leveler. I mean no offense in this, stranger. I state the obvious that you might identify someone to claim your body when the contest has concluded."

"If I am defeated, then only death awaits us all."

The guard grunted, a sound of boredom and exasperation. "More work for the carters, then? Very well. You may enter with armor and a set of weapons of your choosing. That short staff strapped to your back might not be the best choice. There are standard-issue weapons and gear inside. B'vakla's double quad is short a man; you'll do to complete their numbers for the Nines."

Tarkannen folded his arms together. "I need no such preparations. Let's begin."

The shearing of oiled metal bars accompanied the ascent of the portcullis, and the guard led him through. The corridor descended as a ramp for a dozen paces. Inside, ten-foot-wide halls crisscrossed each other in a labyrinth. Torches guttered and provided poor illumination, but the acrid smoke dissipated the pervasive reek, a strange mixture of wet stone, blood, and offal. The muted cheers of the crowd echoed through the chamber, a roaring cacophony that Tarkannen found more annoying than rousing.

The guard led him past several alcoves filled with tables displaying weapons and armor. He stopped and tapped a finger on a table of swords, then shouted above the din, "Last chance, stranger. You might want to give them a show, at least?"

Tarkannen lifted one of the weapons by the hilt, inspected the grip, then let it clatter to the table. "I don't expect you to understand. But you will."

"Suit yourself. Ancestors guide your path. This way." The guard led him to a ramp that climbed out of the shadows and toward the center of the coliseum. A group of eight, a mix of men and women, stood at the base of the ramp. They each wore a unique mixture of fitted leather armor, some with metal bracers, others with buckler shields, and each holding a short sword. All of them gripped their weapons in anticipation, except one.

A woman leaned a shoulder against the wall, her folded arms revealing a tapestry of silvery scars intermingled with black, lacy tattoos running over corded, lean muscle. A single black sash wrapped around the bicep of her left arm. Her kinky, black hair was braided in intricate patterns, one of which accentuated a ragged scar across the temple. Delicate tattoos with thorny barbs climbed across her collar bones and wreathed the base of her jaw, as if a briar patch supported her head.

The guard leading Tarkannen approached and dipped his head to the woman. "Reiner B'vakla, this man is to join your group for the Nines."

The woman walked her eyes up and down Tarkannen's frame before turning back to the ramp leading up to the arena floor. "No. We will enjoy more honor without him. He will only make work for the carters."

The guard cleared his throat by way of apology. "It's not a request, I'm afraid. General Havka's orders."

B'vakla's jaw muscles clenched a few times, and she sighed, turning to give Tarkannen closer consideration. She walked a slow circle around him, and he thought to warn her against touching the nadrean, but his patience for the charade was limited, so he settled for maintaining his protective coating of nadir under his clothing. Volencia enjoyed such games of manipulation, and a part of him hoped this woman would grasp the weapon. Her agonizing death might be just the thing to disrupt the thin veneer of peace and allow a portion of his wrath to pour out on them all.

Instead, B'vakla rounded to stand before him, staring into his eyes, no doubt intrigued by the subtle shifting of his sigils about his skin. She leaned in close enough that he could smell the not-unpleasant fragrance of a scented oil. "He will do," she said to the guard.

To Tarkannen, she spoke in quiet tones as she affixed a black sash to his left upper arm, matching the eight other combatants preparing for the contest. "You're more than you seem. Those are not tattoos. What are you exactly, and why has Havka sent you to die with us?"

Tarkannen nodded, considering her words. Since arriving in Kreeg, this woman was the first person to show him an ounce of respect instead of dismissing him outright as a substandard foreigner. "For a woman anticipating death, you don't seem too nervous."

She continued to gaze, unflinching into his eyes. "I've cheated death more times than I can count. Above though, it's a numbers game. Each group to enter the Dalkreeg has the same weapons, the same training. With you, we make a full nine, but you are not Kreeg."

He shifted the matrix of nadir that formed his shadow armor, allowing the protective veneer to caress his face. Her eyebrows twitched in mild amusement. "No, I'm definitely not Kreeg. I'm something much more."

She exhaled through her nose, sharp and curt. "We'll see. Is that supposed to be a weapon? That . . . baton?"

Before he could explain further, the small portcullis at the top of the ramp screeched into place. "Come then, painted man. Let's see if you can die as bravely as you stand. Form up! Flanking quads, center on me!"

B'vakla led them up the ramp and onto the arena in time to witness the victors trot off at the far end of the Dalkreeg. Of the original nine, only four made the exit, and two of these leaned heavily on their group members. The stadium, shaped like an oval, stretched out at least three hundred paces. Every fifty paces, an arched passageway with an identical portcullis bored into the circular plaza, and no fewer than ten of the openings dotted the walls. At the farthest point of the oval wall stood a lone, black steel door.

Six pillars of stone, each standing over ten feet high, formed a ring in the center, with enough space for four people to stand in between the columns. Broad bands of white and black stone formed concentric rings on the floor of the Dalkreeg, each separated by a strip of sand. The pattern repeated three more times, white, black, then sand, until only a central pitch of sand remained. Light shimmered off the glistening black pools of blood staining the stone paths and central sand pit.

Carters meandered around the arena in three-man teams, picking up the bodies of the dead and collecting their weapons. Other workers busied themselves sweeping the stone rings free from sand and debris. Behind them, the metal gate slammed shut. Around the arena, three similar teams walked out, their presence punctuated by the clanging of metal grates. At their collective arrival, the clamor of the crowd blossomed.

Tarkannen watched as the members of B'vakla's group settled themselves in units of four to either side of her. He stepped into position to her right side, where he assumed the ninth team member would stand.

"Are there any rules?" he asked.

"Not really. Don't fall onto the stabby end of things. Every ten minutes or so, the outermost rings will flare. It forces combatants to the center, though contests rarely last more than two flares. We fight as a group on black. Black or sand."

"Why is that?"

She lifted her chin, surveying the other teams. "Because white drains the soul, steals your will to fight. Still, everyone must cross the white rings four times and meet in the center."

"Do the black rings do anything?" he asked.

"Not to anyone in these games. The last Mogdurian child died centuries ago. When the contest begins, we will race over the white and charge the group to the left."

Before she could explain further, a man's voice erupted across the din from a raised platform near the center of the arena. General Havka stood beside a shaded throne as he announced, "Citizens of Kreeg. Witness the last glorious Trial of Nines! And today a special combatant steps onto the great leveler. Joining Reiner B'vakla's team is Tarkannen, slayer of my cousin, high abrogator, and conqueror of Dernegia!"

B'vakla turned her full attention to him, a genuine expression of alarm evident. She shouted above the jeering crowd. "Is that true? Are you a child of Mogdurian?"

"I am not familiar with that term," he shouted back.

She cursed something guttural and drew her sword, gesturing to her team. "Place him on the edge! He's no good on black. Keep to the sands!" She grabbed him by the shoulder and yelled in his ear, "If you really are an abrogator, then whatever you do, try not cross the last black ring! Every time you cross a black ring, that black steel door opens a bit farther."

B'vakla shoved him into place just as a resonant gong echoed through the arena and the crowds erupted with a deafening roar. He followed as his team sprinted across the white stone and sand. He waited for the fatiguing or draining sensation to sap his strength, but felt nothing as they passed over the first white stone ring. Currents of nadir flowed across his sigils, encasing him in dense, shadowy armor and evoking a nadir blade in his hand.

He sensed the team cut to the left and could see that B'vakla intended to strike the flank of another group of nine who had their attention trained directly ahead. As he sprinted along, he considered blasting them all with a single detonation. A sphere of deadly onyx shards coalesced in his other hand, but just before he released the summoning, one foot stepped onto the black ring. The vibrations of metal grating against metal screeched throughout the arena, drawing everyone's attention to the far side, where the black steel door shuddered. Before he could make sense of the phenomenon, the currents of nadir slipped through his fingers like smoke.

He strained to direct the power into his sigils, but the sphere of nadir, his shadow armor, and even the nadir blade all vanished. His steps faltered, boots plodding in the sand as if weighed down by mud, and he collided with the ground, knees, then chest, and even his face striking the black stones. He became immediately aware of a naked emptiness inside himself. Nadir swirled in oily, palpable currents, but where the force should saturate his sigils, it slid off, oblivious to the efforts of his siphoning.

His group sprinted ahead on the black ring, leaving him rooted to the spot in abject surprise and confusion. Havka's voice boomed in laughter overhead. "Welcome to the great leveler, painted man. Let the contest begin!"

Chapter Twenty-Five: Melting Barriers

Ranika sat on the ground, her saddle draped over a log that served as a backrest. The urn holding Reddevek's ashes rested between her knees, but with no Luna Rova in sight, she began to wonder how she would ever deliver them to his ancestors. A shadow fell across her shoulders, and Zippy whickered a soft greeting. She stood and placed her temple against his jaw, taking comfort in his warmth and familiar smell.

With Laryn preoccupied sorting out everyone's injuries, the Aarindin was pretty much her only companion of late. Her isolation had intensified since the others realized she could wield nadir. They had to know that she was an abrogator, right? By the way Savnah nodded now instead of offering her usual toothy grin, Ranika felt like things had changed, though maybe not as much as she feared.

The young men—Nolan, Tovnik, and Dexxin—still regarded her like a kid sister. Baccal threw herself into the mission with professional detachment, and Amniah was as stone-faced as ever, but that was no surprise. Their opinions mattered little to her compared to what Karragin and Lluthean might think.

After the weeks of travel before arriving in Stone's Grasp, she felt a kinship with them, especially Lluthean. "Life was a lot more fun back in the Bend, Mr. Zip."

The Aarindin swiveled his head in the direction of the cliffs and the cave where Laryn was recovering. Though Zippy's nostrils flared, his ears twitched, and his tail swished a lazy cadence, Ranika knew he was acting out of curiosity and not fear. She shaded her eyes in time to see Lluthean spiraling down like a leaf caught on currents of air. Scintillating sparks of zenith flared from underfoot until he hopped onto the ledge before the cave.

"Lutney's dice, there's something you don't see every day." Several minutes later, Karragin quite literally skipped out of the cave, then hopped down the trail with all the exuberance of a toddler.

Zippy blinked and shifted his gaze to Ranika. She thought by the way his muscles tightened at the back of his deep eyes that he must be smiling. "Don't ask me, Mr. Zip. I don't know either, but I suppose I can go find out. I'll see you in a bit."

She retrieved the urn, placed it in a satchel, and hoisted it over her back, then began the hike up the switchbacks to the cave. Karragin flashed her a rare smile when they passed and clutched something to her chest.

"What have you got there?" signed Ranika.

Karragin reined in some of the enthusiasm that had affected her descent. "Neska found me a moonwing egg. If I can hatch it, I might be able to use the hawk to hear again. Nika, do you have anything I can use to hold it?"

"I heard Nolan talk about them on the way to Callinora once. He said the people in the highlands call them riftwings. In the bottom of my saddle pack there's an empty leather coin purse," she signed. Karragin squinted and turned her head to the side, her cheeks flushed. *"Nevermind, follow me."*

Ranika walked back to her saddle and pack, retrieved a leather coin purse, and handed it to Karragin. The egg fit snugly through the drawstring, and Karragin produced a leather cord, then fashioned a crude necklace and pulled the strange egg purse over her head. The woman adjusted the cord to allow the rounded parcel to rest at mid-chest, then, as if handling a delicate piece of crystal, tucked it under the front panel of her uniform.

"How long before it hatches?" signed Ranika.

"I don't know. Hopefully not until we return home." Karragin stopped signing and tongued the scar of her upper lip, then spoke out loud. "There's a falconer in Stone's Grasp. If all goes well, I can get his help."

"I bet you could use that fountain room with the blue dome to start with," signed Ranika.

"The Founder's Memorial? You're right. That would be perfect. I hadn't thought of that." Karragin tapped at the slight bulge under her uniform, then exhaled and seemed to retreat back into herself, reassuming her detached, professional demeanor.

Where others might find the woman's stiff affect off-putting, Ranika relaxed with Karragin's easy banter, and the fact that she could provide the coin purse didn't hurt. Still, she wondered now if Karragin had turned her thoughts to darker concerns.

"Did you see Llu float down from the cliffside?"

Karragin frowned and shook her head but offered no further response.

Ranika struggled to think of something to direct the conversation to anything but her use of nadir. *"Is Laryn awake? I thought to pay her a visit. I'm not sure what to do with this,"* she signed, tapping Reddevek's urn.

Something softened in Karragin's bearing. "You can talk to me about it if you want to, Nika."

Ranika's thoughts hopped from one issue to another, struggling to land on anything but the fact that she was an abrogator. A long silence drew out as she considered how to reply. *"Thanks. Ever since Red died, I haven't been myself."* She stopped signing as Karragin held up a hand in a gesture of peace.

"Not that, well . . . yes, that. You can talk to any of us anytime about that." Karragin lifted her eyes to the horizon and Ranika followed, feeling secure in their privacy as the others in their company attended to the tasks of patrolling the area.

"Nika, I can't imagine what it's like for you, not really, but sometimes us motherless types have to stick together, you know? I've still got Nolan and even Savnah I can trust with my secrets. I know Red was family to you, more than any of us. Did he know? Was he aware that you could channel nadir?"

Ranika dropped her eyes to the ground, uncertain how to respond. *"Yes,"* she signed at last.

Karragin released an audible sigh. "That sort of feels like the hand of the Giver in all of this. I mean, if Red of all people trusted you . . . who else knows? And what I mean is, do you have anyone else you can talk to?"

"Bryndor, Kaellor, and Laryn are the only ones. Besides them, nobody else has ever seen me do it."

"I see," said Karragin.

Ranika wanted to make eye contact, to feel a sense of understanding in Karragin's expression, but feared what she might discover if she lifted her eyes from the ground. In the moment, it felt easier, safer, to avoid the condemnation she knew the woman must be harboring.

Without explanation, Ranika began to shuffle off. She had no idea where her feet might carry her, but anywhere away from the scrutiny of Karragin's prying questions felt safer than standing in the woman's company. Before she got three steps away, Karragin placed a soft hand on her shoulder.

"Nika, you can talk to me about it. Any of it, all of it, or none of it, if that's what you want. It's good that you have the others, but I can imagine that getting alone time with any of them these days is a rarity."

Karragin walked to stand in front of Ranika, but all she could do was stare at the woman's boots until Karragin placed a knuckle under her chin, drawing her eyes up. With reluctance, Ranika drifted her focus up from the woman's casual palm resting on her sword hilt, to her shoulder, then her chin, and eventually her eyes. But instead of anger, she sensed . . . nothing. Karragin remained as unreadable as ever until a soft smile graced her face and she winked.

Ranika felt the rush of emotion swell the back of her nose and cause her eyes to sting, but smothered the sensation before it overwhelmed her and instead threw herself into a giggle. *"Thanks. Maybe someday, when I'm ready."*

"Of course, but when you are ready, you can trust me. Now come on; we should see what's going on up there. I think Baccal discovered something in the cave, but I was too distracted to pay her much attention."

"Alright," she agreed, and they climbed back along the trail leading up to the cave, arriving to find Lluthean, Baccal, and Laryn running fingers along the expansive smooth stone that formed the back of the cave.

Baccal stepped back, staring with intensity into the stone. "Some of them are awake. I think they can hear us but they're just sitting there, waiting. I don't see an obvious way to move the barrier."

"What's going on?" asked Karragin.

Laryn turned and signed a response. *"There are Moonies trapped inside, behind this wall. Karra, see if you can punch through maybe?"*

Karragin stepped up to the stone and used the pommel of a dagger to tap along the breadth of the wall. "Any idea how thick it is, Baccal?"

"At least three feet. That's why I didn't see them at first. But in the middle it thins a bit, right here," said Baccal. She picked up a small stone and outlined an oval section in the middle of the wall.

Karragin lifted the cord holding the egg pouch and handed it to Ranika. "Keep this warm for me?"

"Of course." Ranika bent her head forward to receive the burden, then tucked it against her bare skin. Even through the leather pouch, she could feel the egg radiating its own warmth.

Karragin rolled back her sleeves and considered the wall. "This would be easier with a maul. I don't suppose anyone brought one along?"

Without waiting for a response, Karragin walked out of the cave only to return holding a large boulder over her shoulder. "Everyone, get back to the mouth of the cave."

Once they backed out to safety, Karragin launched the boulder, hurling it directly in the center of the target Baccal had outlined. A painful and deafening clack echoed from the cave, and fragments of rock and dust billowed out of the entrance. Ranika buried her nose under her tunic, but didn't have to wait for the dust to settle before Karragin uttered a curse.

"Grind me. I'm sorry, Laryn. The boulder crumbled apart, but there's barely a scratch in the wall."

Lluthean fanned a hand in front of his face to clear the dust, then signed. *"I can try."*

"With rune fire? Are you sure? In a closed space, a munition would be ill-advised. Your power might bring down the entire mountainside," said Karragin.

"I can reshape it, maybe make it into a thin stream instead of an outright blast," he signed.

Laryn considered them both a moment. *"Do you really think you can alter the release to avoid harming yourself? Karra is right. A detonation would affect everything inside a small space."*

"Bryndor shaped a small ember once when starting a fire, and he could shape zenith into an orb to dry out my rain-soaked cloak. Maybe you can focus it into something small like that," Ranika suggested.

Lluthean shook his hands out, then clenched his fists a few times. *"It's worth a try. I can stand in the back and direct the force outward. It should be fine. Let me give it a try."*

Laryn shook her head but held up a beseeching hand. "Giver guide the rest of my day, because I'm surely walking off the path this morning. Alright, give it a try, but be careful."

Karragin and Lluthean switched places, and he positioned himself in the back of the cave but still facing the polished stone wall. He stood for over a minute in concentration, then turned to them all. "Best . . . back up several more paces, just in case. And keep Neska back with you."

They each did as he requested, Ranika retreating the farthest back down the trail. Even the wolvryn came to sit next to Karragin. "Here goes!" shouted Lluthean. In the next moment, a vacuum sucked pebbles and air into the cave, only to be blasted out as a funnel-shaped cloud of debris under a thunderclap of power as rune fire exploded.

Ranika turned her back to the entrance and tucked her head on instinct. While the debris flew far overhead, the force of the detonation threw her to her hands and knees. In the next instant, Karragin was at her side, helping her stand and adjusting the shoulder pack holding Reddevek's ashes.

"Are you hurt? Is anything . . . broken?" asked Karragin.

Ranika's hands flew to the egg pouch, finding it intact. "I'm fine, I think everything is fine, but you should take this to be safe. If anything happened while I wore it—"

280

Karragin's focus trained on Ranika's lips, but it was clear she understood as she reached forward to assist in removing the cord from around her neck. With uncommon caution, the woman opened the pouch and massaged the egg into her palm. Finding it intact, she replaced the thong around her own neck and secured the egg under her uniform.

They turned back to the cave entrance to find Lluthean dusting off his pant legs. His windblown hair gave him a comical look of surprise, but otherwise he appeared without injury.

"Taker's teeth, what is going on up there?" signed Savnah. The other Outriders had gathered as well, drawn by the commotion.

"Baccal found the Moonies. Some of them are alive but trapped behind a barrier of stone at the back of the cave. I tried to break through, but couldn't even crack it. So Lluthean gave it a try," said Karragin.

"With rune fire? He knows rocks don't burn, right?" signed Savnah.

"Come on then, let's have a look. Maybe you can think of a better way in," said Karragin.

The group marched up to the cave to survey the progress and found the strange smooth-walled portion unmarred.

"If anything, your rune fire just polished the surface to a sheen," said Baccal. "But you got their attention. There's more people than I can count sitting just inside now."

"Sorry, that's the best I can do. Maybe if I had time to practice, I could figure out how to channel it differently. What's next?" asked Lluthean.

"Send Nolan and Dexxin to scout out the backside of these cliffs. Perhaps there's another passageway in," said Karragin.

"Good idea; send word if you break through. We'll do the same if we find another way in," signed Savnah. She turned and gathered the quad, and they left without further debate.

"Now what?" asked Lluthean.

"Unless you've got a way to melt stone, we wait," said Karragin before she sagged down to sit with her back against the wall.

The prince looked like he was going to respond to her comment, but signed something to Neska instead, and the two of them left without further words. Ranika replayed the conversation in her mind, sifting through the words, but couldn't find anything off-putting. She would have to ask Lluthean about the strange turn in the conversation.

Before she could consider the matter further, Laryn approached and leaned in close, speaking in hushed tones. "There might be a way to safely melt a portion of the stone away, Nika."

Ranika looked past Laryn to see if anyone overheard. Karragin sat with her eyes closed, and Amniah and Baccal stood at the mouth of the cave in quiet conversation. "They already know, Nika. You were amazing against the rumblers. Without you, I don't think any of us would be alive, and on some level they know that. They have questions, but I reassured them you're still the same person who joined us in the battle against the Lacuna. I've seen the Cloud Walkers use tiny bits of nadir to remove diseased tissue. Theirs was but a fragment of the strength you possess. If there is a way for you to use your gift to melt the stone, the others might begin to see—"

"I'll do it," said Ranika. "I mean, I'll try. It's what Red would want me to do. If his people are trapped in there, I'll see if I can get them out."

"Alright. Do you need anything from me, from us?" asked Laryn.

"No. I don't think you can help me really, just stay back for now, and maybe warn the others so they aren't surprised."

Laryn nodded and stepped back, giving Ranika the space she needed. She sighed inwardly. She had never willingly displayed her gift for anything other than conflict. The shoulder harness felt heavy, and she lowered Reddevek's urn to the ground and considered his words, his growly voice echoing in her mind. *Remember, Nika, gifted, not cursed.*

Siphoning nadir to her bidding was easy. Shaping it to her intent would be the challenge. She rested both palms flat against the stone and drew out the force, creating dense clusters of nadir in her fists. She tried to press the black globes into the stone, but they met resistance.

After several minutes and failed attempts to breach the stone, she dropped the globes to the ground and stifled a curse on her lips. Where the small spheres dropped, they seared into the stone floor and left shallow deposits of melted stone. All at once, she recalled the innate way her stingers burrowed through her foes. They didn't so much pierce into flesh as they melted it away, reducing any resistance to their passage.

That must be the trick. She drafted the nadir into palm-sized spheres and held them to the stone once again, but this time allowed the globes to blend into the rock, overcoming its nature and dissolving it away. Galvanic vapors rose from under her hands and she removed them to reveal two hand-sized oval depressions set more than four inches into the stone.

Building on her progress, she reshaped the next sphere of nadir into a single larger globe and melted it into the stone in the same fashion, letting the nadir have its due, but coaxing it to dissolve and reduce the substrate. The effect was astonishing, and she gasped, standing back to assess the rather large, elbow-deep hole left behind.

"The Taker never makes it easy, but the Giver always finds a way," said Karragin. "Ranika, that's amazing. Can you do it again? If you enlarge the hole, I might be able to break through, but at the rate you're going, you won't even need that."

Laryn stood beside her smiling and Baccal stepped close, her eyes ablaze with the light of zenith. The woman stared into the stone depression for a moment before turning her gaze on Ranika.

"What does your gift tell you when you look through me, Baccal?" asked Ranika.

"Apparently not half as much as it should," said the woman. She turned her focus back to the wall. "You're more than two-thirds of the way through. I've been watching from behind. I think if you give that area one more go, then move below and do it again, you should be able to remove a large section all at once."

Ranika inhaled a breath, finding confidence in the unexpected acceptance of the three women. She brought forth another globe of nadir and eroded several more inches from the initial depression, then moved and began anew in the area Baccal indicated. As she worked, Baccal gave her updates on her progress, and Ranika found that when she set her intention into the nadir, then released it to carry out her bidding, the natural expression of her gift removed stone with far more efficiency than if she tried to force the issue.

At last, she stepped back, a tingly, buzzing sensation swirling in her forehead. The hole she had created sank well past her elbows into the stone and could accommodate a small adult. Ranika paced back and forth across the cave, feeling restless and edgy.

"Nika, are you alright? What is it?" asked Laryn. She moved to wrap her arms around Ranika, but the urgency of the buzzing in her head caused her to quickstep to the side and continue her agitated pacing.

"It's my . . . buzzing. When I use too much nadir, it makes my head buzz and I get all wound up. I won't be able to sleep for at least a day. I'm sorry, I just need a few minutes, then I can finish."

Ranika tried to slow her breathing and paced with her hands clasped over her head. Behind her, Karragin grunted, and the sound of crumbled stone falling to the ground followed.

"Giver, you made that easy, Nika. Everyone, come have a look," said Karragin.

Ranika pursed her lips to dissipate a subtle wave of nausea, then stepped in front of the hole to peer into the darkness. She thought something shifted in the murky shadows, so she pulled out her moonstone and held it high. In seconds, the glow of countless eyes peered back at her.

"Hello in there. My name is Ranika. I'm with friends. I suppose we were all friends of Reddevek Taim. You can come out now. The rumblers are gone. It's just us, and it's safe."

Chapter Twenty-Six: Honest Work

The bustling sound of cheerful patrons filled the air, but the merriment did little to soothe Valdesta's mind as they arrived for their evening meal. The enticing aroma of freshly baked bread and the savory scents of spiced stew wafted through the space, drawing her down the stairs of The Kettle and Pot, one of her few honest businesses. Nestled just a block away from Hawker's Row, adjacent to the vibrant market district, and shielded from the chaos of the Sprawl, the tavern had thrived in the aftermath of the Reckoning, when many of her other ventures fell victim to their ties with the Lacuna and her identity as Tixon B'gin.

She stopped midway down the steps to survey the crowd. Not a single seat remained open as locals mixed over food and ale. Several families even crowded around two of the larger round tables, lending a certain honorable authenticity to the establishment. Taking a cue from Kunzi's refined establishment in the Delve, she had replaced the barmaids with a mixture of young men and women required to dress in formal uniforms. The staff kept busy refilling drinks, collecting payments, and clearing tables.

She had to admit her surprise when she reviewed the books from last week. The investment in higher caliber staff and a simple menu was paying dividends that rivaled her brothel. It didn't come close to the take from the gaming halls, but she entertained a fleeting notion that she could rebuild a portion of her holdings with similar adventures in time.

Just as quickly as the idea entered her mind, it dissipated. She had other matters to attend to this evening. Her gaze swept across the crowds, searching for her contact, but he was late, and that fact alone took up residence in her thoughts.

She caught the eye of one her runners and signaled the young man over. "Hello, Camber. Any news from Stone's Grasp today? Any announcements?"

"Nothing unusual, Val. The ordinary proclamations following the regent's hearings were posted, but none of my contacts had anything to report."

"I see. Well, if you learn of anything unusual, you know where to find me," said Valdesta. She turned to retreat up the stairs to her private suite.

"Shall I send up your usual?" asked Camber.

"Yes. Leave it at the door, thanks."

Valdesta climbed the stairs and walked along a narrow balcony to her suite, eyes searching one last time for her contact and the telltale flash of color that might reveal her presence. The crowd blended into a uniform sea of common, drab clothing.

"Grind it all."

She reached the door to her suite and set the key in the lock, but found it already unlocked. Her hand patted against a dagger secreted under her blouse, but instead withdrew a separate weapon stowed under a bench beside the door. With the knife gripped in one hand, she backed down the hall.

Camber met her at the top of the steps, holding a tray of food. "Val, is everything alright?"

"Have you seen anyone enter my rooms this evening?"

"No, Val. Just you." He eyed the knife gripped in her hand and set down the tray. "Want me to grab a few men and have a look?"

She nodded once, but kept her gaze trained on her door. Camber returned a minute later with two broad-shouldered men. All three held cudgels and moved about their business with a casual ease that indicated their familiarity with such tasks.

She followed behind them, knife gripped in a fist, and grumbled to herself, "Nobody takes from the house."

Camber signaled with his fingers, then pushed into the room on three, the other men in close pursuit. The thudding of feet moving with purpose was met by silence. Valdesta peered over their shoulders. Her eyes adjusted to the dim illumination to see a woman sitting behind a small table in the far corner of the room, her black hair swept up in layers to reveal a high forehead. "Good evening, gentlemen, Valdesta," said Endera.

"Taker's sauce, woman. Why can't we ever meet like regular people? How did you even get in here?" she growled.

Endera reclined into the chair's back and looked out the window. "Lots of things can slide under the shadow of the moon."

Valdesta blew air through her nose. "It's fine, Camber. She's a friend of sorts. Thanks all the same, but you fellas should return to minding the security downstairs."

Camber nodded once, folded his cudgel against his forearm, and signaled the others to leave. "All the same, I'll post up here. Holler if you have need."

Endera waited for the men to depart, then cleared her throat. "I came to find out how your foray into the castle went. My sources inform me that the dark presence haunting the corridors of Stone's Grasp has vanished. I assume your team was successful?"

Valdesta set her knife down on a bureau beside the door, retrieved a flask of resco and two glasses, then took a seat at the table. "If I ask how you know about that, will you tell me, or speak in more riddles?"

Endera tilted her head, acknowledging the request for a truthful dialogue. "The foreign mercenaries you recruited are known to me. I assume they have already fled the kingdom? The regent has access to trackers, one in particular that would be capable of sourcing their whereabouts if they attempt to remain in Aarindorn."

Valdesta unstoppered the flask, and volatile caramel and oak aromas wafted over the table. The familiar sound of the amber liquid splashing into the cup eased her nerves. She poured two fingers in each glass, pushed Endera's across the table, then clinked them together before sipping at hers. She blew off the fumes and let her shoulders relax. "They lost two men inside, but otherwise made it out unharmed."

"And the abrogator?" pressed Endera, sipping at her own cup.

Valdesta took a larger gulp, shook her head, and refilled her glass. "She wasn't even there. Years of developing contacts on the inside and cultivating reliable informants, all spent to breach the royal suites only to find them empty. Well, empty is not exactly the right word, I suppose. Two of the Baellentrells rebuffed the attack. We nearly had that Balladuren scribe as well, which would have been compensation enough for all that the little grinder cost me in the past year."

Endera's brow creased, and she ran a finger over the rim of her glass. "That's puzzling. You said the abrogator was a girl. You're certain that she wasn't killed in the chaos of the assault?"

"As sure as I can be, but then the royals have played the entire affair close to the vest. It's been difficult getting any news from beyond the curtain wall, but what news there is makes no mention of the conflict."

"Well, one way or the other, I suspect that your abrogator troubles are solved," said the duchess.

"How so? That cursed girl is still on the loose."

"Perhaps, but even if that's so, she can't hope to return to Stone's Grasp as long as Kaellor Baellentrell maintains the wards encompassing the city. And from what I know of the man, and his respect for Tarkannen, he will not take that risk, at least, not for a long time."

"So, you believe that rubbish about the return of the usurper?" asked Valdesta.

Endera stared into the depths of the amber liquid swirling in her glass and took another sip. "Where is Chancle?"

Her abrupt change in topics seemed evasive, but Valdesta played along. "He escaped over the walls on the night the Baellentrells returned. You know that."

"Yes, but do you know of his whereabouts? Surely, after all that the Lacuna accomplished together, you must have some idea?"

"For a woman who is supposed to know everything, you've sort of missed the point that our inner circle tried to depose the man. If I knew where he landed, I would have tied up that loose end already, but I don't. What does that have to do with anything we've been talking about?"

Endera sighed. "It's the big picture, Val. You're a smart woman. Think outside the walls of Stone's Grasp, outside of Aarindorn even. Kaellor and his family were doing fine in the Southlands. They were happy and never would have returned, but for two things. First, the Lacuna, governed by your council, sent an assassin who botched the job. Second, they learned of Tarkannen's resurgence. One of those things alone might have brought them to your doorstep, but the two taken together guaranteed their return. Disbelieve the usurper's threat at your own peril. Regardless, Kaellor and his family believe in the threat and, for now anyway, he maintains powerful wards around the entire city, barring the entrance of abrogators."

"Why tell me any of this?" asked Valdesta.

"Maybe I think you deserve to know. Maybe I wonder if there's a spark of the young woman who knew how to lift the oppressed before becoming one of the oppressors. Use the information or don't. I've got other things to contend with."

Never one to squander an opportunity, Valdesta pressed, "Is it anything I can assist with? I've reorganized considerable resources within the city."

"I appreciate the offer, but there's no need, and besides, you appear to have your hands full. I like what you've done with the tavern."

Valdesta bobbed her head back and forth. "It's working for now, I suppose."

"Don't sell this place short. It's honest work for decent people. But I'm not here to tell you how to run your affairs," said Endera. She pushed her glass forward, leaving most of the resco behind.

"One last bit of advice before I go. Tarkannen's threat is real, and the ward surrounding Stone's Grasp might be the only thing keeping the usurper at bay. Run your businesses as you see fit, but try not to do anything that would jeopardize the only thing protecting all of us from the return of the abrogators."

Valdesta harrumphed, considering the warning, retrieved Endera's glass, and poured the contents into her own. She felt the gentle vacuum of zenith as the woman channeled. When she looked up, a curtain billowed out into the night air through an open window, but Endera's seat was vacant.

She strode to the window and craned her neck out, but found nothing unusual in the comings and goings of the common folk. The window lowered into place, and she secured the lock, only to find the clasp loose where it had been jimmied open. "So, you rely at least a little on mundane trickery to support your smoke and mirrors."

A knock at her door interrupted her thoughts. Camber spoke through the door. "Val, I felt someone channel. Is everything alright?"

"I'm fine, but come in all the same, Cam." She waited for the young man to enter. He held the platter of food with steady hands, but she still caught the glint of a knife blade under the tray. His eyes searched her room, and she snapped to get his attention. "For the next week, position watchers at each of the city gates. Tell them to keep a watch for the girl with the frizzy, straw-colored hair, and also any information on the comings and goings of Ksenia Balladuren. She's a scribe in the regent's offices."

"If we find either of them, how do you want the men to respond?" asked Camber.

"If either is alone, and the opportunity is safe, take them out. But they are connected, so be sure to place our best people on the job. Anyone who succeeds will receive twice the usual going rate for proof of the deed carried out with no witnesses."

Camber dipped his chin, registering the significance of the contract. "I'll see to it at once. Will there be anything else?"

"Yes, two things. See about getting a man inside Endera's court at Beclure again. I need more information about their duchess. If that doesn't work, I know that three or four of their men visit my girls regularly. Work that angle if you need to. And send for my daughter, Vinnedesta."

"Doesn't she work as a scribe for the regent as well?"

"She used to, but we moved her into the offices of the new prima dicta. She's likely to come across more meaningful information there now that the regent has shuffled off the petitioners to a panel of judges. Anyway, tell Vin I expect her for supper tomorrow."

"At once," said Camber. He set down the tray of food.

Valdesta spread a bit of cheese on a cracker and plopped the entire bite into her mouth. The sharp tang drew her cheeks to a pucker. She waved a hand, dismissing Camber, and polished a drab metal spoon with her napkin. She lifted the cover of a rounded crock, and the savory aroma of peppered stew made her stomach gurgle.

She stirred the contents, lifting a bit of carrot in her spoon. *Run your affairs as you see fit. Well, Endera, I intend to do that very thing. And who knows—if things work out, whether by the Giver's touch or the Taker's grip, we might get a run at more than just the Balladuren woman.*

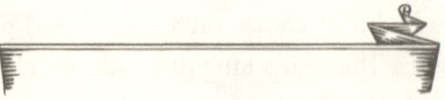

Chapter Twenty-Seven: A Painful Channel

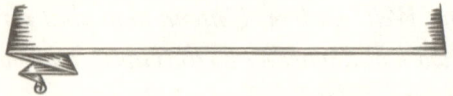

Bryndor squatted down to peer out of the secret passageway on the backside of Stone's Grasp, waiting for Boru's return. He pressed his back against the cold stone, aware now of the faint buzzing of zenith through the veining. The thought reminded him to maintain a trickle of zenith into the shek, but the device had remained dormant all day.

The late afternoon sun cast a dappled patina of light on the forest floor, and the scent of wet leaves beckoned him out. But after the events of the previous week, Kaellor had made him swear he would not leave the castle grounds without an escort, and if he were honest, his muscles ached in places too numerous to count to seek much adventure.

During their encounter with the invaders the night before, he acquitted himself well enough, he supposed, but he felt like he got lucky in several of the exchanges. His assailants had worked to injure and disarm, not kill. Regardless, the myriad of welts and bruises on his arms, ribs, and legs served as ample reminders of just how intense the fighting had been.

He eased into a sitting position and replayed several of the exchanges in his mind. His forearms had threatened to fail with fatigue as he parried and blocked, but his footwork had remained sound. After only a minute of reliving the encounter, however, his breaths came rapid and shoulder muscles tensed. Boru saved him from wading further into the chaotic memory by loping into the passageway.

The wolvryn cocked his head to the side, giving Bryndor the unmistakable feeling that he was being scrutinized. Boru took a few steps forward, then eased belly to the ground before rolling onto his back. His massive head shifted onto Bryndor's lap, beckoning to be scratched, and so he obliged.

The shek vibrated on his chest and Kaellor's voice carried out clear, as if he stood beside them. "Bryn, are you there? Is anyone listening?"

Bryndor startled at the way Kaellor's voice broke the silence, but then, that's why he'd kept the communication open, he supposed. "I'm here, Kae. Boru and I will make the climb back to you shortly."

He considered telling Kae exactly where he sat, but wasn't sure how many others in the closed council might be listening and preferred to maintain the secrecy of the passageway. Keeping secrets still felt like a burden, but after the attack the previous night, he understood the need for such things.

None of the others chimed in to announce their presence in the conversation. "Any word from the others?" asked Kaellor.

"Not so far."

"And you've kept the shek primed with zenith?" he pressed.

"Yes, but I've not heard anything."

After a long pause, Kaellor sighed through the device. "If we don't hear from them all soon, we might have to task the Outriders with a rescue mission. You might as well let me man the fort, so to speak. You've kept the shek open for several hours. Has it taxed you in any way?"

"Not really. My aches are more from the bruises I developed after sparring with those invaders. Makes me wish Rona was here with one of those foul-tasting herbal remedies, you know?"

"Mmm. I've had that same thought before. If you could choke down the cup in one or two gulps, it was worth the relief. You could present yourself to the healers in the House of the Moons. There is a branch on the lower level of the castle."

"I know. I don't think I realized how sore I was until I made the trek down here. But they've likely got people with actual injuries to attend to," said Bryndor. "I think of her now and again, Aunt Ro."

"So do I, son . . . all the time."

The admission made Bryndor smile, and he realized that, other than a conversation with Ksenia, this was the first time he'd talked about Rona without a heavy, hollowed-out sensation growing in the center of his chest. There was still a pain there, a scar that reminded him of the loss, but it felt good to talk about her, to remember her. "Do you remember the tidy rows of herbs she would plant on the south side of the barn? I was thinking last week that this was the time of year she would have Lluthean and me covered to our knees and elbows in mud, pulling weeds and preparing her garden for the next rotation."

Kaellor laughed softly through the shek. "Every now and again I catch myself making a statement that Rona or one of the Tellends might have uttered. It usually has something to do with the weather, gardens, or using simple common sense. It makes me sound provincial, but I sort of enjoy the strange looks people at court give me when some of Rona's words spill out of my mouth. At first they seem surprised, only to be mollified when the truth of her plain speech cuts to the core."

Bryndor huffed a chuckle. "That's the Giver's truth."

Laryn's voice broke through on the tail end of his comment. Exhaustion flavored her tone. "Bryn? Can you hear me? It's Laryn. Is anyone else listening?"

"Laryn! It's just the two of us for now, love. It's so good to hear your voice. How are you all? What's going on up there? I had half a mind to charge a few Outrider quints to come find you," said Kaellor.

"I'm sorry. I can imagine that our delay has caused some concern. We ran into a bit of trouble up here, but everything is turning out for the best, I think. I'm with Lluthean. We found Reddevek's people, what's left of them."

"That sounds . . . ominous. We've had our fair share of adventure here as well. Are you all safe? Is Ranika with you?" Kaellor pressed.

"Yes, she is fine. She's spending time with their speaker now. The Dev'advari speaker is one of Reddevek's aunts, Sintra Vekkuh Taim."

"It sounds like we've both got some news to share. Tell us about it," said Kaellor.

Laryn spent the better part of the next hour describing their arrival at the Dev'advari camp, the battle against the strange rumbler beasts, and her theory about how they used vibration in their sound attacks.

"How have the others taken to Nika now that they know about her skills?" asked Kaellor.

"Honestly? I haven't had much time to sort all of that out," said Laryn. "She received some strange looks at first, but without her we never would have survived against the rumblers or rescued Reddevek's people. The clan had a stone shaper. They lost several people in the initial attempt to repel the rumblers, good men and women who bought the rest of them time to retreat into a cave high in the cliffs. Their stone shaper sealed them behind a three-foot-thick barrier of stone, but once inside, he perished from the trauma the rumblers had inflicted. The rest of them were stranded inside. Karragin couldn't break through, but Ranika was able to use her gift to melt through the stone. You should have seen her, Kae. It was nothing short of a miracle.

"Anyway, we spent the better part of the last day ushering them out, treating everyone for dehydration, and just helping them recover. Lluthean and Neska, with the aid of Savnah's quad, have already hunted enough game to sustain them for a time."

"It sounds like the Giver had a hand in your timely arrival. How many of the Dev'advari are left?" asked Kaellor.

"We've been able to rescue over two hundred, but many of those are the young and old. They lost a good number of their able bodied adults in the initial fight against the rumblers."

"Would they accept a charitable mission from Aarindorn?" asked Bryndor.

"It's possible. They're all in a state of shock. They seem more aloof, more suspicious than the Luna Rova from the low country, but their losses were significant, and it's still early."

Kaellor grunted in agreement. "I wonder if a word from Overwarden Kaldera would ease the situation. He might even be able to get them to allow the support of soldiers from Stone's Grasp to aid in their recovery and defense."

"It's possible, I suppose, but the clans are nomadic. Despite all that they have lost, the speaker made it clear that they will continue to follow the moons, migrating to the southeast corner of the Great Crown. The only people who might be able to lend them aid are Outriders and, as I understand it, their ranks are already pressed into service at the Pillars."

"That's true enough," said Kaellor.

"That about sums up our grand adventure into the Great Crown. Tell me what kind of trouble you two got into while I've been away."

Bryndor chewed on the inside of his lower lip, waiting for Kaellor to take the lead in the conversation. The shek remained silent for long moments until Laryn spoke again. "Kae? Bryn, are you there?"

"Still here. Can anyone else overhear our conversation?" asked Bryndor.

"I'm alone up here for the moment. None of the Luna Rova had any desire to remain up here after being trapped inside," said Laryn.

"Alright, then," said Kaellor. "There was an attack, a breach into the castle. A capable group of assassins broke through the defenses and into the wing housing the royal suites."

"Were either of you hurt?" asked Laryn.

"We're fine. Bryndor and I managed to take out two of their members. We lost a sentinel, and several others recover from nonlethal wounds," said Kaellor.

"I see. Was it the Lacuna?" asked Laryn.

"We don't think so, not directly anyway," said Kaellor. He went on to explain the nature of the attack, the professional demeanor of the group, and their subsequent escape, including how they'd left behind a haze of vellevlin.

"You lost me there, Kae. Why would they go to all that effort to break into Ranika's rooms?" asked Laryn.

"Vellevlin is basically aerosolized Eldrenol's solution. It likely stifles an abrogator's ability to channel nadir. We think the group came specifically for Nika."

Ranika's voice echoed through the shek as if speaking from the other side of a thick door. "That sounds about right," she said.

Laryn sighed. "How long have you been listening? Never mind, you may as well get over here. This affects you as much as anyone else."

The sound of Ranika grunting, then shifting about on the cave floor gave Bryndor the impression that she sat down next to Laryn. When she spoke, her voice rang as clear as the others. "Sorry. I came up here to talk to you, Laryn. Anyway, the last time Bryn and I ran into the Lacuna, they had set a trap for me and painted everyone in a cloud of that purple stuff.

It made me feel sick, and I couldn't touch nadir for a bit. It's clear that they were expecting me. Maybe it was only a matter of time."

"I'm glad you're safe, both of you," said Kaellor. "Hestian has already commissioned an investigation into how the invaders came by the vellevlin. We should have it sorted out by the time you return. When will you start back home? We'll need to coordinate your arrival. I've adjusted the wards over Stone's Grasp, but I'm confident that I can lift them to allow you safe entrance, Nika."

"We'll wait another day," said Laryn. "There's a Giver's Stone here. Lluthean is going to use rune fire to cremate the dead in a ceremony tonight. Speaker Vekkuh said that once the ashes were placed on the stone, they would strike camp. It's a small kindness, and Llu is happy to help. Besides, I need to rest before we head back. I promise to do a better job communicating through the shek. We can plan to speak two or three times a day. If we keep you apprised of our progress, it should not be difficult to coordinate our arrival."

The sound of Laryn's muffled voice carried through the shek. Though Bryndor couldn't understand the words, a definite tone of surprise carried through the commotion. At last, a clear voice returned to the conversation, but instead of Laryn, it was Ranika who spoke. "I said, I'm not coming back. Not yet, maybe not ever, I don't know. But these people need someone like me, and I can help them, protect them if anything like those rumblers shows up. They don't care that I'm an abrogator, and we're about as far removed from the Lacuna as we can be here."

Bryndor thought about Ranika's position and tried to imagine settling in with the nomadic clan in the mountains. While he intuitively understood that such a life would shed the comforts of a warm hearth, soft bed, and good food, he envied her for the simple freedom of her decision.

Kaellor spoke, a softer resonance in his baritone. "Nika, the Giver knows we've not done a very good job of keeping you safe before now. But I'm confident we can get you inside, keep you safe, and be the family Red would want you to have."

There was another long silence, and Bryndor imagined his friend shaking out her spirals of straw-colored hair, gathering the spun glass into one hand, and deftly depositing it all under an oversized hat. The thought drew a smile to his face.

"You've already done more for me than anyone should have a right to ask. All of you. But, I think it's best if I stay with the Dev'advari, at least for now. Besides, you guys don't need me, not really. And if word got out that you threw in with an abrogator? Well, I don't think that would make for pleasant conversation at your coronation. But these people need me. It's for the best, so . . . for now anyway, goodbye, both of you. Bryn, squeeze Boru for me."

The wolvryn rose to his feet upon hearing his name and licked Bryndor on the chin. He cleared his throat to dismiss the heavy feeling gathering there. "He says he'll miss you too. Maybe we can try to come find you later this summer. Pay a visit."

"I would like that, but don't make promises a king can't keep. Eyes to the horizon, Bryn."

Kaellor tried once again to engage the young woman. "It sounds like you've made up your mind, Nika, and I can understand why you might feel that way—"

"She's gone, Kae," said Laryn. "I'm sorry, I had no idea. I'll speak to her in the morning. For now, I've got to get some rest to shake off the draft, especially if we are to head back soon."

"I understand, love. I'll keep the shek open. We can talk tomorrow. Let's make it midday so you don't rise early," said Kaellor.

"That sounds perfect. Until tomorrow," said Laryn.

Bryndor rose to his feet and stretched sore back muscles. "Are you still there, Bryn?" asked Kaellor.

"Yes, Kae. What is it?"

"I've been thinking. Until we are certain about your safety, you should bring Boru into your sleeping chambers. He and Neska have warned us of danger on more than one occasion in the past, and their presence alone might deter any other threats."

"Fair point, but I don't think he is going to like it. It's . . . quiet down here, isolated from the overwhelming sounds and smells."

"Perhaps you and Lluthean, maybe even Ksenia, can alternate bringing them to the passageway every day."

Bryndor nodded to himself. Ksenia had already entered through the passageway, and with her unique connection to the wolvryn she could easily assist in managing their comings and goings . . . and if he were honest, it wouldn't hurt to have more opportunities to spend time with her.

"I can speak to her about it," he said.

"Good, that will set my mind at ease a bit," said Kaellor. "I've been thinking, I want you and Lluthean to resume sparring sessions in the morning when he returns, and I asked Therek to round up a few tutors to see about training you in your rune craft."

"I expect we can use all the help we can get. Now that we are not attending court to hear the petitioners, we should have a bit more time to manage it."

"I agree. Therek has also agreed to take the lead in schooling both of you in Aarindorian customs and law, with lessons to begin tomorrow afternoon. We have a lot of ground to cover before your coronation, and I can't think of anyone more suited to the task."

Bryndor sighed with resignation, turned, and bumped his forehead against the cold stone. He pushed back and clenched a fist, then lightly rapped his knuckles against one of the silver veins traversing the wall. Instead of the familiar buzzing sensation, a throbbing ache spread across the runes on his forearm, as if he and Lluthean had crossed swords and the force of the blow reverberated through the weapon and deep into bone.

"Grind it." He sucked at his teeth and shook his hand to dissipate the painful sensation.

"Bryn?"

"I'm fine. Just a pulled muscle. We'll be up in a bit. I'm going to let the shek fall dormant for now."

"That's fine. I'll see you soon."

"Yes, soon," he said and continued to shake his forearm as if to remove hot wax. The intensity of the achy feeling persisted, and he rolled back his shirtsleeve to study the runes. Flickers of zenith rippled back and forth, building in intensity that flared in concert with the bone-deep aching feeling.

Giver, I can't even channel safely. You should do it, Kae. Train in your gift, school with Therek, wear the crown . . . all of it.

And just as quickly as the thought popped into his head, so too did the achy feeling in his forearm vanish. He tapped a single finger on the silver veining to test if the strange pain would return. Boru sat on his haunches, mouth slightly open, the corners withdrawn in a smile.

Right, that's rather something Lluthean would do.

He withdrew his hand, holding it up in a gesture as if to show the ward he meant no harm. When nothing happened, he reached out, sensing the ambient currents of zenith, and realized that even though he had silenced the shek, he had still been channeling right up until the moment that the rune on his forearm, and the associated pain, fell dormant.

"Come on, Boru. As much as I might hate it, Kae is right. I need a lot of practice, and we're going to be late to meet Ksenia."

He backtracked his steps through the secret passages, careful to use the placards now attuned to the Baellentrell gift, and securely closed each door. Eventually, they emerged into the broad hallway before the inner sanctum. Though he had passed by the entrance many times, he avoided entering the sacred hall where the statuesque remains of his parents had stood through the years.

The grand double doors stood slightly ajar and Boru loped ahead, nudged his nose through the door, then disappeared inside. At the threshold, the light fragrance of winter night's asylum lifted to his awareness and removed any hesitation he felt about returning to the sanctum.

He pushed through the doors, pulling his gaze from the towering statue of Eldrek Baellentrell and searching the room. Ksenia sat cross-legged on one of the benches, frowning at pages of loose-leaf paper. Bryndor sensed a delicate tug on the currents of zenith. Like the subtle draft of air through a room with a cracked window, Ksenia's channeling rose as a slight tickle to his awareness.

She looked up as Boru lapped at the surface of the clear pool in the center of the room. "I wonder what the regent would say if he knew Boru was slaking his thirst down here."

He sat down on a bench beside her and studied the patina of freckles across the bridge of her nose, accentuating her cheekbones. For a moment, all he could manage was the simple act of observation. His thoughts seemed to suspend, unable to find purchase in his mind. Then she squinted. "You're doing that thing again," she said, then leaned forward and pecked a kiss on his lips.

Their fingers interlocked and heat rose to his cheeks. A soft smile found its way onto his face. "Sorry, I know. I can't help it."

He wanted to say: *Whenever I walk into a room and see you, it's like I'm looking at you for the first time, and it always muddles my thoughts.* Instead, he drew his attention to the papers she held in her hand. "What are you working on there?"

"I can't remove *The Tome of Nivosh* from the archives, so I asked a friend of mine, Veeble, to copy some of the pages." She pinched what appeared to be no fewer than fifty sheets of paper between thumb and finger. While Bryndor recognized most of the symbols, he did not know what to make of the actual words.

"All of that is copied? Why didn't he make a draft in the Kindred speech?"

"He can't. I have to decipher the text with my gift, and High Aarindorian is tricky. The context and juxtaposition of phrasing can completely alter the meaning. So Veeble copies the words with expert precision and sends them to me."

"That must have taken a long time," said Bryndor.

"Mmm, I assumed as much, but Veeble is different; special."

"Gifted?" he asked.

"No, actually, he's runeless. But I don't think his mind works like other people." Her focus pulled away as she searched for the words to describe the man. "He's a very odd man with a complete disregard for social decorum. I can't explain it, but whenever I talk to him, he seems oblivious to the normal flow of a conversation, and I think he's pathologically unable to bathe. But despite all that, he has an uncanny memory for symbols and figures. I'm not explaining it very well."

"I think I understand. Lluthean is that way with maps and directions. He can get lost three times riding across foreign land in a single afternoon, then sit down and accurately record the details of the journey on a map."

Ksenia nodded. "That's impressive. Could he do that before you both had access to your gift?"

"Yes, and it was maddening!" He laughed. "But amazing at the same time, you know?"

"Don't tell Llu I said anything, but that does sound a little . . . Veeble-ish."

Her thumb massaged the center of his palm, and the small gesture overwhelmed his awareness, reducing his focus to the intimate touch, the flecks of pigment in her eyes, and the upturned curve of her upper lip. Without words, the space between them dissolved, and they shared a passionate kiss. His free hand wrapped behind her shoulders, pulling her close, and their breaths drew heavy. After a few seconds, her papers clattered to the floor, and she grabbed the back of his neck, drawing him further into the embrace.

He became intimately focused on every alteration in the pressure of her touch, the depth and speed of her breath, the press of her chest to his. They lingered oblivious to the world until something cold and heavy dropped onto his lap. He pulled back with abrupt surprise to find Boru's massive head. The wolvryn rolled his ear onto Ksenia's lap, but allowed his dripping wet chin to drape across Bryndor's thighs.

Bryndor dropped his head forward, long strands of dark hair obscuring the flush on his face. He finger-combed them back to find Ksenia's bright smile, and as one, they fell into a fit of laughter. She pressed her thumb into his palm once and squeezed her fingers before letting go to retrieve her papers.

"Sorry for the . . . wet, I think he tried to bathe himself in the pool there," said Bryndor.

"If I didn't know better, I would think your aunt and uncle tasked Boru as our chaperone," she said.

"I had a mind to wonder if it was your mother."

She righted herself on the bench. "Oh, I hadn't even considered that angle. Yes, that makes much more sense."

"Beyond coordinating the governance of Stone's Grasp with the regent and managing the defense of Aarindorn, I think Kae and Laryn have too much to contend with to give much thought to our supervision." He puffed out his cheeks and exhaled.

"That doesn't sound so bad. What's underneath that serious frown, my prince?"

He hadn't realized the tension that gathered between his brows and forced his face to relax, then shared the details of the conservation through the shek, recounting what he could of the attack by the rumblers. He maintained Ranika's secret as an abrogator, stepping lightly around the topic, then divulged her decision to remain with the Luna Rova. Finally, he reviewed Kaellor's plan to redouble the efforts to prepare him and Lluthean for their roles in governing the kingdom.

Ksenia leaned in, listening intently to all of his revelations. At last, she cupped his cheek in one hand, the fingers of her other hand tracing around Boru's ear. "That's a heavy burden, Bryn. I don't understand why those assassins used vellevlin or why they sought Nika's rooms. What are you not telling me?"

His next words came slow and clumsy as he struggled to string together an apology without divulging too much. "Before we met, I made Nika a promise. The promise of one friend to another, and I don't know how to tell you more without breaking that promise."

"It's alright. I mean it's not like she's an abrogator or anything."

At her words, his shoulders slumped, and he dropped his gaze to Boru. When he looked up, Ksenia had a calculating expression and searched his eyes.

Without words, color flared her cheeks, and her mouth dropped open. "But the Lacuna must believe she's an abrogator. Why else would they use vellevlin?"

"Kess, as much as I want to, I can . . . neither agree with nor deny any conclusions, so—"

Her expression softened, and she grabbed the front of his tunic, pecked him once on the lips, then pushed him back. "It's alright, Bryn. If you told me, if you broke your promise, then you wouldn't be the man I . . . well, the man I know you to be."

He sighed with relief. "Well, Boru and I should begin the long climb back up. Care to join us?"

She gathered all her papers into a folio and tucked it under her arm. "He and Neska don't like it up top much. They say it's too much of us in one place, the smells, the sounds."

"I can imagine, but Kae asked me to keep them in our suites at night. He figures their presence will deter any other attacks and help keep us safe."

She stood. "That makes sense, especially if he is as good at protecting you from enemies as he is at protecting your virtue."

"I think . . . I think," he stumbled.

"You think what?" she teased.

"Well, didn't he sort of interrupt both of us?"

She chuckled a throaty laugh. "Maybe, my prince. But if you try to tell anyone, I'll deny it, and since I'm the only one who can speak to Boru directly, I'm pretty sure I could set the record straight before another sympath had the chance to question him."

She raised an eyebrow, challenging him to question her resolve. He responded with a laugh in kind and held up his hands in submission. "I yield to your wit, your talent, and your beauty . . . I am clearly overmatched."

They walked out of the inner sanctum and began the long climb back to Stone's Grasp. Boru kept pace between them. "You know, Nivosh wrote that several members of the royal families bonded with wolvryn hundreds of years ago. To accommodate them, the hallways of the lower levels were built extra wide."

"What else have you learned from the writings?" he asked.

"Squeeze me into your busy schedule, and I'll let you know."

They reached the top of the landing, breathless from the long climb. Bryndor held open a door and Ksenia looked through, but drew up short as a woman wearing a formal grey doublet and skirt embroidered with the purple insignia of the offices of the prima dicta stepped forward. She appeared of a similar age to Ksenia and, by her reaction, the two were acquaintances.

"Vinn, how have you been?" said Ksenia.

"Happy to escape the offices of the prima dicta, if I'm honest. It's stiflingly hot in there, and I can't say the company is much better." The two embraced a moment, and the clerk eyed Bryndor over Ksenia's shoulder.

"Are you going to introduce me to your friends?"

"Of course," said Ksenia. "I think the climb stole my wits. Vinnedesta, may I introduce His Highness, Prince Bryndorllean Baellentrell and his faithful wolvryn, Boru. Your Highness, this is Vinnedesta, a dear friend of mine. Vinn taught me everything I know about scribing before she left for the offices of the prima dicta."

"Nice to meet you, Vinn," said Bryndor.

Vinnedesta placed a hand over her chest, made eyes at Ksenia, then pulled a face of exasperation. "Nice to meet me, goodness no. The honor is mine, Your Highness, really such a pleasure."

"Well, any friend of Ksenia's is someone I should likely worry about," said Bryndor, and then immediately wondered where the comment came from. It felt like a flirty line Lluthean might quip in a tavern full of strangers. Thankfully, both women laughed at the jibe.

Vinnedesta played along and leaned in conspiratorially. "Yes, well, you can pick your friends but not your family, nor those assigned to mentor you in the regent's court, I'm afraid. You will have to give me a chance to prove my value as a loyal subject of the kingdom before associating me with someone of such dubious character."

Ksenia playfully slapped Vinnedesta on the shoulder. "You two. Had I known where this conversation was going, I would have stayed in the sanctum, just me and the papers from Nivosh."

"Still at it with that old thing?" asked Vinnedesta. "I wondered if you still tortured yourself with that epic piece. I miss you, Kess. Maybe we could meet for a night out and catch up soon?"

"I'm free this afternoon?" Ksenia suggested.

Vinnedesta deflated. "I can't. I'm due back in the offices after running this errand. In fact, I should take my leave."

Vinnedesta curtsied. "Your Highness, Kess. It has been a true pleasure."

Bryndor tilted his head, acknowledging the greeting. "For me as well."

They watched her disappear around the corner, and Bryndor held the door open. Ksenia placed a hand on the door and looked back down the long spiral stairs they had ascended. Her eyes glinted with a mischievous expression, and she stepped in close. When their lips touched, he barely registered the sound of the door slamming closed.

Chapter Twenty-Eight: Two Forks from the Same Stream

A weary Karragin settled down against a boulder nestled close to a campfire. A cascade of embers sparked across the top of her boot, and though she couldn't hear the crackling flames, the familiar alpine scent of woodsmoke reminded her of survivor's essence. As she leaned back, the heat from the fire that had radiated onto the stone enveloped her in a comforting warmth. The fading light of the setting sun cast a subtle hue over the horizon, there one moment, then abruptly gone as it dropped below the western peaks of the Great Crown. With only the delicate crescent moon of Baellen, the sky transformed into a velvety darkness punctuated by a dazzling array of stars.

She closed her eyes and massaged her temples, trying to ease the throbbing ache in her head. She had spent a significant part of the day rounding up the horses of the Luna Rova. In the attack by the rumblers, the mounts had broken free in a panic. Neska and Nolan had joined Lluthean in hunting herd animals to replenish the food stores of the Dev'advari. That left Karragin to rely on her Aarindin, Trini. Though more than capable of finding the lost mounts, Trini's talkative nature tried Karragin's patience.

It was the Giver's good fortune that they'd found the horses grazing together only a few miles away. Still skittish from the panicked flight, they initially resisted Trini's lead. Karragin had to provide constant reassurance to the small herd, offering soothing images and redirecting any that wandered away. What should have taken a few hours took most of the day. She had never needed to rely on her sympath ability for such a continuous period of time and felt surprised that she had not dropped into the draft.

On top of that, she was still recovering from the cumulative trauma of the rumbler attacks. Laryn suspected her stamina would return only after several days of rest, but nobody else in their group had her sympath ability, and sitting idle in a camp of busy refugees was simply not in her nature.

Savnah plopped down beside Karragin and handed her a waterskin and a kerchief folded over something warm with a savory aroma. The prime scooted so close that their hips touched, and Karragin gave her a sideways look.

Savnah kicked off her boots and wiggled her toes. *"You took the best spot. I share my meat pies, you share the spot?"* she signed.

Karragin nudged her hips to the side, inviting Savnah to a more comfortable reclined position against the warmth of the rock. She unfolded the kerchief to find six half-moon shaped pastries. She took a bite to discover a chewy meat, chopped tubers, and some kind of pepper spice.

Karragin held the kerchief out, and Savnah retrieved a pastry, raised it in a toast, and sampled the fare. Her eyebrows rose in appreciation. After finishing one, she wriggled her shoulders against the boulder and reclined further with fingers interlocked overhead.

"Long day?" asked Karragin.

"I've had better," she signed. A distant look washed over her face, and then she smiled. *"I've also had worse. This job can be a real grot grind."*

The two of them laughed together. "Don't we know it," Karragin said. They stared out across the Luna Rova camp. Where before the conical tents were scattered across the mountain valley, now everyone clustered together against the defensive backing of the cliffside. Individual members of the Dev'advari went about their business with heads hung low, and Karragin didn't need to hear their collective silence to perceive the somber mood that permeated the clan in the wake of the rumbler attacks.

"How do you think they'll do?" asked Karragin.

"The Moonies? Who can say, but I'll wager Ranika will see them through any trouble if more rumblers show up. Girl's made of tougher metal than I gave her credit for," signed Savnah.

Karragin briefly considered the bodies of the slain Lacuna she had investigated with Laryn. It was not hard to puzzle together Ranika's motivations for hunting the rebels, but the insidious way she had single-handedly disrupted the organization still seemed like more than the young woman should be able to accomplish.

"Is she really is staying behind then?"

Savnah shrugged her shoulders. *"It's probably for the best. Even though Her Radiance swore us each to secrecy, things like that have a way of getting out."*

A distinct vacuum pulled at the currents of zenith, and Karragin reached out her fingers, as if to better understand the disturbance. A strobe of brilliant blue light flared, followed by the palpable vibration of rune fire in the distance.

Karragin sat forward in alarm until Savnah placed a hand on her shoulder. *"Sorry, I should have warned you. It's Lluthean. He's burning the remains of the rumblers. The speaker, Vekkuh, asked him to leave no trace of the things."*

Karragin thought back to the ceremony at the Giver's Stone the night before. Lluthean used rune fire to cremate the bodies of those lost to the rumblers. Afterward, the survivors gathered the Dev'advari ashes and deposited them on top of the bowl-shaped depression in a somber ceremony. Amniah then gusted the ashes into the heavens. "Did you have the chance to dissect the rumbler corpses? A record of those things could prove valuable."

"Tovnik, Dexxin, and I got it done. Tov made drawings and notations. It's not something a scribe in the regent's offices would be proud of, but good enough for now."

"Where do you think they came from? I've never heard of anything like that in any of the Outrider histories."

"The rumblers? Who can say? Somewhere beyond the Drift, I hope. That way, we aren't likely to run across more. Can you even imagine how much damage one of those things could do in a crowd of people?"

"I know what you mean. Those creepy tail-swatters are one thing, but we underestimated the effect of their sound attack," said Karragin.

"Well, some of us more than others, but we did alright seeing as we had no understanding of them. If there is a next time, we'll be ready."

Another surge of zenith and detonation of rune fire lit up the valley. Several minutes later, Lluthean walked across the camp. His shoulders slumped, and he lacked any of the mirth that usually permeated his nature. "If he's that tired, maybe he shouldn't show off using rune fire," Karragin muttered.

The words were out of her mouth before she could edit her thoughts. Where had that come from? She must be more fatigued than she realized.

Savnah retrieved another pastry, crammed the whole thing in her mouth, then dusted off her hands and signed, *"He's given more than most today, Karra. Go easy."*

Savnah could embellish a story as good as any gleeman in a tavern, but something in her friend's gestures gave Karragin pause. *"How so?"* she signed back.

"He hunted and field dressed three crown rams, walked each one back here on a horse-drawn litter, butchered the meat, then helped a good number of Luna Rova widows move and assemble their tents. You can't tell in the shadows, but his leathers are covered with more blood, sweat, and dirt than anyone else."

"I'm an absolute monk," she muttered. She watched as Neska padded along beside Lluthean. The wolvryn lifted her nose to the sky in greeting, and Karra palmed the leather bag holding the riftwing egg against her breast. She kindled zenith into her sympath rune and reached out.

"Hello, Neska. You two have done a lot today. Is Lluthean well?"

Neska's response echoed back through the link, a familiar mixture of images, scents, and sounds. *"My Lluthean tries to be, he . . . thinks he is well."*

"You don't sound so sure."

"He is always busy, restless. Of late, he searches for ways to fill his day."

"Everyone knows he's done a lot today. The people are grateful. Make sure that he rests."

Neska gave no further reply, and Karragin severed their link. She thought back to Savnah's last remark. Not for the first time that month, Karragin appreciated her friend's command of the hand signing. "Savnah, how are you so good at the sign language?"

Savnah heaved a shoulder into her. *"We made the lessons part of our evening ritual. I know you've been invited, but it's like you almost refuse to practice. You could use it with me, you know? Anyway, between Ranika and Lluthean, we've had sessions every day, sometimes two or three times a day. But you're changing the subject. It doesn't take someone with your father's gifts to see things between you two are colder than fish tits in the middle of winter. Care to explain?"*

Karragin allowed a half-smile to blossom on her face. "Fish don't even have—never mind. You were right; on the ranging to Stone's Grasp from the Borderlands, he took a fancy to me, but I couldn't see it going anywhere. So, I asked him to find other things to do with his time and treat me as any other member of the kingdom."

"Asked him or told him?" pressed Savnah.

She tried to recall their conversation, but her exact words didn't rise to the surface of her awareness. Instead, she recalled feeling like he understood her wishes and that they'd laid the issue to rest. "I don't know, but he's given me the space I need to do my job, and that will give him the chance to find his place in the kingdom."

"Keep telling yourself that and maybe the Giver will see fit to make it come true," signed Savnah.

"It's true enough."

"Karra, there's how you want things to be and then there's how things are. It's easy to get the two mixed up. Don't believe me? Then, consider this; Baccal saw our young prince risk his life to scramble to the top of that column of rock. You think Neska retrieved that riftwing egg all by herself? Think again. He's not done anything like that for any of the rest of us."

Karragin swore under her breath. An anchor of self-deprecation tugged at her midsection and threatened to roll her into a ball. "Well, if that's true, I am grateful, but it also means he needs more time to come to grips with his role in the kingdom. When the two of us stand on solid ground, I'll thank him, but right now I don't want to do anything to lead him on. You know?"

Savnah reached for the waterskin and took a long draw. *"Is that why you haven't joined us to practice the hand signing?"*

Karragin bobbed her head side to side, considering her own motivations, then eventually nodded. "Yes. But I will come. After watching all of you, I can see that I've fallen behind, and let's face it, standing downwind of a Derrigand is flirting with disaster."

Savnah spluttered and choked on the water. She lightly tapped a knuckle on the side of Karragin's temple. *"I was beginning to wonder if you were still in there. Welcome back."*

Baccal and Amniah wandered over to sit beside them and share the warmth of the campfire. Laryn had dismissed them for the night and held council with the speaker, Vekkuh. In time, Nolan, Tovnik, and Dexxin joined them. They shared an easy banter with each person using the sign language for Karragin's benefit. While she caught most of the exchanges, she could tell by the occasional outburst of laughter that she still missed some of the more subtle parts of the conversation.

Ranika eventually found her way to the group, and where Karragin might have expected awkward looks, they received her with a warm welcome. Dexxin, of all people, stood and offered the young woman a seat beside him. Savnah beat a hasty retreat, only to return with a flask of resco.

She held the flask up high, then stored it under one arm and signed, *"There is only enough here for each person to take a sip, but it's the least we can do. Nika, it's been a pleasure. I call on those who would call me friend, to remember those who've met their end. Though our paths diverge under the light of the moon, may the Giver grant that we meet again. Moons!"*

Savnah took a sip, grimaced, then blew out the fumes before passing the flask to Ranika, who repeated the gesture. She stared into the flask, then placed it under her arm to sign as she spoke. *"Red would like that. He might say something like, 'take your sword to bed and not a woman so you wake up on the right side of the dirt.'"*

By the way everyone chuckled, Karragin guessed that Ranika had attempted to imitate the warden's gruff voice. Not for the first time, memories of the man flashed through her mind, and a wistful smile found its way onto her face.

"I'll miss you, Red. I'll never stop missing you. Moons!" Ranika tipped the flask up for a long swig. To her credit, the young woman only wrinkled her nose after imbibing the volatile spirit. She passed it along and, in turn, each Outrider took a sip.

Baccal stood up when the flask reached her. *"Nika, I said once that my gift didn't see half as much as it should when it came to you. I can't see things like decency or bravery. Reddevek was the best of us, and he likened you to a daughter. I count it a blessing of the Giver that our paths crossed. Moons!"*

In turn, the flask found its way to Karragin. She sloshed the contents around to judge how much was left just as Lluthean approached. Nolan was first to welcome the prince, joined by the others, who pounded fists to knee or chest. Their welcome seemed to lessen Lluthean's fatigue, and with a visible effort, he straightened his shoulders. He nodded his appreciation of the welcome and held his hands to the flames in strained silence.

Eventually, his eyes found Karragin's, and she stood, choosing to speak instead of sign. The inability to hear her own voice, especially when speaking to her friends, still felt alienating, but she pressed on. "You're just in time, Llu. We are toasting friendship and asking the Giver to place us in each other's company once again. To friendship, to Reddevek, to Ranika. The Luna Rova are lucky to have you, and you will always have a sister in Stone's Grasp should you choose it. You will be missed. Moons."

Karragin took a sip, then handed the flask to Lluthean, who maintained a somber expression. He turned to Ranika and signed as he spoke. *"You absolutely will be missed. To friendship, to Reddevek, and to you, Nika."* He held the flask up to take a sip, then muttered, "Umm, moons." Lluthean tossed back the flask and spluttered, causing everyone to laugh as he choked on the harsh spirit.

After wiping away tears, a smile found its way onto his face and he signed, *"You can't warn a man? That's worse than Malvressian honey-cut and that stuff is awful!"*

His response caused everyone to break into fits of laughter. Karragin shrugged and patted Lluthean on the shoulder. "Think of it as surviving shared misery. That's the stuff that makes a tighter bond than most things."

Lluthean coughed one last time into his fist and croaked out, "Shared misery, I get it."

The conversation lingered into the night for several more hours, with each of them retreating to their tents as the embers faded until, at the last, only Savnah and Ranika remained.

"I can take first watch," offered Savnah.

"I'm not in a mood to argue; are you sure?" asked Karragin.

"You both may as well get some rest," signed Ranika. *"I'm spending this last night with Neska."*

On cue, the majestic wolvryn padded out of the shadows to sit beside Ranika. Savnah stretched her arms overhead and yawned. *"I can live with that."*

Savnah stared across the camp, then turned and winked. *"Maybe Nolan or Dexx could use some company,"* signed the prime. She stood and walked toward Nolan's tent with a light bounce in her step.

Karragin watched her go, knowing it was not the first time the two had sought one another's company. How did her brother manage it? They seemed so different. She dismissed the thought and turned back to Ranika. "You don't need sleep for the journey tomorrow?"

"I'm fine, still buzzing from melting that hole through the cave," signed Ranika.

Karragin found her feet as well. "Buzzing, what does that mean?"

Ranika sighed, then signed as she spoke, *"Red explained that when he channeled too long, it made him feel sick. It's the same with me, only instead of tired, I get all wound up inside. I won't be able to sleep until tomorrow night. Besides, you look about as perky as Lluthean. Two forks from the same stream, if you ask me."*

"How so?"

"Neither one of you with enough common sense to stop before giving too much of yourself. Red could be that way too, though."

Karragin didn't feel like she could argue the point. *"Wake me if you need a break or if you sense any trouble?"*

"I'll think about it," signed Ranika. She started to walk off into the shadows, but turned at the last moment. *"I can tell things with you and Llu have changed. You don't have to tell me any of it, but know that he sees you . . . different from other people."*

"Different, how?" asked Karragin.

"It doesn't matter, and it's not for me to say. Just maybe get out of your own way once in a while? You might like what comes across your path when you do. Good night, Karra."

Karragin watched Ranika depart and considered the young woman's words. Her first inclination was to take offense that someone of Ranika's age was offering her advice. But she felt too tired to invest further in the feeling. The young abrogator and Neska slid into the shadows, and Karra wondered if she ever would see her again.

"Grind it, I don't get in my own way." She spoke the words out loud, but drew up short upon being confronted once again with her complete inability to hear anything.

By the dim light of the moon, she approached her tent set adjacent to Laryn's. She turned at the last moment and walked to the other side of the camp, where a different tent stood. She dropped to a knee and pushed the tent flap open. The top of the bedroll shifted, and Lluthean's bewildered eyes appeared in the opening.

"What's wrong?" he signed, then scrubbed fingers into his light brown curls and tried to stifle a yawn.

She considered him for a long moment. *Do I get in my own way?* Lluthean started to crawl forward, and she set a hand on his shoulder, easing him back inside the tent. Doubt began to erode the motivation that drew her feet to his tent.

He looked up in confusion and signed, *"My Karragin? What is it?"*

The gesture was ever so subtle, a curl of the little finger, but he had signed the words as naturally as he breathed, and any of the reservations she had melted. She stared up at the twinkling patina of stars. *Moons Karra, get inside or leave him be, but make a grinding choice.*

She searched his face once again, then nodded. Somewhere beneath the fatigue and self-deprecation, she needed this. She just hoped that he did too. "Did you know that it's not uncommon for Outriders to share a bed after a day like today?"

He shook his head in the negative.

"Do you want me to leave?" she asked.

He paused with uncertainty, then shook his head once again in the negative. *"Is this something to do with shared misery?"*

Now it was her turn to shake her head no, and the muscles of her face relaxed in a smile. "It's because of our shared misery that we seek each other's company, but my feet would likely have found their way here, regardless. Now, Giver's truth, Llu. Have you ever . . . been with a woman before?"

He dropped his head and even in the shadows, she could see his face flush, but he inhaled a breath and lifted his eyes before shaking his head no once again.

"Are you sure then? I mean, your tent does seem somewhat small."

His head tilted, he smiled, then shifted himself to the side, leaving plenty of room on the bedroll for her.

"Right then. If we do this, it will not change anything between us. You are the prince and need to focus on your duty to the kingdom. I have my responsibilities to Her Radiance. Tonight, for a spell, we can choose to leave the world outside this tent. Tomorrow, though, we have to lift those burdens again."

Lluthean shrank back a moment, apparently considering her words, but eventually conceded the point with a nod. He then patted the empty space on the bedroll.

"Good." She crawled in and pulled the tent flap closed, searching through the darkness until their lips touched. It took only a moment for him to respond, pushing into the kiss and exhaling a heady breath through his nose. Together, they surrendered to the moment, to the need, and to one another.

Chapter Twenty-Nine: Reshaping Barriers

Therek lay on his back, his chest heaving as he gasped for breath. The sickly sweet scent of his sweat stained the air, causing the bedsheets to stick to his wiry torso. He struggled to regain his bearings, his disorientation amplified by the poor illumination of morning's first light filtering through the curtains. In his mind, afterimages danced like fleeting bolts of lightning, their vivid streaks making sense one moment before dissolving into a jumbled, bewildering mishmash the next.

Zenith tingled along his arca prime, and he pushed up to a sitting position despite the lingering stiffness of age. He forced the current into his runes of sapience and discernment, then sifted back through the images he could recall, diving into the muddled memories. A vision of the barrier surrounding Stone's Grasp materialized as a resolute, shimmering blue dome, barring entry to any affiliated with Tarkannen. Kaellor stood in the inner sanctum before the statue of Eldrek Baellentrell. The prince remained steadfast, empowering the defenses, and then it seemed he didn't . . . and all manner of terror broke loose.

The chitinous clawed limbs of umbral clattered through the streets, scarring the very stones with their deployment of nadir. Moonlight glinted off the strange sigils enslaving the flatheads. They led scores of grotvonen who ran amok, slaughtering the citizens. The clamor of chaos and smells from the Abrogator's War flooded his awareness: people moaning, soldiers shouting commands, the ring of steel on steel, the stink of flesh melting under nadir burns mixing with the char of smoking timbers.

He stumbled out of the sundered gates of the inner curtain wall, climbing over twisted metal and the rubble of broken stone. Though he left behind the possible safety of the royal grounds, fear for his family drove him onward. The low rumble of raging grondle stampeding up the major streets diverted him to the relative shelter of smaller roads and back alleys. He raced through the smoke and shadows, dodging fleeing citizens and marauding patrols of grotvonen in a desperate attempt to reach his family.

A meat cleaver and bread knife materialized in his fists. He avoided direct confrontation, stabbing and slashing at enemies as he sprinted past, finally reaching their estate in the high district. Flames and smoke poured out from broken windows on the second floor, and the front door lay splintered on the ground.

Inside the common room, his wife lay sprawled in an unnatural position, draped over the arm of a chair with her head hovering inches from the floor. Dark blood dripped from her nose, and her lifeless eyes were fixed on his feet. Karragin's scream propelled him upstairs, and he arrived in time to see a thick-necked grotvonen towering over his child.

Coarse hair bristled across the back and shoulders of the beast, and it twitched an ear as it considered the little girl. She brandished a knitting needle and stood crouched before Nolan, who peeked out behind her. Before he could act, she lunged forward and plunged the needle deep into the hairy thigh of the grotvonen. Therek hesitated a moment and watched the beast howl in rage, then swing a stout club, catching Karragin across the side of the face.

A sickening crack of bone preceded the tumble of her limp little body into the corner. Therek swung the meat cleaver like an axe, burying it into the back of the grotvonen's skull. He leaped onto its back, stabbing over and over, knife blade rising and plunging into the thing's neck and back as he rode the beast to the ground until at last his hands, slicked with blood and cramped with fatigue, dropped the bloody utensil to the floor.

Annoying pinpricks tingled on his fingertips and around his mouth, the byproduct of his hyperventilation, and he released his hold on zenith. He swiveled his feet to the floor, allowing the cool stone to ground him in the room. The images lost their cohesion, and he wondered how much, if any, of the visions were from the spontaneous flare of his arca prime. Certainly the back end of the dream sequence accurately captured his memories from that terrible night when he lost his wife in the Abrogator's War.

He had made peace with that trauma years ago though, so something else must have triggered the dream sequence. Kaellor had allowed the barrier surrounding Stone's Grasp to fail. That began the nightmare. But was that something his restless mind created, or an actual manifestation of his arca prime? The disorienting dream left him uncertain.

He pushed the thoughts from his mind. *You have enough trouble sorting out your gift when you're awake. Don't go looking for the Giver's light in the Taker's shadow.*

An hour later, he stirred a cup of tea and pressed the tip of a bony finger onto a plate, collecting the last few crumbs from a crownberry muffin. A knock on his door preceded the arrival of Hestian Lellendule. The ginger-haired man puffed out a breath of air through ruddy cheeks.

"You're late, my friend. I'm afraid all I can offer you is a cup of tea," said Therek.

Hestian waved him off and took a chair beside him, drumming thick fingertips on the small table. "I can't stay long, but thanks all the same. I came to talk to you about our resident prima dicta."

"What has Endera's puppet done now?"

"Several things. First, he implied that the western duchies would fall well short of expected contributions to the military defense of the kingdom. He claims that the bulk of the soldiers we expected to join us at the forward base camp are required for the patrol and defense of the Endulian Pass. He's even diverted some of the regiments here to Stone's Grasp under the auspices of making a formal inspection, but anyone can see it's a delay tactic."

"I expected as much, and am prepared to offer a course correction this afternoon. Kaellor and Bryndor intend to join me for the meeting," said Therek.

Hestian's brow creased. "You think that's wise? Their presence feels like an acknowledgment of Edlemund's authority."

Therek nodded, conceding the point. "I agree, but Bryndor needs to be there to continue to learn how to manage the concerns of the nobles, and Edlemund is at least a predictable adversary. As for Kaellor, his glower can always be called upon to intimidate the young prima dicta. And don't worry overmuch about the soldiers. The pass is not the sole property of the Endules. It's a resource for the kingdom. I've already tasked Overwarden Kaldera with appointing Outriders to garrison and patrol the area."

Hestian pursed his lips, considering the revelation. "That should free up Edlemund's resources to bolster the forces between the Pillars of Eldrek. I still question the wisdom of allowing the Endules to profit from control of the trade route."

"Consider this then. The Endules will reap the reward of taxation for a season or two, but as people come to see that the Outriders, a neutral kingdom element, are providing security, while the Endules tax the passage of goods . . . well, it will only be a matter of time before even Edlemund understands the loss of goodwill and political capital such a position places them in. Besides, the Outrider garrison will require support. At least a portion of the tax revenues will be required to pay for that support."

Hestian arched an eyebrow, and a savage grin caused his beard to flare. "I am reminded why I stopped playing games of chance with you when we were younger. There is something rather poetic in watching an Endule fashion the noose, then place it around his own neck."

Therek grunted with agreement. "We just have to ensure that they only choke on the trap without feeling the drop, so to speak. Endera needs to know that we value the contributions of the western duchies, and that is the Giver's truth. However, their personal concerns will always be tempered by the greater good of the kingdom."

Hestian leaned forward with hands on his knees, as if ready to stand. "Thanks for putting my mind at ease. Have you any need of my services this morning?"

"I can't think of anything. Let's keep our meeting set for two days from now. Laryn and her funeral entourage should return this afternoon. I should like to have most of our closed council present to strategize about the months ahead. We can receive reports on the status of the troops at that time."

Hestian slapped his thighs and stood. "Agreed. I'll see you in two days."

After taking only a few steps, Hestian paused and turned. "Have you and Kae discussed preparations for the princes and their Rite of Revealing?"

"Only briefly," said Therek. "We agreed that they should have every opportunity to develop their other skills before attempting the trial. Why do you ask?"

"You read Overwarden Kaldera's latest report?"

Now it was Therek's turn to push air through pursed lips. "I did."

Hestian shoved his hands into pockets. "It can't be a coincidence, the increased encounters with grot and grondle at a time when the usurper's threat looms on the horizon. Japheth and Nebrine's sacrifice bought us time, but there's nobody in the kingdom with their knowledge. If we are to walk down those dark roads once again, I would prefer to have as many Baellentrells in full command of their martial talents as possible."

"Their command of rune fire doesn't set your mind at ease?"

"Oh, it's impressive to be sure," said Hestian. "But after witnessing the tapestry of their runes, I can't help but think that theirs will be a generational gift. Like the kind referenced in *The Book of Seven Prophets*."

"I never took you for a student of old prophecy, Hes."

"I've never forgotten, my friend. Chancle did. He let his grief alter his focus, turned it too far inward, I think. I don't know, maybe that's not fair. There's so much about him I never saw. But, regardless, I've not forgotten the old lessons."

"I understand, but the trials can be unpredictable. The princes are as likely to survive the Rite of Revealing as anyone else, but there are no guarantees as to the nature of their arca prime."

"I know, I know," said Hestian. "Have you . . . seen anything of their future, of our future?"

"Nothing of consequence, I'm afraid. But if anything important changes, rest assured you will be one of the first to know."

Hestian dipped his head. "You ever think it's strange that after centuries of sending our youth through the Rite of Revealing, that none can ever recall much detail about what happened? Not beyond the simple notion of sacrifice?"

Therek smiled wistfully. "Before Karra sat for her trial, I spent years trying to force an answer to that mystery. Eventually, I surmised that some things are beyond our understanding."

Another knock at the door interrupted further discussion, and Kaellor stuck his head inside. He appeared unburdened, entering the room with a lighter step than in the prior few days. Bryndor followed and closed the door behind them, looking far more haggard than his uncle.

"I hope we're not interrupting?" asked Kaellor.

"Just two old men ruminating about things they can't control," grumbled Hestian.

"And you started without me?" jibed Kaellor.

"I would ask what brings you, but I gather your training and sparring sessions for the day have concluded?" asked Therek.

Bryndor nodded agreement and pointed to the chair Hestian had vacated. "Do you mind, my lord?"

"As long as we can agree to drop the silly titles behind closed doors, you can be my guest. It's all warmed up for you," said Hestian.

Bryndor collapsed into the chair. "My thanks. Sparring with Kae is one thing, but the tutors in rune craft are another. I've channeled enough zenith to choke on it for the next several days."

Therek leaned forward with interest. "It can be frustrating, trying to push zenith into a rune that hasn't revealed its full purpose yet. Even worse if you're trying to make up for lost time, I imagine."

Bryndor's head sagged enough that dark bangs fell before his eyes. He sucked at his teeth. "I feel like I might have an easier time trying to bash through the walls of Stone's Grasp with nothing but my head."

"A piece of advice, then?" asked Therek.

"Sure, anything," said Bryndor.

"Don't force the issue. Hold the runes, the . . . undeclared ones, not your rune fire. Hold the others primed as much as you can manage it. Not enough to slip into the draft, mind you, but as much as you can allow. Don't try to force it, just keep them awake if you will. The habit will develop your tolerance for channeling, but more than that, it's quite possible that a situation will arise where necessity demands that an ability reveal itself."

"Like with Lluthean and his gliding thing?" asked Bryndor.

Therek placed a finger to the side of his nose, then slid it forward. "Just so."

Bryndor chewed on the inside of his cheek, taking the advice under consideration. "Thanks. I'll keep at it. If I may, while you're all here, have you any thoughts on when Llu and I might attempt the Rite of Revealing?"

Therek glanced once to Hestian, then to Kaellor. "We thought to give both of you as much time as possible to learn more of your gift before you sit for the trial," said Kaellor.

"Do you think we should attempt it before the coronation in the fall?" the young man pressed.

"It's possible, but let's see how your skill set progresses in the months ahead. It's not as if we don't have enough to keep you preoccupied until then," said Kaellor.

"That's the Giver's truth, I suppose," said Bryndor. He turned his attention to Hestian. "I appreciate how fast the sentinels worked to secure the castle since the attack. I paid a visit to the healers at the House of the Moons. There are still a few men and one woman recovering from their injuries, but I'm told all are expected to return to full duty soon."

"Have you learned anything else about those who made the attack?" asked Kaellor.

"Our best tracker is still a half day's ride away from returning with the funeral escort, but I spoke to Salveen," said Hestian. "She assures me that the breach was made by professionals who have since left the kingdom."

"Their leader indicated as much," said Kaellor.

"Have you had the chance to reshape the definitions to the ward protecting Stone's Grasp?" asked Hestian.

"No, and I'm not sure how safe that will be," said Kaellor.

"I don't understand," said Hestian.

"I think I do," said Therek. "He's concerned that if the ward is altered, if the definitions are too broad, then innocent people might be harmed."

Kaellor ran knuckles against his bearded chin. "Wishing us harm and committing to action are two completely different things."

Hestian paced a slow circle. "That makes a certain kind of sense, I suppose. We can learn to adjust our defenses for similar future attacks. What about the girl, Reddevek's ward?"

Therek watched as Bryndor and Kaellor shared a look, and both smiled. At last, the young prince spoke up. "Ranika decided to remain with the Luna Rova, at least for now. I'll miss her more than most, but I don't think we need to worry about her safety. Red taught her more than self-reliance, and I pity the assassins who make the mistake of tracking her down."

"One last thing before I go," said Hestian. "Savnah and her quad preserved a few samples from the creatures that attacked them at the Moonie camp. I was going to have them all sent to the docent for further study, but it might make sense for you and maybe Laryn to assess them first, Kae. Perhaps you could ensure that the barrier allows those items entry as well?"

"Of course, Hes. That makes good sense, my friend," said Kaellor.

"Well, if there is nothing else, I will leave you to it and see you in a few days at our next closed council meeting," said Hestian. When none of them spoke up, Hestian bowed and took his leave.

"I should take my leave as well," said Bryndor. "As I recall, we have a date to join you for a meeting with the prima dicta this afternoon?"

"Yes, and there are a few details I should like to review with you before we do," said Therek. He spent the next twenty minutes reviewing what he knew of Edlemund's stance as it pertained to the Endulian Pass and its management. Bryndor and Kaellor both asked insightful questions, demonstrating a solid understanding of the salient details.

"Alright," said Bryndor. "So, direct the placement of a flank of Outriders to be garrisoned in the Endulian, but somehow frame it as a suggestion designed to convey consensus with the western duchies?"

"That sounds about right," said Therek.

"What if he refuses?" asked Bryndor.

"Oh, he most certainly will, initially," Therek said with a wink. "Count on it, in fact, but think of his confrontation as an opportunity to reshape a barrier. And if you can't get him to concede the issue, we have a few other points of leverage. We'll remind him that though he serves at the behest of several high houses, he is nonetheless a steward of the kingdom. A kingdom which you will be governing. He can choose to become your rival, or he can find ways to seek profitable consensus."

"And if that doesn't work, bring Boru. We're meeting in the regent's receiving hall. There's plenty of room, and it never hurts to remind the prima dicta who wields the actual power in Aarindorn," said Kaellor.

Bryndor stood, appearing more exhausted than when he had entered, but Kaellor's last suggestion evoked a smile on the young man's face. "I might need Ksenia's help, but I think we can do that."

Kaellor turned as well. "I have a few things to attend to before Laryn returns. I'll meet both of you in a few hours, then?"

"Until we meet the prima dicta!" said Therek with fake enthusiasm.

He watched them leave and considered the strange way that his dreams had foreshadowed the conversations about the ward protecting Stone's Grasp. Once again, he wondered if his gift had manifested through his arca prime while he slept. Was the hand of the Giver directing his thoughts, or was it all a simple coincidence? He wondered at the strangeness of it all, like working his tongue through the fresh socket of a newly shed tooth.

After several minutes of contemplation, and with no obvious answers forthcoming, he sighed and pulled himself upright. "Get your eyes to the horizon, old man."

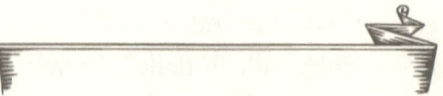

Chapter Thirty: Out of the Archives, into Darkness

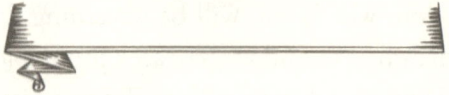

A simple rhythm organized Ksenia's days now that the regent no longer held long court sessions. Though she still retained her status as a scribe, her direct responsibilities with Therek amounted to an hour of work three days a week. Sometimes the sessions took place over crownberry muffins and stout tea at the start of the day. Other encounters occurred as the situation demanded, but she shared these responsibilities with several others. That left her more time to spend with *The Tome of Nivosh*, and with the aid of archivist Veeble Hebben, she made significant progress.

Veeble's uncannily accurate ability to transcribe the dead language onto fresh parchment allowed her to leave the confines of the archives to continue the work. With her new freedom, she often spent hours outside of Stone's Grasp. She and Winter found and followed different paths into the Great Crown, sometimes accompanied by the wolvryn, sometimes alone. When she returned, Veeble reserved a secluded desk in the archives where the two of them could record her progress.

When she first met the strange man, his odd nature nearly ruined the friendship before it could blossom. His understanding of social graces and customs was off-putting, but also charming. There was simply no pretense and no filter to his expression. If Veeble noticed something unusual or strange, whether it be a random stain on her blouse or a bit of cabbage between her teeth, he indicated each with stark austerity. On occasion, his comments made her cringe, but more often than not, they made her laugh with appreciation for his simple truth.

"Riding again I see, with the wolvryn no less," said the man as he sat down beside her.

Ksenia arched an eyebrow and playfully challenged his assertion. "We're not supposed to speak so loud. I might have been riding. What makes you so certain?"

Veeble patted the flat of his hands against his ribs as if he were attempting to put out a flame, and huffed a breath, then spoke with his unusual, pressured speech. "For now, you're the only one here so we can talk as LOUD AS WE LIKE."

The incongruity of his outburst with an absolutely flat expression almost caused her to break into a fit of laughter. He considered her a moment, then continued, "You leave clues, lots of things. Your footsteps were quiet today. You're wearing riding boots and not those noisy stiff shoes. It's a nuisance how those clatter through the halls. I like your boots. These are better. One set of footwear is simple, and simple is always best. Also, you smell like horse."

He paused a moment and plucked a small twig with pine needles from the back of her hair. "And this came from out there." He pointed out the window with a view of the Great Crown. "Unless you spent all day in the Founders Memorial. Then maybe . . ." His eyes squinted as he considered the proposition. "No, you went riding again, I think."

"You have the right of things, Veeble." She reached into her travel bag and set the transcribed papers on the desktop. "I finished these today. Can you add them to our collection?"

The sides of his mouth drew up into a smile, but the middle of his upper lip dipped down, giving the man a comically frog-like expression. With a flurry, he swiped her papers, exchanging them for the next chapter of the ancient tome. "Raise one, see one."

Ksenia puzzled over the expression, but couldn't quite place his meaning as she gathered the untranslated pages. "What does that mean, exactly?"

"Like in the game halls, when people bet on cards."

"I think you mean see one, raise one, yes?" she asked.

His eyes lost focus for a moment. "Yes, maybe. I'm not sure. They don't let me go there anymore. I miss going there."

"Why would you want to go to the gaming halls, Veeble? All people do there is lose their hard-earned coin."

"Some people lose their coin when they give it to me. I never lose. I keep track of the numbers. Numbers, and suits, and colors. Also, I can tell when people lie about their cards."

Ksenia sat back and considered the savant. "Veeble, are you saying that you can count the cards and tell when someone is bluffing?"

"Oh yes. Every time. Well, eighty-two percent of the time. But that's too much, so nobody will play with me and they don't like it when I go there."

"Moons, and they say you're ungifted," said Ksenia.

"Runeless for sure." He pulled up the sleeves of his archivist robes to reveal pale, unadorned forearms.

She began to place the new pages he had transcribed into her satchel, but noticed that under each line, he had already recorded a second script in the Kindred tongue. "Veeble, what have you done here?"

Her linguist rune ignited and sifted the ancient text under the scrutiny of her gift. He had accurately recorded the main body of the work, missing only subtle contextual connotations, which made sense when she considered the way he seemed to see the world: all numbers and processes. She lifted her eyes from the pages to find him studying his feet in a rare display of chagrin.

He held out a hand without looking up. "Sorry, I'm sorry. Those are the wrong papers. I tried to do what you do. It's not right, I know. It was something fun to pass the time. I can get you the other copy."

Ksenia clutched the papers to her chest. "Veeble, I don't know what to say."

For the first time she could recall, the poor man's face flushed crimson. He began to pat and then rub the flat of his palms on his rib cage, as if trying to wipe off an offending stain. "I know, I know, I know."

"No, you misunderstand. I think what you did is wonderful, and it's so close to perfect. How did you ever—and you drafted two copies? That's . . . I'm amazed, honestly."

The content of her words melted his agitation, his flapping slowing, and he lifted his eyes. "Truly?"

"Giver's truth." She wanted to reach out and lay a reassuring hand on his forearm, but knew that he did not appreciate intimate gestures, and thought the move might cause him to retreat like a frightened rabbit.

Instead, she shook her head in wonder. "So, it looks like we've translated enough of the High Aarindorian for you to translate the language yourself."

"No, not me, you. You translated the work. I used your words to make a tri-layered cipher. I understand the tense, dates, numbers, the gender, and most of the terms. But sometimes the phrases, the way she says things, it is confusing."

"Well, keep it up. What you've done will make the rest of this go much faster; you nearly got it all perfect. I can show you how to understand the unusual phrases and figures of speech Nivosh used."

He patted at his rib cage, but the gesture seemed more playful, less intense. "Nearly perfect? More than eighty-two percent?"

"More like over ninety percent. And I think we should make plans to list you as the co-author for the final translated work when it's complete."

Veeble's mouth hung open for a few seconds, then snapped shut, and the froggy grin sprouted on his face once again. "I see. I see see see. I need more paper, more paper and pens and pens and pens."

The staccato clatter of hard-soled shoes preceded a familiar woman's voice. "I should have known to find you here. Still slaving through ancient Aarindorian history?" asked Vinnedesta.

Ksenia had not seen her friend since their chance meeting in the halls. The young woman wore a uniform similar to Ksenia's formal scribe attire, but instead of the delicate insignia of the regent's office, a purple insignia surrounded with gold and silver embroidery perched across the breast panel of the tunic like a garish spider.

Vinnedesta fanned at her face. "Giver, it's stuffy in here, but not so bad as the prima dicta offices."

"Vinn, this is Veeble, a master archivist. He's been aiding me in the research of *The Tome of Nivosh*. Veeble, this is Vinnedesta."

Veeble retreated a few steps, patting nervously at his ribs, and bowed. Before he could say anything, Vinnedesta set a hand on his forearm. "Oh, we've met before, isn't that right?"

Veeble stood frozen, like a deer transfixed by the gaze of a predator. Ksenia stood from her chair, threw her satchel over a shoulder, and looped an arm through Vinnedesta's, pulling her away from the poor man.

"So. How is it being the lead contact for the prima dicta?"

Vinnedesta withdrew her study of Veeble, and the archivist wilted back a few steps, then retreated down the hall. She huffed a breath in exasperation. "Honestly? It's . . . amazing! I was hoping to pull you away for a drink so we could catch up."

Ksenia looked over her shoulder once to ensure that Veeble had recovered, running his hands over a stash of books that needed to be reshelved. Her first inclination was to decline the invitation, but Veeble's breakthrough left her feeling like celebrating, and she knew that the archivist had no desire to leave the security of his halls for a bit of unbridled frivolity. "You know, that sounds like just the thing. What did you have in mind?"

An hour later, they sat at a cozy booth on the second floor of an upscale tavern. Tables with comfortable chairs stood empty in the center of the room, but Ksenia wanted to sit near a window. Aside from the staff and a family of four taking an early meal on the first floor, they were alone. The open room added to her sense of freedom and escape.

The furnishings smelled of new leather, and the aroma of survivor's essence carried over the rafters. She ran her hand across a polished and unmarred tabletop. "This place is lovely. I'm afraid to ask how much a simple glass of wine might cost."

"Relax, it sounds like we both deserve it," said Vinnedesta. "Besides, I have it on good authority that the proprietor purchased the tavern for three barrels of resco."

Ksenia leaned forward, speaking more with her eyes than her words. "Really?"

"Well, something like that. Apparently, this building was a major holding of Tixon B'gin, one of the last Lacuna leaders unaccounted for. Anyway, being in the offices of the prima dicta allows me certain discretionary eavesdropping, shall we say? A minor lord from Beclure bought the place on the cheap, overhauled the furnishings, and just opened the doors a few days ago."

A young man dressed in a pressed tan doublet and pants approached with two glasses, filled them with water, and stepped back. "Ladies, my name is Toff, and it is my sincere pleasure to see a member of the regent's staff here. I'll admit, though, that I am intrigued by the purple emblem on your tunic."

Vinnedesta's back arched with pride. "I'm on staff in the offices of the new prima dicta. I am his lord's personal envoy."

Toff whistled with appreciation and even had the good manners to blush. "Well, there's me looking like the polished rock in the bowl of gems!" He looked over his shoulder at the bartender, who watched the interaction with a discerning eye. The young man pitched his voice low. "If you don't mind, and apologies, I was bid to make a bit of a show presenting you with your options. Can two of the kingdom's esteemed women humor a struggling young server today?"

They both nodded, happy to play along with the performance. Toff rubbed his hands together and winked at Vinnedesta, then mouthed the words "thank you." He cleared his throat and assumed a theater voice. "Ladies, it is my pleasure to welcome you to the Twisted Cork. The evening meal is still a few hours away, but I can provide you with a tray of breads and fine cheese. We have a selection of Stellancian reds, a winter white, or if you prefer, the bartender offers an array of resco and similar spirits."

"The bread and cheese plate sounds perfect, and I'll try a Stellancian red. Not the top shelf stuff, middle of the road if you please," said Vinnedesta.

"Very good, and for you, miss?"

Ksenia's misgivings about the oddity of such a formal interaction withered under the man's polite flattery. "Can I ask, how much is a glass of the winter white?"

Toff dipped his head. "Certainly, apologies. Our signage arrives next week and will display the prices for all to see. As we are still in the business of building relations, word of mouth you know, each glass is but a half sun, and the bread and cheese are on the house today."

Vinnedesta's eyes shot up in surprise, and they shared a giggle. Ksenia nodded. "Well alright, I'll try the winter white please."

A moment later, Toff placed a plate set with three small loaves of bread, an assortment of cheeses, and their drinks. "If I may, the breads each carry a deliberate, slightly bitter taste. It's a contrast to the cheeses and opens up the palate to better enjoy the different flavors."

Ksenia sipped at the delicate glass of wine, finding it fruity and slightly sweet, but light. "So, tell me all about the prima dicta. What's it like? What is he like?"

Vinnedesta took a small loaf of bread, dividing it and handing a portion to Ksenia. "Edlemund? He's not bad, actually. He puts on a good face whenever interacting with anyone from the duchies or trade guilds. He's always trying to work one of them with an angle. But once all of that is done, he seems nice enough, I suppose."

Ksenia echoed her statement. "Nice enough, I suppose. Is he married?"

Vinnedesta sipped at her wine and made a show of struggling to swallow. "Yes, but even if he were not, he's far too rigid. Besides, I'm not ready to settle down just yet. I would rather take my chances with someone like Toff over there."

Ksenia turned to catch the server and Vinnedesta sharing an openly flirtatious moment. "Well, I don't know why you shouldn't." She raised her glass in a toast. "To seeking adventure, in whatever or whoever it presents itself."

They clinked glasses and continued their friendly conversation, Vinnedesta describing her new role and activities, Ksenia sharing her new discoveries with *The Tome of Nivosh* and her changing roles as a scribe. She considered revealing the nature of her romance with Bryndor, but thought the better of it. She sat back, feeling more relaxed than she had since possibly arriving in Aarindorn. "I think, with Veeble developing his cipher, that I can see an end to *The Tome of Nivosh*, and maybe an opportunity to return to the ranch."

"Really?" gasped Vinnedesta. "You would actually leave everything Stone's Grasp has to offer?"

Ksenia wondered at the thought. Could she leave now? Did she truly want to leave? Maybe it would be easier to get out as soon as the translation was complete and before things . . . developed further with Bryndor. The wine went to her head and made her feel more giddy than she expected. A chuckle escaped her mouth. "Honestly? I don't know anymore."

Ksenia became aware of the need to edit her words, but also took comfort in the realization that Vinnedesta seemed to be enjoying the effect the wine was having as well. Her friend chewed a piece of bread, frowning in concentration at the odd taste, then nibbled at a bit of white cheese with red flecks. At once, Vinnedesta's face turned from serious concern to playful elation. "Woe, woe, woe, woe, woe. That might be . . . a few too many woes, sorry. But that is crazy. It's like someone shoved a crownberry muffin into a block of cheese, only you can't taste it without the bread first. Really, try it."

Ksenia repeated the sequence, struggling through the odd-tasting bread, then taking a generous bite of cheese and indeed finding a playful explosion of sweet and sour crownberry melting through the white cheese.

Vinnedesta tore into the other samples with reckless abandon, and soon they were competing over giggles to see who could ingest more of the delicious combinations. A somber expression stole across Vinnedesta's face, and she leaned in with a stage whisper. "You might be able to leave everything the city has to offer, but could you really leave him?"

Ksenia's mind raced back through the hazy jumble of conversation. Had she divulged her relationship after all? She leaned forward, feeling slightly wobbly. "Who?"

Vinnedesta's eyes flared wide a moment, and then she seemed to try her very best to not look mildly inebriated, but the dramatic way she switched her expressions betrayed her giddy nature. "Come on. I might be locked away with Edlemund all day, but that doesn't mean I don't manage to keep up on castle gossip."

Ksenia tried not to smile and plopped some of the herby, bitter bread into her mouth to allow herself some time to think. She grabbed another piece of cheese, but frowned when the expected rush of flavor failed to surprise her. She tapped at her lips and then her teeth, noticing a numb sensation.

When she spoke, her words sounded slurred to her own mind, but instead of sensing the danger, she worked to stifle a giggle. "Vinn, I think I'm sauced!"

Vinnedesta must have felt something similar. She slumped into the plush leather backing and smacked her lips a few times, eyes hooded and droopy. "Absolutely marinated!" she slurred. "I think I juss need a mo-mo-ment."

Vinnedesta pouted out her lower lip, crossed her arms, and closed her eyes. That was smart. Vinn was a smart friend. Ksenia mirrored her friend, folded her arms, and leaned to the side, fading into the inevitable pull of sleep. She had a fleeting thought that more than half of her wine still remained in her glass.

KSENIA AWOKE TO A DISTANT, rattling, bouncing sensation. The sound of creaking wood and the vague scent of horse took several minutes to lift her from the drug-induced haze, but eventually the endless rhythm of a horse-drawn wagon penetrated her awareness. She lay on her left side and shifted to her back to ease a blossoming ache in her hip and shoulder. The motion seemed all that she could accomplish, as her limbs felt heavy and weak, clumsy even.

There was a vague awareness that her hands were bound. She lifted them up only to smack herself in the nose with abrasive cords of rope. She spent the next several minutes—or maybe hours, she couldn't be sure—drifting in and out of sleep, startled each time by the discovery of her surroundings and the realization that while the fingers of her hands were interlocked, she couldn't tell which fingers belonged to which hand. The notion was at once disconcerting and humorous, and more than once, she felt herself giggle.

Light, harsh and blinding, interrupted her mirth as a tarp was lifted from her face. A man's unfamiliar voice, gruff and flat, carried over the constant din of the wagon. "How's the cargo?"

The tarp dropped, returning her to the blessed, warm darkness. "She's still in the thick of it. How much longer?" asked a second man. Ksenia knew the voice and sifted through confusing memories. It was Toff. She tried to say his name out loud, to ask a question, but her mouth wouldn't work right.

"By wagon? Another day at least, maybe two," replied the first man.

"Why don't we just dump her anywhere here? It's not like anyone is going to know."

"Boss wants to send a message. She wants her found in the range above their family ranch near the spot they killed the Leech."

"I still think we should have brought the other one. She took a shine to me. Might have been fun."

"I know. But nabbing a scribe is one thing. Nobody is going to miss her, not with everything that's coming. Nabbing the personal assistant to the prima dicta would draw more heat than the boss wants."

Trickles of fear worked their way through her confusion like a trail of ice melt dripping down her back. The unpleasant sensation gave her something to focus on, and she reached out for zenith. If she could control her gift, she could easily control the horse. The ambient currents lapped against her, teasing, but when she tried to beckon the flow, it passed over her with all the penetration of a soft wind.

The realization fueled a surge of panic, and she struggled against her bonds, trying to roll and kick, but either she was too clumsy, too weak, or too bound by rope. She cried out, and the tarp pulled back, exposing her to the blinding light once again.

"Hey now. There's no need for that. All this will be easy with just another drop of this," said Toff. A hand gripped her jaw, and she turned to bite, but was too slow. Toff swore something guttural, and the wagon drew to a lurching stop.

She strained to focus her vision, but Toff's image was a watery outline at best. A calloused hand smelling of leather gripped her forehead and pinched her nose closed, while another held her jaw. The gruff man's voice spoke with a detached, calm cadence. Droplets of liquid spilled on her lips, and Ksenia struggled to turn her head, keeping her mouth closed.

"Grind it, Toff. Stop wasting the stilben. That tincture is all we've got, and she'll need at least four or five more doses before we get there. Just give it a moment."

Ksenia's lungs flared hot as her heartbeat throttled inside her chest, pounding in her neck. At last, she gasped her mouth open to take a breath. She vaguely sensed the taste of anise as more than one drop hit the back of her tongue. The hands released her and in moments, the wagon returned to the steady cadence of motion. Ksenia felt herself plunge into the depths of darkness once again.

SHE CLAWED BACK TO wakefulness, stiff, achy and cold, still lying on the wooden cart. With an effort, she turned back to her side and wriggled under the edge of the tarp, low enough to search her surroundings. Stars shone overhead and the scent of a campfire carried thick and heavy on the air, but the absence of any flickering light meant that either the fire had died out or was located farther away than it smelled.

She lay searching the silence for any sign of her captors, but beyond the chirping of crickets and frogs, the only other sound came from the creaking wagon as she shifted about. One at a time, she worked her legs back and forth, relieved to discover that only her hands remained bound.

Zenith flowed around her, teasing and still beyond reach. *Stupid monk. There must have been veramanth in something you ate. Probably that bread.*

Every muscle in her low back and core protested when she tried to sit up, and she had to latch her hands onto the side of the wagon to manage it. A shard of wood splintered off as she hoisted herself upright. The sharp crack silenced the night creatures all around. Ksenia sat there, holding the piece of wood and waiting to be discovered, until the sounds of crickets returned.

Faint embers, from the campfire, she assumed, glowed only twenty paces away. With painstaking slowness, Ksenia rocked her hips back and forth, inching toward the end of the wagon, the wood shard still in her grip. At last, her ankles caught purchase on the end of the cart, allowing her to scoot with better progress.

The work of it caused her breaths to come rapid and labored, the steam of her exhalations fogging the night air. She waited in silence and gathered her strength. Just when she thought to drop her feet to the ground, one of the men rounded the side of the cart and placed a hand on her shoulder.

Though she couldn't see him clearly, Toff's voice froze her in place. "Time for more stilben then. I wondered how long it would last. Look, this can go easy or this can go hard. What's it going to be?"

Ksenia dropped her head and her shoulders, feigning a shudder, and sobbed.

"Right, easy then. It's better that way. You won't feel nothing. Just tip your head back and it will all be over soon."

She sensed him step closer and leaned to the side, then threw all her weight into a clumsy swing, gripping the splintered wood in both hands. The shard bit into something soft. Toff grunted and staggered back a few paces. He coughed a gurgling, wet sound, and Ksenia wasted no time dropping to her feet.

Though her mind seemed clear and focused, her body responded poorly, made all the worse by stumbling along in the dark. After no more than ten lurching strides, the ground shifted underfoot, and she fell to the side. A shout of alarm from the other man fueled her purpose, and she struggled to stand. His vague silhouette shambled forward, and Ksenia turned to run.

Her steps came awkward and lurching, and she sensed the panting breaths of the man just before he knocked her to the ground. Rough hands turned her onto her back and he straddled her, pinning her and trapping both her arms under his girth. She tried to buck and writhe, but he held her fast. The edge of a knife blade pressed up under her jaw, its icy burn putting a stop to her struggles.

"Toff? You alright, man?" No response came after, and the big man shifted his weight, careful to hold the knife blade in place. "Grind it, lass. I think you might have killed Toff. You have no idea how much work that's going to make for me."

"To the Taker with Toff, and you too!"

The man leaned forward, his breath warm and foul. "You first."

She felt his weight shift, and he rested a hand on the center of her chest, preventing her from drawing breath. He lingered there, allowing her to struggle, and delicate stars began to swim at the edges of her vision. Her pulse beat a frantic drum in her head. Vaguely, she felt the knife slice deeper into her skin, searing a burning pain under the edge of her jaw. There was a lurching sensation, a strange grunt, and the man's weight lifted, allowing her to draw in a full breath of air.

After several exaggerated breaths, tremulous fingers probed her jaw, tracing a flap of skin. She could feel her pulse deep beyond the wound and sighed with relief, though the sticky wet of blood clung to her fingertips. She lay there, waiting for the man to return to finish his grisly work, when something massive plopped down beside her in the grass.

Coarse hair tickled at her nose, and the unmistakable panting breath of a wolvryn eased her mind. She turned into the creature with a genuine sob of relief and received a lick on the forehead. By the wolvryn's length, she thought it must be Boru. She spider-walked her fingers into his fur and tried to heave herself to a sitting position, but once again, the stars of the night sky streaked at the edges of her vision, and she sank into darkness.

Chapter Thirty-One: The Fear of Failure

Kaellor closed the door to the suite previously reserved for Ranika. Ksenia Balladuren slept in the bedchamber, recovering from effects of veramanth and what Laryn described as an expert distillation of stilben root. Bryndor kept a wary vigil with Boru in the front room and, he suspected, there was no safer place for the young woman to recover.

Stone and metal crafters had made quick work of fortifying the windows against intrusion from the outside. The sharp smell of oiled metal hung in the air and might have been off-putting were it not for the sense of security it fostered.

He walked to the end of the hall, finding the charred door already removed by castle craftsmen. In its place stood a thick timber door reinforced with four metal bands. Heavy duty steel bolt locks at the floor and ceiling kept the door secured from the inside. He unbolted the locks, and the door swung out on silent hinges to reveal two sentinels.

A young man and middle-aged woman snapped a brisk salute. He initially thought Hestian's choices in picking the two seemed unusual, but learned that the young man possessed a gifted ability to hear, while the woman had acquitted herself admirably in the attack by the invaders, holding the stairs for a time until becoming overwhelmed when three of the assailants turned their full attention on her.

The man wore a standard short sword and dagger, while a bandolier accentuated the woman's black sentinel uniform. Oiled leather straps crisscrossed over her shoulders, and the tangs of more than a dozen throwing knives studded her ensemble. Both carried vials of Eldrenol's solution, a recent addition given the strange creatures encountered by the group returning from Reddevek's funeral procession into the Great Crown.

"Your Highness, how can we be of service?" asked the woman.

"Call it the musings of a restless mind. I just came to check on you both. What are your names?"

The woman tipped her head. "I am Sentinel Vatha. This is Sentinel Kade."

"You don't favor the sword, Vatha?"

"Field Marshal Hestian has each of us play to our strengths, Your Highness."

"I see. I would still trust the length of a sword over those knives of yours." He offered the comment not as an insult, but as a test of the woman's competence.

Vatha stared at Kaellor for a few seconds until understanding flashed across her brow. Her hands flowed across the bandolier in a blur of motion. Almost faster than he could register, she withdrew three of the knives and flicked them across the room, where they embedded one on top of the other into the edge of a rounded table.

Vatha retrieved the knives, sheathed them, and returned to stand by her colleague on silent feet. Kaellor tilted his head in approval. "What's the rotation? How long are you posted here?"

"Our shift here lasts six hours, but there are constant overlapping patrols," said Vatha.

Kaellor knew that Hestian had markedly increased the security presence, but seeing someone of Vatha's professionalism and experience quieted his sense of unrest. "You have my thanks for your service. It's possible that one of Ksenia's brothers or her parents might arrive in the night to check on her. Beyond those immediate family members, Hestian Lellendule, or the regent himself, we are not to be disturbed."

Vatha snapped a curt nod of agreement.

"I bid you both a good night." He closed the door, secured the locking bolts, and returned to the suite he shared with Laryn. She sat at a side table, looking out a window at the night sky. "How is my patient?" she asked.

He walked behind her and massaged the muscles of her shoulders. "She is resting well enough. I don't even think the wound will leave a scar thanks to your gift. Now she just needs to sleep off the veramanth."

Her shoulders heaved, then relaxed with a sigh. "We've seen worse, but that woman is touched by the breath of the Giver. If Boru had been but a second later . . . I should not like to be the one to break the news to her parents."

"Nor I," Kaellor agreed.

"How is Bryn?"

The weight of her question caused him to drop into a chair beside her. "It's a lot. One moment he's riddled with guilt, and the next anger sharpens his tongue. But I can see that underneath it all, he's uncertain."

"The uncertainty I can understand. Stone's Grasp is a world away from Journey's Bend, and he's shouldering it all, Kae. All of the kingdom's expectations for a stable future, then there's Tarkannen's looming threat, and the Lacuna. Sometimes I wonder if it's too much for him."

The weight of her words came as no surprise, but still drew his breath out like the last sigh of a fading bellows. "I know, love. If we can just get to the other side of it all, I know he'll be every bit the leader that his parents were. He just needs a chance. It's not even that, though. Tonight, I think, he struggles with guilt."

"What does he have to feel guilty about?"

Kaellor shook his head and gazed at the stars. "Nothing, but he doesn't see it that way. Apparently, he crossed paths with the other woman who was drugged, Ksenia's friend. Vinnedesta. She was a scribe before becoming the personal envoy to the prima dicta. Anyway, Bryndor thinks that something of his gift triggered when he met them both, as if it tried to warn him of the danger, only he couldn't make sense of the images. It wasn't until the archivist, Veeble Hebben, tracked him down that Bryn realized Ksenia was in danger."

"That's why he ignored your request to remain inside Stone's Grasp and rode out with Boru to find her," said Laryn.

"Indeed."

"What happened to the other woman? This Vinnedesta?"

"The thugs who kidnapped Kess dumped her in an alley. A patrol found her drugged and gagged, suffering from mild exposure, but she's expected to make a full recovery under the care of the healers here at the castle. Tomorrow, Hestian plans to question the woman. According to archivist Hebben, Vinnedesta was instrumental in filing affidavits for the acquisition of several Lacuna properties in the past few years."

"That feels like more than a bad coincidence," said Laryn.

"Hestian and I thought the same. He already raided the tavern, the Twisted Cork. From what we can tell, an agent of the Lacuna rented out the top floor for the entire week."

"Life a rock, find a snake, follow it to its den. Sounds like a promising lead," said Laryn.

"It is, and it isn't. While it proves that remnants of the Lacuna still exist, the payments were given up front and in coin by a man using an obvious alias. The tavern proprietor has been cooperative, and neither Therek nor I could sense anything duplicitous in his statements."

"That fits with the conversation Ksenia overheard. She said that the men were hired to make an example of her. Her body was supposed to be found near the same place Reddevek killed the Leech."

They sat in silence for a time, and Kaellor rubbed a chill from his arms. "Mind if I chase away the cold?"

"As long as you do it with an actual fire. I like the smell of the woodsmoke as much as you."

Kaellor lit the kindling and warmed his hands as the flames crackled.

"I gather by your silence that Nolan wasn't much help, either?" she asked.

He stood and arched his low back, then turned a slow circle in front of the flames. "He found bits and pieces of their trail here in Stone's Grasp, but nothing that allowed us to place them in a residence. We even spoke to Salveen through the shek to see if anyone from the Spicers knew of the two men, but so far there's nothing."

A soft knock on the door interrupted his thoughts. Kaellor placed a hand on the pommel of his guardian sword; the weapon was always at his side now. "Who is it?"

"It's me, Kae. I'm with Llu. Can we come in?" asked Bryndor from the hallway.

Kaellor opened the door to see both of his nephews standing expectantly. Neska padded behind them to sniff at the base of the far door where the sentinels stood guard, then returned, tail wagging. He stepped aside and welcomed them in. Neither took a chair, so he remained standing as well. Something in the decisive nature of their collective bearing put him on edge.

The brothers shared a look of unspoken commitment. Bryndor tucked his hair behind his ears to reveal a serious expression that looked so much like his father that Kaellor felt his breath catch. "Apologies for the late hour. Given everything that's passed in the last week, we wanted to talk to you both about a decision we've come to," said Bryndor.

Kaellor stepped beside Laryn's chair and placed a hand on its back. "Please. You know you can come to us with anything."

"We know," said Bryndor. "Look, we've been talking and . . ." he inhaled a deep breath before continuing, "we think it would be best to sit for the Rite of Revealing soon."

Kaellor studied the young men. Bryndor held his stance at ease, eyes unwavering. Even Lluthean remained still, with none of the fidgeting he usually demonstrated. The silence drew out between them as Kaellor weighed their words. Eventually, Laryn leaned forward. "The Rite of Revealing can be treacherous. That's why we proposed you wait until you have a better sense of your other gifts, but your proposal is not without merit. We've all endured more danger than we expected since returning to Stone's Grasp. Help me understand what brought about your decision."

Lluthean withdrew three billow seeds, their soft rattling a welcome break in the silence. "It's just that. All the dangers. Tarkannen's threat, the pressure of grondle in the Borderlands, and twice now we've encountered strange beasts in the Great Crown. Whether it's all related or not, it feels like it's all related, and it's getting worse. If that's the case, I, we, would prefer to meet those dangers with the full measure of our gifts."

"Kae, you've always taught us to meet challenges head-on. This business of waiting, trying to develop a better understanding of our other gifts, it could take years. I can't help but think, if I had full use of the gift, then Ksenia never would have been placed in such danger. It was the same for Llu in the mountains," said Bryndor.

Kaellor pulled a chair to sit beside Laryn, using the moment to gather his thoughts. Any number of sharp retorts entered his mind, but Laryn had already set the tone, and something in the easy way the conversation was unfolding appealed to him more than a confrontation. He sat bobbing his head as he considered the implications of their decision.

It seemed clear that the brothers had already given the decision a lot of thought, and why wouldn't they? He remembered thinking about his Rite of Revealing every day for years, and that was in a time of relative peace in the kingdom. *Giver, is it really any more of a gamble than any of us accepted?*

Lluthean cleared his throat as he rolled the billow seeds across his knuckles. "Rona and the Tellends always said you don't put off a chore just because it's unpleasant. You pull the weeds when you find them, whether the ground is hard or—"

Kaellor held a hand up. "Not everything can be reduced to a Southlands metaphor, but your point is well made, son."

"We know there is risk involved with the trial," said Bryndor. "But you've never spoken of what's involved. None of you, not even Kess, will tell me anything about the process."

"That's because nobody truly knows," said Laryn. "We know that the ritual must be initiated by five others who have completed the trial. Once begun, the process is governed by forces we don't entirely understand, but the complex runes on the statue of Eldrek are involved, and we're pretty sure that the reflection pool acts as a conduit, empowering the rite. The adept is placed into something like a dozenth, and beyond that, nobody knows what happens."

Bryndor chewed on the inside of his lip. "What happened to you once you were inside the dozenth? What kind of challenges did you face?"

"That's just it, son," said Kaellor. "None who emerge ever recall what happened. Whether the rite takes a few days or a few weeks, either you wake up from the zentrist or you don't. All anyone can recall is the notion of making some kind of sacrifice, some kind of choice."

"How would you know if someone failed the trial?" asked Lluthean.

Laryn picked up the conversation. "In the histories, there have been adepts who simply vanished, there one moment and gone the next. More often though, when a gifted fails the rite, the dozenth withers, leaving nothing but a desiccated corpse already long dead and well beyond the ability of any healer to revive."

"How often does that happen?" asked Bryndor.

"It's uncommon, but not rare. In truth, the risk is small, but it's not zero, and neither of you completely understand your value to the kingdom," said Kaellor.

"You're talking about assuming the throne, but Kae, any of you are more qualified to wear the crown than I am," said Bryndor.

"Don't sell yourself short, either of you. But it's more than the crown. You are the last surviving Baellentrells and, as such, our bloodline rests with you. The ability of future Aarindorians to receive the benefits of the Baellentrell gifts, their martial talents, the defense of the kingdom—all of that rests with you both. And whether you sit for the Rite of Revealing or not, you can always pass on your gift to your children."

"But not if we fail in the trial," said Lluthean.

"Exactly," said Kaellor. "It's not that we don't think either of you is worthy or prepared. You've both already faced down more adversity than I ever did at your age, but the risk of your loss tips the scales in favor of waiting."

"What about you and Laryn? Is there any hope that I'll have a young cousin or two to call on someday?" asked Bryndor.

"Kaellor and I are a marriage discouraged by the founders," said Laryn. "There was always meant to be a division of power at the changing of the moons so that no single family could ever hold sway over the kingdom. With the shifting moons, every hundred years, the seat of power shifts from one family to the next, Baellentrell to Lellendule, and succession is guaranteed as a peaceful process. While a Lellendule and

Baellentrell can marry, something in the gift's restriction prevents the union from ever producing children."

Bryndor interlocked his fingers overhead and puffed out his cheeks. "I think I recall Kae explaining that some time ago, but I forgot. I'm sorry for that, for my forgetting. Still, it doesn't change the dangers that we face now. For all we know, I might never have children, then we would have wasted all that time on a different gamble."

Kaellor considered bringing up the old prophecy. Its words echoed in his mind. Laryn must have sensed as much, for she searched his eyes, waiting to see if he would broach the subject. How could he, though? He never believed in the power of prophecy, and if he made a decision now out of superstitious fear, wasn't that the same thing as giving in to belief?

He pulled at coarse beard hairs, using the discomfort to distract his mind from wandering into convoluted and dark corridors. Instead, he committed to action before his fears made him say something he would later regret. "When?"

Bryndor shared a shocked look with Lluthean, who fumbled a billow seed and had to lurch forward to collect the errant bobble. He shoved them back into his pockets, appearing chagrined.

"When what?" asked Bryndor.

"When do you want to sit for the rite?" asked Kaellor.

"The sooner begun, the sooner done," quipped Lluthean.

Kaellor shook his head, amazed that he was even considering their proposal. "No, we'll need at least a few days to set contingency plans with Therek. There will have to be legal documents drafted in case either of you is incapacitated for a time. The . . . affairs of the kingdom will roll forward whether you're stuck in a zentrist or sleeping in your bed."

"I would like the attendance and added security of the Mirrare, and they have the next two days off. Besides, Karragin's egg hatched a few hours ago, and she will need time to train with the falconer," said Laryn.

An unusual frown creased Lluthean's face, but he kept his tone lighthearted. "That's good news, I hadn't heard."

"How long do you imagine the Rite of Revealing will take?" asked Bryndor.

"Successful trials have been completed in as little as a few days or as much as a few weeks. It's another mystery of the process," said Kaellor.

"What's next then?" asked Lluthean.

"You two should try to get adequate sleep," said Kaellor. "Resume your training and tutoring tomorrow. I'll set a meeting with Therek in the late afternoon. Make no mention of this to anyone, and especially not through the shek. If word got out that you were both sitting for the rite, I don't know what kind of unrest that might invite. Think carefully about your decision. Therek might have further council about the matter."

"That sounds like good advice. Until tomorrow then," said Bryndor.

"One more thing, boys," said Kaellor. "By convention, the king, or in this case the regent, and your closest family members initiate the Rite of Revealing. If you sit together, which is frankly the simpler option, we can round up the principal members we need, but you will each need to recruit an instigator. Someone who you trust who is both meaningful and who will keep the secret of your trial."

Lluthean's eyes flared with mock exasperation, but Bryndor nodded understanding. "Good night," they said in unison.

After they departed to their private suites, Laryn swiveled in her seat and placed both her hands on his thighs. "You managed that much better than I imagined, and you didn't mention the prophecy."

There was an unspoken question in her statement. Kaellor glanced to the bookshelf behind her, where he kept a copy of *The Book of Seven Prophets*. "I think that the constant flow of your good graces has worn smooth the rough edges." He shook his head, baffled at how calmly he had received the boys' request. "They have no concept of the cost if either were lost, but then neither did I and . . . how can I refuse them after how they've persevered?"

She waited for him to say more. He sensed it by the space she held between them, gentle, supportive, patient. "What?" he asked.

"Why don't you admit what's really troubling you? It's only you and me."

Kaellor sucked at his teeth, then released a sigh. He retrieved the book and turned to a well-worn page, finding the passage marked from the Abrogator Derivation, and squinted to make out the text in the dim light. "When the wild wolvryn scars the highborn one, the channelers of nadir will arise." He looked up and shrugged. "That sort of fits, right? Bryndor survived an attack, and that same season we had our first encounter with abrogators."

Laryn shrugged her shoulders, neither agreeing nor disagreeing. Kaellor grunted. "Right, then it reads on, 'the tethers that bind can leech or sustain,' whatever that means. 'The chance for confluence emerges, but only from balance,' more gibberish." He sighed again. "Here though, 'the sundered bindings will unleash one who rules from the void.' That sounds like Tarkannen's return, right?"

Again Laryn remained neutral, beckoning him to continue.

"Right, so here it is. 'Seek the bearer who carries the burden, then look to reveal the Eidolon, but only after the sibling passes to the Drift.'" Kaellor snapped the book closed and replaced it on the shelf, then returned to his chair, feeling more exhausted than at any part of the week.

"I've been denying the way those words feel for a long time now. I told myself I never believed in prophecy, never understood it anyway, not like Japheth did," he said.

"What about now, Kae?"

"I think it's obvious that I must have believed my brother at least. Japheth and Nebrine sacrificed everything. They bought us time, and I've wasted it trying to convince myself that the prophecy holds no truth. But it feels inescapable now, like we've been dumped into a river with no recourse except to let it drag us over the falls. If I'm honest, the very fact that I've kept that Taker-cursed book is proof enough that I must believe in at least the possibility of the words, even if I don't understand them all."

He sat back, and the sting of tears filmed his eyes and tingled his nose as he considered all that his admission meant.

"Do you know what I think, love?" she asked. "I think that as long as they remain here with you, you can act to . . . be the guardian Japheth charged you to be. But once they enter the rite, you can't control what happens. There is no recourse for either of us to intervene. It's not that you think they will fail, it's that you fear failing them."

Chapter Thirty-Two: Rings and Circles

I set a bouquet of crownberry blossoms in a vase in the window of my suite in honor of my friend's birthday. Vexine was a daughter of the 'fo and ever a dear friend. She and most of her immediate family joined the Luna Rova, following their visions and the cycles of the moon. Those who remain in Aarindorn carry but a fragment of their gift for prophecy. I tried several times to recruit members of their clan to return to Aarindorn, but our sedentary life, it seems, was never one they could abide.

—The Tome of Nivosh, 75 PC, translated by Ksenia Balladuren

ZIPPY LOWERED HIS HEAD, his warm breath puffing a cloudy mist in the cool morning mountain air. The smell of oiled leather mixed with his musky scent, and Ranika grounded herself in the comfort of the familiar. The fingers of one hand tangled through his forelock while the other caressed his thick-muscled jaw. With his bangs pushed back, the Aarindin stared at her without blinking. She gazed into the smoky depths of his eyes, captivated by the intense feeling that he was giving her all of his attention.

"What are you thinking this morning, Mr. Zip? Looks like it's another day of just you and me. Nobody else to talk to. No wonder Red was such an acorn. Lutney's dice, I would gamble a lot to be able to reach you like Karragin. As it is, we just have to read each other, I suppose."

She wished one of the brothers traveled with them. Bryndor made her feel safe and comfortable; Lluthean made her laugh. At night, one of the wolvryn had always kept her company when she couldn't sleep, and ever since joining the Luna Rova caravan, sleep was elusive. The remnants of the buzzing disturbed her nights almost as much as a fear that the rumblers might return.

Trail dust painted her tongue as she tried to stifle a full-mouthed yawn. The shuffle of horse hooves drew her attention as several riders in the Dev'advari clan started out on caravan. Some nodded politely as they rode by, but none offered any words. Compared to the lowland Rovinary clan, Reddevek's people traveled in stoic silence by horseback. They seemed polite enough, the young assisting the old with breaking down tents, and the old in turn consoling children who struggled to find their way as newfound orphans.

Women used sashes and kerchiefs of indigo to tie their hair back while the men often sported similar neck kerchiefs. The absence of any cheerfully painted wagons made sense, as the clan traversed rocky trails unfit for wagon wheels. As nomads, they traveled with stark, utilitarian possessions, but she thought it also reflected their collective somber mood. Though, she supposed, they were a people in mourning from the losses of the rumbler attacks less than a week ago.

Sintra Vekkuh rode by and called out over her shoulder, "Best mount up, Nika. We've a long ride today before we make camp. I know Zippy will have no trouble, but I thought to have words with you as we go."

"Yes ma'am. We'll be right there." Ranika watched as the blind woman rode on, an indigo sash covering her eyes. She leaned in to whisper to Zippy, "She's blind, right Zip?"

Instead of an answer, the Aarindin lowered belly to the ground, waiting for her to mount. She stepped back. "You know I can climb up from the stirrups, right? You don't have to do that for me, Zip."

Zippy turned to regard her, then stared forward at the passing riders. "Alright, alright." She tossed a leg over the saddle and, once situated, Zippy lurched forward, trotting a few paces to fall in line with a comfortable walk.

She blended into the train of horses, some loaded with tents and packs, others carrying riders, as the clan wound a serpentine path across the Great Crown. They roamed in a counterclockwise pattern that Sintra Vekkuh insisted followed the moons. Ranika had attempted to track the moons across the night sky, but couldn't discern any relationship to the course they now followed.

By midday, they stopped to water the horses at a shallow stream of ice melt that cut along the upper ridge of the Great Crown. Ranika hopped down and massaged muscles in her thighs and low back. Riding Zippy by saddle was more comfortable than bareback, but she was unaccustomed to spending so many hours in continuous travel.

She splashed water on her face and arms. The ice melt numbed her fingers and caused her to gasp. After filling a waterskin, she walked a short distance before climbing the bank. A young boy wearing a faded indigo kerchief skipped along the rocks. He carried a bundle of something in a weathered orange kerchief and held the parcel out to Ranika. She collected the gift, unwrapping the cloth to find six marbled berries. "Thank you. Edible, I assume?"

The boy nodded and held up one finger. Before she could ask, he plucked one of the berries from her clutch, popped it into his mouth, and chewed. He smiled and pointed back up the hill where Sintra Vekkuh sat on her mare, appearing to survey the clan despite her blindness. Ranika removed one of the berries and chanced a bite. The fruit popped but had none of the berry taste she expected. Instead, a faint licorice flavor coated her tongue, followed by a tingly sensation. While the flavor was lackluster, when she exhaled, a pleasant herbal aroma fumed through her nose.

She walked over to Vekkuh. "Can I interest you in one of these berries, Sintra?"

Vekkuh shook her head. "Pepperbark berry? No thanks. More than one a day is a waste. They should relieve your sore muscles, so make them last. Those are for you and will keep."

"Thank you," she said and folded the kerchief before placing it into a breast pocket.

More riders in the caravan arrived as others moved on, all in relative silence. Individuals watered their horses, shared trail rations, and departed. Today marked the third day of travel, and Ranika found the silence bewildering.

"Your people don't talk much. Do the Dev'advari use a hand language?" she asked.

"Tonight will be different. We travel in relative silence for three days after the death of a Luna Rova. Speech is not forbidden, but the silence is a sacred time. It frees the mind to remember those lost."

Ranika felt her face flush. "Oh, I didn't know. I like that." As she watched, men, women, and children arrived and carried on without words. She wondered how many of them must look on her as a braying mule. Then again, she felt relieved that the strange social isolation was perhaps just a reflection of the collective mourning, and not from some offense she had given.

"I taste ice crystals on the wind. When you turn your gaze to the northwest horizon, tell me what you see, child," said the speaker.

Ranika turned a slow circle. The sun sat high overhead, and she had not paid attention to its path across the sky. "Which way is northwest?"

Vekkuh pointed across the mountains. Ranika turned, orienting herself. "I can't make out the end of the mountain range. A layer of fog or maybe distant storm clouds obscures the horizon. There's a light mist, I guess?"

"Can you see the ocean, the Rodendian Sea?"

Ranika shaded her eyes and strained her senses. She considered pulling the shadows to enhance her vision, but that trick only worked at night. "No. The mountains end in clouds or maybe a dense fog. I can't explain it, but it's like nothing I've ever seen. Whatever it is reflects the sun, makes it hard to look for very long."

Vekkuh's lips tightened, causing wrinkles to gather around her lips. "It should not be so for months now. The sky you describe, the air I taste . . . it is what one would expect before winter. The next camp is another six hours' ride. Once we arrive, there is a trading post and a House of the Moons. We will spend a few days there. Use the time to think on those you have lost, and keep a wary eye on the coastline as we travel today. Come find me in the healer house when we stop to camp. I want to hear of all that you see."

With that, the speaker nudged her horse forward and joined the train of riders. Ranika rushed up to Zippy and hopped into the saddle before he could lower to the ground. The Aarindin turned an eye to regard her, causing her to stifle a giggle. She whispered back, "I told you I can do it."

Zippy chuffed by way of response, a soft rumbling sound, and once again they melted into the train of Luna Rova winding across the Great Crown. The rest of the day felt more like two as the silent isolation led to boredom. She thought of her mother, the memories but a silvery scar on her heart. Her thoughts drifted to Reddevek, and she tried to imagine what he must have been like as a boy growing up among these nomadic people.

She bent her mind to the task of recalling her favorite memories of the man: their first meeting in Callish when she swiped the ruby-hilted dagger, then following him to Journey's Bend and all the woodcraft he taught her in the months after. She remembered their tracking games and the day she revealed herself as an abrogator.

The caravan moved ahead while she lingered. But it gave her little concern, as she realized that, for the first time, she could think of him without becoming overwhelmed by the need for vengeance. A hollow, vacant pit still threatened to tip her stomach with unease, but today at least, the sensation was manageable, and she didn't feel the need to fill the vast chasm with retribution and anger.

The sun settled low on the horizon, obscured by the distant haze that made gazing at the bright light manageable for a few seconds, anyway. A strange white halo sparkled around the burning orange center. As she approached the camp, the sound of merriment and music filled the air.

She dismounted and saw to Zippy's grooming needs, then retrieved a tent from a packhorse and staked out her spot at the periphery of the camp. By the time she finished, however, more than thirty similar tents had sprouted up around her, and she found herself in the middle of a crowd. After stowing the saddle inside, she removed the drab orange kerchief holding the pepperbark berries. When tied to the front panel of the tent, the kerchief made an adequate flag, marking it from all the others.

The smell of cookfires made her stomach gurgle and drew her into the center of camp. A youth turned a flank of meat on a spit, while steam carrying the scent of roasted vegetables wafted up from a cauldron set over a semi-permanent hearth of mountain stone. Beyond the center of activity stood a small stone shelter with a blue roof. Smoke drifted up from the single chimney stack.

She turned to check on Zippy. The Aarindin eyed her once, then dipped his head low to crop the grass, his tail swishing back and forth. Something in his bearing put her at ease, and she made her way through the crowd to the House of the Moons. A broad covered deck ringed the single-story building, and she shivered as she stepped into the shade.

Crafted from mountain rock and thick timbers, the structure had a single window on each wall. Ranika stood on tiptoe and peered inside to find Sintra Vekkuh seated at a small table. She walked to the door and knocked. A middle-aged man wearing the faded robes of a healer of Callinora opened the door. A wiry salt and pepper beard framed a weathered face set with deep wrinkles accentuated by sun and wind.

"You're not a Luna Rova. You the girl Vekkuh is expecting?" snapped the old docent.

"Yes, I mean, I think so. My name is—"

"Don't matter to me none, lass. See to it she drinks every last drop of that tea. There's warm bread and fresh goat's milk in the back room, but don't let her have any of it before the tea. Do that for me and I'll be back soon with stew for you both."

With that, the odd man stepped off the covered porch and meandered through the crowd.

Vekkuh's voice beckoned her inside. "Don't mind Havish. He spends more time with his goats than other people. We're lucky to have access to him, but like his medicine, he's an acquired taste."

Ranika stepped inside and shut the door. Long wood benches filled the room and small blue crystal sconces hanging from the rafters bathed the room in pale, sterile light. Vekkuh sat at a small table beside a hearth. Knobby, arthritic hands grasped a cup of tea. She sipped the brew and pulled a face, then smacked her lips. "I never get used to that, but it does ease my aches after a day like today."

Vekkuh tipped her cup upside down. "There, all gone. Now be a dear and fetch the bread and milk."

Ranika found the food in a small back room, returned to sit beside the speaker, and filled two cups with the milk then divided the bread, wasting no time and chewing a mouthful. Ranika realized that the speaker, in her blindness, might not be aware of the food and gulped down a barely chewed mouthful.

"Sorry," she mumbled, then led Vekkuh's hands to the cup and bread.

Vekkuh nodded. "It's no bother. Every gift has a toll, and I suspect you're still paying for the help you gave us."

Ranika took a long drink from the milk, the creamy liquid slightly sweet and tangy on the tongue. For the first time that day, her stomach settled and her shoulders relaxed. "It's not that. I'm just hungry."

Vekkuh tore a small piece of bread and chewed the morsel. "I assume you've been the one patrolling at night? Is that because of your gift?"

"Sometimes, yes. I haven't been able to sleep. When I channel too much, it can take a while for things inside of me to settle. But I should be fine tonight."

The speaker grunted and rubbed at her knees. Ranika began to wonder how the woman managed the long trip when she, herself, felt exhausted from the travel. "Were you able to view the sea today?" asked Vekkuh.

"No. All day the entire western horizon shimmered with a white fog, and this afternoon you could look at the sun for three or four seconds before having to look away. There was also a white ring around the sun most of the day."

The speaker sipped at her milk and nodded. "Out the south window, the blue moon should be above the horizon. Can you see it now?"

Ranika leaned back in her chair and found the blue moon, proud and full. Just like with the sun, a shimmering halo of dim light formed a corona around it. She eased back onto all four legs of her chair. "Voshna—sorry, the blue moon, is full, and just like the sun, there's a ring around the moon. Why is that?"

"Water," said Vekkuh as she chewed another piece of bread. "Water, or maybe ice crystals. If we're lucky, it will hold off until we move south. If not, we're on high ground and can wait it out, I suppose."

They ate in silence for a time, and fatigue settled into Ranika's aching back muscles. "Why did you call the blue moon Voshna?"

"In the Southlands, where I came from, people call the blue moon Voshna. I forget sometimes that it's different up here."

"Do they have a name for the red moon, then?"

"Sure, that's her sister, Vaeda."

Vekkuh removed the indigo sash covering her eyes and rubbed at her eyelids, then opened them to reveal milky white orbs. She blinked a few times and shook her head. "Do they ever say fo'Vaeda or fo'Voshna?"

"No, but there are other gods down there, Lutney, Mogdure and the like," said Ranika. "Why?"

Vekkuh sighed and sank back in her chair. "In our histories, fo'Vaeda and fo'Voshna were two of the founding sisters of the Luna Rova. We can trace the lines of all the major families back to their children. To hear them deified as sisters feels like more than coincidence."

Havish barged into the room carrying two bowls full of stew. He set the bowls down, retrieved a few spoons from the back room, and unceremoniously plopped them into the broth. The savory aroma of wild onion caused her to salivate.

"You have our thanks, Havish. Might we use the room for a bit longer?"

"I would think you need to mind your clan. Making a ruckus out there tonight. Unless I'm mistaken, there's more than a few broken families that need mending," growled the docent. Beyond the healing house, the music of drums and flutes combined with a strumming lute, all of it whipping the clan into a chanted song.

"We're all one family in the Dev'advari, you know that old man. But there are more than a few grieving widows who could use someone to keep them warm tonight."

Havish had opened his mouth in rebuttal but snapped it shut, eyebrows raised, as he set his hands on his hips. "Widows, you say? Well, sometimes the Giver gives, I suppose. Take your time then, but be sure to come see me by midday tomorrow. You need a realignment before you sit the horse if you intend to make it all the way to Stellance."

Without waiting, Havish tossed open the door. He two-stepped to one side and then the other in time with the music from the camp before disappearing into the night. Ranika rose and closed the door behind him, and when she returned, she and Vekkuh shared a giggle.

"You can't blame the man. He's stuck up here all alone with only his goats for company most of the year," said Vekkuh.

"Yeah," said Ranika. "Poor goats."

At that, Vekkuh cackled and slapped the table. By the time she recovered, she put palms to her eyes to dry the tears. "Oh Giver, I needed that, my dear."

Feeling more comfortable in the woman's presence, Ranika cleared her throat. "Sintra Vekkuh, can I ask . . . why am I here? Why did you agree to let me travel with the Dev'advari?"

Vekkuh nodded to herself as if confirming a suspicion. "Laryn said you were clever and carried yourself like someone well beyond her years. So let me ask you, why did you ask to join us?"

Ranika removed her hat and scratched at her scalp, the frilly spirals of hair tickling her neck. She picked up a spoon and blew on the steam. "Lots of reasons. If those rumblers come back, Red taught me how to deal with stuff like that. And right now, there's people in Stone's Grasp that . . . it's a mess, and I'm in the middle of it. Mostly, I wanted to feel closer to Red."

"It's no secret that the clan would benefit from your gifts, Ranika. The question is, how can the clan help you?"

"I'm not sure what you mean."

"I know Reddevek allowed himself to be read by Speaker Movshka of the Rovinary clan. But there's still so much that's been lost to us. We're his family, his blood, but so are you. If you would allow it, I can read you, Ranika, but in doing so you would be party to everything we know about Reddevek's past, how he grew up, who he loved, and why he left us. Think of a reading as a conversation. I get to learn about your past, your experiences with Reddevek, and you get to learn just as much from me."

She sipped at the soup and used the time to consider her words. The proposal was intriguing, but her walls were not so easily breached. "I saw Red when the speaker read him. It looked like it hurt."

"That's likely because monks like Movshka and Red tried to cram a few decades of history into a few minutes. It can be done, but it taxes the mind. What I'm talking about would be a gentle exchange of stories, a way to bring Reddevek's history full circle. You think on it, and if you want more answers about the Rovinary, and Reddevek, maybe even about yourself, come find me."

Chapter Thirty-Three: The Instigators

Lluthean awoke to discover that the silky sensation intertwined with his legs was not Karragin's calf, but rather a tangled bedsheet. He tried to force his mind back into the depths of sleep, to recapture something of the intimacy he recalled from their single night, but inherent restlessness, and his appetite, dashed away the fleeting images.

He slapped the mattress with the flat of his hand in frustration. Ever since Callinora, restful sleep seemed impossible to capture. All too often, he dreamed of umbral, with their voices shifting from a shrill screech to a raspy whisper. They called out to him from beyond the dark portal in the basement of the Sanitorium as oily rivulets of power siphoned into the vortex, caressing his skin, beckoning him to step inside.

The unrelenting allure to drop through, to answer the call of the creatures from the Drift, drew something out of him, like a faint tether anchored to his core, dragging him into shadowy depths. Yet, amidst the haunting nightmares that plagued him, his memories of the night with Karragin provided a lone sanctuary, a mental refuge from the horrors that besieged his mind.

A sigh loud enough to disturb the curtains escaped his lips and Neska padded close, the bed frame creaking under her weight. He rolled toward the depression she created and came nose to nose with her. The heat of her breath rushed over his face, and he stared into the depths of her eyes, crystalline shards of blue. She licked him once, covering him from chin to forehead, and he laughed.

"Alright, alright. Let's get you outside. I've half a mind to go with you."

An hour later, he wandered the halls of Stone's Grasp, billow seeds clacking as he rolled them around in one clutched hand. Kaellor had begrudgingly proposed that he and Bryndor begin the Rite of Revealing tomorrow. As such, his uncle had suspended their sparring sessions and lessons with tutors. A formal evening meal was the only thing on his schedule today.

Yet, none of that occupied much of his thoughts compared to the strange behavior of Karragin. The woman was an enigma. She had sought him out that last night in the Great Crown. They spent hours first succumbing to absolute need and desire, then exploring the intimate curves of one another and the different ways their bodies could intertwine.

She had told him nothing would change between them, and in the heat of the moment he'd understood the words, but he hadn't thought that she was serious—not until he awoke the next morning to find her attending to her duties as Laryn's Mirrare. The ride back to Stone's Grasp had not afforded them the chance to speak beyond cursory greetings, and the closer the party drew to the castle, the more focused she and the Outriders became regarding their safe arrival.

It felt like all of them were paranoid. Clearly, the greatest danger lay in the creatures they'd fought in the Great Crown. Why couldn't everyone relax and give the two of them the chance to talk? Taker's grip. All he wanted was to talk to her, alone. And yet, in the week since their return, sparring sessions and long lessons with tutors occupied all of his time, while attending to Laryn's security monopolized hers.

In his restless wandering, he arrived at the threshold of a door leading to the royal plaza. His gaze wandered across Stone's Grasp. The city stretched out well beyond the tiered castle in a labyrinth of districts. Close to the inner curtain wall sat the affluent estates and manor houses with blue, slate-tiled roofs. A broad road divided these estates and led down to a mismatched cluster of market and merchant districts, interspersed with neighborhoods and private dwellings. Well beyond the outer curtain wall, sunlight glinted off the shores of Lake Ullend.

A faint breeze lifted from the city, and Lluthean wrinkled his nose against the offensive smell of too many people in one place. He considered muttering an oath against the Taker, but stifled any comment upon discovering that two sentinels stood at attention beside the door. Both men wore the formal black uniform and snapped to attention as he turned to them. "Hello. Um, at ease I suppose?"

At his suggestion, the guards relaxed their posture. "Your Highness," one of them said.

He knew the sentinels would refuse to break protocol, and nodded. He had become used to the stiff formalities, but still didn't care for the sense of distance it created between him and basically anyone he encountered in Stone's Grasp. "Every time I step out here, I'm taken aback by the view. Do you ever get used to it?"

After a moment of silence, one of the sentinels ticked his head to the side. "Your Highness?"

"There is not a city in all the Southlands that rivals the size of Stone's Grasp. Well, maybe Callish, but I never made it that far east. Still, to see it all from up here . . . it's really something."

One sentinel looked to the other, and eventually the first man cleared his throat. "I suppose it's all we've ever known, but you're right . . . it's a good view, Your Highness."

Lluthean sensed he was unlikely to draw either man into conversation and stepped out onto the royal plaza. "Right then, well, good day."

The sentinels responded in unison, "Good day, Your Highness."

He walked over to the northwest edge of the plaza and leaned on the balustrade, shoulders and back achy with fatigue. He searched the timberline of the foothills climbing into the Great Crown. In moments, slashes of silver and grey flashed under the canopy as Neska and Boru struck out for the afternoon. He and Bryndor, sometimes with Ksenia's aid, took turns leading the wolvryn back and forth between their lair at the back of Stone's Grasp and the royal suites at nighttime.

While Boru seemed to be adjusting to the new sleeping arrangements, he felt pretty certain that Neska disdained the close quarters. Most nights, Bryndor lost at least a half hour coaxing Boru off his bed. The wolvryn had each surpassed the height of the Aarindin, and Boru in particular was beginning to fill out with more muscle. He often sat with his haunches on the floor and half of his body draped over Bryndor's sizable bed.

Neska, though, always lounged in the anteroom under an open window that faced the Great Crown, refusing to join him in the bedchamber until morning. Given how restless his sleep had been of late, that was likely more peaceful, he supposed.

"Catch a moment of freedom from the tutors today?" asked Nolan from behind him.

Lluthean startled and turned to see his friend approach. Nolan's quad walked across the royal plaza and down the steps to the green below. Savnah, Tovnik, and Dexxin each waved as they descended to the lower tiered green.

"Yes, I guess. I should be grateful but can't seem to find anything to keep myself busy. But, ahh never mind, how are you? Off on some grand mission for the kingdom?"

"No, we were just checking on Karragin. The bird hatched, you know, the riftwing you found."

The revelation washed over him, and he couldn't decide whether to feel happy or relieved. "Laryn told me as much. That's great, really great. But truth be told, Neska found it. I didn't even know what it was at first."

Nolan tipped his head forward and squinted, considering him through a jumbled coif of cinnamon curls. Then he smiled. "You can tell yourself that, Llu. But Baccal saw you up there, on top of that column of rock. Neska's amazing, but she can't fly."

Lluthean pushed hands into pockets. "That's true enough, I suppose. So, is it working? Can she hear through the riftwing?"

"Not yet, but she's hopeful. The royal falconer said he's never worked with a riftwing, but apparently a few centuries ago, one would visit the Founder's Memorial every summer for more than eighty years." Nolan shook his head and laughed. "Moons, I've never heard of such a thing. I mean, having a pet is one thing, but for eighty years? We had a cat when I was a kid, and Mom, she couldn't stand that thing. Good mouser, but never stayed off the tables."

"I don't follow," said Lluthean.

"We had that cat for four miserable years. It always chewed holes in my socks, or Karra's blankets. Mom threw a small celebration the day she pawned it off to an orphanage in the Sprawl. Anyway, the falconer says there will be none of that between Karra and the riftwing, since it's imprinted on her. So, for better or worse, she's got a shadow for at least eighty years."

"Ah. I didn't know any of that. Is it going alright?"

Nolan waved a hand, deflecting any concern. "Of course. Karra is absolutely smitten with the thing. I've never seen her smile so much. It's . . ." He shook his head in disbelief. "Dad and I, we can't thank you enough, Llu. It feels like I might get back the sister I knew before the Abrogator's War."

"That's, wow, that's good. I'm really happy for her."

"You haven't seen her yet with the bird, have you?"

Lluthean's face flushed. "Between her duties as a Mirrare and everything Kae has us doing, there hasn't been time." He stopped and nodded to himself. "But you're right, I should stop in."

Nolan studied his face and smiled once again, waiting expectantly, as if Lluthean might say something else, and the moment drew out with an awkward silence. "Are you alright, man?" asked Nolan.

"Me? Yes, not sleeping so good, maybe, that's all."

Nolan bobbed his chin up and down. "Can I . . . can I say something, as a friend, and not make it weird?"

"Well, it's already a little weird, so, yes, why not?"

"If you like Karra, and I think you do, you can't let her push you away. She's good at that . . . an absolute expert, actually." Nolan leaned in, conspiratorially. "It's the Giver's mystery what you see in her, but don't give up. She'll get out of her own way eventually and see everything you've done for her. Some people are just slow learners, you know?"

Lluthean took a deep breath, then exhaled, feeling suddenly a little better than he had all day. "Right, I appreciate the advice."

"Well, I should run along before Savnah invents some new curse to pickle my name with."

"Say, before you go, I wanted to ask you something, confidentially?"

"Alright, shoot," said Nolan.

"Bryndor and I convinced Kae to let us sit for our Rite of Revealing. We start tomorrow morning."

Surprise lifted Nolan's eyebrows under his curls. "Moons, that's brilliant!" His focus withdrew, and he nodded to himself. "It's because of everything that's happened of late, isn't it? I mean, the usurper's return is one thing, but the Lacuna, the things we found in the mountains. Giver knows we could all benefit from your arca prime."

"That's the hope. Anyway, I wanted to ask if you would stand beside your father as my instigator. You know, to help start the ritual. Kae and Laryn will be there. Bryn asked Ksenia, and I'm to find the last."

Nolan crossed his arms. "I would be honored, Llu. But are you sure you don't want to ask Karra?"

"I considered it, but she's been pretty preoccupied, and now with the riftwing, I don't want to add to her responsibilities. Besides, I think I would prefer a good friend to be there, and I'm not sure your sister thinks of me that way, not yet, anyway. So, what do you say?"

Nolan shook his head from side to side as if to say no, but smiled. "Absolutely, yes. I'm honored, man. I'll be there. Inner sanctum it is, bright and early!"

Savnah's voice echoed from the green below. "If you gossip girls are done grindin' about, we could use our scout down here!"

"Sorry, our search for the invaders that broke into Ranika's suite turned up empty. Now Hestian has us tracking down leads on the thugs that tried to nab Ksenia the other night. Savnah gets grouchy when we fail to finish a mission. I should get going, but I'll see you tomorrow!"

With that, the ginger-haired man took the steps two at a time to catch up with his quad. Lluthean lingered a while longer, and eventually his feet seemed to walk of their own accord, following the path back inside to Karragin's suite. He lingered at the door and lifted a knuckle to knock, but couldn't bring himself to do it. He stood there, heart pounding, billow seeds creaking together under his grip.

The clatter of crockery falling to the floor broke his trance, and he finally knocked on the door. He realized that she might not have even heard him and was turning to leave when Karragin opened the door. She looked curious. "Llu, was that you, knocking just now?"

Her sudden appearance left him bewildered. He began to sign, *"Yes, sorry, I was coming to check on you and the bird."*

She reached forward and grabbed his hands, the warmth of her touch further addling his mind. "Don't sign it. Say it out loud."

He spoke the only things that came to mind. "Hello, my name is Lluthean. I'm the coward standing outside your door, but I heard something and wanted to see if you were alright."

Tears brimmed in Karragin's eyes, and she clutched her fists to her mouth, turned a slow circle, then retreated into her room. She lifted a finger to the fledgling hawk sitting on the post of her bed and placed it on her shoulder, then returned, wiping tears from her face.

"It's working, Llu. It's really working, I can hear you. Say something else, say anything."

Something in her exuberance, the raw emotions shifting across her face, caught him utterly unprepared, and he stammered, finding clever words elusive. "Karra, that's wonderful, really. I'm so happy for you, for both of you. Does it have a name?"

Karragin beamed a smile at him. "She's a girl, and her name is Iska."

Lluthean studied the fledgling. Already larger than his hand, the creature sat stoically on Karragin's shoulder, a downy white chick with dark eyes and a slash of blue at the base of a beak that curled into a black point. Silvery-white scales ringed its talons. Iska turned to gaze at the window.

"Iska seems preoccupied with staring at the blue moon," he said.

"Well, she is a moonwing. Riftwing is the slang from fairy tales. Anyway, I considered Baellen, but she likes the softer sounding name, so Iska. What do you think?" Karragin ran a finger across the hawk's beak and along its spine.

"It sounds perfect." He looked past her into the room to eye a broken vase on the floor. "What happened there?"

"I've not had the chance to bird-proof my rooms yet and Iska was exploring," she said, as if that explained everything.

"She's already twice the size of the egg. What does she eat?"

Karragin gestured for him to step inside. "Come in, I'll show you." He stepped inside and closed the door while she retrieved a cup and waved it in front of his nose. The ground food gave off a less than pleasant odor. "It's a mixture of rat and chicken meat, plus crickets and things. In a few weeks, she'll be able to eat without having to tear up the food. The falconer says she's maturing faster than anything he's dealt with."

Karragin lifted her finger to Iska, who hopped on, and she set the moonwing on his shoulder. The creature gripped his tunic and fluttered her downy white wings a few times, tickling his ear. She settled and stared unblinking at him. Up close, he could tell that the chick's eyes held deep navy blue hues. "Hello Iska. How long until she can fly?"

"We're not sure. The falconer has never raised a moonwing. Probably before she's three months old, but time will tell."

"I saw Nolan this morning. He tells me Iska might live over eighty years."

Karragin laughed. "I'm sorry. It's just, after all this time, being able to hear you, through my link to her, it's the most amazing thing, and so clear . . . I can't explain it."

"Is it anything like talking to Neska?"

Karragin walked over to a small table and pulled out a chair, inviting him to sit, but Iska flapped her wings in irritable rapid succession. Her talons bit into his shoulder, and he winced.

"It's alright, Iska. I'm not going anywhere," she said.

Karragin held her hand out, and Iska hopped off his shoulder. Lluthean lifted the material of his tunic, noting that the chick's sharp talons had drawn blood. Karragin frowned upon realizing she had caused him injury. "Grind it, I'm so sorry. I had no idea she would get so irritated."

She rushed over to a cabinet and returned with a clean cloth. "Let me see. Turn your head."

He removed the top three toggles at the neck of his tunic and craned his head to the side. Karragin leaned in close, smelling of leather and mountain heather. She tsked and blotted the cloth over the wound.

"Taker's grip, Iska. Hold one moment, Llu."

She stepped back to the cabinet with the cloth in hand, several dots of blood visible. Her hands moved swiftly and she doused the cloth with a clear liquid, then returned. Her face resumed its usual placid expression, and she considered him for a moment. She reached a hand to tangle her fingers through the back of his hair, and his entire world focused on the warmth at the nape of his neck. She leaned in to kiss him, but just as their lips brushed, a searing pain flared in his shoulder where Iska had clawed into his flesh.

Lluthean inhaled and instinctively pulled away, but she pressed herself close, her strength holding him immobile despite his struggle. "I know it burns, but take two breaths, in and out, in and out, and it will fade."

He searched her eyes, but felt completely overwhelmed by the pain, her unrelenting strength, and the feel of her torso pressed against his. He struggled to make sense of her words, and still, she held him in place. Finally, he took a ragged, full breath, and then another, and just as she said, the pain dissipated.

He relaxed his body and dropped his forehead onto her shoulder, panting as the last bit of pain subsided. "It's not as bad as devil's tail, but you could warn a guy."

"You managed well, my prince. Your tunic will need mending, and see Laryn within the hour. She really got you good, but at least it will not become infected. Take a seat, but keep the cloth pressed on it."

Lluthean sat down, an achy throb already cramping the broad muscle that ran from his neck to shoulder. Karragin took the only other chair beside a small wood table and stroked a finger over Iska's neck and spine once again, but her brow knitted in a frown as she seemed to consider something.

"Nolan said she imprinted on you. I imagine that to her, you're her entire world."

"That's just it. She did fine being passed around to Nolan's quad just before you got here."

"Did she tell you anything through your gift?" he asked.

"No. She doesn't communicate like other creatures. Moonwings are mute. I think maybe that's why when I link to her, I can hear what she hears."

"What about other senses? Can you see through her eyes as well?"

367

Karragin shrugged. "I don't know. I haven't tried that yet."

"Well, I'll be sure to wear a leather jerkin before she perches on my shoulder again."

"Yeah, not a bad idea. I have to get ready for my rotation with Laryn in an hour. Why aren't you sweating it out in sparring sessions with your uncle today?"

"Bryndor and I have this one day of reprieve before we sit for our Rite of Revealing tomorrow morning."

The announcement caused Karragin to lean back in her chair. "Is that wise? I mean, you've both only begun to discover your other gifts."

"Oh, it's definitely something a monk would do, but if the boot fits. Anyway, given everything that's happened, it sort of feels necessary. Do you remember anything from your trial? Any hints you can give me?"

She shook her head. "Not really. I woke up like most, feet wet and feeling lucky to have escaped something."

"Why were your feet wet?"

"The ritual is governed by the power of the runes inscribed on the statue of Eldrek, but it is also powered by the reflecting pool in the inner sanctum. Anyone who sits for the Rite of Revealing has to submerge something in the pool. Usually it's easiest to drop your feet in."

"That's more than anyone else has been able to tell me. You don't remember what happened once the whole thing began?"

"Nothing else, I'm afraid. Kae and Laryn will be your instigators, I assume?"

Lluthean felt a prickly heat rise from his neck and couldn't tell if it was because of the wound he nursed on his shoulder or the awkward way he now felt. "We need five in total. Your father will attend, of course, and Kae, and Laryn. Bryndor asked Ksenia. I . . . asked Nolan to stand for me. I was going to ask you, but didn't want to burden you with everything you have to deal with."

She held up a hand to forestall his explanation. "Nolan was a good choice. You two have shared more than most in the last few months. He'll be honored and besides, if Her Radiance will be in attendance, I'll be there in an official capacity to make sure nobody grinds it all up."

The cramp in his shoulder blossomed into a deep ache, and he pushed to his feet. "That sounds good. I think I may need to pay Laryn a visit sooner than later for this. I'll see you tomorrow morning then? In the inner sanctum?"

She stood and escorted him to the door. "I imagine that all the Mirrare will be in attendance. Llu, you don't look so good."

A light sweat had gathered on his forehead and between his shoulders, and he had to resist a wave of lightheadedness. "Woozy. What was in that tincture?"

She frowned once again and placed a hand for support under his uninjured shoulder. "Diluted embertang. Come on. We're going to see Laryn now."

Iska hopped onto her shoulder, and she escorted him around the corner and down the hall to the royal suites. The sentinels standing guard saluted as he pushed into the restricted hallway reserved for the royal family. A few more steps brought them to Laryn's door. Karragin pounded a fist three times, and Laryn pulled the door open. She tucked locks of white hair behind her ears and considered them both.

"Your Radiance. My moonwing punctured his shoulder, an accident. I cleaned the wound with embertang but perhaps you should take a look."

Lluthean felt himself ushered inside as the whir of the healer song filled the chamber. Karragin walked him over to a couch and within seconds, Laryn had him reclined, one hand on his chest and another on his forehead. The pain subsided, and he nearly drifted to sleep before the healer song faded.

"Sit up, Llu. See how you feel," said Laryn.

Lluthean looked at his naked shoulder, expecting to see puncture wounds, but Laryn's art had completely removed any sign of the injury. He turned his neck from side to side and stretched his arms overhead, then sat upright.

"Better?" she asked.

"Yes, thanks." He sighed. "Again."

Karragin spoke from behind Laryn. "The wound seemed shallow. Did I miss something?"

Laryn turned and began to sign, but tilted her head to the side. "Can you hear me? Is it working?"

A smile as pure and genuine as the sunrise blossomed on Karragin's placid face, there one moment and gone the next. "Yes."

"Well, promise me you'll still practice the hand language," Laryn suggested.

"Of course," said Karragin.

Laryn nodded agreement. "Good. As for the wounds, you cleaned them well, but two of the punctures compromised the muscle sheath along his shoulder. He started to develop a pocket of blood in the muscle. That's enough to make most people faint and vomit from the pain. You should be fine now, but no more adventure before tomorrow morning, for either of you."

"Certainly. I'll take my leave," said Karragin.

Lluthean waved as she departed. Laryn escorted her out of the suite and returned with arms folded. "Why am I not surprised that the one person Karra's moonwing wounds is you?"

Chapter Thirty-Four: Eldrek's Arca Prime

B efore the Great War, the Giver saw fit to bestow arca primes on a good majority of gifted, but something changed immediately after the conflict. I was one of the very few gifted to inherit my arca prime, while most developed accessory runes, but failed to inherit anything resembling a primary rune. Nearly an entire generation failed to manifest the full power of their gift.

All that changed about twenty-five years ago, when we unveiled a statue of my father and placed it before the deepening well. The project was the culmination of years of augury and divination. Our most skilled artisans relied on visions from the Giver in the creation of the monument.

In addition to serving as the focus of the castle defenses, the statue now serves as a conduit to initiate the Rite of Revealing. Though the process is not without its dangers, nearly all our gifted endure the trial and inherit their arca prime.

Neldrek says Father would have bristled at the grandiosity of the effigy, but I'm grateful to have an accurate reminder of his face. Most of the paintings recording the Great War show Father's back as he faced the abrogator forces. In those artistic murals, I can see the faces of fo'Vaeda and fo'Voshna, my mother and aunt, but only when I visit the monument can I see the determination in his expression.

—The Tome of Nivosh, 75 PC, translated by Ksenia Balladuren

LARYN AWOKE UNDER THE warmth of her covers and stretched a tentative foot, probing for Kaellor, but found his side of the bed empty.

She rubbed the sand from her eyes and made her way to the front room of their suite to find him standing at the window, steaming cup in hand, gazing out across the Great Crown. He wore formal attire with a midnight blue tunic tailored to accentuate his shoulders, light blue embroidery at the shoulders and cuffs, the moon of Baellen on the left front chest.

Already up and at it. Did you even come to bed, I wonder?

The previous evening, they had shared a meal and finished the last of a spirit called Malvressian honey-cut. She'd tried a tiny sip and spluttered when a single drop of the liquid evaporated in the back of her throat. That led to much-needed laughter and a recounting of stories from their time in the Southlands. They were well into another round of memories when she retired for the evening.

Though Kaellor had tried to hide his reservations, she found it no surprise that sleep eluded him. She walked behind him and wrapped arms around his abdomen, interlocking her fingers. "I can still smell the musk of the wolvryn in the room. How late did you three stay up last night?"

His hand rubbed across her forearms, warm and calloused. "Later than we should have, but maybe not half as long as I would have liked."

She reached up and massaged his shoulders and the back of his neck. Only after a few minutes did he relax his posture, eventually setting his cup down to turn and embrace her. They stood like that for more than a dozen breaths.

"Whatever you are thinking, they are more prepared than either of us were at this age," she offered.

"I know. I've challenged my gift more times than I can count, looking for a reason to contradict the decision to move forward."

"And?"

"And, sometimes the Giver gives, but if she has anything to say against their Rite of Revealing, she isn't saying anything about it to me or Therek."

"Mm. If I could get a sense for the Giver's hand in decisions I made, I would likely walk around with those runes primed all day long."

In answer to her response, Kaellor leaned back and revealed the runes on his forearms, both imbued with the unmistakable blue currents of zenith. She shook her head and smiled. She wanted to scold him about the risk of developing the draft, but he conceded her point before she could speak. "I know. I'll let it go."

"How much time do we have before everyone gathers for the ritual?"

"About an hour. In fact, I should go check on the boys. I left a warm crownberry muffin in the basket by the teakettle there."

She rose to her tiptoes and kissed him on the lips, a fast peck. "Thanks. I'll see you in a bit."

Kaellor belted his guardian sword and left. After devouring the muffin and a stout cup of tea, she washed up and set her hair in a loose braid that added the illusion of depth and height, with the back end of the braid held up by a circular, silver clasp. Some of the white locks of hair framed her cheeks, and others mingled into the weave.

She wore the simple yet elegant attire of Her Radiance: rich, double-layered ivory silks accented at the wrists and ankles with silver filigree. A thin, gold cord accentuated her waist and completed the outfit. She was turning back and forth in the mirror, inspecting her appearance, just as the door knocked.

Bryndor's muffled baritone voice, resembling Kaellor's more and more this year, sounded from beyond the door. "Aunt Laryn? Care for an escort?"

She opened the door to find him standing in a simple fitted shirt and pants. "Thank you. I would love nothing more. Lead on."

She followed him through the common hall that joined the royal suites and out into the larger atrium where the sentinels stood guard. Her Mirrare stood ready with Kaellor and Lluthean. As a group, they descended to the inner sanctum. Though the journey took well over a quarter hour, none in the group seemed inclined toward idle conversation.

When they finally passed through the double doors to the sanctum, the light, clean fragrance of survivor's essence burning from oiled sconces welcomed them. Therek stood beside the reflecting pool chatting with Nolan and Ksenia, his words lost in the vastness of the great chamber.

The wolvryn bookended the statue of Eldrek, Boru preoccupied with cleaning a front paw and Neska yawning with casual boredom.

Laryn turned to her Mirrare and signed, *"We're safe in here. Assume security in the hall. Until the ritual is complete, no others may enter."*

Karragin dipped her chin and signed to her sister Mirrare, *"Choose your post."* Baccal hitched a thumb over her shoulder, indicating that she preferred the far side of the hall. Amniah reflected Karragin's stoic expression, then turned without words and walked to the other side of the hallway.

Karragin stood a moment at the doorway. Her moonwing gripped its talons into a strap of leather on the woman's shoulder, and the two surveyed the chamber like predators in waiting. Her surveillance complete, the young woman signed, *"I'll be just on the other side of the door if you have need."*

Once the doors were closed, Therek cleared his throat. "I appreciate everyone's prompt arrival. Before we begin, does anyone have any questions?"

"I've got loads, but I think we've learned all that there is to know," said Lluthean.

"Agreed. The sooner begun, the sooner done," said Bryndor.

"Very well. If each of you would remove your boots, lie down on the mats beside the pool, and drape your feet in the reflecting pool," the regent directed.

The oval pool stretched out before the statue of Eldrek, and a padded mat was set on either side. Without question or words, each brother followed Therek's directive, rolling up their pant legs and situating themselves on the mats. The surface of the pool rippled as they each placed their feet in the water.

A half-hearted laugh born of surprise and possibly a little anxiety escaped Lluthean's lips, and he reached a hand into the water. "Woah, tingly."

Kaellor looked as if he might reprimand his nephew's lack of decorum, but instead he inhaled and took a knee beside Lluthean. "That's normal, Llu. The reflecting pool enhances your gift, allowing you to channel without the effort of drawing on the ambient currents of zenith. Don't let it distract you. Just like we spoke of, focus your intention."

Lluthean lay back, squirming on the mat into a position of comfort. He reached into a back pocket and withdrew the three billow seeds. They rattled together when he deposited them into Kae's hand. "Hold them for when we get back? Otherwise, see you on the other side, Kae."

Kaellor rolled the billow seeds in one hand. "Eyes to the horizon, Llu."

He stood and nodded at Bryndor, who had already positioned himself on the mat, reclining on elbows. "All set?" asked Kaellor.

Bryndor looked at Ksenia and winked, then turned back to his uncle. "Eyes to the horizon."

Therek walked to stand in front of the statue of Eldrek. "In times past, the Rite of Revealing was preceded by years of training, a formal petition to attempt the trial, and an entire week of preparation and celebration. Though necessity circumvents all of that pomp and circumstance, know that your efforts here are no less critical, no less meaningful. In fact, your accomplishments in the trial will likely shape the kingdom for years to come. Bryndorllean and Llutheandellen Baellentrell, are you prepared to begin your Rite of Revealing?"

"Yes," they said in unison.

Therek smiled and held his arms out, his vast wingspan beckoning them forward. "Very well. Would the instigators join me around the statue of Eldrek? Bryndor and Lluthean, may the Giver see you safely through and light your arca primes. Suspend any channeling, and we shall begin."

Laryn took her place between Kaellor and Ksenia. They each held hands, with Ksenia grasping Nolan's hand, and he, in turn grabbing Therek's. Together, the five of them formed a half circle facing the statue of Eldrek.

She had not instigated a Rite of Revealing before, but Therek had prepared them well. Still, for a moment, her heart hammered inside her chest. She turned to Kaellor, wondering if he felt the same sense of anticipation. He offered a soft smile that seemed born out of trepidation more than enthusiasm.

Laryn winked at him and turned to Ksenia, who trained her focus on Therek's instructions. "Now then," he said. "Each of us must channel zenith into our arca prime, but instead of activating your rune, hold it charged. Kaellor and I will complete the circle by touching the statue of Eldrek. You will sense the zenith being pulled from you. Don't resist it; rather, allow the current to flow out. Our success will initiate a cascade of runes along the statue which will, in turn, suspend the princes in their own zentrist. Think of it as a magic-laden cocoon in which their Rite of Revealing will take place. Let's begin."

Therek placed his free hand on the statue, and Kaellor mirrored him on the other side. Laryn siphoned zenith, directing the flow into her arca prime. The soft, whirring murmur of the healer song filled the chamber. The intricate tapestry of runes carved into the statue of Eldrek flared from drab stone to iridescent hues of blue. Laryn felt the strange tug as zenith flowed out from her arca prime and into the statue. The sensation was not unlike the feeling when Kaellor siphoned on the ambient currents, but where his actions felt like the whisper of a soft wind, the ritual felt like the steady, unrelenting tug of a river pulling her downstream.

Arcing streams of zenith flickered all about the statue. They began at the feet as slow rivulets of power that wound up the torso, down the arms, and to the head, even twinkling in the eyes. A deep tone echoed in the chamber, then another layered on top, and another, as if a chorus of otherworldly spirits supervised the ritual. In moments, the intensity and pitch of the echoes rose, and all the runes on the statue glowed with a steady current of zenith.

Laryn felt her head swim and wondered how much zenith she had donated to the process. The sounds of the ritual drowned out her healer song, but still she siphoned zenith, keeping her arca prime charged. Finally, Therek released his hand from the statue, breaking the circuit.

Therek panted and staggered back a step, then raised his voice to speak over the moaning chorus arising from the statue. "It is done. You can stop channeling now. The Eldrek runes will move forward of their own accord. It's no small miracle, though. Watch."

Laryn watched as the runes pulsed like a heartbeat, never dimming, becoming ever more intense, ever brighter. The droning chorus rose in volume until the resonance tingled through her feet and in her core. Then, all at once, the Eldrek runes flowed into the arca prime on the statue and, in a single brilliant pulse, zenith flared out into the room.

A shock wave pulsed through each of them, and Laryn felt invigorated to the point that she couldn't help but release a giddy laugh. She looked at the others in the half circle, and each of them wore expressions of astonished surprise. Therek's wispy eyebrows rose with a knowing smile, and he clasped his hands over his chest. Nolan dropped to his knees, giggling, and Ksenia laughed into cupped hands. Even Kaellor chuckled.

"I had no idea that Eldrek's statue could do that," she said.

"Every time," said Therek. "I think it's the Giver's way of rewarding those who contribute to the ritual by returning their zenith . . . twofold." Therek's last words trailed off as a look of confusion wilted the exuberance from his face. He stared back in the direction of the reflecting pool.

"What is it, Therek?" Kaellor pressed.

"The zentrists, I've never seen any so misshapen, or so massive," said the regent.

"When was the last time you supervised the trial for a Baellentrell? Maybe the greater the arca prime, the greater the zentrist?" suggested Nolan.

Therek walked over to the blue cocoon covering Bryndor and rapped a knuckle on the barrier, then pressed his nose to the surface and cupped his hand over his eyes, attempting to see inside. He pulled back, appearing even more bewildered. "I understand the logic, but I've attended numerous Rite of Revealings over the decades, and nobody from house Baellentrell or Lellendule has ever been encased in anything like this. Also, I should be able to see inside, like a dozenth, but this barrier is more like stone."

Laryn studied the oversized cocoons of zenith shrouding each of the brothers. The constructs did resemble a dozenth, with dense strands of zenith forming a complex latticework. But she could tell at a glance that something seemed off.

They each approached and tried to peer through the barriers. She even placed a hand on the surface. Where a dozenth felt malleable and spongy, the surface of the zentrist tingled under her touch, and static charges of zenith flared from under her palm, yet the construct had a density not unlike solid stone.

Therek gasped and took two steps back, then stopped, turning to search the room with a wild expression on his face. "Merciful Giver. Where are the wolvryn?"

As one they all searched one another's faces, looking for clear answers where none were forthcoming. Kaellor inhaled a deep breath and held up a hand. When he spoke, his voice held the edge of deadly purpose. "They were lounging behind the statue when we started. Did anyone escort them out?"

"Let me see," said Laryn. She began to walk toward the doors, where Karragin maintained a guard.

"Your Radiance, I have them. A moment," said Nolan. The young man appeared entranced, his attention monopolized by the information his arca prime transmitted. He knelt at the base of Lluthean's zentrist, then stepped around the pool to Bryndor's.

At last he stood. "They're in there, with them. Boru with Bryndor, Neska with Lluthean. That's probably why the zentrists are so big, because of the wolvryn."

"You're sure?" asked Therek.

Nolan tilted his head and looked about to offer an apology. "I wish I wasn't, but yes, I'm sure."

Kaellor paced around the edge of Lluthean's zentrist, running a hand along its surface. He clawed his fingers into the barrier, grimacing as sparks of zenith showered in the wake of his touch. He lifted his hand and shook it. "Has anything like this ever happened before?"

Therek pinched his lower lip between thumb and forefinger in concentration. "Never in our recorded histories that I know of."

"Do we know if it will alter their chances of success, or change the mechanics of the rite?" Laryn pressed.

"Who can say? Again, I'm not aware that anything like this has ever happened before," said Therek. The sagely man took three lurching steps to collapse onto a bench at the room's periphery. He looked utterly defeated and seemed to have aged a year in the space of a few minutes.

Kaellor took a seat beside him, and they sat in silence. Laryn and Nolan sat down on the bench behind them, as if their proximity might offer some relief from the oppressive weight that permeated the room. Only Ksenia remained standing beside Bryndor's zentrist.

The young woman placed her palms flat on the barrier. "I can sense Boru with my sympath ability. I think I can even hear faint echoes of his thoughts, but it's not like before. It's hollow, bereft of other sounds or scents, more of a feeling, really. Perhaps you could try the shek devices? Maybe see if one of them can hear you or respond?"

Without waiting, Therek activated his shek and spoke into the device. "Bryndor, Lluthean, if either of you can hear me, please respond."

His voice echoed through Kaellor's shek, but otherwise the device remained silent. "It was worth a try," said Laryn. "Remember, they might not hear anything if they are not channeling into the shek. Kess, if you can hear Boru, can you try to talk to him, send him a message of some sort?"

Ksenia stared into the depths of the zentrist. After a few minutes, she withdrew her hands and looked up. "I don't think he can hear me, but I did sense something. He's at peace."

Therek stared at the floor. "Sometimes the grinding Taker takes."

Laryn laid a hand on Kaellor's shoulder and waited. It took a moment for him to come around, but at last he relaxed and rubbed the top of her hand. His soft baritone voice broke the awkward silence. "Did I ever tell you about the time Boru nearly tore my arm off when we were sparring in the Valley of the Cloud Walkers?"

Therek lifted his eyes, appearing more hopeful now that his friend had adopted an air of forgiveness. Kaellor continued, "Well, it was a lesson I swore I would never forget, and somehow, in the stress leading up to all of this, I did. What happened today, it's not anyone's fault. And none of you is more accountable to the oversight than me. Ever since they found each other, back in the Southlands, the boys and those . . .

magnificent creatures have been inseparable. Maybe this is exactly what the Giver intended."

"Quoting the Giver's designs? You sound more and more like your brother the older you get, my friend," said Therek.

"Don't go expecting those kinds of miracles from me. One world saving martyr per family seems like enough," said Kaellor.

"Excuse me," said Ksenia. "Might I be excused? You said none of our recorded histories mentioned anything like this before, but what about *The Tome of Nivosh*? Veeble and I have made a lot of progress this past month. It couldn't hurt to see if we can learn anything new."

"By all means. We've basically done all we can for now. I might advise that we all keep the events of the ritual a secret, for now at least," said Therek.

"I agree," said Kaellor. "The last thing we need is for someone like Edlemund to use the information to undermine the crown."

"Kess, have the Mirrare come in," said Laryn. "We are going to have to establish a rotation of watchers to see when they emerge from the ritual. This could take days or weeks."

"Certainly," she said. As she left the inner sanctum, Karragin, Baccal, and Amniah presented themselves.

"Why does the zentrist look big enough to hold four or five people?" asked Karragin.

"Close," said Kaellor. "One person and one very motivated wolvryn."

Karragin's face shifted into an uncharacteristic expression of surprise. "Woof."

Kaellor stood and puffed air through his cheeks. "Exactly. So look, here is what we are going to need from you three."

Chapter Thirty-Five: The Trial of Nines

Tarkannen staggered a few steps, sand kicking up from his feet, then dropped to his knees. His single step on the black stone ring had leeched away all of his strength, and he fell behind the others in B'vakla's group. He clenched the sand in anger, self-loathing threatening to overwhelm him. Never again would he leave others to wonder about the severity of his intent or the authenticity of his might. He should have arrived wreathed in overwhelming power and subdued the nation on his terms; now he was subject to theirs.

The sound of footsteps pitching through the sand gave him a brief warning of the approach of someone from behind. He dove belly to the sand as a combatant struck. The shearing sound of a sword careening off the nadir rod strapped to his back rang out, but he felt no pain.

He looked up to see his assailant, a man wearing leather armor similar to what those in B'vakla's group wore, but he had an orange sash tied to his upper arm. The man twirled a short sword with casual ease and turned to face him. "This one's not even armed. Hold him up!" he shouted to someone else from behind.

Another combatant grabbed Tarkannen by the shoulders, wrenching him upright, and set a knee into his back. The first man cocked his arm to deliver a killing thrust but stopped as a look of revulsion erased his battle rage. The nadrean throbbed once, and the assailant holding Tarkannen in place crumpled to the ground. A single glance at the withered husk of the man told him all he needed to know.

Before the first man could come to his senses, Tarkannen withdrew the nadir rod in a single swipe. The man deflected the strike, but not before the weapon struck his thigh. The blow seemed underpowered, yet the man crumpled in on himself, folding over the rod. Tarkannen checked his surroundings. B'vakla's black team had already dashed off into the melee. Two others wearing orange sashes sprinted toward Tarkannen.

He stepped onto the next ring of white stone, placing himself squarely in the middle. B'vakla had said that they fought on black because the white rings leeched their strength, but Tarkannen felt no change in his stamina. The black ring, however, had completely disrupted his ability to channel.

The creators of the Dalkreeg must have meant to pit zeniphiles and abrogators against one another without access to their gift. He had dismantled his ability to channel zenith years ago, but still, he should feel something while standing on the white stone path—shouldn't he?

Before he could unravel the puzzle, the next two combatants, female warriors wearing orange sashes, arrived. They fanned out, apprehensive about approaching him on the white ring. Their delay gave him time to collect his thoughts, and he siphoned on nadir once again. This time, it felt like his fingers swept through currents of water instead of vapor, but still, the power did not engage his sigils.

One of the women lifted her sword and pointed it at him. "Nobody can stand long on the white. Come meet your end!"

"Leave him, Szikes!" hissed the other woman. "The rings are soon to collapse. We can find others."

Tarkannen picked his moment. "Are you afraid to test your stamina on the white? I didn't think Kreeg bred cowards, but now I see I was wrong. Run past me then, and show all in the arena how brave you really are."

The simple goad was all Szikes needed. She snarled and raised her weapon overhead. Tarkannen hesitated a moment, then backstepped out of reach of her swing. Before he could jab in with the nadrean, her partner lunged at him from the side and he retreated again, but now both women stood in front of him. They each began to pant, and appeared as weary as he had felt only moments before.

He feigned similar fatigue, dropping to a single knee and holding the nadir rod over his shoulder. As one they charged, two lionesses sensing wounded prey. Tarkannen rolled to the side, catching Szikes on the calf. As with her teammates only moments before, the nadrean required only a touch to snuff out her life. She squelched in surprise, sword and body collapsing to the white stone ring.

Her partner, surprised by the leeching effect of the stone and the abrupt death of Szikes, paused a moment, then pivoted to run away. Tarkannen simply tossed the rod underhand like a stick. It struck her lightly on the back, yet she reacted as if impaled by a ballista bolt. The woman's arms lurched out, and she gasped once before crumpling boneless to the white stone ring.

The clanging sounds of steel on steel rang out from across the arena. The crowd roared, though whether the cheers were for him or the others, he couldn't tell in the cacophony of voices. He retrieved the nadir rod and a sword from the fallen, then searched the arena. Six of B'vakla's blacks engaged the reds, fighting on the next black ring. Fortunately, a group of blue-sashed fighters engaged the reds from the opposite side. For now, at least, none of the combatants could break away to give him any of their attention.

Tarkannen surveyed the next black ring. It was too broad to leap over, but he could probably cross it with only a single step. He grasped the nadrean at its midsection and trotted across the white ring, then the strip of sand, then leaped. A flicker of nadir engaged one of his sigils, and his shadow armor materialized. He bound over most of the black ring, placing a foot down, then falling and rolling into the next ring of sand. Another wave of exhaustion came over him, and once again, his sigils fell dormant.

Two competing sounds rang out across the Dalkreeg. The outermost rings flared with strobe-like pulses, and he saw the bodies of the women burst apart. A low rumble, as if thunder had detonated underground, accompanied the ring's detonation. At the same time, from across the arena, the black metal door lurched upward once again, lifting a third of its height from the ground.

Clanging swords, screams of agony, and the muted grunts of the combatants rose above the crowd, which fell abruptly silent. He sensed all eyes searching the far end of the arena, trained on the black metal door. He understood now that surviving the Dalkreeg meant reaching the central circle of sand, and that he would have to cross two more rings, but every time he set foot on a black stone, it stole his ability to siphon nadir.

While everyone had their attention diverted, he could reach the center and maybe even have enough time to recover before the other combatants turned their attention back to him. He committed to action and rose to his feet. After gathering his muted strength, he inhaled a few breaths and sprinted toward the center. Someone in the crowd must have sensed his intention and cried out in panicked alarm, "Don't do it! Stop him! Stop him!"

Tarkannen crossed the third ring, barely managing to keep his feet. A lone combatant in a red sash stepped forward to engage him. If the man thought Tarkannen was easy prey, he wasn't wrong. Instead of chancing a direct encounter, Tarkannen stumbled along the next white ring. With every step he took, his strength recovered, while the red-sashed man fell behind.

His path brought him up behind two reds fighting two blues standing half on sand and half on black. Tarkannen pushed past his fatigue, thighs burning and arms aching, heart throttling in his chest. He reached out as he ran by, and the tip of the nadir rod rattled off the backs of the two red fighters. He didn't pause to watch them drop, hoping only that the blue fighters would engage the red-sashed warrior who gave chase.

For good measure, he adjusted his grip on the nadrean again, holding it mid-shaft, and ran another thirty paces along the white. The reprieve allowed something resembling normal weariness to displace the utter fatigue caused by crossing the black rings.

Now or never then.

More people in the crowd cried out, and even General Havka's voice carried out, magnified somehow, "Stop him, stop the painted man!"

They were too late or already engaged in their own struggles. He stumbled onward, over the fourth black ring, then dropped to his hands and knees in the sandy center. In the periphery of his awareness, he sensed the metal door screeching one last time as it lifted. Fighting against cramped muscles, he raised his head to see what danger had everyone on edge. The world tilted, or maybe he did, and another vibration rumbled through the arena as the next set of rings flared with deadly purpose.

The fallen, wounded and dead alike, undulated, then sundered apart into pieces. Tarkannen drew his focus away from the metal door, searching for any threats. Footsteps approached, and he shifted his grip back to the base of the nadir rod, though he wasn't sure that he had the strength to wield it. The combatant stopped several paces away, breathing heavily, and took a knee.

"Taker's grip, man. What did you do?" asked B'vakla through panted breaths.

"Survived."

B'vakla ushered a few commands, and three blacks stepped forward to dispatch the lone remaining fighters, an orange and the two blues he had passed earlier.

"You tipped the scales in our favor. The blacks have won the Trial of Nines, but none of us will likely live to speak of it. You crossed the last ring."

Tarkannen found the strength to push back onto his knees. Of the thirty-six who had entered the arena, only six remained, all wearing the black sash. "What waits behind the black metal door?"

B'vakla shook her head and shaded her eyes, staring at the far end of the Dalkreeg. "Something born of shadow, but it hasn't been loosed in my lifetime."

A low-pitched rasping growl echoed from the door, and thudding, irregular steps resonated even through the sand. "What's it waiting for, then?" asked Tarkannen.

"The beast in there . . . it's supposed to be cunning. We have a minute, maybe more, before the last set of rings flare. I suspect it's waiting. Form up, blacks! We'll meet it between two of the pillars."

Tarkannen remained, knees in the sand, weight balanced back on his heels. He strained his senses, urging the flows of nadir to saturate his sigils. The inky markings shifted across his skin, but the power failed to gain purchase.

The last of the rings flared, and the beast from beyond the black metal door issued a reverberant, pulsing growl. Three black appendages flowed forward, wrapping around the stone arch, and the monster slingshotted itself out onto the arena.

As one, the crowd gasped at the sight of the thing. It rolled forward ten paces, then lurched to a stop, limbs stretching out, searching the environment. Its central segmented torso barely cleared the ground. Sunlight glistened off rows of rippling bumps. The creature inhaled through a round mouth, screeching into the air instead of howling, and Tarkannen felt sure by the appearance of the thing that it had originated in the Drift.

The sound of scuffling and grunting caused him to glance to the side. Three of their black-sashed team had removed their boots and were scurrying up the shafts of the stone columns. Only B'vakla stood her ground beside him.

She spat to the side. "It's not a bad idea, really. I mean, they've managed to keep that thing in here for years, so it must not be able to climb out. Right?"

"You have time to reach one of the vacant columns."

She spat to the side. "Those three will never ascend in the Kreegorian. I would rather die fighting than live craven."

The beast rolled forward with alarming speed, halting again and sending its three limbs flowing out. B'vakla shifted her feet in the sand, and Tarkannen stood, wringing his hands over the nadir rod with enough friction to cause his palms to burn. He had come too far to see it all end this way.

"I did not survive the Drift to be consumed by a creature born of the void."

The creature rolled in a circle, stopping at one of the stone pillars. Two of its appendages lashed out, elongating into whiplike structures that probed a column of stone. The black-sashed man cowering on top clanged his short sword against the pillar in an attempt to frighten the beast away. Instead, one of the limbs formed a tentacle and lashed around the man's ankle. He toppled to the ground with a frantic scream that was immediately muffled, then suffocated as the beast pulled him under its considerable bulk.

It hovered a moment, body shivering in place, and when it rolled away, only the stain of blood and two disembodied appendages remained. Black limbs shot out into the air, like a lizard tasting the scent of its prey. The thing seemed to gather itself to roll forward, and Tarkannen willed the sigils on his left palm to recede, leaving bare skin. If his assault on the creature failed, he would surrender to the power of the nadir rod before he allowed that thing to claim him.

B'vakla screamed in rage, likely at the futility of fighting the beast, but kicked sand to the right, then rolled to the left, placing a column between herself and the creature. The beast hovered, its strange limbs probing at the ground and the air. The surface of its black hide rippled, and a low rumble vibrated through the sand.

Tarkannen used the momentary distraction to siphon from the nadrean. He gripped his right hand around the rod and beckoned the sigils to consume the force, while keeping his unprotected hand free. Instantly, a deluge of nadir flooded his senses and primed his sigils. He devoured a quarter of its length, then shoved the rest through a belt loop.

Sigils danced to his bidding, and a crescent-shaped barrier of whirling shards of nadir surrounded the beast. It must have sensed his power, as it screeched in a higher-pitched echo of what sounded like fear. It shot out its appendages, testing the nadir barrier, recoiled in pain, then tried to roll back and retreat.

Tarkannen formed two lashings of nadir and wound them around the creature, anchoring it in place. It tried to spin and roll, but he drafted hooks into the tethers, and the beast only managed to ensnare itself. The inner surface of the onyx crescent barrier churned with frenzy, and slowly, with theatrical purpose, he collapsed the construct onto the beast.

At first, only flecks of oily material scattered to the ground, but the creature wailed an almost mournful sound as he enveloped it inside the death sphere and pressed the whirling shards into its flesh. In moments, chunks of black hide and ichor splashed to the ground, and in less than a minute, he had reduced the thing to a tumbled mass of glistening, black meat.

The entire crowd stared in silent captivation. Tarkannen shrouded himself in shadow armor once again, the ambient flows of nadir flooding his sigils with familiar purpose.

"B'vakla. If we cross back over the rings, will they continue to steal our strength?"

The woman approached him with a hesitant step. "No. The Trial of Nines is complete."

Tarkannen strode with casual purpose to the edge of the Dalkreeg, where General Havka stood on a raised, shaded platform beside a lavish, throne-like chair. The general bent to whisper something to the man he assumed must be Zsheck, the krug rai'al. The king of Kreeg leaned forward, elbows on knees, studying the scene before him. Time peppered the man's braided hair with grey and cast furrowed wrinkles about his eyes. Yet his brawny, bare shoulders showed he'd weathered the changes of age better than most.

Before Tarkannen could address the man, he stood and leaped down to the sand. His descent seemed unnatural, augmented by zenith perhaps. The king wore a fitted leather vest trimmed with silver filigree that exposed his chest and shoulders. An onyx scepter with symbols carved along the shaft rested in the crook of one arm, and a short sword was sheathed at his hip. The remaining black-sashed warriors took a knee and bowed their heads, but Tarkannen remained standing.

From overhead, the general shouted down into the arena. "Bow before the honor of Zsheck the krug rai'al, painted man!"

Tarkannen grunted once and tilted his head in respect to the king, but turned his attention to Havka. "I came seeking an audience to forge an alliance, but without any consideration for diplomacy, you tossed me into your arena to die. I am told the Kreeg respect strength, and you have witnessed but a fraction of mine. Address me casually and with disregard again at your peril, Havka."

The krug rai'al turned a questioning look back to his general. Havka's face darkened with a ruddy hue. "Your blood is not worthy to stain the holy sands upon which you stand!"

In the seconds that Havka bellowed, Tarkannen considered the myriad of methods he might employ to kill the man, but most of them involved a colossal detonation of his rage that would also kill many innocent dignitaries standing behind Havka. He settled on something more pragmatic, something the crowd could both relate to and witness, and drafted a single, four-foot-long shaft of nadir.

Without waiting for permission and seeking none, he hurled the onyx shard. The missile flickered through the air like a flash of lightning and speared Havka in the chest. The man grunted once in surprise, looked down at the black shaft embedded in his chest, then wore one last expression of befuddlement as the nadir vanished, leaving a hole burned through his torso. He collapsed without words.

The crowd gasped, and all through the arena, the hiss of swords rang out. Multiple gates lifted around the Dalkreeg and soldiers streamed forward to protect their king. Tarkannen waited and fingered his control of the ambient currents of nadir, finding security in the familiar way the power permeated his sigils.

Zsheck stepped forward and lifted his black scepter high in the air. Flickers of light, possibly zenith, flared along the shaft, and some property allowed him to magnify his voice. "Silence!" he boomed.

Though Tarkannen had long ago lost the ability to perceive the ambient currents of zenith, he realized the scepter resembled the fabrications of the Dernegians, and was likely the source of the man's parlor tricks. "Champions of the Nines, you honor all of Kreeg by your valor this day. Not since the days of my forefathers has the caligot been released. Tarkannen, is it? Your power is matched only by your restraint, for Havka's actions do not represent the ideals of Kreeg society. Warriors of Kreeg, sheath your weapons. I would have words with our guest."

The king turned and held his hands up, signaling the hundreds of soldiers to keep their distance. He lowered his scepter, dropping it back into the crook of his elbow, and spoke without the artificial amplification. "My scouts inform me you ride at the head of an army of beasts. What brings a man with such power at his command to my doorstep?"

"Your armies are a vast weapon poised to strike, but have no target upon which to vent their rage. Some of your generals whisper that the krug rai'al has failed to provide them with the opportunity to find the glory they spend their entire lives training for. I offer you a solution to these problems."

Zsheck's eyes narrowed. "You are remarkably well informed for one who has only been in my city but a day."

"The wise man prepares. I am not here as a conqueror, Zsheck. I came in person as a courtesy, something none in your kingdom have returned to me. My forces will either pass by Kreeg or, if need be, ride over it. You are not my enemy, and I have no cause to consider you so. An alliance could prove mutually beneficial."

"I am listening."

Tarkannen considered the man and the venue. Though he disdained theatrics, he understood that sometimes Volencia's machinations delivered results. "Grant me a boon as a champion of the Nines and amplify my voice. I would address your people this one time."

Zsheck looked around, considering the request, then shrugged as if the matter was of little consequence. He stepped close and lifted the scepter high overhead. "The champion of the Nines wishes to address the people of Kreeg. We will hear him on this day of days!"

Zsheck bowed once, and Tarkannen cleared his throat. "Mighty warriors of Kreeg. Stories of your might are not exaggerated. I have walked your streets, survived your Dalkreeg, and find your kingdom unrivaled on Karsk. You don't know it yet, but we share a common enemy. Far to the east, beyond your border kingdoms, the sorcerers of Aarindorn hide in their mountain kingdom and dabble with forces beyond their control. They have upset the natural balance, and a drought sweeps across the plains. Within a year, it will lead to the starvation of your people and all others across central Karsk unless we confront them and put an end to their black magic. I ride to put down this evil and invite Kreeg to all the spoils of war. What say you?"

B'vakla rose to her feet and stepped closer, lifting her fist into the air. "For the glory of Kreeg and the krug rai'al!" She drew out the last word, screaming for several seconds. When she took a breath, others joined her in chanting. "Krug rai'al, krug rai'al!"

In moments, the entire crowd joined in, repeating the chant, a deafening echo rising out from the arena. A gleam sparkled in Zsheck's eye and he tipped his head, shouting above the din, "It seems you have your answer!"

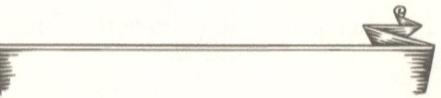

Chapter Thirty-Six: The Rite of Revealing

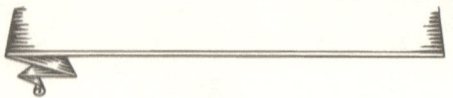

A young woman stood knee-deep in the shallows of the nameless river that cut through the Great Crown. Sunlight filtered through her light brown hair, accenting a hint of auburn that resembled her mother. She held a delicate fly rod in her right hand and swished the tip back and forth overhead, the susurrations creating a rhythm that cut through the tranquil air. The silky line billowed out, and she released the fly upstream.

She nibbled at her lower lip in silent concentration, waiting, biding her time. Mountain jays chirped in the distance, and a gentle breeze sifted through the green canopy, giving her line a bit more play. The fly drifted downstream without notice from the mountain trout. She allowed the lure to continue to float past for more than thirty paces before reeling in to begin the process again.

A dry twig snapped, and Boru's muzzle poked out from tall grasses on the bank. The first traces of silvery-white hairs peppered the edge of his snout and chin, but the wolvryn's eyes maintained a sharp, vigilant expression. Bryndor sat on the bank, watching his daughter practice her craft. He lifted the basket of fish, setting it to the side, and patted the grassy bank, welcoming his companion to sit down.

He walked his fingers through the fur behind Boru's ear. "You're losing your touch, old man. Times past, you would have snuck up on me. Did Kess send you to fetch us already?"

Boru dipped his chin, then swiveled his broad head, craning his neck back toward their home. Bryndor turned his attention back to the young woman. Already her arms flowed through the motions, gracefully arcing the line upstream and delivering the fly into the shallows.

He took it all in, her lean silhouette framed by the golden sun, the babbling water, the earthy scent of the mountain water cutting through the Great Crown. He set his mind to the deliberate task of framing the image, setting it in his memory. The solitude of the moment broke as a large trout flopped into the air and the woman squealed with delight.

The wolvryn huffed once, echoing her excitement, and Bryndor grunted against the protest of stiff muscles in his low back that ached from prolonged sitting. He retrieved a net and stepped beside her into the cool water, waiting. She played the trout with expert patience and he dipped the net under the fish.

He deftly removed the hook and held the fish by its lower lip, measuring it against his forearm. Faint ribbons of blue wove under a patina of silver scales. "Is that a king trout?" she asked, wonder accenting her question.

Bryndor opened the basket and removed one of the smaller mountain trout, holding them side by side for comparison. "It is! Nicely done, Ro."

He felt the gentle tug of zenith as she siphoned from the ambient currents and knew she employed a measure of her gift. She spooled out a bit of line in anticipation of another cast. "There are at least three more up there, in the eddy above those rocks."

Acting out of habit, he kindled zenith through the sagacious rune on his left forearm, weighing the possibilities, the pros and cons of whether to stay or go. He already knew the answer, but a little of the Giver's validation never hurt. After confirming his thoughts, he set the king trout in the basket, then hoisted the strap over his shoulder. "Leave them for another day. We've got plenty. Besides, your mother sent Boru to retrieve us, and if I've learned one thing in all our years, it's that you don't keep a good woman waiting."

Rona sighed. "This would all be a lot faster if you let me use the gift. I could probably charm them into the net. Moons, Dad, Uncle Llu told me how you two used rune fire once to shock a dozen of them up to the surface."

Bryndor nodded and struggled to master a grin, the memory rising to his awareness with clarity. "We had to feed two quads that night, and your uncle embellished that story like he always does. Besides, you know the rules up here."

Rona hopped out of the river and unrolled her pant legs before stomping her feet into a pair of worn boots. She dipped her chin and pitched her voice low, attempting to imitate her great-uncle, Kaellor Baellentrell. "Don't abuse your gifts. Take only what we need, and never more than the Giver grants. Save some for next time."

"That's a pretty good Uncle Kae," he had to admit.

As they walked up the winding path that led to their home, Rona continued to offer epithets while attempting to reproduce Kaellor's baritone. "Sometimes the Giver gives . . . keep your eyes to the horizon except when walking through a cow pasture, unless you want the Taker to sully your boots."

Bryndor chuckled out loud. "Uncle Kae never said that."

"Did too, only he said maybe not to repeat it around Great-Aunt Laryn."

"Alright, I stand corrected, that does sound like something from our time in the Southlands. What else have you got? Get them all out before we get home."

Rona considered for a moment. "Let's see, something to do with your days in the Bend." She cleared her throat. "Everybody gets weather, hoe when it's dry and pull when it's wet, and don't listen to the rector 'cause he's windy as a sack of farts."

That last one gave him cause to stop, set hands to his knees, and roar with laughter. He had to admit that in his age, Kaellor had lost some of his regard for courtly decorum. "Do not let your brother hear that one; not until he's your age, anyway."

"Why not?" she asked.

"If you honestly think he can keep that one under wraps, go for it, but I suspect your mother will track down the origins of that phrase and—"

Rona altered her voice in a perfect imitation of her mother. "Elbend Kae Baellentrell, since you like fart jokes so much, go muck out the stable with your bare hands, and Rona, since you saw fit to sully your brother's vocabulary, you can join him!"

Bryndor lurched sideways, bumping his hip into his daughter's to emphasize his point. "Exactly."

The path wound out of the woods and onto a rocky ledge that allowed a panoramic view of the kingdom as the sun dropped below the Great Crown. To the southeast, the towers of Stone's Grasp melted into a low-lying bank of clouds. The flowering herbal fields outside Callinora rippled like blue waves, and the Balladuren Aarindin herds kicked up dust on the plains below them. Rona stepped beside him and locked her fingers through his.

"Do you ever miss it?" she asked.

"I miss your great-aunt and uncle, and time with Uncle Llu. Sometimes I miss the food, but that's really about all, I think. Attending the assembly twice a year is more than enough exposure to the nobles in Stone's Grasp. Between the visits from the Luna Rova and trips to your mother's ranch, I hear enough about the world as it is."

"Are you ever sad that you don't get to be the king?"

"Moons, no. Abdicating the throne to your Great-Uncle Kae was the fifth best thing that ever happened to me."

Rona's head bent to the side. "Why fifth?"

"One was your mother. Two was you, and three your brother. Four was finding Boru," he said.

She leaned her head against his shoulder and looked up. "I wish another wolvryn would wander down from the mountains and give me a chance."

He winked at her. "You never know. Sometimes the Giver gives. Come on then, we're losing daylight, and these fish won't clean themselves."

A broad slab of mountain stone served as their front porch. Rona kicked off her boots and made her way inside. Bryndor sat to work at his laces, and the front door slammed open as Elbend hopped out to greet them. At the budding age of twelve, Elbend's curiosity had already landed him in more trouble than Bryndor and Lluthean combined had ever managed.

"How'd you do?" he asked.

Bryndor held the basket forward and lifted the lid for him to peek inside, then clapped it shut as the boy's nose drew near.

"Caught a king and two mountain trout," he answered.

"Giver's truth? A king? Can I see again?" pressed Elbend.

Bryndor removed the shoulder strap and set the basket down for his son to make a safe inspection. Elbend whistled, then appeared crestfallen. "Wish I could have been there."

"I know, son," said Bryndor. "Me too. But your mother still hasn't forgiven you for sleeping with those cave larks."

Elbend lifted a finger into the air. "Greater cave larks!"

"I stand corrected, greater cave larks. You're just lucky Boru found you before she did."

Elbend sat down, pulled his knees to his chest, crossed his arms, and bounced his chin on his kneecaps. Bryndor felt like he was looking into a mirror as the boy's straight black hair draped in front of his eyes. Somehow, the Giver saw fit to give the boy Bryndor's physical characteristics but Lluthean's penchant for causing trouble, and he loved his son for both qualities in equal measure.

Rona reappeared on the front porch. "Where is Mother, El?"

He pointed at the stable. "She thinks Winter is finally going to drop her foal. I filled the stall with fresh hay. They've been in there a while now."

"How long?" asked Bryndor.

Elbend shrugged. "A couple hours, at least."

Bryndor nibbled on the inside of his cheek. "Tell you what, fire the oven, then clean these and spice them like I showed you. Wrap a few yams in the sweet leaf and set them in the oven. Be sure to turn them every quarter hour or so. For the trout, use the herbs your mother likes. It's the only way she'll eat fish. They're in the blue tin beside the salt. Pick enough greens for a salad, and we'll see if she can be persuaded to lift your grounding."

Elbend frowned in concentration, as if calculating the task for the reward he might earn. "Giver's truth?"

Bryndor held his hands out, palms up. "Why would I lie, son?"

"Alright. Oven, yams, spice the fish and greens. Got it." Without further comment or complaint, Elbend hopped up, grabbed the basket of fish, and disappeared inside. Bryndor relaced his boots, stood, and stretched his back. "Keep an eye on your brother. I'm going to see if your mom needs a hand."

Bryndor grabbed a waterskin, then walked the short distance to the stable to find his wife standing knee-deep in fresh hay beside her Aarindin, massaging her flank. Both of them looked exhausted. Ksenia's hair was matted to her forehead, and Winter panted lightly.

"Oh, thank the Giver," said Ksenia.

Bryndor stepped inside and handed his wife the water. "What can I do?"

Ksenia tipped the skin up and took a long drink. "Rewind time and convince the two stubborn women standing in the stables not to walk down this road. Father warned us labor would be a challenge at her age."

At her words, Winter craned her neck around and chuffed. Experience had taught him something of the Aarindin's body language, and he understood the sound as a mixture of fatigue and agreement. He stepped behind Ksenia and massaged her shoulders for several minutes. Remnants of a wild vine that offered mild pain relief sat in Winter's trough, and he knew Ksenia would have already done everything to attend to the Aarindin's needs. So he stood in silent support.

Sometimes the simple act of being present was enough. Sometimes, it was all one could offer. He thought back to the times in his life when that simple truth had upended all of his motivations: the birth of his children or watching his brother survive a near-death illness under the ministrations of his aunt. Life was not always about taking action or fixing a problem; sometimes life was about simply showing up for the people that mattered.

"I wish I had Laryn's gift and could ease her labor. I would even settle for a visit from Ranika to remove her pain," she said.

She reached up and wrapped the fingers of each hand around his wrists, her touch warm as she wrung her grip around his forearms. He kissed the back of her head. "What is it?" he asked.

"Her water broke a few hours ago and I can't get her to lie down. She's as stubborn as I am sometimes."

Winter panted and grunted for several more minutes and eventually, the glistening forelegs and head of a foal presented at her backside. The albino Aarindin dipped her head against Ksenia's shoulder, and the two stood in silent communion for several long moments.

Ksenia walked to the horse's flank, and the mare nipped at her. "Grind it, Winter. Let me check."

He watched his wife. After only a moment, she quickstepped back and pressed her cheek to Winter's. "You are so close now. Push girl, push for all you're worth. Come on! Push, Winter!"

The Aarindin responded, huffed a few deep breaths and contracted, her muscular core quivering in place. Despite her labor, nothing changed, and the foal appeared lifeless, failing to advance.

"Can I help? Want me to?"

"Yes love, grab its legs and pull with her next contraction. Pull for all you're worth when I tell you to," said Ksenia.

Bryndor rolled up his shirtsleeves and grabbed at the ankles of the foal, finding them less slippery than he imagined. He found purchase when Ksenia yelled, "Now love, pull!"

Bryndor braced one leg behind himself and slowly eased all his weight back. They remained locked in place, Winter tremulous with all the effort of pushing and Bryndor pulling. His arms began to fatigue and grip weaken just as the foal seemed to cross over some internal resistance and slowly, with the inexorable drift of a glacier down the side of a mountain, the baby emerged.

He stumbled, and the delicate creature, as pale as its mother, spilled onto his lap with the remnants of the birth sac clinging to its backside. Surprisingly little fluid spilled, and he brushed bits of hay away from the foal's mouth. "Kess, it's done, she did it!"

The foal heaved its lungs and twitched its neck. Pink lashes blinked, and it opened eyes of crystal blue. Bryndor eased the foal off his lap and onto the hay just as Winter settled onto her flank, turning to be nose to nose with the little creature. The two sniffed at one another, and Winter licked its nose.

Bryndor studied his wife and became lost in the simplicity of her beauty. Sweat-matted brown hair flecked with auburn highlights framed a face with a patina of freckles across her nose and cheeks. The glint of her sympath rune peeked out along the top edge of her hip bone, showing flickers of zenith. Ksenia stood enthralled in the moment, as if she had just conceived and delivered her own child. Tears streamed down her cheeks, and she reached to haul him to his feet. "Come here, you."

With her help, he rose to his feet, his damp clothes sticking to his chest and thighs. She leaned in and pecked him on the cheek. Then, oblivious to the mess, embraced him. They stood, arms encircling each other and rocking side to side, watching Winter bond with her foal.

"Boy or girl?" he asked.

"Filly," said Ksenia. She craned her neck back and brushed the hair from his face. "You always come at the right time and do what needs doing, Baellentrell."

"*Balladur cor delledence*, right?"

She huffed a giggle and nodded. "True enough. Come on, let's get you cleaned up."

"Does she need us anymore?"

Ksenia nodded. "No. She knows what to do. I can check on her in a few hours."

They walked hand in hand back toward the house. Ksenia sniffed at the air. "I smell recompense."

"You're going to have to let the boy out of the house sometime. He's trying to bake his way to amends."

She sighed. "I know. What's he up to?"

"Dinner, if my nose has the right of it."

Boru trotted over and sniffed at the two of them, sneezed once, withdrew his head in revulsion, then trotted off.

Bryndor considered his soiled clothes. "I should clean up first."

A mischievous glint sparkled in Ksenia's eye. "If you heat the pool, I'll bring soap and towels."

"I'll see you there."

A short walk from the house, a stream of water trickled into a saucer-shaped depression in the mountain stone that created a pool of water large enough for two before brimming over the edge and splashing down the mountain as a gentle waterfall. The moon of Baellen would rise full and bright in the night sky, but only a sliver yet crested above the mountain peaks.

Bryndor wasted no time and stripped off his clothes. He waded into the icy waters and summoned rune fire, releasing it as a continuous, controlled flare and directing the current into the mountain stone. In moments, the pool steamed, and he lowered chest-deep into the water.

He eased his head back and closed his eyes. Minutes later, the sound of fresh clothes and towels dropped behind him. He turned in time to catch the naked silhouette of his wife sliding into the water.

"Ooooh, you did good, love."

"Far be it from me to refuse the suggestion of a good woman."

She arched a single eyebrow, a wicked expression playing across her face. "And what about . . . the provocative solicitation of a woman with something nefarious on her mind?"

"I suppose that would depend."

She dipped under the water and pulled her hair back, then swam to him, chest to chest, pulling herself up to straddle him. With her nose only inches from his, she spoke with a breathy voice. "On what would that depend, exactly?"

He swallowed once. "On how long it takes Elbend to burn the fish."

She pursed her lips, frowning, and shook her head from side to side. "Rona is overseeing dinner and knows not to rush things, love. For the next half hour, you're all mine."

"If I can last a half hour, then I suppose I am at your mercy."

"Mmmhmm." Her chin rose and fell in agreement.

She eased closer, her hips resting on his thighs, and tilted her head to the side. "Why, Prince Bryndorllean, it feels like you've been expecting me."

He kissed her and pulled her tight, relishing every touch of their pressed skin. The sound of their breaths rose with their ardor. She gasped for a breath and tugged at the hair on the back of his head. "Is the water too hot?" he asked.

"It's perfect." She returned his kiss, and they collapsed into the rhythm of their lovemaking. He lost himself in the subtle aroma of her fragrance, enhanced by the steam rising from the pool and the way her sighs carried him away. The only other sound came from the occasional splash of water lapping over the edge of the pool. When the full breadth of the blue moon shone over the mountain summit, they separated with laughter, and finally the soap found its way into the pool.

Ksenia lathered her hair and then dropped underwater, rising to spit a fountain of water in his face. "The water's getting chilly, lover."

He turned and released another flare of rune fire against the mountain stone, causing the water to bubble and roil. As he finished, she pressed herself against him, wrapping her arms and legs around his torso, her chin resting on his shoulder. She nibbled on his earlobe.

"Hungry?"

She sighed in his ear, the heat of her breath sending a fresh thrill down his neck and spine. "Yes. As much as I would love to remain here all night, we should probably go see what that boy of yours has accomplished."

They dried off and dressed, then embraced once more, standing at the pool's edge. A nimbus of light haloed Stone's Grasp to the southeast. Moonlight shone across the mountain valley with uncommon clarity. A soft rustle announced the arrival of Boru as he padded over to sit beside them. He moaned a low, melancholy howl across the horizon, and from somewhere across the valley, Neska returned his greeting.

Ksenia hugged him tight, then placed the bare palm of her hand against his chest, where his arca prime would have been if he had compelled his Rite of Revealing. "You didn't have to leave it all behind to choose this life, to choose me. But I'm sure glad you did."

"Every time, Kess. I would choose you every time."

She stepped back but held his hand. "I believe you. Come on, then, I'm famished."

They walked the familiar path back to their home, where Elbend, with not a little help from his sister, had set a perfect table. Herb-crusted fish steamed near a basket of fresh-baked bread, and bowls of salad greens and yams adorned the table. The boy had even managed to gather a fresh vase of wildflowers.

Elbend held the chair out for his mother, and Ksenia took her seat, allowing him to dote on her. He served her generous portions, and they settled in for a perfect evening. Any conversation dissipated as they filled their mouths with the savory food, but eventually Elbend couldn't resist.

"There is crownberry-brickle for desert?" he asked of no one in particular, but cast a sidelong glance at his mother.

Ksenia sat back in her chair and dabbed at her mouth. "It sounds wonderful, but maybe after this meal settles, El."

Elbend pushed his chair back and removed her plate, taking it the few steps into the kitchen area. Bryndor looked to Rona, who used her napkin to hide her smile, and he forced himself to chew on the inside of his mouth for fear of releasing a giggle. He turned his eyes to Ksenia, and she nodded once, understanding.

She waved a hand at their son. "Come here, El."

He walked over with a hesitant step and stood beside her, eyes downcast. She pulled him close and kissed the top of his head, using the fingers of one hand to finger-comb his hair from his face.

"What you've done here tonight is wonderful. If you can see to spending more time with this family and less time with smelly cave larks, I think we can lift your grounding. What do you say?"

He chewed the inside of his lip and bobbed his head up and down in agreement.

"Do you know why you were grounded, El?" asked Bryndor.

The boy sighed. "Because I never told you where I was going, and it took Boru to find me."

Ksenia grabbed his chin and brought his eyes up to meet hers. "I know you can speak to them, just like me. But it's important that you spend as much time with people as you do with the animals. Understand?"

He nodded again.

"Alright then, I should go check on Winter and her filly," said Ksenia.

"We'll get this, El and I. Ro, go with your mother, and when you get back, we'll have the brickle ready," said Bryndor.

Rona pushed her chair back and stretched her arms overhead. "You don't have to tell me twice."

Elbend stepped over to his sister and hugged her around the waist, then whispered in a stage voice, "Thanks for helping me tonight, Ro."

She ruffled his hair and joined Ksenia as they retreated to Winter's stable. Over the next half hour, Bryndor and his son divided the tasks of clearing the table, storing leftover foodstuffs, and cleaning the dishes. When they were done, Elbend removed a reed flute and sat on the porch chirping a merry melody.

Bryndor walked out to take in the night sky. The blue moon hovered so close and bright that stars were difficult to see except on the distant horizon. He stared at the moon's surface, noticing how cerulean currents flowed with mesmerizing lethargy across its surface.

In the corner of his eye, scintillating lights of zenith skittered across the surface of a full barrel of rainwater, reflecting the moon's silhouette. He stepped close and stared at the moon's reflection. The appearance of the moon rippled, and he saw the reflection of his face, only not his face. Gone was the hint of grey at the chin of his beard and the shallow crow's feet accenting his eyes. The face he gazed upon was that of his youth.

He stared at the image, thinking that the water must not offer a clear rendering, when he realized that their surroundings had fallen into complete stillness. Elbend tipped back on a chair, defying gravity and holding the flute in perfect stillness but making no sound. In the distance, Ksenia and Rona stood frozen in mid-step, exiting the stables hand in hand, mother and daughter sharing a laugh over a private joke.

Tension gathered between his shoulders and he siphoned on zenith, prepared to break the uncanny spell, when the face in the water spoke. "Bryndor, you have come to the end of your trial and now you must choose. Stay here in this idyllic place and live this life, or return to your station and complete the trial."

Bryndor grabbed the edges of the barrel, but the surface remained as clear and still as a mirror. "What? What is this? Who are you?"

The younger image of himself offered a soft smile. "I am a construct of the Rite of Revealing. The confrontation of your own image is the only way to enable you to see the truth of your situation. You must choose.

Inheriting the arca prime requires sacrifice. Stay and live this life here bereft of the full measure of the gift the Giver intended, or leave them behind and return now to embrace your destiny."

Bryndor's fingernails cracked as he gripped the barrel's edge. "What becomes of them, of my children, my wife?"

"I do not have those answers."

"Will they just think I disappeared? Will they—will they even know?"

"Those are not answers I can provide," said the reflection.

"Then . . . what happens to the real Kaellor and Lluthean if I stay here?"

"Again, those are not answers I can provide. I am just a construct. I can, however, give you this."

Memories of the last eighteen years arose, unbidden, in his mind. He relived his courtship and marriage to Ksenia, abdicating the throne to his uncle, the life they crafted in the mountains, and the births of their children. Between these major events, the countless precious moments that made up the magical fabric of domestic life eddied about in his mind.

Bryndor sobbed and dashed a fist into the water, but the image reformed. "Stop, stop, you're making it worse. I'll do it, I'll do it. Just stop and tell me what I have to do."

"When you are ready, make your choice. Let go of the barrel and remain here, or drop your head into the water and return."

Bryndor stood beyond the measure of time, wrestling with indecision. Stay and cherish the people he loved, or leave them and return to other people who loved him with equal measure. Stay . . . go . . . the scales of each life tipped gently back and forth in his mind, over and over. Eventually, Boru padded across the stone porch and looked into the pool, sniffing with curiosity, then startled back in revulsion or surprise.

He wondered at the wolvryn's odd behavior and the strangeness of his movements in this otherwise still and silent world. The realization pulled Bryndor from indecision. He wiped his nose on his sleeve, blinked away tears, and shook his head with disbelief at what he was about to do. "Can I at least tell them goodbye?"

"If you release the barrel, the trial is over and you will remain here," said the construct.

"Grind your grinding trial!"

Bryndor summoned rune fire in preparation to incinerate the barrel. The heat and pressure gathered along the runes at his shoulders, surging with an utter need for release. He wouldn't just release the barrel, he would annihilate the construct and everything it stood for. He took a breath and prepared to unleash his power when Boru licked his cheek.

He turned, and the wolvryn blinked once, tipped his nose to the water, then looked back expectantly. Bryndor held himself, primed for release, but the wolvryn stared back with knowing empathy. "How can they ask me to do this, Boru? It's too much, and it's so . . . absolutely wrong."

The wolvryn sat down beside him and lifted one massive paw to the barrel's edge. Eventually, Bryndor allowed his shoulders to sag and stifled his connection to zenith. Before he could torture himself with any more deliberation, he dunked his head into the pool and screamed.

He emptied his lungs, then tried to push back for another breath of air, but something anchored him in place, tugging at the tapestry of his runes. A blinding kaleidoscope of lights flooded his awareness, and he became weightless. His stomach lurched, and he propelled forward, landing with hands and knees on a solid stone floor.

He lifted his head, images of his family still careening through his mind. It took him some time to orient himself to the space, but eventually he realized that he was kneeling before the statue of Eldrek in the inner sanctum. Boru walked forward and met Neska in the center of the room. They stood nose to nose in silent reunion. Behind her, Lluthean rested on one knee, head bowed, one palm resting flat on the stone.

When his brother looked up, Bryndor was confronted anew with the realization of what he had left behind. He'd expected to meet eyes with Rona's adult Uncle Lluthean, not the youthful younger brother he had not seen for nearly two decades. And yet, despite his physical appearance, Lluthean appeared every bit as wrung out and bereft of joy as Bryndor felt.

Bryndor turned to survey the room, but beyond the wolvryn, they stood alone. "How long?" he rasped.

Lluthean held up one hand and signed, *"Peace, Bryn. Give me a moment."*

His brother breathed in through his nose and out through pursed lips, the action strangely invoking a moment of solitude in which Bryn took stock of their situation. When Llu spoke, his voice was ragged, as if from disuse. "I arrived but a moment before you."

"Not, not that. Do you remember? How long were you in the Revealing?"

Lluthean's lips drew to a thin line, and he shook his head. At last he spoke softly, seeming almost haunted by the revelation. "Too long."

Bryndor paced the room and realized that smooth stone covered the place where the large double doors should stand. He tapped a finger along the silver veining and received the familiar thrill of the castle wards Kaellor had erected when they first returned to Stone's Grasp.

"I think I was there nearly twenty years, Llu. Twenty years with them, and it's all gone. I had a family, named my oldest after Rona."

Lluthean nodded as if he understood. "I'm so sorry, Bryn. I . . . had a Rona in my time as well. I think I might still linger there were it not for Neska showing me the way back," said Lluthean.

Anger threatened to overtake him for all that he had sacrificed, and he summoned zenith, feeling it course over familiar runes . . . familiar runes and nothing else. He walked over to Lluthean and hoisted him up by the tunic. His brother stared at him in confusion but didn't resist his inspection as Bryndor ripped open his shirt, finding his brother's chest empty of any runes.

Bryndor cursed and tore open his own shirt, finding his chest just as bare. The naked absence caused tears to well up once again, and a hollow dread sucked at his core. Utter grief overwhelmed him, dropping him to his knees where he sobbed and shuddered with self-loathing and complete emptiness.

Eventually, Lluthean walked over and crouched down. His brother seemed oddly composed, calm even, and rested a hand on his shoulder. He left it there, massaging achy muscles and eventually pulling Bryndor into an embrace, offering comfort. They huddled together for time beyond measure until Bryndor looked up. Lluthean gave him a sad smile that spoke of understanding, of shared loss.

His brother lifted his chin. "Come then, Bryn. Lift your eyes to the horizon, brother. We're not done, and we didn't come through everything to quit now."

Chapter Thirty-Seven: Startling Revelations from Nivosh

I struggle to record the events of the past week and wonder if any of this should be documented, but there can be no greater danger than hiding from truth and reality. The Council of Elders met regarding the restriction of The Book of Seven Prophets. It was by a thin majority that the text remains in publication, though all known copies are to be stored in the archives at Stone's Grasp.

Against my warnings, it seems, several noble houses from the Lellendule, Endule, and Llentrell lines have attempted to trigger the rebirth of the Eidolon. Seeking higher status and power, I suspect, they have each secretly placed not one, but two family members into the same Rite of Revealing. I should have seen this, I suppose, given the recent attrition among the gifted, but those in power have ignored my warnings for over a decade now and seek my council only on rare occasions.

If only we had made better efforts to maintain open communication with the descendants of the 'fo sisters, perhaps we would better understand the words of prophecy. To this day, their children continue a nomadic existence as the Luna Rova and resist attempts to integrate with common society. My research has shown that those few left in Stone's Grasp with the gift of foresight and prophecy command but a limited version of what the founding sisters could manage.

I was additionally able to confirm that the process of selecting the Eidolon will require great sacrifice, indeed quite possibly the death of a sibling. I conveyed this information to Her Majesty, Queen Brekka. She has issued a strict edict that any future Revealings may only occur as solo endeavors, and yet I wonder how many lives, how much potential, was lost in attempts to force a prophecy that might not come to fruition for hundreds of years. May this folly be a warning to generations to come.

I record again the Abrogator Derivation, from The Book of Seven Prophets, lest it be lost or restricted: When the wild wolvryn scars the highborn one, the channelers of nadir will rise. The tethers that bind can leech or sustain. The chance for confluence emerges, but only from balance. The sundered bindings will unleash one who rules from the void. Seek the bearer who carries the burden, then look to reveal the Eidolon, but only after the sibling passes to the Drift. For a time shall come again when the forces of zenith and nadir are magnified into opposition. Hear me then: channel zenith to save the world or nadir to destroy it. Channel confluence to become the Eidolon reborn.

—The Tome of Nivosh, 75 PC, translated by Ksenia Balladuren

KSENIA SAT ALONE IN the inner sanctum, stunned by the revelations of her latest translation from *The Tome of Nivosh*. She and other instigators took turns waiting for the brothers to awaken from the Rite of Revealing, but after more than two weeks, neither had emerged from the process. In her lifetime, she had never heard of a trial taking so long to complete.

The realization, along with the discoveries from her recent translation work, threatened to overwhelm her ability to synthesize the text. The sound of her zeniscrawl hitting the floor echoed in the room as she clenched her fingers around her wrist, desperate for a new interpretation. A cold perspiration gathered on her chest and the small of her back as she severed her connection to zenith with frantic intent. Her linguist rune fell dormant, and she labored to master her breathing, then began translating again, feeling the weight of the words as they synchronized into the same unmistakable pattern.

"Oh Giver, Bryn. What have we done?" She spoke the words out loud, and in the same breath, her brother's voice echoed in her mind. *The Giver can be a tricky bitch.*

Tricky indeed. Self-recrimination occupied her mind as she realized that an earlier translation of *The Tome of Nivosh* might have prevented the danger the brothers now shared. The doors to the inner sanctum opened and Karragin walked in, the downy riftwing perched on her shoulder.

The Mirrare sat down beside her and studied the room. A latticework of delicate fibers of zenith covered each brother and their wolvryn in broad cocoons. They remained in companionable silence and Ksenia carried out one final translation of the ancient writing, releasing a sigh when she came to the identical outcome.

"Ever since finding Iska, I've been delighted to rediscover all sorts of sounds. Sounds and speech. But that particular sigh gives me pause. Care to explain?" asked Karragin.

"I've been working on translating an ancient text for your father. *The Tome of Nivosh* was recorded by Nivosh Baellentrell. She was a daughter of Eldrek Baellentrell and the 'fo, one of the original founders of Stone's Grasp. She recorded this late in life. It's one part diary and one part historical record. I just finished this today."

Ksenia placed the paper on Karragin's lap and waited for her friend to read through the translation. Karragin's relaxed posture shifted to one of vigilant awareness as she read, then reread, the words. "And you are certain of the authenticity of this?" she asked.

"Yes. It's authentic and accurate. I have a friend in the archives, Veeble. He's something of a savant with symbols. I think the work is actually pretty easy for him, but he still takes great pains to record the symbols and check their accuracy before giving them to me. I translate the words, then return the work to him to collate. It's a strange system, but it allows me the freedom to work outside of the archives."

"Have you shown this to anyone else yet?" she asked.

Ksenia rolled her left wrist back and forth inside the grip of her right hand, attempting to collect her thoughts and dissipate her sense of dread with a full breath. "You're the first. I thought if I relaxed and tried again, maybe I would find a different meaning to the words, but every time I engage my linguist rune, I end up with the same result."

"How do you want to proceed?" asked Karragin.

"What do you mean?"

Karragin turned to face her for the first time, and a softer expression eased onto her face. "Bryn loves you, Kess. And it's plain to see you feel the same. None of this is easy, the waiting and now this," she said, and waved the paper in the air. "It's a lot. If you need, I can be there when you tell everyone else. We can go about things however you want, but they need to know, and as soon as possible."

Ksenia knew she was right and nodded her head in agreement. "We should probably tell your father, Kaellor, and Laryn first, don't you think? Maybe call them down with the shek?"

Karragin bobbed her head. "The problem with the shek is that you never really know who else might be listening. Better that I gather them in person. It's late afternoon already. I imagine I can have them here in a few hours, if you can stand to wait until then?"

"Yes, that would be good, I think."

Karragin bobbed her head once. "Right then." She held her wrist forward to Iska, and the hawk climbed on, then hopped over to Ksenia's knee. "Careful Iska, go easy."

Ksenia studied the creature, surprised by its weight. Iska settled onto Ksenia's knee and flapped her wings, releasing a few downy feathers. In the weeks since hatching, she had shed much of her downy coat. Silvery-white feathers edged with a subtle blue sheen now complemented alert, blue eyes. Where before, Iska's eyes appeared dark, the pigments had matured and seemed to swirl with pigments of zenith. A sharp white beak edged with the same blue pigmentation tapered to a dark point.

"She likes you. Go ahead and run a finger over her head. She won't bite."

Ksenia lifted her hand and Iska ducked her head, then leaned into the caress. When Ksenia's hand ran along the creature's back, she flared her crest of head feathers.

"I think she knows you're a sympath. She doesn't do that for anyone else but me," said Karragin.

Ksenia allowed herself the freedom to marvel at the creature's intricate silvery scales, the pigments of her eyes, and the way Iska tipped her head as if considering Ksenia in equal measure. "Sometimes the Giver gives."

"Well, the Giver and Neska with a little help from Llu, I suppose," said Karragin.

"If anyone ever doubted the brilliance of the Giver, all they need to do is spend but a moment with Iska," said Ksenia. "How long until she can fly?"

"The falconer doesn't know. She's already exceeded all of his predictions. But at this rate, he thinks another week, two at the most."

Karragin held out her wrist, and Iska hopped off Ksenia's knee to resume her perch on Karragin's shoulder. "I intended to relieve you from the obligation of watching. As it is, I can likely round up Father, Laryn, and Kae faster than you. So, will you be alright until I return with them in a few hours?"

"Yes, thanks. I can wait until then."

She watched Karragin leave, then walked around the zentrists. Currents of zenith wove in listless flows and prevented her from seeing either brother with any clarity. "Giver, if only there was a way to warn you, both of you."

A thought rose to her awareness, and she ignited her sympath rune, casting out her awareness in search of the wolvryn. There was a faint, familiar reverberation through her link, just enough to sense Boru's presence. But after several minutes of focused intensity, she realized that either her gift failed to penetrate the construct of the Rite of Revealing, or some property of the zentrist prevented the wolvryn from responding to her pleas.

She stood by the edge of the reflecting pool and lost herself in the swirling currents of zenith. Not for the first time, she wondered how deep the pool ran. Certainly, it extended far beyond the range of her sight. It was taboo to treat the pool with anything short of reverence and yet still, she had to resist the urge to dive in and seek the bottom, if there even was one. Maybe that action would allow her to warn either of the brothers, maybe it would disrupt the ritual and bring them back, or maybe it would end in disaster.

An odd restlessness took up residence in her mind, preventing her from concentrating on solutions. Eventually, she resumed a slow pace around the hall. The fourth time she walked past the statue of Eldrek, she made herself reread the inscription at the base. "*Balladur cor delledence.*"

Therek had told her once that he thought it meant, "without condition, wield your greatest power," but after mastering the subtleties of High Aarindorian, she felt certain it meant something else: unconditional love wields the greatest power. The truth of the words both elated and shattered her, because a part of her understood, like never before, what they meant.

"If only there was some way for my love to tip the scales in your favor, Bryn."

The doors swung open and Karragin ushered Therek, Kaellor, and Laryn inside. Therek took a seat, panting lightly. The whirring hum of Laryn's healer gift filled the chamber as she assessed the integrity of the cocoons. Kaellor waited expectantly for his wife to finish her survey.

After a few minutes, Laryn stilled her gift and gave Kaellor a reassuring nod. "Nothing seems out of the ordinary, beyond the wolvryn, of course."

"You were rather cryptic, my dear," said Therek. "Care to explain why we are gathered here?"

Karragin retrieved the translated papers Ksenia had left on a bench and handed them to Kaellor, then stepped beside Ksenia. "Kess made a discovery of significant import. Kess?"

Ksenia took a deep breath. "I've been making regular progress through *The Tome of Nivosh*, and only just today translated the pages you hold. I found the text troubling, so I suspended my gift and tried to . . . arrive at different words. But every time, I arrived at the same conclusion."

Worry pressed down on Therek's wispy brows and he stepped to Kaellor's left shoulder while Laryn stepped to his right. Together, they read the words recorded by Nivosh hundreds of years ago.

"Taker's breath, what have we done?" whispered Kaellor.

"I don't understand how knowledge of this was withheld. Why wouldn't our ancestors codify something like this to prevent unnecessary risks?" asked Laryn.

Therek deflated onto a bench. "I can imagine that they tried to. To my knowledge, only a few copies of *The Book of Seven Prophets* exist. Far better to bury the truth than admit such an embarrassing and tragic loss of life. Especially given the nefarious motives and the high families involved."

"Therek, is there any way to contact them, to warn them?" pressed Kaellor.

"Not to my knowledge. I know that you already tried the shek." Therek nodded with appreciation. "That was smart, actually."

"I couldn't reach the wolvryn either, with my sympath abilities," Ksenia added.

"Iska can sense that they are both alive, all four of them actually, but I can't get a message out through her," said Karragin.

Kaellor sighed. "It's of small consequence, I suppose. We have no idea what they are facing and any warning we might send would likely only make their trial more difficult."

He squatted beside Bryndor's zentrist and ran the flat of his palm over the construct before resting his forehead against the magical barrier. The pressure of his touch caused zenith to swirl in wisps of indigo and cerulean until he leaned back. "What happens if we suspend the trial, sever their connection to zenith?"

"I would not recommend it, Kae," said Therek. "Once begun, the definitions of the trial are shaped by the runes on Eldrek's statue. Hundreds of years of study have taught us that the complex mechanics are well beyond anything we understand. For all we know, stopping the trial could cause the death of both of them."

Ksenia stammered and took a lurching step forward. "I . . . I should give the papers to Veeble. Perhaps I've made a mistake. And while he checks my work, we could send for my mother. She could try to reach the wolvryn with her abilities. The sympath rune is her arca prime," said Ksenia. "Anything we can do, name it, I'll do it. Just tell me what to do."

Tears spilled down her cheeks as she pleaded with each of them. At last, Kaellor sighed and stood. Something in his bearing shifted. He walked over and took her hand between his. "Your work is sound, Kess. Don't let fear give you doubts. I recognize every word from the Abrogator Derivation. There is no need to question the accuracy of your translation. I'm sorry, but sometimes the hardest thing to do, is nothing."

Laryn rubbed her back in sympathy. "We have to place our trust in the what the Giver bestowed on them, all of them, together. Think of all that they accomplished before they inherited their gift. Words penned by a scholar hundreds of years ago won't be able to stop them from returning to us."

Ksenia wiped at her tears. "I keep trying to tell myself the same, but it's Nivosh, a daughter of Eldrek. And . . . I can't get past it."

Kaellor shook her shoulder, a soft gesture meant to convey confidence. "We are all Eldrek's children in one way or another. I think Laryn has the right of it, Kess. I'm confident that whatever the Taker sets before them, the Giver will see them through. Besides, I doubt anything in there has had to tangle with a wolvryn before."

"So we just . . . continue to wait, then? Watch and wait?" she asked.

"It's all we can do, I'm afraid. But from now on, we'll continue to share the burden. Things like this are always managed better together," said Kaellor, and he pulled her into a warm embrace.

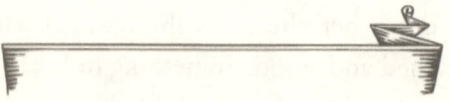

Chapter Thirty-Eight: Drifting

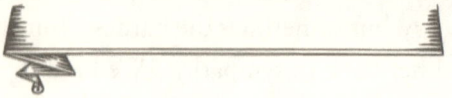

Lluthean remained a comforting presence at Bryndor's side. The transition had left his older brother shaken by all he had been and everything they had left behind. He studied Bryndor's face, absent the scars of time and wisdom of experience. In Lluthean's version of the Revealing, Bryndor had been King Baellentrell, the unifier. There was no conflict in Aarindorn he could not mollify, and nothing undermined the king's steadfast and compassionate rule. But now, as the silence drew out, it became clear that Bryndor needed time to reckon with everything that had changed.

If Lluthean had been ripped from his . . . experience after only twenty years, he would likely be equally broken. But something about being removed in the twilight of his life gave him a different perspective. As Bryndor worked his way through the vast chasm of loss, Lluthean thought back to the decades, the lifetime he had spent in the Rite of Revealing. And for the entire experience, he felt a sense of peace and gratitude.

Is that all it was? An experience? Giver, if I knew then what I know now . . . I wonder, when we come out on the other side of this thing, if all of it will be erased from our memories.

Neska padded over and sniffed at his ear. He turned to embrace her, taking a moment to stare into the depths of her zenith-laden eyes. Before arriving in this room, her fur had faded to that of a ghost, and age had withered some of her muscular frame. But now the wolvryn moved with agile grace. A vibrant silvery coat of fur framed a youthful jaw. He signed to her, a test to see if she recalled as much from the experience as he did, *"Did you always know? Were any of them real to you?"*

In answer, she tilted her head to the side and then lifted her nose, her sign of affirmation. Lluthean ruffled the fur behind her ears. "The Giver saw fit to bond us together, but didn't think to imbue me with a sympath rune. No justice for the wicked, I suppose."

He huffed a laugh at the youthful timbre of his voice. When he was propelled through the Revealing and back into the inner sanctum, he'd half expected his arthritic knees to shatter on impact and for his raspy voice to barely fill the chamber. He clenched fists, happy to discover the regression of a lifetime of wear and tear, then reached up to his face, surprised by the absence of spectacles.

The wonder of the discovery caused him to turn in place, ready to share the revelation. Bryndor remained on his knees, eyes vacant and distant. His heart ached to rescue his brother from the depths of that kind of despair. But if he had learned anything in his trial, it was the value of patience. And even more, he knew that processing grief, weighing loss, and finding a sense of closure were not things he could rush.

He sat down cross-legged beside the reflecting pool and practiced the meditative breath work that his wife had taught him in his version of the Revealing. Five seconds in through the nose, then ten seconds out through pursed lips. His senses cast out, gaining a better understanding of their isolation. He smelled the wolvryn and his brother and heard their breathing, but the chamber seemed empty of anything else.

Memories of the extended family he had left behind tumbled in his mind, and he knew that if they persisted beyond his own imaginings, they would be fine. *They are fine.* And in that moment, instead of despair, he offered thanks to the Giver for the moment of solitude. "And for second chances," he said aloud.

The stone floor felt cold against his flat palms, but connecting to the resolute surface failed to ground him further in the meditative trance. Instead, his fingers traced etchings, symbols carved into the surface. Shifting his weight back, he discovered an inscription. Standing up, he followed the words around the edge of the pool.

"Every journey begins with a single step. If a single sacrifice can yield miracles, what of the force of unconditional love? Choose wisely, but know that when two gifted enter, only one may depart. Channel zenith to save the world or nadir to destroy it. Channel confluence to become the Eidolon reborn."

Lluthean walked the perimeter, mulling the phrases over in his mind. Neska set her head on the top of his shoulder, her tail wagging enough that he felt the rhythm of her body through their touch. Her muscles tensed as if she meant to leap into the pool, and her breath quickened, eyes focused on something unseen.

He placed his hand between her shoulder blades and synchronized his breaths to hers, feeling his senses melt into her perception. He became intimately aware of the limited stimulus of the inner sanctum: his brother's shallow breathing, the musky scent of the wolvryn. Gazing into the reflecting pool revealed lazy currents of zenith swirling in boundless depths. But he sensed that Neska perceived something more, something beyond even their shared perception.

"Every journey begins with a single step." *How much faith are we supposed to place in this trial? Wasn't the return trip enough of a test?*

He puzzled over the meaning of the words from the inscription, repeating them mentally and waiting for the enlightenment of some logical path forward, but no simple action came to mind.

"This feels like something Lluthean the monk would do, not Grampa Llu," he muttered to Neska. "What's the worst thing that can happen? We get a little wet?"

The wolvryn seemed oblivious to his angst and remained poised to leap into the water. He found comfort in their connection and sighed, then stepped out into the pool, feeling surprised when his foot met resistance. It felt a little like standing on a frozen pond in the dead of winter. There was a subtle give to the surface, but also the sense of depth beyond his ability to break through.

The words from the inscription around the pool circulated in his mind, and he dwelled on the notions of sacrifice and unconditional love, and what those concepts meant to him. A glance over his shoulder showed that Bryndor remained oblivious to his movements. He didn't like the ominous portent, and whispered to himself, "When two gifted enter, only one may depart. And so, what if only one gifted enters?"

Channel zenith to save the world. Lluthean separated from Neska's senses and reached out to the ambient currents. The wolvryn stood beside him and stared down into the pool, tail wagging. She looked up to him once, as if waiting for a fish to swim up from the darkness.

As soon as he allowed the flows of zenith to filter through his runes, the surface of the reflecting pool shifted beneath his feet. Where before he gazed upon a glassy barrier over delicate flows of zenith, now a vast, empty blackness opened up. Terror swelled as an unwelcome tide threatening to overwhelm his senses. The shearing, ripping sound of nadir streaming into the void drowned out any other sounds from the room, and he was reminded of standing before the portal in the basement of Callinora when the umbral had beckoned him to step inside.

He sank slowly into the murky depths. An ice-cold vise gripped at his legs. One of his hands gripped Neska's fur, and the other flailed out to grasp the side of the pool. For a moment, his fingers found purchase, and he tried to pull himself free, but something inexorable tugged at him, pulling him farther into the void. When he lifted a leg, it felt like painful wires were searing into his flesh wherever his runes lay.

In a gasp of panicked pain, he stopped channeling and released Neska's fur. She plummeted like a rock tossed into water, sliding down without resistance. Her silent and abrupt departure left him reeling. What had he done, and how could he get her back? He attempted to claw through the pool, waving frantically in hopes of discovering her fur, a paw, anything to indicate that she was still with him.

The searing, biting cold leeched up into his core. He thought to release a blast of rune fire to break free from the trap. With an effort, he siphoned on the flows of zenith, but as soon as he primed the runes, his entire body lurched down, propelled into the shadows.

IMMENSE AND ALL-CONSUMING pressure, cold and biting, caused Lluthean's breath to seize, stinging his face, torso, and limbs all at once with disorienting agony. The faint scent of decay filled his nostrils, but he refused to draw a breath, the experience reminiscent of sinking to the bottom of the Shelwyn River. There was even the sensation of being tumbled along by an unseen current.

His heart began to hammer inside his chest, and a starburst of scintillating lights sparkled in the periphery of his vision. A cascade of urgency mounted inside him as he clenched his mouth, refusing to draw breath. At last, when the burning need to breathe overwhelmed him, Lluthean unclenched his jaw to scream. Instead of the sweet relief of air, something palpable and slimy invaded his mouth, worming its way inside him with the rancid taste of decay and filling his chest with more of the stinging agony.

In the periphery of his awareness, the last vestiges of zenith slid from his control, and with it, he felt himself give up and accept what felt like an inevitable death. Would it really be so bad? He hovered at the precipice now, and in a moment longer, there would be no pain, no absence, no loss.

He fluttered a hand to feel the wispy currents of zenith one last time, and something warm and vaguely familiar clutched at his wrist. A ripple of zenith flared, a nimbus of blue light revealing Neska soft-mouthing his forearm.

In the instant of their connection, the oily black currents leeched away, receding beyond the halo of light that gathered around them. The unrelenting and pervasive weight of the atmosphere shifted, the biting cold dissipated, and together they floated, hovering in an eddy of zenith.

Lluthean reached out and siphoned a trickle of the constructive force, enough to prime his runes, and realized that he felt no compulsion to draw breath. The discovery was unsettling, and he removed his forearm from Neska's jaw to check his own pulse. At the moment their connection severed, the black currents of the void rushed back in a torrential deluge to claim him.

Instinctively, he grabbed her foreleg and then wrapped his arms around her flank. Once again, the reductive substance seeped back into the shadows beyond the scope of his vision.

It's nadir, that has to be nadir. And we are in the Drift, not dead, but not entirely alive either, just . . . drifting.

Lluthean migrated his fingers through Neska's fur and found he could pull himself, weightless, to straddle her back. They lingered in that position, Neska standing or floating and him lying prone, unwilling to allow any separation between them and fearful of the sense of isolation and loneliness. He remained content to hover there with her, drifting in the place between places until a maternal voice broke into his awareness.

"My Lluthean. Are you ready?"

Lingering there, in the emptiness of the void, surrounded by an ocean of nadir waiting to consume him, a connection he had sought for years buoyed his courage and sharpened his focus.

"Neska? How?"

"In this place, you call it the Drift, the barriers between us erode. In this place, my Lluthean, we are nearly one. We have been this close before."

"I don't remember being anywhere near anything like this."

"When we first arrived at the Valley of the Cloud Walkers, you hovered near this place. I tried to guide you back, but Laryn returned you to me."

He slid forward across her back and pressed his cheek to hers. "Nes, you are a blessing of the Giver, the Taker, and all the Seven in the South."

"Yes, I am. But then, this is what we are to one another."

If he felt surprised by her command of language, her ability to convey humor and emotion left him too amazed to form cohesive thoughts.

As if in answer to his befuddlement, her voice resonated in his mind. *"One cannot live a lifetime in your company without picking up a few things."*

At that he barked a laugh. "I suppose that's true enough."

He considered their situation, the way they arrived, and his utter relief at having someone to confide in. "This whole thing, the Rite of Revealing, it's madness. First, the sacrifices required, and then this one-way trip to the Drift. If we find the grinder responsible for all of this somewhere in here, we're going to have more than words."

Neska remained silent for a time, and he realized he couldn't discern if the silence had stretched out for a few seconds or an hour. In the moment of that revelation, he also understood that he didn't seem to care. Her voice lifted him from dwelling on the unnerving uncertainties. *"I knew it was not real. That is why I never mated."*

"So, none of them, not even the grandchildren, were real?"

"Your love for them was real, your investment was real. The world inside the Rite of Revealing was almost real, but the creatures there had no depth, no—"

"No soul." He pushed to a sitting position and stared at the vast emptiness around them.

His last words lingered, and he relived key moments from the Revealing, trying to dissect the memory and see where he had been so misled.

"Why do you cause yourself such pain?" she asked.

"I don't know. If you could tell it wasn't real, it seems like I should have been able to as well."

"You misunderstand, my Lluthean. It was not real to me, but it was very real to you."

"Is that why you waited so long to show me the way? You pulled me over to stare down into that well, and that's when I was confronted with the choice. Without you, I would probably still be there."

"Yes. You were not ready to make the right choice before that day."

"Moons, Nes. You waited over sixty years for me to, what? Mature? Figure myself out?"

"I waited for you to feel free to choose. Before that time, you would have remained. By the end, you knew they would be fine without you. I am sorry, my Lluthean, for taking that peace from you, but there are things you must do."

For the first time since orienting himself in the Drift, his shoulders felt heavy, and he seemed to sag into her. "I have so many questions, but I don't know where to begin. Do you know if we can return, and if so how? How do we get back?"

"No. I do not know these answers, but I can still sense Boru. I can still sense our pack."

"Alright, that seems like a good thing. Can you tell how long we've been in here? Is it days, or months?"

"I do not know."

"So it's not just me then." He spread his fingers apart and combed through the fur on her back, hoping some idea would manifest in his mind, but his thoughts seemed to always wander back to the Revealing and everything he had left behind. Eventually, a sense of self-loathing returned. "I'm sorry. If the words around the reflecting pool simply said 'beware, this is a portal to the Drift,' I never would have taken that first step. How did anyone think Bryn and I would survive in this place?"

"Your shared connection, I suspect, would have enabled you to survive for a time."

"I don't know. I would rather cross back over the Korjinth. At least then we had some idea about the variables or direction."

"Why are we doing any of this? What is it all for?" Neska asked.

"I'm trying to remember, but I keep getting lost in the other life. It feels like it all started, like . . . like it was a long time ago."

"It was, and it was not. Before Boru and I awakened, we lived only in the present moment. Can you do that?"

"I can try." He began sifting back through the years of memories, before children, before marriage, but every memory threatened to mislead him into convoluted and tangential mental corridors.

What would Bryndor do? The question brought the image of his broken brother to mind, slumped on the floor of the inner sanctum. Concentrating on that image felt right, and somehow, he could see the dividing line between that real life and the construction of the Rite of Revealing.

He focused on Bryndor's youthful face and his brother's anger as he wallowed in the grief of all that he had given up, then the way he'd torn open Lluthean's shirt, and his mind settled into focus. "It's no easy thing, trying to live only in the present. It feels wrong to abandon everything we did there, but I understand. It's for the arca prime. We're in a test. This whole thing is a test to see if we're worthy of bearing that kind of power."

"I can sense the source of your power in the currents of the Drift. Perhaps if we search out those distant stars," said Neska.

"You can see stars? Where?"

A maternal sigh rippled through their conversation. *"Don't be a monk; attune to me."*

"Grind it. Sorry." He began the mental task of attuning to her senses, but found the connection elusive without the ability to focus on their breathing, the synchrony of their heartbeats.

"All these years and you still haven't figured it out?" she asked.

"I'm trying. It's not easy here. You aren't even breathing. That's how I start. Old habits, you know?"

"It was never about the breath. You assume, when we attune, that I give something to you, but my Lluthean, it is you who gives something of yourself to me. Forget about the breath. Still your mind and send me a push."

"A push?"

Neska growled. *"That's what Boru calls it. Send me a bit of zenith and keep the connection open. I can do the rest in this place."*

Now that he thought about it, her explanation felt so obvious and natural that he wondered how he had never realized before that simply connecting a current of zenith to her triggered their shared senses. He drafted a small current, ushering the flow into her, and in an instant, a miasma of lights flared all around them.

"Now you see? Stars."

Lluthean craned his neck, and the countless lights shimmered not only above but beside, below, ahead, and behind—an ocean of stars unmoored from any sky. They pulsed faintly, like lanterns glimpsed through deep water, yet offered no warmth. The currents of the Drift brushed against him with a sterile hush, stripped of the rustle of leaves, the murmur of voices, or salt tang of the sea.

Beyond Neska's voice in his mind, absolute silence pressed against his ears, a void where even the echo of his voice refused to dwell. The air carried no tang of smoke, no sweetness of blossom, only the pallid neutrality of nothingness.

He shivered, but gratitude for Neska's presence displaced any fear. "How do we get a sense of direction in this place?"

He sensed by the drifting pattern of lights that she allowed herself to tip forward. His stomach lurched until she brought their rotation to a stop. *"There, in front of my nose, that distant star, the blue one."*

"How do we get there?" he asked.

"I'm not sure."

REVEALING THE ARCA PRIME

Lluthean strained his senses, casting out his enhanced awareness. Barely discernable amidst the myriad of brighter stars, a blue light twinkled. He brought his entire focus to bear on the phenomenon and willed them closer. At first, nothing changed, but vaguely, in his peripheral vision, he understood that many of the stars passed around them, some diverting to the side, others above or below. Soft and wispy currents, like silky ash flowing against his skin, gave him the vague sensation of movement.

"It's working. Whatever you are doing is working," said Neska.

Out of curiosity he scanned to the side, wondering at the source of the lights or stars. All at once, the patina of lights froze in place, indicating that their progress had stalled. "I lost it, Neska. Can you sense where the blue star went?"

Before she could respond, an amorphous, oily black cloud rippled in the shadowy void in front of them, obscuring some of the distant lights. As it approached, a myriad of eyes sprouted within it. Lluthean primed his rune fire, and the creature blinked a rapid succession of misshapen globes, then dissipated, fading from view.

"What just happened?" he asked.

"We . . . drifted into a different current. The spirits of the dead from our world and others migrate through the Drift. You need to move us before—"

Below them, a strange vacuum sensation tugged at Lluthean's awareness, and he leaned out to look below Neska. A roiling mass of something resembling a serpent, coiling in and out of itself, blossomed into being. As it approached, a central circular maw opened and closed, pulsing with the rhythm of its muscular undulations.

An acrid odor permeated the space between them, so strong it stung his eyes. Lluthean released a surge of rune fire, a controlled burst that allowed him to rapidly re-prime his gift. The detonation caused the creature to burst apart, but he sensed it also hurtled them backward as the stars and lights streaked by them.

When they came to a stop, he sensed movement all around them. From every direction, shifting shadows obscured the distant stars. The denizens of the Drift raised their voices in a collective shriek, paralyzing him in a moment of awe-inspired fear.

Neska's voice broke into his consciousness, an unmistakable sense of urgency affecting her tone. *"They're everywhere, closing in. Fix yourself on something, a distant star, anything. Pick one and bring us to it. Now!"*

Lluthean startled to action and released three different globes of rune fire, sending them to the farthest reaches of his awareness. The years in the Revealing had taught him how to compress a globe of rune fire, send it on a trajectory, and cause its detonation by releasing the constriction. The creatures of shadow gave chase, crisscrossing in the streamers left behind by the globes.

There was no rumble of thunder, no reverberation or gust of wind, but mixed among the shimmering lights, three separate bursts of cerulean blue rune fire erupted in the Drift.

"I think I bought us a chance!" He picked out a point of light brighter than the others. Against the wailing and shrieking, he concentrated. With painfully gradual progress, they seemed to migrate through the voids, the susurrations of the current against his ears imparting a sense of movement. The screams faded to echoes, and the echoes faded to sighs. In what he could only discern as a strange flicker of brief moments, they arrived before the bright star and hovered at the outer edge of a spiral corona of light.

Neska's voice eased into his mind. *"We should be safe here. Whatever gives rise to this also manifests zenith. Whatever you do, do not lose our connection here. I don't think I could find your essence among so much life."*

"I'm not sure I understand."

"Before, when I found you, your zenith was a beacon in the darkness. I think that's why your release of rune fire attracted so much attention. But here, close to this, we are but raindrops in the sea."

"If this isn't a star, if it's alive or emitting zenith, what exactly is it?" he asked.

Neska had no answers, and he willed them to hover about the spiral, finding it at once immensely massive and inconceivably convoluted. As they approached, the arms of the spiral extended beyond his awareness, which struck him as odd since he remembered seeing it from a distance.

With caution, Lluthean willed them closer, and he discovered that a fine glittering dust flowed in lazy currents, emitting light and constituting the substance of the spiral. Some of the curves seemed impossibly dense, while others tapered to paper-thin concentric rings.

Sensing no danger, they floated closer. A stream of glittering particles formed a thin tentacle that undulated toward them, probing, searching. From the leading edge of the tentacle, a single grain of the crystalline dust popped free and burst. A creature with two sets of delicate wings appeared, shedding a faint aura of the same light that had birthed it.

Vertical rows of eyes lined all sides of an oblong head that tapered into a tubular body. The creature waved delicate, jointed arms about its body and seemed to use the limbs, more than its wings, to direct its circular migration around them.

"What do you make of it?" he asked.

"I think I understand. This is the remnant of something that once lived. All of these particles of light are just how we see those who have crossed over. But their world is not our world."

The creature twirled in a tight circle and waved its arms in a beckoning motion, leading them away from the spiral of light. "What do you think? Should we follow?"

"Yes," said Neska.

Lluthean willed them closer to the creature, and it flitted in a lazy spiral. In moments, the eternal black void of the Drift reappeared, punctuated by countless points of light. The creature led them past worlds with unique and varied shapes. Some appeared like the brilliant spiral, composed of currents and particles of light. Others possessed a mixture of ribbons of nadir intertwined with zenith. And as they navigated through the Drift, he came to appreciate that where no points of light existed, there must be whole worlds composed of unopposed nadir.

Abruptly, a new beacon of blue light manifested in his awareness. The creature leading them through the currents of the Drift paused, arms waving toward the blue light.

"There. Take us there. The resonance of zenith is familiar," said Neska.

Lluthean willed them closer, leaving the winged creature behind. For an immeasurable span of time, the beacon seemed unchanged, and just as he began to wonder about its distance, a brilliant sphere of blue particles erupted before them. The outer corona held loose clouds of particles that created a light blue haze. He could see that if they continued toward the center, the material condensed into darker hues of blue, reflecting the concentrations of zenith permeating the region.

The particles before them began to swirl and eddy with rising frenetic activity. In a burst of light, an expansive field with long grasses sprang up before them, ringed in the distance by the shadow of mountains. Iridescent crystals floated by and popped, some exploding into butterflies or birds, others giving rise to trees, and still others shifted into vestek that bound away through the grasses.

He tracked the arrival of a single grain of light as it reached the strange environment and popped into a hawk, only to dematerialize back into a scintillating particle as it rose above the plains and into the miasma of light forming what he could only describe as the sky.

He willed them forward onto the plains, and as Neska's feet reached what appeared to be solid ground, he sensed a portion of his weight return. A gust of humid air, redolent with the scent of midsummer flowers, carried across the grasslands, undulating the field of green like an ocean wave. For the first time since entering the Drift, Lluthean inhaled.

"This is the Valley of the Cloud Walkers, Nes, or a version of it, at least."

"I think you are right," she replied.

He was just about to ask Neska what to make of it all when a strange voice from behind him broke through his astonishment. Though human, the voice echoed with multiple resonances, as if several people, men and women, spoke the words with imperfect unison. "Lluthean, my son, you do not belong here."

Chapter Thirty-Nine: The Other End of the Tether

Zsheck, the krug rai'al, kept a palatial estate in northern Kreeg. Though the building stood only a fraction of the size of the Dalkreeg, the vistas offered unparalleled beauty. To the northeast, sunlight shimmered on silvery fronds topping the grasslands. Winds from the Torgrend Range, shaped by a harsh passage over ice and scree, whipped white caps across the lake north of the kingdom. Volencia lifted her chin, relishing the novel sensation of the breeze. After depositing the nadrean rods, and enduring a solo ride across the stagnant northern coast, the wind reminded her what the world was supposed to feel like before her master imparted his will.

The royal palace, a sprawling structure in its own right, straddled the headwaters of the Rodemar River. Stone conduits divided and reconnected streams of water, channeling currents through rooms on the lower levels. Where other parts of the city buzzed with the cacophony of the military schools or the cheers of crowds attending competitions at the Dalkreeg, the palace offered a peaceful retreat.

Volencia strolled along one of the waterways cut into a mezzanine, the babbling water failing to mollify her restless mood. Colorful fish fluttered in lazy circles and reminded her of the luminous schools of fish that thrived in the grotvonen caverns.

Unbidden, the rancid taste of the warrens polluted the back of her nose and caused her to draft a thin mesh of nadir to dissipate the odor, only to realize that the sensation was a scent memory. With disgust, she climbed several sets of stairs until she found her way to an open-air balcony.

In a rare moment of immodesty, she lifted her veil, allowing the fresh breeze to touch her face. The late-morning sun felt warm against her marred cheek. Shading her eyes, she gazed to the northeast, where she had deposited the nadrean rods. Nothing appeared amiss on the plains. She half expected the crystallized nadir to generate ominous storm clouds. But then, that was rather the point, she supposed. If a drought was to befall the region, then there would be no storm clouds. Just the arrival of a slow death from an invisible foe.

At first, the notion left her dissatisfied. How would anyone ever know what they had accomplished? The entire affair lacked any of the grandeur of surprise. The revelation of an act of sabotage well executed was more than half the fun. And yet, there was something to be said for the insidious way that fear wormed its way into the hearts and minds of lesser men.

In the weeks since her arrival, merchant caravans whispered of an eerie stillness that settled across the region. Streambeds normally bursting to overflowing ran as shallow brooks at the bottom of dried gulleys. Herd beasts, vestek and the like, collapsed dead in record numbers.

Tarkannen wasted little time in laying blame for the natural disaster at the feet of the "sorcerers in Aarindorn." As the two kingdoms had little to no exposure to one another, weaving the lie, filling in the vacancy of the unknown, was more than palatable to the Kreeg citizens. People always searched for explanations for any unnatural phenomena that devastated a region, and he'd provided one. In but a matter of weeks, the gossip in communal houses shifted from wagers at the Dalkreeg competitions to discussions on provisioning the army for direct military conflict with Aarindorn.

Everything seemed primed. So, what were they waiting for? What was he waiting for? She pushed back from the balcony and retreated deep inside the palace to the library. Tarkannen sat at a table surrounded by stacks of books and a sprawling map of Kreeg.

She closed the door and stepped inside. "I didn't take you for a student of local history."

The master abrogator lifted one sigil-stained finger but continued to read until he reached the end of the page. At last, he lifted a purple ribbon attached to the book's spine, marked his page, then closed the tome. The title read, *A Contemporary Treatise on the Founding of Kreeg.*

Tarkannen sat back, the sigils on his face shifting in slow patterns. "Matters of local history often bisect events affecting the entire world. What do you know of the Great War, Volencia?"

"Enough to know that we should never hesitate to seize the battle when ours is the superior force."

Tarkannen's eyes narrowed. "You grow frustrated by our delay?"

Volencia took a seat at the table and leaned forward on her elbows. She dropped her head a moment, biting back a frustrated retort, then said, "Mogdurian had one dissenting adviser, Lutn Egaine. His council of abrogators urged action, but Lutn sued for peace, for dialogue. And while the abrogators eventually went to war, the delay allowed Kal'Malldra to marshal the zeniphile kingdoms, bringing people like Eldrek Baellentrell to the conflict. Mogdurian's delay cost him everything, and the disaster that followed reshaped the face of Karsk."

Tarkannen considered her words, eventually nodding with agreement. "I apologize if I misjudged you."

"You didn't. We should have left weeks ago. Verrador said as much in his reports of the grondle herds. The umbral keep them in check, but that kind of aggression needs an outlet. And the grotvonen haven't wandered under an open sky in generations."

"I agree, to all of that and more. The umbral are managing the grondle as they have done for over a decade now, and the grotvonen are using this time to become acclimated to life beyond the confines of the Torgrend caves. I want them motivated to conquer Aarindorn, not run away cowering for their homeland at the first sign of resistance. Besides, the Kreeg armies will require another week to arrange stable provision lines. I intend to use that time to learn all I can about their Dalkreeg."

"Why?" she drew the question out with genuine curiosity.

"Because of the caligot, the creature I destroyed in the Trial of Nines. I never pulled anything like that from the Drift the last time we assaulted

Aarindorn. Which means it was most likely trapped in there for decades, possibly hundreds of years."

"We've already bumped into other things, like that mursk in Dernegia. Maybe it slipped in recently."

"I don't think so. Zsheck made it sound like the creature had been held captive for over a generation, but that's not the only thing that should concern us."

He left the statement hanging, waiting for her to find that missing puzzle piece. An idea coalesced in her mind. "If I had been held captive for years, my first instinct would be to seek revenge on my captors or escape."

"Precisely," said Tarkannen. "The Kreeg, at least those walking the streets today, possess no skill with abrogation. Beyond Zsheck's scepter, I've recognized no deployment of zenith. How would they subdue, let alone cage, such a creature?"

"And why did it choose to fight instead of run away? Unless, maybe, it couldn't. Do you think it was anchored to the Dalkreeg? Maybe there was something preventing it from leaving?"

"I think we must consider the possibility before we leave this place. I would know if the people of Kreeg possess anything that could trap an abrogator in one place. And if so, how to defeat such a device. Since we have a week, we should at least investigate the possibility." He sighed and eyed a rather daunting pile of books.

She leaned back, considering the statement, then nodded with understanding. "Alright. I'm interested. Are they at least translated into Kindred speech?"

"Some are, but the older tomes, the ones most likely to provide the insights we desire, require more work. A translator is supposed to provide assistance this afternoon."

"Is that wise? I mean, if we uncover something unknown to the ruling class, they could try to use it against us."

"It's a minor risk. I imagine if we discover something about the caligot's captivity, between the two of us, we can ensure that the information never leaves the library."

That was true enough, she supposed. The puckered scar on one side of her face pulled taut as she sneered. "The entire thing, the Dalkreeg, the caligot, make for a troubling set of circumstances. At the very least, we would likely learn more about the Dalkreeg's construction, those rings . . . and the way they stifled your ability to channel."

"Good. You agree then." He stood and waved a hand across the table. "I shall leave you to it. Let me know if you find anything useful."

A startled gasp escaped Tarkannen's lips. At first, she assumed he was gloating at assigning her the mundane task of working through the tomes, but a bone-aching chill stole across the room, followed by a pervasive, otherworldly ripple that stifled and corrupted the very atmosphere. Where before the scent of leather-bound books filled the room, now the complete absence of any smell betrayed the work of abrogation.

Tarkannen threw his arms forward, leaning on the table, panting in pain. Crystals of ice coalesced between his fingers, spreading out across the surface of the map, and his breath escaped in ragged, frosty gasps.

Without waiting, Volencia siphoned deep on the currents of nadir and wove a dense sphere around them both. She intended to prevent further attack or at least perceive if someone else, another abrogator, worked against them. Yet her shielding remained sound, and she identified no others siphoning from the ambient currents.

Tarkannen arched his neck in pain, ice crystals flowing up his forearms and appearing now on his cheeks. Acting with frantic effort, Volencia sundered her sphere and swept two sickles of nadir down beside the desk and into the carpet below, cleaving nadir burns even into the stone floor.

"It's not like the Dalkreeg! There are no rings in the stone, so what is it?" she demanded.

Tarkannen pulled his hands from the table with a pained grunt and wove them through complex circular patterns side to side, then up and down, the gestures an artful display contradictory to the usual employment of nadir. He repeated the maneuvers with greater alacrity, and the ice crystal receded from his face. With a third and then fourth recreation of the intricate motions, his hands seemed to blur and flow until finally, he reached forward as if to grasp at some invisible rope and tie it off.

He collapsed back in his chair, and the dead smell of abrogation dissipated. The faint aroma of old leather and candle smoke returned, accompanied only by the sounds of her master's panted breaths and the cracking, receding crystals of ice from the table.

Volencia turned to secure the door against intrusion, even wedging a plank of nadir against the doorframe to prevent any disturbance. She poured a glass of water and held it out. Tarkannen stared at the offering, eventually leaning forward to receive the meager gift.

"That didn't seem like anything to do with the caligot or its cage," she said.

"No. That was a prison of an entirely different design. A . . . noose of my own making."

She searched his eyes, eventually understanding his meaning, and guffawed. "Your tether? To the Baellentrell?"

Tarkannen's eyes narrowed. "Yes. Somehow, our young prince has found himself on the wrong side of the dirt. He's in the Drift, but he is not dead, and so he siphons from the other end of the tether."

"How can that be? He has none of your mastery. There is no possible way that he could survive there, even with the tether."

"I don't know. I can think of a few ways, but they beg the question, why? Why would he travel there in the first place?"

He stood and paced a slow circle around the table, grimacing as his knees bent. "It's not a puzzle we will solve today. I was able to tie off the tether. I can't prevent him from leeching a portion of my essence, but I can make sure he only receives a trickle. It won't change things and shouldn't affect our progress."

"Are you sure?" The question, asked out of fear, escaped her lips before she realized her mistake.

Normally, anything that questioned his absolute strength triggered his anger. As it was, he took a breath and seemed to take a mental inventory of himself, shaking his head from side to side. "Yes, I'm fine, but I will have to be vigilant."

The fact that he didn't berate her left her unconvinced. "Of course. Just let me know if there is anything I can do to help. I'll get right to these books."

He smirked, and the gesture eased her nerves. "Your talents are wasted here, cousin. I have a different task in mind. General Thuum is a trusted adviser to the krug rai'al. Zsheck holds him in high esteem. The general is the lone voice of dissent against a war with Aarindorn and constantly whispers into Zsheck's ear."

Volencia inhaled and bided her time, waiting for a clear delineation of her mission.

"While the general is an old man and would not likely survive the campaign, I would not make the same mistakes as Mogdurian."

Tarkannen waved her back to the table and flared a delicate sheet of nadir across the map, dissipating the pooled water left from the thawed ice. He tapped a finger on the southwest quadrant of the city, where a manor house stood. "This is Thuum's estate. You should have little trouble accessing it. Find the man and pith the gourd, but make it delicate. He could appear to have had an age-related brain malady. If your nadir picks are fine enough, nobody will know."

"When would you see this done?" she asked.

"Tonight. That will leave an opening on the krug rai'al's inner council of advisers, one which I intend to fill."

A genuinely wicked smile stretched her face, making her momentarily aware of the scars under her veil.

"I didn't realize you detested reading so much," he chided.

"It's not that. I was just thinking that the Kreeg seem clannish. They might replace a dead old general with a new younger one from Kreeg. And so, I was wondering, how many generals will I get to remove from service?"

"We will only need the one."

"Was your performance in the Dalkreeg really that heroic?" she asked.

"That bit of theater did open a few doors, but no, I think we have our predecessor, Mogdurian, to thank. I couldn't remember why I had designs on Kreeg, on recruiting this kingdom to our cause. When I crossed over from the Drift, I was not able to retain everything I had learned there. But I had this nagging feeling that they could be valuable to our plans."

He reached over and retrieved the book he had been reading when she entered, then recited, "And so, in the years before the Great Cataclysm, our esteemed krug rai'al, Mogdurian, gathered unto himself all the abrogators of the nation, the young and the old, and set out on the grand crusade to rid the world of the zeniphiles, those anarchists to natural order."

He snapped the book closed. "If one of their founding kings was himself an abrogator, how do you think they'll respond to me?"

Chapter Forty: An Unexplained Variable

The Luna Rova caravan continued a serpentine path around the Great Crown. Ranika took solace in the daily routine: the rustling of the caravan, the crisp alpine scent of mountain air, and Zippy's surefootedness. In the weeks of travel, they passed by several village communities carving out a living in the highlands, each offering a glimpse into a different way of life.

Necessity trumped the cultural norms present in Stone's Grasp. Families were as like to be composed of women as a mix of men and women. If illness or tragedy stole away the members of different families, they simply merged into one new clan, finding security in their shared struggles. The people here lived hard lives and valued a quality axe or a warm coat that reliably shed the rain. Lean frames and calloused hands were common, but their smiles were as open as the mountain range.

Some evenings, the Luna Rova camp swelled as mountain folk joined the festivities. Ranika kept a vigilant eye on the outsiders until she confirmed they had arrived in good faith, bartering goods for services and rekindling obvious friendships. They were as varied as any other people across Karsk, but all possessed a similar desire for friendly conversation, news from the lowlands, and honest trade for services rendered.

Eventually, she felt comfortable enough to insert herself into some of the conversations, listening at first as a shadow, then an interested party, and eventually engaging the highlanders in questions. To her surprise, they appreciated conversation with a young woman as much as anyone else from the group. If this were Callish, men would hold most of the authority and respect.

But this was not Callish—this was anything but. And so she sat in idle conversation for over an hour with two young men and their sister. She left their campfire with a belly full of stew and the reassurance that the family had seen nothing resembling the rumblers.

Zippy cropped the grass beside her travel tent, and she gave him the ends of some leftover mountain tuber that resembled a sweet carrot. The Aarindin chuffed with pleasure and soft-mouthed the morsel from her palm.

She stroked her other hand across his forehead and ruffled his forelock, stifling a yawn. "The day's getting on, Mr. Zip. See you in the morning."

The tapping of Speaker Vekkuh's guide cane announced her arrival from the shadows. "For as much as you talk to that horse, it was good to see you interacting with folk your own age. How did you find the Stokers?"

"Zippy is more than a horse, Vekkuh. What are the Stokers exactly?"

The crone cackled and patted Zippy on the rump. "That he is, and I meant no offense. The Stokers were that family you spent the last hour with. They have kin scattered across this side of the Great Crown. I've known them for years. The father died young, some kind of rock fall. The mother succumbed to a sickness of the mind. Sad thing really. But she made it long enough to raise those kids and give them a fighting chance, which is more than I can say for some."

Ranika wondered if Vekkuh was referencing her own childhood, and whether the speaker knew more than she let on. "They were nice. Pretty much all the people we've met up here are nice."

Vekkuh searched the ground with her cane until she discovered a boulder large enough to use as a seat. She grunted as she lowered to a sitting position. Ranika gave brief consideration to aiding the blind woman, but the speaker always rebuffed her offers of assistance. "And why would you be surprised by the kindness of the people up here? What exactly do they say about us in the lowlands?"

"It's nothing like that," said Ranika. "I just didn't expect it, is all."

The speaker nodded her head and blinked pale, milky eyes. "So young and already as hard as the mountain stone. Why do you think that is?"

They sat in silence for a while longer, Ranika tracing the outlines of constellations known by other names in Callish. Memories of growing up on the streets of the seaport rose to her awareness. "I've only met really nice people in a few places. Journey's Bend in the Southlands, a few villages when we traveled to Aarindorn, and now people like the Stokers. Everywhere else, the cities especially, people are different."

"How so?" asked Vekkuh.

"I don't know. It seems like, whenever there are too many of us, we don't act so good. It's like all the bad stuff inside of people takes over and buries all the good stuff. Does that make sense?"

"It does, but you sound surprised."

She removed her hat and allowed the breeze to gust through her curls while she scratched at her scalp. "Well, in the cities, folks go to church or to school. So it's weird, you know?"

"I don't follow," said Vekkuh.

"I suppose those are places where people go to learn things, learn about life or learn about how to be good," said Ranika.

"But that doesn't match what you've seen?"

"Not at all. Journey's Bend only had a rector. There weren't any schools or churches, and those were some of the nicest people I've ever met."

The speaker pressed her hands to her knees and stood with a grunt. "Have you thought any more about a reading, Nika? You could learn more about Reddevek, but also, I think you would find explanations for some of the things we've talked about."

Ranika yawned, a genuine gesture that brought tears to her eyes. "Can it wait for another time?"

"Absolutely, dear. I don't know if you are aware, but we crossed a pass that leads beyond the Great Crown a few days ago. As I understand it, the lowlanders are calling it the Endulian. They ought to call it Moonies Run for as many times as I've walked its path. Regardless, it means that after another day, we won't encounter other highlanders for three or four days."

Ranika frowned. "Was that the winding trail between those duchies?"

Vekkuh smiled. "So, you did notice. The nobles believe they are the only ones who know about the route, but highlanders have walked those trails for generations. We might have taken it to travel the Borderlands, but the western outlet is already snowed in."

Ranika wondered how the woman could possibly know that but felt too tired to give it much thought. Vekkuh turned and tapped her way back into the shadows. "I've got to share words with a young man goes by the name Balladuren—up here on some errand for your Prince Kaellor. Anyway, come find me when you are ready for a reading, Nika. Bring a few sprigs of the purple flower. It makes good tea. Giver bless your dreams, child."

Nika considered pressing Vekkuh for information about the man from Stone's Grasp, but the anonymity and open acceptance she enjoyed among the Luna Rova felt more important than reconnecting with anyone from the city. So, she retired to her tent and attempted to use Vekkuh's blessing for sound sleep.

If the Giver had anything to do with a good night's rest, she withheld her favor. Stressful dreams of fighting the shapeshifting beast with Reddevek disrupted her sleep. She awoke before dawn cloaked in a veil of nadir, hair matted to a light sweat on her brow. The swelling restlessness infused by the beginning of the buzzing kept her from getting back to sleep, so she walked the perimeter of the camp, returning as the caravan broke with a clutch of wild berries and mountain tubers.

After greeting and saddling Zippy, she fell in line for another day of travel. They crossed paths with a family of six traveling north, exchanged pleasantries, and continued. Beyond that, Vekkuh's predictions proved true. They encountered no other highlanders.

The farther south they traveled, the more temperate the climate. Carpets of green ivy splashed with blooms of red and purple covered the mountains. Ranika pocketed handfuls of the fragrant flowers. Zippy gorged on the fare, so she nibbled on a few of the yellow-green leaves, finding them sour at first, then subtly sweet. Wild rabbits, birds, and a herd of some kind of mountain goat crossed their path. When the caravan stopped, Ranika sought the speaker's tent.

Vekkuh sat by a kettle of water suspended over a small cookfire, clutching an oversized metal bowl of stew between gnarled hands. "Good evening, Vekkuh. I brought you some of the purple flowers, for the tea?"

The speaker reached into a pocket and withdrew a fenestrated metal tea infuser and satchel of dried tea. "Take this," said the speaker, handing Ranika the bowl.

The savory aroma made her stomach gurgle. Vekkuh emptied the last of her dried tea leaves into the infuser and dropped it into the kettle of water, then sat back. "Well, don't wait on my account. I've kept that bowl warm for you."

"How did you know I would make my way here tonight?" Ranika asked.

"Sometimes the Giver gives." She tapped a bony finger at her temple. "My gift sifts through likely variables, shows me things that are most likely to occur."

Vekkuh patted her empty satchel. "Seems I'm all out of tea. Can you do me a favor before you wade into that stew? Dry the flowers for me."

Ranika set down the bowl and began to tie the small bouquet over the fire to dry. "Not that way, girl. Do it fast, with your gift."

"Oh. I've never really done that before."

"You never used abrogation to dry your clothes or remove a dirt stain?"

"Never had the need, I suppose."

"You mean, never had the imagination," said Vekkuh. "Go on. Give it a try. The worst thing to happen will be you dissolve the flowers and have to pick more."

That seemed true enough. Ranika looked around to see if any of the Luna Rova watched her, but this night, they left the two of them to eat in peace. "I don't exactly know how."

"I imagine you have to remove the water, girl. Try removing some of the water from the kettle, maybe. Once you get a feel for that, try the same thing on the flowers."

Ranika channeled nadir and drafted a thin tentacle, the extension of her power, into the kettle of water. Her connection lingered for several minutes until at last, she thought she could reduce away the water without causing damage to the kettle. In seconds, the water level dropped a few inches.

"Here goes nothing," she said, and focused on the bouquet, holding it in her hand. Instead of unleashing her power to obliterate, she divided the tentacle into filaments and entwined them with the stems. But all she managed to do was crush them. She released the tentacle and instead brought forth a trickle of her gift. Inky shadow painted across her palms, and she labored to siphon away that part of the flowers that felt like the water from the kettle. At first nothing seemed to happen, then abruptly the plants withered, browned, and desiccated, emitting a floral fragrance.

"I did it!"

Vekkuh held open her small tea satchel. "Good. Place them in here, if you don't mind."

Ranika deposited the dried tea, then retrieved her stew, noting that Vekkuh had assumed an air of satisfaction. "Vekkuh, you see things before they happen, right?"

"The Giver shines a light on some things, but the Taker hides others under his shadow. Such is the gift and the curse of our people. Why do you ask?"

"You knew I would come tonight, and you knew I could do that with my gift, didn't you?"

"I had an idea."

"So, what else have you seen about me?"

"You have questions, Nika, and I do have some answers. The best way would be a—"

"A reading," Ranika finished. She set the bowl of stew down on the ground. "Alright, then. What do we do?"

Vekkuh rose to her feet. "You eat the stew. When I get back, we'll talk."

Ranika eased into a comfortable position and reclaimed her bowl, cupping it in two hands and tipping back large gulps. She bit into something resembling spiced potato, and the aromatic flavors caused her nose to tingle. She drained the last of the bowl just as a commotion disturbed the camp. From beyond the dancing light of another campfire, shadows flickered, and someone shouted. A young man raced over to stand before Ranika.

She rose to her feet, prepared to summon nadir in defense of the camp. "What is it?"

"It's the speaker. She's hurt and sent me to fetch you. Please come."

Ranika followed without question, arriving to find a small crowd gathered around the speaker. Vekkuh lay on the ground propped up on her elbows, staring at her right leg, where shadows obscured her foot. She spoke in quick breaths, splintered by pain. "Nika, come here, girl."

Ranika pushed forward and dropped to her knees beside Vekkuh, eyes trained on something wriggling in the shadows. "What happened?"

"Crown snake got me. Tenacious grinder, still latched on to my ankle. Taker's bitter breath," she groaned.

"She's been bitten by a snake. Someone get a healer!" she yelled, but none of the Luna Rova moved, and after a moment Ranika leaned closer to Vekkuh. "Let me guess, you folks don't have a healer, do you?"

Vekkuh shook her head. "That we do not, girl. This is likely to be my last night, Nika. Crown snakes feed first, but it's impossible to remove them before they release their venom and up here, there's no cure. Even with a gifted healer, recovery is never guaranteed. We don't have a way to remove the venom. But I wanted to offer you my reading before it's too late."

Ranika gave brief consideration to the strange way everyone stood around. Something felt off. Why had the speaker wandered into the night in the first place, knowing full well the dangers of the Great Crown? Why wasn't anyone trying to help her?

Acting on instinct, she flared her vision into the ethereal, pulling currents of nadir through her eyes. A familiar crisp, cold sensation flowed into her face, and the details of the world resolved into clear shades of silver and grey.

A fat snake coiled around Vekkuh's foot and ankle. Its mouth gaped impossibly wide and its teeth were latched deep into the front of the woman's lower leg. With sickening rhythms, the thing constricted and undulated, the peristalsis of its feeding drawing a wave of nausea to Ranika's throat.

"Promise me this isn't some kind of trick," said Ranika.

In answer, Vekkuh involuntarily craned her neck back, stifling a moan of agony. "No tricks. The Taker blackened the gift of the 'fo. We speakers are cursed with glimpses of our last days. This is to be mine, Nika. If we are going to read one another, it has to be now, dear. I just want Reddevek's story returned to our people. Please, before I can't manage it."

Before she could question herself, Ranika gathered a ball of nadir in one fist, shaping it to her intention. She roiled the current into a knot, concentrating her intent for several seconds. With deliberate, delicate purpose, she released a lone tendril against Vekkuh's skin, committing the feel of the woman's flesh to her mind.

Vekkuh groaned again, and one of the Moonies grabbed Ranika's shoulder, trying to pull her away. She resisted the urge to flare her power with violent intent. Instead, she folded a current of nadir around itself, creating a roiling barrier that pushed everyone back several paces without causing them harm. With a perimeter established, she refined the force into a protective sphere of the same substance around herself and the speaker, preventing any others from disturbing her efforts.

She devoted a small portion of her channeling to maintain the barrier and redirected her focus to the probing tendril in Vekkuh's leg. They lingered there together; the speaker moaning softly, panting through pained breaths, and Ranika attempting to direct her power with infinitely delicate control.

Once she felt certain that she could reliably identify Vekkuh's flesh, she committed to action. Like the crack of a whip, the force sprang from her hand, striking the serpent on the snout. Instead of releasing the current as a missile, Ranika maintained her connection and followed the essence of the snake.

Through her threads of nadir, she sensed the reptilian quality of the thing, even tasted its oily musk. Once she had a solid feel for it and how different it felt to the probing fiber she maintained with Vekkuh, she unleashed the current.

A loud hiss, like water hitting the bottom of a griddle, broke the strange silence and in seconds, the crown snake dissolved. Vekkuh gasped a breath, though whether from pain or relief, Ranika couldn't tell. Yet, in the darkness, she identified a lingering problem. From a set of small puncture wounds, she sensed the acrid taste of the venom, felt how alien the substance was as an infiltrative toxin in the speaker's flesh.

"Hold still, Vekkuh. I'm not done."

She divided the currents of nadir into multiple thin fibers and probed the area around the wound. Her assessment took several painstaking minutes, but eventually she found a region above the speaker's knee that was free from the taint of the venom. Starting with the unblemished flesh, she directed the flow of nadir along strange, branching pathways just beneath the woman's skin.

It took all of her concentration to follow the myriad divisions, redirecting the reductive flows to burn away the toxin. She sensed that her efforts damaged and scarred some of the surrounding tissues, but she had no idea how to remove the venom without the collateral trauma.

In the periphery of her awareness, she sensed Vekkuh cry out in pain, accompanied by the concerned mutters of the Luna Rova. She pushed all of it to the back of her mind and maintained her focus on searching out the last vestiges of the toxin. Only when her probing failed to identify any remnant of the acrid venom did she dissipate the tendril of nadir.

Vekkuh lay back, her milky eyes searching the darkness, a confused expression playing on her face as her panting slowed. Ranika sensed torchlight from beyond the barrier of nadir she had erected and dismissed her ward, finally allowing her vision to return to its normal spectrum.

Several Moonies crowded forward, anger affecting their posture and gestures, but everyone drew up short when the speaker began to cackle. The sounds began as a wheezing rasp but grew to full-throated laughter as Vekkuh recovered. Eventually, several others began to join her with nervous laughs of their own.

Ranika's head thrummed with a light buzzing, and she didn't trust herself to understand the strange turn of events. She had been in the throes of the buzzing before and knew it muddled her ability to think clearly, so she waited.

Eventually, Vekkuh sat up under her own strength and wiped tears from her eyes, still giggling. She ran fingers along her right leg, where a pink, lacy scar with countless feathery branches ran from thigh to ankle. The woman wiggled her toes with an exaggerated nature. She lifted her foot into the air, showing the rest of the Luna Rova for good measure, and laughed again.

"I don't see what's so funny, Vekkuh."

The speaker shook her head. "The irony, child. Everyone thinks abrogation is a curse from the Taker, but you've shown it anything but. I'm a daughter of the 'fo, blessed by the Giver with foresight and premonition, but cursed by the Taker. That crown snake was supposed to be my end, but you used a reductive force to cancel his plans."

"I'm not sure I understand what you mean."

"I mean, child, you're a rare and unexplained element. You single-handedly shifted the trajectory of my life. Nika, to my people, that's nothing short of a miracle. You're truly gifted, my dear. You just don't completely believe it yet."

Ranika smiled at last. "Red used to try to tell me that. I never really believed it, but then a friend of mine, Bryndor, tried to get me to see the same thing."

"Is it so hard to believe, child? Look what you did for me."

"Until a little over a year ago, nobody ever thought much of me. It's taken some time, I guess, to see how all those people were wrong."

Vekkuh held her hand up. "Help me to me feet, Nika."

Ranika hoisted the woman to her feet, finding her lighter than she expected. Vekkuh pitched her voice low and leaned in close. "Am I right in assuming that when you channel that much nadir, you won't be able to sleep for a day or so?"

"Maybe two," said Ranika.

The speaker pulled Ranika into an embrace, then turned her by the shoulders to face the gathered crowd of Luna Rova. "Moonies of the highlands, gather up for a moot. Tonight, we celebrate the return of Reddevek's daughter to our fold. As speaker of our clan, I claim Ranika Taim as a sister of the Dev'advari!"

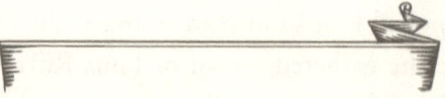

Chapter Forty-One: The Silence of the Moonwing

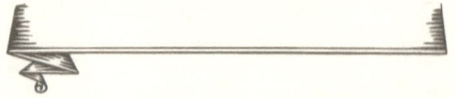

The lively jingle of a doorbell preceded Karragin's entrance to the provisioner's shop. The rich, sweet aromas of oiled leather displaced the acrid smoke from the smithy next door. Iska shifted on her shoulder as she stepped inside. The moonwing's feathers tickled Karragin's left ear. A quick surveillance revealed a vaulted open room with ordered rows of leather goods.

The first few rows displayed common items of utility: straps, gloves, belts, and the like. She walked forward down the center aisle, passing two rows of saddles and tack, rows of leather breeches, coats, and gear crafted to resist rain and snow. Finally, she passed by stands of leather cuirasses of variable quality and make. The simplest versions offered hardened leather vests that could deflect the swipe of a blade.

Barton Sparks, the proprietor, parlayed his gift in a secret process to refine and harden the leather. His methods required none of the chemicals that tanners from the poor quarters employed. While his creations cost a bit more, the armor, in particular, resisted the elements as much as the blow from a weapon, and with far superior results when compared to standard leather goods. As such, Barton enjoyed the loyalty of discerning customers like members of the Outriders.

Karragin continued to peruse the wares, stopping at a row of mannequins displaying more refined, and more costly, sets of armor. Here, the models displayed reinforced leather cut in overlapping scales. She fingered the rugged stitching along the armhole, admiring the craftsmanship. These afforded improved mobility and adequate protection. She had ruined a few sets of similar gear delving into the grotvonen warrens or simply ranging on Aarindin.

To her far right, an entire set of hardened leather cuirasses set with intricate metal studs, rings, and even plating lined the wall. Mercenaries, guards, and members of the city watch often sought such heavier protection.

None of these met Karragin's needs. Several weeks ago, she had requisitioned a modification designed to allow Iska to comfortably perch on her left shoulder without ruining her uniforms. While the moonwing had learned to ease her grip, the creature's talons ended in sharp points that had shredded no fewer than eight tunics in the past month.

As Karragin approached the sales counter, she signed to Iska in the Cloud Walker hand language and reinforced the command through their sympath link, *"Post up top, Iska."*

The weight of the moonwing lifted as Iska hopped from shoulder to her forearm. In a move they had practiced to near perfection, Karragin tossed Iska high into the air. The bird held her wings close to her body until the apex of the ascent, flapped once, and landed on a rafter overhead.

Over the past six weeks, while training with Iska, Karragin had stressed her tolerance for channeling by maintaining her sympath link for as much of the waking day as she could manage. The first week she'd nursed a continuous headache and nausea, but by the end of the second week, she'd honed the skill.

Instead of broadcasting her gift to any sentient creatures in the vicinity, she restricted the connection to Iska, on the bird's awareness. She began to understand Iska's moods and needs. The moonwing never used words to communicate, but flawlessly amplified sounds from the environment through the link. The unique connection allowed Karragin to channel her sympath rune almost without effort for hours on end. In the past week, she had managed the connection from sunrise to sunset without incurring even an inkling of the draft.

Still, a backup means of communication seemed wise. So, for the time being, she issued every command first in the silent hand language.

When Iska seemed uncertain, a simple reinforcement of the concept through their sympath link clarified the order.

With the moonwing situated overhead, Karragin wrapped her knuckles on the countertop. Barton shouted in a gravelly voice from a back room, "Be a minute!"

The man eventually made his way forward, resting the edge of a somewhat rotund belly on the edge of the counter. Wire-rimmed spectacles stood on the tip of his nose and a toothy grin split a salt and pepper beard. Tannins and conditioner stained his fingers and a leather apron. He wiped beefy hands with a cloth and, after recognizing Karragin, peered up into the rafters. "She learned that trick fast!"

"Morning, Barton. She's a clever one. How are you today?"

"Oh, I'm not as happy as a bear with a fistful of honey, but I manage. How are things inside the high walls?"

"It's not the adventure of an Outrider, but I manage."

He peered at her over the top of the glasses and leaned in conspiratorially. "I don't suppose you've any news about how the princes progress in the Rite of Revealing?"

"Tell me you didn't waste good coin in one of those betting pools. You know the only person to win one of those is the man running the game."

"Actually, a woman runs the game, Valdesta." He sighed and made a pretense of cleaning his spectacles. "But I imagine you have the right of things. Still, she gives better odds than most and I might be in a position to walk away with a few coins if either of the boys wakes this week."

Karragin shook her head. "If I did, you know I couldn't tell you even if I wanted to."

Before she finished, he waved a hand and smiled, already guessing her response. "Can't blame a fella for trying. The entire city is talking about it. Nobody's ever heard of a trial taking so long. I think I dipped under for maybe an afternoon before I came to. Of course, that was a few decades ago, and my gifts with leather shaping don't amount to much compared to the martial talents of a highborn."

"Don't sell yourself short. All the Outriders know to come here for the best gear."

He received the compliment with an appreciative nod of the head and patted his belly bulge along the front of his apron. "Well then, in keeping with expectations, let me retrieve your order. Take off that shoddy thing you're wearing and I'll be right back."

Karragin began to unbuckle the boiled leather cuirass she had walked in with. Though simple in design, it was one of the few things she owned that stood up to Iska's grip. The man returned a moment later with two sets of armor. He laid each of them on the counter for her inspection and stepped back.

She lifted the first, a remarkable matching set of leather pauldrons and cuirass. She had no doubt of the quality and studied the pieces with a genuine appreciation for the man's craftmanship. Oiled hazel-brown leather segments fell in fitted sections over both shoulders, adorned with steel rivets both for protection and embellished with engravings for the simple art of the piece. An eight-inch-long steel bar sat along the ridge of the left shoulder.

"Taker's teeth, forgot the vambraces!" Barton scurried into the back room and produced two sets of the forearm guards, crafted from matching materials.

Karragin set down the brown leather armor and inspected the second suit. The design and fit appeared similar. The left shoulder held the same metal bar Karragin intended for Iska's perch. But where the first set was crafted from some kind of treated leather, the second set appeared cast from the hide of a black-scaled animal. She ran her fingers over the pauldron, where black scales the size of a thumbprint gave the armor a supple quality.

Something about the material seemed familiar. The scaled edges shone, but the hide underneath absorbed the window light. She lifted the matching black cuirass, expecting it to weigh more, and grunted in surprise. "Barton, this is not what I ordered."

The man dropped his head, appearing ashamed. "I know, I know. I couldn't give it any of the artful embellishments and none of the metal reinforcement. But the truth is, it doesn't need it. That scaled hide is better than anything my gift can reinforce. It wouldn't accept any engraving. I cursed the Taker's name more times than I can count trying to figure out how to get that shoulder bar through the material. Must have ruined four sets of shears trying to cut through the hide. But he said he wanted each of you Mirrare to have a set and brought me just enough hide to manage it."

Karragin fell back into her resting asshole gaze to hide her surprise. "Who brought you the material?"

"Prince Lluthean. He said it came from the hide of a beast slain in the Great Crown."

Karragin realized why the scaled hide seemed so familiar. Lluthean must have recovered it from the carcass of one of the rumblers. She couldn't think of any animal native to Aarindorn with black-scaled hide.

Barton stepped around the counter and twirled his fingers. "Well, turn around, try on each piece. Let's see if they need adjusting."

Karragin followed his directives and allowed the man to show her how the cuirass, pauldrons, and forearm pieces fit together. She stood in the brown set, finding the tailoring and fitting quite comfortable. He made her twist and bend, twirl her arms overhead, then flow through a few sword stances, testing the malleability and fit of the suit.

"How does it feel? Pinch anywhere? I can make adjustments easy enough."

"As usual, it's perfect," she said.

"Now for the final test." Barton walked behind the counter and retrieved a spear. He held it forward and tilted his head, an unspoken question on his face.

Karragin fingered the tip of the spear, finding it sharp enough to pierce the lower-quality boiled leather piece she had walked in with. "You sure this is necessary?"

"Well, maybe not, but you've always humored me before," said Barton.

"Alright, but if you ruin it, the repairs on are you."

"Hah!" Barton exclaimed and rammed the spear forward. Karragin felt a dull thump across her chest. Somehow, the armor deflected the blow, diffusing the force. She shifted her weight back a step and looked at the armor, unable to find even a scratch. "Impressive."

"Just wait until you try the other set."

He waited for her to unbuckle and remove the brown armor pieces, then she donned the set crafted from the black rumbler hide. The armor allowed her an economy of movement so unrestricted she doubted the ability of the pieces to provide much protection. It felt more like ornamental clothing than anything protective. She looked up to Barton in question, and he held a small sledgehammer in one hand with a gleam in his eye.

"Are you sure?" she asked.

He lifted his eyebrows twice in rapid succession.

"Give me a moment," she said, and kindled her arca prime, then set her feet in a stance prepared to receive a blow. "All set, go."

Barton wound up and delivered a blow to the shoulder, then the chest piece, then the other shoulder. All Karragin felt were muffled taps. Next, he grunted and stabbed with a knife over and over again, failing to leave a scratch in the armor. He stepped back, panting, and wiped at his brow. "Moons, that's remarkable."

"You sound surprised," said Karragin.

"I admit, I might have gotten a little carried away, but I thought I could at least scratch it. Still, I shouldn't be surprised, I suppose. I had to channel three times as much effort to shape those pieces. I'll have the other Mirrare suits ready in a week."

"What do we owe you, then? What I paid you won't cover the extra work," said Karragin.

Barton readjusted his spectacles. "With what I'll earn from word of mouth and what the prince already advanced, we're square. Though you could do me a favor?"

Karragin signaled, and Iska swept down to perch on her left shoulder. The moonwing gripped easily around the metal bar and perched comfortably. She looked up to hear his request.

"I'm helping my son. He's opening an upscale resco bar in the Delve. I'm to be his 'rescologist.' We've even procured a few bottles of prewar resco to commemorate the grand opening. Stop by. Bring some of your friends, maybe."

Karragin thought it unlikely that she would attend, but knew Nolan and others might have an interest. "I'll think about it. What's the place called?"

"Sipseys in the Delve."

"Sipseys?" she asked.

"Yeah, you know, like sip easy, Sipseys!"

"We'll see," said Karragin. "Can you deliver the other set to my rooms? I'll pay the courier fee."

"Consider it done," said Barton.

She thanked the man and left the establishment, the clanging noise of the neighboring smithy an immediate assault on her senses. "To the air, Iska. Meet me up top."

She ran her fingers through the gestures and sent images of the royal plaza to Iska through the sympath link. Iska hopped onto her forearm and hunkered down, legs tucked for the launch. Karragin flared her arca prime and tossed the moonwing into the sky. Once again, at the apex of the trajectory, Iska opened silvery-white wings and glided into the clouds, then off toward the castle.

Karragin stifled her sympath rune, relieved to lose all perception of the painful rhythmic metal clang of the smith's hammer. Over the next hour, she navigated the streets of Stone's Grasp, finding comfort in the isolation of her silence. She made her way past the inner curtain wall, past the checkpoints, and up the tiers of the castle to find Iska perched on the edge of a parapet.

She opened herself to the sympath rune. *"To me Iska."*

As the moonwing landed and secured its talons around the metal bar on Karragin's left shoulder, someone whistled from the green below. Karragin turned to see the other Mirrare accompanying Laryn.

"A little light shopping on your day off?" asked Baccal.

"Something like that. Good day, Amniah, Your Radiance."

Laryn stepped forward and ran a finger across the top of Iska's head, then down her back. The moonwing flared the crest of her feathers with a pleasurable response.

"The armor suits you, Karra. How does it feel?" asked Laryn.

"Like a burden I can't repay."

Laryn frowned. "I don't understand."

With an uncharacteristic loss of control, Karragin's face flushed. She didn't really desire to reveal the details of her one-night stand with the prince, especially not with his aunt. "Well, Llu it seems, retrieved the carcass . . . from one of the rumblers and commissioned Barton Sparks to craft three sets of armor for the Mirrare."

"And that's a problem, why exactly?" asked Laryn.

Amniah looked on with her usual distant expression. "Karra is worried that the prince thinks the gesture is given with romantic attachments. But that would imply he shared his bedroll with each of us, which is either silly or prolific, maybe both, I'm not sure."

The guster always spoke in naked truths, but Baccal worked to stifle a laugh and school her face to neutrality. For her part, Laryn nodded as if understanding and continued to caress the moonwing. "I see. Well, put your mind at ease. I commissioned the armor and asked Lluthean to deliver the hide to Barton. How does it fit?"

Karragin felt grateful not only for the gift but also for the opportunity to talk about anything other than her dalliance with the prince. "Honestly, it's the most remarkable thing I've ever worn, Your Radiance. Compared to standard armor, it is practically weightless. The combination of mobility and protection is unparalleled. Thank you."

Baccal stepped close, eyebrow raised in question, and Karragin held a forearm out for inspection. Zenith rippled in the depths of Baccal's eyes as she scrutinized the material with her gift, finally grunting in approval. "I can't penetrate it. It's more dense than plate. Did Barton make you test it out?"

"Of course, he's Barton. He wouldn't let me walk out of the shop until he dulled a dagger blade trying to puncture the vest. I barely felt the hammer blows."

"When do we get ours, and how much do we owe the man?" asked Baccal.

"End of the week. No charge, thanks to Laryn."

Her Radiance stepped back and tilted her head. "I only commissioned the pieces. Lluthean must have paid for them."

Karragin tucked that last fact into the back of her mind. "We can settle up when he wakes, I suppose. Anyway, Barton did have a request. His son is opening up a resco bar in the Delve, calls it Sipseys."

"Sipseys?" asked Baccal.

Karragin shrugged with indifference. "It's supposed to be a play on words since you sip resco. Sip, easy, Sipseys, or so Barton said. Anyway, he wanted me to pass the word around."

"Are you going to the bar? I don't care for resco. It doesn't cure the rot or make you brave. It burns like fire and tastes like ash, and then it makes you stupid," said Amniah.

"No," said Karragin. "I'm due to relieve Ksenia for a shift watching the brothers in the inner sanctum. It's boring, but allows me to continue training Iska."

"We should take our leave as well. I have been asked to attend a meeting with Edlemund, the prima dicta. I think your father wants to make sure someone in the room buffers any tensions."

"That sounds frankly awful," said Karragin.

"Care to trade? An afternoon of quiet sentry duty over a set of petitioners in the inner sanctum sounds lovely," said Laryn.

"Honestly, I don't think I'm equipped for that kind of constant tooth grinding, Your Radiance."

"Nobody ever is," said Laryn. "Well, the sooner begun, the sooner done."

She gestured to the door, and Karragin held it open, allowing her sister Mirrare to pass with Laryn. They turned to the right, but Karragin wound around to the circular stairs that dropped to the inner sanctum. Several minutes later, she entered the sacred chamber.

The zestrils shimmered adjacent to the reflecting pool, maintaining the princes and their wolvryn in a strange state of magical hibernation. The only sound came from the clatter of a zeniscrawl as Ksenia set down her writing instrument.

"Working hard or hardly working?" asked Karragin.

Ksenia stretched arms overhead and yawned. "A little of both, I imagine. How are you?"

"Well enough," said Karragin.

"I've seen Iska fly over Stone's Grasp more than once this week. I tried to use my gift to send her a greeting, but it didn't seem to stick."

"I'm not surprised. I've kept my sympath rune active for most of the day. She will not likely receive another person's connection at the same time."

Ksenia looked wistfully at Iska and smiled. "What's her voice like, then?"

"It's different. Moonwings don't communicate like other creatures. I can sense her emotions and her needs. There is . . . body language, to be sure, and she is capable of understanding complex directives. But when it comes to sending information back, she is more of a mirror, reflecting the surrounding sounds through our link."

Iska leaped from Ksenia's shoulder, glided around the spacious chamber, and landed on one of the outstretched forearms of the statue of Eldrek. She paced back and forth, settled into a comfortable position, and began preening her feathers.

Ksenia stood and walked to the front of the statue. "Eldrek's statue holds a small dragon in one palm and a hawk in the other. But now that I see her sitting so close, I'm not sure the sculpture didn't mean for that to be a moonwing."

Karragin joined her, even standing on a bench to get a closer view. "You might be right. Have you found anything in your translation work that speaks to the significance of Eldrek's statue? Specifically, the runes or these effigies in his hands?"

"Not yet, but I've mastered a cipher that my colleague can use. Together, we're bound to uncover something. So far, *The Tome of Nivosh* has been a history of the kingdom, its first seventy years, and their struggles after the Great War."

Karragin wrinkled her nose. "That sounds . . . tedious."

Ksenia laughed. "To say the least. For as different as they were back then, they shared much of the same struggles we do today: clannish rivalries upending years of cooperation, petty power conflicts between the prominent families, and the Merc War of the sixties."

"I've never heard of that. The Merc War?"

"It wasn't a real war. Families of influence spread across the Great Crown claiming lands thought to be rich with silver mines. They used the predicted proceeds from silver exports to hire mercenary gifted to fill the ranks of their private household guard and militias."

Karragin tongued the scar of her upper lip. "Aarindorn doesn't have a thriving silver industry."

"That's right. The mines failed to produce, exports dropped, and within two seasons the gifted mercenaries returned to their homes, leaving many prominent families in financial ruin. The Endule and Llentrell branches, in particular, never fully recovered. Ever since, they have been relegated to second-tier status. After that, the first prima dicta was elected to represent the interests of the nobles in Stone's Grasp. The position was one that gave representation but also bound the families to cooperate in a more civil discourse."

"I wonder what the new prima dicta intends these days," said Karragin.

Ksenia yawned and removed her shek from the front of her tunic. "Giver only knows. Here, take this. When they emerge, you can use it to inform the others."

Karragin eyed the stickpin. "Just channel and speak? How do I know who is listening?"

"You don't, not really I suppose, not unless someone speaks to you first or in response. But even then, you won't hear anything unless you keep it primed with zenith," Ksenia explained.

Karragin gave the item back. "I have enough keeping my sympath link open to Iska. You keep it. I'll manage without."

Ksenia replaced the shek, then collected a bundle of loose papers. "Suit yourself. I'm off to meet with Veeble in the archives. Holler if anything changes down here."

"Will do. Eyes to the horizon, Kess."

The young woman smiled back, as if hearing the words for the first time. "You too, Karra. Eyes to the horizon."

Karragin walked about the sanctum, her mind reviewing conversations from the day. She ran fingers along one of the cocoons, swirls of zenith tingling under her touch. She stopped and turned to find

Iska staring at her. "What do you see when you look at that hawk beside you? Is it a moonwing, or something else?"

Iska rotated her head in that strange way only birds can.

"Is that a yes? No? What, Iska? Tell me."

Iska quirked her head to the side and lifted one leg, holding it in a strange posture. Karragin searched for any feeling through their link but sensed no confirmation or emotion. She was just about ready to recline back on one of the benches when she realized Iska was holding two digits of the lifted talon in a curled position and had flared the other forward.

Karragin made a fist, then extended her index finger, mirroring the moonwing, and recreating the Cloud Walker sign for "Yes."

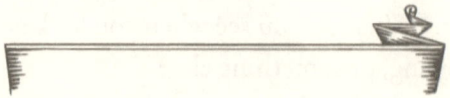

Chapter Forty-Two: The Tether Revealed

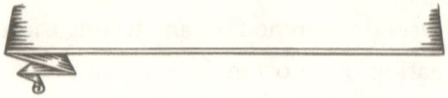

Lluthean reviewed the words in his mind, their subtle meaning disorienting him as much as anything else they had encountered in the Drift. "My son."

Only a few people could address him so. His parents, of course, but also Kaellor. If he turned to see who spoke the words, would he find his uncle in this place, and if he did, what did that mean? Was Kaellor dead? What did any of that even mean as he sat astride Neska gazing across this strange version of the Valley of the Cloud Walkers?

He bristled at his indecision. He had learned better than that in his time in the Revealing. And yet, his restless fingers tapped intervals, counting numbers against his thigh. *Taker's breath, I haven't done that in years.*

He shook his hands in anger to dissipate the fidgety sensation, then twisted around to see who stood behind them.

Standing on the grasslands that stretched out to the far horizon, an apparition waited not ten paces away. The outline wavered, shifting in height and breadth, until the features resolved into something humanoid, but it still felt like looking at a person lying under several feet of rushing water.

He lifted a hand. "Hello?"

The figure remained in place, poorly resolved, its edges rippling like waves of heat rising from stone baking in the midday sun.

"My name is Lluthean, but I guess you already knew that. Who are you?"

"We are . . . the intermingled parts of many, my son." An overlapping chorus of voices responded with a haunting cadence, a mixture of masculine and feminine personae.

"That's the second time you've called me your son. What does that mean, exactly?"

The apparition remained still, and a vacant silence stretched out between them.

"If this is part of the Drift, can you tell me about this place, or how we can return?"

The phantom turned to survey their surroundings, as if seeing them for the first time. Overhead, streaks of light plummeted, materializing as a bird or flying insect. The creatures flitted about for several seconds, then soared up from the grasslands, flaring back to light. Similar larger foci dropped to the ground like shooting stars, streaking light in their wake. These took the forms of mice and rabbits, even vestek.

"What you do here . . . should not be possible," rasped the incongruous voices. It felt like some responses were made of curiosity, some of anger or condemnation, and still others of wonder.

Lluthean's head recoiled with mild discomfort from the shearing quality of the speech. "Is it possible for you to speak with one voice?"

The outlines of the apparition sharpened, and Reddevek's scarred face resolved. "Of course," said the warden. "Is this better?"

Before he could answer, the warden's silhouette softened and shortened, and Rona's kindly round face appeared, wearing a drab apron and dress. "Parts of me are here as well, Llu. But there are others, more . . . integrated that you should speak with. They have been waiting and watching. A moment, dear."

Rona's chin dipped, and the phantom elongated, growing in height. A slender arm reached forward, and sharp features resolved on a face with piercing eyes that twinkled with hues of zenith. She lifted her gaze and his breath caught. Standing before him, in sharp relief, was Nebrine, his mother. She wore silks of white held in place with silver clasps, the look evoking a sense of timeless elegance. When she spoke, a woman's confident alto voice resonated. "How is this, my son?"

461

Colliding emotions threatened to befuddle his mind—surprise, wonder and even a tinge of anger. Lluthean swallowed back all of it, struggling to make sense of the development. "Much better, thank you, Mother. Is Father in there with you as well?"

Nebrine's focus glazed over as if she were attending to some private, inner conversation. After only a moment, her eyes sharpened, and she smiled. "He listens, but allows me this chance to speak with you. Come down from Neska." She held her arms forward, welcoming an embrace.

Lluthean shifted his weight, reluctant to be separated. "I tried that once and the Drift nearly claimed me; currents of nadir rushed in. Somehow, my connection to Neska keeps them at bay."

"That was before you arrived at the nexus to our world. Now that you are here, in this specific . . . current of the Drift, zenith reshapes to conform around you, the definitions becoming something your mind can comprehend. Now that the construct, this valley, is stable, you can safely step down."

"What do you think, Nes?" he whispered.

Neska's maternal voice resonated in his mind. *"The ground is solid, and the air reminds me of the Valley of the Cloud Walkers. The resonance of her, the way zenith sheds from her, reminds me of you."*

Lluthean gripped a fistful of Neska's fur and swung a leg over, setting his weight onto the ground. He used the toe of one boot to bend stalks of grass to the side and watched as they sprang back into place. It felt real enough. He released his grip, then lifted his hand inches from her neck, prepared to slam it down and rekindle their connection if the biting cold of nadir swept in to claim them. But nothing happened.

A small flock of starlings swirled behind Nebrine, swooping low to the ground, then rising to dissipate in the air in a swish of light that vanished into the ether. Lluthean stepped forward and took her hands, the two studying one another's expressions before closing the distance with a long embrace.

She stood only a few inches shorter than him, and the fragrance of her hair reminded him of the flowers from the Founder's Memorial. "Bryn is never going to forgive me for keeping him from all of this."

They separated, but she clasped his hands, her thumbs caressing the tops of his knuckles. "This is your Rite of Revealing, isn't it? You two were never supposed to begin the trial and yet, the only way for you to arrive here is . . . accompanied by the unconditional love of another. That's one of the few ways for anyone to resist the tide of nadir."

Nebrine's gaze shifted to Neska who lounged while surveying the horizon, nose lifted into the wind. Nebrine released his hands and approached the wolvryn, bending only slightly to bring herself nose to nose with Neska. "It's because of her. Why did your elders place her into the Revealing? How would they even know to do that?"

"I don't think they intended for either of the wolvryn to join us," said Lluthean. "But if you are suggesting that she saved me, I can't say that I'm surprised."

Nebrine straightened to her full height and paced a slow circle in contemplation. At last, she threw her head back. Laughter, full-throated, warm and genuine, echoed across the valley. When she regained her composure, she shook her head in disbelief. "Sometimes the Giver gives."

"Care to elaborate?"

"Your father and I thought we had all the answers. We became convinced that were you to remain in Aarindorn, fate would snag you in an unrelenting current, pulling you unerringly toward the day when you would sit for your Rite of Revealing. In every computation, every foretelling, you entered the Drift together, to seek the means to become the Eidolon, and in so doing, one of you perished. We couldn't abide that. Especially since your uncle also neatly fits some of the parameters of the prophecy. And yet, despite our sacrifices, fate brought you here."

"That's why you placed the mantle on us. You wanted to give us a chance at a normal life without the risk of all this." He waved his hand in an arc, indicating their surroundings. He stooped and picked a few stones from the ground, rattled them in his fist, then threw them, one at a time, above the plain. Each pebble flared to light at the peak of its flight, only to fall back as a dull stone.

Nebrine stepped beside him. "No, not this. This is something entirely unexpected."

They stood in quiet vigil, each watching the other. Eventually, a look of concern furrowed her otherwise flawless brow. "You have questions."

He gathered a few more pebbles, finding comfort in the way they rattled inside his cupped hand, and nodded. "So many, I don't know where to begin. Questions about you and Japheth, about this place, the Giver and the Taker, how to get home, maybe? All of it."

She placed a hand on his shoulder and lingered there, as if studying him. After a moment, she gasped. "There is an emptiness inside of you where I expected to find joy. My boy, what happened to you?"

He threw the pebbles at the ground. "Grind it, lots of things, not the least of which is that after surviving the Revealing, Neska and I are now apparently standing on some alternate version of the Valley of the Cloud Walkers inside the Drift!"

Nebrine raised a hand to forestall further comments. "Forgive me, I assume overmuch. I am not used to being separated from your thoughts, from the thoughts of others who have passed on. But now I understand . . . I am required to be more specific. I shall endeavor to do so. What I meant to ask is: Why does my young son carry the burden of a lifetime of loss?"

In through the nose, five seconds, out through the lips, ten seconds. He repeated the mantra. "Back where Bryn is, in the . . . living world, do you watch us?"

"Not in the way your mind will understand. We are always with you." She shook her head. "No, that is not the way to explain it. We sense your life, but it would not be correct to say that we watch you."

He resisted his first impulse and bit back a sarcastic response. He understood enough about himself now to know that stress, anger, and loss affected his mood. Still, he felt the prickly heat of anger climbing up his neck, flushing the skin at his jawline.

Some part of his mother must have recognized his inner turmoil. "There is a merging in the Drift. You become connected to everything. It's an evolution I cannot explain in words that will mean anything to you."

He exhaled through his nose. "Look, I'm walking around in the body of a young man, but Neska and I? We just left the Rite of Revealing, where we lived for more than six decades. I had a wife, children, and grandchildren. Kae and the others said we wouldn't remember any of it. But I remember pretty much everything."

Nebrine inhaled sharply, tremulous fingers lifting to her chest. "Giver's last breath, that should not be possible. Your mind is not equipped to manage that kind of loss. The parameters of the Rite of Revealing should have protected you, stripped that from your memory."

"What do you want me to say? Sometimes the grinding Taker takes. At least Neska led me out when I was ready to go. I can probably make peace with that some day. But Bryn was still in the thick of it. Leaving like that left him devastated."

He paced a circle, uncertain how to manage the conversation. He had not thought about a reunion with his mother in years, quite possibly decades. However he imagined the conversation, he felt certain it wasn't supposed to be laced with anger. Now he grew even more frustrated by the futility of it all, by the way events conspired to place him before her here.

The silence between them stretched on. Ethereal currents of zenith swirled down to the plains and rustled the grasslands as gusts from the mountains. Nebrine's haunted expression melted and her focus turned inward once again, her eyes darting back and forth as if sifting through images. Lluthean contended himself to wait and walked back to Neska, massaging the fur behind her ears.

"What do you think, Nes? Might be that you and I only have each other out here unless we can find a way out."

The wolvryn blinked once and followed the flight of a dragonfly that sped by her nose. "When they first appeared, there was joy. Now there is pain. Whatever they are, whatever this is, quiet the storm inside you. Give them a chance to help."

"Lluthean." The strange ethereal chorus of dissonant voices spoke his name, and he turned. The phantom shifted, resolving again into the shorter stature of Rona. She smoothed down the front panel of her apron. The gesture, so hauntingly familiar, caused something inside his core to ache.

"This is better, we think," said Rona. Tears brimmed her eyes, and she smiled, shaking her head from side to side. "Your mother and father sense something of the pain they have caused you, something we all caused you simply by leaving. But oh my boy, they are so proud, we all are."

Something in the pureness of her voice, her patient mannerisms, chipped through the ice of his angry resolve and allowed him to feel something of the young man who'd entered the Rite of Revealing. He staggered a few steps forward and dropped to his knees, embracing his aunt. She smelled of lavender and herbal tea and combed fingers through his hair just as she had done countless times before when giving him a spring cut.

He dwelled in that familiar embrace for a time. At last, when it felt right, he stood up.

"Thanks for coming, Ro. I don't know if it's easy or difficult, but thanks all the same. I named a daughter after you. So did Bryn."

Rona cocked her head to the side. "You're talking about your time in the Revealing?"

"Yes. Neska already told me they weren't real, not to anyone else but me, but I have this huge empty chasm inside. If they weren't real, I shouldn't feel that way."

She inhaled and sighed. "I can only imagine. It's a terrible burden you carry, but we think there is something you can use here. Indeed, something that you must use to begin to fill the vacant hole inside."

"Alright," he said, but his intonation left no doubt that he found her proposal suspicious.

"You are not meant for this place, not yet. Because of that, when you return to the living world, your mind will struggle to remember all of the knowledge you amass while you are here."

"How does that help me, exactly?"

"We think it might be possible for you to displace some, perhaps even all the memories from your Revealing if you deliberately flood yourself with other memories while you dwell here."

"I've got less than twenty years in the real world to fall back on, Ro. I don't see how that is going to replace the sixty or so I spent inside the Revealing."

She smiled knowingly and adjusted her dress to allow her to kneel in the grasses. "In the original Valley of the Cloud Walkers, there was a small pool of water, clear water with flat grey stones lining the bottom. A spring bubbled up from under a boulder just a few steps away and gave rise to the pool and then a shallow stream. Do you remember it?"

Lluthean dropped to his knees beside her. "Yes, it was in the western reaches, near Mahkeel, the handler."

"Good. Now picture that boulder and the pool in your mind and so it shall be."

Lluthean closed his eyes, imagining the pool she referenced. He remembered the wolvryn pups splashing through the pool, then spraying him with water as they whipped their fur back and forth to dry.

"That's it. Now, open your eyes."

He obeyed, surprised to find a shallow pool just as he remembered. A subtle current bubbled up from the spring underneath a large boulder, filling the six-foot-wide pool before it meandered through the grasslands as a small brook.

"In this place, the nexus of our world, water is a powerful spirit medium. As such, you can cast your awareness into the surface and conjure up reflections of the past. Kae always used the expression 'eyes to the horizon.' And most of the time, I suspect, he meant to convey a sense of looking forward. But what about the horizons you've left behind? Think of a pleasant memory from our time in the Bend."

Lluthean brought to mind a midsummer day at their home. Images coalesced on the surface of the pool. Rona clipped flowers of Maedra's pitchers from her herb garden. A goat goaded Bryndor into a game of play by threatening to headbutt him, and Kaellor sat on the covered porch peeling potatoes. The surface of the water stilled, then manifested the images in perfect clarity, even producing sounds as Bryndor swore under his breath when the goat rammed his backside.

"Good," said Rona. "Now think of something from the past, a day from history, but a day in which you were not there."

"I wasn't much for history, Ro, you know that."

"It's not so hard. At least, it shouldn't be for someone capable of so much wanderlust as a child."

"Alright, show me the start of the Great War."

He stared at the images on the surface of the pool. Two armies darkened the horizons, squaring off across an expansive grassland. Black lightning, reminiscent of the nadir strikes from the summit of the Korjinth, skittered in the skies above the army to the north. Instead of striking the ground, the wild currents warped and deviated with unnatural bearing, becoming tendrils of nadir that whipped out before the abrogator forces.

To the south, similar flickers of zenith streaked overhead to be harnessed by one of the gifted below, empowering runes and coalescing as a protective dome before the zeniphile forces. A woman wearing ornamental armor with gold and silver filigree walked her mount before the zeniphile forces, rallying them to her cause.

Lluthean focused on her efforts, and her words rang out from the reflecting pool as she punched a fist into the sky. "Today we stand against the oppression of Mogdurian! Fight for those you love, fight for yourselves, fight for your freedom!"

All along the line, zeniphiles of mixed bearing brandished weapons. Some kept warhorses in check, the steeds stamping at the ground. Others waited on foot, arranged in groups with sword and shield reinforced with pikemen.

Lines of archers formed up in strategic locations at the rear and sides, and a lone zeniphile strode to the front of the army. He turned to the leader, who acknowledged him with a simple nod of her head. A vortex of zenith swirled about the man, funneling into his channeling, and he summoned a roiling ball of rune fire in the middle of the battlefield.

The globe hurtled toward the abrogator lines, erupting in a colossal detonation that scalloped the surface of the reflecting pool. Lluthean placed a hand on his stomach to still the tickle from the vibrations and watched as the zeniphile forces charged.

A hand on his shoulder and Rona's gentle voice lifted him from the scene. With reluctance, Lluthean sat back and allowed the images of conflict to disperse. "Was that Eldrek standing before the zeniphiles? The man wielding rune fire?"

Rona tilted her head forward. "The very same."

"Who was their leader, the woman addressing the troops?"

"That was Kal'Malldra. You can redirect the images to learn more about her should you desire. You can look in on practically any element from the past."

Lluthean had never been a student of history, certainly nothing as ancient as the Great War, but easily recognized the similarity to the Southland goddess the All-Mother Malldra as more than coincidence. "I will."

He turned his attention back to the pool, intending to manifest the conclusion of the war, but instead, his mind drifted to her, the woman he had built a life with in the Revealing. The images shifted and blurred for a moment, until a bird's eye view of Stone's Grasp appeared. Along the streets of the manor district, just outside the gates to the castle, movement drew his attention. Lluthean leaned in out of curiosity and found a procession of Outriders walking through the streets of Stone's Grasp.

Crowds of Aarindorians lined the streets, tossing floral wreaths and offering cheers. A young Therek Lefledge towered above the crowd, and on his shoulders sat a slate-haired adolescent girl with a serious intensity. Karragin leaned down and whispered something to her father, who smiled and nodded. He waved a hand and a young Outrider deviated from the procession.

Therek's voice rose above the din as Lluthean concentrated on the interaction. "Elbiona, I would like to introduce my daughter, Karragin. She thinks of all the Outriders attending the king's procession today, that you are most likely the toughest in the lot."

Elbiona's cheek hitched up in a smile. "Sounds like she inherited something of your wisdom, my friend."

The Outrider removed a claw from a belt loop and handed it to Karragin. "This is from a grot shaman. You hold on to it, and when you become an Outrider someday, you can give it back to me."

The girl fingered the sharp tip, then wedged it between two knuckles and raked it through the air as if brandishing a weapon. Her nose wrinkled up and a feral expression glazed her face as she growled. Elbiona chuckled. "They don't sound anything like that, but you've got something of their savage nature down."

"We'll see," said Therek.

Elbiona leaned back on her Aarindin and nodded. "Is she gifted?"

"I can talk to your Aarindin," piped Karragin. She pulled back the sleeves of her shirt to reveal the runes on her forearm.

"Giver's truth, a sympath? We can always use someone with that kind of skill. Come see me when you inherit your arca prime."

Rona's voice removed him from dwelling on the images. "She would be a worthy match for you if you think you can keep up."

Lluthean stood and considered the specter of his aunt. "If, or when I return, she won't recall any of it, will she?"

Rona's eyes lifted with renewed understanding and empathy. "From your time in the Revealing? No, my boy, she won't."

Lluthean looked back at the pool, now returned to the placid body of water lined with stones. "Can I use this to look into the future?"

"I wondered how long it would take you to ask me that. Time has little meaning here, but you are not of this place, not yet, and so you can only perceive events from the past, I'm afraid."

"What about Bryn? Can I see what he's doing right now?"

"That should be possible. Give it a try," she said and gestured back to the pool.

Lluthean tried to think about Bryndor, crumpled into a kneeling position alone on the floor inside the inner sanctum. His brother must have sensed something and walked forward to peer into the reflecting pool inside the sanctum. As he did so, the images shifted, and he stared back at the haunted expression of his brother as if looking at him through a window.

"Bryn? Can you hear me?"

Bryndor's head tilted, and he leaned forward, nodding. "I hear you, Llu. Where are you?"

Relief washed over him, both at hearing his brother speak and at realizing that he was not so alone. "It's a crazy story, but I'm in the Drift. Neska and I sort of crossed into this place."

Bryndor shook his head in mock disbelief. "Why does that not surprise me? How are we to get you back here?"

Lluthean shrugged and looked to Rona. "Can I use this to hop back through?"

"That is a likely consequence of such an action, but you should consider your next steps carefully."

"Why?" asked Lluthean.

"Because you are tethered to the usurper, my boy. If you cross back now, Tarkannen might have access not just to his power, but to the full measure of your gift as well. You would practically deliver Karsk to him on a silver platter. Nothing could prevent him from assuming control of the entire world with that kind of power."

"What are you even talking about?" asked Lluthean.

Rona waved a hand over the pool, finding the day that Lluthean accompanied Kaellor, Laryn, and the Outriders into the basement of the Sanitorium in Callinora. She paused the images just as the umbral stepped through the dark vortex and into the room. "You remember this day, yes?"

"Of course. Who could forget?"

"You were there to prevent the theft of the vessel, the life-form that Tarkannen had tethered himself to while he lingered here in the Drift. Now watch and see what happens."

She moved a hand over the pool, and he watched as a version of himself stabbed through the umbral and into the body of the burn victim. The memory of that moment leeched the heat from his core and gave rise to ripples of icy dread. Rona slowed the images and shook her head. An expression of utter discontent marred her otherwise peaceful face.

As Lluthean's image plunged the knife through the umbral, a flare of shadow, absorbing all light, rippled from the point of contact. When the images resolved, a thin smoky tendril rose from his apparition's back.

Lluthean hovered over the pool for time beyond measure. "How does a thing like that even happen? Wouldn't I at least have some awareness of it?"

"We aren't sure. Maybe it has something to do with your shadow mark, the scar on your shoulder. Maybe it has something to do with the mechanics of being in contact with the umbral and the vessel all at once. What we do know is that the tether connects your life force to Tarkannen's."

Rona passed her hand over his head as if to remove a strand of spider silk, and Lluthean felt an unpleasant vacancy hollow out his stomach, steeling his breath. "Taker's grip," he gasped.

Eventually, he turned to Neska. "You could sense it, couldn't you? That's why you seemed so distant after Callinora."

In answer, Neska lowered her head onto her front paws.

"Guess I'm just a slow learner," grumbled Lluthean.

Bryndor's voice echoed through the surface of the water and he reappeared, pressing himself against the other side of the water as if trying to push through a glass window. He pounded a fist, and the water rippled. "Grind it, Llu. Just get back here, and with Kae's help, we can sort this all out."

Lluthean turned to Rona. "What happens if he comes through, if both of us are in the Drift?"

In an instant, Rona's apparition elongated, and Nebrine assumed control of the phantom. "You must prevent that at all costs! If you allow Bryn to step through, only one of you will survive. This is the very outcome we sacrificed everything to avoid!"

"And yet, if I go back, Tarkannen might have access to the full measure of my gift."

Nebrine turned sad eyes to her oldest, peering at Bryndor through the reflecting pool. "Bryndor, my son, you must not enter the Drift, please. I beg you. Instead, you must seek the Ilovesh in their tree kingdom far to the east of Aarindorn. They hold the secrets of the tether and its deconstruction. Lluthean should remain here."

The shade of his mother turned to consider him directly. "Lluthean, only you can close the way, my son."

A shearing, rasping sound, like thick fabric being ripped apart, tore through the pool as Bryndor's fist appeared. The surface of the pool flowed back, and a portal began to open. Bryndor grasped the edges and wrenched the opening wider.

Lluthean dropped to his knees, but instead of shouting and berating his brother, he reached one hand forward to grasp Bryndor's wrist and the other to cup his cheek. The gesture was at once intimate and disarming. "Bryn, brother, stop. You have to leave me here for now and find the Ilovesh. You heard Mother. Travel to the east, find the secrets of Tarkannen's tether. If you come through, one of us, maybe both of us, will die."

Bryndor chewed on his lower lip in anguish, clearly considering all that had been revealed. Something dark passed across his expression and he shook his head. "Grind all that. I'm done watching things happen to us. Give me your hand and come back."

Lluthean looked back at his mother's phantom. "He'll never stop. What should I do?"

"You have to dismiss the pool from this side. Place your thoughts elsewhere, and the connection from this side will leave him back in the inner sanctum."

He turned back to Bryndor. "I'm sorry, Bryn. You can't come through and I can't go back, not yet. But you'll find a way. You always find a way."

The angry look of determination on Bryndor's face melted, his shoulders slumped, and he exhaled a heady breath. "Please, Llu, don't you leave me. I can't do it, not alone."

The authentic distress in his brother's voice almost forced Lluthean to jump through the pool. Instead, he lifted his hands from Bryndor's cheek. His brother continued to plead, but the words now echoed as if from a distance, and Lluthean sensed him falling away as he drew his focus to Neska. He stared overlong into the depths of her blue, zenith-laden, unblinking eyes.

"You did well, Lluthean. He's gone now," said Nebrine.

Lluthean allowed his gaze to drift back across the placid surface of the pool. A mixture of emotions warred to preside over his thoughts, fear and anger chief among them. He remained there, one hand at the edge of the pool, the other clenching his brother's tears in a tight fist.

Chapter Forty-Three: The Taker's Embrace

Embers popped and hissed from a burning log as Ranika used a stick to push the coals of a small campfire closer together. A small eruption of sparks spewed up into the night sky when she tossed a new log onto the fire, the sweet smoke of green wood flavoring the air.

"That should do for a while," she said.

From the opposite side of the fire, Speaker Vekkuh sat on one of two bedrolls lying side by side. She held forth her palms, warming her hands. "Be sure to bank the coals together, dear. The last time I took a reading, the fire died, and it took me two days to get the aching cold to leave my joints."

"Just how long does a reading take?"

"A proper recounting of events takes a few hours," said the speaker.

Something in the notion that she would be linked intimately to this woman for several hours set Ranika's mind on edge. "Red's reading only took a few minutes."

"I know, and he and Speaker Movshka paid a price. The reading was incomplete and, I suspect, both men nursed headaches for days. That's what happens when you try to cram a lifetime into a few minutes. Can't say I'm surprised really, Red was never one for such things and most men don't have the patience for the work. But you and I? We're better than all of that, don't you think?"

Ranika couldn't rightly decide if the woman was patronizing her to begin the reading or speaking plain truths. That bit about Red felt right, and the woman seemed genuine in her desire to recover something of Reddevek's history to be included in the recorded traditions of the

Dev'advari clan. If Ranika, in turn, glimpsed something of Reddevek's past, she could live with the discomfort, for a little while at least.

She moved around the fire to sit down beside the speaker on the vacant bedroll. "So, what do we do? How do we begin?"

Vekkuh lay back on the bedroll, adjusting a bundled cloak as a support under her neck. She shimmied back and forth, then frowned and sat up, turning to remove a small rock from under the bedroll. She tossed the rock to a collection of others ringing the fire, then once again, she lay back, this time finding what appeared to be a restful position. "First, I get comfortable. I suggest that you do the same and don't cross your legs. When I took Dergan's reading, the boy sat cross-legged. We came out and he couldn't walk right for a few days."

Ranika knew the young man of whom she spoke. He still walked with a limp to this day, which made Ranika wonder once again how long the reading would actually take. Regardless, she had agreed and couldn't see to refusing the woman now. So, she did as instructed, removed her hat and lay back, situating herself comfortably on the bedroll, mindful to keep her legs uncrossed. "Alright. Now what?"

Vekkuh patted the back of her hand on the bedroll between them, palm open. "Now you place your hand in mine. Close your eyes and I'll create a link between us. There will be a warm sensation. It shouldn't hurt, not if you don't resist it. Once we are connected, I could push into your mind, but I'm tired and frankly don't have the patience for that kind of struggle. When you feel my hand and the warmth, just settle your thoughts there and then we'll begin."

Ranika scrubbed fingers once through the spirals of her hair, finding comfort in a soft gust of wind that lifted the curls from her face. She closed her eyes and grasped Vekkuh's hand, interlocking with the woman's withered, cold fingers.

After only a few breaths, a warmth kindled in her hand, spreading into her arms and across her chest. She inhaled, finding the sensation pleasurable, and relaxed into the flow that washed over her. Wispy images of Reddevek materialized in her awareness: the last time she saw the man among the Rovinary clan, sharing space beside him at meals by campfire, fighting beside him on the plains south of Stone's Grasp.

She realized that Vekkuh was directing the images, considering them one by one, as if sifting through cards on a deck, but always tracking back through time until the first day Ranika set eyes on the man disembarking from a ship onto the streets of Callish.

Ranika watched the scene play out, noting the way the appearance of the Aarindin first caught her attention. Zippy stomped onto the gangplank more majestic than anything she had seen in all her young days. Reddevek had curt words for one of the deckhands who threatened to whip the Aarindin, and she'd considered the man for the first time, wondering if he could be her next mark.

She could sense at first glance that he was wary of the busy surroundings. He didn't carry much, and looked ready for rough travel. She could likely filch the dagger at his hip and wondered if the dirt over the hilt covered a metal pommel or something more substantial. Regardless, he had a belt pouch and something that could pass for saddlebags, but no saddle, which Ranika found odd at the time.

She kept her distance, studying him while leaning against a wood post supporting the awning of a port side tavern. She thought to allow him to pass, then follow from a distance, but the man turned to glare directly at her. "Boy, you know the city?" he asked, and so it began. The scene unfolded with Ranika asking all sorts of questions, leading them through the rough parts of Callish and deftly removing the man's dagger, then darting off into the twisted back alleys.

Once she felt safe, she considered the prize, rubbing off the dirt with elation to discover a ruby set into the pommel. She knew there was no easy way to offload the item. Its quality and make were far beyond anything she had delivered to the black-market fences. Just owning the trophy would make her the target of any number of thieves. She held the dagger blade, tapping the pommel into her palm, and weighed the options in her mind.

She had scratched out a meager life on the streets. Nobody had connected her to the death of Lord Drassle, the man who had murdered her mother in a drunken rage. But over the past several years, she had escaped more than a few close calls with rival gangs and pickpockets, relying more and more on her ability to slip into the shadows.

Street justice was brutal, plain, and efficient. Get caught operating on rival gang turf and they would claim the loot and at least one finger. Get caught a second time, and they removed an eye. Not many thieves made it long without all their fingers and even fewer without an eye.

Ranika had evaded no fewer than three close calls in just the last few months. The city was getting crowded, and she didn't care to join a gang. She saw what happened to most girls in gangs and didn't like the way they stared out at the world with lifeless eyes.

She'd thought about striking out. How much worse could her fortunes be if she followed a man who traveled with a ruby-hilted dagger? She reasoned that if he treated such a valuable item with casual regard, he must be connected to wealth, right? Besides, what did she have to lose?

Without further thought, she grabbed a travel sack and pulled her shadow like a protective cloak around her, disappearing from view. Using her innate gift, she maneuvered through Callish, pilfering sausages, hard cheese, and some dried fruit for the road. It wasn't hard to find the man. The mount was as distinctive as his callous bearing.

Contemporary Ranika felt herself giggle as she watched Vekkuh sift through her memories, studying the scenes as Ranika followed Reddevek on his solo travel to Journey's Bend. The young abrogator separated her awareness from the images and Vekkuh's probing inspection. Revisiting her past was fun, to be sure, but also oddly tedious.

Vekkuh shuffled through the memories forward and back, obviously inspecting them for minute details. She had a clear sensation that the older woman was somehow recording all of the events. Beyond her control, the speaker left the current set of memories and sifted back in time to Ranika's interactions with her mother, Silvy.

Ranika considered watching, but all too often she had dreamed of her mother's last night, and she had no desire to watch the scene unfold again. She gently pushed back from the imagery and reached out with her awareness. The sensation was disorienting, like stumbling along a forest path under a new moon.

In the periphery of her awareness she sensed movement, a flickering in the shadows. She urged herself to the disturbance, curiosity overwhelming any sense of caution. Fog and mist seemed to obscure her ability to focus on the movement, but she leaned in, waiting, patient, and all at once an image of a young Reddevek materialized.

He and a woman ran headlong down a steep mountain path, skidding and stumbling over rocky ground, barely keeping his feet by the light of the full moon of Baellen. He looked to be no more than fifteen years old but gripped the ruby-hilted dagger and an axe with all the grim determination of the man she remembered. Sweat glistened on his bare chest, bereft of any arca prime.

Reddevek hopped into the washout of a dry streambed and sprinted for the better part of a minute, craggy brush and thorns scraping open cuts on his arms and face. He skidded to a stop when the streambed forked and shouted over his shoulder, "Grind it, which way, Vekkuh?"

Ranika realized she had become so enthralled by the events, that she'd failed register that Vekkuh, a younger version of an adult Vekkuh, was running with Reddevek. "Left. They're down that way," a younger, more robust sounding Vekkuh panted.

Reddevek spun the axe in his hand, using the seconds to catch his breath, then prepared to set out. "Wait, Red. What are you gonna do?"

A malevolent darkness passed behind Reddevek's eyes. "Your gift doesn't amount to much if you don't know that already."

"It doesn't work that way and you know it. If it did, I would have stopped them. So, I'll ask again, what are you gonna do?"

"I'm going . . . to settle a score. The Church of the Giver never should have sent poachers after Voosh, or any of the wolvryn. He never hurt anyone. We never even ventured into the lowlands! They came up here, into our land, sat at our fire, ate our food, baited him, then slaughtered him!"

Reddevek's face darkened with purple hues, and spittle flew from his lips as he spat the words. "I know. I know they did, Red. And I know you're the Wolfespark. You returned the wolvryn to the clan. But the king refused to decree protection for the wolvryn and people . . . people are scared. Besides, there are six of them and only you. You're running into the Taker's embrace."

Reddevek shook his head, refusing to be mollified. "Maybe so. But these people made a choice. I didn't choose this path. They did. You can either come with me or run back to the speaker and tell her what I'm about. I'm grateful you gave me this chance, but I'm done talking, Vekkuh."

Reddevek turned without waiting and jogged down the path to the left. Vekkuh stood and watched him leave, then paced back and forth, staring at the ground as her feet wandered with indecision. Hovering unseen, Ranika fretted with anxiety, silently urging the woman to follow Reddevek, and at last, she did.

As Vekkuh ran along the streambed, the shouts and screams of men engaged in combat became louder and louder. Vekkuh scrambled up the steep bank and peered through the grasses to see three dead or incapacitated bodies strewn about a campfire. Two burly men held Reddevek by the arms as a third advanced, brandishing a flaming log from the fire. Without preamble, the last man grabbed a fistful of Reddevek's hair, forcing his head back. "You attacked my men like a wild animal. We brand animals where I come from, boy."

Reddevek released a feral scream that sounded more rage than pain as the man swung the stout, burning log like a cudgel, causing a wound that both splintered and seared the side of his face. The man stepped back and grabbed at the waist of Reddevek's trousers, tossing the burning log aside and removing a knife from its sheath. "Hold him still boys, I'm going to geld him."

The younger Vekkuh looked down and shook her head. "Taker's bite, Red. I saw it and you still brought me here. You're still gonna make me do it." Vekkuh plunged her hands into the sandy bank as if she knew right where to excavate a sharp-edged, wedge-shaped river rock. She sprinted out of the shadows toward the man holding the knife.

A sickening sound, a short crack followed by a splatter of soft meat being cleaved, split the night, followed by a single grunt, and the man fell dead. Vekkuh withdrew the rock and dropped to her knees, slamming the makeshift implement onto the foot of one of the burly men holding Reddevek in place. The distal half of the man's foot lopped off, dark blood shooting out onto the soil. He collapsed to the side, howling in pain.

Reddevek used the surprise of the moment to twist out of the last man's grip. He darted to the ground and popped back up, chest to chest with his foe and brandishing the knife of the dead man Vekkuh had brained. The last man grunted, mouth agape and eyes wide in shocked horror as Reddevek plunged the knife deep into the man's lower belly, then ripped upward, opening a rent up to the bottom of the man's rib cage.

Vekkuh regained her feet and stared at the blood on her hands. The man Vekkuh had wounded continued to scream in pain, clutching at his ankle. Reddevek turned and nodded once, then stalked into the shadows to end the man's misery. There was a squelching, wet sound from the darkness, then the sound of an axe chopping into something that was definitely not wood. Reddevek took his time, finding each incapacitated foe and bringing the mountain's justice to them.

When he finished, only the occasional crackle of the campfire broke the somber silence. The moon shined down on the young man to reveal a face bloodied and burned. He shook his head at the ground. "I'm sorry you had to do that, Vekkuh. Did you know?"

"I had an idea it might happen. Perhaps if I had said something—"

"It wouldn't have changed anything." He wiped blood from his axe and dagger. "We should get back before anyone notices we're gone."

"No. I've seen this moment. You can't go back, Red. You lose yourself to vengeance every time the caravan encounters missionaries or pilgrims from the Church of the Giver, and they're not all bad people, but they drive you to do bad things. You become something the king cannot abide and meet your death at the end of the king's justice. Tonight, this one skirmish, was justice for Voosh, but it has to stop here. It stops or you die."

Reddevek probed fingers at the fresh wound on the side of his face and forehead. He stared at the ground for several minutes, but eventually inhaled once and holstered his axe. "Did you see another path?"

She nodded and swallowed to clear phlegm from the back of her throat. "I did. You must follow your brother into the Outriders. It will tear your mother apart, but you'll have the opportunity to do great things. And one day, if you play your cards right, you'll meet a wolvryn again. Moons light your path, Red."

Ranika withdrew from the memory and cast out her awareness. If Vekkuh continued her reading, Ranika couldn't tell. None of the images that took shape before her seemed familiar, which was more than strange because the apparitions that materialized next were people that she knew, people that she knew very well.

Bryndor's silhouette clarified through a haze of images. Ksenia knelt just behind him, her hand set oddly on his thigh, as if the touch was one of reassurance and not intimacy. A concussive pulse originated between the two of them, and the environment illuminated in a flare of zenith.

They stood on a cliffside surrounded by dense currents of what she assumed must be zenith. A tall pillar of rock rose from the mountains to stand in stark relief behind them. Roiling storm clouds of the arcane power gathered in a massive vortex overhead, blotting out the stars. Chaotic eruptions of zenith flared and ignited high above in the night sky, appearing as striations of blue lightning. Bryndor held his hands out, gesturing as if calling more and more of the power into himself.

The surrounding air rippled, becoming super-heated, even painful. As she observed the moment, she instinctively erected a globe of insulating nadir around herself. And then, as if somehow pulled into the vision, she was standing not twenty paces behind him on the mountainside.

Bryndor continued to churn the vortex, runes pulsing across his skin with blinding intensity, flaring from cerulean to brilliant white. Boru whimpered in pain, and somehow she knew to extend her null field, and the great wolvryn dropped belly to the ground, seeking shelter within her protective globe of shadow.

A hand, cold and bony, clutched at her shoulder, and Ranika startled awake. "You've seen enough, Nika. The reading is over."

Ranika fluttered her eyes open, and awareness of the weight of her body on the bedroll returned. Her arms and legs felt heavy, as if she had slept in the same position overlong. The sweet smell of woodsmoke aided her reorientation, and familiar constellations twinkled overhead in the night sky.

"Did you get what you need?" she asked.

"That and then some. It was a good reading, Nika, and Reddevek's story can take its place among the Luna Rova. For that, you have my gratitude."

She struggled to a sitting position, and Vekkuh handed her a waterskin. "Here, drink. It's water infused with lammen berry leaf."

She turned up the waterskin and gulped several mouthfuls. "I saw Reddevek, after he lost Voosh. I saw what you did for him."

"Not my finest hour, but not my worst. Weeks before that day, I had a vision. The Giver saw fit to show me a fork, but I didn't trust my gift and missed my chance to direct him down a different path."

"I . . . what?" she asked, befuddled by the woman's casual references.

Vekkuh sat forward, hands clasped around her knees. "My ancestors joined the Luna Rova hundreds of years ago. They emigrated here after the Great War. The gift of prophecy ran strong in their bloodline, but over the generations, the purity of that gift has been diluted. Anyway, on occasion, some of us still inherit something of the gift."

Ranika recalled the strange vision in which she saw herself standing behind Bryndor on the mountainside, and nodded, understanding beginning to settle in place. "You pulled me from the reading just when I was seeing the future, didn't you? That place I saw, those events—they haven't happened yet, right?"

Vekkuh's milky white eyes stared absently into the night, and she reached out with one hand, gesturing for the waterskin. Ranika placed it into her grip and waited. After drinking her fill, the woman answered, "You glimpsed but one of many possible futures. Although, I have to admit, that one feels more likely the closer we get."

"Why didn't you let me see how it ends?"

Vekkuh remained silent for long moments and muttered something to herself, then shook her head. "I can't tell you everything, but I can tell you this. Before that day even has a chance, your fate will be decided by the love or the venom of two brothers. The older one, he wants to protect you, but the younger one . . . there is a darkness shrouding the younger one. I—I can't say more."

Ranika stifled a desire to swear at the speaker and rose to her feet. "But why? Why tell me even that? Just tell me all of it!"

Vekkuh dropped her head. "I'm not what my ancestors were, girl. Prophecy is never absolute and is often laced with hidden meanings, misunderstood outcomes. If you see too much of it, you might commit to an action that provokes the very thing you were trying to avoid. Understand?"

Ranika nodded as if the crone's words made sense, but they really didn't. Vekkuh must have sensed something by her noncommittal gesture. "Look girl, I've seen numerous futures, and you are in all of them. That scene you started to observe, though?"

Vekkuh shook her head and pressed her lips to a thin line. "If that day comes to pass, you'll witness terrible power and... the worst kind of loss. I pray to the Giver none of those events unfold as you saw them."

"I think I was standing in the Great Crown, not twenty paces away from Bryndor, but I don't think he knew I was there. Can you at least tell me if I am supposed to help him? Is there anything I am supposed to do?"

"I cannot. Not because I don't want to, but because I don't know. I'm an observer to possible events as much as anyone else. Even if I felt certain of the outcome, it's like I told you when you healed me from the bite of that crown snake. You're the unexplained element, remember? Your presence alone could unravel the tangled events. All I can say is that this caravan has to drop out of the Great Crown, skirt the Borderlands, and arrive on the southeastern slopes of the mountains by midsummer. Whatever else happens, I do know that you have to be there. If he needs your help, you'll know it, I imagine. But you can't do that if we don't arrive in time."

"Why don't we cut across instead of trekking all the way around the mountains? Surely we could make better time."

"Can't do that for several reasons. First, is that we're highlanders. We have a tradition and an obligation to follow the moons in the highlands. Second, we would never pass through now that the kingdom prepares for war. We'll never be granted access through the Pillars of Eldrek, and the army has fortified a palisade we can't cross. Finally, if we arrive too soon, it's liable to be as catastrophic as arriving too late."

Ranika stood and fluffed fingers through her hair before gathering the loose spirals under her wide-brimmed hat. Pervasive fatigue seeped into her bones, and she struggled to stifle a yawn. "If we are done, I'm for bed. You coming?"

"No girl, I think I'll sit with it all for a time. I have a lot to consider and even more to record. You get to sleep, though. We've a long day tomorrow, and the day after we drop into the Borderlands. If I'm right, the caravan will need you more than ever once we leave the safety of the mountains."

"Good night, Vekkuh."

"Eyes to the horizon, Nika."

Chapter Forty-Four: The True Purpose of the Revealing

I nearly forgot to write about the strange visitors we had when I was still a young, bare-chested runeling. A Leandurian man and Vellendarian woman both possessed of uncommon height and slender grace and marked with peculiar color patterns arrived from the east to consecrate our deepening well. I can close my eyes and still recall how the moonlight fell upon their beautiful dark skin, illuminating purple birthmarks. Their smallest member still dwarfed our tallest men by more than a head. And their voices? I can't begin to describe the simple, breathtaking beauty of their song. Tree singers, my sister called them.

—The Tome of Nivosh, 75 PC, translated by Ksenia Balladuren

BRYNDOR CLUTCHED AT the edges of the portal that had appeared on the surface of the reflecting pool inside the inner sanctum. Instead of dipping into the water, his fingers found purchase, an edge, and he sensed that by infusing his grip with zenith, he could force the opening wider.

As he did so, a cold, biting wind carrying the stink of things long dead and moldering began to numb his fingers. He flared zenith into his grip and the leeching effect of the Drift dissipated. He wrenched the portal open even further.

He could do this. He could make the opening wide enough and hold it open for Lluthean to dive through. Muscles in his shoulders strained, but the opening failed to move until he allowed more zenith to flow into

485

the window-like opening of the barrier. Any resistance melted, and the portal stretched even more.

From the other side, Lluthean dropped to his knees and reached one hand forward to grasp Bryndor's wrist and the other to cup his cheek. "Bryn, brother, stop. You have to leave me here for now and find the Ilovesh. You heard our mother. Travel to the east, find the secrets of Tarkannen's tether. If you come through, one of us, maybe both of us, will die."

Bryndor chewed on his lower lip in anguish, considering all that had been revealed. Behind Lluthean, an apparition of his mother watched with a clear look of concern on her face. But the whole mess was too much. Too much left to the unknown, too much left for him to manage alone.

He flared zenith into his sagacious rune, hoping to force a clear sign of the correct path. To his dismay, the rune resonated with passivity, leaving him with the notion that he should be a patient observer. He shut down the flow.

"Grind all that. I'm done watching things happen to us. Give me your hand and come back."

Lluthean looked back at his mother's phantom. "He'll never stop. What should I do?"

The shade of his mother responded. "You have to dismiss the pool from this side. Place your thoughts elsewhere, and the connection from this side will leave him back in the inner sanctum."

He turned back to Bryndor. "I'm sorry, Bryn. You can't come through, and I can't go back, not yet. But you'll find a way. You always find a way."

Bryndor prepared to unleash a controlled burst of rune fire into the pool, sensing that his action would be sufficient to bolster the opening and retrieve his impulsive brother. But something in Lluthean's bearing, the calm manner in which he tried to get Bryndor to understand, made him falter. So, at the last, he suspended his channeling and watched, dumbfounded and defeated.

The righteous determination he felt only a moment prior vanished, and he felt his grip on the portal loosen. "Please, Llu, don't you leave me. I can't do it, not alone."

The firm edge he had gripped dissolved, and Bryndor tumbled headlong into the reflecting pool. He lingered in the depths, confused, watching bubbles rise, and eventually kicked up to the surface. When his face broke the surface though, instead of the expected sensation of matted hair clinging to his face, Bryndor sat bolt upright, as if waking from a vivid dream.

Zenith-laden filaments tingled as the zentrist of the Revealing fell away. Confused, Bryndor patted at his clothing, surprised to find it dry. Beside him, Boru lay on his side and stretched all four legs, mouth agape in a full-throated yawn. He searched the room, finding it much as the one he had left, with two exceptions. The massive double doors now stood in plain relief on the far side of the room, and a lone figure sat dozing on one of the benches. What he assumed must be the construct of Lluthean's Revealing, a strange oval cocoon woven of iridescent blue fibers, sat adjacent to the reflecting pool.

The woman sat with arms folded across her chest, head bowed, and the sight of her displaced any confusion he experienced about leaving the altered reality of the Rite of Revealing. A familiar patina of freckles adorned the upturned nose and cheeks of the woman. Bryndor rose to his feet and took a few staggering steps against a rising tide of uncertainty. He swallowed hard, trying to reconcile the young woman sleeping before him and the myriad of fresh memories from a life he had left behind.

His feet felt heavy, mouth dry, and his heart hammered in his chest. He couldn't bring himself to say anything. What if he spoke, and she never awoke? What if this woman didn't love him the way he loved her? *Balladur cor delledence*, right? Would she even know what that meant yet? Giver's last breath, did she actually love him at all? It felt difficult to separate what he expected of the woman he remembered, and this woman sitting here.

Boru padded forward, and before Bryndor could signal him back, the wolvryn sniffed at Ksenia's ear, causing her to awaken. Loose papers fluttered off her lap to the ground, and she bent to retrieve them, then shot bolt upright, a look of exuberance and surprise on her face. "Boru? What?"

She turned to him, quivering fingers held to her lips for a moment, then began to ring her left hand around her right wrist and smiled. "Welcome back, Bryn. Giver's tears, I've missed you. How are you?"

Something poignant and bittersweet broke inside him at hearing the authentic timbre of her voice, at sensing the reality not just of her presence but her excitement to see him, and tears fell in abundance down his cheeks. He swallowed back the full feeling gathering in his throat. "I'm not sure exactly, but I'm so glad you're the one I get to come back to."

Her face flushed, and she rushed into his arms. Her total commitment to the embrace, the smell of winter night's asylum lifting from her hair, the press of her body to his—all of it erased any misgivings he had about the sacrifice he made in the Revealing. This was the woman he loved and would love. She was here; she was real. He pressed his hands into the familiar musculature of her back and exhaled with utter relief. *I didn't leave her behind.*

The simple joy of that notion caused him to gasp once with a sob, and she held him for long moments as they rocked back and forth. When it felt right, she leaned her head back and finger-combed the hair from his face. "What's wrong?"

He laughed and sniffed back the swollen, congested bogginess in the back of his nose. "Nothing. I'm beyond words, Kess. I thought I lost you, I thought I lost everything. Seeing you here, it's the best second chance ever. This is it, right here, this is my Revealing. You and me. I'll never need anything else."

"I'm going to kiss you, Baellentrell. Is that alright?" she asked.

He nodded. "Yes, I would like that. I would like that a lot."

With a natural tilt of his head, he found her lips and pressed into the kiss with intimate need, the sensation at once novel and yet a reflection of the familiar. Afterward, they renewed a tight embrace.

As if in comical protest to their intimacy, Boru grumbled from the back of his throat and tried to nose in between them. Bryndor rested a hand on the wolvryn's head. "And you too, Boru. I'll always need you."

A tentative inflection altered Ksenia's tone. "Why isn't Lluthean waking from the Revealing, Bryn?"

"Because he's the Taker's grinding ass," said Bryndor. "I have to find a member of the Ilovesh to untether him from Tarkannen before he can come back."

Ksenia leaned forward. "But he can come back then? He's not dead?"

"Not in the sense that you mean," he said. Ksenia arched an eyebrow, expecting a more thorough explanation, so Bryndor obliged. "Let's sit and I'll explain what I can. I just need a moment to think."

He considered telling her everything about the life they had lived, their idyllic home in the mountains, but he knew this woman, her desires and her fears, and he felt certain that if he unloaded all of the details about the life they had lived, that she would feel trapped by the expectation to be some reflection of that person. He imagined how she would receive the information and intuitively knew that telling her would be disastrous for any future they might have.

Her warm touch on his left forearm brought him back to the room. "You're channeling this rune. That's new."

Bryndor looked down, surprised to discover that he had indeed been channeling into one of the delicate runes. "In my Revealing, I learned that this is the rune of sagacity. It's much like Kaellor's runes of judgment and balance. I think it overlaps with Therek's runes of sapience. I probably fall back on it too much and was trying to get a sense for where to begin."

"We are taught that no one has ever remembered anything from their Revealing. What else can you recall?"

With deliberate effort, he suspended his channeling. "Not much, really. I do remember seeing Lluthean, though. Somehow, he crossed with Neska into the Drift. I was stuck on this side, in a different version of this room. There were no doors though, and the surface of the pool acted like a window, allowing me to see and speak with him."

Bryndor proceeded to describe the conversations he observed with the apparition, the different forms it took, and the revelations about Lluthean's tether. He concluded with the mandate from his mother to find the Ilovesh. "When I say it all out loud, it sounds about as nonsensical as a fever dream. Does any of that make any sense?"

Ksenia frowned at him. "I've never heard of the Ilovesh, but it's not completely foreign sounding either. In fact it sounds very High Aarindorian. No matter, we can check the archives. If anyone knows the histories, it's my friend Veeble. He might be able to help. It's the middle of the night, but he keeps odd hours."

Her disclosure of the hour made him realize how disoriented he still felt since emerging from the Revealing. "How long has it been on this side of the Revealing?"

"I've been waiting six weeks for you to shed that cocoon. Your aunt and uncle should be notified at once. I may have given them some misleading information."

Now it was Bryndor's turn to effect an expression of question, so Ksenia explained her work translating *The Tome of Nivosh* and their collective concern that one of the brothers would perish.

"That squares with what the apparition of my mother said in the Drift. She seemed convinced that were I to cross, one or possibly both of us would die."

"Moons, Lluthean is alive in the Drift," she said.

"I think it's the wolvryn," said Bryndor. "Somehow their presence altered the experience. Then again, Llu's tether might enable him to endure where others would perish. I don't know."

Ksenia nodded, frowning and considering the puzzle. "Well, we should definitely share all of this with Kae and Laryn."

Bryndor held up a hand, forestalling her suggestion. "In time. I think I need time to adjust; maybe by morning, if that's alright."

"Of course, whatever you want."

"Has anything happened since we began the trial? What of Tarkannen? Any news I should be made aware of?"

"I admit that I am a little outside the loop of information regarding the usurper. But the steady caravan of supplies and troops being sent to the forward staging area between the Pillars tells me they anticipate something big. Kaellor and my father have been rather busy with minding the concerns of the high families. They will both welcome your return, I suspect, as a sign that the crown is secure."

"I was afraid of that," he muttered.

Instead of asking the obvious question, she studied his face, waiting for him to continue. "Leaving the kingdom to find the Ilovesh would be a difficult request during peacetime. Kae will bristle at any suggestion that I leave now. No matter, a problem for later."

"Can't someone else go? Send an Outrider diplomatic mission or something?"

"I don't think so, and I'm not sure why, but my mother said I have to be the one to find the Ilovesh. I don't know, maybe it's the conclusion of the trial."

Ksenia cocked her head, and he pulled open the top of his shirt to reveal a bare chest. She placed a warm palm where his arca prime should reside. "I see."

Her touch aroused his desire, and he searched the room, thinking to kiss her again, when his eyes fell across Lluthean's cocoon. He held one hand to hers, holding her touch on his breast, and with the other cupped her cheek. "There is nothing I would love more than to ride out of here under cover of darkness into the mountains with you."

"But you can't. Lluthean needs you. The kingdom needs you."

He released a heavy sigh and walked back toward the reflecting pool to inspect his brother's hibernation. "Yes."

Tingly static strafed across his palm as he ran fingers over the zentrist. Faint, sterile, galvanic vapors rose from the surface. He rapped a fist lightly against the blue fibers and thought one more time about the life he had left behind. Perhaps this was all meant to be. When he had entered the Revealing, he possessed the maturity of a man nearing twenty. He understood now that the trial demanded sacrifice for the potential of the arca prime, a rune he had yet to obtain. But had he not inherited something nearly as valuable?

He considered the problems before them with all the confidence of a man in his prime, a man who had lived and lost. He had a much better command of at least some of the runes on his arms. Sagacity on his left and perception on his right. "Huh," he said out loud. "I don't even recall when I learned to use that."

He realized then that maybe that was the true purpose of the Revealing: knowledge, maturity, and a sense of perspective that made him feel grateful for the woman standing across the room.

He whispered to the cocoon. "If that's the case, how much better prepared will you be when you finally return, brother? And how different will you be?"

"What's that?" asked Ksenia.

"I was just talking to Llu, but I'm pretty sure he can't hear me." He turned to face her. "Before we wake up Kaellor and the others, do you think we could stop in and visit your archivist? Anything we can learn of the Ilovesh would be helpful."

She stood and gathered papers under her arm. "I can drop these off to Veeble, but I warn you, he's an acquired taste."

"How so?"

"I can't explain it. He's gifted with some things, numbers, names, symbols and such. But he's not a gifted, he's runeless."

"I think I met him once, before my Revealing. But it was brief. Can we trust him? He's not with the Lacuna, or . . . ?"

"He's about as driven to deceit as a hitching post."

"I don't follow."

"Veeble is, I can't put it into words, but he doesn't really care about the things others care about. Kingdom politics, gossip, the allegiance of the prominent families, none of that matters to him. He finds joy in an organized set of archives, or solving the translation of *The Tome of Nivosh*. While I rely on my gift, he created a mathematical cipher to translate High Aarindorian. It's the puzzle he loves, but not the picture that the puzzle reveals. If you can get past his strange mannerisms and the fact that when he smiles, he resembles a frog, you'll find he's one of the most refreshing, honest people in Aarindorn."

As they exited the inner sanctum, Boru padded to the right, to the end of the corridor where the hidden passages led to the lair he and Neska preferred. Bryndor considered signing to him.

"He wants to see the stars, the real ones, not the ones from the Revealing," said Ksenia with a tone of curiosity.

He understood she must be employing her sympath gift. "What is it?" asked Bryndor.

"I can't be sure, but he's different from what I recall. It's his voice, maybe or . . . it's like his thinking is much more linear, less whimsical. And it felt like Boru was trying to say that he's not seen the night sky for years."

Bryndor nibbled on the inside of his cheek. He didn't want to lie to Ksenia, but he wasn't sure yet how she would react to the knowledge that he had spent nearly two decades of life inside the Revealing. "Our time in the Revealing was a particularly long row to hoe. Let me get the doors, see him out, and then we can visit the archives."

He found the placard at the end of the hall, recognizable by the dense cluster of silver veining on the stone. He set his palm to the surface and felt the vibration as the castle ward recognized his identity and intent. Familiar crackling noises skittered across the wall and blue lines of zenith outlined the stone door. It opened on silent hinges, and Boru padded through.

Bryndor reached into his pocket and removed one of the petrified wolvryn eyes, holding the orb high to cast light into the dark corridor. Boru walked ahead without him and a strange desire to accompany the wolvryn nearly pulled him through the doorway. As if he understood, Boru turned and swiveled his neck around, blinked once, then continued down the hall.

"He said to tell you, you're going to be fine and"—she laughed—"you are supposed to enjoy some alone time with me."

"I think he has the right of things," said Bryndor. He resealed the door, assuming the descent down to the secret passageway on the backside of the castle would be unobstructed.

They navigated through the castle, finding the halls empty except for the occasional patrolling sentinels. Fortunately, the soldiers were easy to identify by their strict dress code and the clatter of boots over stone. They considered evading the patrols, but Bryndor decided that an escort might prove the most efficient means of getting to the archives. After a brief introduction in which there was the exchange of formal greetings and salutes, the sentinels delivered them to the archives without delay.

He followed Ksenia through several long rooms lined with desks and towering shelves of books and scrolls. Once they were in the great hall and had found it empty, she cleared her throat. "Veeble? It's Ksenia. I've got some more translated pages for you, and I brought a friend."

From a balcony overhead, a wiry man wearing the black tailored garb of an archivist poked his head out. "Just finishing up here. Be right down."

A minute later, the clerk whirled down a tight spiral staircase, stopping just two steps away. The clerk rubbed the palms of his hands against his ribs in a strange, repetitive fashion. The gesture seemed to exacerbate the release of a pungent body odor that caused Bryndor's head to withdraw.

"Veeble Hebben, master archivist of the first order, may I introduce His Highness, Prince Bryndorllean Baellentrell. Prince, this is my friend, Veeble."

The odd man's hands stopped their patting a moment, then he tapped them with light repetition. "Oh my, oh my. Yes, yes, yes. We have met."

"Really? When was that?" asked Ksenia.

Veeble flushed and stared at his feet, circling his ribs with the flat of his hands. "I'm the one who . . . reported Vinnedesta's affiliation with the Lacuna to you, Prince. It's nice to see you again. Welcome to the archives, Prince Baellentrell. Yes, welcome indeed. Anything you need, I can get. You name it, I can get it very fast, very easy."

"It's a pleasure to see you under less dire circumstances, Veeble," said Bryndor. He considered offering the man his hand, but sensed that the gesture might scare him off. "Ksenia tells me that if I am interested in finding information about one of Aarindorn's neighbors, you might be the man to speak to."

Veeble rocked back and forth, his hand resuming the rhythmic patting gesture across the front panel of his uniform. "Mmmm. It's not the thing I am best at. You really should ask me something I am best at.

Then I can get you the answer very fast and very easy. Fast and easy is always the best, you know."

Bryndor smiled at the clerk's plain, yet earnest, odd nature and looked to Ksenia for confirmation that the man wasn't acting a part. She winked, so he continued, "Yes, well, all the same, I'm looking for any information you can find about the Ilovesh. Apparently, they are a people who reside far to the east. If there is anything you can tell us, I would be grateful."

Veeble looked once to Ksenia, then back to Bryndor. The man's eyes squinted, and he gave them both a smile that did, in point of fact, look more than a little frog-ish. "Follow me, this way."

Veeble led them up a different set of spiral stairs to a restricted wing of the archives. He donned cloth gloves and removed a set of four silver discs that looked like coasters for a fine glass of wine. Next, he removed a large scroll, taking great care to unroll it across the surface of a table. He used the weighted silver discs to anchor the edges, then stepped back and rubbed absently at the front panel of his uniform.

"This is one of the oldest maps of the Northlands, drafted in the time of Nivosh, after the Great War. You can see the northern range of the Korjinth Mountains. Those were not there before the Great War. That place used to be called the Plains of Jintha."

Bryndor studied the map, finding it reasonably well rendered and exceptionally well preserved if Veeble's indication of the age was accurate. He identified Aarindorn easily enough, with its distinctive ring of mountains. Far to the east, a massive tract of forest arose, and the names Leandur and Vellendar were penned with symbols.

"What do you know of these cities, Leandur and Vellendar?" he asked.

The archivist continued to pat down the front of his uniform and stared at Ksenia as if waiting for her to comment. Bryndor chewed on the inside of his cheek, considering the time that had elapsed since the map was recorded. "By now these might be cities or kingdoms or even ruins. Who can say after so much time?"

"I know those names. Why do I know those names?" asked Ksenia.

Veeble rose up and down on his tiptoes and bobbed his head. "Yes you do, yes you do!"

Ksenia's eyes widened. "One of the last entries from Nivosh mentioned emissaries from Leandur and Vellendar." Her gaze became unfocused as she tried to recite the translation. "A Leandurian man and Vellendarian woman both possessed of uncommon height and slender grace and marked with peculiar color patterns arrived with tidings from the tree singers." Her expression returned to the room. "I can't recall what she recorded after that. Veeble?"

The clerk cleared his throat, inhaled a deep breath, and recited the translation in a monotone voice with oddly pressured speech. "They held council with Queen Brekka and blessed the reflecting pool of the inner sanctum. They arrived on druska, strange mounts resembling a cross between an Aarindin and a moose. After a turn of the moon of Baellen, the druska migrated east, and the emissaries revealed that they could travel through the deepening well, their name for the reflecting pool. After the Ilovesh departed, scholars from across the kingdom were summoned to study the well. Aquamancers plied their gift in failed attempts to travel through the well. After the deaths of three gifted, the queen wisely suspended all efforts to use the well for that purpose."

Veeble gasped for air, having recited the entire entry with a single breath. Bryndor had to admit, the man's ability to recall the entire text was nothing short of remarkable. It reminded him a little of how Lluthean could travel the wilds, then accurately record a map of the region.

Ksenia nodded, showing no surprise at Veeble's skill. "That's right. I've been so focused on recording individual phrases that I think I didn't really pay attention to what Nivosh was saying."

"So, there are people and places to the east, but no reference to the Ilovesh?"

Veeble held both hands out before him, palms up, and flapped them up and down as if waiting expectantly for Ksenia to deliver a package. She stared at him a moment, then smacked her forehead. "Taker's breath, of course. Ilo . . . Vesh . . . those are High Aarindorian words for tree and singer."

"My codex indicates that the word vesh can be applied to mean singer, speaker, one who mumbles, or one even one who whispers. It changes depending on the context," said Veeble.

Bryndor made the connection as soon as the archivist made the clarification. "Alright then, we have a notion of where to begin. Veeble, is this map to scale?"

"As far as we know, but we don't know very far," said the archivist.

"Let me guess, Aarindorn never explored that far to the east? Why wouldn't they at least reciprocate with emissaries of their own?" Bryndor hovered a palm over Aarindorn without touching the ancient map, then estimated the distance to Leandur. "How long does it take to ride from Callinora to Stellance?"

"That depends on a lot of things. Aarindin or wagon, hard travel or easy. The seasons can affect it all," said Ksenia.

"It's early summer. If we left in a few days and rode with purpose, how long would it take?"

"At least ten days on Aarindin, maybe more," said Ksenia.

Bryndor puffed out his cheeks and pursed air through his lips. He gripped the edge of the table and dropped his head, muttering in frustration, "Grind it, Llu. Forty days to get there, forty to get back. I just found her and now I have to leave? You pop over and I'll hang out in the Drift for a bit."

Ksenia massaged an ache in his shoulder he didn't know existed. When he pushed back from the table, her warm fingers interlocked with his and his frustration melted. "You can't go alone, and I'm long overdue to get out of Stone's Grasp. Besides, you might need an above-average translator once we find them."

He realized at that moment that while he had every desire for her to join him, he couldn't ask her to assume such a burden. "You would do that? I could never ask that, but . . . are you sure?" he asked.

She shrugged. "It would mean that Veeble would have to finish the translation of *The Tome of Nivosh*, and it might mean—"

"It would mean everything," he broke in. "Sorry, it would mean everything to me, Kess. I can't explain what happened to me in the

Revealing, but I don't think I can reconcile what I have to do for my brother and separate from you."

"Then don't," she said, and kissed him lightly on the lips. "Don't leave without me."

A rustle of feet preceded a baritone voice breaking the relative silence of the archives. "Bryn? Bryn, it's me, Kae. The sentinels informed me of your awakening. Son, are you alright?"

There was an awkward silence as Bryndor walked around the table to lean out across the balcony. Kaellor stood below, barefoot and in rumpled sleeping clothes. He appeared to be rolling three billow seeds in his hand. A pillow crease marred his face, and the back of his hair betrayed where his head had lain on the pillow. "I'm up here, Kae."

His uncle looked up, a mixed expression of elation and concern on his face. "Giver's mercy. It's true then. Son, where is your brother? Where is Llu?"

Chapter Forty-Five: The Giver Gives and the Taker Takes

As Bryndor finished his recounting of the events of the Revealing, Kaellor found himself utterly at a loss for words. The three of them sat in the seclusion of Bryndor's suite, Ksenia having taken her leave to catch a few hours of sleep. His nephew had offered an explanation that strained all credibility, except that it was Bryndor and, compared to Lluthean, he never embellished a story, ever. Still, the entire thing was beyond Kae's initial comprehension. Nearly twenty years in the trial? What did that mean for the young man sitting across the table?

Kaellor had sensed at once that his nephew had emerged from the Revealing a different person. Bryndor was always introspective, but now that introspection was coupled with a stronger sense of self, as if the lad really had amassed a certain amount of authentic life experience. The revelation was at once both miraculous and troubling.

Kaellor drummed fingers on the tabletop and glanced to his wife, who sat equally perplexed. More than once, Laryn had readjusted the front panels of her sleeping robe. While she listened intently, her restlessness betrayed her concern. Bryndor, appearing to have come to terms with some part of the experience, sipped on a cup of stout tea.

Several questions formed in his mind. How did he remember any portion of the trial? Why didn't he inherit his arca prime, and was it still possible to claim that last part of his inheritance? What would happen if Lluthean remained in the Drift and how, exactly, did he plan to free his brother?

Laryn's steady voice broke through the parade of warring questions. "I assume you chose not to tell Ksenia about . . . what you left behind?"

"I gave it consideration, but . . ." He shook his head, staring into his teacup. "There might be a time in the future when I can tell her all of it. Right now, though, I'm still struggling to separate what was from what is. And I know Kess. She hates being defined by other people's expectations. I don't want her second-guessing my motives or her own by comparing herself to the woman from my Revealing."

Kaellor growled in self-deprecating frustration. For the last hour, he had listened to Bryndor's narrative, but questions continued to break into the surface of his awareness, distracting him from engaging in the conversation. With renewed effort, he set all his concerns to the side and tried to focus on the issues before them. "Does Ksenia know about Lluthean, about the apparitions he interacted with?"

Bryndor nodded. "Most of it. We didn't have time to get into specifics, but she knows about the tether, and Llu's choice to remain behind. That's why we went to the archives first. Her contact there, Archivist Hebben, I believe, was helpful."

Laryn set her forearms on the table and leaned forward. "Are you certain about the tether? I can't understand why Docent Venlith or myself never detected the strain of carrying the usurper's tether."

"Fairly certain," said Bryndor. "I could see a remnant of it floating up from Llu like a wisp of smoke. And if I understood the conversation between Llu and the spirit of our mother, Neska sensed something of the tether from its inception."

Kaellor rubbed a hand down past his eyes and tugged hard at the edges of his beard. "And the ghost of your mother, she said that you must be the one to seek out the Ilovesh? You and not someone else?"

Bryndor sat back and nodded slowly, appearing to consider the question. "Look, I can understand that all of this is a lot to digest all at once. I had twenty years to learn something of my gift and how the Revealing changed me. You look at me and see the same young man who entered the trial six weeks ago. But Kae, I had a life inside the Revealing, an entire, complete happy life. Giver, you both were basically grandparents to my kids."

He swallowed and blinked a single set of tears. "I've loved and lost more than most. They might not have been real to anyone but me, but I can feel the raw emptiness of the scar it left behind."

Kaellor held up a hand. "I'm not questioning any of that, son."

Bryndor nodded. "I know, believe me, I know. What I am trying to say, is that I understand more of your motivations than you realize. I understand." He let the words linger in the air. "I know that your desire to protect all of us is your chief motivation. But I am absolutely convinced of the need to set out for the Ilovesh as soon as possible. We can't leave Llu in there. And if any part of that journey gives me a second chance with Ksenia, then I'll take it. I'll walk through the worst the Taker sets before me for that kind of opportunity."

"The Borderlands are riddled with roving grondle herds. There have been sightings of more beasts from the Drift breaking through to our world. It's such a gamble," said Kaellor.

Now Bryndor held up a hand, mirroring Kaellor's earlier gesture. "Heard. But even if I didn't believe that seeking the Ilovesh was the right action, my gift confirmed it. Take a moment and challenge my proposition with your own gifts. If I can't convince you, maybe the Giver can."

Kaellor sat back in his chair and tilted his head, agreeing to Bryndor's proposal. He reached out, embracing the flow of zenith, and felt warmed by its caress across his runes and in his core. Answering his bidding, the flow naturally infused his runes of judgment and perception, reviewing the quest Bryndor proposed and the potential to not only find the Ilovesh but to return Lluthean from the Drift during the current turmoil.

A distinct image of Bryndor riding beside Ksenia across the plains toward the sunrise materialized in his mind. A calm breeze gusted over the plains, and on the wind a strong, maternal voice whispered, "You cannot shackle this man. Set him free and let the world see all that he can become, my child."

Rarely did the Giver speak to him with such clear declarations through his gift. All of Kaellor's rebuttals drained away like so much water in a bucket full of holes. He sensed Laryn's eyes on him and muttered a curse under his breath, but found he had no choice but to begrudgingly agree. "I can't say that I would act any differently were I wearing your boots. I don't like it, but you're right."

"When do you propose to leave?" asked Laryn.

"That depends on how fast we can gather a group of Outriders. Are there any to spare?" said Bryndor.

"We'll make it happen. Overwarden Kaldera has pressed most of them into service supporting the army mustered at the Pillars. Others provide ongoing reconnaissance of the Borderlands," said Kaellor. "We can either use the shek or one of the sender triplets to send word. The road from here to the forward base camp is well maintained. It will take you less than a week to make the Pillars, but that should be enough time to assign a quad or two to accompany you."

"Ksenia mentioned that you and Therek have had your hands full managing the nobles. I assume that means neither of you could join us? I know that the timing of all of this is awful. It was a risk, I suppose, when we started the trial."

Kaellor studied his nephew. The young man seemed possessed of unnatural maturity, and yet, it was clear that his newfound perspective was a sword that cut both ways. While he could draw on his experiences to help him manage difficult situations, his awareness also meant that he now understood the full weight of the burdens thrust upon him. His comprehension was at once a blessing of the Giver and a curse from the Taker.

Kaellor sighed. "It is a lot, Bryn. All of it. The power struggles of the nobles, the remnants of the Lacuna, and these attacks from creatures born of the Drift. But none of that is your fault. I can't say it won't be more difficult without you here, but with your aunt and the regent, we can maintain stability within the kingdom while the army defends us from the dangers without. But even if none of those problems existed, I would still need to stay within Stone's Grasp. It's the only way to maintain the barrier preventing Tarkannen's return."

"Is there a chance that the barrier will hold if any Baellentrell resides within the confines of the castle, or is it tied to you?" asked Bryndor.

"In the past, your father could leave the city and travel to the duchies or Stellance. As long as I remained within Stone's Grasp, the barriers did hold. But I'm not clear if that was something unique Japheth did when he created the barrier, or if it was a natural consequence of the castle defenses."

"And of course, now would be one of the worst times to test the theory," said Bryndor.

"Exactly," said Kaellor.

Bryndor chewed on the inside of his lip. "Well, you heard all about my time in the Revealing. Tell me more about where things stand with the usurper."

Laryn reached for the teapot and refilled their cups as she spoke. "Before we returned to Stone's Grasp, Therek sent emissaries to the border kingdoms of Faltusch and Norfold. Their mission to initiate trade discussions failed miserably."

"What happened?" asked Bryndor.

"Both kingdoms received the diplomats with professional decorum, but neither could commit to trade discussions. A drought has affected the plains west of these kingdoms and that is one concern. The other is that their own scouts report an army amassing in Kreeg. The Sea King of Faltusch gave lip service to sending a delegation to Aarindorn, but the words were offered with little commitment. At any rate, all reports are that the Kreeg, supported by a horde of grotvonen, prepare to march east. We only learned of the development a few days ago."

"If Therek sent diplomats months ago, why did they only just return with this news?" asked Bryndor.

Kaellor tilted his head, acknowledging Bryndor's reasoning. "We anticipated that our diplomats could return through the Endulian, a pass through the western edge of the Great Crown. When the pass is open, one can make the journey from Beclure to Faltusch in about five days. But freak snowstorms have made the Endulian Pass impassable. It's like all the water left the plains, only to deposit on our western slopes. The diplomats were forced to skirt the Great Crown and approach through the Pillars of Eldrek, but ran afoul of a crush of grondle. Four Outrider quints accompanied the diplomats. A total of twenty-four left for the border kingdoms, but only six returned."

The news gave Bryndor pause. "I don't suppose we've had scouts in the field east of Aarindorn?"

"All scouts report that the majority of the grondle attacks are to the south and west of Aarindorn. We suspect that Tarkannen has directed them to disrupt trade in these areas," said Kaellor.

"And do we also suspect that since a horde of grotvonen accompanies the army in Kreeg, that Tarkannen must somehow direct their forces?" asked Bryndor.

"We do," said Kaellor.

A heavy silence blanketed the room as they each considered the import of Kaellor's statement.

"How long will it take his army to reach the Pillars?" asked Bryndor.

"Who can say?" answered Kaellor. "Armies move with much less agility and grace than a small company of Outriders. But our best guess is that they could be on our doorstep within three months, assuming that they bypass the border kingdoms and approach us directly."

"That's cutting it grinding close," said Bryndor. "If the maps in the archives are accurate and if we manage to find the Ilovesh, the ride there might take the better part of five weeks, maybe six. It makes me question the wisdom of leaving."

"It's a gamble either way," said Kaellor. "I would rather face Tarkannen's forces standing beside both of you. If your gift gave you as much confirmation as mine did, then it's a gamble well placed."

"I know, but like you said, I don't like it. Still, I'll plan to leave tomorrow morning. Can you see to connecting us to a group of Outriders?" he asked.

"Consider it done," said Kaellor.

"Does Dexxin still ride under Savnah's command? I would prefer to have the backup of a sender in case the sheks fail," said Bryndor.

"If they are available, we will put them at your service," said Kaellor.

"What about Karragin? None were more formidable in a scratch," said Bryndor.

"She resigned her commission in the Outriders and serves as one of my Mirrare, my personal guard," explained Laryn.

Recognition flashed across Bryndor's face at her words. "That's right. I forgot about her hearing deficit. She was different in my Revealing. But then, I suppose everyone was. Moons, that's a lot of cards to reshuffle."

He stretched back and yawned for the first time, the gesture at once infectious to Kaellor and Laryn. "We should take our leave. I've a meeting with the regent and can inform him of your experience, if that's alright?"

Bryndor waved his head side to side. "It's information he should have, I think, but swear him to secrecy about, well, everything I suppose. I don't want Kess to hear about those things from anyone but me, and . . . I'm not ready."

Kaellor pulled his nephew into a warm embrace. "Have no worry. We need everyone in Aarindorn working for the common defense of the kingdom. I don't think that the people are ready to grapple with all the transcendental ramifications of the things you witnessed. Better to keep our eyes to the horizon."

"Eyes to the horizon, Kae," said Bryndor.

They took their leave, retiring to their own rooms, and Kaellor walked to the window to clear his head and consider how he would approach Therek. Laryn embraced him from behind, her touch at once disarming and comforting. She laid her cheek on his back and he allowed his senses to become momentarily lost in the warmth of her body pressed to his. "Your mind wanders a long way from this room, love."

He inhaled and released a deep breath. "I can't help thinking that we pushed them both into the trial before they were ready. Maybe that had something to do with the strange outcome."

"Or maybe it was the wolvryn, or Lluthean's tether, or any number of variables you could neither foresee nor control. But you know that already, so what's really bothering you?"

What was bothering him? They had spent the last month sleepless, convinced that one of the boys would perish in the Revealing and now, at least, there was a chance that both might emerge. Wasn't that reason enough for celebration? If that were the case, why did he feel as if he'd lost something?

"He's not Bryndor anymore. I mean, he's not the young man who entered the trial," said Kaellor.

He felt her shake her head against his back. "No, he is not, my love. He's something more."

"I know, and I think I'll be grateful for that someday, but right now, all I can think about is the time I lost with him. The Giver increased his empathy, and now he carries a certain awareness that he never demonstrated before. But the Taker robbed us of the chance to watch him become the man he is."

"He's still Bryndor, love, you know that."

Kaellor sighed, then turned to face her and returned her embrace. "I know. But I can't help thinking that if Bryn survived a lifetime of experiences in the Revealing, how much different will Llu be if we can get him out?"

Chapter Forty-Six: Possibilities in the Stillness

A heavy fog blanketed the ground, muffling sound but failing to dissipate the pervasive odor of rotting detritus. Seldora had pushed well beyond the western edge of the ursulu forest, beyond the plains and down the rolling hills to explore the moss-covered bog the Ilovesh called the Stillness. He shifted forward on his mount's thick shoulders, peering between Kadra's stout antlers.

Now that he'd reached the edge of the bog, alone but for Kadra's company, he understood the reason for the term. No life stirred in the brackish pools. No animal life, anyway. And as such, the region remained free from birdsong and other creatures who made a home among the resolute trunks of the ursulu forest.

More than that, though, the Stillness exuded a palpable feeling of emptiness. He pulled his fingers through the air, trying to better understand the sensation, and abruptly realized the change. Ahead of him, across the bracken waters, the land lay devoid of the current of zenith.

He dismounted, and Kadra grunted a sound of displeasure through black, fleshy lips. Then the great druska trotted back uphill and nibbled leaves from a stunted bush. The flesh on his bald head tightened as if struck by a cold wind, and Seldora retreated to stand next to his mount.

What are you eating this far from the forest?

Closer inspection showed that the briars grew around a stunted ursulu sapling. The displacement of even a single seed of the sacred ursulu tree seemed a mystery eclipsed only by the fact that it grew at all. The unnatural fog and cloud cover obscured any direct light.

How then did the young tree thrive? He rubbed fingers over one of the leaves, and without thinking, siphoned for zenith. A faint wisp of the power tickled his fingers. He knelt down by the sapling. "You're living solely on the meager flow of zenith, but that will never be enough. You need rich soil, exposure to the sun and moons, and the company of your ancestors if you are to survive."

Kadra leaned his snout forward to pluck the last few leaves from the tree and Seldora tapped a single finger on the druska's nose. "Kadra, you know better. I can save this one. Besides, it marks the boundary where zenith stops."

The druska snorted a deep sound of disagreement, but wandered back up the hill in search of other shrubs to nibble. Seldora considered his options. He could manifest zenith into his fingers, elongating and strengthening them, then carefully remove the soil from the roots.

He removed his sheff, the loose-fitting shirt covering his torso and arms. Woven from the fibers of discarded ursulu leaves, the material was lightweight but resilient. Depending on the size of the root bulb, he could use the sheff to protect and carry the roots. With Kadra's help, he could probably transplant the sapling back to the ursulu forest within a day.

He jabbed the point of his kesak into the ground, then opened his senses, searching for the faint currents of zenith. In the lush forests of his homeland, the transformation he intended took seconds. Manifesting the changes here, at the edge of the Stillness, took nearly an hour. He could call upon his inner reserves, but that practice would tax him severely.

With the patience known only to the Ilovesh, a race that lived well beyond a turning of the moon cycles, he altered his hands. Eventually, his right hand resembled a curved trowel, and the left a rigid clawed implement with curved tines.

He went to work, excavating the thick layer of moss that covered the ground, then carefully removing the briars choking the tree, and finally the soil. All the while, he was mindful of the delicate roots. While tedious, the work was a welcome distraction from his established routine. In the last ten years, he had scouted in isolation all the lands south of the ursulu forest.

After all that time, he'd come to the conclusion that any foreign travelers would arrive from the lands to the west. Improbable as it might seem, those who could offer him the opportunity for redemption must cross the Stillness. Kadra had become his lone companion in the last few years. Kadra and the ghost of his sister, Sephora.

Her voice sheared through the fog. "Why do you spend yourself so? The chances of this sapling making any meaningful recovery are slim."

He sensed her form disperse some of the fog to his left, but kept his eyes on his work, separating soil from the tender rootlets. "Hello sister. Meaningful labor may be separated from futility by nothing more than the breath of the Giver."

She hummed a response, neither agreeing nor disagreeing. Her wispy silhouette floated around the sapling, as if considering his probability of success. "You speak a truth, brother, but hear my truth as well. You are no tree singer. Even if this sapling survives the trip back, the forest may not accept its return. Without a connection to the others, it will perish in time."

Seldora kept digging and freed enough of the root structure that the small tree listed to the side. He knelt back, allowing the tension in his shoulder muscles to disperse. "Are we still talking about saplings? I do not care to revisit old arguments."

"Nor do I, but all this wandering has left you even more separated from our people, brother. It's not too late to accept your place, to live your life among the Ilovesh."

The rune marks on Seldora's scalp burned with heat. "An unresolved life is no life at all."

"The resolution you seek is a dead branch and will not bear fruit. You think destroying Tarkannen will change things, but only when you stop living your life for my failures will yours amount to anything."

"It is inevitable, and I told you, an old argument. I've not seen you for months. Why are you here today?"

Again, her voice became a shearing, ethereal melody. "Do not be less than you are, brother. You know that time is meaningless here."

That was a fair rebuke, he supposed. From earlier conversations, he knew Sephora found the concept of time meaningless. "Thank you for the opportunity to improve, sister. I will speak with clarity. Was there anything in particular that drew you to me today? I know it is not easy for you."

"Better," she said.

He continued to free a particularly long and stringy section of roots. When she spoke no more, he began to wonder if she had faded back to the Drift, but her silhouette remained in his peripheral vision. He sat back and gave her his full attention.

Sephora dipped her chin. "I came to tell you about a disturbance in the Drift."

"I know. You already told me he escaped."

"I'm not talking about Tarkannen. Another has arrived, a human. He is connected to us and Tarkannen. I'm going to reveal myself and teach him our ways."

The news gave Seldora pause. Sephora had learned a bitter lesson when her intentions for Tarkannen soured. Surely she would not make similar mistakes. But even if she did, what would it harm if she shared the secrets of the Ilovesh with another who had passed into the Drift?

"I hope he brings you peace, sister."

"I do not seek your blessing in this. I come to tell you that his brother—"

Schlock! A wet, popping sound, as if something heavy was plodding through the brackish water, echoed through the fog. Another followed, and several more. Whatever created the disturbance was close and getting closer.

Seldora stood and reached for the haft of one of his kesaks, but his rigid fingers failed to find a grip. He trapped the haft under one arm and used the crook of his other elbow to support the weapon, then backpedaled up the hill. He glanced to the side, hoping Sephora might give him some insight, but her visits were becoming more and more ephemeral, and she had already faded back to the Drift. All he could see was the sapling, listing to the side, in the hole he had carefully excavated.

A head materialized through the fog. Its broad, scaled snout traveled back and forth, sweeping in arcs. Another series of noises echoed, and he now understood they were from the heavy footfalls of the creature lifting in and out of the bog. The reptilian thing stepped closer, its size rivaling the druska. A patina of glistening grey and green scales covered its thick neck and torso. A tongue flicked out in rapid succession, and matched sets of beady black eyes set to the back and sides of its wide head stared, unblinking.

Seldora thought the creature likely had his scent, but he didn't think it had seen him yet. There was a detached vacancy in its eyes. He chanced a slow step backward, and the beast remained still but for the flicking of its tongue. Eventually, it snorted and stepped closer, then turned in a serpentine circle. Through the fog, a long, scaled body supported by three sets of stout legs emerged.

He continued a cautious retreat, his nimble feet lifting and dropping without a sound. He had no desire to find conflict with the beast, and by its girth alone, he didn't relish his chances of surviving a skirmish. The lizard plodded forward, nose sweeping back and forth, until it approached the ursulu sapling. It stopped and hovered over the area, tongue flicking in and out with a frenzied tempo.

The Ilovesh remained still, studying the thing. He considered making a noise, anything to draw the beast away. Before he took action, the lizard lifted its head to stare directly at him. Corded muscles around its front shoulder rippled, and one clawed foot dropped unerringly down onto the ursulu, grinding it back into the mud.

As a people, the Ilovesh had little cause to swear. Their vocabulary made no such accommodations. But all Ilovesh knew the harsh sound of a dead ursulu leaf releasing from the parent tree and Seldora inhaled, the sound involuntarily escaping his lips, "Fths!"

The lizard hissed and clawed at the ground, preparing to charge. As it did, his misshapen hands fumbled his kesak to the ground. He left the weapon and crouched with anticipation, then rasped the implements of his hands together in challenge.

The lizard surged forward with surprising speed, clawed feet churning up moss and mud. Seldora leaped, arcing over the beast's head and twisting to rake his tine-shaped hand across the cluster of eyes on its left side. The flat of his other hand smacked against its snout for good measure, a painful vibration burning up his forearm as he contacted solid bone. He kicked off, landing in a roll, then turned to watch as the lizard swept its head back and forth, hissing in pain.

Blood ran freely down the left side of its face and from its snout. The beast lashed a thick tail back and forth. Seldora circled as the lizard turned, keeping to its blind side. All around the thing, great patches of brown appeared as it displaced clumps of moss.

Seldora tried to channel zenith, but found the source too weak, so he drew upon a small portion of his innate stores, refining his left hand, giving it an edge.

He bent down and retrieved a bit of dirt, flinging it to the far side of the beast. Before he could leap onto its back and attack its remaining set of eyes, the lizard tucked the limbs on that side and log-rolled, attempting to crush him under its weight.

You are capable of learning. Then I shall be your teacher, and you shall learn to respect the ursulu.

The lizard tumbled back and forth over the ground, attempting to crush him, and Seldora used the opportunity to step forward, knowing it would flick its tongue out on instinct. He understood that standing so close, even on its blind side, was a risk, but before he could reconsider, the pink tongue lashed out, and he sliced his right hand through the air, lopping off nearly a foot of sinuous tongue, which fell to the mud.

Reptilian muscles spasmed from the front to the back, the tail stiffened, and after several seconds of silent agony, the lizard roared a keening rasp of pain. For the first time since the encounter, it dropped its head and backtracked, slowly at first, then all six legs clumsily backpedaling. A musky, oily scent rose into the air. Seldora remained still, watching, listening, and waiting.

The lizard made no attempts to hide its pain, hissing, wailing, and stamping its heavy clawed feet into the mud. The Ilovesh stood as immutable as the great ursulu and maintained a vigilant observation.

Finally, he ushered in the subtle flow of zenith and returned his hands to their native shape, but enlarged the lobes of his ears to better capture any sound should the beast return. Over time, even with the auditory enhancement, he lost the ability to sense its footfalls, and eventually even the hissing stopped.

He retrieved his kesak, finding comfort in the way his fingers gripped the haft. He chided himself. *You allowed your sister to distract you and made mistakes. Do better.*

He turned to walk back up the hill, intent on finding Kadra and returning to the safety of the ursulu forest. A single bead of sweat ran down the middle of his back and he shivered, topless. He turned to find the sheff discarded on the ground near the sapling. After recovering the garment, he inspected the damage the lizard had caused.

Where he thought to find the sapling broken or splintered, instead it had molded into the boggy soil. The last of its broad, waxy leaves appeared covered in mud, but remained attached. He used the blade at the tip of his kesak to scrape the mud away, and the tree sprang back to a perky, erect position.

His own words echoed in his mind, and he crouched, speaking with reverence to the sapling. "Meaningful labor may be separated from futility by nothing more than the breath of the Giver. A small possibility is not the same thing as zero possibility."

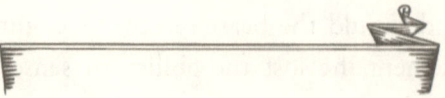

Chapter Forty-Seven: All the Variables

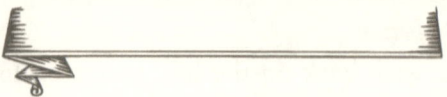

Ksenia's eyes fluttered awake with stinging protest against the bright, late-morning sun. She desired nothing more than to bury her face under her pillow, but the knock at her door recurred, accompanied by a muffled voice. Was that Laryn?

She sat upright, head swimming as she struggled to rise. Her balance floundered as she walked out of her bedroom, then across the generous receiving room to the door. She had become accustomed to the lavish quarters vacated by Ranika, and sidestepped a chair and table before reaching the door.

The knock rapped out again, more insistent. "Kess, it's Laryn. Are you well? May I come in?"

Ksenia opened the door to find Laryn standing alone in the hallway of the royal suites. One hand held a platter of tea on one hip and her other was balled into a fist as if to pound on the door. "Apologies, I'm fine, mostly. Sleep was just evasive. I think it was Bryndor's return and everything we learned, you know?"

Laryn's shoulders relaxed, and she stepped inside, closing the door behind her. "Yes, that's . . . well, that's why I wanted to talk to you before you set out. Can we sit?"

"Please," said Ksenia, gesturing to a small table. "I just need a moment to answer the call of nature. Make yourself comfortable and I'll be right back."

When Ksenia returned, she took her seat while Laryn poured them each a cup of black tea.

Ksenia gripped the fingers of her right hand around her left wrist, rolling it back and forth. While the gesture stilled her restless mind, it appeared fidgety, like something Lluthean might do. With an effort, she clasped the teacup and inhaled the fragrance. "My thanks. I'll need about three more of these before we leave."

Laryn filled her own cup, then sat back. "I know what you mean. Kae and I had half a mind to cancel our obligations for this afternoon and spend the day in slumber. But needs must, I suppose."

"I can only imagine."

"Bryndor told us that you will be joining him on his journey to the east, to find the Ilovesh?"

Right to it then. Ksenia acknowledged the question with a simple nod of her head, and her face flushed under the strange, direct nature of the inquiry.

Laryn must have sensed her discomfort and held up a hand. "I apologize. Don't misunderstand my intentions. Kae and I think it's a wise choice. We're happy that you will accompany him. We know that you can handle yourself on the trail. Nobody is better with the Aarindin, and your linguistics skill might be required for the mission to succeed."

"Alright, though I sense a but coming in."

"But I wanted to talk to you about a few things first." Laryn sipped at her tea, her expression becoming introspective. "Did you sense that anything had changed with Bryndor, when he emerged from the Revealing?"

Ksenia searched Laryn's face for some hidden meaning. Sensing none, she replied truthfully, "No, nothing one couldn't explain by waking up from such strange circumstances. Why do you ask?"

"He's been through a lot, more than anyone that we are aware of. I think it's a reflection of the potential power of his arca prime. Great power requires great sacrifice, it seems. Anyway, when you travel with him, if you notice that he seems different or even distant, I want you to know it's not you. It's Bryndor getting used to all the changes. He's still Bryndor, the young man who loves you. Whatever happens on the ride to the Ilovesh, promise me you'll remember that and give him a measure of the Giver's grace if he seems different."

Laryn's dual blessing and acknowledgment that she and Kaellor were well aware of their feelings for one another put Ksenia's mind at ease. "I appreciate the advice, and I will—be patient with him, I mean. Is there anything more specific you can tell me about what he's been through? Is there any way I can help him?"

Laryn smiled and shook her head side to side. "Nothing specific. Your commitment to joining him, just being present really, it gives him more strength than either of you realize. I'm glad that he has you, Kess. We both are."

Ksenia wrinkled her nose to prevent the tingly sensation from building into tears. "That means the world to me, honestly. Thank you so much."

She sipped at her tea to give herself time to recover from the poignancy of the moment. "So, what other kinds of advice do you have for traveling beside a Baellentrell prince?"

Laryn answered her with a soft giggle. "It's not so difficult or grand as most might imagine, but you know that already. Be yourself, speak to him with honesty, tell him the things he needs to hear, but more, the things he doesn't want to hear. Be his confidant, but never forget to be yourself. I suspect it's what drew him to you in the first place, your strong sense of self."

Their conversation shifted to discussions about Ksenia's preparations for the journey and she found that instead of any sense of trepidation, she felt excitement. The freedom to ride Winter across the kingdom, far away from the politics of Stone's Grasp, was reward enough. That she was on the adventure with Bryndor only raised her expectations.

Laryn finished her tea and stood. "Well, I should leave you to it, then. We both have many things to accomplish today."

They shared an embrace, and she walked Laryn to the door. As she did, she ticked off a mental list of the things she had accomplished already. *Penned a letter to Mother and Father, spoke to Veeble about finishing the tome, and gathered supplies; now to collect Winter and head out.*

Though her final tasks seemed simple enough, she felt the need to jog to the stables. Her step quickened both from the press of time and her anticipation of the journey. She rounded the corner to Winter's stall and there Bryndor stood, arms draped over Winter's gate, talking to the Aarindin as if they understood one another.

He wore a leather vest over a white shirt and leather breeches. His pack and bow rested beside the stall. She couldn't resist and snuck up behind him, slapping him on the butt cheek.

Bryndor's head dipped, and he chuckled. "Ksenia Balladuren, you haven't done that in a long time."

Ksenia stepped back and assumed a look of mock indignation. "My prince, you must have me confused with someone else, for I've never properly slapped you on the ass before."

"I meant sneak up on me. But that too, I suppose. Are you ready, then?"

"I am. What were you and Winter conspiring about?"

Bryndor rested a hand on Winter's forehead. "I gave her a carrot, one of the purple ones from the larder."

Winter blinked her pink lashes and looked guilty. "How did you know that those are her favorite? I don't think I have shared that with anyone. It's how I bribe her when she's feeling obstinate."

Bryndor grunted once, a sound of surprise, and turned to face her, leaning a shoulder on the stall. He searched her eyes, and she held his gaze, doing the same. A flicker of zenith flashed behind the blue of his eyes, and he assumed a mischievous expression. "Let's chalk it up to one of the things I learned in my Revealing."

"Hmm . . . alright, Prince Bryndor, man of secrets. But just know that anything you tell Winter in confidence is eventually likely to find its way to my ears. She can't help it. She's terrible with secrets, you know."

His eyes lingered on her face longer than she expected. "What is it?" she asked.

A pensive, even haunted expression passed over him, and he chewed on his lower lip. "Nothing. I suppose we should be off. I . . . nothing."

Laryn's advice echoed in her mind. She dropped her saddlebag and stepped forward, grabbing him by the front of his vest. "Hey Bryn, whatever it is, it's all going to be alright. You and me, together, okay? We've got this, all of it, the ride there, the Ilovesh, anything between here and setting Llu free."

He nodded agreement but held the somber expression on his face, so she rose to her tiptoes and kissed him, a deliberate, wet, lingering kiss full on the lips. She stepped back and grabbed her saddlebags. When she met his eye, he seemed oddly relieved.

Bryndor cleared his throat. "I wanted to do that from the moment you surprised me."

"I know. But we've got a bit of a schedule to keep, right? I mean, a girl on a mission to rescue the second son of the kingdom can't wait around all day."

He chuckled, and the smile reached his eyes. "No, I imagine she cannot. I'll grab Tacit and the packhorse and meet you out front."

"You recruited Tacit? Ooo, does Karragin know? He's one of her favorites."

"I already spoke to her this morning. She recommended Tacit over Trini. There weren't any other Aarindin to choose from." He started to walk down the row of stalls.

Ksenia set her small riding pack across Winter's hips and signaled the Aarindin out of the stall. "What about Boru?"

Bryndor stopped and unlatched the gate before Tacit's stall, then led the majestic Aarindin out. "I sent him to hunt this morning. He's going to meet us outside the Timber Gate."

They rode out without any of the formal ceremony one might expect for the departure of a highborn son. "Do you think it's strange that nobody came to, you know, see us off?"

He chewed errantly on the inside of his cheek. "Not really. I spent most of last night with Kae and Laryn, and I spoke to the regent and Karragin this morning. Other than you, there's not anyone else I care to spend my time with, and it's probably better if we slip out of the kingdom unannounced. Anything else would cause delay."

He shifted his weight on Tacit's back and met her eyes again. "Besides, other than you and Boru, I don't think I need much more to mark the start of a good day."

"I figured as much, but it's still nice to hear," she said.

"Kess, can you maybe talk to Tacit for me? See if you can convince him to grip me? I tried the carrot bribe, and he's responsive enough, but it's going to make for a long few days without his grip."

"Surely, give me a moment."

Ksenia kindled her sympath rune on instinct, linking Winter and Tacit into a conversation. The shared conversation always made for faster bonding in the past, and Tacit took little convincing.

Bryndor's posture eased back.

"Better?" she asked.

"Much better. I don't think I would weather a full day riding ungripped with very much grace."

He signaled, and Tacit fell into a comfortable canter, following the trail through the Crown's Timber and to the Timber Gate. Bryndor nodded at the trio of guards posted at the gate and drew Tacit to a halt. The trio stood at attention and offered a formal salute with fists pressed to chests.

"At ease, I'm only here to collect Boru," said Bryndor.

"What's a boru?" asked one of the guards.

Skirting the outer walls, the great wolvryn loped forward on silent paws. He stopped a few paces away to scratch his flank, and Ksenia noted that Boru's head eclipsed Bryndor's as he sat on Tacit. *Moons, is he ever going to stop growing?*

All three guards stepped back into the gate, hands nervously resting on sword pommels. "That's Boru. Have a good day, men. The kingdom is blessed by your service."

Bryndor signaled Tacit back into a canter, and Boru fell in beside them as they circled around the city, eventually finding the road leading south toward Stellance. He signed for Boru to follow at a distance, both to avoid attention and, she supposed, to prevent the wolvryn from startling any of the citizens using the road for similar travel.

She rode beside him in silence, taking in the sights. They passed several small caravans: vendors carting all manner of goods, families traveling in wagons to and from Stone's Grasp. The late afternoon sun glared off the rippling surface of Lake Ullend and warmed her cheek. She wished she had a hat like Ranika's shielding her eyes.

A few hours later, Bryndor slowed the pace. "Does the kingdom still maintain groundings along the outskirts of Lake Ullend?" he asked.

"You mean the camp shelters? I'm not sure, but this close to Stone's Grasp, it's a fair bet."

He chewed on the inside of his cheek. "What do you think? Pull up at one of the established camps with a view of the lake, or find a place more secluded and off the beaten path?"

"I haven't camped on the shores of Lake Ullend in years. If it's our safety you're concerned for, I'm pretty sure that Boru's presence alone will discourage anyone from approaching. Besides, it will be easier for the mounts to graze and water there."

"Sounds good." They passed by several occupied campsites, stopping at a vacant spot on the southeast edge of the lake.

Bryndor made quick work of removing their gear from the packhorse. "There are two small tents here. If you can set them up, I'll curry the packhorse and Aarindin, then we can see to supper?"

Ksenia nodded her agreement and unrolled the tents. Both were woven from the familiar lightweight oil cloth Outriders used and provided enough room to sit. She assembled the first one without difficulty, but struggled to unroll the second one. After lifting and folding the corners back and forth, she discovered that a large tear in one sidewall had compromised the integrity of the structure.

"Well, that's not a promising omen," she muttered.

Bryndor stepped alongside her, recognizing the defect, and clasped his hands overhead, pulling his hair back. "Huh. Well, that one will suit me fine until we rendezvous with the others at the Pillars. I can exchange it for a good one then. It's only a few nights. I'm sure it will be fine."

He retrieved a small pot and waved it at her. "Help me with supper?"

Her stomach gurgled in answer, and she clutched her abdomen in surprise. "Absolutely. What can I do?"

"Come on, you bring the water. I'll grab some rocks."

She followed him to the lake edge, where they both took the opportunity to wash the trail dust from their face and arms. He gathered an armful of small rocks, and she filled the pot with water. "What are those for, exactly?"

He smiled. "Another trick I learned in the Revealing. Give me a moment, I'll show you."

He knelt down, organizing the rocks into a stacked ring. The hairs on her forearms rose as the ambient currents of zenith responded to his channeling. A moment later, a soft pressure wave and low-pitched thump pulsed from his hands. It sounded like a cork being removed from a fat-bottomed glass vase.

An intense burst of rune fire roared under his palms for almost a minute before he stopped. A wave of heat rolled out from the rocks, which now glowed like hot embers. Without waiting, she placed the pot on the bed of rocks. Water from the outer edge immediately sizzled and hissed.

"That's a pretty good trick, Bryn. Very little light and no smoke. What else did you learn while you were away?"

He inhaled as if to respond, then seemed to reconsider, chewing on his lower lip and frowning. "I'm still sorting it all out in my head, you know?"

Instead of explaining further, he rose to his feet and retrieved a parcel from the packs. He scooped out two handfuls, dropping the contents into the pot. She recognized dried lentils easily enough, but the aroma was beyond anything she had imagined.

She inhaled with exaggerated pleasure. "Giver's blessings. Where did you get this?"

Bryndor smiled. "I thought you might like something more than bean soup and bread. It's a long trip, so I stopped by a vendor in the lower commons. It won't last the whole journey, but it's better than nothing."

She considered him with renewed appreciation and studied the pack and supplies. Other than two bedrolls and some blankets, waterskins, and a quiver of arrows, it appeared that most of the weight that had burdened the packhorse was from pouches of dried lentils and similar foodstuffs. "You didn't pack anything extra for yourself, did you?"

He shrugged and tilted his head. "Boru and I can hunt game later, and we can forage when there is time, but I thought it would be better if you had alternatives."

Ksenia shook her head in wonder. Where did this man really come from, and how did the Giver ever see fit to place him in her path? She stepped forward and wrapped her arms around his waist. He placed one arm around her shoulder, and they stood in silence as the night stars began to twinkle over the surface of Lake Ullend.

Eventually, they separated, and he divided the stew into portions. She considered pressing him with more questions, but before she could ask him, a yawn overtook her, and then another. She giggled despite herself. "Taker's breath, I'm sorry, I didn't sleep well last night."

Bryndor held up a hand. "Me either. Let's turn in for the night and make an early start tomorrow?"

He reached for the pot and began to walk toward the lake, but she stopped him and grabbed his wrist. When he turned back, she stepped in close and kissed him on the lips. He leaned into the kiss, drawing her in, and a firm hand pressed against the small of her back. Her lips explored his, and her senses focused on the way he responded when she nibbled and caressed, on the feel of him and the pressured exhalation of breath through his nose, even on his scent. All of it was intoxicating, and her breath quickened.

The urgency of the kissing slowed, and for that she was relieved, for if they continued, she wasn't at all certain where it would stop. In synchrony, they withdrew and settled for a long embrace, comically ending only when he dropped the pot to reach both arms around her.

They separated after the onslaught of another wave of yawns, shared a laugh, and retired for the night. So ended day one of their journey to the Ilovesh. *And if the rest of this adventure is similar, I don't think we're ever coming back to Aarindorn.*

They awoke early the next morning and pressed on, keeping mostly to the road, finding another grounding. The third evening placed them in Stellance, where a bit of coin provided care for the mounts and lodging. Bryndor even managed to take a ground-level room and snuck Boru inside for the night.

Ksenia awoke early on the fourth morning to the rumble of thunder and flashes of lightning. The steady rattle of rain heralded a long day if they chose to venture out. She wondered if Bryndor would delay their departure, but when she entered the common room, he sat at a table drinking hot tea. Two oil cloth ponchos draped over the bench beside him.

Well, rain it is then.

She took a seat beside him and helped herself to a serving of cheese melted on toasted buttered bread. She thought back to the short time they had traveled together in the Great Crown. "Are you always the first one to rise and the last to bed? Doesn't seem natural."

He blew steam from his cup of tea and winked. "And why not?"

"Well, you're either a morning person, you know, to bed early and up early, or you're a night owl. You can't be both, not for very long, I expect."

"Which one are you?" he asked.

"Hmm. That depends on all the variables." She lifted her hand, splaying her fingers and folding down each finger one at a time as she explained.

"How good is the food?" One finger folded down. "How good is the company?" A second finger folded down. "How comfortable is the bed?" Three fingers folded. "What have I got to do today and who am I going to do it with?"

She made a fist and shook it once in the air.

"So, you're a night owl," he surmised.

She tossed a piece of bread, bouncing it off his shirt, then conceded, "Most of the time."

He waited for her to finish, then stood and donned one of the ponchos, holding the other up for her. In minutes, they rode out of the sleepy border town. The noisy patter of rain on her shoulders and hood made conversation difficult. She passed the time by periodically linking to the Aarindin. She even tried communicating with the packhorse, but found the gelding's thoughts unsophisticated.

The endless rain cleared the roads of other travelers, and Boru loped alongside them. His fur gathered in wet locks that only accentuated the muscles along his chest and shoulders. She thought to reach out to him and see how he fared, but realized that Bryndor was carrying on a conversation with him by signing.

Her chin poked out from under her poncho and she tilted her hood back, watching as the two communicated.

"Have you sensed any others? Any danger?" Bryn signed. Boru tilted his head to the left.

"We will not make the Pillars today. I would like to press on, find shelter near the rim of the Great Crown. Can you continue?" he signed. Again Boru tilted his head to the left, but only after lifting his nose to the air.

"I understand. It's been nearly three days. You should find something to eat. We will be safe enough. Find us camped near the Great Crown directly south of here."

Boru tilted his head to the right, a gesture Ksenia understood for consent or agreement. The great wolvryn lurched ahead in three bounding hops and disappeared into the timber.

The rain settled into a soft drizzle, so she left her hood down and pulled up alongside Bryndor. "When did you two learn all of that?"

Bryndor turned his head to the side in confusion. A rivulet of rainwater streamed down the poncho and along the short beard covering his jaw. He shook his head once, dispersing water, then pulled his hood back. "I don't actually think that these ponchos have been rain-tested. There isn't any part of me that isn't at least a little bit soggy."

"It's the same with me, but you're avoiding the question, Baellentrell. Forgive me for watching your conversation, but Boru understood some really complex signing there. When did you two sort all of that out?"

Bryndor nodded to himself, as if just becoming aware of the miraculous conversation he had shared without using zenith. "Kess, the Revealing . . . changed me in some ways. Some that I'm only just beginning to understand. Boru was in there with me, through it all. I think it changed him as well."

"So, you're not a sympath then?" she pressed, but her tone made it clear that she was teasing.

"No, nothing so grand as all that. Remember, I left the Revealing with the exact same set of runes that I started with, though I might . . . understand things a little better. Boru and I certainly understand one another better. And I learned a lot more about how to employ some of my gifts. But I still have a lot of questions."

She walked Winter directly to the south, heading into untamed forest when the road doglegged to the west.

"Where are you going?" he asked.

She yelled over her shoulder, "You told Boru to meet us at our camp directly to the south, near the mountains. I don't know about you, but I'm ready for that rock-fire trick of yours and some hot stew."

He followed without protest and within the hour found a stream to set up camp by. The rain abated, and they made quick work of setting the tents, grooming the packhorse, and preparing the stew. The sun fell below the summit of the Great Crown and the entire valley plummeted into darkness as clouds obscured the moon and stars.

They finished their meal just as Boru returned to camp. He plopped down to lounge near the hot rocks, appearing content. Bryndor draped their ponchos over his tent, effectively covering the large rent in the side. He assured her he would make do through the night. She crawled into her tent, feeling soggy and exhausted.

Slipping off her boots without soiling her bedroll and blanket was a challenge. Her clothes came next, unforgiving and sticky with the weight of the endless drizzle. She lay back and shimmied out of her pants, panting from the exertion. She hadn't realized, but in the struggle to disrobe, the temperature dropped. Wind buffeted her tent and large drops of rain began to batter the ground.

Through the clamor of the storm, she could hear Bryndor utter a curse. She poked her head out of the tent and a flash of lightning showed him standing shirtless, trying to secure one of the ponchos to the tent, which now sported a tear more than twice the size.

"Grind it," he muttered and siphoned zenith, pulsing rune fire from his hand into his chest. Instead of causing any damage, the runes visible on his shoulders and arms flared with the blue light, casting enough illumination that she could see steam rise from his skin.

"Moons," she said out loud.

Bryndor turned at her sound, still wrestling with the unruly poncho, trying to make it lie flat when it was clearly designed to do anything but. He flapped the oil cloth, sending a spray of rainwater against his face, and grinned despite himself. "What?"

"You can spend all night fighting the rain and, I suspect, trying to respect my virtue. Or you can shimmy out of those rain-soaked clothes and get in here with me. The choice is yours, my prince."

She ducked back inside the tent, replaying the words in her mind. *Taker's twisted tongue, did I really just say all that?*

With knees pulled to chest, she wriggled her feet under the lone blanket, now shivering in part from the cold and in part from the angst of the moment. She strained to hear beyond the persistent pattering of rainfall.

Perhaps if she kindled her sympath gift, Winter could reveal something of his movements. But she knew that the Aarindin had wandered to the cover of the trees. From the darkness, Bryndor cleared his throat, his voice soft and pitched low. "Kess, it wouldn't be the first time I slept in the rain. But if you don't mind, I would prefer to share your tent."

Her head shot up from her knees, eyes wide, and her mouth dropped open as she shook her head to nobody in particular that she did not, in fact, mind. "The offer still stands. Come inside."

Bryndor poked his head in, and she scooted to the side. He removed something from a pocket and tossed it on the bedroll. The petrified wolvryn eye gave off a soft blue radiance. His shoulders shimmied back and forth and he frowned, grunting.

"What are you doing?" she asked.

"Trying . . . not to soil your bedroll . . . with my boots! There, grind it."

He climbed farther into the tent, working his pants off until only his smallclothes remained. He bunched the wad of rain-soaked clothes into a pile and kicked them out of the tent.

His scent and the smell of wet leather permeated the tent. He sat with awkward formality staring forward, arms wrapped around knees.

"This is not exactly the way I imagined our adventure rolling out," he said.

She leaned a shoulder against his. "I don't know. It's not so bad in here. But I do wonder what you think you are going to wear in the morning."

He rested his head on top of hers. "I've got another trick. I can dry them out in the morning, boots and all."

They sat in awkward silence for a moment, the crackle of lightning and patter of rain the only sound between them. He inhaled a deep breath and swept the wolvryn eye under the blanket. He kissed the top of her head, then lay back. She settled onto her left side, resting on his shoulder, and struggled to find a place to rest her right hand. She draped it on her own hip, but that felt beyond awkward, so she rested her palm on his abdomen.

In the silence, he swallowed once. *This man. He's never going to make the first move, Kess.* She brought her hand up to cup his jaw and turned him to face her. The tempo of his heartbeat quickened, a palpable drum inside his chest.

"Kess, I'm having trouble sorting out things, from before the Revealing and—"

"What is it?"

A serious frown creased his forehead. "Have we done this before?"

She returned his frown for a few seconds, then smiled. "Bryndorllean Baellentrell. Are you saying that you can't recall if you've shared my bed?"

She kissed him on the neck, and he moaned a response.

"Because a woman might take offense to having something so memorable forgotten because of something as trivial as a mystical and unprecedented Rite of Revealing." She kissed him on the breast and swept her hand along the muscles of his flank, tracing the edge down and resting her fingers on the front of his hip bone.

His stomach muscles contracted, and he giggled in the darkness. "Woman, you are not making this easy."

She threw a leg over his hips and straddled him, finding him more than eager for the gesture. His hands found the small of her back, and she relished the warmth of his touch, then reached behind and interlocked her fingers into his and pinned his hands over his head. She leaned forward to kiss him, finding his lips instinctively in the darkness.

"One thing I am not, Bryn, is easy." She kissed him again. "But one thing I am, and will always be, is yours."

She nibbled his earlobe, and he responded with a soft growl. She whispered hot words into his ear. "Since this is, in point of fact, our first time, let's make it memorable."

Chapter Forty-Eight: Burning the Taker's Shadow

Therek drummed his fingers on the tabletop, listening to Kaellor's latest update. Laryn sat beside the prince, silvery locks of hair framing the curve of her cheek and chin. On Kaellor's other side sat Field Marshal Hestian Lellendule, and the man's broad-shouldered girth dwarfed the royal gardener and speaker for the runeless, Fagle Hoff. Others of the closed council listened through the sheks.

The utilization of the speaking devices proved invaluable not only in tracking Bryndor's progress but also in coordinating with the council members. The senders offered a degree of efficient communication, but the ability to speak and strategize contemporaneously allowed Therek to solicit different opinions and judge the merits of the suggestions. *How might the world change if Sheklith invented a device that allowed even the runeless to communicate?*

He looked across the table, first exchanging glances with Laryn, and then Fagle Hoff. Already the man's keen and unique insights had proven as rare as the plants he cultivated. While Fagle could not activate the shek, his perspectives already allowed for more inclusive strategies. *If only our wives could see us now, old friend.*

Thinking of his wife always brought Karragin to mind, and how could it not? His daughter was every bit as fierce and determined as her mother, twice as obstinate and, by the Giver, twice as beautiful. He allowed his eyes to drift to the corner of the room. Karragin stood adjacent to a window, attentive and listening through Iska no doubt. The moonwing rested on the clever shoulder perch Karragin had fashioned.

The late-morning sun highlighted a blue sheen at the edge of Iska's crest feathers and betrayed the creature's innate affinity for zenith.

The guster Amniah entered the room with relative anonymous silence to relieve Karragin's rotation. His daughter departed without a word but managed to wink once on her way out. Therek still questioned Amniah's ability to offer any meaningful protection against a serious attack, but then chided himself for allowing such a nuisance idea to take up residence in his mind.

He understood all too well that half of Amniah's ability to overwhelm any adversary lay in the misconception that she could not protect herself. But more than that, if his daughter trusted Amniah, then the guster should have the benefit of his trust as well.

His wandering mind returned to the conversation at hand as Kaellor continued. Bryndor and Ksenia had reached the forward base camp with exceptional time given the weather and rendezvoused with Savnah's quad. The group encountered half a crush of grondle and three times that number in grotvonen the first day beyond the Pillars of Eldrek. Therek worried about their chances for surviving the mission, let alone returning before the full might of Tarkannen's forces arrived. Yet, the party had made stealthy progress in the past three days and now traveled unmolested across the plains known as the Vastlands.

The Docent Venlith chimed in through the shek, "I thought the Outriders traveled as quints or double quads these days? Did they lose a man already?"

Overwarden Kaldera responded, both his gruff voice and the unvarnished way he spoke plain truths a bittersweet reminder of Reddevek. "We're spread thin at the border fighting the grot and grondle. While the Outriders acquit themselves well, I don't have the bodies to spare a double quad. I need every seasoned Outrider bolstering the ranks of the common soldiers or scouting for grotvonen incursions. Savnah's group had a fifth man, but in the initial skirmish with the grondle, he took a spear to the chest and lost his grip."

The sheks fell silent as each of them considered the overwarden's report. Therek thought about Nolan, riding at the head of the group. The news of the group's progress eased any sense of anxiety he felt. And if he were honest, a part of him found comfort in the notion that Nolan would be traveling well beyond the daily encounters with grondle and the like.

Kaellor cleared his throat to continue, "Thank you for the clarity, Overwarden. What else can you report on the situation at the Pillars?"

"Benyon Garr is a tactical genius. Under his direction, we completed the palisades weeks ago. Stone masons now reinforce the wooden barrier. Construction of ballistas and catapults began in earnest this week."

Hestian Lellendule sat back, arms folded across his rotund belly. He fingered his shek. "I sent reinforcements to prepare the ground outside the Pillars. Have they arrived?"

"Yes, my lord," said Kaldera. "Just this morning, Garr deployed them as teams of gifted and runeless to dig trenches and deadfalls in the forest south of the Pillars. Any meaningful future travel, trade and the like, will need to stick to the road or make accommodations for these obstacles, but once complete, these measures should mitigate the brute force of any grondle charge. I will take any questions or suggestions."

Therek leaned forward on the table, a silly gesture he knew, but somehow it felt natural, like he was engaging the overwarden despite the distance of the shek. He channeled into the device. "Warden Elbiona, was she able to use Salveen's premonition and make contact with the delegation from Faltusch?"

"She did. If there are no questions for me, I will cede the shek so you might hear from the warden herself," said Kaldera.

There was a scuffle of voices, muted and chaotic, then Elbiona's voice carried through the shek. "Am I doing this right? Can anyone hear me?"

"We can hear you plain as if you stood in the regent's hall, Warden. This is Kaellor Baellentrell. You address the closed council."

Elbiona muttered something about the Giver's anatomy, but her tone was one of wonder. "Apologies, Your Highness, and members of the closed council. Salveen's information led us to the Faltuschian delegation just in time. We found them, or what was left of them. Yugan the Sea King sent his fifth wife as part of a diplomatic effort."

"Did she say fifth wife?" asked Fagle.

Therek nodded, speaking without engaging the shek. "Faltuschians revere the number five. As such, the fifth queen consort will be a skilled and educated politician, but we can speak more of this later." He kindled zenith into the shek. "Elaborate please, Warden. Is the queen consort unharmed? It would not bode well if she incurred injury."

"Queen Fenna arrived with two advisers and several guards. They are all that's left from a party of twenty-five. We are treating their wounded, but Fenna is well enough if not a little shocked," said Elbiona. "They were attacked by a scouting band of grot and grondle. She is recovering behind the safety of the palisade but came to no physical harm."

Salveen's voice echoed through the sheks. "I foresaw that Fenna carried information of great import. Have you been able to learn anything in that regard?"

"I'm not familiar with these devices, the sheks," said Elbiona. "Is it safe to divulge what I learned?"

"The only people listening are all members of the closed council. Speak your piece, Warden," said Kaellor.

Elbiona continued, "Yes, Your Highness. Fenna carries ill news from the west. The Faltuschian scouts report that a great host is on the move. An army beyond counting currently, composed of the Kreegorian and flanked by an army of grondle and grotvonen working in concert with a host of umbral. An unnatural drought plagues the lands between Kreeg and Faltusch. Tarkannen has convinced anyone who will listen that the blame for the natural disaster should fall at our feet. Even if the army was not enough, villagers and townsfolk from across the region flock to their banner in pursuit of our destruction and the promise of salvation at our demise."

More silence stilled the room as the full impact of the usurper's machinations settled on them. Therek cleared his throat. "The nobility of people withers when faced with thirst and starvation. A man struggling in the desert easily finds justifications to stab his brother for a full skin of water."

"It's a gamble. His forces will be completely dependent on a stable supply train. We can use that to slow and deter their advance," said Hestian.

Laryn rapped a knuckle on the table. "Elbiona, is there any sense that Tarkannen's propaganda has infected Fenna or her people? We've seen how a good lie, whispered over and over without rebuttal, can take root in the hearts and minds of people."

"No, Your Highness," said the warden. "Quite the opposite, I think. She seems quite aware of the convenience of the drought and the way the Kreeg weaponized the disaster to their favor. She carries a request for aid, military support mainly, as their attempts to engage the Kreeg in diplomatic negotiations have fallen on deaf ears. Marauding herds of grondle already disrupt trade between the border kingdoms of Millstone, Norfold, and Faltusch."

Kaellor grabbed the edge of his beard along the side of his chin. "I wondered if our plan to barricade ourselves behind the Great Crown would mean our neighbors suffered. Now I guess we have our answer."

Hestian growled. "Can't the Sea King simply avoid conflict by escaping across the Rodendian Sea?"

Overwarden Kaldera's voice chimed in with unusual caution. "We have a theory on that front, but it's only speculation."

"You are on the front lines, Overwarden, and your insights are likely more accurate than anyone sitting around a table in Stone's Grasp," said Kaellor.

"The regent recommended we carry out reconnaissance of the Great Crown. I sent scouting parties along the western edge of the Great Crown as far north as Beclure. Their mission was twofold: first identify and report any grotvonen warrens. Second, assess the viability of the Endulian Pass. We've made no further discoveries of the enemy. But whatever force gave rise to the drought seems to have displaced all that weather to the east. The mountain pass out of the Great Crown is impassable with drifts of snow and ice like nothing ever recorded in our histories."

"By our histories, do you refer to the Luna Rova?" asked Therek.

"Just so, Your Grace. Anyway, to the field marshal's question, great slags of snow and ice have encroached from the northwestern region of the Great Crown and begun to drop into the Rodendian Sea. These . . . ice barges have drifted as far west as the mouth of the Faltuschian Bay.

The queen consort referenced the loss of not only safe sea lanes but also any meaningful wind to carry their ships to safe harbors."

Hestian sat forward, fists tapping lightly on the table. "Taker's grip. It's like he knew we would take defensive actions and works to draw us out. But we have no idea about the size of his forces, their capabilities, or their demands. All our efforts should focus on fortifying and defending the pass at the Pillars."

"I fear that, if we do not render aid to our neighbors, they are all the more likely to be ground under Tarkannen's boot or worse, forced to join him out of a sense of self-preservation," said Therek.

He pressed a hand back against his wispy eyebrows, considering the different ways that they might be able to aid the border kingdoms. So much of Kaldera's information confirmed portions of his visions, and yet, despite the confirmation, he remained uncertain as to how to proceed. "Please pass along our collective admiration for the heroic service of our forces, Overwarden. This information arrives not a moment too soon. Do either of you have anything else to report?"

"You have the full measure of our limited information at this time," said Kaldera. "Based on the revelations shared by the Faltuschian delegation, we will task long-range scouting parties of Outriders. When we learn more, I will notify you at once."

"The sheks are only valuable if someone is listening. Let's schedule formal communications at dawn and dusk," said Therek.

"Understood."

"One last thing, Kal," said Therek. "Faltuschians, especially nobles, are rumored to possess an ability to read your thoughts, but only if they maintain physical contact. See that Fenna and her dignitaries keep their gloves on."

"Sound advice. Until this evening then," said Kaldera.

Docent Venlith addressed the council through the shek, "My time is best spent with patients. I will leave military strategy and the defense of the kingdom to you all, but I will attend the meetings."

"Unless there is anything required of my services at this time, I am needed elsewhere as well," said Salveen.

"Not at this time, but thank you both for attending. Salveen, let us know if your gift imparts any fresh developments," said Therek.

Kaellor grabbed fistfuls of beard along his jaw and looked ready to shave his face with his knuckles. His tension eased when Laryn spoke softly. "So, we can either dwell on the diagnosis or formulate a plan of treatment."

"This does go a long way to explaining the impasse at the Endulian," said Therek.

Hestian glowered. "If the Endulian Pass is not serviceable as a means of egress, then that prima dicta has some explaining to do."

"Not that I enjoy Edlemund's company, but care to explain, Hes?" asked Kaellor.

"Despite your previous conversations, he's acted in the interests of the minor nobles of the western duchies to limit contributing to the military under the guise of maintaining and guarding the Endulian Pass," said Hestian.

"Hmm, well, don't dwell on the Taker's shadow when the Giver shines a light," said Therek.

Hestian rubbed at his temples as if to ward of an ache. "Grind it, speak plain Therek. None of that rubbish ever gets through my thick head."

Therek gave his friend a reassuring smile. "If Edlemund has been holding back reserves, now we have unanticipated reinforcements to tap, and there will likely be a significant mixture of gifted. We meet with his excellency this afternoon and I will be only too happy to explain the way of things."

"What do we know about the Kreeg? Are they gifted? Do we know anything about their military capabilities?" asked Kaellor.

"Not as much as we should like, which is another reason we need to interview Queen Fenna as soon as possible," said Therek.

"So," said Kaellor. "Tarkannen has started his march across Karsk and we don't have a sense for the size of the army he is mustering, but he leads the Kreeg forces bolstered by grondle shock troops, grotvonen marauders, and who knows how many umbral. Our neighbors in Faltusch are bottlenecked by ice floes, and escape by sea is unlikely. If we fail to reinforce Norfold and even Millstone, they might fall under Tarkannen's banner."

"Which means that we would have to contend with an even larger force. And who knows how such transgressions would affect future relations between our kingdoms," said Therek.

"Tarkannen wants something here in Stone's Grasp. He tried to access the city on the night of the Reckoning, after the mantle around the boys fractured. Maybe all of this could be avoided if I dropped the barriers here. We could prepare, and even set a trap?" suggested Kaellor.

Therek sifted Kaellor's words through his gift. Kaellor was serious and clearly laboring to find a peaceful resolution to the conflict. Yet, despite the integrity of Kaellor's suggestion, Therek knew that inviting Tarkannen into the halls of Stone's Grasp would be an enormous misstep.

He thought about how to counsel his friend, a reactive rebuke forming on his tongue. Then he softened his response. "Kae, that's a gracious offer and none more than you understands the risks involved, to be sure, but after everything your brother and Nebrine sacrificed to prevent that very thing, I think we can all agree, while it might lead to a swift conclusion to the conflict, it will not provide a beneficial outcome."

"I agree," said Hestian. "It's a creative solution, Kae. I don't know why that grinder set his sights on us again, but after everything the usurper put this kingdom through, I personally kind of relish the notion that no matter what, he can't gain access to Stone's Grasp so long as your wards remain."

Kaellor inhaled, appearing at first relieved, but then aggravated. "Which means I am stuck here in the city, days away from the front lines and unable to reinforce the troops."

Hestian turned and placed a beefy hand on Kaellor's shoulder. "One man, even one so great as yourself, is unlikely to turn the tide of this battle. But a sound strategy might see the Giver shine her light on us when it's all done."

"I believe I know the answer to this question, but do we have the resources, the human bodies, to reinforce the kingdoms of Faltusch, Norfold, or Millstone?" asked Laryn.

"We do not, cousin," said Hestian. "We will need every capable man and woman acting in mutual defense of our own kingdom."

"We could offer refuge to any seeking to avoid conflict. It's a minor risk to be sure, but I would rather harbor friends behind the safety of the Great Crown than see them bolster Tarkannen's forces," said Therek.

Therek stood and retrieved a map of Karsk and the border kingdoms, unrolling it on the table. Together they stood, considering the situation. Bryndor's group was making swift progress across the Vastlands, but how they would find the Ilovesh and return before Tarkannen's forces was anyone's guess.

"We can't remain hidden behind the security of the Great Crown," said Fagle. "If we do nothing, innocent people will be swept into his army. The way I see it, we need to resend emissaries to Norfold and Millstone, gain their trust, and bolster their ability to defend themselves. Otherwise, those two kingdoms will simply become stable points that reinforce the enemy lines, not just with troops, but with supplies too. We might hold out a year against those odds, but if Tarkannen conquers those nations, he could wage war for years."

Hestian turned to consider the slight man. "By all the dead in the Drift, what if that's his plan? It does seem like he's taken his time mustering the forces in Kreeg. What if it's all designed to force a long campaign of attrition? If I were in charge of Kreeg and coming this way, knowing that the Great Crown served as an impenetrable wall, I would seek to coordinate logistics and draw from all three kingdoms. Who cares about supply lines if you've got access to those kinds of resources?"

"I agree," said Kaellor. "While it feels safe to bolster our defenses behind the Great Crown, I think we need to support the border kingdoms where we can, weaken the Kreeg as they approach, and offer sanctuary to any who would flee before the armies of Tarkannen."

"I don't disagree," said Therek. "Are we committed to this action, then?"

"I would rather use the Giver's light to burn the Taker's shadow than wither in the darkness," said Laryn.

He searched the faces of them each, finding confirmation. "Alright. A course correction, then. Hestian, you have the unpleasant task of replacing me in the meeting with Edlemund."

The field marshal began to protest, but Therek held up a hand. "I will decree that until the end of hostilities with the Kreeg, the kingdom shall be placed under martial law and, as such, the offices of the prima dicta are to be suspended. Edlemund will return home at once and the western duchies will provide an equal measure of support to the war effort or face severe penalties. You, my friend, get to cut the legs out from under Endera's puppet. I'll need you to personally pay a visit to the Beclurian court to see that the duchess capitulates."

Hestian nodded with approval.

"Laryn, see about rounding up as many able-bodied healers as possible, any that we can spare. The border kingdoms are not without their own abilities to defend themselves, but none of them have access to that kind of talent. The miraculous healing of any royals afflicted or injured in the battles ahead could be the very thing that engenders loyalty beyond measure."

He turned to Kaellor. "Can you travel beyond the curtain wall of the castle? Will the ward drop if you are in the city itself?"

A puzzled expression played across Kaellor's face. "You know, I'm not entirely sure. I've not had the chance to step beyond the curtain wall since I first activated the ward."

Therek's wispy eyebrows drew down. "Now is not the time to put that to the test. I have a proposal. How would you feel about assuming the regency of the kingdom?"

Kaellor's eyes narrowed. "It feels like an unnecessary risk. Why create uncertainty at a time when we need the kingdom to unify behind our common cause?"

Therek nodded knowingly. "Because the nobles and high houses were willing to accept my leadership during peacetime, but they need a more formidable leader as the kingdom prepares for war. They need to see a Baellentrell holding the seat of authority."

"Actually, Kae," said Hestian. "It's not a bad idea. Therek is right. Edlemund and his ilk respect the regent, but they fear you."

Kaellor appeared about to respond, but Laryn's hand on his forearm quelled any rebuttal. "When would you see it done?" she asked.

Therek exhaled. "Today, my friends."

The muscles at the side of Kaellor's jaw tensed and he stared at the table, contemplating the suggestion. By the gentle draft of zenith, Therek knew that he primed his gifts to discern the merits of the proposal. At last, the prince lifted his eyes. "I have a few conditions."

"As you should," said Therek.

"First, I will accept the role so long as you accept the title of prime adviser to the regent. Second, I will handle Edlemund. Let's not drop the weight of martial law across the kingdom just yet," said Kaellor.

Therek considered the request. Any fears that he had about Kaellor refusing the regency dissipated as his friend shifted easily into the leadership role. "I accept. I was scheduled to entertain a small assembly of guild leaders on the lower green this afternoon. We could use the opportunity to announce your regency," said Therek.

Kaellor nodded but held up a hand. "You're awfully eager to be free of the office."

"It's been more than twelve years, longer I think than any of us expected when I agreed to the role," said Therek.

"Fair enough, my friend." Kaellor turned to Fagle. "Master Hoff, I would make a request of the runeless. Gather volunteers, men and women knowledgeable in the harvest and distillation of embertang and brittle amber. I intend to deploy them with diplomatic missions to the border kingdoms. That particular weapon might be the difference in their confrontations with grondle."

"I will see it done, Your Highness," said Fagle.

Kaellor smiled, appearing genuinely appreciative of the man's confident response. "Hestian, I would still see you ride to the western duchies. I don't think I'm speaking out of turn when I state that I don't trust Edlemund's ability to deliver anything that he might promise. I would like you to carry out Therek's original mandate to recruit able-bodied soldiers for the war effort."

Hestian dipped his head. "I can leave tomorrow."

"Therek, can you organize a reception for Queen Fenna?" asked Kaellor.

"Of course . . . Your Highness," said Therek.

Kaellor sighed. "Watch it, old man, or I'll abscond into the Great Crown, become a Moonie, and leave you holding the reins once again."

Therek held both hands up in submission and chuckled. "I yield to the gravity of your threat."

Kaellor tilted his head with a smile and stood. He leaned over the map. "Perhaps with our aid, Faltusch can withdraw to safety. I intend to have the overwarden send reinforcements to Millstone and Norfold, accompanied by as many healers from Callinora as we can spare. I expect that the leaders of Millstone, in particular, can be convinced to use the wooded terrain to their advantage."

"Elbiona's report made it sound like Faltusch was frozen in place. How do you expect to change that?" asked Hestian.

"I might have a few ideas in that regard," said Therek.

"Good. We can adjourn for now, but plan to meet for closed council meetings through the sheks twice a day," said Kaellor.

A commotion disrupted any rebuttals as Karragin stormed into the room. She slammed the door closed with uncharacteristic thunder but must not have been linked to her moonwing as she seemed ignorant of the loud disturbance. The number of times Therek had witnessed his daughter act with unbridled enthusiasm counted less than his fingers and he held his breath, waiting for her to explain.

"Apologies, I have . . . news," she said.

Laryn signed and spoke to Karragin at the same time for the benefit of all. "Karra, where is Iska, your moonwing?"

Karragin took a deep breath, and a lightness seemed to lift her eyebrows. There was also the slightest pressure in the cadence of her speech. "I've only heard rumors, I'm . . . we're still learning about each other, Iska and I. In the highlands, the Moonies call them riftwings for a reason."

She shook her head. "I'm sorry, I'm not explaining this well. Iska can . . . become zenith or become something else, I don't know. I was in the inner sanctum, on my watch over the prince, and Iska seemed restless.

She normally perches on the statue of Eldrek, but today she took to wing and shifted into zenith, then disappeared into Lluthean's zentrist."

Therek replayed the words in his mind, trying to make sense of the speech and assuming he didn't hear his daughter correctly. Before he could ask for clarification, she continued.

"Iska is fine. She's with them, Lluthean and Neska, and when I reached out to her with my sympath gift, I spoke to them both. I spoke to Neska in the Drift."

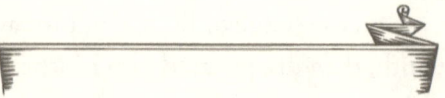

Chapter Forty-Nine: Neska's Obligation

A current of zenith washed down onto the plains, shifting into a warm breeze rich with the fragrance of summer and ruffling Neska's fur. She flared her nostrils and inhaled, sensing something of her mother. The feeling more than the smell was there one moment, then gone in the next, replaced by the rich patina of life that continued to manifest in this altered reality.

She intuitively understood that the creatures, the people, the flowers, and the plants that appeared were ephemeral manifestations of what Lluthean needed them to be. Somehow, his presence here gave the energies in the Drift the ability to become something of what they were before merging into the Drift.

The sound of splashing water drew her from speculating on how long this place would remain after they returned to the waking world.

Lluthean slapped the surface of the water, then sat back, panting. Beads of sweat gathered on his brow, and he exhaled through pursed lips.

She sent her thoughts to him. *"You look like Boru after eating three-day-old organ meat."*

Lluthean nodded and pushed back from the edge of the water, propping himself on bent elbows. "I was watching the Great War again. At the end, something massive spilled out of the sky. Just . . . monstrous. The two sides, zeniphiles and abrogators, had to work together to destroy it and seal up the breach it came through. It was a lot to take in."

"Do you recall why you push so hard? Why you bear witness to everything?"

Lluthean nodded, a sad expression on his face. "It feels wrong, you know? Like I'm displacing people on purpose, forgetting them with deliberate intent."

"They were not real. You remember that part, yes?"

Lluthean dropped his head back. "Yes. I know that now. But I can't help the way I feel."

She walked over and licked the sweat from his brow. Even though neither of them had consumed food, she sensed the right mixture of salty and tangy minerals, with no sign that he required sustenance or drink. She sat back. *"You are ready to continue, I think."*

He chuckled. "You're the expert now? As much as I love hearing your voice in my head, Nes, I think it sounds an awful lot like my mother's."

"If that's what it takes, I'm happy to imitate Nebrine. Anything to prevent you from breaking, like my mother."

"I know, Nes, I know. If we get back, I want to be . . . Giver, I don't know, but not broken would be a nice start, I suppose."

"When we get back," she intimated.

He lifted one hand, surrendering to her point. "Yes, yes, when we get back."

He remained unusually silent. Normally, when separating himself from viewing the past, he required minutes of conversation. *"What is it?"*

Lluthean shook his head. "Nes, you and me, we had a lifetime together there, in the Revealing. I mean, Karra and the kids, they . . ." He couldn't bring himself to finish what he was thinking. "But you and me, that was real. What if everything I'm doing here to reset my memories erases the good stuff? How different will I be? I mean, I kind of like who I am now. How much of that is going to change?"

Neska strode behind him and lay on her side. He reclined back, using her flank as a pillow. The intimacy and warmth of their physical connection set her at ease. *"You will be who you will be, my Lluthean. And we will be together with the pack, and you will be whole. Isn't that enough?"*

"It has to be, I guess. Are you worried that you will be hurt by all of this? I know that the spirit of Rona told us I have to do this, but what about you?"

"It is different with me. She was not my mate. They were not my pack. You are my source, my Lluthean."

"Moons, Nes, that is deep."

She puzzled over the expression. Having the ability to engage him in transparent conversation was both joyous and bewildering. "That is truth."

He chuckled, and something inside her core flared with pleasurable vibrance at the sound. She sniffed at his forehead. Where before vigilance and fear flavored his scent, now he smelled content. "You are ready to begin again. I think you should not spend so much time watching Karra when she was young. Maybe get to know your enemy."

"Tarkannen? What has he got to teach me?"

"You will only know if you observe."

He sat forward and looked back at her with that twinkle that usually preceded hopping onto a log and falling into the river. "I was going to say that sounds like something Aunt Ro would say, and that she is usually right."

"Rona was a wise woman, but I am always right."

"Fair enough. I'll get to it, then." He tilted his neck to the side, stretching, then shook his hands fast and leaned over the pool. Images coalesced over the surface of the water, and Neska directed her attention across the plains.

Another flare of zenith dropped out of the voids, coalescing as a brilliant falling star, unusual in its approach. Scintillating streamers of zenith trailed in its wake, shedding iridescent blue sparkles. Instead of colliding with the grasslands, wings unfurled and the form of a riftwing swept low over the grasses before coming to rest only a few paces away.

Neska was aware that the creature would not divulge its thoughts, not in the way that she did with Lluthean or Boru. The hawk tilted its head and flared its crest feathers up in a playful greeting.

"It's you, little sister. Well met. Did Karragin send you here?"

In answer to her question, an echo of sound rippled through the riftwing, and Karragin's questing voice called out from beyond the void. Neska recognized the resonance of the communication as Karragin's unique gift. She considered remaining silent, but fear and wonder mixed in equal measure vibrated through the link as Karragin called out.

The riftwing flapped her wings with irritation, obviously waiting for Neska to respond. She huffed a breath. *"Iska is with me. She is safe. We are safe."*

The sensation of gasping and surprise flowed through the connection. *"Neska? You can hear me? Giver, I've tried so many times to reach you."*

"It is because of Iska. She is here with us, in the Drift. How is the pack?"

"The pack? Oh, the pack is separated, but I think we are all safe, for the most part."

"We should not have split up the pack, child. Now you divide yourselves again? What can you tell me of Boru?"

"He's with Bryndor, of course, and Ksenia. They travel to the west in search of the Ilovesh and a way to bring you both back, but without the tether."

Neska pondered her words. Bryndor's immediate reunion with Ksenia troubled her. What strain would such a reunion have on the young man? Would Boru be enough to keep him from breaking? What would happen to Boru if the young man became feral?

"Neska, are you still there?"

"I am thinking, child. Still your mind."

"I apologize. You sound different, your voice is different. And I only hear you. I can't sense any of the other things you sense."

"Much has changed and much has not. Iska is our tie and, as such, in this place, my voice is limited to her perceptions."

"Are you with Lluthean? The others will want to know of his condition."

"We are safe in this current of the Drift. He is learning about the tether, where it came from, and how to defend the pack."

"Moons, the Drift, really?"

"Yes."

"Can you tell me more about it? What's it like there?"

"It is the Valley of the Cloud Walkers, more or less."

"I see. Well, will you tell him that I, that we, miss him and work to return him safely?"

"*Yes,*" said Neska, but she sensed that Karragin had not expressed the full measure of her request.

"*I need to go tell the others about this. Will you ask Iska to come back? Can Iska come back?*"

Iska preened the feathers along one wing and flared her crest feathers again. "*She will return when she is ready. It is her way. Riftwings need to replenish here, and she was with you for too long.*"

"*I didn't know that. Thank you for telling me. If Iska remains or if she returns, would it be alright if I check on you again?*"

"*Or course, child. We are pack. Tell my brother not to be a hoof.*"

A strong ripple of mirth emanated from Iska. "*I like that . . . when I see Boru, I will send your greetings. Is there anything else I should convey to the others about Lluthean? Anything you have will give them peace.*"

"*When we return, know that he will be different. He has endured and lost more than any of you. He has sacrificed more than anyone will ever know.*"

Heartache returned through the link, and Neska began to wonder if she had conveyed too much about Lluthean's Revealing. "*Oh Giver, Nes, I can feel it, the pain. I don't know what he gave up or lost, but the way it pulls, so much loss . . . how does he stand it? How do either of you?*"

Karragin severed her gift, and Iska continued her casual preening. When the riftwing flapped her wings, zenith puffed into the air in a haze of blue dust. Striations of zenith gathered into balls, remnants of creatures that dropped to the ground to frolic about as rabbits, or sweep the grasslands as birds before merging back into their origin.

Eventually, Karragin's voice echoed from Iska once again. "*I'm back, Neska. I'm sorry, I wasn't ready for that. It's the first time I could feel what you feel. I'm . . . Giver, there are no words. I'm glad that you have each other. Get back here together. Reunite our pack, Neska; we need you.*"

Neska considered how to respond. She had not meant to share how much pain her Lluthean experienced. She did not care to feel again how much it really affected her. Instead of answering, Neska huffed and tilted her head at Iska. The riftwing hopped into the air and took flight, shedding a brilliant cascade of zenith, then evanesced into shimmering particles that dispersed into the void.

A woman's voice, calm and reassuring, caused Neska to turn. "That was a kindness."

A shapeless phantom walked across the plains, but instead of resolving into Rona's familiar form, a young woman, tall and lithe with unusually long limbs, approached. Her gait was at once alien and graceful. Where Karragin walked with dexterous litheness, this figure approached with something hinting at a more exquisite nature.

Long filaments of black hair with a purple sheen hung from her shoulders, and strange rune marks shifted under the surface of her dark skin. A wispy garment covered her torso. She lifted slender fingers into the air as if catching a current of water, and emitted a spray of zenith like the trailers Iska left behind.

For all that Neska appreciated in the figure, she also sensed a subtle taint, something that reminded her of the tether leeching away at Lluthean's core. The awareness of the corruption caused a rumble to gather in Neska's chest.

"Peace, sister," said the phantom. The voice was at once clear and understandable but also enriched with everything the wolvryn used to communicate. Memory, sight, sound, and even smell permeated the expression of the spoken word. The phantom stopped several paces away and sat on her knees.

"What are you? Why are you here?" demanded Neska.

The figure held up a hand. "I am the remnant of Sephora. I was an Ilovesh. A member of your pack seeks to find my people, no? Anyway, we must speak of your burden."

Neska withheld any confirmation and tilted her head. Clear imagery and meaning rippled through the conversation. *"You are more than you say. Why do I sense the taint of the tether on you?"*

Sephora remained still but blinked once, a slow, deliberate gesture. "You sense with more than your eyes. That is good. He will need you in the days ahead."

Her gaze drifted past Neska to linger on the images Lluthean studied in the reflecting pool. "Did you guide him to that time and place? It's from my past."

"He seeks to learn of our enemy."

Sephora nodded, as if understanding. Her hands folded together, and she stared down before responding. "He will learn of my betrayal, then. I would have at least one of you hear it from me."

The phantom stood and swept a casual hand into the air. Where her fingers passed, globes hovered, some swirling with zenith, others shadowed in nadir, and still others a fluctuating maelstrom of the two currents. A few lingered as shattered, inanimate globes. "Most of these worlds have settled, declaring either for zenith or nadir. They are safe, locked into their pattern, but protected from outside invasion."

She pointed to one of the worlds in which zenith and nadir shifted about. "This is our world. One of the last to remain unsettled. The forces of zenith and nadir struggle for dominance. While this struggle is allowed to carry on, the veil protecting our world thins, and creatures from the Drift gain entrance. You are aware of these? You know of what I speak?"

Neska remained aloof, keeping her thoughts concealed until she had a better sense for the woman.

Sephora sat back down and continued, "I think yes. Regardless, only an Eidolon, one who can wield both zenith and nadir in concert, with confluence, can seal any breach and settle the world. Tarkannen and I saw the signs. We tried to provoke, to instigate, the Eidolon. The tether was supposed to be our answer, but we miscalculated."

Still, Neska chose not to reciprocate the conversation. This phantom, this Ilovesh remnant, communicated with convincing clarity, but that only made Neska more suspicious of her motives. Neska licked lips. *"Are you going to make me ask?"*

Sephora's eyebrows lifted. "You speak, then? Good. For a moment, I thought you were a hoof."

Neska rumbled something softer than a growl that still indicated she was not impressed.

"Alright, not a hoof then," said Sephora. "Tarkannen was a creature of zenith. We thought that if he could acquire the ability to wield nadir, he could become the Eidolon. We thought that by creating and then deliberately breaking a tether, his soul would be so wounded as to become aware of nadir."

Her gaze drifted back across Lluthean's pool once again. "He was so convinced of the righteousness of the cause, and we . . . fell in love. The tether was a natural extension of our connection. But he feared that his tie to zenith would prevent him from inheriting the ability to sense nadir. And my people needed to believe in the authenticity of his devotion. So, before we broke the tether, we bound his ability to wield zenith. We thought, once he had nadir, he could bathe in the waters of a deepening well, reclaim his native gift, and wield both together."

Sephora sighed. "We were blinded by our convictions, we were . . . hooves. My people saw the breach of trust and the dark creature he became as an affront to everything they hold sacred and barred him from gaining entrance to our deepening well. They hunted him to the borders of our lands. His own people went to war with him for much the same. And he . . . he became something different, altered by the power of nadir. He lost his compassion, his empathy, becoming something I struggle to recognize today. His banishment in the Drift only made that worse. He is not a creature we can trust to become the Eidolon. If he were to inherit this power, he would surely declare our world for nadir, and more than ninety percent of all life on Karsk would end."

"Why don't the Ilovesh make their own Eidolon? Why bring in an outsider?" asked Neska.

"Ilovesh do not feel as humans feel. Severing a tether is like cutting off an arm or a leg. It's a wound from which one never recovers, but an Ilovesh does not become irrevocably sundered in the way that is required to sense nadir," explained Sephora. "Besides, an Ilovesh never intentionally severs a tether."

Neska stood and stretched back. *"There is one in my pack who was born with nadir."*

"You speak of Ranika. Yes, we are aware. She is the first true-born abrogator since the Great War. But, like all abrogators before her, she will never inherit the Giver's blessing to control zenith. At least, we have not discovered a means by which one might acquire such a gift."

Sephora sighed and cocked her head, strands of hair lifting into the air as if seeking something on the wind. "It's strange. There are remnants of trees and grasses here. I can sense their song, but it's not the song of the ursulu. I miss the song. I was hoping he would bring even one of the ursulu to this place, but he has never seen them before, so it is not to be."

"Why did you come to this plane, Sephora?"

"To teach him about the tether. He will need this knowledge to defeat Tarkannen. If Karsk is to survive my mistake, he must succeed. He pushes himself hard, your Lluthean. But it is not enough. He can try to displace the experiences of the Revealing. Maybe it will work. But something of that experience will always remain. Humans hold such things deep within them. Their sense of love is not so easily cast aside. It is at once their greatest strength and their greatest weakness. *Balladur cor delledence*, right?"

Neska sensed that the woman had shifted something in the phrasing on her tongue, but by the way she perceived the meaning of the words, she knew at once what Sephora meant, for it was the unspoken code of the pack. *"That is right. How will you teach my Lluthean? And what will he become?"*

"I will remain here with you, guide him when he is ready, and teach him what I remember about the tether. As for what he will become? I cannot say, Neska, which is why you must watch him. If one day he gains access to nadir and fails to become the Eidolon, you must see that he does not become corrupted like my Tarkannen. He would destroy Karsk."

Waves of empathy slammed into Neska's core as the full implication of Sephora's words broke across her mind. Genuine compassion, empathy, and lastly, obligation permeated the statement. "None of us should be less than we are, but the Eidolon must become all things to all life. Anything less will mean the destruction of Karsk. I am sorry, but this is your burden, Neska."

Chapter Fifty: Approaching the Stillness

Queen Brekka is in mourning, and a piece of my heart is torn. A delegation tasked to travel east in search of the tree singers met disaster. We hoped to persuade a cultural exchange, for we learned so much from them when they last visited. Unfortunately, the emissaries were forced to return. My great-nephew, the queen's grandson Dobrek, and several others perished in the attempt. The dangers of the Vastlands and the territories beyond decimated three out of four in their number. If a well-provisioned group of gifted were not able to make the journey, Brekka assumes that the tree singers must also have perished. Regardless, she has banned any future expeditions.

—The Tome of Nivosh, 75 PC, translated by Veeble Hebben

NOLAN SAGGED ON THE back of his Aarindin, waiting for the rest of the small company to arrive. The late afternoon sun burned on the back of his neck and magnified his weariness. The sound of an approaching Aarindin shuffling through the grasses gave him no cause for alarm, and at this point in their journey, fatigue eroded any sense of propriety or professional decorum. So, he remained seated, eyes glazed, staring east down into the valley of a shallow river.

"You pushed a mean pace today. How are you holding up, Nolan?" asked Bryndor.

Something had changed since his friend left the Revealing. He seemed more aware of the group morale, or maybe he was always aware and only now took the initiative to inquire. He was definitely more . . . something, and it had nothing to do with an arca prime. Whatever had happened, Bryndor now stepped with comfortable grace in the leadership role.

His words brought a smile to Nolan's face. "I haven't lost my grip. I'll be better after a dip in that river, I think."

"As will we all. You figure we could camp on the bank down there?" asked Bryndor.

"It's safe enough. The Vastlands are thick with herd animals and nothing else, thank the Giver. No grondle, no umbral, no sign of anything from the Drift. There's a game trail off to the right. The first bit is steep, but after that it levels off. I think the pack horse can manage."

Bryndor drank long from a waterskin, then handed it to Nolan. "You coming down or waiting for the others?"

"I'll stay here and mark the way." He slaked his thirst and returned the skin.

Bryndor twisted back to the west, shading his eyes. "She'll appreciate that, even if she doesn't say it."

Though the sun warmed Nolan's back, it felt like the Taker blistered his face, and he couldn't help but grin. He offered a coy response. "I'm not sure what you mean."

"Well, I'm not talking about Kess. She shares my tent." Bryndor scratched at his beard stubble. "Actually, that's not true. I share hers."

Both men chuckled at that.

"I suppose you're right about Savnah. She doesn't mince words when she's hungry or there's a score to settle. As for the rest, we're figuring it out."

Bryndor clapped him on the shoulder. "That's all we need most days. I'll get a fire going and set a kettle. That river is calling my name. See you down below."

He signaled and led Tacit off to the right, pack horse in tow, and they disappeared down the hillside. Minutes later Boru swished through the grasses, tongue lolling out and panting, followed by Tovnik and Dexxin, who rode in silence, appearing every bit as fatigued as Nolan felt.

The men pulled up to stare down into the valley. "Sweet breath of the Giver," said Tovnik. "You think he'll let us get a full night of sleep?"

"Doubtful," said Dexxin. "If only we knew a medic who could dose him with a hint of stilben root? Just enough to sleep in?"

Tovnik threw his head back and laughed. "Something tells me it wouldn't work. I do have a flask of resco. I was saving it for the end of the mission. We could try to get him sauced, but he's a purpose-driven man these days."

Nolan sat in silent agreement, even bobbing his head up and down. Purpose driven did describe Bryndor these past weeks. By his estimate, they had already shaved off two days of the journey. Outriders were no strangers to ranging and hard travel, but Bryndor had put that notion to shame. The strangest thing was that he did it all without words. Every night, the prince saw to setting up camp and contributing to meals. Every morning he rose early, broke camp, and rode out regardless of whether anyone else was ready.

Well, that's not true. He always makes accommodation for Ksenia. But so far, she's been as bad as him.

Moments later, Ksenia and Savnah joined them and together, the group cast long shadows down into the valley. Savnah chewed on a sprig of grass, the reedy stalk bobbing up and down. She studied the terrain, looking to the north and south. "Taker's twisted bits. Can we cross here, or does it run deep?"

"We can cross. The far bank is obscured by fog, but I waded past the middle," said Nolan.

Savnah spat to the side, then turned. He expected a rebuke, but instead, she arched a scar-furrowed eyebrow. "If you never got to the other side, Tracker, how do you know you reached the middle?"

"The current slowed, and I shot an arrow across. It hit the far bank not more than ten feet in. I couldn't see it, but by the sound I could tell."

None of the others spoke. Eventually, Bryndor walked Tacit onto a sandy bar beside the river. The tone of Savnah's voice shifted. "Are we sure he didn't inherit some rare arca prime of endurance? Grind me twice if he's not worse than Karra."

"That's a bit of the Giver's truth," said Dexxin.

Even the mild-mannered Tovnik chimed in. "I cheated trying to keep up with him but ran out of lammen berries yesterday. A dip in that river and a solid night of sleep seem like just the thing."

"Kess, I don't suppose there's any way you could talk some sense into him. Get him to sleep in a bit?" suggested Savnah. She wriggled her fingers as if casting a spell. "Maybe work some of your Balladuren charms to keep him occupied longer than usual?"

"You think I'm managing any better? I'm asleep before my head hits the bedroll most nights," said Ksenia

Savnah shrugged. "Yes, but most nights is not the same as all nights, right?"

Ksenia giggled. "I'll see what I can do, but I make no promises. Nolan, care to lead the way?"

Nolan dipped his head and signaled his Aarindin down the game trail. Over the next hour, they set camp. Nolan was staring at the bedroll inside his tent, tempted to crawl inside and collapse, when something pale and fleshy flashed in the corner of his vision. Savnah Derrigand, prime of the Outriders, waltzed through camp naked as the day she was born. Scars of various ages mapped across her muscular arms and thighs. Some appeared as thin silver strips, others as deep-set and ruddy furrows. Most remarkably, Nolan noticed, her left butt cheek remained unmarred.

Without concern or ceremony, Savnah walked right into the river. She dipped under, then floated with only her head and toes visible above the water. "Ahh, that's the Giver's blessing it is. Come on in all, the water is perfect!"

Nolan stood and noticed for the first time that Bryndor and Ksenia hovered in the water close together, their heads bobbing not twenty paces upstream. Even Boru waded belly-deep into the current. Dexxin and Tovnik wasted no time shedding their clothes and trotting to the water's edge. Nolan raced to join them, kicking off his boots, shimmying out of his leathers, and running headlong toward the water. He splashed in, ran a few clumsy steps, then collapsed.

The icy cold current caused his muscles to seize up, and that was perhaps the only thing that prevented him from inhaling a lungful of water. His head broke the surface, and he heard a girl scream in pain, then realized that the involuntary screech came from him.

"Taker's grinding bite, Savnah! You c-c-could warn a guy."

Savnah dipped her chin in the water and gulped a mouthful, then spat it out in a fountain. "Lefledge, this is nothing. In Midrock, most folks don't have fancy zenith-powered devices to heat the water. Every bath we take there is near cold as ice. Give it a few minutes and you'll be fine."

Tovnik and Dexxin waded in slower and both men whooped nearly as loud as Nolan, a fact for which he was grateful. Several minutes later, Nolan's rattling teeth settled, and he relaxed in the bubbling current. They lounged in the water until well past sunset, climbing out only when their skin pruned.

Somehow, Bryndor had managed to save half a loaf of black bread, and it made the perfect complement to a bubbling stew. After the meal, they succumbed to exhaustion. Nolan laid his head back, thinking briefly of his rune father, Chancle, and how different their travels had been in the relative luxury of a wagon caravan.

And yet, despite the misery of ranging with little sleep, pushing beyond the point of physical exhaustion, he wouldn't trade a single day of it. Some part of him was aware of the kinship fostered by the simple act of enduring together. Memories from the week floated in and out of his mind: he and Dexxin waxing their bows, Tovnik healing minor injuries, and the way Bryndor checked in on him throughout the day.

The only thing he missed was seeing Karragin smile or hearing her praise his progress. He vaguely wondered how she was getting along with Iska when the wispy rasp of his tent flap caused him to crack an eyelid open. Savnah's head poked in, silhouetted by moonlight. She crawled forward and collapsed onto her side, then snuggled up against him. She had sought him out on a few other occasions, but never in the middle of a ranging. Just when he began to wonder where the night might lead, she draped an arm and leg over his body, effectively using him as a human pillow.

"Sorry, I pitched my tent on rocky ground and you're better company than Boru."

He couldn't help but chuckle. "You've got pretty low standards. I think we need to get you out more."

She pecked him on the cheek and wriggled into a comfortable position. "Shush it. No grinding about, not tonight anyway. Get some sleep. We have no idea what time Bryn will start out."

He ran fingers across her arm and rubbed his cheek against the side of her head. "You notice anything different about him?"

"Yes, he's comfortable in his own skin. Kess noticed it too," she said. "Before he sat for the Revealing, I don't think he would have dared to share a bedroll with her. He's more like his uncle in some ways now. It took me a few days to figure him out, but it's been nice, having him basically lead the mission. It lets me focus on being a prime without all the trappings of worrying about our progress, minding everyone's morale, or whether they like my cooking."

"I love your cooking," he whispered.

"You like everybody's cooking. Now get to sleep before either of us decides we need to do more than talk."

He opened his mouth but couldn't think of a witty retort and fell into a fit of yawning. He startled awake the next morning, blinded by the sun and the sounds and smells of someone working a cookfire. Savnah must have vacated the tent only recently, as the spot where she'd slept still felt warm.

After pulling on his boots and attending to morning ablutions, he walked back to the camp where Tovnik, Dexxin, and Savnah sat beside the cookfire. Nolan activated his arca prime, expecting to find Bryndor's trail somewhere across the river. Instead, the strongest resonance indicated that the prince remained in his tent. As if in confirmation, Tacit strode several paces away, nibbling at grasses.

He joined his quad and sat down by the fire. "Don't fret," said Tovnik. "You're not the last to rise."

"That's good. Even so, it's weird. Should we make sure they are alright?"

Savnah snorted. "If you care to interrupt what's going on behind the tent flap, be my guest!"

Dexxin handed Nolan a bowl of leftover stew. "I saw Kess an hour ago. I gave her a thumb's up, and she bowed before ducking back inside."

After another hour, Ksenia exited the tent, followed by Bryndor. She joined the group while he collapsed and packed up the tent. When he finally strode over, something resembling a deep pillow crease still indented the skin across his face.

"Anything left for me?" he asked, pointing at the small kettle.

"You're just in time," said Dexxin, ladling out the bottom of the kettle.

Bryndor stirred at the bits with a wood spoon. "I'm sorry for how hard we've pushed. I can't shake the feeling that the longer we are away, the closer Tarkannen creeps toward Aarindorn. It feels wrong striking out to the east, like we're running away."

Bryndor stared into the bowl and sucked at his teeth.

"It will all be worth it, especially if it leads you to revealing your arca prime. And regardless, we'll get Llu back," said Ksenia.

"I won't say we didn't need the rest," said Savnah. "And I get it. We all do. There was nothing that held me back from literally running through a burning building to find my brother, Kovesk."

"My sister, Mullayne, is posted at the forward base camp as a liaison to the overwarden," said the sender. "As they understand it, the army crawling out of Kreeg is pretty massive, but it's also making slow progress. It feels like we've got time."

Bryndor nodded appreciatively. "Thanks for that. I spoke with Kae through the shek a few minutes ago and he basically said the same thing. Look, as we go, don't hesitate to tell me if we need to break or change tactics. I'm no Outrider, and we're in this together. I might act otherwise, but I can't do this alone."

"Outrider or no, I'll range with you any day. We all will," said Savnah.

Boru loped forward, sniffed at the cook pot, then sneezed. Bryndor signed and spoke in unison. "Did you eat?"

The wolvryn lifted his nose to the right, apparently answering the question. Nolan glanced at Savnah from the corner of his eye. Neither said anything, but by her expression, he knew they shared the same thought. *That's new.*

"Boru's good for at least three or four days. Everyone ready to push on?" asked Bryndor.

The air filled with groans as they stood and stretched. After stowing their gear, they mounted and Nolan led them across the shallow parts of the river. The zigzag pattern kept the waterline below his mount's belly for all but about ten feet. As they approached the east bank, the strange fog continued to obscure the far side. He waited as the others approached.

"Anyone else think it's a bit unnatural that the fog hovers on this side, but not the other? Is that a Northlands thing, or something worse?" asked Bryndor.

"I don't want to be the voice of undue alarm, but I think it's worse," said Nolan. "And my gift isn't picking up any signs of life. Whereas all the normal tracks crisscross the western shore."

Bryndor chewed on the inside of his lip. "Give me a moment; I'll sieve the events, see if I get a feel for anything."

"When you say 'sieve the events,' what exactly does that mean?" asked Savnah.

"Sorry," said Bryndor. "I did learn some things from my time in the Revealing. The runes on my forearms, they're similar to my uncle's and Therek's. Sometimes, if I pose a question in my mind, like a mental rehearsal of our next steps, I get a sense for whether we are on track or whether there is danger. I can't think of any other way to describe it, but it's like straining through the possibilities."

They sat in the river, Aarindin occasionally shuffling their weight in the ankle-deep water, while Bryndor fell into his gift. After a few minutes, he sighed. "Sorry, I got nothing."

"It's my job. Wait here, let me check things out, and I'll return once I know it's safe," said Nolan.

"We can go together," suggested Bryndor.

"I appreciate it, Bryn, but like it or not, you're still our prince. I'll defer to whatever form of address you want out here, but none of us can abide you taking unnecessary risks. I won't lie and say I like it any more than the rest of us, but it's what I do," said Nolan.

Bryndor frowned and considered the words, then looked to Ksenia, who nodded agreement. A sour expression possessed his face. "Alright, Nolan. You have the lead. But call out if there's any trouble."

"Will do," said Nolan. He signaled his Aarindin to walk forward and disappeared into the blanket of fog. The mists cooled his skin, causing his flesh to dimple. After several shuffled steps, he felt his mount climb the opposite bank. Nolan was certain that they were out of the water, but the Aarindin kept lifting first one foot and then another, like a dog standing overlong on a patch of ice.

He called out, "I made it fine. Give me a moment!"

He lifted a leg over and dropped to the ground, finding it covered with a carpet of moss so dense that the ground felt springy. Searching under the Aarindin showed that even the weight of the mount failed to leave a depression.

Using a belt knife, he cut a generous circle of the moss, lifting it out. Where he expected to find sold ground, there was only more moss, and as he watched, tendrils and rhizomes began to knit across the hole he had created. He reached out to the currents of zenith, intending to ignite the glyphs on his forearm and study the properties of the strange material, when it struck him: he couldn't sense zenith. The discovery was at once unsettling and bewildering.

He signaled to his Aarindin, intending to throw a leg over its back when it dropped to the ground, but the mount whinnied nervously, actually refusing his command. "Woe. Alright, I get it. Come with me then, let's return to the others."

He gathered up a chunk of the moss he had cut away, collected the thin reins, and led the Aarindin back toward the water. Sliding down the bank, he nearly twisted an ankle when he stepped onto slick rocks. The others must have heard his splashing.

"Nolan, is that you?" Savnah's voice called out.

"Yes, I'm coming back. Sorry, I got distracted. Be right there!"

Several clumsy steps later, he felt the warmth of the late-morning sun and led the Aarindin through the shallows.

"Why aren't you mounted?" asked Savnah.

Before answering, Nolan reached out, finding a palpable current of zenith. He charged his runes and sighed with relief. "Giver's sweet breath. It's the Taker's grip in there. Give me a moment."

He drew his focus to the moss in his hand, only to discover that it had withered and fallen apart. The material had the appearance of delicate, hollow tubes that crumbled into dust. To his awareness, the moss held no nutritional value and seemed oddly inert, absent any trace of zenith or nadir as far as he could tell. He washed his hands in the river, then explained his findings, the strange carpet of moss, and the discovery that he couldn't siphon zenith.

"Was it the sun? What made the moss wither to dust?" asked Bryndor.

"I really don't know. Maybe it can't survive being separated, maybe it's the sun. The fog filtered out all direct light, so sun exposure makes as much sense as anything else. It's completely dormant to my gift. I couldn't sense that it was ever plant material. The whole thing is really weird," said Nolan.

"No zenith, none at all?" said Dexxin. "I've never heard of a place like that. Any guess how far we'll have to travel without it?"

"Who can say? All of this is new," said Bryndor. "Maybe we can ride around. Would you be comfortable if we divided? Half ride north on the west bank, half ride south. Return here by sunset?"

Savnah hooked her thumbs over her belt. "Splitting up to carry out reconnaissance feels like a good use of our time. I would rather not be separated from the full measure of our gifts if we can help it; best to do it on this side of the river. I'll take Nolan and Dexx. Boru can find us if we have need and since you have the shek, Dexx can report anything we discover to Mullayne. I would prefer to have Tovnik remain with you in the event of any unforeseen injuries."

"It's a good plan," said Bryndor. "Don't lose your grip, and keep your eyes to the horizon."

"You as well," said Savnah.

They separated, and Nolan finally remounted, then led his small group north. Periodically he sent his gift out, casting toward the east bank, attempting to penetrate the fog. And each time his surveillance failed to identify any signs of life on the eastern shore. After traveling well past the middle of the afternoon, Savnah cursed.

"I've not seen a break, and we'll have to pick up the pace to get back by sunset. I don't suppose you found anything? Either of you?" asked Savnah.

"Nothing from me, and I've been checking," said Nolan.

Savnah hocked spit to the side and shook her head in frustration. "Alright, Dexx, if you haven't already, contact your siblings and make a full account of this place. Tell them we will press on tomorrow morning but that we have no idea if any of our gifts or even the shek will be of use. It's possible they will not hear from us for several days, depending on how far this anomaly stretches."

"I've been updating Mullayne. They are aware. Overwarden Kaldera says that if we have to chance moving forward without zenith, we should press on as hard as possible, get through it, and recover on the far side," said Dexxin.

Savnah's eyes searched the sky, and she shook her head as if bewildered the overwarden would bother to render such obvious advice. "Did his excellency want to tell us anything else about the obvious? Maybe that we should never stand downwind of an Aarindin with the trots?"

Nolan nudged his Aarindin forward and retrieved a hunk of dried meat from his travel rations, portioning out a piece out to each of them. Savnah chewed with anger for several minutes, then washed it down with water. Eventually, she sighed. "My thanks. The thought of crossing through that place makes me feel itchy and scratchy."

He chewed the last bit of jerky and swallowed. "I know, and hunger only makes it worse. Better now?"

"Much. Let's get back before the others become worried," she said.

They made good time, returning to the camp from the prior night before sunset. Nolan continued to cast out with his gift, hoping for a break in the wall of fog. None of his searching and probing found even a crack in the strange barrier. By the silent way Bryndor, Tovnik, and Ksenia went about minding camp, it became clear that their travels south had also failed to discover anything new.

Fortunately, Bryndor discovered a patch of wild yams, and the prize sat roasting near the fire. Despite his good fortune, the young man seemed preoccupied. Nolan saw to his Aarindin, then joined his friend near the fire with the others. The prince was considering the stickpin, rolling it between his fingers.

"Any news from Stone's Grasp?" asked Nolan.

"Some," said Bryndor. "Your sister has been able to communicate with Lluthean, well, with Neska."

Nolan pulled his head back in surprise. "Really? How did she manage that?"

"It's complicated," said Bryndor. "Apparently, they are both still in the Drift, and alive by all reports."

"That's good. Did anyone have any advice for us?" he asked.

Bryndor stared into the flames and shook his head. "I took a reading with my gift while you were out. Our plans to cross the river feel right. I mean, I get a sense that we are supposed to make the journey."

Nolan shrugged. "So, we're in the right place. Why so glum?"

Bryndor tapped the stickpin. "Ksenia's friend, an archivist named Veeble, translated an ancient tome referencing the Stillness. It's what folks back then called the land on the far side of the river. Apparently, hundreds of years ago, explorers from Aarindorn tried to reach the Ilovesh by traveling across the region, this . . . Stillness."

"That sounds promising. What did any of them have to say?" asked Nolan.

"Nothing good," said Bryndor. "None of them made it through."

Chapter Fifty-One: Something to Aspire to

Tarkannen stood alone on the floor of the Dalkreeg before the empty chamber that had caged the caligot. He drafted probing tentacles of nadir and searched the polished black stones that lined the interior of the space. Through the extensions of his will, the surface felt smooth, flawless even, until he surveyed the threshold. Carved into the stone, in archaic script, words of power scrolled along the stones marking the entrance to the cell that had imprisoned the beast.

Beyond the script, his investigation failed to reveal anything arcane. No pulse of power, no leeching effect, nothing he could sense that would prevent the creature from flight once released.

The pitch of footsteps caused him to turn, and Volencia crossed the sand to stand beside him. His pupil adjusted the veil covering the marred portion of her face. "One last inspection before we ride out?"

"Something like that. It does not sit well with me knowing that these people possess the means to cage a creature from the Drift."

"I admit, I was reluctant to cross the rings to get to you. I thought they might leech away my abilities," she said.

He nodded with understanding, recalling the vulnerability he felt in the Trial of Nines. "It's something to do with Zsheck's scepter. It's an artifact, but one crafted for a zeniphile and as such, I can't sense anything of its making or use."

She puzzled over his words, a crease between her brow, the question unasked. "There are several references to the Kreegorian scepter in their histories. But the stories are long on drama and short on any meaningful information as to its creation."

A slithering hiss cut the air as he dissipated the nadir tentacles. Volencia stepped closer to take a look. He wondered briefly what would happen if she went inside. A simple push would cause her to stumble. Would she remain trapped? Would the confinement prevent her from accessing nadir?

The sigils on his forearm shifted, preparing to draft nadir into another tentacle. A subtle ripple, like a faint breeze over water, betrayed her employment of nadir. Perhaps she understood his intent and prepared to defend herself. Tarkannen lingered in the moment, waiting to see what she would do, and realized that she had drafted a thin current of nadir across her eyes. He stifled his sigils, one part disappointed that the mystery of the Dalkreeg would continue, one part thankful that his pupil remained loyal. In the days ahead, he would have need of Volencia's talents.

"When you look through the ethereal, what do you see?" he asked.

"There are words set into the stones around the threshold, some kind of ancient script. They don't resemble Aarindorian runes or any language I've encountered."

"If we had more time, I would summon linguists. As it is, I assume you were sent to fetch me for one last war-council meeting?"

Volencia turned to face him, the lingering shadow of nadir retreating from her eyes. "I was sent to invite you, yes."

"Does Zsheck still intend to accompany the army across Karsk?"

Volencia nodded. "He does. He is leaving his second son in charge of Kreeg. Each of his generals will march as well. They are committing everything to the war we fabricated."

"Are you concerned?" he asked.

"Not really," she said. "I think it's an odd strategy, though. They have bold confidence that no other nation will strike against them. Their assumptions leave them vulnerable. I do wonder, though, how much of Aarindorn will remain after the forces of Kreeg take their due."

It was a valid concern, he knew, but one of little consequence to gaining access to the deepening well. Once he was restored to his full and rightful power, he could stabilize Karsk as a world governed by abrogators, then set about shaping the world to his desires.

"Don't let it concern you over much, Vol. Let us turn our attention to the issues before us. Zsheck and his generals will pose no threat once we access the inner sanctum. Come then, let us not keep the krug rai'al waiting."

They walked with silent purpose across the arena and summoned a carriage, making swift progress through the streets of Kreeg before arriving at last at the palatial estate of the krug rai'al. A house servant led them to Zsheck's war room, a private mezzanine of utilitarian design. Chairs ringed a large stone table topped with a map of Karsk.

Verrador stood in the periphery of the room and tilted his head in silent greeting. Zsheck and his generals hunched over the map. The king looked up, acknowledged their arrival with a nod, then turned to address his advisers.

The king clasped the shoulder of his closest adviser. "We don't need to send more scouts into the field to confirm what has already been confirmed. Prepare the forces to leave at once. While the supply lines should be sufficient to support this campaign, I would prefer to bolster our resources once we conquer Millstone. From there, Norfold will serve as our forward staging area. Any questions?"

One of the generals, Kilken if Tarkannen recalled, spoke up. A thick central braid offset by hair shorn to short stubble above her ears revealed a scar that furrowed a groove across her temple. No less than three knives and a single saber hung from her belt. "Will the high abrogator send his bestial forces ahead of the main host? Our troops are as like to engage them with hostility as the enemy."

"Don't concern yourself with High Abrogator Tarkannen's forces. He has assured me that they will remain on our northern flank, only to engage when summoned. Besides, Kilken, your forces will travel the Rodemar to approach Millstone from the west. You will be as far removed from the bestial army as possible."

As Zsheck spoke, Tarkannen sensed eyes from the other advisers on him. "Now then, any other meaningful questions?" asked the king.

None of his advisers commented further. Zsheck tilted his head. "Good. See to your forces. We leave within the hour and will rendezvous at my tent in two nights' time."

The generals departed and Zsheck turned his attention to Tarkannen. The king of Kreeg wore ornamental shoulder pauldrons over fine silks. His entire ensemble, bejeweled with rare gemstones and gold bangles, made for ostentatious show more than any sense of martial protection. He bore no weapons except for the black scepter, and even that seemed less formidable than a good knife. But Tarkannen knew well that appearances could be deceiving.

"High Abrogator Tarkannen. Some day you are going to have to teach me how to arrive late and yet completely captivate the room," said the king.

"Apologies, Your Majesty, I came as soon as the summons arrived," said Tarkannen.

"No apologies. In fact, you have my thanks. Your arrival likely prevented another meaningless round of strategy and plotting."

Verrador stepped forward. "The prepared mind is unlikely to be surprised, Your Majesty."

Zsheck rested a hand on his scepter. "Preparations will only take us so far. Training in combat is a poor substitute for experience on the battlefield. Eventually, one has to unsheathe the sword and start swinging. Otherwise, we're nothing more than a bunch of old generals sitting around a map and plotting. I appreciate the sentiment, my friend, but we've promised the Kreegorian a war, one that they are overdue to experience, I might add. Any further delay and I might start swinging my sword just to slake my thirst."

Tarkannen considered the map, adorned with the strategic placement of small metal markers designating the forces. The onyx sigils covering his face shifted, masking his surprise by the sheer number of pieces on the board. A single piece designated his bestial forces and no fewer than ten other pieces dotted the map. He began to wonder if Zsheck sent even children into battle.

General Kilken's forces held the relatively inglorious but critically important role of bolstering the supply lines south on the Rodemar River, then west through Millstone and to Norfold. A cartographer had taken artistic liberty and shaded the plains northeast of Kreeg with a brown cloud depicting the drought that plagued the region. Tarkannen tapped the map, noting that the blighted section spread farther east than he anticipated. "Is this an accurate record of the effects of the drought?"

"Unfortunately it is," said Zsheck. "Numerous reports from people forced to vacate the area have been confirmed by our own scouts."

"Has the Rodemar been affected? If supply lines are dependent on the water table, should we not have a backup plan?" asked Tarkannen.

Zsheck waved a hand. "It should not be a concern. Even if the river ran dry, Kilken is a capable strategist and would redesign the supply effort to travel by ground. The rest of our forces will skirt the wilds north of Millstone and approach on foot."

Tarkannen stepped back. "What are your plans for dealing with Faltusch?"

"Our nations have enjoyed years of favorable trade. I expect that the Sea King will remain neutral, or possibly flee across the Rodendian Sea. If he chooses to join the battle, we would call upon your forces to engage, thereby protecting our northern flank. At the end of the campaign, Faltuschian plunder would only enrich Kreeg's coffers."

Since assuming his new role as a trusted adviser, a position offered only upon the untimely death of General Thuum, he recognized that the king had embraced the decision to wage war on Aarindorn as a means to an end, rather than a righteous cause.

Zsheck knew well the ramifications of unleashing his troops. Beyond the immediate plunder and spoils of war, the effort would ensure his hold on power for years, decades even, and could solidify his expansionist ideals. If the king possessed enough cunning to view war through that kind of lens, what else could the clever man accomplish?

Tarkannen's gaze fixed on the ebony scepter and the delicate runes running along its surface. He thought again of the Dalkreeg with its leeching rings capable of draining an abrogator's ability to channel nadir. He wondered, not for the first time, if Zsheck understood the secrets behind caging a creature of abrogation. And if he did, would he not closely guard such information?

He imagined lashing out with a sickle of nadir. How silent would the man remain if he sliced off an arm? He could sense the sigils thrumming for release, but stilled their restless shifting. He needed a unified Kreeg marching across Karsk to confront the Aarindorian forces. But perhaps one day, once he'd reclaimed the full measure of his power, they would revisit the conversation.

After a rather unnatural break from the conversation, Tarkannen bowed. "Your forces are well prepared, and your cause a righteous one. We will keep the grondle armies under tight rein, protecting the northern flank."

Tarkannen turned to leave, intending to reunite with his consort of umbral. Zsheck's voice gave him pause. "I do wonder about your motivations. What plunder does Aarindorn hold that motivates a high abrogator to leave the confines of the Torgrend Range?"

Tarkannen turned to address the man directly. Zsheck matched his gaze, inquisitive to be sure, but fearless in his probing. "Have no fear, Zsheck. You are the krug rai'al. I have no desire to sit in your chair. With all of its power comes all of its responsibilities. I do have a score to settle with the rulers in Aarindorn. See that we breach their walls, and my needs will be met. I leave the governance and spoils of war to you and your generals."

"Really? That seems awfully altruistic of you," said Zsheck. "I've never trusted altruism. Never understood the premise."

"Nor should you," said Tarkannen. "Any man who expects someone else to give him what he can rightly obtain is a man waiting to inherit a debt he can never repay. I don't expect either of us to be indebted to the other when all of this is through. But if we have mutual respect. Well . . . that's something rare enough to aspire to."

Chapter Fifty-Two: Moondancer

"**R**anika Taim . . . Ranika Taim." Ranika lay in her tent, repeating the name over and over to herself, pleased with the way it felt on her tongue. The fact that it matched "Reddevek Taim" in tone and tempo magnified her sense of satisfaction. While she would never forget her mother or the name deChance, something about embracing the name of the man who'd led her out of the Callishite gutters felt like finally setting her feet on solid ground.

The moot, a night and day celebration, lasted two days. There was dancing and singing, feasting and ceremony. In that time, quiet strangers became familiar faces, and familiar faces became friends. She hadn't realized how lonely the ride had been until then. But after Speaker Vekkuh announced Ranika's new status as a daughter of the Dev'advari clan, she rarely had a moment of solitude.

A silken indigo scarf replaced Ranika's oversized hat. One of the women had showed her how to fold the scarf in a band, trapping fragrant flowers in the wrap. She used it to pull the hair back from her face and draped the tail down the nape of her neck and between her shoulders. She was still getting used to the change, but had to admit there was something freeing about feeling the sun on her face and the wind in her hair.

The scarf, like so many other things, was a gift given freely by another daughter of the clan. The girl could not have been more than six years old, and it struck Ranika that parents trusted their children with her company. As the migration out of the Great Crown progressed, more and more people approached, making polite conversation, offering her food or drink, even checking on Zippy. For his part, the Aarindin received so many treats that he became selective, only nibbling on choice bits of fruit or sweet mountain tubers.

Over the past few weeks, the caravan had wound out of the southwest edge of the Great Crown, following narrow switchbacks. The loose scree and steep terrain proved far too rugged for anything beyond a horse in single file, and she realized why the highland clans chose not to utilize wagons. More than once, when the narrow rocky trail twisted in a hairpin descent, Ranika chanced a glance down the cliffside. Heights had never particularly bothered her before, but she felt an earnest sense of gratitude that Zippy traversed the terrain with all the confident grace that she had come to expect from her companion.

Where before the mountains obscured the setting sun, outside the Great Crown it lingered on the far horizon, an unwelcome burning ember adding hours to the end of their travel. When the clan had finally stopped for the day, fatigue and the oppression of travel under the relentless sun dampened their collective mood.

Mounts were groomed, tents erected, and cookfires lit with a silent efficiency that reminded her of an Outrider camp. After grooming Zippy and stowing her saddle, Ranika had accepted an invitation to join two families for a meal of roasted mountain goat and vegetables. Afterward, she'd sat in a circle of eight women, each braiding the hair of the one before her. Dania, a young woman of similar age and sharp wit, sat beside her, showing her how to gather thick strands of hair, then divide, fold, and flip to braid the hair in the Dev'advari fashion.

She thought back to the evening, to the humorous stories and gossip shared about potential romances. They'd all burst into a fit of laughter upon hearing about the misfortunes of a young man attempting to whisper romantic solicitations through a tent. After making some rather embarrassing promises, the girl's father had popped his head out to accept the proposal.

That was when Dania shouldered into Ranika. "And what about you, sister? Has anyone tempted you on this journey?"

Ranika had continued her braid work, laboring to gather a thin plait of hair, twist, and push it through with her little finger. The intricate task resulted in an ornamental braid getting swept up and over the main cluster. She was so focused on the maneuver that she spoke without overthinking. "Boys have never interested me much. Getting them to stop being monks, it's too much work, you know?"

As one, the entire circle had devolved into laughter. Ranika lost her hold of the fine braid, but Dania reached in to rescue the final twisting maneuver. The woman's hands were warm, soft, and dexterous. "So close. Here, like this. Let me guide your fingers."

In motions too swift for Ranika to follow, Dania had finished the braid but allowed her fingers to linger in place. Ranika usually resisted unsolicited attention, but even now, as Dania slept beside her, their fingers interlocked, she couldn't recall a time when she felt so content.

The images of the evening replayed in her mind until her awareness began to slip. Her peaceful descent into dreams stopped when the pressure shifted, as if someone had opened a window only to have the air in the room sweep out into the night. She sat up, fearing she had slipped into one of those nightmares when she inadvertently channeled nadir.

A quick draft of nadir set her vision into the ethereal, and her surroundings flared with clarity. Beside her, Dania slumbered, the young woman a vibrant shimmering patina of silvery lines. She carefully unlocked her fingers from Dania's, secured her ruby-hilted dagger to her belt, and crept headfirst out of the tent.

As she could already perceive the world through the tent, the gesture was more instinctive than necessary. Nothing seemed off, but now that she'd opened herself to the flow of nadir, she could sense that something else was siphoning on the current.

"Foden's teeth. I wish Neska were here."

The moon of Baellen sat full in the night sky, bathing the mountainside in pale streaks of silvery light when filtered through her gift. She cast out her awareness, feeling for the ambient currents without drafting the power into her core. Her senses registered the familiar sights and sounds of the Luna Rova camp. Tents too numerous to count occupied the plateau. Tendrils of smoke from cookfires and the occasional whicker of a horse were all that disturbed the night.

After a few minutes of concentration, she sensed a directional current to the strange siphoning pull. Something drafted nadir farther down the mountainside, beyond the edge of the plateau. Stepping forward, Ranika realized that the moon cast her shadow out before her. She considered using nadir to step into the shadows and conceal her appearance. *But if I can sense someone or something using nadir, could they not sense me?*

She approached the edge of the plateau, dropping belly to the ground and crawling the last ten paces so that she cast no shadow over the ledge. Like an ambush predator, Ranika hunkered down, ethereal sight swinging back and forth across the valley below. Whatever was siphoning on the ambient flows of nadir had stopped. She could sense that for certain now. *Perhaps whatever it was has moved on.*

But she knew at once that the idea was wishful thinking. The night grew unusually still, absent the chirping sounds of frogs and droning calls of cicadas, reminiscent of the night she and Reddevek fought the greater feign. She waited awhile longer, chin resting on her forearms as she lay prone.

Finally, when the muscles in her neck grew stiff, she decided to return. She was pushing back from the ledge when the feathery edge of a shadow passed over her fingers. Without waiting, Ranika pulled hard on nadir, encasing herself in a tight protective web of tiny filaments. At the same time, she rolled to the side.

Something like a heavy pick struck the ground where she had lain only moments before. Bits of rock and stone scattered against her nadir shielding in a staccato pattern, and she turned to see the strangest creature. Moonlight shined on bone-pale leathery flesh and a saucer-shaped, eyeless, faceless head with barely visible sigils engraved around the edge. It stood on two legs that bent at all the wrong angles and ended in sharp, tapered limbs that stabbed into the ground.

"So, you're an umbral. Gotta say, pretty ugly."

She felt vulnerable with the cliffside behind her, so drafted more nadir and encased herself in shadow. With her hand clutching the hilt of her dagger, she prepared to creep behind the beast. But when she tried to sidestep, the umbral clacked its teeth, hissed, and matched her step. She felt it siphon nadir, and sensed a focus of power gathering in its hand.

Before the umbral could attack, Ranika gave in to her instincts. She dropped out of the shadows and poured her focus into a single tentacle of nadir. The appendage speared forth, puncturing the umbral in one of its clawed hands. Another ropelike extension of her gift shot out to immobilize its other arm, but the umbral wrapped her lashing around its arm and began to pull her close.

Acting as much from fear as anything else, she failed to dissipate the tendrils of nadir that now anchored her to the creature. Frantically, she scrambled back, kicking at its feet as it stabbed at the ground. It attempted to impale her and root her to the spot. For a frenzied half minute they danced in place, the umbral trying to stab its feet into her, Ranika dodging and kicking, all the while the two jostling one another through her tethers of nadir.

She gave some slack to the ropes and leaned back, her shoulders now well behind the edge of the cliffside. If she released the tentacles altogether, could she gather them up to protect herself from the fall?

Before she could take action, a woman cried out in rage, and the glint of moonlight caught the blade of a shovel. A sickening thwack followed, like an axe embedding into wet wood. The umbral toppled back and to the side, dragging Ranika away from the cliffside.

She struck the ground hard and lost her grasp of nadir. When she rose to her feet, the umbral turned to face its new assailant, the wood handle of the shovel swinging about like the boom of a sail caught in a chaotic wind. The creature screeched, a sound of anger and pain, and attempted to remove the shovel blade from its flat head.

As it thrashed about, she saw Dania standing barefoot and wide-eyed, backing away from the thing. Ranika darted forward, rolling under a wild swing of the shovel handle to stand between Dania and the umbral. As she came to her feet, the shovel dropped to the ground. She felt the beast siphon nadir, but before it could attack, she screamed in rage and throttled the umbral with no fewer than a dozen stingers. The onyx shards of nadir peppered the umbral's head and torso.

The flathead tottered a few seconds. Rancid smelling ichor streamed from countless nadir burns and fouled the air. It swayed a step to the side, emitting a keening screech of haunted pain, then lurched in a drunken circle and careened off the ledge.

Ranika filtered nadir across her eyes, shifting her sight once again into the ethereal. Far below, the shattered remains of the umbral lingered in faint silver outlines that lost cohesion, melting and dissipating into liquid nadir.

"Taker's tiny twisted bits," said Dania. The woman stepped forward to stand beside her.

"Are you hurt?" asked Ranika.

"No, but that was my best shovel," said Dania in a completely impassive tone. "What was that thing, Nika?"

Ranika held up a hand and turned her ear to the wind, searching for any disturbance. "Umbral, I think. They're like, slaves to Tarkannen, from the Drift. I can't figure what one of those things would be doing out here and all alone."

"You've fought them before?"

"No, but my friends did, Karra and Savnah, Outriders. Only, the one they fought led a whole group of grot," Ranika explained.

Echoes and patterns of unnatural clicking rose up from the valley below. "What do grotvonen sound like?" asked Dania.

Ranika sighed. "I don't have any experience with them either, but I'll eat my hat if that's not them."

The sounds grew louder and eventually, with her augmented sight, Ranika saw more than twenty creatures shambling close to the ground. She reached into a pouch and removed her moonstone, handing it to Dania. "This will give you some light, but not enough. Go sound the alarm. Wake the clan. Make fires. They don't like light. Get the hunters up here. The only way up is the steep trail against the mountainside. I can hold them there."

If Dania was surprised, she hid it well. Instead, she shook her head. "Moons and stars, Nika. Vekkuh told me I would fall for someone who danced under moon's shadow, but I never thought she meant anything like this. Be careful."

"I can handle myself," said Ranika, though the statement sounded more defensive than assured.

"See that you do," said Dania, and she turned to run back to the camp.

Ranika trained her sight below and crept along the cliff ledge until she reached the rocky trail. Behind her, others added to Dania's shouts of alarm, and within minutes the flicker of light from fresh fires scattered dancing shadows against the mountains. The commotion drew the grotvonen in.

Like before, Ranika crouched low against a boulder, a predator watching, biding her time. The gangly beasts flowed across the ground below, some loping on all fours, others lumbering forward with athletic hops that covered nearly as much ground. They stopped at the base of the cliff, roaming back and forth for several minutes until, at last, one of the smaller ones screeched with excitement, and the grotvonen gathered directly below her at the bottom of the trail.

There must have been some discussion as an argument seemed to break out, the clicky speech devolving into growls and savage roars. As they huddled together, a thought struck Ranika. If she acted quickly, perhaps she could eliminate most of the grotvonen where they gathered, instead of waiting for them to swarm onto the plateau.

She siphoned nadir, coalescing it between her hands. As she forced her intent into the construction, the roiling currents felt slippery, resisting the confinement of her will. She redoubled her effort, compressing the nadir into a dense sphere. Onyx shards and thorns bubbled up from the surface, and she forced them back inside, then hurled the globe into the mass of grotvonen below.

The object plummeted, growing in size as she released her control. When it struck the ground, it erupted with the strangest detonation. Rather than a colossal eruption, all light and sound sucked into the center of the globe. What looked like a burst of shadow discharged, sending jagged shards of nadir in all directions.

Ranika ducked her head behind a rock as errant projectiles rattled against the mountainside. When she chanced a look, nearly all of the grotvonen, more than twenty of the beasts, lay dead or twitching under the moonlight. Two of them howled in pain or fear, or both maybe.

She didn't really speak grotvonen. They scurried back down the mountainside and beyond her enhanced vision.

Ranika stood waiting to see if any more threats, umbral or grotvonen, appeared. With an effort, she released the gathered power, and maintained but a fragment of her gift to enhance her vision. Dania found her pacing along the cliffside not long after, the glow of the moonstone announcing her arrival.

Four men and two women, all familiar faces armed with bows, followed the young woman. Three others held torches high. "Did you leave any for the rest of us?" asked Dania.

The hunters carried themselves with vigilant apprehension. Ranika couldn't tell if they were on edge because of the grotvonen or scared of the abrogator in their midst, so she downplayed the encounter. "I think I scared most of them off."

Dania walked to the cliff edge and held the moonstone out, searching below. The woman looked at Ranika once and shook her head in disbelief, then handed the moonstone back. She retrieved a torch and tossed it below, highlighting the absolute carnage. Grotvonen bodies lay sundered in a circle, the limbs of one tangled over another. Torsos twisted at impossible angles, holes gaping where holes should not be, and all of it mixed in a soup of blood and gore.

"Moons," said Ranika. "I didn't think it would do that."

Dania patted her on the shoulder. "Makes me glad you're a Moonie. Come on then, Moondancer, let's go tell the speaker. She's going to love this."

Chapter Fifty-Three: The Stillness

Bryndor lay on his back listening to Ksenia's breathing, finding comfort in the familiar cadence. For every two breaths he took, she took three, as had always been her nature both inside and beyond the Revealing. He turned his head, nose but a breath away from her neck, and inhaled. The complex, sensuous fragrance of winter night's asylum rose to his awareness. The comforting reality of her presence, the fact that she was here beside him, not lost inside the Revealing, brought a stinging sensation to his eyes. And he knew what he had to do.

Taking great pains to move without waking her, he sat up, waiting to see if her breathing changed. She turned toward him, no doubt sensing the loss of his warmth, so he tucked a blanket around her. Moonlight fell on the angle of her jaw and cast a delicate shadow under the upturned tip of her nose. When he got back, she would give him the rough side of her tongue, and he would deserve every last bit of her venom, but at least she would be safe. Giver help him, they all would.

He sighed, then inch-wormed himself out of the tent. Outside, he collected his gear, then walked barefoot several paces. Boru padded over, silent as a shadow but easy to spot by the light of the full moon of Baellen. Bryndor signed, *"I'll grab Tacit. We are leaving. Meet near the water."*

Boru sniffed once at his ear, then pointed his nose back to camp.

"I know. It's just you and me. I can't put the others in danger."

The wolvryn inhaled, sounding every bit like a massive bellows when he sighed a response. But without further protest, he turned and loped off toward the shore.

Bryndor found Tacit standing near Winter and feared they would alert the others, but the Aarindin seemed agreeable enough, and Bryndor walked him back and away from camp before mounting. They circled north in a generous berth around the camp, finally turning east. The gentle rustle of shallow river water drowned out the sound of Tacit's hooves over the sand and pebbles.

He searched through the moonlight, looking south, then back to the north, waiting for Boru to join them. Silent minutes passed, and he tried to settle his mind and appreciate the serenity of the moonlight shimmering over the river, the peace and solitude of the night. But his mind grew restless.

At last, Tacit whickered, a pleasant sound Bryndor knew for a greeting. He turned, and Boru crept out from the shadow of the trees . . . followed by four Outriders and, by the stiff way that she sat Winter, a very angry Ksenia.

Boru's body language betrayed what had happened. The wolvryn kept his nose to the ground, pretending to find something intriguing about the smells there. The sight of the great wolvryn moping about, fearful of reprimand, was too much. Bryndor swallowed his frustration, dismounted, and walked over to his friend.

He stood not two feet from the wolvryn, waiting for him to lift his nose. At last, Bryndor ran fingers through Boru's fur, caressing his neck with reassurance. Finally, the wolvryn looked up. *"Let me guess,"* he signed. *"She made you promise not to leave without her?"*

Boru listed his head to the right.

"All is well, Boru. I wouldn't want to cross her either," he signed.

Bryndor began to feel something of Boru's guilt as Ksenia rode Winter close enough to make eye contact. "I can explain," he began, but she held up a hand, cutting him off.

She sat on Winter, the tempo of her breathing betraying her anger, right hand ringing circles around her left wrist. The five of them, Bryndor and a seasoned quad of Outriders, waited for the sympath to vent her anger. Even Savnah sat stoically, waiting for Ksenia's lead.

He had a thought that she hadn't been this mad at him in years, and then the inconceivable tragedy of those memories collided with his reality and threatened to make him laugh. But he smothered that sensation the moment it bloomed, knowing full well it would only magnify her rage. Without words, he remained still and tried to assume a contrite expression, but Taker bite him if the entire situation didn't threaten to make him grin.

He hid his smile by sucking at his teeth. After mastering his emotions, he lifted his face to meet her gaze. Moons, was she angry. "I owe you all an explanation, so here it is, as much as I can tell you, anyway. In the Revealing I . . . lost things, and it nearly broke me. Crossing the Stillness is my burden, and I would not add to it by chancing any of your lives. The risk is real, and my brother's freedom is worth it, but not at the price of any one of your lives."

He forced himself to look into Ksenia's eyes as he spoke, watching her body language. Hoping she would understand. Nothing softened in the rigid way she sat astride Winter, but at last, she turned to Savnah and nodded once. The prime nudged her Aarindin forward, stopping only for a moment. "She's got your measure, Bryn, and we all have your back."

Nolan, Dexxin, and Tovnik followed Savnah into the river. Each of the young men rode by in silence, offering sympathetic glances as they passed. Somehow, they had managed to break camp and grab the packhorse. Bryndor waited for Ksenia's rebuke, but it never came. Instead, she surprised him with a soft chuckle, head swinging side to side, then said, "A measure of the Giver's grace."

"I don't understand."

Zenith flickered behind her eyes and Tacit knelt to allow him to mount. "Mount up. The others are getting too far ahead."

Not wanting to provoke an argument, Bryndor threw a leg over and Tacit rose, gripping him in the process. Together, they rode into the shallow river, clearly visible under full moonlight. "Your Aunt Laryn warned me you had endured a lot, so much that at times you might seem different. And I understand a little of what she meant."

"I'm trying to remember what I was like before I left, but sometimes it feels like I'm wearing somebody else's skin, or I'm trying to be something I'm not sure I'm meant to be. If I've done a poor job sorting myself out, I'm sorry. I can do better."

Ksenia pulled a lock of hair behind her ear and turned to face him. Both their mounts stopped midstream, clearly under the direction of her gift. "All of that is understandable, Bryn. But do you know why I am so angry with you? Why any of us are?"

"I tried to leave without telling—"

Her head cocked to the side, an obvious dismissal of his simplistic explanation, so he began again. "Right, don't be a monk. So first, by leaving without you all, I removed the respect of your consent, and that devalued your input, your freedom of choice. But . . ." He sighed. "It also cheapens how much . . . you love me . . . doesn't it?"

Her head drew back in surprise, and the Aarindin began plodding through the water again. "I didn't think you would get there. Maybe there's hope for you yet, Baellentrell."

He winced at that. The last time she took to referring to him by his last name, she had remained angry for a week. And again, the surreal nature of it all, the life he had with her before, the life they shared now, dissolved any misgivings he might have felt. He signaled Tacit to follow, the plopping sounds of Aarindin hooves in water his only companion.

As they approached the far side of the river, the Outriders disappeared into the fog bank. Ksenia drew Winter to a halt when a commotion broke out. Moments later, the packhorse whinnied and toppled back into the river, only to right itself. The contents of their food pack drifted downstream, but the horse trotted toward the camp they had just vacated, bedrolls and blankets still strapped to its back.

Nolan reappeared from the fog on his mount, shaking a hand in pain. "Sorry, I don't know what got into him. One moment I was pulling on the lead rope and the next he seemed crazed. Kess, you think you can get him back?"

"Actually no. I tried," she said. "He's mad with fear and . . . Giver." She paused and placed fingers to her mouth. "I think he just ran headlong into a ravine. I can't even reach him. The last time I sensed that kind of panic was during the stampede. The others, the Aarindin, are only barely managing. We need to regroup quickly and see what has them all so spooked."

Nolan turned and led them into the fog. Tacit followed Bryndor's urging, remaining sure-footed, but the Aarindin's ears perked forward, attentive and vigilant. Bryndor felt more than saw the mount climb the far bank. The temperature dropped in the foggy mists, and a shiver stole across his back.

The very feel and sound of the Aarindin walking on the strange moss-laden surface gave him pause. The normal vibrations one felt when a mount stepped onto something solid were simply gone. Instead, Bryndor felt Tacit shift nervously from hoof to hoof, his steps emitting a strange squelching sound.

The Outriders sat their Aarindin in a circle, waiting for them to arrive. Each Aarindin appeared stressed, as if expecting an attack of some kind. Boru paced nervously, nose to the air, then the ground, then back to the air. The great wolvryn even released a whine that hollowed out his core with a wave of fear.

"What is it?" Bryndor spoke and signed the words together, but Boru was too preoccupied to respond.

Ksenia nearly swooned in her saddle. "Taker's breath. There's nothing in here," she said.

Savnah released the locking straps over her twin moonblade axes. "What do you mean, exactly?"

Ksenia lifted a hand and closed her eyes in concentration. After a few minutes, she inhaled and seemed to regain a comfortable position. As one, each of them shifted on their Aarindin as the mounts released their grips.

"Grind it, a little help here, Kess?" said Savnah, shifting her hips back and forth to right herself over the Aarindin.

Ksenia lifted a hand, gesturing for peace. "It can't be helped. Nolan was right. There's no zenith in here. Reach out, see if any of you can prime your gifts."

"Nothing for me, she's right," said Tovnik.

"Giver, it's like we've been ranth'd. Unless I push hard, I can't even sense my siblings," said Dexxin.

"Yes, well, I don't recommend it," said Ksenia.

"She's right," said Tovnik. "We each possess innate zenith stores, so you could likely use your gift, but at great cost."

Ksenia nodded agreement. "It's the same with the Aarindin. So, I told them to release their grips until directed otherwise. If we try to ride like usual, gripped, I don't think they will make it more than half the day before falling to exhaustion."

"What's going on with Boru?" asked Bryndor.

"I've never heard a wolvryn swear before, but I think he came close," explained Ksenia. "He can see and smell us, but his inability to sense at his normal range leaves him feeling blind. It's an adjustment for all of us."

"That's about as welcome as a turd that toppled into the water trough," said Savnah. "Speaking of, how many waterskins do we have?"

They took a fast inventory of their meager supplies. Tovnik had his medic pack. They each had a full waterskin. Savnah had managed to retrieve a single small satchel with one change of clothes and a rough spun blanket. Bryndor's pack held enough rations to last four days . . . for one person.

"How far can the Aarindin range like this, ungripped and without food or water?" asked Bryndor.

"If this cool weather holds, we've got three days, four if things are dire," said Savnah. "After that, we'll all need to forage and find fresh water. That sound about right?"

"Yes," said Ksenia. "What about Boru?"

"It's the same for him. He ate his fill last night. Thirst will be the challenge before hunger," said Bryndor.

"Do we have any idea how far the Stillness goes?" asked Savnah.

"Nothing reliable," said Bryndor. "So, we either push on, or regroup back at camp. We could probably forage for a day, stock up on a few things."

Savnah hocked a glob of spit to the side. "It's all speculation though, right? I mean, if we find game, it will need to be consumed within one or two days, and who is to say that will make any difference? If the Stillness only takes two or three days to cross, it won't matter," said Savnah.

"And if it takes seven?" asked Bryndor.

"It still will not matter," said Savnah. "The way I see it, we have two choices. Stop now and return home and do what we can to prepare for the war, or push on. I can't say that I like it, but sitting here whining about it isn't helping. I know I can be prickly sometimes, and riding ungripped isn't going to be fun, but I say we push on."

"What about the rest of you?" asked Bryndor. "Now's the time to speak your piece."

"I go where she goes," said Dexxin, nodding at his prime.

Nolan and Tovnik shared Dexxin's sentiment. Ksenia leaned forward, patting Winter's neck with affection. "This effort is bigger than any of us. When we free Lluthean, there is every chance that one or both of you will inherit your arca prime. We'll need everything in the fight against Tarkannen. It's worth the risk, Bryn."

"Stubborn as monks, the lot of you," he mumbled.

"Stubborn and stupid are two very different things in the Derrigand house," said Savnah.

He had a thought that most of them, himself included, had likely inherited both in equal measure. "Let's hope the Giver can see through this fog and prove you right. You have the lead, Savnah. Set the pace," said Bryndor.

They set out in a modified quad formation, with Nolan on point, Bryndor and Ksenia sandwiched between Dexxin and Tovnik, and Savnah on the rear. The oppressive fog obscured their sight beyond twenty feet. Within only minutes, they realized the importance of riding in tight formation. Even Boru, who often loped off into the countryside, remained close on Tacit's heels.

Over the next few hours, the sun rose, but the fog only seemed to shift, refracting the light and taking on the appearance of dense white clouds. If anything, their visibility became more limited.

They pushed on, the mounts taking a fast walk. While the buoyancy of the moss took some adjusting to, it did seem to allow the Aarindin to travel with less fatigue. Bryndor only wished the muscles in his hips and back felt the same. They stopped to attend to the call of nature, then remounted and continued without the need for further words or encouragement.

Beyond stifling the light and zenith, the fog seemed to depress their collective mood. The absence of any visible horizon caused the hours to roll on with mind-numbing tedium. He searched the sky, trying to get a sense of the passage of time, but found it impossible to discern where the sun lay.

"How does Nolan know which way is east? What prevents us from walking in circles?" he asked.

"I'm cheating," Nolan called out. "I prime my gift once every hour or so. I confirm where we have been and can sense that we make straight east."

"Every hour or so? We've only been riding for a few hours, right?" asked Bryndor.

"Someone get that man a bit of jerky," teased Nolan. "It's been ten hours already."

Bryndor turned to face Ksenia. "That's not possible, is it?"

Ksenia rubbed at circles under her eyes. "I think he's actually right."

He handed her a waterskin. "Did you stifle your gifts like the rest of us?"

"Mostly," she said.

"Mostly? Kess, what does mostly mean?" he pressed.

She yawned. "About the same as Nolan. I have to check in with the Aarindin, and even Boru. They're barely keeping it together. All any of them want is to scatter and run back, even Winter."

"I didn't know. You should have said something. Would it help if we talked to them?"

"It can't hurt. Anything to help ease their fears."

Bryndor leaned forward. "Tacit, my boy, you're . . . doing great. Karragin would be proud. Just . . . keep it up!"

He turned to look at Boru, who kept pace on his hind flank. The wolvryn appeared weary, but lifted his head. *"Are you able to continue?"* he signed.

Boru flipped his nose to the right with quick affirmation.

"Let me know when it is otherwise."

Another fast acknowledgment, and the wolvryn dropped his head. Bryndor worried for the morale of the group. Even Savnah rode slumped on her Aarindin, keeping her own counsel. He wished, not for the first time, that Lluthean was already free and riding in their company. His brother would surely know how to lift their spirits.

He cleared his throat and began to sing a tavern song from the Southlands. "There once was a maid in Journey's Bend. She filled all the mugs without an end. For wink and a smile she would never fail, for a silver mark she would make a man wail! Oh bring . . . me . . . another round lass! I've a need for the ale so fill my glass! When the day's all done and the sun sets low, it's the ale my boys, makes the good times flow!"

Bryndor rode on. The squelching sound of Aarindin traversing the moss-covered ground was the only response from the group. "Nothing?"

Ksenia bobbed her head from side to side. "It wasn't bad. I didn't know you could sing."

"He can't," chirped Savnah.

"Ha ha, alright, let's hear something from the critic, perhaps a ballad sung at the taverns in Midrock," he challenged.

"Tell you what, when we stop for a break, I'll sing Rubik's song. It's about a man who mistakes a goat for his lover. It doesn't sound like much, but after a few drinks, it's pretty funny," said Savnah.

Bryndor thought to goad her further, but instead tried to recall the second verse to the tavern song, defaulting to humming, even whistling. But after an hour of the solo performance, and with none of the others joining in, he began to wonder if his efforts were only adding to their collective misery.

The oppressive fog leeched any vitality he felt, until all he could do was focus on not sliding off Tacit's back. And so, the hours rolled on in relative silence. Eventually, the sun must have set as the mists resumed their subdued, blue-laden hue. Still, they pushed on, stopping infrequently.

Bryndor realized that he had failed to communicate with Kaellor and the others through the shek. The only way to hear anything from them required him to prime the device with zenith. He felt for the inner reserve Ksenia had referenced, but couldn't see how to use that on the external device, so left it dormant and resigned that he would only be able to reach out once they emerged from the Stillness.

Oddly enough, travel by night was easier, somehow less oppressive. During the daylight hours, the endless confrontation of dense, white clouds became an almost suffocating experience. Which was why, on the following morning, Bryndor suggested they stop for a break.

Boru had loped forward to trot beside him, looking weary and exhausted. *"I could rest. How about you?"* he signed. After receiving confirmation, Bryndor drew them to a halt.

No one, not even Savnah, suggested otherwise. He watched as they each dismounted with groans. Though he had little desire to experience firsthand how stiff and sore his muscles were, Tacit had done his part, so instead of directing the Aarindin to crouch, Bryndor slid a leg back and flopped to the ground without ceremony, his own moan of pain escaping his lips.

They tethered the Aarindin together and Ksenia felt fairly certain the mounts would remain. Nobody volunteered to set a watch, and that seemed like a reasonable concession to their collective fatigue. After all, they had encountered no living creatures in the last day and a half.

He found a spot on the ground beside Boru and when he lay back, the spongy, plush bedding offered by the carpet of moss was a welcome reprieve. His mind, numb from the long journey, collapsed into sleep.

SOMETHING JERKED AT his shoulder, a persistent tugging sensation, and Bryndor tried to wake. It felt like climbing out of layers of heavy bedding. His physical and mental fatigue threatened to pull him back under, smothering him in the world of dreams. But the tugging sensation became more violent, and in the periphery of his awareness, he realized that Boru growled. Not the threatening, angry growl of the predator, but a growl of annoyance.

Bryndor's eyes fluttered open, and he tried to orient himself. Scratchy fibers pressed in all around him, weaving over his limbs, the bare front of his neck, between his fingers, and encroaching on his ears and nose. The stink of dirt and moss filled his nostrils as a carpet of rhizomes cocooned him in a smothering web.

The filaments wove over his chest, making breathing difficult. Still, Boru labored to pull him free, tugging at Bryndor's shoulder. The wolvryn thrashed his head back and forth until something, either his tunic or the mossy fibers, gave way. The wolvryn returned, sniffing and whining, sounding utterly defeated.

Bryndor yelled out, "Can anyone hear me? Kess? Savnah! Anyone?"

Faintly, Bryndor sensed muffled, frantic voices, and then a scream born of fear and despair. Ksenia's scream. Unbidden, zenith flared into Bryndor's shoulders. "Boru, get back! Back Boru!"

Bryndor briefly sensed he should not attempt anything like he was considering. He had used controlled bursts of rune fire to warm his core, but fear and mental fatigue caused him to act beyond caution. He drafted a ball of rune fire, detonating the power directly over his chest. A thunder crack erupted, followed by a pressure wave and a throbbing, painful pulse. Rune fire flared all around him, singeing the meshwork of rhizomes to ash. He sat up, gasping, ears ringing, and searched around, barely registering his tattered, burned clothes falling away.

The carpet of moss around him fell to ash. Boru paced in a circle around four mounds, Ksenia and the Outriders, he assumed. The Aarindin nearby, recognizable by their thrashing, also struggled under layers of green and tan. Bryndor stood and coalesced another ball of rune fire. The accompanying boom of thunder registered as a palpable pulse more than any sound to his deafened senses, and he divided the ball into two blazing spheres. He stood enthralled in the euphoric sensation of his power and rolled the spheres in opposite directions, burning away the moss and undergrowth in a controlled fashion.

Ksenia was the first to emerge, spilling out onto hard ground when the side of her mossy prison withered to ash. One by one, the Outriders spilled out of their tombs, coughing, waving at smoke and ash, but alive. Bryndor maintained his concentration, whirling the balls of rune fire in larger and larger concentric circles, burning the Stillness to ash.

Ksenia ran at him, waving her arms and screaming, but his ears still rang from the initial detonation. Another wave of euphoria caused his head to swim. Flickering lights in the periphery of his vision caused him to look down at the runes pulsing in tempo with his heartbeat, visible across his naked body.

Without warning, his command of zenith winked out, his runes faded to dormancy, and the ground rushed up as he fell into darkness.

Chapter Fifty-Four: Resco to the Rescue

Ksenia writhed against the coarse bindings, the dense fibers abrading against any exposed skin. Her wrists, ankles, and neck burned, but panic caused her to thrash despite the pain. She nearly exhausted herself until a reverberant pulse followed by the unmistakable thunderclap of rune fire stilled her restless mind.

A wave of heat rolled across her side and the fibers of moss evaporated as much as they burned to ash. She spilled out of her confinement, coughing soot and blinking against the stinging sensation of air heavily laden with ash.

A roiling ball of rune fire left streamers in her vision, and she realized what he was doing. *No, stop Bryn, rein yourself in!*

She screamed the thought in her mind but stood rooted to the spot by the wonder of watching him channel. Somehow, Bryndor had summoned enough zenith to obliterate an entire field of moss, releasing them each from their entombment. Brilliant, cerulean currents flared across the tapestry of runes covering his body.

"It's too much, too much!" she shouted and ran at him, waving her arms. But she was too late.

Zenith pulsed out from his runes in a tempo that started fast, then slowed. He swayed, and the rhythm of the pulsing zenith slowed more, fading to an anemic light blue before winking out as he collapsed into the ash.

"Giver please," she blurted in a panic, and raced forward. Bryndor lay lifeless, face buried in ash. She placed two hands on one of his shoulders, finding him cold to the touch, but when she rolled him, a gentle plume of ash puffed from his nose. Though he drew breath, the effort seemed feeble.

From behind her, the Aarindin whinnied. "Nolan, Dexxin, gather the mounts. Keep them calm. Tovnik! Savnah! I need you here, now!" she yelled with unnatural authority.

The medic and Savnah dropped to their knees beside her, each looking bewildered and dusted in a powder of white and grey ash. "He's breathing, but only barely," she explained.

Tovnik wiped at the debris covering his face and blinked in rapid succession, squinting through the haze of ash. "Get him on his back, carefully. Savnah, get the spare clothes. We need to conserve his heat."

The medic cleared ash from Bryndor's mouth and tilted his head back. The maneuver allowed a deep breath to fill his lungs, and he drew several more in rapid succession.

"What can I do?" she asked.

"He needs heat, zenith and heat. Try to warm him, get him covered. I'm going to see if anything else is damaged," said Tovnik.

Without further words, the medic dropped into the healer trance, the murmur of his gift lifting as a hauntingly stifled and muted sound in the fog. Ksenia pulled her shirt overhead, disrobing down to her smallclothes, and pressed her body against his, even entangling their legs.

She pulled herself to him as tight as possible, and it felt like squeezing cold stone. Ignoring the discomfort, she vigorously rubbed an arm and leg up and down to generate heat. His flesh felt stiff, and in moments she shivered as her body heat leached into his. Savnah dropped to the ground, rummaging through the lone pack to find a set of clothes. "Give me a hand, Kess," said the prime.

While Tovnik carried out his assessment, they labored to dress Bryndor in a set of breeches, socks, and two tunics. They reached for his boots but found them scorched beyond use. "Right then, let's sandwich him until Tov says otherwise. He's cold as butchered meat."

Without words, they rolled Bryndor to his side. Savnah spooned him from behind, and Ksenia wriggled until her backside pressed into his front. She pulled his arm over and entangled her fingers through his, cupping her mouth to blow heat into his palm. Despite her effort, his fingers remained stiff and ice-cold. Her teeth began to chatter. "I can't stop shivering."

Savnah's hand rubbed vigorously over her shoulder. "I know, it's like sleeping with the dead. Nope, sorry, scratch that, poor choice there. Grind it, but this isn't working."

"I know. I have an idea. Turn him onto his back," said Ksenia. She stood on wobbly legs and looked about. Nolan and Dexxin held the Aarindin in check, though they walked in restless circles. Boru lay not two paces away, head on forepaws, eyes sharp and focused on Bryndor.

"Here Boru, he needs you." And before she could prime her gift, the wolvryn lurched forward. A gout of ash billowed out in a cloud as he approached and settled himself onto Bryndor, draping over him and licking the soot from his face. Ksenia checked that Boru's tremendous weight didn't prevent him from drawing breath. Somehow, the wolvryn understood what Bryndor needed and kept his weight on his knees and elbows.

She found her clothes and dressed, accepting Savnah's embrace to warm herself. At last, a bit of color returned to Bryndor's face, and Tovnik's song ceased. The medic fell back, panting.

"That's as far as I can go. I'm sorry," he said. "Any more and you'll have two of us to carry out of here."

"What did you find?" pressed Ksenia through chattering teeth.

"There's no injury, nothing I can heal anyway. But it's clear he overextended. His breaths are shallow, thready pulse. I've heard of people burning through their reserves. I've just never seen it before. We'll all have to be careful."

"Will he wake up?" asked Savnah.

Tovnik nodded, but the gesture seemed noncommittal. "Maybe, I think so. I just don't know when. It's this place. We need to skin out. The sooner the better."

"Let's get him mounted. The Aarindin could grip him. If we alternate which mount carries him, maybe no more than an hour or so, how long do you figure they can manage it?" asked Savnah.

"I can't say. A day, I imagine not more than two hours at a time," she said.

"All we can do is try," said Savnah.

Ksenia triggered her sympath gift, linking to Tacit. Her instructions were firm and direct, and the Aarindin responded, dropping belly to the ground. She stifled her gift after only a few seconds, fearful of the consequences. Savnah grabbed his arms, lifting Bryndor like a floppy rag doll to a sitting position, then pulled one arm over her shoulder.

"Grab the other one, Tov. Let's lift him up. Kess, you get a leg over," said Savnah. The prime waited for them to assist and grunted with the effort. "Moons, but he's some kind of slim-thick, heavy . . . grinder."

They lurched to the side, nearly dropping him, but eventually hoisted Bryndor up and flopped him over Tacit's back. The Aarindin rose easily, keeping Bryndor mounted even when he slumped forward.

A faint popping, hissing sound rose to her awareness, and Ksenia searched the ash-laden clearing. Bryndor had burned a swath in a circular pattern. She kicked a boot at the ground, disturbing rocky soil and ash. A flicker of movement, like wriggling worms, caught her eye. Closer inspection at the edge of the moss showed spiraling tendrils and shoots weaving across the burn-scarred ground.

Nolan cleared his throat. "I probably should have mentioned that. I cut a patch out the other day and the stuff began to knit across the hole I made."

Savnah exhaled through her nose. Ksenia could already imagine the prime's berating. *Nolan, what kind of monk forgets to report that the grinding man-eating-moss-carpet is alive and seeks to devour us whole?* But instead, the prime signaled her Aarindin and mounted.

"That bit of information would have been valuable. Just . . . do better. We're all tired, but none of us have lost our grip. Come on, I don't care to be standing here when that circle of moss closes in. Nolan, you have the lead."

Without further words or discussion, they each mounted and followed the scout. The Aarindin trotted eagerly out of the burned area, their hooves once again creating the odd squelching noise as they traveled over the unusual terrain. Ksenia spent the first hour leaning forward to accommodate her achy back and hip muscles and leech

Winter's warmth. After another hour, Tacit's head drooped, and she called a stop.

They switched mounts, and Dexxin rode Tacit while his mount gripped an otherwise lifeless Bryndor. After another two rotations, as they hoisted Bryndor onto Nolan's mount, he flickered his eyes open and moaned.

"Tov, he's waking," said Savnah.

The medic walked over and placed fingers on Bryndor's wrist, assessing something though his healer song remained dormant. Eventually Tovnik nodded, then slapped Bryndor lightly on the cheek in rapid succession. "Bryn, come on man, wake up. Bryn?"

Bryndor's eyes fluttered open, and a collective happy gasp erupted from the group. He convulsed with dry heaves but remained prone over the Aarindin.

Ksenia leaned down to make eye contact. "Bryn, it's me, Kess. How do you feel?"

He panted for several breaths, tried to lift his head, then slumped forward, wincing in pain. "Not good. Everything hurts."

"Anything you can do, Tov?" she asked.

"Not in here. But we can see if he keeps this down. I've got two lammen berries left. It's better than nothing. Open your mouth, Bryn, and whatever you do, don't spit these out. It's maybe the only thing that might restore some of your strength." Tovnik wedged a fat berry into either side of Bryndor's cheek, using the flat of his thumb to smash the fruit against his teeth.

Bryndor clenched against another spasm of retching, but kept the substance inside his mouth, mostly. "That's worse than any of Rona's teas, but thanks, Tov," he croaked.

Boru had wandered ahead and now reappeared from the fog. He plodded over and sniffed at Bryndor, licking him on the face, and finally drawing a smile as Bryndor lifted clumsy fingers to touch the wolvryn's ear.

"Is it just me, or do Boru's feet look wet?" he asked.

Ksenia looked, and indeed, the wolvryn's fur appeared muddy. She searched inside herself, finding the strength to awaken her sympath rune, and opened herself to the wolvryn. *"Is there water near, or only mud?"*

Instead of the vibrant and rich response, Boru's voice echoed through the link with none of the sensory detail to which she had become accustomed. *"Ahead, the way drops to mud and old water. We cannot drink it."*

"You and the Aarindin, can you cross it?"

"Yes," he said, head tilting to the right.

Ksenia stifled her gift. The brief conversation caused the muscles between her shoulders to cramp, and a throbbing ache settled in her forehead. "Boru says the path drops ahead; maybe this becomes a fen. The water sounds brackish, but he thinks the Aarindin can walk through it."

Savnah mounted her Aarindin. "Form up. I'll take the lead for a bit."

She waited for each of them to mount and Ksenia wondered how long the Aarindin would last before needing rest and access to zenith. She worried even more how much longer any of them could go on. Looking back, she couldn't recall if this was the third day or the fifth. Winter was the only Aarindin of the group who had not yet gripped Bryndor, and even she walked with her head dipped lower than usual.

A fast click of her tongue directed Winter to fall in behind Bryndor's mount before he disappeared in the fog. Her weight shifted forward, and for the next hour, the Aarindin trudged along a decline. The air became sticky and humid, feeling even more oppressive as the squelching of moss gave way to sloshing and splashing hooves through stagnant and shallow water. Before long, her feet, made wet by the splatter, became cold and numb.

She alternated between staring at Bryndor's back, waiting to watch him breathe, and staring at the ground. Their journey led through shallow pools, over soggy, moss-covered ground, and back into stagnant water. The smell of rotting vegetation, revolting for the first hour, became only something she was vaguely aware of if she put her mind to it.

Movement caught her eye, and Bryndor pushed himself to a sitting position. She urged Winter to come up beside him. Dark circles ringed his eyes, and his face was gaunt. Even his broad shoulders appeared withered. Soot and ash dappled his skin in grey and white patches. She handed him a waterskin, and he took a cautious sip. "Thanks. You can tell this one to release the grip. I think I can manage."

Ksenia studied the Aarindin, Tovnik's mare. She did appear exhausted, hooves shuffling through the water rather than stepping with Winter's grace. Ksenia clicked her tongue, then gestured to the Aarindin. Bryndor listed to the side, and she placed a hand under his arm, helping him find his balance.

He righted himself and rode slumped, fingers splayed across the Aarindin's withers for balance. "So, did I actually burn off my boots?"

She suppressed a snort. "You burned off more than that, and nearly killed yourself in the process. But." She sighed. "I can't say that we wouldn't be fertilizing the Stillness if you hadn't acted. So, there's that. But Bryn, you can't push that far."

He nodded and lifted one hand, surrendering to her point. "I lost myself in it. It's been years since I really unleashed my gift, you know?"

The oddity of his statement, spoken as a raw, unvarnished truth, caused her to inhale in surprise. She thought back to some of their conversations since he emerged from his Rite of Revealing: how attentive he seemed, his familiarity with his gifts, even the remarkable way he and Boru were able to communicate. Self-awareness governed his actions, and he seemed comfortable leading the mission. A subtle realization rose to her without calculation, more as a statement of wonder. "Bryndor, how long were you in there, inside the Revealing?"

He slumped forward, forearms resting on the Aarindin's shoulders, staring at the ground. She thought to retract the question, but his voice rasped a response as tears streamed down his cheek. "It was years, Kess."

"Moons. How many? Five?"

He shook his head, face obscured by a curtain of black hair.

"Ten? More than ten? Giver's last breath, Bryn. More than ten years?"

He righted himself. "It was more than ten, but less than twenty. I wasn't alone. I had Boru, and we managed, but still, it was a lot."

595

"So you . . . remember it? Laryn said you would be different. That explains what she meant, doesn't it?"

He chewed on his cheek as the mounts continued to slog through the fen. "What is it? You can tell me," she offered.

He seemed about to reply, but shook his head. An ash-painted hand pulled back his hair, and he turned to fix his gaze on her face. They rode that way for nearly a minute, and she sensed his eyes travel across her face, tracking from one eye to the other, studying her delicate, unique features as she did the same to his.

Skin pulled tight across his cheekbones and jaw. The muscle there contracted a few times. His eyes, so penetrating and serious, seemed almost grey in the Stillness, like the first time they met, before his mantle fractured. His tears were gone as fast as they had appeared, leaving streaks through the white ash.

At last, she inhaled a breath and held out a hand, which he took. "It's alright. Someday maybe, when you have it all . . . sorted out, if you want, you can tell me all about it. Until then, I suppose we should focus on getting out of the Stillness, together."

"Together," he agreed, squeezed her hand, then let go to shift his weight back to the center of the Aarindin's back. He pulled at his tunic and looked down at the several inches of exposed leg and ankle protruding from the spare trousers that were obviously not his. "I'm wearing two shirts and . . . are these Savnah's britches?"

"I'm not sure. Yours burned off, and the pack horse lost the others over the river. The only thing of yours that survived was that bow and the wolvryn eye, but it's been dormant here. Nolan's carrying your things," she said.

They rode in silence, and she knew by the way he sucked at his teeth that the full implication of her statement rose to his awareness. Behind a curtain of black hair that fell forward, a smile found its way to his face, and his chin sank toward his chest. "Did you get me dressed in Savnah's breeches all by yourself?"

"Moons, no. She helped me. Nolan and Dexx were busy minding the mounts, and Tovnik was lost to the healer's trance. But don't worry. We had your bum covered up pretty quick, and she's got eyes for Nolan these days."

He released a soft giggle. "She's never going to let me hear the end of how I got into her pants, though, is she?"

"Probably not."

They pushed on until the color of the fog shifted from the stifling bright white of day to a muted blue. Still, the moon and stars remained obscured. Another day had passed and, without debate or question, when Nolan's mount climbed up a small rise, leaving the soggy fen for dry moss-covered ground, they dismounted. Boru paced in a slow circle, then sagged to the ground and fell asleep.

"If I sit or lie down, I'm not sure there's any getting back up," said Dexxin. The sender wobbled on his feet, and Savnah placed a hand on his shoulder, keeping him from collapsing.

Dexxin looked every bit as haggard as Bryndor, perhaps even more. "You've been trying to reach them, haven't you, Dexx?" Savnah chided.

"I wanted them to know about this place in case things go sideways," said Dexxin.

"Were you able to reach them?" asked Nolan.

Dexxin just shook his head. "Well, thanks for trying all the same, Dexx," said Bryndor.

They all stood in exhaustion, and Bryndor dropped to his knees to cut away at a few strands of moss that had already crept over Boru's hind paw. The wolvryn drew deep, easy breaths, oblivious of the offending rhizomes.

Bryndor held out his palm, and she watched as the severed moss withered and browned in seconds, dissipating to fine tubules and then fragmenting to dust. "I wonder if we could use our weapons and carve out a section. Maybe we could claim enough ground to get a few hours of sleep?"

"It's not the worst idea I've heard all day," said Savnah. She removed her moonblade axes, handing one to Nolan. Without further encouragement, they dropped to knees and sliced away at the thick carpet.

Ksenia found the work fun at first. She grabbed a fistful of the offending material and cut away large swaths. A small pile formed from the discards and browned almost as fast as the remnant Bryndor had held in his palm.

However, after a few minutes, the muscles in her forearms cramped, and despite what appeared to be easy labor, she panted hard. In fact, they all did. More discouraging was the meager patch they had cleared for all their work.

Bryndor sat back on his heels and tossed his knife into the moss, blade first. "I'm nearly out of water, and we could all use three meals and two full days of sleep. Maybe we should push on, walk the mounts."

They each ceased their labors and sat, deflated. Even Savnah, who was more stubborn than most, seemed at a loss. Tovnik rummaged through his medic pack, tossing out bandages, delicate instruments, a few small flasks, and satchels before producing a bottle of resco.

He unstoppered the bottle and waved it forward. "I was saving this for the end of the journey, but, well . . . anyone?"

Savnah reached out and accepted the bottle, taking a small sip, lips pulled back. "Taker, that's got more of a bite than I expected."

Tovnik nodded. "Sorry, it's higher proof than regular resco. In a pinch, I can use it as a disinfectant."

The bottle passed around, each person sniffing nervously at the top, then taking a tiny sip. When it fell to Ksenia, her stomach gurgled. With shaky hands, she tipped the bottle back, receiving a rather large gulp instead of the sip she intended. The liquor splashed like bubbling fire onto the back of her throat and she lurched forward, spraying the contents onto the ground.

Tears brimmed her eyes and her nose stung. Giver, it felt like her entire head had been reduced to vapor and ash. She spluttered and coughed, wiping her face in her shirt sleeve, and when she recovered, they all stared, transfixed, on the ground before her.

"Are you seeing this or did that stuff muddle my brain?" asked Savnah.

"I see it too," said Bryndor.

Ksenia recovered enough to look down. Where the spray of resco landed, a fan-shaped wedge of moss melted away. The recession continued such that they each had to scoot back several feet. In just minutes, a bare patch of muddy ground more than ten feet wide stood ringed by a blackened edge of moss.

Nolan placed a hand to the charred edge, then tapped the blade of his knife against it. It emitted a sound not unlike striking stone. "It's some kind of replicating, transfusional reaction. I've never seen anything like that before. Have you, Tov?"

Tovnik shook his head and retrieved the bottle, taking a large mouthful, then deliberately spraying the contents as a fine mist in a circle. He stoppered the bottle, and they all watched as the moss dissipated and crackled away, retreating another twenty feet.

After ten minutes, the reaction stopped and the Aarindin, Boru, and their small party stood on bare ground ringed by a three-foot-high wall of blackened moss. A giddy mood settled on them all and Ksenia wondered if it was relief or the effects of the resco.

Savnah leaned down, turning her head to the side. "Shush a moment. Let me listen."

She remained bent to the side and ran her fingers up and over the blackened edge of the moss. "Well, pickle me in the Taker's sauce if that isn't the Giver handing us a minor miracle. I think we can rest here, sleep even. The fibers aren't trying to regrow across this black scar."

"Seriously? Are you sure?" asked Nolan, his voice carrying all their hope.

"As sure as I can be in this crater on the backside of the Taker's ass. Check for yourselves," said Savnah.

Ksenia walked over, inspecting the rough edge where the moss had curdled into something resembling plants carved into black stone. She allowed a hand to rest on the edge, fingers draped onto the softer plant carpet, and waited for the fibers to begin to wriggle and try to trap her there. But nothing happened.

Eventually, they all reached the same conclusion.

"Alright," said Savnah. "I don't have to tell you how precious that bottle is, Tov. Keep it safe and secure. I'll stay awake for a bit to be sure.

The rest of you get some sleep. When Boru and the Aarindin are ready, we'll set out again."

Chapter Fifty-Five: Lluthean's Why

Lluthean pushed back from the edge of the reflecting pool, and the images of Bryndor's party struggling through the fen dissipated, resolving into an overland map of Karsk. He drew his focus to Kreeg and the army that was dividing its forces there. A train of wagons and mounted riders snaked across the terrain to the east of Kreeg while a fleet of riverboats traversed the Rodemar River to the south.

A cloud of grondle and grotvonen migrated like a black shadow on the army's north flank. Lluthean was all too familiar with the fate that befell any humans caught in their wake and had long ago stopped watching the atrocities perpetrated by the usurper's minions.

Back at the Pillars of Eldrek, the Aarindorian forces bolstered their wood palisade with mountain stone. They tested the distance and accuracy of siege engines and stockpiled supplies in anticipation of Tarkannen's arrival. Outriders led patrols skirmishing with roving crushes of grondle. The elite forces met with little success in direct conflicts, but had developed clever feigned retreats, baiting the creatures into munitions traps or pincer movements.

He studied the battlefront and tapped at his shek, wishing the device would activate in the Drift. But so far, his efforts in that regard had proved pointless. The images on the surface dissolved as he lifted his eyes to gaze across this version of the Valley of the Cloud Walkers. As before, a myriad of life-forms streaked out of the voids of the Drift like so many comets from the night sky. Their brilliant and multicolored embers flared with tails of zenith as they fell to the valley to relive ephemeral echoes of the lives they had before.

The helplessness he experienced while watching the people he loved struggle without him undermined any of the wonder at the miracles to which he bore witness. Neska must have sensed as much. She watched him with all the patience of a stone in a river, head cocked to the side in silent contemplation.

"I feel like I need to warn them, at least Kae. Is Karra with you just now?" he pressed.

Neska rose to all fours and stretched, then walked over to sit beside him. Her voice, resonant with motherly authority, filled his mind with a chorus of the surrounding sights and smells. *"You know that she is not, or I would tell you. Show me what things darken your mood."*

Lluthean reformed the images in the pool, pointing out Tarkannen's troop movements. "He's going to conquer Millstone, plunder its resources, and then wage war on Norfold. He'll use that as his staging area to approach Aarindorn at the Pillars."

"Such things are not in your control and not your concern. You have done well shaping your mind in this place, but you resist becoming more."

"You're talking about Sephora?" he asked. A ripple of cold dread chilled him. "What if, after everything she teaches me, what if I go back and can't remember? What if I'm never ready to face Tarkannen?"

"These questions you ask are like chasing shadows. Even if you catch one, your teeth will never find purchase," she admonished. *"But you are not being honest with me, my Lluthean. There is a part of your mind that I don't recognize. It's like a scared rabbit."*

Her words sounded terse, but there was a kindness in her probing that took a moment to saturate into him. "Never could hide much from you, Nes. I'm afraid of what this place is doing to me. I'm afraid that when I finally get back, I won't remember who I was, or who I am. Adjusting to change is one thing, but what if I forget you?"

"You mean her." The intensity of the word, her, rushed through him and his breath failed him, suppressed by the vacant sensation in his chest. Her fragrance, the silent athletic grace when she slid into their bed, the way she challenged him and inspired him, the light in her eyes when he earned a genuine smile, how she tongued the scar of her lip

whenever she considered one of his proposals . . . all of it enriched Neska's communication.

The wolvryn eased down, belly to the ground, and draped her head in his lap. Though Neska rarely conveyed frustration to him, he sensed her concern now. He massaged over her ears and across her forehead, her soft fur tickling the web space of his fingers. He cleared his throat, dismissing the gravel that had gathered there. "I don't want to forget either of you, but yes, I worry about forgetting what I had with Karragin."

She rolled onto her back, and he scratched her chin and jawline. *"Do you remember your Revealing? The time we spent there?"*

"Yes, some parts of it, I think. But it's like remembering parts of a recurring dream. Does that make any sense?"

She yawned and rubbed her head against his thigh. *"Why are we here, my Lluthean?"*

He pondered the question, knowing full well that she meant for him to see beyond the simple answer. "You're really asking me, what is my why, aren't you?"

The lids of her eyes sank, but he sensed she waited attentively for his response.

When she offered no further prodding, he spoke. "In the Revealing, the pack, the people I loved became my why. You have always been my why. Kaellor and Bryn are my why. And . . . I imagine that if we get back, I might find a new why."

"It is good for you to know your why. And it is good to accept that you will find a new why when we return from this place. But these things are not enough."

She rolled to sit and brought her nose up to his, deep crystalline blue eyes searching his. *"She might be your why once again. But stop chasing shadows, and stop acting like prey. Become Tarkannen's predator, my Lluthean, and then you can focus on your why."*

The emotion and conviction, the unconditional belief Neska conveyed through their link, caused something inside him to break, as if a shackle of doubt had fractured and he finally stood free from the chains. "Alright, my Neska. Call Sephora. I'm ready."

His mind, accustomed to the disorienting way that events in the Drift seemed to both linger and yet abruptly culminate, waited in the stillness. In the space before Sephora manifested, he settled his intent, focused on his breath, and released all other concerns.

"I sense that you are ready. Shall we begin?" asked Sephora in a melodic voice.

Lluthean opened his eyes to consider the apparition. She hovered above the ground, taller than him by a head. Thick black hair with indigo and violet undertones swept over her shoulder and caressed around her waist. Rune marks shifted under her dark skin and accentuated her alien features: high and impossibly angular cheekbones, slanted, penetrating eyes, and a sharp nose.

Gauzy fabric wrapped around shoulders chiseled with lean, hard angles. Her limbs seemed longer and slightly out of proportion compared to a human's. When she reached forward, the gesture seemed even more elegant by the graceful, sweeping arc of her arm.

He stood and tilted his head. "Neska tells me that you can teach me about the tether and how to stop Tarkannen."

Sephora looked past him, making eye contact with Neska. Her hand flowed forward, and she plucked at something in the air behind him and just out of sight overhead. "This was never supposed to be."

A sharp pain lanced between his shoulders and flared down to his navel, there and gone as she dropped her hand to her side. Lluthean grunted in pain. "I take it you mean the tether."

"Of course. The odds of this are so staggering . . . that you, one who bears a shadow mark, might interact with an umbral!" She spat the words, her face flaring with ruddy-hued runes for a moment before settling to a placid expression that would make Karragin envious. "And at the precise time it held Tarkannen's vessel. I can't help but think that a higher power directed this to be so."

"Do you mean the Giver?"

"I'm not sure. Giver, Taker; my people use these terms, but they are different to the Ilovesh. Regardless, you bear the tether, and now we must prepare."

"Where do you want to start?" he asked.

"I need to understand the limitations of your power." Sephora appeared to withdraw into herself, then nodded as if confirming a suspicion.

"Where did you go just now?" he asked.

The Ilovesh walked a slow circle around him. "Humans believe they are fragmented or isolated. It's not until your forms cross into the Drift that you appreciate the interconnection of all life. Tarkannen knew this once, but his banishment in the Drift destroyed his ability to sense those connections. Tragic irony really, since he is connected to you by the tether. We can use that. But again, I need to understand the limits of your capabilities. Prepare to defend yourself."

The Ilovesh swept her arms in artistic circles, fingers sweeping through air as if gathering strands of spider silk. Lluthean sensed the subtle shift in the currents of zenith and primed his gift just as a fissure ruptured across the ground. A familiar fell wind, shearing and harsh, swept across the plains as oily currents of nadir corrupted the grasslands, rushing into the dark crevice.

The taint of decay and rotting meat corrupted the air. Lluthean swallowed hard against the burning sensation of vomit that burned at the back of this throat. Unbidden, memories of standing before the dark portal in the basement in the Sanitorium at Callinora filled his mind. And just as before, three flat-headed figures crawled out of the fissure. Though eyeless and faceless but for malformed mouths cast in rictus snarls, the umbral tracked his movements as he sidestepped.

One of the creatures began to gather a ball of nadir, but Lluthean committed to action. He flooded zenith into the runes on his shoulders, the surging power a pleasurable heat. He held it there a moment, and the runes vibrated, building in strength. Before the umbral could attack, he unleashed a torrential gout of rune fire.

The column shot out parallel to the ground as searing blue flames that warped the air. The umbral screeched in pain, and he felt a resistance to the flood of zenith as one of the creatures erected some kind of shielding. He siphoned hard, reinforcing the rune fire, and poured a furious effort into the channeling.

The flames intensified, filaments of zenith shifting in a kaleidoscope from indigo to light blue and roaring out as a burning deluge. He felt the nadir buckle underneath the continuous onslaught and one of the umbral crumpled, but the other two sprang away on gangly limbs. A small globe of nadir streaked toward him, and Lluthean had to suspend his channeling and dive to the side.

He recovered in time to see more globes of nadir hurtling toward him. He met these with dense foci of rune fire that shot out from his hands. The globes of nadir and zenith collided, erupting in small explosions.

To his right, an umbral charged, propelled on legs that bent at odd ankles. Lluthean drafted zenith into a continuous barrage of small spheres of rune fire. The first few sizzled into the ground, and the umbral leaped forward, dodging the missiles until, at the apex of its leap, Lluthean redirected the trajectory of the projectiles, catching the creature in the chest.

The umbral tumbled to the ground beside him and rolled in a feeble attempt to evade the constant barrage. His shoulder and arms pulsed in time as he continued the relentless attack, shredding the umbral into a formless pulp.

Neska's voice filled his head, shouting a warning. *"Move!"*

He dove to the side and felt the vibration as the third umbral fell from overhead, wielding a saber of nadir. The blade crashed into the ground, searing away the valley floor and opening up a second dark rent in the ground. Lluthean rolled to his feet and sensed movement from within the new crevice. Clawed hands reached through, followed by a saucer-shaped head as another umbral prepared to join the conflict.

"A little help?" he yelled at Neska.

"Stop acting like prey."

"Like prey? Grind it, Nes!" He swallowed any further retorts as the umbral wielding the nadir blade spun and leaped with more adroitness than he imagined possible from the gangly creature. Lluthean backpedaled and stumbled as the creature pursued. He lashed out with a wild spray of rune fire, spewing multiple small globes. The umbral deflected these with its blade and lashed out with a fan of nadir, dissipating others, but the pause gave Lluthean time to rise to his feet.

More rune fire flared between his hands, then detonated in another burst, catching the umbral in a crescent of blazing zenith. He folded the edges around to form a suffocating envelope. Without allowing the creature to escape, he collapsed the edges inward. The umbral thrashed inside, screeching and striking out with the nadir blade, but Lluthean reinforced the construction, tightening the confines.

From the original fissure that Sephora had created, two more umbral emerged. Still another began to crawl out from the crevice created by the nadir blade. They each formed ebony blades of nadir and fanned out to surround him.

"Sephora, how do I seal the breach?" he yelled.

Lluthean glanced about, but the Ilovesh had turned her attention to Neska, who sat on her haunches watching the conflict with casual disregard. Sephora reached out, tugging at the flows of zenith once again, and Neska tilted her head to consider the apparition. The two remained entranced by one another, as if locked in some kind of silent contest.

The umbral stopped their advance, instead turning their attention to the wolvryn. They screeched and clicked at one another. One of the creatures pointed and gestured. Lluthean set his feet and siphoned once again on zenith, ushering in more and more of the power.

He gave definition to the force, shifting and dividing it into five equal columns. His stomach lurched, mouth watering with the threat of retching, and a wave of vertigo caused him to stagger. At last, he released the rune fire, directing it into pillars of continuous, roaring, cerulean flame: one for each umbral and one for each fissure.

The inferno splashed over each flathead, holding them in place and consuming them outright. The dark crevices melted back together, sealing closed under the intensity of the blaze. At last, he stifled the flows of zenith and dropped to his knees, panting. The silent, sterile scent of galvanic vapors dissipated any lingering odor of corruption.

As one, Neska and the Ilovesh turned to face him. Before Sephora's challenge, the valley appeared kinetic with the frenzy of life as spiritual energies dropped to the plains to frolic about the grasslands. Now, even the ethereal winds stilled, and the horizon appeared bereft of any streaks of zenith.

Sephora folded her hands, and a single wrinkle of concern creased her otherwise flawless brow. "Your control needs work, though your capacity is admirable. But . . ." She shook her head.

"But what?" he gasped, then dropped to his knees before a small pool of water.

Instead of answering, the Ilovesh turned back to Neska, who finally answered his question, *"She fears you will only fully commit yourself to the task of defeating Tarkannen if your why is placed in mortal danger."*

He reflected on the statement and understood that he did hold something of himself in reserve. His memories of Karragin and his family in the Revealing were familiar, comfortable. And even while he understood they were not real to anyone but him, the thought of losing them, of more than that, of taking deliberate action to displace them from his mind, was a bridge he still felt nervous about crossing.

His focus drifted back to the surface of the pool. Unbidden, images of the people he loved manifested on the surface. Karragin stood outside on the royal plaza under moonlight and tossed Iska high into the air. The hawk rocketed into the clouds, propelled by her gifted strength.

The riftwing dropped into view, moonlight shimmering over her wings, and circled over Stone's Grasp. He tracked her course over the Sprawl, the lower commons, and merchant districts.

Finally, Iska passed over the Crown's Timber, then came to rest on the balcony outside Kaellor and Laryn's private suite. He thought to listen to their conversation, but the intimacy of their embrace left him feeling voyeuristic and intrusive, so he withdrew from those images and focused on Bryndor.

His brother rode Ksenia's albino Aarindin, Winter. Mud stained the mount's belly and flank, a visual testament to the obvious misery of their journey. Bryndor swayed on her back, bootless and dressed in someone else's clothes by the way his wrists and ankles protruded. Boru slogged through the swamp, head bowed and nose lifted only inches above the water. Ksenia and the Outriders walked alongside the other mounts, each waste-deep in brackish water.

Something drew the company to a stop, and the Outriders stepped forward, weapons brandished. None of them looked prepared for a fight. Savnah held both moonblade axes with a weariness he had not thought her capable of demonstrating. The crescent of one blade dipped into the water. The men each knocked arrows to bowstrings, but none of them wasted the energy to pull back.

Boru slogged a few steps forward to stand behind the Outriders, and the great wolvryn listed to the side when he stumbled on something unseen under the stagnant waters. Neska's head pressed against Lluthean's shoulder as she leaned in close. A low rumble gathered in her throat, and her muscles tensed as if she intended to leap through the pool.

"Whatever they face, they look ill-prepared to defend themselves," said Lluthean. He trained his focus on the scene to keep their surveillance active, but lifted his chin to Sephora.

"Is there anything you can do? Any aid you can give them?" he asked.

The Ilovesh sauntered closer. "Perhaps," she purred.

At the edge of the fog, something massive and reptilian disturbed the mists as a muscled tail armored in shiny scales whipped in and out of the fog, making irregular ripples travel across the fen. Lluthean set his mind to the task and lifted his gaze. "Then do it. Send whatever help you can, and I promise to commit myself to your training."

"I can do this thing, but it will alter you. I am not sure that you are willing to pay the price."

Lluthean lifted his eyes from the pool to settle them on the apparition. She returned the stare with equal intensity, at last tipping her head forward. "As you wish."

Chapter Fifty-Six: Driven by Different Convictions

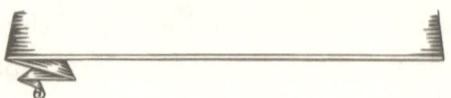

A chill seeped into Laryn's bones and she shivered despite the covers pulled high over her nose. The persistent discomfort finally broke through her sleep. With a groan, she stretched a leg out, searching for Kaellor. Her foot ran across cool, empty sheets and she sat up, surprised by the vacancy.

Or maybe not that surprised. What she initially mistook for the draw of the chilly night air, she now understood as a perception of Kaellor's channeling. Like a gentle breeze, she sensed him siphoning on the currents of zenith. And if she knew her husband, he would readily marinade himself with the draft in search of answers about Bryndor's safety, the kingdom's welfare be damned.

She found him standing alone at the balcony, head bowed, hands gripped on the rail and mumbling. She placed a hand on the small of his back and ran it up between his shoulders, where the tight muscles betrayed his stress. "Are you talking to the moon now?"

"Sorry, love. Therek and I, neither of us could sleep. He's worried about Nolan, and—"

"And you're worried about Bryn, but neither of you has the good sense to claim rest when you can."

Therek's voice echoed from the shek. "Sorry, Laryn. She's right, Kae. I will keep the shek active for a few more hours. You should get some sleep. We can review any communications at the closed council meeting in the morning."

"Let it go, Kae," she encouraged.

"I don't think I can. And even if I do, I don't think I can sleep."

"You both have to trust that Bryn will reach out when he can, but it won't be in the dead of night."

His hands gripped the railing one last time, then he pushed back. "Good night, Therek." And at last she sensed him release his command of zenith. He turned to embrace her, his head heavy on her shoulder. "I wish that archivist, Veeble, had never disclosed his translation about the Stillness. It's all I can think about these days."

"I know. But have you met anyone with as much capability as our nephew?"

"Not really. Bryn's always managed to rise to any challenge," said Kaellor. "But I still can't escape the feeling that I should be there, helping him."

"That's natural." She interlocked the fingers of one hand through his. A fluttering sound drew her attention to the shadows. Iska landed on the balcony, and Laryn knew Karragin kept a vigil through her intimate connection to the riftwing.

She gripped Kaellor's hand, pecked him on the cheek, and pulled him back inside. "Come on. If you're going to keep me awake, you might as well catch me up on kingdom business. Tell me about the meeting with the diplomats from Faltusch."

He followed her inside. "Fenna is a capable negotiator. We're lucky she survived the grondle attacks, otherwise I'm not sure we could rely on the Sea King."

"Elbiona made it sound like the Faltuschians had already sided against Tarkannen's forces from Kreeg."

"I'm not so sure," said Kaellor. "I think they would have been happy to remain neutral in the conflict, but after witnessing the bestiality of the grondle, Fenna and her advisers are convinced that they will have to take action."

"That's to our benefit, I suppose, but she's either brave or foolish if she intends to travel back to Faltusch without the safety of the Endulian Pass."

"I thought the same, but Therek thinks he might know of a way to open the pass," said Kaellor.

"The old lynx still has a few tricks, I imagine," she said.

"If we can get her safely back, she believes she can organize the Sea King's forces to sweep down and disrupt the supply lines. Facilitating that effort would slow the approach of Tarkannen's forces, maybe long enough for Bryn to return."

Laryn sensed the way Kaellor carried the weight of responsibility for the whole kingdom on his shoulders and wondered if she should change the subject, but sometimes her husband was like a dog with a bone, and neither of them was likely to rest until he settled his mind. "What have you learned about our renewed efforts to reach Norfold or Millstone?"

"Our envoys to Norfold were turned back. Apparently, the king of Norfold has no interest in receiving foreign influence or aid. Their fields lay fallow, livestock slaughtered by grondle attacks, but they have withdrawn behind the safety of their walls. It's a foolish gamble, one born of fear, I imagine. We haven't heard from the Outriders sent to Millstone, but it's several more days away and through dangerous territory."

"How has Hestian fared with the western duchies?"

"Your cousin is not a man to be trifled with. He might very well be the one person in the entire kingdom capable of putting Endera Endule in her place. Reinforcements to the Pillars should arrive within a few days. If he can manage that, the kingdom will owe him a debt."

"Bringing Endera to heel is not a task I would enjoy. You'll have to source a bottle of prewar resco to make it up to him."

Kaellor tugged at the edge of his beard and nodded in agreement. "I've thought the same. Thanks, love."

"For what?" she asked.

He shook his head. "For just, letting me get it all out, I suppose. We've spent all this time talking about my troubles, and I haven't even asked about you. You had two meetings set yesterday. How did they unfold?"

"The recruitment of more healers to the Pillars of Eldrek went fine. That's one group of people eager to help where they are most needed. But I left the meeting with the textiles guild realizing why I remain forever grateful that we found each other."

Kaellor lifted a shock of white hair from her face and tucked it behind her ear, then caressed a thumb over her cheek. "That bad?"

Laryn puffed out her lips. "After the Abrogator's War, the family business only survived by the good graces of Chancle and Hestian. We merged our financial interests and diversified into mining, medicinal precursors like embertang, and textiles. In the past, Hestian oversaw our small mining interests. I was the logical choice to coordinate any endeavors with medicinal production and distribution."

"And Chancle managed the textiles side of things. Let me guess, in his absence, the guild doesn't care to offer favorable terms?"

Laryn tilted her head, acknowledging his deduction. "Let's just say that they suggested favorable terms in exchange for face time at the next assembly."

Kaellor grunted. "I suppose I would rather rub shoulders with guild leaders than mingle with the highbrows from the duchies."

Laryn leaned back, surprised to find him so accepting of the guild's demands. "I thought we agreed not to engage in those kind of relationships. Accepting a bribe, even for something as innocent as time and consideration, feels like stepping onto a slippery slope. I told the guild leaders as much and left without concessions."

Kaellor shrugged. "It's not like you and I will be running things. Bryndor's official coronation is this fall. If the guild leaders have a desire to mingle with discerning company, I can't begrudge them that."

Her eyebrow arched involuntarily. "Discerning or nefarious—I'm not sure which category we might fall into if we make those kinds of agreements."

Kaellor chuckled and held his hand up. "I yield to your wise and ethical decision, love."

They sat beside each other on the edge of their bed, fingers of one hand interlocked. He turned to her. "I've half a mind to pour a finger of resco just to get back to sleep, but it's never quite the rest you hope for. Any chance you might use your gift to help me?"

She stretched her arms overhead with a theatrical yawn. "I don't feel like channeling this early in the morning, but I can think of a few things for us to occupy our time."

AFTER THE MORNING'S closed council, Therek excused himself and escorted Fenna and her small surviving entourage. He found it more difficult than he imagined to dismiss the various sentinels, city guards, and even a double quad of Outriders, all of whom insisted on accompanying him. In the end, he feigned a meeting in the archives, snuck through the offices of the regent, and made rather secretive egress through the castle and to the royal stables, where he rendezvoused with the Faltuschian queen.

He rode an Aarindin beside Fenna's saddled mare, and together they passed through the Crown's Timber. They circled around Stone's Grasp on the road south toward Stellance, but instead of turning to the west, they continued along the road for an hour. Fenna made polite conversation until Therek directed his mount to the east and onto a small road that rose into the foothills of the Great Crown.

"Forgive me Regent Lefledge, but one cannot help but notice that we left by rather secretive means today, and now you divert us from our intended destination. The Endulian Pass lies to the west, toward Faltusch." Fenna left the obvious question unspoken.

Therek's mount trotted down a gentle slope, then returned to a walk on the next rise. "You are quite correct. But the Endulian Pass is blocked by unseasonal snow and ice."

The young queen narrowed her eyes, considering his explanation. "This is known to me, but you said you had a means to open the pass."

Therek nodded but kept his eyes on the path ahead. "I said I might have a way. We're going to meet someone who might be able to help us return you safely to Faltusch."

Fenna drew her mount to a stop, and Therek signaled his Aarindin to do the same. She removed a glove from her hand and held it forward, waiting. Therek pulled back his sleeve and consented to her probing. A not unpleasant warmth flowed from her touch, lasting only a few seconds before she withdrew and replaced her glove. "You gamble our safety with a criminal?"

Therek sighed. That was certainly a reasonable conclusion. "You are not entirely wrong. The man we are going to meet is not someone who can readily show his face in Aarindorian society, and yet, he owes me a favor or two."

They rode on in silence, but her stiff posture and steely gaze communicated volumes about her apprehension. "Queen Fenna, I mean no disrespect, but why did the Sea King choose you for the diplomatic mission to Aarindorn?"

"The high queen is too old for the journey. The next two queens were dispatched to Millstone and Norfold. The fourth queen is expecting child within the month. That left me."

"Well, I think it is to our mutual advantage that he chose you. The journey I propose is challenging, but you are more than capable of completing the task."

"That is obvious, but I fail to see how my fitness for this endeavor dismisses the fact that you pin our hopes and my safety on the company of a man of dubious reputation within your own kingdom."

Therek nodded. "I am only trying to point out that these are desperate times, and we need to take advantage of any tool the Giver provides us. To that end, I would like to tell you about the man who styled himself the Aspect of the Lacuna."

They rode for the next several hours, climbing higher into the eastern rim of the Great Crown, traversing paths seldom trafficked and far from any significant human settlements. Therek spoke of Chancle Lellendule, the man he was before the Abrogator's War, the widower afterward, and how he became the architect of the Lacuna. He held nothing back, understanding that any obfuscation would only undermine Fenna's trust in the man and likely prevent the success of their mission.

As they emerged from a tree-shaded trail onto a clearing of rock and mountain scrub with delicate yellow flowers, he brought them to a halt. "So you see, he never was an evil man, just a man driven by different convictions."

Fenna lifted her chin ahead to a small cabin. "You jailed him all the way up here?"

"I did not. Chancle is a broken man, and placed himself here, in a self-imposed isolation. He stifles his gift by ingesting veramanth. It's the herb with the yellow flowers growing wild all over this valley."

"My people call it severance. The tea prevents one from channeling for days," said Fenna.

Therek nodded. "When ingested in its raw form, veramanth doesn't just stifle your connection to zenith, it leeches all traces of it from the body. My own son, a gifted scout, can follow a person's zenith trail weeks after passing, but could not find Chancle here without a detailed map. We just have to hope he has not ruined himself and that we can convince him to come to our aid."

"Is his command of wind and weather really strong enough to re-open the Endulian?" she pressed.

"I'm not actually sure, but right now it's the only option the Giver granted us."

A rhythmic sound of chopping wood echoed from the far side of the cabin. Therek signaled his Aarindin forward and led the procession around the backside of the modest dwelling. As they approached, Fenna held back, and two of her guards interposed themselves between their queen and whomever was making the ruckus.

Therek rounded to the back of the house where a gangly, malnourished man lifted and dropped an axe, sending chips of wood spraying from a thick stump he couldn't possibly hope to defeat. Sweat stained his trousers, glistened on his bare back, and matted a scraggly beard to his face. Therek began to doubt that the man before him was Chancle, but his vision had been so clear, and his conversations with Salveen had confirmed this very meeting.

"Chancle Lellendule, my friend, the kingdom has need of your gifts, and you owe the kingdom a terrible debt."

When Therek spoke, Chancle held the axe at the apex of a swing, panting. He allowed the blade to wedge into the stump and turned, lifting grey eyes. Everything about the man appeared to be wasting, from his sunken cheeks and the hollow above his collar bones to the way his paper-thin skin clung to every single rib and draped over sharp hip bones.

"Chancle Lellendule died. And anyone who would call him a friend is likely to be stoned or worse." The voice came out raspy from obvious disuse, but Therek recognized it, nonetheless.

"I understand the risks, and I understand the need. The scales have tipped beyond my control, and needs must."

"You understand very little if you think I am able to offer anything that would benefit Aarindorn, old man." Chancle collapsed to sit on the stump and stared at the ground for long moments. He grabbed a fistful of wild veramanth and chewed on the flowers, grimacing. When at last he spoke again, his voice was flat. "Therek, I'm not even sure I can channel. Even if I wanted to help you, I am not sure that I could. Just leave me to die up here. I'm close now."

Fenna walked forward. The lithe woman had dismounted and stalked behind Therek to stand beside Chancle. She placed a hand on his shoulder, and the flows of zenith shifted ever so slightly. She held the contact for more than a minute, and Chancle stared at his feet. When at last she released him, she squatted down to make eye contact. How she could stand the pervasive stink of the man was a wonder.

"Your son's name was Eidan. You will accompany me to the Endulian Pass and use your gift to open the way. You will leave this kingdom and never come back, serve as the Sea King's adviser, and deploy your gift to the advantage of our navy. We will never ask you to act against Aarindorn. Do these things, and my soul singers will let you speak to your wife, your daughter, to Eidan."

Chancle picked another fistful of raw veramanth. "I'm days away from seeing them as it is."

"No. You are not. If you enter the Drift stripped of yourself as you are now, you will merge on, unaware of their presence even should they reach out to you. But if you come with me, become more than what you are now, you can speak to them again one day."

Chancle crushed the veramanth in his yellow-stained, calloused hands. "I don't know if I believe . . ." He shook his head. "I don't deserve what you offer."

"No, you do not. But I tell you this, Chancle. As a scion in the Sea King's house, I am forbidden to lie, and I do not embellish my truth in this. Use this second chance. Come with me. Make amends in our common struggle against Tarkannen, and I will see that you meet your loved ones again."

The bent stalks of veramanth fell to the ground, and Chancle lifted his face. He wouldn't meet Therek's eyes, but acquiesced with a single, silent nod.

Chapter Fifty-Seven: Strangers in a Strange Land

Our greatest strength is revealed to be our greatest weakness. Queen Brekka convened a panel to review the failed mission to reach the tree singers. The expedition attempted to cross a territory bereft of zenith. Their stories seem fantastical in nature. Some, it seems were consumed by the wildlife there; others perished from abject exhaustion. Still others fought with predators in the mists. Perhaps there are some obstacles that even the Giver's gifts cannot overcome.

—The Tome of Nivosh, 75 PC, translated by Veeble Hebben

BRYNDOR LAY ON HIS back, listening to the slow cadence of Boru's breathing. The ground pressed into him, causing everything to ache, and he fluttered his eyes open but remained still, knowing that any movement was likely to trigger spasms of pain. To his side, Ksenia stirred.

She must have known not to move him by the cautious way she lifted one leg across his torso to straddle him without actually touching him. She shook her head back and forth, allowing her hair to tickle the front of his face. It smelled of smoke and ash.

"I would say good morning, but I think I've lost all track of time in this place," he said.

She turned her head and scanned their surroundings. "Early morning, I would guess. The fog is starting to shift from grey to white."

His stomach gurgled and pulled with a vacant, drawing sensation. "Any chance someone was hoarding crownberry muffins? I would even settle for hard tack."

"No such luck, I'm afraid."

Boru's muzzle leaned into view and he licked Ksenia on the cheek, then offered the same greeting to Bryndor. She giggled. "That's one way to get rid of all the soot."

Savnah spoke out from his left. "Everyone awake then? We should push on. Tovnik says the rest we think we are getting is actually sapping our strength. Something about not replenishing our stores of zenith."

Bryndor inhaled and tried to project his voice. "Tov is right. I can feel it. Help me get to my feet."

Ksenia's face darkened with concern. "Do you have enough strength to stand?"

Bryndor engaged the muscles of his arms and legs. His limbs moved with sluggish response and pervasive, bone-deep achy pain flared whenever his joints moved. "Taker's grip," he panted.

"That bad?" Ksenia asked.

"Maybe if you can turn me to my side," he suggested.

She unstraddled him and placed one hand behind his shoulder and the other at his hip. "Ready when you are."

Bryndor inhaled a breath, then nodded. Ksenia pushed as he rolled, and pain flared anew from the base of his skull down to the small of his back. Without exhaling, he drew up his knees and pushed to his elbows, then his hands. He remained frozen on all fours, each breath a wave of pained exhaustion.

The tip of Savnah's boots appeared on the ground beside him, Ksenia's on the other side. They each placed a hand under his arm and the prime counted, "One, two, three."

Together, they pulled him to his feet, and he gasped. His head swam a moment but then cleared, and he staggered a cautious step, then another, the ground cold under his bare feet. He limped a slow circle around the clearing made by the resco, stopping to stand near Boru.

"Sorry for all of this, my friend," he signed. Boru lifted his chin, inviting a scratch, and Bryndor obliged, knowing the simple gesture was all his friend required.

"Did the moss ever push back in?" he asked.

"Not so far. But if you can manage it, I should not like to test how long we can remain," said Savnah.

"I'm not going to get any better standing here. Lead on," said Bryndor.

When none of them moved, he searched their faces. Eventually, Ksenia stepped forward. "None of us has the strength to continue, Bryn, so we're all riding ungripped. You'll take Winter. She has the most stamina left. But when the mounts fail . . ."

She couldn't finish the statement. "I understand. Let's keep going for as long as we can."

Nolan stepped forward and offered the Logrend bow. Bryndor held up a hand. "Keep it. I don't have the strength to use it."

Without words, the scout slung the weapon over his shoulder, then stepped close to Winter and cupped his hands. Bryndor sucked at his teeth. "Are they so tired that they can't lower to the ground?"

"Yes," said Ksenia.

"Alright then. I might need a hand." He set his left foot into Nolan's hands, hopped on the other a few times, then clumsily tried to toss the right leg over Winter's back. Fresh pain flared in his ankles, knees, and hips, causing him to gasp. Giver, even the small bones in his hands ached when he gripped the Aarindin's withers. He began to slide off, and only when Savnah and Dexxin pushed at his hips did he manage to situate himself.

Over the next few minutes, they each managed to mount, and Nolan led them out of their camp and in what Bryndor could only assume was an eastern direction. The mosses gave way to stagnant pools of water, and occasionally Bryndor's toes broke the surface. Instead of offering any refreshing reprieve, the fetid liquid only left his toes feeling oily, and he did his best to lift his legs.

They continued for the next several hours, the Aarindin grunting and struggling to climb out of the stagnant water and onto small stretches of mossy ground, only to drop back into the brackish liquid. Bryndor's mind retreated, focusing on the minute shifts of his weight on Winter's back. The muscles in his thighs cramped, and he leaned forward just as Winter drew to an abrupt stop. He barely recovered without falling forward and bit back a curse.

They stood at the top of one of the moss-covered hills, each Outrider staring down into the fog. Those that had bows held arrows knocked to the string, and Savnah ran her palms over the hilt of her axes. Boru stood pensive, nose searching the air. Before he could ask about the source of their vigilance, the sound of something plodding through the water carried up to his position.

Whatever creature made the noise, it was clearly large and gave little concern to moving about in silence. They held their position, and the splashing, sloshing noises carried around them in a perimeter to the north. He allowed a wave of relief to ease the tension in his shoulders, but then his flesh tightened like goosebumps when he sensed more danger still downhill and to the east.

He chanced a hissing sound, and both Boru and Nolan turned. *"There is still something down there, to the east, where the sound started,"* he signed.

Nolan nodded once, and Boru blinked, then trained his sight down toward the water. They remained in place, fanned out across the mossy rise, until Savnah sighed. She turned as if to speak when something charged out of the water and up the hill. The fog stirred to reveal a broad, reptilian head perched on a thick, scaled body propelled by three sets of limbs that churned up moss and mud. The ridged shoulders rose only half as high as the Aarindin, but its rear feet and tail extended several feet longer than any of the mounts.

Bows twanged and arrows sprouted from the snout and shoulder of the beast, but the lizard charged into the group, heedless of the wounds. The Aarindin whinnied with uncharacteristic fear and scattered, but not before the beast lurched in a tight circle, bringing its tail around and knocking both Nolan and Dexxin from their mounts. Tovnik's Aarindin reared back, and it was all the medic could do to drop and roll to the ground.

Bryndor struggled to remain mounted as Winter pranced back and circled behind the lizard. He strained to keep his eye on the beast and hold on to her mane, registering that at least three of the unmounted Aarindin had trotted off into the fog.

Savnah dropped from her mount and charged the beast from one side while Boru growled, hackles raised in challenge from the other. Before either could attack, the beast charged at Boru, lowering a shoulder and lashing out with one of its clawed feet, then spinning in a tight circle to swat its tail at Savnah.

The wolvryn tumbled down the hill, and Savnah lost her footing but rolled to stand in front of Winter. Though brief, the skirmish left the prime panting. She brandished her weapons and crouched in anticipation of the next charge. The beast flicked a tongue in and out, swinging its broad snout back and forth, stopping as if frozen to glare with rows of unblinking, beady eyes at Ksenia.

With a trembling hand she signed, *"Trying to cloud its mind with my gift. Can't do it much longer."*

"Now, Savnah," Bryndor hissed.

Savnah took two lurching steps, clearly planning to bring both of her moonblade axes down onto the neck of the lizard, but her foot slipped and she only managed a gash along its side. The momentum of her swing caused her to topple to the ground, and the lizard turned to face her. It lifted a muscled, clawed front limb when something caused it to lurch forward.

Boru growled as he tried to sink his teeth into the scaled shoulder of the beast. The wolvryn scrabbled and clawed for purchase, standing on the lizard's back. Boru's effort was furious and savage, but his teeth couldn't penetrate the thick hide, and in seconds, the lizard rolled, coming deftly to its feet while the wolvryn tumbled back into the fog, splashing into the brackish water below.

Ksenia slumped forward on her mount, Savnah staggered to her feet, and Nolan and Dexxin nocked arrows as the lizard recovered to consider them all, red tongue flicking in and out. Each of them looked spent beyond the point of simple exhaustion. Only Tovnik seemed to possess any vigor, and the medic walked calmly and directly forward, approaching the lizard.

The beast hissed and clawed its feet into the ground as if to charge when Tovnik bent forward at the waist and spewed a mouthful of resco. The cloud of volatile spirits caught the lizard full on the snout, and it recoiled, curled into a ball, then flailed on the ground. Tovnik took another swig from his bottle and waited, cheeks puffed out, eyes watering.

Angry hisses gave way to rasps of pain, and the lizard clawed at its nose. The medic took careful steps around the beast, biding his time, and when the thing chanced a glance his way, Tovnik spewed another gout of resco, catching it on the side of its broad head.

Thick muscles along its neck shuddered as it shrieked and rolled away down the hill and into the fog. By the receding sounds, it retreated somewhere deep into the Stillness. Bryndor looked around, taking stock of their situation. Ksenia slumped forward on Tacit's shoulders, and Winter shifted her weight nervously. The other three Aarindin had scattered into the fog.

Boru plodded back up the hill. Each of the Outriders knelt or sat on their heels. Bryndor cleared his throat. "At least—" he began, but stopped when the familiar plodding, sloshing sound from the north returned.

"Grind it. That would be the other one. Tovnik, be ready with the resco."

The medic turned with a rueful expression and tipped the bottle upside down, indicating that it was empty. He dropped the bottle and retrieved his bow, nocking an arrow to the string. The insidious, plodding, sloshing noises got louder and louder as it became clear that another lizard climbed toward them. And something else pierced the smothering blanket of fog: the rhythmic sound of a creature cantering from the east.

Nolan, Dexxin, and Tovnik stood facing the east one moment and north the next, uncertain where the next attack might come from. Even Boru seemed befuddled, and the great wolvryn backpedaled to stand beside Bryn. The pounding canter drew his focus, but then the head of another swamp lizard appeared from the north.

Before he could shout a warning, something much more nimble but equally alien resolved from the fog. A muscled, antlered beast charged directly toward the lizard, stopping several paces away. It lowered its head and issued a deep grunt of challenge as a man wielding a set of short spears spilled forward between the antlers and slid across the ground on his knees.

His trajectory carried him along the reptilian beast's flank, where the points of his weapons carved deep gashes into the front shoulder of the lizard. Bows twanged, and once again arrows sprouted from the beast's head and torso, but it turned, oblivious, and faced the stranger holding the spears. Its tongue lashed out in rapid flickers.

With uncanny composure, the man used the butt of one spear to tap at the ground several feet away, distracting the beast. He even flicked mud at the creature, who whipped its tail at him, then tried to roll him over. The stranger danced back, then to the side, and brought his weapons around in a blinding arc that plunged into the wound he had already made.

The beast lurched forward, collapsing on its ruined front limb, and Savnah used the opportunity to heave one of her axes. With two hands around one hilt, she delivered an overhand strike that sunk deep into the lizard's neck. In a frantic attempt to escape, the lizard rolled back down the hill, splashing into the water and taking her axe with it.

The stranger stood his ground, considering them, then sprinted down the hill after the lizard. Through the fog, Bryndor heard thrashing noises, then a man's deep-voiced grunt, then silence. A moment later, Savnah's axe twirled through the air to land on the ground, followed by the stranger, who climbed the hill, panting.

He walked forward, and Bryndor took in his appearance as he removed a swath of thin fabric from his shoulders, wringing out the muddy water while standing only in tailored pants woven from the same material. His plum-hued skin was pulled taut over corded, lean muscles and his limbs, though gangly and long at first glance, moved with unusual grace. Slanted eyes over high cheekbones stared back and considered them all.

"You have our thanks, stranger. My name is Bryndor, and we're searching for the Ilovesh—"

The stranger held up a palm and pointed to his ears, then to the fog. Somewhere in the distance, an Aarindin whinnied in pain, followed by the sounds of thrashing and struggle. With a thick accent augmented by an oddly lethargic cadence, the man spoke in a bass voice that seemed to resonate from his chest and not his mouth. "There will be time for introductions later. I would not have your friend's sacrifice be in vain."

"What do you mean? All our friends are alive," said Savnah, her words laced with suspicion, and she gripped her axes as if expecting an attack.

The muscles around the stranger's slanted eyes tightened. "Your . . . mounts. Those who scattered are lost. Blood will distract these lizards but attract others. Follow me if you wish to live."

"Three of our group are on foot. There is no way they can keep up through the water," said Bryndor.

"If fear for your lives is inadequate motivation, then perhaps you are not the ones I seek. I will set a gentle pace, but we must leave," he said, then turned and whistled a short, sharp trill.

His mount, looking like some strange combination of an Aarindin and a moose, dipped its thick rack of antlers. The stranger grabbed one side and used it to leap up onto its back. Without waiting, he led them down the mossy bank and into the fog. Bryndor checked on Ksenia. She slumped forward on Tacit's back, eyes open, but a slick of drool ran over Tacit's shoulder. He knew well that feeling of overextending.

He placed a reassuring hand on her shoulder. "Hang in there Kess, we're not done yet."

They followed the man as he wound a serpentine path, keeping mostly to banks of moss and avoiding the brackish water. The stranger offered no words except to his mount, but stopped occasionally to ensure that the weary party kept pace. Somehow, whether mounted or on foot, the exhausted company kept up, slogging through the fen.

After several hours, they climbed a gentle slope. Bryndor expected the mossy knoll to drop back into the swamp, but realized with no small relief that they kept climbing. The fog thinned, and familiar yellow sunlight broke through in golden shafts.

At last, as if shrugging off a tremendous set of weighted chains, Bryndor felt it: zenith. Though the currents ran thin, he drew in the essence of the power. It felt like taking a fresh breath after remaining underwater for too long.

The vitality of the current infused his core, spreading into his muscles and dissipating the profound fatigue. The others sensed it as well, and as one, they collapsed to the ground, laughing. Boru wagged his tail, and the Aarindin lifted their heads. Ksenia pushed back to a sitting position.

"Are we through the Stillness?" Bryndor asked.

The stranger answered with his patient, slow rhythm, as if unfamiliarity tempered the pace of his speech. Yet his diction was crisp and his meanings clear. "Yes, but here is not safe. Restore your reserves, then we should press on. We are at the edge of the fen. Ahead is food and water."

Bryndor dismounted and wiggled his toes through tender shoots of grass. Winter's warm breath exhaled near his dirt-stained ankles as she cropped the grass. He patted her once on the neck, then stepped around her in time to see Ksenia slide down from Tacit's back. A tension had gathered between his shoulders, and it finally eased at seeing her walk with purpose. She set Tacit to grazing and stepped close for an embrace.

He rested his cheek on the top of her head and offered a silent thanks to the Giver for seeing them through it all. "I'm so sorry about the other Aarindin."

She leaned back, then pecked him on the cheek. "Me too. I tried to reach them, but I was spent, and my gift failed me."

He nodded with understanding. "Surviving the Stillness took everything we could give."

Bryndor surveyed the group. Nolan paced a slow perimeter, appearing to survey the ground. Savnah grabbed fistfuls of moss and used it to clean the blades of her axes. Tovnik sat in silence beside Dexxin, who seemed lost in a trance. Bryndor fingered the shek, but knew that if he made contact with Kaellor now, they would be conversing for hours. "Tov, is Dexxin speaking to his siblings?"

Tovnik smiled and nodded.

"Ask him to pass along a message to the regent and my uncle that I will reach out through the shek this evening," said Bryndor.

Tovnik leaned in and spoke in Dexxin's ear, relaying the message. Boru rested his sizable chin on Ksenia's shoulder, inserting himself into their embrace. Ksenia giggled and released her grip around his waist, then gave the wolvryn the affection he craved.

Bryndor approached the stranger, who stood beside his mount. The antlered beast nibbled at the ground with dexterous, fleshy lips. "We were ready to give up back there. I don't see that we would have made it out if not for your aid. You have my sincere gratitude."

Subtle hues, like shifting birthmarks, migrated under the surface of his skin, most notable across his bald head. He tilted his head but made no further comment. Instead, remounted and walked several paces east, obviously waiting for the rest of them to catch up.

Savnah approached, thumbs tucked over her belt. "He's not much for small talk, is he?" asked Savnah.

Bryndor sighed. "We are strangers to him and approached uninvited. Who can say what their customs are? Lluthean and I have been treated far worse and with a lot more suspicion by people in the Southlands."

Zenith filtered into the tiny pockets of his lungs when he inhaled a deep breath. He turned and looked to the west, shading his eyes against the late-day sun. A blanket of grey fog obscured the ground, and he shivered. "I'm due to walk for a spell. The Aarindin can likely manage two at once now that we are out of the Stillness."

"I'm . . . actually not going to argue the point. We can all feel it, the return of zenith, but my feet have blisters on blisters," said the prime.

Dexxin stood, released from the trance of his communication. "Dexx, any news from home?"

"Stone's Grasp still stands and my sister is as cheeky as ever," said the sender.

"I imagine I'll get the full story tonight when we stop. I think our guide is ready to push on. You three alternate two at a time on Tacit. Savnah and Kess can ride Winter. I'll walk for a spell," said Bryndor.

With no argument, they set out, following the stranger across a grassy plain, the sun setting on their backs. Instead of any sense of fatigue, Bryndor only felt renewed and restored the farther they traveled from the Stillness. At last, they stopped beside a stream with clear, fresh water.

The stranger dismounted and waited for them to approach. Bryndor resisted every instinct, wanting nothing more than to strip naked and drop into the current. "You have a command of the Kindred speech."

The stranger nodded.

"Are there any customs we should know about before we partake of the stream?"

The question seemed to catch the man off guard. Again, the hues of purple and burgundy shifted under the surface of his skin. "You are wise to ask, but we are well outside the ursulu forests of the Ilovesh. You may enter the water as you will."

Bryndor tilted his head in respect. "Again, you have our thanks. You mention the Ilovesh. We are on a journey to seek their aid."

"This is known to me, for your people owe mine a great debt, and I mean to collect. My name is Seldora, of the Ilovesh. Rest here, manling. I will return with food and supplies, and then we can speak of compensation." The Ilovesh twirled the haft of one of his short spears, bringing it to rest under his armpit. He picked his way across the stream and disappeared up the far hillside.

Savnah grunted as she struggled to stand on one foot while removing the boot from another. "Did he say compensation?"

"He did," said Bryndor.

"That sounds ominous," said the prime.

Without waiting for comment, Savnah flopped back to the ground, wriggling her toes in the open air. Bryndor sighed. "I was thinking the very same thing."

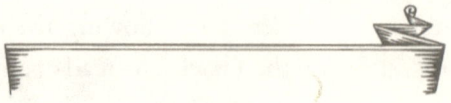

Chapter Fifty-Eight: First Contact

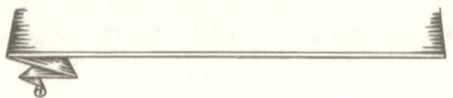

Morning dew gathered on the surface of Ranika's tent, and the musty, oil-slicked fabric sagged over the support poles. Acting more on instinct than any deliberate thought, she flared a web of nadir across the surface, drafting it into fine filaments. Once she discerned the feel of the fabric underneath her gift, she used the reductive fibers to dissipate the slick of water.

In moments, the offensive odor dissipated, and the fabric fluttered in the breeze. It took her no time to dismantle the dwelling; the dry panels rolled up easily. Zippy nickered, and she greeted the Aarindin with affection, running one hand across his jaw and the other across his forehead.

"Good morning, Mr. Zip. I'm out of treats this morning, but I'll make amends before the day is through." She stared down the western side of the Great Crown and inspected the trail she assumed the caravan would take. In the last week they had climbed up and down, sometimes riding north only to turn south, but always journeying farther and farther to the west.

"I don't know how she did it, but that blind woman got us on the outside of the mountains. It looks like we drop out of the highlands today."

The Aarindin whickered, then dropped his head to crop the grass. She left him to graze and studied the western horizon. Motion caught her eye as the unmistakable and rather ominous appearance of smoke rose to underline and darken the clouds.

The smell of roasted flatbread caused her to turn. Speaker Vekkuh stood fanning a generous portion. "Eat your fill, then tell me what your young eyes see this morning."

Ranika accepted the flatbread, tearing off a hunk and chewing. Oil and spices leaked from the morsel as she chewed, and she released an involuntary groan of pleasure. "Oh moons, that's good. I can see the trail we'll take to drop into the foothills. We should be out of the mountains by midday. There's smoke on the far horizon, maybe a forest fire."

Vekkuh grunted and nodded, as if expecting the report. "Good. We're not too late then."

"Late for what?"

"If I read the signs right, that's no forest fire. That's the forward element of the Kreeg army marching this way. We made good time getting this far. We'll drop out of the mountains and skirt around the Pillars before they arrive."

Ranika followed the ominous dark underline of smoke from the north far to the south. "All that smoke is from an army? Vekkuh, just how many people are the Kreeg bringing to Aarindorn?"

The speaker shrugged. "I can't really say, but as long as we get the caravan around to the east side of the Great Crown before they arrive, I think we'll be safe enough."

"Should we warn Kaellor? Do you think they know?"

"They are aware," said Vekkuh.

"How can you know that?"

"My cousin, Salveen, sits on their closed council. Her command of our gift is perhaps the strongest in a generation. If I could see that army coming, she is more than aware of its pending arrival. Besides, I don't expect that the good people from Stone's Grasp have been laboring to erect a defensible wall between the Pillars just to govern trade."

Vekkuh set hands on her low back and stretched her hips. "Life gives you choices, Nika. Most are small, everyday, trivial things, but some are big. Regardless, all of them shape the future we live in. Right now, I choose to live in a world where we are not fighting for our lives against the Kreeg army."

Ranika held up a hand in submission, then scoffed at the silliness of gesturing to a blind woman. "I understand. I'll get Zippy saddled."

"Good girl. I'll see you on the trail. Mind your tongue today; we have company."

"What do you mean?"

"The Kreeg have scouts combing the area. Our caravan isn't that hard to discover. One of them will likely follow us for a time. I expect we'll meet whoever it is in the next few days."

Ranika stared at the woman who had become her counselor, her friend. "What?" asked Vekkuh, well aware of the silence.

"If you aren't as gifted as Salveen, how is it you know about the scout?"

Vekkuh scowled. "I honestly can't be sure, but the signs indicate that strangers track our journey, and it doesn't take much imagination to consider that an approaching army would send scouts."

"What should I say if I cross paths with one of them?" she asked.

"Taker's grip, I don't know. But play nice, or dumb, or maybe a little bit of both. I would rather someone like that underestimate us."

Ranika turned in a slow circle, searching the surrounding cliffs for any sign that someone followed the caravan. She wished, not for the first time, that Reddevek rode alongside her, or maybe one of the Baellentrell brothers and their wolvryn; anything to shed the feeling that a rat had crawled behind her bedroll. That had happened once on the streets of Callish, and she had spent most of the night searching for the hidden invader, convinced it would start to chew on her toes the moment she drifted to sleep.

"Whatever the day brings, you are more than up to the task, Nika. Find me at day's end."

With that, the speaker turned and received help from one of the Luna Rova to mount a horse. Ranika made quick work of saddling Zippy, who had become accustomed to the routine. Within ten minutes, the Aarindin trotted to fall in line with the caravan. They dropped into the foothills and made swift progress compared to the winding route of the previous week.

By the day's end, they found a valley nestled against the cliffs of the Great Crown. Ranika slid from the saddle, shoulder muscles achy with fatigue from riding with the apprehension of being tracked. While she saw no direct signs of their shadow, Vekkuh's warning had left her nervous enough that she'd repeatedly checked over her shoulder or craned her neck to peer down the mountainside.

When they stopped for the day, she almost forgot to remove Zippy's saddle in favor of slipping into the shadows to see if she could find their would-be pursuer. The Aarindin nipped the shift at her shoulder, quickly disabusing her of the folly.

"Grind me, sorry, Mr. Zip." She unsaddled, brushed, and groomed Zippy. By the time she finished and set up her tent, twilight had settled across the foothills. The rich aroma of stew tugged at her stomach, and she wandered through the camp in search of Vekkuh. The speaker could usually be found in the center of the caravan.

As Ranika approached, she sensed an odd stillness among the Luna Rova. In the distance, children giggled and played, but as she walked toward the center of camp, a blanket of silence stifled even idle conversations. She met the eye of a Luna Rova tending a cookfire, posing an unspoken question by the tilt of her head. The woman flicked her eyes to an adjacent fire, and Ranika turned to see the speaker in conversation with a stranger clearly not of the Luna Rova.

The middle-aged man wore leather gear, weathered from rough travel. He sat with lean, muscular arms resting on his knees. Grey stubble peppered his jawline. When he spoke, his thick accent made the Kindred speech difficult to understand. "How is it that your caravan avoids the grondle? They patrol these areas. I had to be careful to avoid them, and I am only one man."

Vekkuh rubbed arthritic hands over a bony knee. "We keep to the foothills. Maybe the grondle don't wander this close to the mountains?"

The man considered her words with a hard look. Eventually, he grunted and seemed to accept her answer. "What can you tell me of these mountains? Is there a means to enter Aarindorn without passing through these . . . Pillars?"

"If there is, we haven't found it. That's why our caravan migrates along the foothills," said Vekkuh.

Ranika approached to stand behind Vekkuh, resting one hand on the speaker's shoulder as an announcement of her arrival. She looked around the campfire at the faces of familiar Luna Rova, who went about the business of preparing stew in relative silence. "Good evening, all. Smells good."

Vekkuh reached up and patted a reassuring hand on Ranika's. "Coglek, this is Ranika. Ranika, Coglek is an emissary for the Kreeg. Apparently, they have sent several emissaries. He was hoping to find a way past the Pillars of Eldrek, but I was just explaining that he arrived about two months too late."

One of the Luna Rova dipped a ladle into the stew, handed a serving to the stranger, and then to Vekkuh. Ranika received hers in turn and blew at the steamy surface, watching Coglek from the corner of her eye. It wasn't until well after she and Vekkuh had taken several bites of the stew that he sampled the fare.

"My thanks," said Coglek, the words heavy in the back of his mouth. "A meal befitting the krug rai'al."

"What's a krug rai'al?" asked Ranika.

Coglek wolfed down a few more spoonfuls, then paused. "Krug rai'al is Kreeg for supreme leader, what we call our king. You will see. The krug rai'al will arrive soon, and all of this will be placed under his control, saving the people of the region from the witch-king of Aarindorn."

Ranika puzzled over the words and was going to ask what he meant, but Vekkuh spoke first. "The Luna Rova are nomadic. We have little direct contact with the people of Aarindorn except to trade now and again. We see little and hear even less from their king."

"Witch-king," Coglek corrected.

Ranika couldn't help herself. "Have you met the king of Aarindorn?"

Coglek shook his head and busied himself scraping the bottom of his bowl. "Would that I could dirty my blade with the witch-king's blood. Great would be my honor under the krug rai'al."

"So, if you've never met the king, why do you think he's a witch?" asked Ranika.

"Is simple. We have an adviser, a painted man, a child of Mogdurian. He wields nadir like none in a generation, and once lived in Aarindorn. He's the one who explained how the witch-king set a drought across Karsk. But before he tries to conquer the free people of Kreeg, the krug rai'al will arrive and conquer him. Then all of this, everything you see, will be called Kreeg."

"What happens to people like the Luna Rova when the Kreeg arrive?" asked Vekkuh.

Coglek picked at a bit of food caught in his teeth. "I followed you, tracking your clan for the last part of the day. Your people have no warriors. Maybe you become cooks. Maybe not, maybe something else."

The man leered at Ranika like one of the lecherous customers from Felpinge House, the Callishite brothel from her childhood. A flare of anger colored her cheeks when their eyes met and he refused to look away.

"So, let me get this straight," said Ranika. "An abrogator, I'm guessing Tarkannen by your description, someone who by all rights really *is* a witch-king, tells you lot a story about a decent man, and you swallow that bit of rubbish like it's the Giver's truth, then march all the way across Karsk without stopping to think for yourselves about the lie you've been fed?"

Coglek rose to his feet with slow but dexterous purpose, appearing less like a tired traveler and more like a snake poised to strike. With theatrical intent, he withdrew a wicked knife, brandishing the weapon only a few feet before Vekkuh's face. "I don't like your girl's questions. You need to teach her manners before her betters."

Ranika watched the man, a palpable flow of nadir held at the ready. The speaker sighed. "Every life is the summation of choices made, Coglek. Are you sure this is the choice you want to make?"

"You people are weak. Just parasites on this land," he spat. "When the rest of the army arrives, we will sweep over you as an ocean across a pond. I think I'll take my due before they get here." He pointed the blade at Ranika. "Stand up girl, you're coming with me."

Ranika set her bowl down and dusted off her hands, then swathed herself in nadir, stepped back into the shadows, and vanished from the man's sight. Coglek blinked once, then swept out with his blade. "Witch," he hissed, pivoting.

Ranika considered toying with the man, but he remained within striking distance of Vekkuh. She walked several paces away, then released her command of the shadows. "Psst, over here."

Coglek turned to see her and flipped his knife into a throwing position, but before he could launch the blade, Vekkuh stood up and brained the man with her bowl of stew. A wet *thwack* split the night as she dented the man's skull. The Kreegorian grunted and staggered a few steps to the side, but turned and raised to strike the woman.

Before Ranika could act, two bowstrings twanged and a pair of arrows sprouted from the man's chest. He gasped once in pain, drew a ragged breath, and fell dead. Ranika shifted her sight to the ethereal in time to see a group of five Outriders descend on Aarindin. She turned to Vekkuh. "You knew someone trailed us and thought it was an enemy scout, but couldn't think to warn me we had Outriders watching our backs?"

Vekkuh grunted. "Until just now I wasn't actually sure who dogged our trail, girl. Just be thankful for small blessings, like stew served in stone bowls instead of wooden ones."

Ranika used the cover of darkness to pull threads of nadir across her vision, shifting her sight into the ethereal. Coglek lay dead on the ground. If the arrows hadn't killed him, Ranika felt certain that the unnatural depression on the backside of his skull eventually would have.

Small blessings indeed.

The five Outriders approached, their nimble-footed mounts descending the craggy terrain with relative ease despite the darkness. The group fanned out without formally entering the camp of the Luna Rova. They held themselves at a distance, seeming more preoccupied with surveillance of the shadowed cliffs than the Moonies below.

Their leader approached on foot, and Ranika dismissed the nadir. In the firelight, she could see he wore a short-cropped ginger beard.

"Good evening. Are you the speaker of this Luna Rova clan?" he asked.

Vekkuh sighed, shoulders sagging with weary fatigue, as if the question reminded her of a forgotten burden. "The last time I checked, I still wore the title. Name's Vekkuh."

"It's an honor, Speaker Vekkuh. My name is Larik Lellendule. We have nothing we can trade or offer as a gift, but you've picked a dangerous time to travel beyond the Great Crown, and my quint could be of service."

Ranika nodded inwardly, now placing the prime as the son of the field marshal. He must have sensed her eyes upon him, as he turned to meet her gaze. "You're here. That explains a lot. I thought I recognized an Aarindin, but you rode with a saddle, so I was not sure. Still, I should have realized. Reddevek's mount is one of the few removed from service in the Outriders."

"I'm not gifted like that, so Zippy can't grip me. But even so, I think you'll find you have a difficult time separating the two of us," said Ranika.

Larik gave her an easy smile and held up a single hand in peace. "I wouldn't think of dishonoring Warden Reddevek's service, or yours."

"I never served in the Outriders. I've thought about it, but my place is here, with the Luna Rova."

"I understand, but we can speak of these things later." He turned his attention back to Vekkuh. "I thought the Dev'advari were a highland clan?"

"We are that and more, young Lellendule," said Vekkuh.

He chewed on his lower lip, causing the ginger hairs on his chin to stand on end like prickly barbs. "Did you come through the Endulian Pass before it iced over?"

"We followed the moons. Our path was long and winding. I don't think you need to worry about enemy scouts discovering a passage to the interior, at least none that an army could use," explained Vekkuh.

If her explanation reassured the prime, he gave no immediate indication, instead searching the dark ridgeline from which they had just descended. Eventually, he brought his focus to Coglek's corpse. He bent to retrieve the arrows, finding both lodged deep enough that he had to push them through. He stabbed both into the ground near the fire to dry, then wiped his hands on the ground.

"Do you plan to lead your caravan back to the interior of the Great Crown?" he asked.

"We go where the moons lead us, young man. For the foreseeable future, our path winds outside the Pillars to the east side of the Great Crown," said Vekkuh.

Larik searched the faces of the Luna Rova scattered around the campfire. "We were sent to hunt grondle but encountered other Kreeg scouts. That's the third one we've killed in the last two days. More will come, and in larger numbers. If they don't harass your clan, the grondle surely will. Then there are the traps. You'll never make it to the east side."

"What do you mean, traps?" asked Ranika.

"The Aarindorian military set all kinds of traps before the Pillars: deadfalls, snares, and the like. I swear there's enough munitions rigged to blow another passage through the Great Crown. There's no help for it; we'll accompany your caravan to the far side or through the Pillars, should you change course."

"There's no need. We have the guidance of the moons and other ways to protect ourselves from danger. But you are welcome, all the same," said Vekkuh.

"I appreciate that. Speaker, if I'm honest, I can't take the chance of the Kreeg army following you back into Aarindorn." He glanced back to Ranika, and their eyes met. "While I know you have some means to protect yourselves, it's not enough to avoid the traps. We'll ride along for now, offer our protection when we can, and give you our counsel, if you will have it. Do my Outriders have your blessing to enter your camp?"

"You and yours are welcome among the Dev'advari, young Lellendule. You may approach with your mounts and rest among good company," said Vekkuh. "Moons light your path."

Larik whistled three sharp, shrill trills, and the rest of his quint approached on foot, leading their Aarindin. He stepped closer to Ranika and Vekkuh and pitched his voice low. "We should dispose of the body. Is that something your gift can help with?"

A wave of nausea rippled across her stomach. "You want me to dissolve Coglek?"

Larik puffed out his cheeks. "We dropped the other two corpses into ravines. It would help our progress if we could somehow hide this one too."

"Do you remember that trick you did when you dissolved the stone and freed us?" asked Vekkuh.

"You want me to do it too?" asked Ranika.

Vekkuh waved a hand. "Of course not, girl. Wait, could you do that? No, never mind. I was thinking you could melt a small hole in the side of the cliff. We could roll him in and backfill it with stones."

That notion felt more appealing to Ranika than using her gift to completely erase any trace of someone's existence. "Alright. I can do that. I'll get to it straightaway."

"Don't overextend yourself. We'll need you fresh in the days ahead. It's not likely that our first contact with the Kreeg will be our last."

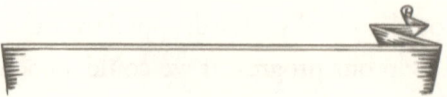

Chapter Fifty-Nine: The Generosity of the Ilovesh

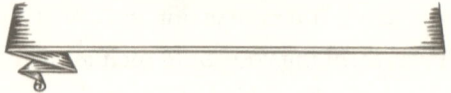

The hindquarter of a herd animal sizzled and popped as Savnah turned a makeshift spit over a cookfire. After the Ilovesh departed, Boru had struck out hunting while the exhausted party rested near a small stream. The wolvryn, having slaked his hunger, provided them with the leftovers.

Ksenia warmed herself by the fire, knowing that she would likely have to consume the meat. If so, it would be the first time in years. But the journey had stolen all the energy required to forage for alternate sources of sustenance. She wondered whether she could even consume the meat. Was her mouth salivating because of the aroma of the cookfire, or in anticipation of vomiting? She couldn't be sure.

Hunger drew the others to the fire in anticipation of the sustenance. They sat together in weary silence except for Bryndor, who paced in a slow perimeter. Ksenia stared into the crackling flames and listened as he employed the shek to make a full report to his uncle, the regent, and other members of the closed council. "I can't say that we know yet. As soon as the Ilovesh made the statement, he left with the promise of food and supplies."

She turned to consider him, walking barefoot through the grasses. He seemed relaxed, listening as Kaellor offered suggestions through the shek. Each time Bryndor nodded or shook his head, she couldn't help but think that between him and his uncle, Bryndor sounded like the calm adult in the conversation. Eventually, he sighed and stared at the sky, as if searching for patience. Yet when he spoke, his tone was tempered. "I'm aware, Kae. I don't like it either, and I agree it's a strange coincidence that he speaks the Kindred tongue. Try not to worry. Together, we'll sort out his motives soon enough."

Bryndor nodded a final time, then offered one last response. "Until tomorrow eve, eyes to the horizon."

He gripped the shek with white knuckles, then slipped it into a pocket and took a seat beside her. "You handled that well. He sounded pretty worried," she said.

Bryndor nodded and stared at the flames. "It's understandable. We missed too many check-ins through the shek, and when Dexxin couldn't access his gift to send to his siblings, they must have thought the worst."

He chuckled and stretched his arms overhead. "But even if we had crossed the Stillness in relative safety, he would still worry. He's always been able to step in and protect us. I think it must drive most parents mad to feel helpless to intervene."

Before she could consider the strange perspective his response seemed to indicate, her stomach gurgled, and she clutched her forearms to her midsection. Savnah carved a strip of meat from the spit and waited for it to cool before taking a bite. Her jaw muscles flexed and her head bobbed as she worked to chew the meat, at last swallowing with a dip of her chin. A dissatisfied expression furrowed her brow. "I can't say any of us will enjoy it, but it fills a hole. Anyone?"

Nolan stabbed a knife into the meat and waited for Savnah to cut a wedge free. He gingerly fingered the cut, eventually chancing a large bite with his back teeth, grimacing and laboring with concentration. After swallowing, he pursed his lips as if exhaling the fumes from a rather volatile splash of resco.

"That bad?" asked Tovnik.

Nolan shrugged and took another bite. "It's gamey, but we've had worse. I'll take it over grot rations."

"Can't argue that, I suppose," said the medic, and he stood to receive a portion. Savnah sliced off more for Tovnik, Dexxin, and then Bryndor. Ksenia stared at the ground but could tell by the orientation of Savnah's feet that she waited. Eventually, Savnah crouched down. "Kess, you look about as green as the swamp water from the Stillness. I know it's not your preference, but you've got to eat something if we are to continue."

A wave of nausea swelled at the back of her throat, and she swallowed, nodding her consent. Savnah must have already removed a portion as she pushed a palm-sized wedge of meat off her blade into Ksenia's hand. She tried to focus on the smell of the fire, the char, anything but the aroma of cooked meat.

Just when she worked up the courage to lift her hand to her mouth, Bryndor smothered his palm over the meat and took it from her. Her shoulders sagged with the release of tension, and she met his eyes. "We have time. Besides, I think Seldora returns."

Boru rose to his feet and stretched, tail swishing at a slow, easy cadence, ears perked forward, and stared to the eastern horizon. In moments, the antlered silhouette of the Ilovesh's mount appeared, and not long after she could make out the Ilovesh riding the mount. Seldora dismounted when the creature dropped its head forward. He hopped from the perch, landing over ten feet down the hillside as if he had only taken a small step. Two large sacks, one over each shoulder, held the promise of her salvation.

Bryndor stood and held a hand toward the spit. "Welcome, Seldora. Can we interest you in some food?"

The Ilovesh pulled back his head and the birthmarks under his skin flared a ruddy color on his scalp, there one moment, then fading the next. He spoke with the same strange, lethargic tempo as before. "No. Ilovesh do not eat our friends."

Seldora cast his gaze across the party, and failed to hide a look of disgust until he considered Boru. He studied the wolvryn and his expression softened. "I begin to understand. You consumed what was left behind. This is wise and provokes no offense. But when we cross into the Ilovesh forest, know that the use of fire is restricted, and consumption of meat is a grave offense."

He tossed the sacks forward and turned to walk back up the hill.

Bryndor called out, "Seldora, do you have to leave? I was hoping that we could speak."

The Ilovesh spoke over his shoulder. "You stink of the swamp and woodsmoke. Travel east, and I will find you after you bathe and rest."

Ksenia tucked her nose under the neckline of her shirt and recoiled. "He's not wrong," she said to nobody in particular.

Bryndor sucked at his teeth. "Grind me. We're never going to make it back in time. We should have stayed to join the battle against Tarkannen."

Seldora took three more steps, then stopped. He stood in silence, turning at last to walk back down the hillside. Hues of color, like shifting birthmarks, played across his forehead and cheeks. "This Tarkannen, he is your enemy?"

"You heard that?" asked Bryndor.

"Of course. Perhaps we should sit, as you say, and speak," said the Ilovesh.

Bryndor clasped his hands together. "I apologize for the fire and the meat. We appreciate your warnings and meant no offense. We have a lot to learn about one another. Where we come from, it is considered polite to share the warmth of a fire, good company, and what food we can offer. Meager as it is, what we have is yours to share."

Seldora dipped his head. "We are . . . not so different." He retrieved one of the sacks and removed sets of clothing woven from some type of thin fabric dyed sage green with tan accents. "You are welcome to retain your clothing, but might be more comfortable in these. The sheff, what you call a tunic, is folded like so." He gestured with one long-fingered hand to his own attire, demonstrating how the sides of the top crisscrossed and tucked into the pants.

"And for you, Bryndor, to cover your feet." Seldora handed him a pair of low-cut footwear woven from the same material but somehow reinforced, and with strange pockets for each individual toe.

"We are in your debt, Seldora," said Bryndor.

"Just so," replied the Ilovesh.

Ksenia received the set of clothing, fingering the material. A light, floral scent rose to her awareness. "You have our sincere gratitude."

Seldora retrieved the second sack and removed a dark green cylinder. He cradled the item under one arm. "May I share your fire?"

"Please," said Bryndor.

The Ilovesh dropped to both knees, holding the cylinder in one hand. Ksenia stifled a gasp as he reshaped two fingers of the other hand into a blade, which he used to slice off an end of the cylinder. The fragrant aroma of savory spices displaced her surprise as Seldora used the flames to toast the smaller disc. He turned and offered her the piece. "This is hesk, a staple among my people. It is ground nuts, mushrooms, and smoked tubers wrapped in ursulu leaf."

Without waiting for her to sample the food, he sliced off another disc-shaped wedge and began to toast it. Ksenia bit into the hesk, teeth crunching through the toasted layer, then sinking into something gratifyingly chewy. An alien burst of tangy, salty, and floral spices tingled in her nose and danced on her tongue. She exhaled with unbridled pleasure and kept chewing. "Giver's sweet breath. I might not eat anything else, ever."

"Yeah?" Bryndor asked.

Ksenia kept chewing, swallowed, and took another generous bite. Bryndor tossed his uneaten hunk of meat into the fire and waited for Seldora to offer him a wedge. In minutes, they each sampled the novelty. Savnah initially resisted abandoning her spit, but after one bite of the hesk, she removed the flank of meat and discarded it on the other side of the stream.

She returned, wiped her hands on her soiled trousers, and sat down, content to chew a generous bite of hesk. Ksenia finished hers and thought she would need more to feel satisfied, but her stomach rumbles quieted, and she felt oddly satiated.

With only a third of the hesk consumed, Seldora toasted a disc for himself and then reformed his fingers into the normal if not unusually long extensions of his hand. With their hunger relieved, the mood around the fire improved. Savnah made a show of licking her fingers and began to giggle.

"What's so funny?" asked Tovnik.

The prime patted her belly. "I was just trying to imagine the look on my brother's face when I tell him that the best thing I've eaten in the last year is toasted hesk."

Seldora turned to consider Savnah. Beyond chewing with small, measured bites, his expression remained flat. Savnah looked back, uncertainty evident by her expression, but then filled the awkward silence. "You see, at the Derrigand table, a meal isn't considered complete unless it has at least two and preferably three meat courses. But toasted hesk is definitely something I could get used to."

Seldora gave her a slight tilt of his head. "When we reach Leandur, I can show you how we make it."

"Leandur, is that the name for the Ilovesh territory?" asked Bryndor.

"No, we claim no such title. The Ilovesh live among the ursulu forest. Where the ursulu live, so do the Ilovesh. Leandur is like a city within the forest."

"Seldora, when we spoke before, you mentioned a debt, which implies that we've met before. But nobody from Aarindorn knew about your existence until just recently. Can you sort that out for me?" asked Bryndor.

The Ilovesh placed the last bite into his mouth and chewed methodically. Just as Ksenia began to wonder if the stranger had misunderstood the question, he stood and put the uneaten portion of hesk back into the sack, then withdrew a long gourd with a stopper. He returned to the fire and uncorked the container, holding it forward. "My mentor sent this with me as a token of friendship. Drink first, talk later."

He handed the gourd to Bryndor, but Nolan leaned forward to take the gourd. The scout sniffed at the edge, and Ksenia felt him siphon zenith. After a moment of study, his eyebrows lifted in surprise. "It's resco. Prewar stuff, if my gift isn't failing me."

Nolan lifted the gourd in salute and took a small sip, blowing out fumes that carried the unmistakable aroma of resco. He smacked his lips and nodded with appreciation, but then he coughed once and his eyes watered. He passed the gourd to Dexxin, who took a swig, then Tovnik. In turn, they each sampled the spirit.

Ksenia intended for only a dash of the fiery liquid to splash her tongue, but upon tipping the gourd, she received a rather large mouthful. To her surprise, the resco left a caramel, nutty residue on her tongue but carried none of the burn she expected. She handed the drink to Bryndor. He took a gulp and exhaled, tilting his head in appreciation. "Smooth."

At last, the gourd returned to Seldora. The Ilovesh swished the gourd, testing the volume of the contents, then tipped it to his mouth and swallowed a mouthful. The pigmented markings under his skin flared once again, and he slammed a fist onto his knee several times, blinking away tears.

When he spoke, the tempo of his response betrayed his exasperation. "Moons, I forgot how vile that is," said Seldora. "I never understood why he brought it."

Seldora passed the gourd for another round and turned to Bryndor. "You have questions."

Bryndor frowned but nodded. "I do. Questions about the debt you referenced, how you seemed to know we would arrive, and where this drink came from."

Seldora stared into the flames. "I can answer these things, but first tell me, why did you cross the Stillness?"

Bryndor opened his mouth to speak, then seemed to reconsider his first response, and took a moment to frame his answer. "My parents sacrificed themselves to banish our enemy, Tarkannen, to the Drift, but he has escaped. Before he broke free, my brother, Lluthean, became tethered to him. The forging of the bond was something of a freak accident, and now Lluthean lingers on the edge of the Drift. He doesn't think he can return until we discover how to sever the tether. We were led to believe that the knowledge to break the connection could be learned from the Ilovesh."

Seldora nodded, and once again the markings under his skin pulsed with color, flaring for several seconds and lingering as a flush of color on his cheeks. "Some of these things are known to me and some are not. If I or any of my people are to help you, I must understand more of the bond. Tell me more of how this came to be, and the condition of your brother."

Bryndor grabbed the gourd of resco and took another swallow, then exhaled and began a story that lasted well into the next hour. Despite their collective fatigue, each person leaned in, absorbing the details of how Lluthean likely acquired the tether in the cellars of Callinora after stabbing through an umbral and into the vessel to which Tarkannen was tethered. Without prompting, he then explained what he understood about how Aarindorians inherited their arca prime, referencing the Rite of Revealing and how Lluthean chose to remain behind, alive but trapped within the Drift.

"Your brother feared his power would be subverted by the abrogator," said Seldora.

"Something like that, yes." Bryndor chewed on the inside of his cheek.

Whether fatigue or resco or both loosened her tongue, Ksenia blurted out her confusion. "Seldora, it seems like you are acquainted with Tarkannen. I mean . . . none of us ever mentioned that he is an abrogator."

Her statement, spoken as an unasked question, hung in the air. Eventually, the Ilovesh leaned forward and took another pull from the gourd of resco. He grimaced and smacked his lips once. "I knew a manling named Tarkannen. I once called him friend, then brother, then betrayer. Now I call him enemy. He came to my people before the turning of the moons and befriended my sister, Sephora. As a display of his devotion, he consented to binding his access to zenith. Moved by his gesture and against the wisdom of the Ilovesh, Sephora entered into a tether with Tarkannen. It's a sacred bond that unites the life force of one to the other. They lived among the ursulu for a time; he learning of our ways, and she of yours."

He sighed and gazed up to the stars. "My sister, always training her eyes beyond the horizon of the ursulu. But, if not for her vision, and her guidance, I would not have found you in time."

Purple markings flowed in a rhythm under the surface of Seldora's cheeks, giving him a gaunt and melancholy appearance. "She did not understand the burden of severance on the human soul. When a tether is broken between two Ilovesh, we are wounded, but we mend. It is not so with humans; the strain of severance irrevocably alters your kind. Her death sundered Tarkannen's soul. As he had lost his ability to access zenith, his soul bolstered itself with nadir. In her death, he became at once the cause of my family's shame and the single greatest source of darkness in our world."

"That's what you meant by compensation, and the debt, isn't it?" asked Bryndor.

Instead of answering, Seldora ran a palm across his head and stared at the fading embers of the fire. Savnah used a branch to stir the coals, and a shower of sparks swirled up into the night sky. "Did Tarkannen bring you the resco?" she asked.

"He did. We have no use for it. Ilovesh do not consume spirits as a general rule. My mentor, the Elder Somaya, foresaw this day. She suggested that I offer you the resco."

Ksenia leaned forward. "Do the Ilovesh employ zenith?"

"Why do you ask?" questioned Seldora.

"I saw you alter your hands when you divided the hesk. And you mentioned that your elder foresaw our arrival. There are a few people in Aarindorn gifted with prophecy, but they are zeniphiles," said Ksenia.

"All Ilovesh use zenith, but not in the ways you describe. For us, zenith is a natural part of living, like breathing air. It is the essence that sustains us, heals us, allows us to shape our body in limited ways. Only the tree singers can command the flows of zenith to work outside themselves."

"So, this tether, the one binding Tarkannen and Lluthean, will it have the same devastating effect on my brother if we find a way to break it?" asked Bryndor.

"I don't believe so. Theirs is a parasitic construct, a corruption of everything the Ilovesh hold sacred. Our connection is one of mutual commitment, and as such confers mutual benefit."

"Can you tell us how to break it?" Bryndor pressed.

"Beyond slaying Tarkannen, I do not have the knowledge, but the elder council in Vellendar might. And if they do not, my sister, what is left of her, manifests in the Drift, and might be able to teach your brother how to protect himself," said Seldora.

"You can speak to the dead?" asked Bryndor.

"Those closest to us in this life remain connected beyond. She visits me on occasion, although less and less over the years as she merges on.

I have not spoken to Sephora for weeks now. But the last time she appeared, she told me that she was aware of your brother, Lluthean. She intended to mentor him, teach him something of our ways."

Bryndor grunted. "Let's hope she's a patient teacher. How long will it take us to reach Vellendar?"

"A week, less if I can find more druska." Seldora stood and tilted his head toward his antlered mount. "I will see if Kadra can find friends and return to you after moonfall."

"Moonfall?" asked Ksenia.

"Morning. I will find you in the morning." The Ilovesh retreated up the hillside without further comment.

Ksenia stood and stretched her back, then stepped behind Bryndor, resting her hands on his shoulders. Unnatural tension gathered in the muscles there, and she worked her fingers across them. He dropped his head and rolled his neck back and forth. "Giver, that's a kindness," he said.

After several minutes, he turned his head and kissed her hand. She retrieved the set of clothes Seldora had left and began to walk toward the stream. "Where are you off to?" he asked.

"I smell like something that died in the Stillness, and none of you are any better. I'm for taking a bath in the stream, then I intend to change into these," she said, patting the fresh clothing.

Savnah rummaged through the sack holding the hesk and removed two more gourds of resco and four more logs of hesk. "Moons, he left us enough food for a week. We can thank the Giver for small miracles and the generosity of the Ilovesh."

Bryndor retrieved his set of clothing, and the footwear Seldora had left. When he stood, she expected to see a relieved smile, but he chewed on the inside of his cheek.

She bumped her hip into his as they walked toward the stream. "I'm sure Lluthean's fine," said Ksenia.

"I wager he is. He always seems to land on his feet," said Bryndor.

"Then why the long face?" she asked.

"I was just thinking about Seldora's initial reaction to us. He already considers us in his debt for Tarkannen's transgressions. Relying on their generosity feels like a risk."

"What choice do we have?" she asked.

"None, I suppose. But I don't think I'll rest easy until we learn what we can and are heading back to Aarindorn."

Chapter Sixty: A Promise Made

A most peculiar creature has taken up residence in the Founder's Memorial. A riftwing of all things is roosting in one of the trees. The falconer, a skilled sympath, has failed to entice the creature down, but a few days ago, the hawk perched not two feet from me. I gave it some leftover crownberry muffin, and then the most amazing thing happened. It took to wing, lifting beyond the confines of the memorial, and dissipated into pure zenith. I thought the creature had met its end, but just before I penned these words, it reappeared, beseeching me for another tangy morsel. The Giver's miracles never cease to amaze me.

—The Tome of Nivosh, 76 PC, translated by Veeble Hennen

AS KARRAGIN MADE THE familiar descent to the inner sanctum, the air chilled the back of her neck and carried the faint scent of mildew. Iska gripped and re-gripped the bar at her shoulder, shifting about with restless anticipation. Karragin knew from observations in the past several weeks that the riftwing needed to dissipate and enter the Drift at least once every six or seven days.

Something about ascending to the other plane rejuvenated the creature. Whenever she returned, streaking down from the clouds, Iska seemed more alert, more engaged. Ascension allowed her to master in hours lessons that might take two days near the end of such a cycle. And while she could transform anywhere, the riftwing made it clear by her behavior that she preferred to access the Drift through Lluthean's unique instance.

651

They reached the bottom of the stairs, and Iska spread her wings, buffeting the back of Karragin's hair. The bird's weight bobbed on the shoulder bar, as if she might leap into the air. Karragin spoke through her sympath link. *"Peace, Iska. I know you are excited, but be still."*

She waited for the bird to settle, surprised to discover a swell of anticipation within herself. She pondered the sensation and realized that she looked forward to her conversations with Neska. Through some trick of the Rite of Revealing, or possibly some property of the Drift, Neska's intelligence blossomed. Their conversations always left Karragin feeling as if she had confided in an old friend.

As soon as she pushed open the double doors to the sanctum, Iska took to wing. She glided around the room, gathering speed, soared over the shoulders of the statue of Eldrek, then flared into zenith. Streamers of iridescent blue light trailed behind her as Iska plunged into the zentrist shrouding Lluthean and Neska as they lingered in the Rite of Revealing.

"And that's why you are not just a moonwing; you are truly my riftwing."

Karragin eased back onto one of the stone benches and waited. But for the shifting currents of zenith migrating across the surface of the cocoon, the room remained still. She took advantage of the solitude, retreating to her breath as her father had taught her.

In just moments, the familiar sounds of wildlife echoed through the connection of her sympath link. Wind rustled through the grasses, and a hawk screeched out a greeting. Iska flapped her wings and must have settled, as the ambient sounds stilled, then Neska's maternal voice made her presence known.

"What news from beyond the veil?" asked the wolvryn.

"Hello Neska. I should ask you the same. How is the prince? How are you?"

There was an unusual pause in the communication, but Karragin waited, and eventually Neska replied, *"He is becoming what he needs to be."*

"By your tone, I can't tell if that is a good thing or bad."

"It is necessary. But what he learns comes at a cost."

Karragin puzzled over the statement. *"Iska allows me to hear your thoughts, Neska, but it's not the same as when you are standing beside me. Can you explain what you mean?"*

"He is learning how to be the predator and not the prey, but learning how to hunt his enemy requires . . . sacrifice."

"Most worthy accomplishments involve sacrifice. What can you tell me of his?"

"Inside my Lluthean, his . . . mind, it is an enormous cavern, but the space is limited. In order to learn what the Ilovesh is teaching, he will lose parts of himself."

"Will he lose memories? Perhaps if you can tell me more, we can prepare to help him when he returns, when you both return."

"I do not know. He will need the entire pack to guide him, to fight beside him. He might need you most of all to face the enemy. Will you fight alongside him?"

"Yes, of course," said Karragin.

The sound of a woman's voice echoed through the connection. *"Is someone else there with you? I can hear another, but I can't make out her words,"* Karragin asked.

"Yes. Sephora, the Ilovesh woman, returned. She is teaching my Lluthean her ways."

"Do other spirits visit you there?" asked Karragin.

An image of the countless stars in the night sky rippled through the link. *"We have many visitors here. Some are fragmented, others whole."*

Not for the first time in all their conversations, Karragin shook her head, bemused at Neska's command of complex thoughts. *"What do you mean by fragmented?"*

"We do not belong here, but our presence shapes this current of the Drift into a stable space." There was another long pause in which the ambient sounds of birds, chirping insects, and the lone howl of a wolvryn echoed through the connection. Karragin remained a silent listener.

Eventually, Neska continued, *"I may not have the right words. All life . . . merges on in the Drift, but this space attracts beings, if only for a brief moment. Some separate to experience something of what they once were, but very few manifest whole like the Ilovesh. Still fewer can remain for more than a fleeting experience, at least as I understand it."*

A question hovered at the edge of her awareness, a delicate torchlight dancing in the darkness. Before she could breathe life into the hope, she squashed it. *"I think Iska likes what she finds when she enters the Drift to find you there."*

"Why do you do that?" pressed Neska.

Karragin opened her eyes for the first time and searched the room, expecting to find the wolvryn standing directly before her. *"I do not understand. Are you talking to me, Neska?"*

"Of course. There is nobody else in our link, but there could be if I search for it, if I search for her."

Karragin sat forward, elbows resting on knees, tremulous hands clasped together. *"How can you know that? I've said nothing about her."*

"You are not so mysterious or isolated as you imagine. You think this link only lets you inside my head, but you forget I am inside yours. Some part of her visits this place. All you have to do is ask, and I will seek her out."

"Alright, Neska, yes. If you can get her attention, I would like that very much."

A woman's voice resonated through her connection to Iska, distant and wavering, but oddly familiar. At first, it sounded as if she spoke from beyond a thick door, but eventually the voice resolved into the unmistakable clarity of her mother.

"Karra? What is this? How is this possible? Karra, can you actually hear me?"

"Mother, yes, I hear you, through Iska the riftwing. Mother, is that really you?"

"Sweet breath of the Giver, I understand. Moons, what a miracle this is. Even so, I don't think I can stay long."

The back of Karragin's nose began to sting, and tears dripped freely onto the floor. *"I've missed you, Mother, we all have. Father, Nolan, and I, we miss you so much."*

"Oh, my girl, I know. I can feel you, your love and your pain, in equal measure. I'm so sorry I didn't get the chance to be there longer. But I'm

always there, you know, connected to you all. You don't understand now, but you will."

Karragin tongued the grooved scar of her upper lip, salted by her runny nose. She wiped a sleeve across her face. *"There's so much I want to tell you. I don't know where to begin."*

"It's alright, dear, I know everything already. Part of the miracle of life is how connected we are."

"What does that even mean?" asked Karragin.

"It means, I feel you, Karra. I see you and hear you even when you are not aware of my presence. And oh my girl, I am so proud."

"Thanks. It's amazing to hear your voice. It's just that sometimes, I feel. . ."

"You feel alone, I know. It's one of life's puzzles. But feeling and being are not the same thing. You are never truly alone, my child. You may do things that make you feel isolated, but I'm always here, aware, connected. A little thing like death will never change that."

"I wish we could talk like this all the time."

"I understand, but I don't know if I can do this again. Already I feel myself slipping back. It's the strangest thing; I'm not entirely sure how I got here in the first place. It must have something to do with that young man. For Giver's sake, he's . . . stripping away everything that he was, even the life he had with you. Why is he doing that?"

"Mother, what are you talking about? Do you mean Lluthean?"

Her mother gasped, and her voice rippled through the link, weighted down by unmistakable empathy. *"Oh, Giver's sweet breath, I see now. He's giving it up, everything, to try to save you all, isn't he? That sweet, sweet, stupid boy."*

Her mother's voice receded back to distant echoes. *"Karra, I'm sliding away, dear. If you can still hear me, promise me one thing."*

Karragin flared zenith into her sympath rune, trying to bolster the link. *"Anything. If it's in my power, I'll try to make it so."*

"This is it, your one life. You are never alone, but you hide behind walls. Stop it. Tear them down and get out of your way, dear. You might be surprised by who or what is waiting on the other side."

"Walls? Mother, I don't . . . what do you mean?"

The sounds of a babbling stream, trilling insects, and chirping birds echoed through her sympath rune. Karragin held the link open, her breath quick and shallow, waiting. Neska's soft voice broke the stillness. *"She's gone, Karra. She remained longer than most, as long as she could."*

"Well, can you get her back? Call her back, or can we try again next week?"

"We can always try, but it is not likely she can return, and even if she does, she will be fragmented," said Neska.

"But, why not? That makes no sense! Please, get her back, Neska."

"Nothing I say will make sense. I am sorry. I did not mean to cause you pain."

Karragin paced alone around the inner sanctum, stopping to run a palm over the zentrist. She could just make out the shadowed form where she imagined Neska lay. *When did you become aware of another's pain? That's more than remarkable.*

"It's not your fault, Nes. And . . . I should be grateful, I suppose. It's too bad Father and Nolan couldn't speak to her."

"Your bond to Iska is a rare and precious thing. Without her, none of this would be possible."

Karragin stifled a laugh. *"I know, but thanks for reminding me."*

"Will you be able to keep your promise?"

Karragin thought back to the conversation. *"I will try. I'm still not sure what Mother meant."*

"Not that promise. My Lluthean will need the pack if he is to become what he needs to be, but he will need you more than the others."

"Oh, yes, absolutely. I will do whatever I can. We all will." She nodded to herself. *"In fact, I should probably make a report to the others now. Is there anything else you can tell me about how we can prepare for his return?"*

"Only this: when we finally leave this place, my Lluthean will need all of you to defeat the enemy."

"I understand. Thank you, both of you," she intimated to Iska.

Karragin stifled her sympath rune and redirected zenith into her arca prime. She leaped up the stairs, taking five or six at a time. Her breath quickened just as she reached the top, and she made her way through the upper floors of Stone's Grasp to the royal suites.

Three sentinels with their black tabards draped over chainmail stood guard. As one, they saluted, and Karragin realized how muted the gesture seemed. She should have been able to hear the synchronous rattle of their chainmail. But Iska remained in the Drift, and she had broken their connection. "As you were."

Once inside, she found her way to the suite Laryn shared with Kaellor. She rapped a knuckle on the door and waited. The play of shadows and light under the foot of the door preceded Amniah. The Mirrare studied Karragin's appearance, then stepped back to allow her inside.

"What's wrong?" she signed.

"Nothing. Why do you ask?"

"Because you are without Iska and it's your day off."

Karragin inhaled through her nose. *"Fair point. Iska is renewing herself in the Drift. I have news for Kaellor and Laryn."*

As Karragin entered the antechamber, movement from the balcony caught her eye. Laryn strode in with Kaellor a step behind. A crease of concern furrowed her brow.

Her Radiance signed, *"Is everything all right?"*

"Yes, but I've just left a conversation with Neska. There are some things you should know."

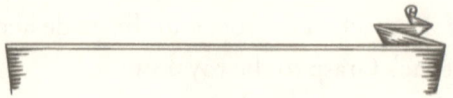

Chapter Sixty-One: Predators and Prevarications

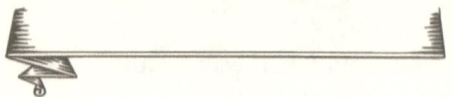

Tarkannen drew his kruga to a halt at the top of a rise. The warhorse released an uncharacteristic grunt of displeasure and shifted its weight from hoof to hoof. Moments later, Volencia rode her kruga to stand beside him. Under the intensity of the late-day sun, they surveyed the sundered gates of Millstone.

The fields before Millstone were animated with the sounds of the Kreeg army: supply wagons creaking, mallets pounding stakes into the ground, and soldiers barking orders. Though they rode just out of sight over the north horizon, the stink of the grotvonen and grondle herd stained the faint breeze with their musk. The scene was familiar, but that's all it was, which troubled the abrogator.

"What do you see, Volencia?" he asked.

"Either the good citizens of Millstone had warning and fled, or someone arrived before we did."

"Someone or something," grumbled Tarkannen.

"More acoustics then?" she asked.

He let the question hang unanswered. Acoustics seemed like such an elegant term to describe the beasts from the Drift. On two separate occasions, the army had run afoul of creatures that employed terrible sound attacks with near-catastrophic consequences. The first encounter decimated a crush of grondle before Volencia and several umbral subdued the beast.

Not more than two days ago, Tarkannen and Volencia dispatched two more of the creatures. They had arrived to find an entire flank of the army in disarray. Kruga and draft animals fled with or without their riders, creating a panic that threatened to spread into a stampede.

Volencia had erected a nullifying barrier that neutralized the rattling sound attacks of the beasts, and Tarkannen made quick work dispatching them, but not before more than sixty Kreeg soldiers fell. Though they managed to blame "the witch-king of Aarindorn" for the otherworldly attack, the subsequent recovery and strategy sessions had set them back several days.

Riders galloped out from the front gates of Millstone. One peeled away, angling toward the krug rai'al's central tent. The other paused, shading her eyes and searching the horizon. Volencia drafted nadir into a broad umbrella, protecting them from the heat of the sun and signaling the rider.

The scout spurred her kruga across the field and approached them directly. She dismounted and stopped at the edge of the shade, eyeing Volencia's construct with suspicion. "There is no danger to you under Volencia's awning. Step forward and relay your findings, Reiner B'vakla."

The woman hesitated a moment, but dipped her head and stepped forward. "It's more of the same, just like the villages we crossed on the way here."

"Are there any survivors to interrogate?" asked Volencia.

B'vakla scuffed the ground with a boot. "Not that we found. A reinforced palisade surrounds the city. It might have been a tough nut to crack from the outside, but whatever killed all those people made quick work of the gates. From that point on, the city became a death trap."

The woman bent down and picked a fistful of wildflowers, crushing and rubbing the blossoms between her hands.

"Speak your mind, B'vakla," said Tarkannen.

B'vakla cupped her hands and inhaled. "Whatever killed all those people smelled as bad as the caligot from the Trial of Nines, and it killed without discrimination. Animals were as likely to meet their end as women and children."

"That explains why the army decided to set up camp well beyond the city walls," said Volencia.

The Kreeg soldier nodded her agreement. "The corpses show the same signs of trauma that we found from the other acoustic attacks: dried blood at the ears, nose, and mouth, diffuse bruising, people dropped where they stood as if a cloud of poison washed over them. It's a bad omen."

"What do you mean by that?" Volencia challenged.

"She means," said Tarkannen, "that the Kreeg march in anticipation of a battle, but looting the corpses of an entire city decimated by the denizens of the witch-king of Aarindorn cannot offer them the glory they desire. Fear not, Reiner; there will be plenty of opportunities to test your mettle when we reach Aarindorn. The Kreeg will be the sword against sword. Volencia and I will defend against this dark sorcery."

B'vakla tilted her head and relaxed her posture, appearing more like the casual gladiator from the Trial of Nines. In the same moment, a commotion broke out at the krug rai'al's tent. Zsheck emerged from his tent, screamed more obscenities, and threw one of his soldiers to the ground, but left him otherwise unmolested.

"Isn't that the scout that entered Millstone beside you?" asked Tarkannen.

"Yes. He's likely reported our other findings. General Kilken's forces, the ones who traveled downriver, beat us here. They were to wait for us to engage Millstone, so that the city could be enslaved with its resources captured."

"Were Kilken's men among the dead?" asked Volencia.

B'vakla set her mouth in a thin line. "Yes and no. None of them entered the city, but whatever destroyed Millstone spilled out into the forest to the west and overwhelmed Kilken's forces. We lost our quartermaster and as it stands, the supply line is severely compromised."

"Is there anything to be salvaged from inside? I was led to believe that our success was predicated on the assumption that the city stores could be sacked," said Tarkannen.

"It's too early to tell. I'm not even sure the water is safe to consume. We found bodies toppled into wells. They've been rotting for days. There might be some grain stores we can salvage, but it's not the windfall we anticipated."

Tarkannen felt the sigils on his neck shift about with a restlessness that reflected his frustration. He stretched to lift his chin and tried not to allow his irritation to show. *A lifetime of sacrifice and I'm reduced to the role of quartermaster for an army that cannot march its way across a defeated kingdom.*

"Volencia, accompany B'vakla into Millstone and find the wells. Purify them if you can, then the two of you make an accurate accounting of any food stores. I will go see to mollifying Zsheck's tantrum before our esteemed krug rai'al loses credibility with his generals."

Volencia adjusted the veil about the marred side of her face and nudged her kruga forward. The shade from her umbrella of nadir dissipated, and the sun warmed his face. Tarkannen walked his kruga toward the central command tent and allowed the hood from his cloak to fall back so that all could bear witness to his sigils.

He dismounted and walked the last twenty paces, stopping before Zsheck's royal guards. The six burly men stood their ground, but considered him with wary respect. Tarkannen waited for one of the guards to announce his arrival. A moment later, Zsheck threw open the tent flap and glowered. He stared at Tarkannen with unprovoked venom and animosity, eventually beckoning him inside.

Tarkannen held his gaze without acknowledging the king's rancor and stepped inside. The tent, opulent by nomadic standards, was a sprawling five-room affair decked out with furniture including tables, chairs, bedding, and more pillows than any reasonable person would require. Zsheck paced the breadth of the entry room, his face a brooding storm waiting to erupt.

The man turned, one hand gripping the neck of the onyx scepter strapped to his waist. When he spoke, his words sounded more like an angry growl than intelligent speech. "In Kreeg, you spoke to me of mutual respect, but the events of the past week leave me wondering if you have not plotted my demise for all the generals to bear witness!"

Tarkannen touched the fingertips of one hand to the other, forming the shape of a sphere. He pulled on the flows of zenith and crafted a nullifying field, setting the edges just inside the walls of the tent and shrouding the two of them in relative silence. "I will give you a moment to reflect on the stupidity of your assertion."

Zsheck held up one finger and inhaled as if to shout. Instead, his eyes narrowed with understanding. He stormed out of the tent only to return several seconds later, and in apparent control of his anger. He retrieved two glasses and a flask from his sleeping room. After pouring a generous amount into each, he handed one to Tarkannen, then welcomed him to a chair.

The volatile aroma of distilled spirits wafted through the room. "My apologies. I spoke in haste." He gestured with one hand at the inside of the tent. "You have acted wisely. My men cannot hear us, cannot hear me, whine like an unbloodied child. For that, you have my thanks. Please allow me first to show you it's not poison." Zsheck tossed back the contents of his glass, then refilled it.

Tarkannen lifted his, clinking the two glasses together. "I was told that alcohol was outlawed in Kreeg."

Zsheck took a sip, blew off the fumes, and stuck out his lower lip. "That's true enough, but then, we are not in Kreeg. So tell me, what do you know about these creatures, the acoustics?"

"In some ways, they are like the caligot."

"That's it? Nothing more?" pressed Zsheck.

"What do you want to hear? They are creatures of nadir, summoned from the Drift. They indiscriminately kill and consume."

Zsheck swirled the amber liquor in his glass and took another sip. "You've dealt with them before?"

"I've dealt with similar predators, but not of this variety. Still, now that we know how to protect ourselves from their unique attacks, any future encounters should pose little threat."

"You said they were summoned? Summoned by whom, exactly? And don't spout that drivel about the witch-king of Aarindorn. I appreciate the need to motivate the masses, but don't insult me by expecting me to swallow that particular prevarication."

Tarkannen sipped at the liquor. The smoky burn lingered on the back of his tongue as he considered how much to reveal to the man.

"Does it suffice to say we will probably randomly encounter similar creatures? At least until we gain access to Stone's Grasp."

"It does not," said Zsheck.

"Alright then, summoned was not the correct term. They are invaders."

Zsheck squinted his eyes and leaned forward, elbows on knees. "Tell me more."

"What do you know about the Cataclysm that divided Karsk?"

"I know that the Great War pitted zeniphiles against abrogators and that Mogdurian, our founding ancestor, led his most courageous against the chaos of the zeniphiles in a war that decimated both sides and threatened to annihilate all of Karsk."

Tarkannen grabbed the flask of liquor and topped off both of their glasses. "That's a start, but your history is incomplete. Have a seat, Zsheck. This is going to take a while."

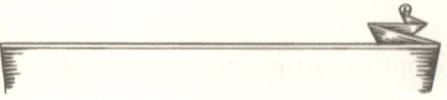

Chapter Sixty-Two: The Song of the Ursulu

Nolan shifted his weight on the back of the druska and had to admit that while the mount failed to offer the same comfort or security of a gripped Aarindin, the creature walked and cantered with unusual grace. Not for the first time, he leaned to the side to make sure the druska actually picked up its feet, as it seemed like the mount was gliding rather than walking.

Seldora had procured mounts for Dexxin and Savnah as well, and the company made exceptional time. By morning of the second day, the dark outline of trees marked the eastern horizon, rising up like a mountain range and spreading beyond the north and south horizons. By that same evening, they had reached the outskirts of the ursulu forest. The majesty of the ancient, towering trees stretched quite literally up into the clouds, defying the elements. It was beyond anything he might have imagined.

Sunlight failed to fall on the shaded ground, wind currents diverted around the resolute trunks, and even water flowed in grooved channels that spiraled around the trees. None of them had words for the sight. Even Savnah stood fish-mouthed and silent as Seldora explained how the tree singers encouraged and maintained the ancient grove.

"There is no higher calling, no greater gift among my people," he explained. "Through their whispers, the ursulu become their best selves."

He signaled, and Kadra dipped its broad, antlered head, allowing him to swing down. Seldora walked ten paces up what could only be described as a broad ramp spiraling around the trunk of one of the ursulu trees. He stopped and placed a palm flat on the tree, standing in quiet communion.

At last, he pushed back and turned to address them all. "You have the blessing of the forest. Come, leave your friends here."

"Perhaps I should remain behind," said Ksenia. "Just to make sure Winter and Tacit are safe."

Seldora gave her an uncharacteristic smile, and Nolan thought it was the first time since meeting the Ilovesh that the expression had touched his face. "I understand your reluctance. But there are no predators who will threaten the Aarindin. We can reach the elders in Vellendar by way of this spring tree and arrive in a matter of minutes. Boru and the Aarindin are too large and will have to remain behind."

"If we travel by ground, how many days would it take to reach the elders?" asked Bryndor.

"More than ten but less than fourteen. It's the best way to experience the ursulu, but—"

"But that would add nearly a month of travel to arrive and return. And we don't have the luxury of time," said Ksenia. "I will need a moment to assure them."

Nolan watched as Winter, Tacit, and Boru turned their attention to the sympath. They stood in silent conversation for several minutes before Ksenia turned and nodded her consent to proceed. "Alright. Boru promised to keep an eye out. I told them we should return within three days. Does that seem reasonable?"

"Yes," said Seldora, and he beckoned them up the ramp.

Nolan slid off the back of his druska and stepped onto the ramp. He grunted with surprise, expecting to find the spiraling pathway tottering. Instead, the path felt like a solid extension of the trunk. Once they all seemed convinced of the soundness of the ramp, Seldora led them up a climb that defied logic.

Every fifty steps, a latticework of branches connected the trees together, forming a living scaffolding between the massive trunks. Seldora stopped to explain how the trees became one living creature instead of isolated, individual structures. Nolan wasn't sure he completely understood what the Ilovesh meant but was grateful for the rest. Each of them labored to draw breath, and Nolan massaged a burning fatigue from his thigh muscles.

With the lesson complete, the Ilovesh led them higher into the canopy. Nolan estimated that one revolution around the trunk took at least forty paces. Eventually, clouded mists settled as a layer of condensation, and the slope of the ramp flattened to accommodate the slippery footing. Grooves funneled the moisture into a trough on the inside of the spiral, and Seldora encouraged them each to take a drink.

Nolan crouched and channeled zenith into his forearms, activating his proof and clarification runes. He sifted through the liquid, assessing its components. To his surprise, faint particles of zenith remained suspended in the water. He cupped his hands and took a drink, finding the liquid slightly sweet and utterly refreshing.

"Well, scout boy, what's the verdict?" pressed Savnah.

"It's good, really good." He reached for a small travel canteen and shook it in Seldora's direction. "I'm unfamiliar with Ilovesh customs. Would it be acceptable to fill my canteen? I don't want to provoke offense."

Seldora tilted his head. "No offense is taken, and no permission is needed. You already have the blessing of the ursulu. Please take your fill. We still have a climb, but the waters, as you say, will refresh and sustain you."

In short order, they continued up the spiral, but the fatigue leeched away from Nolan's legs and his breath came easy. He lost track of how many times they circled the trunk, but at last Seldora stopped when the ramp opened onto a platform. A teardrop-shaped opening appeared in the trunk, and the Ilovesh waited for them to gather.

"Scattered throughout the forest are spring trees. This is one such tree. Once we step inside, the ursulu will transport us to a spring tree in Vellendar, but you will have to leave your weapons here." He gestured to Savnah. "Especially those. While I have seen you wield those blades in defense of your group, others among the Ilovesh would not look upon you kindly were you to arrive in Vellendar with tools capable of wounding our sacred grove."

"We understand," said Bryndor. Without further direction, he unbuckled a sword and knife and leaned them against the trunk of the tree with his Logrend bow. The others followed suit without protest.

Even Savnah, whose mood seemed mollified by the zenith-enriched water, complied without complaint.

"Good. Once inside the spring tree, the song of the ursulu will transport you. Do not access your zenith lest you disturb the process," said the Ilovesh.

"What happens if we disturb the process?" asked Savnah.

"You might end up lost in the ursulu forest, emerging from a different spring tree or, worse, deposited within the trunk, forever trapped. Any questions?"

"Is there going to be pain, or danger? What else can you tell us about the process?" asked Savnah.

A playful expression colored Seldora's face. "No, it's a simple transition. Nothing more."

Savnah began to question Seldora further, but Bryndor rolled up his sleeve, zenith illuminating the runes on his forearm. He studied the Ilovesh with uncommon intensity, and Nolan sensed the currents of zenith shifting to Bryndor's need. Then, without warning, he stilled his gift. "It's fine, Savnah. I'm convinced that he speaks the truth. I am going, but it's reasonable for you to stay here. Either way, I need to find out if the elders can help us free Lluthean. Lead on, Seldora."

Savnah tucked her thumbs over her belt, then slid her hands to her hips, searching for the axes, which weren't there. She cursed under her breath. "May the Giver continue to smile on us monks."

Seldora turned and led them through the teardrop-shaped opening in the trunk. Nolan struggled to adjust his vision in the darkness and ran his hands along the inside of the polished wood surface. He considered reaching for zenith with the intention of keeping track of the others. The currents flowed all around him. All he had to do was let them in, a gentle caress across his arca prime. At the last moment, he resisted the urge.

A distant, ethereal chorus rose to his awareness. It started deep within the trunk as a moaning sound that resolved into melodic humming, resonant and primal, vibrating through the timber and into his core. As the sound rose in intensity, amber light and the aroma of freshly toasted hesk filled his senses.

What seemed to be zenith-laden filaments flowed into his core, reaching inside. For several seconds, he lost the ability to tell where the limits of his senses stopped and where the flows of the ursulu began. The sensation was at once disorienting and exhilarating. There was a feeling of being ushered forward while weightless, and he wondered if somehow he were flying. Just as soon as the sensation rose, it subsided, and his feet found purchase on something solid. Within seconds, the vibrating song of the ursulu dissipated.

Nolan blinked to clear his vision and reached out, placing a palm once again on a polished wood surface. Faint light oriented him to the teardrop opening. "Everyone alright? I think I see the way out."

"I'm good, what say the rest of you?" asked Savnah.

"Nobody back home is going to believe any of this," said Tovnik.

"I bet I can get my siblings to believe it," said Dexxin.

Ksenia's voice quavered. "Bryn? Where did you go?" No answer came forth. "He was right here, holding my hand. Bryn?"

"Grind the Taker's grip. Nolan, see if he's nearby," ordered Savnah.

"On it," said Nolan. He allowed zenith to infuse his arca prime and searched for Bryndor, for anything resembling his resonance. At once the life-forms all around him flared under the filter of his gift. But other than a flicker of recognition on Ksenia's hand, he found no sign that Bryndor was ever in the spring tree.

Shadows flickered from beyond the teardrop opening in the trunk, and an unfamiliar voice called out. The cadence and inflection matched Seldora's odd, lethargic tempo, but with an unmistakable undertone of violence. "You in the spring tree, come out at once or be sealed inside forever!"

Chapter Sixty-Three: The Council of Elders

Seldora felt something resembling peace for the first time in months. Returning to the ursulu, embracing the power of the forest, if even for a brief passage through a spring tree, always made him feel less disconnected.

To transition through the ursulu was to experience the entwining of all life. During the seconds it took to pass from one spring tree to the next, the sense of isolation vanished as the intricate wave of zenith overwhelmed his senses, displacing the awareness of self with the near-infinite consciousness of the forest. For the Ilovesh, the experience of commingling his essence with that of the ursulu could only be described as ecstasy.

Though his senses remained deaf to the song of the forest, the resonance of the spring tree thrummed into his core, pulling him forward to the destination just steps from his dwelling. From there he could orient the manlings, contact Somaya, and petition the elders. Perhaps they would finally offer him the opportunity to restore his honor.

He wondered how the visitors would experience the transition. Would they be moved by the sacred interconnectedness of the ursulu, or was that kind of perception beyond their recognition?

Before he could consider the question further, something shifted within the flows. Where he expected to feel propelled as a leaf in a rushing stream, instead he felt wrenched to the side, diverted. A feeling of dread rose up inside and he resisted the urge to grasp zenith. Only a chendreweh, a tree singer, could manipulate the flows once a person began a transition.

But the chendreweh would have no cause to interfere with his passage. Such action was counter to the Ilovesh. It was a diversion of the natural and, more, it was a violation. And knowledge of that fact only magnified his apprehension, for the tree singers would only act if directed to by the Council of Elders.

He shuddered as the embrace of the ursulu receded, leaving him standing once again isolated but for the presence of one of the manlings, who gasped. The air in the chamber carried heady floral aromas laced with palpable moisture.

"Is everyone alright? Kess? Savnah?"

Bryndor, that was Bryndor's voice. Seldora turned to find him standing unusually close. Zenith flooded into the man, igniting the myriad of runes and scintillating in the depths of his eyes. "Where I come from, you don't separate a man from the people he loves without warning. Some might consider such an action an abuse of trust," growled Bryndor.

Seldora sighed. Their abrupt departure from the spring tree had left him unprepared. His suspicion that they had arrived at the heartwood tree under the direct summons of the Council of Elders left him unable to offer an explanation that would mollify Bryndor's anger. "Ease your storm. The separation was not of my doing. I am as surprised by the deviation in our transition as you are."

"Are they safe? Is she safe?"

"The elders would have little reason to harm any of you."

The young man sucked at his teeth. "Give me your hand. I would learn the truth myself."

Seldora tipped his head and held out one hand. Bryndor clasped both hands around Seldora's. He sensed the man kindle zenith through runes on his forearms, and a probing wave washed over him. At first, the man had inquisitive intent, laced even with a hint of accusation. But as the feeling subsided, Bryndor's aggressive posture withered, and he appeared exhausted by the acceptance of everything that Seldora was.

The man staggered back a step when he released the probing energy. Seldora caught him by the shoulder. "Are you unwell?"

"Nobody has ever let me in to see so much. Are all Ilovesh so . . . vast?"

Seldora considered the words. Kindred speech was functional but seldom conveyed the complexities of the native Ilovesh tongue. "I do not know how to answer that. We should not keep the elders waiting."

Bryndor seemed to recover something of himself and rubbed a hand across his forehead. "I am your guest; please lead the way."

"If I am correct, we are to stand before the Council of Elders. As with the spring tree, inside is for listening. And do not embrace your gift. Not all Ilovesh are as accepting of the lesser races as I am."

Bryndor nodded. "I understand."

"Beyond here is the rostrum. It is a . . . platform at the upper reaches of the heartwood tree and houses the Council of Elders."

Seldora turned to the only light filling the chamber from a teardrop-shaped opening. It struck him that he had never had cause to travel through the heartwood tree and visit the Council of Elders. He thought the thoroughfare would seem somehow more majestic, but even to his Ilovesh eyes, the doorway appeared no more or less than any other he had cause to visit.

He led Bryndor out onto the rostrum. Moonlight filtered through the branches high overhead and shimmered on a dark pool in the center of the expansive chamber. Luminescent flowering vines emitted light in vibrant hues of orange, purple, and green, further illuminating the rostrum.

The heartwood tree swirled in grooves around the pool, and condensation made the surface slippery. Seldora gave the pool a wide berth. "The roots of the heartwood tree surround the Ilovesh deepening well. Do you know this term?"

"No, I don't believe that I do," said Bryndor.

His denial might have been calculated or born of genuine ignorance. Seldora searched his memory for past conversations with the betrayer, Tarkannen. He felt certain that the abrogator had indicated a deepening well lay in the heart of Stone's Grasp.

"The well is the source of all life in the ursulu forest. You would do well to avoid stepping too close to the pool. While it sustains, Ilovesh have drowned in its dark waters."

"How deep does the well go?" asked Bryndor.

"Who can say and know for sure? The column of water must run hundreds of feet down to the source below."

"It's what, fifty paces across? If you fall in, can't you simply swim back out?"

The question drew Seldora to a halt, and he realized how little he knew of the manlings and how little they knew of the Ilovesh. He quirked a smile. "Ilovesh do not swim. If we fall in, we sink."

"But you crossed into the Stillness."

"Whose waters are shallow and brackish. Beyond the predators, there was no risk to me."

Bryndor began to ask another question, but Seldora held up a hand. "Please, there will be time for this later, after we present ourselves to the elders. Any delay might only provoke offense."

The manling dipped his chin and motioned for Seldora to lead them forward. He walked them around the deepening well, passing around and under more of the glowing flowering vines. At last, on the far side of the chamber and elevated on natural shelves more than ten feet above, sat the five elders.

Each elder appeared hewn from the heartwood with furrowed lines of wisdom, hundreds of years in the making, giving unique shapes to their stoic expressions. Seldora searched their faces, each staring out across the rostrum in different directions. Finally, he recognized Somaya, the one elder who might offer a sympathetic ear.

Seldora dropped to one knee, head bowed, and waited. In his periphery, he saw that Bryndor followed his example, taking a knee and bowing in silence. They held their position long enough that Seldora's knee began to throb, and he resisted the urge to summon zenith and bolster the tissues there. To the side, Bryndor panted and rivulets of sweat ran down his face, yet even he resisted the urge to siphon zenith.

Speaking in the dual-tone harmony and language of the Ilovesh, an elder on the far left spoke. "Rise, sapling." The sound vibrated into Seldora as a tickly feeling in his core.

He rose to his feet and helped Bryndor stand upright. The manling limped and rubbed at his knee, grimacing, but spoke no words, which was more than he'd expected.

The elder on the far right spoke, and when she gestured, her limbs creaked like the branches of a tree in a storm. Her voice, also spoken in the Ilovesh tongue, rippled through him with waves of disgust. "Why does the brother of the betrayer believe he can arrive unannounced and uninvited to the rostrum of the heartwood?"

To his relief, Somaya stepped forward on her perch, one hand held forward. When she spoke, the melodious tones put Seldora's tension at ease. He was reminded at once of a soothing breeze through leaves. "I directed the chendreweh to divert them here. You know the truth of my visions and the pain long suffered by Seldora."

The elder sitting in the center spoke, and with his words, another painful chorus washed over the rostrum. "We are Ilovesh. We do not bow to lesser races!"

The first elder echoed an abrasive agreement, hissing, "Lesser races!"

Somaya leaned forward, cantilevering herself well beyond the edge of her platform. Under her authority, a rustling wind swept around the rostrum, gathering fragrant flowers and mist from the deepening well into a vortex that silenced the others. Her alto voice carried, primal and unyielding, like a gale force on the whirlwind. "You diminish yourselves, but I will not be diminished! And you will not make of the Ilovesh what you would of the other races. We will act in this now, or we accept the breaking of the world!"

Her storm eased, and on the currents of air, the subtle aroma of moonflowers conveyed her compassion. "We must send them back to undo the abrogator's folly. Only then can the Eidolon have a chance to heal the world. Only then can Seldora return to us whole."

Something in Somaya's maternal tone mollified the elders, who turned their focus on him. At last, the remaining elder, the one who had remained silent, spoke. "What have you to say in all of this, Sapling?"

Seldora regarded them each. "We are here—"

"We knew all the moment you passed through the spring tree," interrupted the elder to the far right. "Will you accept this burden? Will you risk the deepening well to throw down the abrogator and sever the tether?"

A shiver, rare and unexpected, ran down Seldora's back. If he succeeded, he could set right all that his sister had corrupted. But travel through the deepening well? He had not known such a task was possible. Somehow though, the intimacy of passing through the spring tree had conveyed all the knowledge he required. There was a means to obtain enough strength to confront and throw down the abrogator. He could see it now.

He set his feet and offered a long, low-pitched choral response, pouring honest intent into the simple words. "I will."

Once again, the wind gathered through the chamber as the elders deliberated, speaking their tones into the winds, an ever-rising crescendo of sounds at times harmonious, and at times a discordant cacophony as the storm of their debate raged on. At last, the winds stilled, and Seldora released his breath, waiting.

The room smelled like the forest after a heavy rain, and Somaya's maternal voice hummed throughout the rostrum. "What tongue does the manling speak?"

"Kindred speech," said Seldora.

Somaya's neck creaked as she retreated to a sitting position and stilled the breadth of her communication to the Kindred tongue. Even still, the sibilance and melody with which she spoke evoked a feeling of grandeur that no human could ever hope to match. "Manling, the Council of Elders are prepared to offer you the means to aid your brother's return and sever the tether binding him to the abrogator. But such aid comes at a price."

Bryndor looked to Seldora before answering. "The Elder Somaya poses a question. You should not keep her waiting," Seldora said.

Bryndor spoke, choosing his words with a cadence that resembled Seldora's thoughtful rhythm. "I appreciate the opportunity to receive the council's consideration. What is the price?"

Somaya said, "One in your party must enter the deepening well and relinquish their gift. Such a sacrifice is required for the blessing of the Ilovesh. Only then can Seldora pass through the deepening well and confront Tarkannen."

Bryndor's face flushed, and he searched the ground. "I accept. Let it be me."

A furrow creased Somaya's brow, which emitted a creaking sound as of wood splitting. "Are you so sure? Yours is not a gift to be cast aside so idly."

He nodded. "None of them are. But he's my brother, and I'll not ask anyone else to pay the price. Tell me what I have to do."

Somaya's gaze drifted over their heads. "It's a simple process. Walk into the deepening well. Submerge completely, and swim to the opposite shore. When you leave the pool, your gift and all ability to command zenith will be stripped away."

Seldora escorted Bryndor back through the gardens, across the rostrum to the edge of the pool. The manling stopped only a pace away from the water's edge, staring out across the well. Moonlight reflected off the surface and shone on his face, revealing a serious, committed expression. Seldora began to realize that he had misjudged the young man. Without hesitation, Bryndor had accepted responsibility and was prepared to pay the price demanded by the elders. Would he be able to make such a sacrifice?

"I don't have words. I was not prepared for any of this," said Seldora.

Bryndor inhaled a deep breath. "I know."

Seldora frowned at Bryndor, wondering about the truth of his statement. "I saw more than I bargained for when I read you," said Bryndor. "I think it's better this way. If you had known or told me earlier, the decision would have been difficult. Kess or any of the others would have tried to take my place, and that's not a debt I can repay."

Without further words, the young man crouched down and dove into the pool. The wonder of watching him swim through the water displaced any surprise he might have felt by Bryndor's abrupt commitment to the task. A gentle wake rippled behind him as he sliced through the pool, and on its crest, flickers of zenith reflected the moonlight. At first he thought that was all it was, a trick of the blue moon playing across the water. But as Bryndor continued his solo swim, it became apparent that the deepening well was literally leeching away the prince's gift.

Chapter Sixty-Four: Royal Sacrifices

I've witnessed leaders come and go, but in all my years, those I hold in highest regard, those leaders who drew forth the best from us, in every case they were servants first and leaders second. For only by leading from example, demonstrating that they would not ask anything from their followers that they were not willing to do themselves, only in those circumstances did they become truly inspirational. The rest of them are not worth an empty bottle of resco.

—The Tome of Nivosh, 75 PC, translated by Veeble Hebben

THE FAMILIAR CRASH of water, turbulent and chaotic, rushed past Bryndor's ears as he dove into the pool. He allowed his momentum to carry him forward, slicing down into the darkness. Instead of pulling himself to the surface, he hovered, waiting to feel something, anything that indicated a separation from his gift.

At first there was only the chill of the water pressing in against his skin, shifting the material of the sheff under his arms. But as he kicked to the surface, a distinct tingling sensation sheared across his skin. He first noticed the pins-and-needle prickling on his jaw, but by the time his head broke the surface and he drew breath, the discomfort had spread across every rune on his body.

A distinct leeching sensation took hold of him, and omnipresent fatigue caused his breath to quicken. What seemed like an easy swim across a small pool now felt like a daunting task. He panted several breaths and dipped his head into the water, allowing the achy muscles in his neck to relax, then pulled and kicked for several strokes.

A palpable current resisted his progress as if invisible tethers held him back, threatening to pull him deeper into the depths. His lungs burned, eager for fresh air, and he kicked frantically to lift his head from the water. He chanced a glance and was surprised to see he had crossed only perhaps a third of the distance. Panic threatened to overwhelm his efforts as he began to doubt that he had the stamina to reach the far edge of the pool.

He gritted his teeth and forced his arms and legs into painful but coordinated rhythms, pushing past the increasing, achy fatigue of muscles that felt beyond spent. In the periphery of his vision, delicate, iridescent blue particles stained the water, flowing freely from his runes. The awareness of the loss caused a flush of anger to rise in his chest. *What did you expect, you stupid monk?*

He used the anger to good purpose, pulling and kicking, periodically lifting his nose just above the waterline. With all the speed of dripping sap on a cold autumn morning, he made progress across the breadth of the deepening well. A cramp began in his core, threatening to buckle him underwater just as his fingers brushed the edge of the pool. His nails sank into the rooted edge and found purchase.

He clung there, labored breaths providing poor relief from the severe sense of air famine. He was reminded of the worst parts of crossing the Korjinth. Seldora's deep voice brought him to his senses. "You did well, Bryndor. But the elders cannot stop the deepening well from stealing your essence. If you linger, it will strip away everything."

He tried to pull himself free, but his arm muscles cramped. "I think . . . I might need your help."

Strong hands gripped under his arms and hoisted him free from the pool. He flopped onto his back, boneless, but grateful for the assistance. Seldora sat down beside him, staring back across the water.

"I must admit, I began to doubt that you could make it. No Ilovesh could survive being stripped in such a manner. How did you manage it?"

"Sometimes the Giver gives," he gasped.

"That is a strange expression. Do you also believe that the Taker takes?"

Bryndor shrugged. "Not really. Well, maybe sometimes. I don't know."

He took stock of his body. His breaths finally filled his lungs with air that dissipated the exhaustion of the swim, and the painful prickling that drained his gift had receded. Upon lifting his head, neck muscles ached, so instead he rolled to the side, gazing back across the pool. Swirls of zenith, his zenith, the remnants of his gift, stirred in the water's depths. "Sometimes a man just has to do what needs to be done. I think this was one of those times."

"I owe you an apology, Bryndor of Aarindorn."

A single huff, the incomplete manifestation of a chuckle, escaped his lips at the randomness of Seldora's statement. "I don't follow."

"I made judgments about you and your companions. Even the elders seem impressed by both your sacrifice and your tenacity. You did not hesitate to enter the pool. That kind of commitment is admirable."

"*Ballador cor delledence*, my friend."

"I am unfamiliar with those words."

"It's something Kess taught me. It means—"

The reverberant chorus of Somaya the elder echoed across the chamber. "Do not dwell in the rostrum. You each have your tasks. See them done."

Seldora assisted Bryndor to his feet. "Come, then."

"What happens now?"

"First, we reunite you with your friends."

He led Bryndor back through the spring tree. The immersive experience of transitioning through the ursulu returned a portion of his vigor, and he stepped from the teardrop portal to stand under his own strength. They stood on an isolated platform high in the canopy of the ursulu. Stars, appearing as close as when they stood on the summit of the Korjinth Mountains, twinkled overhead.

Ksenia and the Outriders slept alone in the center of the otherwise vacant deck. Bryndor recognized at once that the unique placement served as an open-air prison. Unless any of them possessed the ability to fly, the only way off the lofty perch was safe egress through the spring tree.

He cleared his throat, and Savnah lifted her head. She nudged Ksenia, and in short order they each startled to their feet. Ksenia ran forward, followed in close pursuit by the others. She drew up short just steps away, an expression of confusion stuttering her speech. "What—your eyes! Grey again? What did they do to you, Bryn?"

"All is as it needs to be. The elders promised us a means to release Lluthean and even thwart Tarkannen, but their aid came at a price," said Bryndor.

Savnah stepped forward and grabbed Bryndor's wrist, pushing back the sleeve of his sheff to reveal barely visible runes that looked more like faint white scars than the clear demarcations of his gift. She spat to the side. "They stole your gift?"

"Not, Savnah. I gave it willingly."

Ksenia danced her fingers through the Cloud Walker sign language. *"Tell me true. Are you well?"*

"I will be," he signed.

Tovnik placed a hand on his shoulder. "Would you mind if I have a look, inside?"

"I'm not injured, but be my guest," said Bryndor.

The soft murmur of the healer song echoed into the night as Tovnik deployed his gift, searching for any injuries. After only a few minutes, the medic released his touch and stilled his song. "That's the most unusual thing. I've never seen dormant runes before. It's almost like you've been ranth'd."

"What do you mean, Tov?" pressed Savnah.

"His innate zenith stores are depleted, but not like in the Stillness. Even so, the source should mingle freely with his runes, and yet . . ." The medic shook his head.

"I can't channel, so I can't prime the runes," said Bryndor.

Ksenia threw her arms around his chest and hugged him tight, but stepped back with surprise. "You're soaked."

"Yes, I sort of fell into the Ilovesh deepening well."

Seldora made a sound and shook his head. "It was so much more than that. But come, time is our collective enemy. I would see you to comfortable lodging for the night. Tomorrow, I will escort you to your friends."

"He means Boru and the Aarindin," said Bryndor.

"Yes, come then, unless you care to sleep on the moon cell," said Seldora.

He ushered them back inside the spring tree, activated their transition once again, and led them out onto a broad thoroughfare that branched from one ursulu to another. Moonlight and luminescent flowering vines lit their way as Seldora led them through what appeared to be a park.

A waterfall roared somewhere beyond the shadows and cast everything in a fine mist. Seldora led them around the trunk of one ursulu, then onto a different branch point, arriving at last before a pointed arched door set into the trunk of a different tree.

He brushed a few desiccated leaves from the threshold and welcomed them inside. Bryndor's eyes adjusted to a lamp that reminded him of the wolvryn eye. A round common room held four doors and one hallway.

Seldora busied himself opening the doors to reveal small sleeping chambers. Without waiting for an invitation, Bryndor pulled the sheff over his head, kicked off the waterlogged shoes and pants, and climbed into the first chamber. He felt Ksenia's arm drape around his midsection before sleep claimed him.

He awoke sometime the next morning to the smell of toasted hesk, and hunger motivated him to push open the door. Ksenia and the Outriders sat around a table in the small common room. Moments later, Seldora emerged from the only hallway carrying a platter of toasted hesk, berries, and a steaming kettle.

Bryndor sat down in the last open chair and helped himself to a portion of hesk. As he chewed, the rest of them stared at their mugs or plates, making little progress in the way of sustenance or conversation. "What did I miss?"

Ksenia placed her hand on his wrist and massaged his forearm. "Seldora told us what you did, Bryn. But it's like when you tried to cross

681

the Stillness without us. It was too much. You should have let one of us pay that kind of price."

He nodded in understanding. "I did think about it. I know my talents in defending Aarindorn are rare, but I couldn't ask any of you to make that kind of sacrifice. And the truth is, none of you have ever lived without your gift. But I have. It will take some adjusting, but I'll manage better than any of you would."

None of them indicated agreement with his statement. Even Seldora struggled to make eye contact, and the Ilovesh usually seemed beyond such emotional concerns. He thought to insert a little levity. "Besides, can any of you imagine what Savnah would be like without her arca prime?"

Savnah threw a piece of hesk at him, and it bounced off his chest. Their eyes met, and she shook her head in disbelief. She pointed a finger at him and appeared about to scold him, but cracked a smile. "I should say something about princes and monkery, but I will not. Just promise me that it's the last risk you'll take between now and when we get home. I don't think any of us can take much more of your royal sacrifices."

"Pass me a mug of whatever that is and you have a deal," said Bryndor.

Savnah passed him a mug of something resembling hot tea but with a thicker consistency and tasting of candied nuts. Her gesture broke the tension, and everyone finally tried Seldora's version of fried hesk smeared with berry paste.

After breakfast, Seldora led them back through the tree city. If the ursulu forest instilled awe by moonlight, by the light of day it became utterly captivating. Both above and below, countless branching thoroughfares connected the individual trees in a dense latticework of timber. Flowering vines with exotic fragrances lent further definition and support to the system of bridges.

They passed a lone tree singer, humming in what sounded like three harmonious voices at once. What could only be described as a current of wood flowed under her touch, shaping into the peaked arch of a new doorway. Once the shape was set, she stepped back and rapped a knuckle on the firm wood structure.

Ilovesh of every age meandered about the city. Some walked in idle conversation, speaking in the melodic dual-toned speech of the Ilovesh. Others leaped off one bridge to drop unnaturally but gracefully down to another thoroughfare.

Seldora led them along the edge of a large platform where crowds of Ilovesh mingled around vendors with stalls set into the tree trunks. The aromas of roasted nuts, baked hesk, and something savory permeated the air. Children sprinted by in games of chase, balanced precariously on the edge of the deck, or dangled from overhanging vines.

The alien appearance of the Aarindorians drew furtive glances, but nobody engaged them in conversation. Bryndor realized that, to a person, even the elders, every Ilovesh wore flowing manes of hair in shades ranging from violet to burgundy. None of them were bald except Seldora, and he covered that fact with a cowled cloak.

Seldora stopped at a hesk stand to negotiate for a sackful of the food supply. Another customer turned, pushed back Seldora's hood, then spoke an obvious curse. Markings under Seldora's scalp flared, but he just stared at the aggressive Ilovesh. After concluding his business, he placed the hesk into a sack while the man continued his berating. Finally, Seldora muttered a few words, and the man drew back, dipped his head, and stepped aside.

Seldora replaced his cowl and led them to a spring tree. Once inside, Savnah broached the confrontation. "What was all that about?"

"He speaks the sentiments of the Ilovesh. Because of my sister's betrayal, I am deaf to the song of the forest. It is the responsibility of all Ilovesh to recognize my family's shame. But today we follow the mandate of the Council of Elders. I simply reminded him of this fact."

Without further explanation, Seldora initiated one final transition through a spring tree, and they emerged at the familiar ursulu on the western edge of the ursulu forest. Once they recovered their gear, they began the descent to the ground. Ksenia used her sympath gift, and in minutes Tacit, Winter, and Boru joined them.

Bryndor wasn't sure what he expected, but the wolvryn nosed under his arm and licked his neck with unrestrained affection. "Some things never change, do they, my friend?"

Seldora placed cupped hands to his mouth and emitted a low-pitched droning noise. In just seconds, four druska pushed into the clearing. The creatures waltzed forward, heavy antlers tilting with their easy gait. A magical silence settled upon them as the Aarindin and druska met, nose to nose, some kind of silent conversation exchanging between them.

The Ilovesh lifted his chin to Ksenia. "They will remain with you until you release them. You must make all haste. Travel north along the western edge of the ursulu. The fog around the Stillness will thin; that is where you should turn northwest. You can skirt a lake and avoid the desolation. Turn west if you reach the mountains."

He handed the sack of hesk to Savnah. "You're not coming with us?" she asked.

"No. Though our goals are the same, I must pass through the deepening well. To that end, I must make of you a request."

"What is it?" asked Bryndor.

"If I survive the transition, I should emerge from the deepening well in Stone's Grasp. I would not desire to arrive uninvited. Can you send word of my coming?"

"We can do that, my friend," said Bryndor. "How long will your journey take?"

"It is a question without an answer. None of my people have attempted passage through the wells for several turns of the moons. I will do my best to arrive before you. That is all I can say."

Bryndor signaled to Tacit and mounted when the Aarindin lowered belly to the ground. To his relief, Tacit had no difficulty gripping him. He situated his bow and quiver over his shoulder and gazed one last time up into the massive canopy defining the edge of the ursulu.

"Eyes to the horizon, Seldora."

"May the Giver truly give," said the Ilovesh.

Chapter Sixty-Five: A Turn on the Mountainside

The Luna Rova caravan made swift progress between the Pillars of Eldrek. By nightfall, Ranika estimated they should camp just beyond the eastern pillar. She coordinated the defense of the column with Larik Lellendule. His Outriders guided the caravan away from the Aarindorian pitfalls and munitions traps, while she provided the rear guard. More than once, a distant eruption announced a detonation as marauding groups of grotvonen or grondle ran afoul of the Aarindorian munitions.

The most recent explosion left a lingering smell of alchemics. Rotten eggs, burned hair, and acrid smoke carried on the wind. Zippy chuffed a sound of displeasure, and Ranika leaned forward, patting him on the neck in reassurance. Without giving much thought to her actions, she drafted a delicate web of nadir, thin as spider silk, and tossed the netting into the air above them. She dismissed the threads before they fell, but her effort dissipated the unpleasant smell.

She drew a long breath through her nose. "That's a little better, I think."

The trail dipped low around rocky ground, then climbed up again, and at the crest, another gust of wind blew the foul smell of munitions in her face. Zippy huffed again at the offensive odor. "Well, I tried, Mr. Zip."

The sun cast a long shadow out before them, and she knew without turning that it lay low on the horizon. "Larik or one of the others should have come to find me by now. Come on, Mr. Zip, let's catch up."

She signaled the Aarindin with her feet and relaxed her hold of the reins, trusting his nose to find the trailing edge of the caravan. Their path wound through the foothills, and the rocky terrain was anything but straight. While the Aarindin navigated the course with sure footing, more than once, Ranika's molars rattled together when he made a last-second correction.

As night fell, she began to doubt Zippy's navigation. To her relief, a lone rider galloped around a hillside angling straight for them. She recognized the young man from the Luna Rova camp but couldn't place his name. He drew his mount to a stop and barely kept the animal in check. The horse panted heavy breaths, nostrils and eyes flared wide.

"Ranika? Thank the Giver! You must come. The Outriders tried to turn the caravan around, but a bunch of those grot things ambushed them!"

Without waiting for further explanation, Ranika kicked Zippy into action. The Aarindin galloped ahead in a serpentine pattern that climbed up into the base of the Great Crown. He skirted a cluster of pine trees and drew up short.

A field of wildflowers and tall grasses stretched up into the foothills. Dense trees and rocky outcroppings hunkered over the edges of the field, funneling everything into a killing zone. At the far end, she could make out the Luna Rova caravan clustered behind a thin line of Outriders. And in between her and them, the dark forms of grotvonen too numerous to count sifted through the grasses.

The beasts hooted and clicked strange calls to one another. To the right, several grotvonen sprinted from cover and hurled spears. The Outriders shifted their defense, and several other grotvonen attempted to charge from the left. Larik barked a command, and three of the Outriders recovered. Flares of zenith erupted from the gifted as they brought their skills to bear. In the strange, flickering light, she could see that they were struggling to repel the advance.

Ranika tried to assess how many of the beasts ranged across the field. "Too many, if I had to guess. Forward, Mr. Zip."

The Aarindin turned to look at her with one ebony orb. "I know, Zip. Trust me. I won't let any of them touch you. We just have to get their attention. Help me do that."

Zippy exhaled, pawed the ground, and surged ahead, an uncharacteristic angry whinny billowing from his lungs. Ranika leaned forward and directed him in a serpentine path. A scream born of both fear and exhilaration roared from her throat. "You little grinders! My name is Ranika Taim! Come get me!"

She wheeled the Aarindin about in a circle, crude spears hissing past them both and into the grasses. When they turned to face the grotvonen horde, she could barely sense their motion in the shadows. The Outriders at the top watched her with the momentary reprieve. Angry hoots and clicks accompanied the susurrations of countless beasts running through the grasses. "Hold here, Zip."

Ranika siphoned the currents of nadir, first shifting her sight to the ethereal. The entire field rippled with movement as a wave of grotvonen descended on their location. To her augmented sight, they poured down the field as a chaotic, rampaging flood.

She called on more and more of the reductive force, summoning it to her bidding. An onyx ring coalesced on the ground around Zippy, but the Aarindin remained still, panting.

"Good boy, Zip!"

Shards and jagged edges formed along the circle of nadir, and she labored to lift it into a barrier. The dark curtain rose up just as the first volley of spears crested in the sky. The missiles fell to the ground, bereft of any force and emitting hissing sounds when they encountered her null field.

The first several grotvonen, those carried forward by bloodlust and governed by their bestial nature, fell dead as they crossed the boundary. Still more tried to leap over the corpses of their ilk, only to screech or grunt in surprised pain as they collapsed, lifeless.

The passage of so many at once diminished the intensity of her barrier, and she opened herself up, inhaling as much nadir as she could tolerate. The force thrummed inside her, a wriggling, torrential deluge of power. Grotvonen farther back began to slow their approach, saucer-shaped eyes searching the night sky, wrinkled snouts sniffing the air.

Several screeched with panic, but their alarm sounded too late. Ranika Taim became the eye of a storm and unleashed angry retribution on the remaining horde. She pulled the nadir into countless blades and shards, then detonated the whirling mass out in a circumference of death. The blast wave pulsed out with a heavy thud that left a vacant hollow in her core.

She stood erect in the stirrups, ruby-hilted dagger drawn, searching for any attackers. But the entire field had fallen dormant. Dismembered and disemboweled corpses lay strewn all about her. A light breeze carried over the field, and individual stalks of grass fell to the ground, scythed along with the grotvonen by the intensity of her fury.

Ranika's scalp tingled, and she drew in more nadir, eager for another confronting wave of grotvonen. Yet the only commotion came from the rise at the far end of the field as men and women began to cheer, and Zippy nickered softly. She sat back in the saddle and slowly, begrudgingly, released her power.

She turned Zippy to the side, and the Aarindin picked up his feet, stepping with caution around the bodies of the grotvonen. Eventually, he left the killing zone and cantered up the field. Larik Lellendule stood beside his Outriders. Just behind them, Dania and Vekkuh stood cheering and hooting.

Larik shook his head in disbelief. "If I hadn't seen that myself . . . that was either some kind of brilliance or some kind of nuts."

Ranika removed her scarf and shook out the spirals of her hair. The breeze cooled her sweat-laden scalp. "A little of both, I expect."

"We're grateful, all of us. Reddevek—he would be proud."

The simple accolade gave rise to a warm swell of emotion. She dipped her head and wrinkled her nose to prevent the gathering sting that heralded tears. A deep breath dissipated the feeling, and she hopped down, then stroked Zippy across the neck. "I couldn't have done it without Mr. Zip here."

One of Larik's Outriders stepped forward, holding a zenith-laced forearm out. Zippy chuffed a familiar greeting and swished his tail. "It's good to see you too, Zip."

"You know each other?" she asked.

Freckled cheeks crested the young man's smile, and he ran his hands through short-cropped honey-colored hair. "Name's Kervin Balladuren. I think you knew my sister, Ksenia? Me and old Zip go way back. If you like, when we get out of this mess, I could groom him later. It would be a pleasure."

He did resemble Ksenia more than a little, and Zippy's obvious recognition quelled her restless mind. "Sure thing. Once we get out of here. What happened exactly?"

Kervin's face curdled and he spat to the side. "The trail leading out of this small canyon broke apart, but by the time we figured out it was impassable, the horde bottlenecked us."

Ranika gazed back down the field, now a shadowed slope dimly illuminated by the blue moon. "What's the plan for tonight then?"

Larik wrinkled his nose. "Moons, but those things reek. I was going to suggest we fortify ourselves up here tonight, but the smell alone would disturb the Taker."

The musky odor of so many grotvonen did challenge Ranika's edgy patience, and she suspected she was unlikely to find sleep after siphoning so much nadir. "How do we find a safe path in the dark?"

Vekkuh stepped forward. "The moons light our path tonight, sister. There is refuge just a little farther to the east."

Larik shouted, "You heard the speaker. Mount up! The sooner we leave this valley, the sooner we can rest for the night!"

The prime turned back to Ranika. "Are you still up for rear guard? It's lonely, but you've shown you're more than capable."

"I'll hang back with you, if that's alright?" asked Kervin.

Zippy swished his tail once again. "If Mr. Zip agrees, it's fine with me," said Ranika.

They waited for the entire caravan of Luna Rova to follow Larik and the Outriders across the field. Ranika cast her gaze to the stars, studying familiar constellations. Kervin removed a flask from his pack

689

and swished the liquid around. "What do you think, give it another quarter hour then head out?" he asked.

She looked at the bottom of the field, where the last of the Luna Rova departed into the shadows. "Sounds good."

Kervin signaled his Aarindin, and the mount lowered belly to the ground, then rose with ease after he threw a leg over. He swished the flask. "Care for a nip before we go?"

"I'm alright, thanks all the same."

He lifted the flask in a mock toast. "Sometimes the Giver gives!"

Kervin tipped the flask back and appeared to take a large gulp, cheeks swollen with the contents. A frown creased his brow, and he clutched at his chest, then fell, ungripped from his Aarindin. Ranika flared nadir across her vision, searching the vicinity for any signs of an attack. She swept her gaze back and forth. With no obvious threats, she began to wonder if the Outrider had been poisoned. She crouched down, keeping a vigilant watch, and shook Kervin's shoulder. "Kervin, are you awake? What is it?"

The Outrider's eyes fluttered open, and he waved her close. As she leaned forward, he exhaled something foul and volatile into her face, even spewing the contents of his drink into her mouth. She recognized the taint of the solution at once from the Lacuna attack in Stone's Grasp, the one time her gift had been nullified.

Violent cramping spasmed in her core, and Ranika doubled over, gasping for clean air. She sensed Kervin approach and reached out for nadir, but the flows evaded her grip, slippery as a snakefish from the Callishite harbor. Even her enhanced vision failed her.

In confused panic, she lashed out wildly with the ruby-hilted dagger, but the Outrider deflected the swing, disarmed her, and kicked her in the gut. She crumpled to the ground, struggling both to make sense of his betrayal and to draw breath. He leaned in and dumped the contents of the flask onto her face just as she gasped for air.

Violent waves of tetany and cramping caused the muscles in her back and arms to seize up. She blinked away tears, gasping in pain, and labored to keep an eye on her attacker. Kervin spat to the side and wiped at his face. "I'm sorry for that. It looks worse than veramanth tea. I've got no choice in all this. It's Tixon B'gin and the Lacuna. There's a price on your head, Ranika, and bringing you in keeps my family safe."

"But . . . Kaellor. I thought he freed you from the Lacuna."

Kervin began tying her hands behind her back, and Zippy whinnied, rearing back. Zenith flared in the young man's eyes and within moments the Aarindin stilled, standing at peace. "My sister got out alright, but it hasn't been the same for me. I'll never be a prime again. But maybe this way I can secure the safety of my family."

Ranika doubled forward and emptied her stomach with violent retching. Somehow, Kervin got Zippy to lower belly to the ground and hoisted her into the saddle, then he tied each leg to the stirrup. She considered resisting, but the Eldrenol's solution leeched away all her strength, and she sagged forward on the Aarindin, intermittent dry heaves her constant companion.

In moments, Kervin mounted and led them down the field, but instead of turning to the east and following the caravan, he led them south. That realization should have given her cause for alarm, but the leeching effects of the toxin pulled her into darkness.

She awoke to the sensation of being suffocated and tried to pull her head back only to realize someone held a rag over her face. Ranika inhaled, then arched back and tumbled out of the saddle. She startled to awareness, blinking away tears, blinded by the sun and gagging on the now familiar taste of Eldrenol's solution.

Her world became one endless episode of dry heaves and violent cramping. Over the next three days, she experienced moments of clarity, usually right before Kervin dosed her with the volatile purple liquid. Even if she had not been separated from her ability to summon nadir, the cumulative physical effects of three days and nights of constant sickness drained her stamina.

She had made water the day before. He'd needed to help her off the mount. *Not peeing for a day, that is probably a bad sign, isn't it?* Still, it was no worse than the isolation she felt at having her only friend turned into a neutral party in the whole affair.

Zippy carried her with all the attention of a packhorse. She had puzzled out that Kervin was a sympath, like his sister. But Taker's grip, why couldn't the Aarindin at least acknowledge her now? She grunted. When did she start swearing like a Northlander?

She lifted her head from the mount's neck; the effort sent a stab of pain between her shoulder blades. "Where are you taking me?"

Kervin rode beside her but didn't glance down. "Back to Stone's Grasp. Back to Tixon."

"Just do it then. End me here. I'm not going to survive. It's the least you can do."

Kervin didn't acknowledge her, and just kept riding. Ranika used the last of her strength to push back from Zippy's neck. "Coward! You're a grinding coward, Kervin Balladuren! Do it yourself, now!"

Both Aarindin came to a stop and Kervin dipped his head. She collapsed forward, returning to the prone position on Zippy's back, and Kervin dismounted. He walked around and bent down so she could see him.

He brandished her ruby-hilted dagger, holding the blade forward as if to stab her. Tears brimmed in his eyes. "You think I want any of this? I don't. You think I want to hand you over to Tixon? You're the bait. Get it? You're the only way I'll ever get an audience with him, and when I do, he's dead. If it costs me everything, I'm taking him out."

Her mind was too addled for a response, but she understood his motions when he sheathed the knife and doused a cloth with the vile purple solution. She tried to pull back, but he gripped a handful of her hair, holding her fast. Just as he reached up to snuff her back into oblivion, a gruff voice called out.

"Kervin! Stop."

The young man froze in place and lowered his hand to his side. Ranika chanced a glance to see a man riding an Aarindin, also bareback, so a gifted if she had the right of things. The newcomer looked older by several years, broad-shouldered, with a black beard and a stern expression. "Brother, this is not the way."

"What are you doing here, Rugen? You're supposed to be managing the royal affairs along the Endulian Pass."

"I was, until a certain speaker approached me back near the Endulian. Vekkuh shared a vision with me, and reminded me what's really important, so I came to find you," said Rugen.

Kervin paced back and forth. "You came all this way for her? That's a grind fest! You dragged me into the Lacuna. You got a royal promotion, while I barely managed to stay in the Outriders, and now you come here for her?"

Rugen held up both hands in submission. "No, brother. I came here for you. You're what really matters. Everything here, it's not your fault, Kervin. It's my fault, all of it. I got you into the Lacuna. This, what you're doing, it's not you. And if you continue, you'll never come back from it."

"They threatened Mother and Father. They tried to kill Kess! I can put it all right if I take her back and deal with Tixon myself! It's the only way!"

Rugen sighed and placed his hands in his pockets. "She doesn't appear likely to survive the trip, not with what you've already done to her. Will you kill me too then? Because, brother, that's what it's going to take. I can't let you do this, but together, there's another way."

Kervin stared at his brother. He gripped the hilt and began to hyperventilate, then lurched forward to strike Rugen in the chest but drew up short, holding the blade a hair's breadth from Rugen's neck. The two of them stood there, Rugen offering his neck, Kervin threatening to strike, until at last the younger man dropped the dagger and dipped his head forward, sobbing.

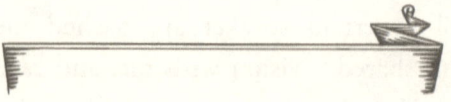

Chapter Sixty-Six: Forgetting to Remember

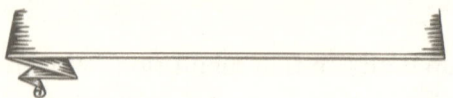

Lluthean clung to the remnant of a shattered ship mast adrift in dark ocean waters. The detritus of the shipwreck floated all around him, smelling of pitch and woodsmoke. A frigid wave washed over him, stinging the back of his nose with the salty tang. His body shivered, fingers numb and tingly, then his arm muscles cramped, and he began to sink. In a panic, he kicked hard, arching his neck to keep his lips above water. Sephora's voice cut through the disorienting predicament. "Find your center. Embrace your power."

Understanding washed over him. This was another test, one of Sephora's creations. At least she had spared him the challenge of surviving the fiery eruption that caused the ship to explode. He had nearly failed in that particular exposure. This was another drowning exercise.

Somehow, the Ilovesh understood that the threat of drowning triggered old memories and tickled a primal instinct in Lluthean: either he would succumb to fear or master it and become even more adept in his gift. Fleeting images of Bruug Hawklin holding him underwater flickered in his mind. The brute held tight, raining blows on his head, his neck, his shoulders. The bully's voice echoed in his mind. "Never should have crawled off your farm, boy!"

Lluthean's feet kicked against sharp rocks, cutting through the tender flesh. His heart began to thrum inside his chest, and lungs burned to draw in fresh air. In an instant, he recognized the trap and smothered the instinctive, frantic part of his mind, the part that became complicit in the struggle.

Instead, he embraced his source, and focused on the flows of zenith in his core. A protective sphere of his gift manifested around him, displacing the water and insulating him in a sterile field with galvanic vapors. He surged the power through his runes, taking command of the ambient currents, reshaping them to the familiar landscape of the Valley of the Cloud Walkers. Wild grasslands sprang up, extending out to the mountainous horizons. Clusters of trees erupted from the ground, and a stream cut around a hillside.

The effort began to tax his stamina, so he diverted his attention to his tether. The manifestation of the leeching and sustaining link hovered in front of his chest as a tangled ribbon of zenith coiled around a solitary strand of nadir. He studied the interlace, the wriggling knot of zenith placed to prevent Tarkannen from leeching his power. If he released the constraints, could he not obtain more power and stabilize the environment?

A smothering force slammed him to the ground, and Sephora's voice vibrated in his mind, a resolute command issued in dual tones, disrupting his concentration. "No!"

Lluthean stopped channeling. The power drained out of him and back into the atmosphere. He sat up, relieved to feel the familiar friction of grass between his fingers. Neska padded over and sniffed his ear.

"You did much better this time," she said.

He rolled his neck from side to side, stretching muscles that had stiffened with the memory of Bruug Hawklin's pummeling blows. "Thanks, Nes."

The Ilovesh stood several paces away, arms folded and head cocked to the side. "She is right; you managed the transformation with adequate efficiency. But toward the end, you chose to gamble instead of trusting yourself and—"

"And I began to reach for the tether," he finished.

The apparition of the Ilovesh turned her back to him and stared up into the darkness of the Drift. "Tarkannen is corrupted. I've told you this. We have no means of predicting how that might affect you if you try to siphon through the tether."

Lluthean tipped his head back, panting. "Understood."

Sephora returned her gaze to study him, her unblinking alien eyes framed by angular features. Purple birthmarks flared across her cheeks and forehead, even under the skin on her neck. Luscious, thick locks of deep purple hair billowed out in the ethereal wind before settling on her shoulders. "Now that you have command of your impulses, show me how you might release the interlace."

He stood and studied the tangled knot of zenith he had woven around the single strand of nadir. His barrier, the interlace, should in theory prevent Tarkannen from siphoning anything but a minute fraction of his power. Current circumstances, with him in the Drift and his nemesis walking Karsk, should dictate that any transfer of power flow from Tarkannen to him. But the abrogator had sealed his end of the tether with his own interlace, and now Lluthean needed to learn the same technique in preparation for his return.

He mentally turned the interlace back and forth, finding the nodal edges, the places where he could unravel the construct. He had only managed four nodes in his original interlace. That first barrier was inadequate to prevent Tarkannen from leeching his power, but easy to dismantle. His current work consisted of more than a dozen nodes, tightly woven in intricate, roiling knots of zenith.

He found the first ten nodes easily enough. They felt like sharp edges, places he could almost physically grasp. The last two remained buried deep within the interlace. He waited for the shifting ropes of zenith to reveal the last two nodes, and then with a sharp tug, he mentally pulled at all the edges.

The interlace frayed apart to reveal the lone tether, a wispy filament of nadir. Now that he knew what to look for, Lluthean wondered how he had never noticed the parasitic line before.

"Good, this is good. Now weave the interlace once again," said Sephora.

Lluthean rubbed thumbs to fingers. First, he primed his runes, then began the arduous task of mentally and physically coaxing the power back out, shaping it into stable ropes of zenith. Finally, he started the complex weave.

Sephora waited for him to finish, then tsk'd. "You still use your hands to create the barrier. I've told you this is not necessary. The construction is in here." She tapped him on the temple.

"I know, but it helps me focus."

She folded her arms and leaned in, studying his interlace. "Adequate."

"Well, don't gush all over me now," said Lluthean.

Sephora's expression remained unchanged while she considered his words. At last, she nodded to herself. "Ilovesh do not gush. Humans gush. Regardless, your interlace is adequate. It should protect you when you leave the Drift."

"I consider that high praise and . . . extend my heartfelt thanks for teaching such an inept pupil."

Sephora tipped her head in a subtle nod. The familiar, distant flapping of wings preceded Iska's arrival. The riftwing streaked down from the dark currents of the Drift and swept over the grassy plains. Iridescent blue particles trailed behind her like sparks erupting from a burning log. She swooped in low, then fluttered her wings, coming to roost on Lluthean's shoulder.

"Hello Iska," he said, then looked to Neska. "Can you tell her I said hello?"

Neska's voice resonated in his thoughts. *"She understands much of what you have to say in this place."*

Sephora inserted herself into the conversation. "What can you tell me of this bird?"

Peripherally, he thought the question seemed strange, but then much of Sephora's mannerisms were strange. "She's a riftwing, more specifically, Karragin's riftwing. As I understand it, she has to periodically return to the Drift to renew herself."

"Who is Karragin?" Sephora pressed.

Lluthean ran a single finger over Iska's head, and the riftwing flared a crown of feathers, shifting the grain first in a vertical line and then horizontal, then back to vertical. The effect caused a tiny cloud of zenith to disperse into the atmosphere, and she hooded her eyes in a slow gesture he understood as pleasure.

"Well, let's see, Karragin is the oldest child of the regent, a talented sympathy, and one of the most skilled Outriders in an age. She's reserved, maybe? She plays it close to the vest. Nobody else I would rather have by my side in a scrap, and she's a good friend. At least, I think we're friends."

"Hm. Nothing else? Can you remember anything else about Karragin? What about her smile?" asked Sephora.

"Her smile?" Lluthean searched his memories. Images floated up to his awareness, incomplete and fleeting. He might as well have tried to grab smoke. He paced in a slow circle. Why did he have such a difficult time recalling his experiences with Karragin? Finally, he thought of her brother, Nolan, and he recalled once that she let her guard down and smiled for him, a full, unbridled smile that reached her eyes and was accompanied by a bout of laughter.

That memory led to others: Karragin riding Aarindin, the prime directing him to take to the trees to escape the bartusk, fighting the Lacuna, fighting the rumblers in the Great Crown. Then the memories became elusive, and he lost his concentration. He focused his attention on Sephora. The Ilovesh stared at him with uncommon intensity. At last, he shrugged. "She rarely smiles and usually only for her brother, Nolan. I tried to get her to smile, loads of times, but I think . . . I don't know, maybe she considers me a nuisance?"

He looked to Neska for confirmation, but the wolvryn chose not to meet his gaze, staring off across the plains. "What is it? What am I missing?" he asked.

"You don't remember anything else about Karragin? What about the child, Rona, or her siblings?"

Lluthean scratched his head and replayed the words in his mind. "If you mean Aunt Rona, she's merged on. She found me in this place when I first came to the Drift."

The Ilovesh tapped her lips and walked to stand beside him. She flared graceful, long fingers, and a pond appeared on the ground. "What can you tell me of the interlace?"

The words rose with stark clarity in his mind. "The interlace serves to restrict the flow of my zenith, my power, through the tether Tarkannen created."

Sephora twirled her hand, and a small pouch appeared. She loosened the cinch string to reveal tiny grains of silver sand. Facets of each grain glittered in the pale light with the telltale blue hue of zenith. "What is this substance?"

"It's crystallized zenith," he replied.

She grasped one of his hands, turned his palm up, and set the pouch in his grasp. "I give this to you freely but know it came at great cost to me. Tell me, will you be able to return from the Drift with the crystallized zenith intact?"

Lluthean put the pouch in his pocket and flapped his hands in exasperation. "Again with this? The universe demands balance. Tarkannen brought forth an equal measure of nadrean, so I should be able to return with this. It can be used to nullify nadrean or restore life to those bereft of zenith."

Sephora nodded but returned her focus to the surface of the pool. She stood in awkward silence, and eventually Neska came to stand beside him. Lluthean cleared his throat. "Did I get it wrong?"

Neska's reassuring voice filled his mind. *It's what you did not say, my Lluthean. We have dwelled in this place for a time beyond measure, and it has altered you. You were made to forget some things, but now you risk forgetting to remember. Some of this was necessary to prepare you for the return.*

Sephora finally turned to look at him, and her eyes softened with an expression of compassion. "I have taught you what I can, what you needed. But that information came at a price. It displaced parts of your past. I fear if we continue, though, you will forget too much of the boy you once were and lose all motivation for the struggle ahead. So, we must stop. And now, your time of return approaches."

Images resolved on the surface of the water. A bald Ilovesh man, lean and muscled, walked with casual grace through a garden under moonlight. Exotic, luminous flowers lit his path, and he stood before a placid pond. He passed a hand over the water and a mirror appeared, except, instead of the man's reflection, Lluthean saw his own. He lifted a hand with a confused wave, surprised to see his reflection mirror his movements. Sephora touched fingers to her lips. The Ilovesh man nodded to each of them. "Is he ready, sister?"

"He is as ready as he can be. Hurry, Seldora; he cannot remain here much longer, and I cannot resist the merging. Even now, it calls to me."

Seldora dipped his head. "You have done all that we can ask and more. Be at peace, Sephora. Forget these struggles and merge on. Leave the cares of this world to those who must suffer it."

Sephora gasped with a sigh of relief and vanished into the ether. Lluthean pulled his gaze across the recreation of the Valley of the Cloud Walkers. Beyond Neska and Iska, he stood alone. He turned his attention back to the pool, where the bald Ilovesh leaned forward, clearly intrigued and assessing Lluthean's surroundings.

"Such a miracle should not be possible. But then, your brother showed me the folly of Ilovesh preconceptions. Humans have," he said, shaking his head, "limitless capacity for commitment."

"My brother? You met Bryn? How is he? Is he safe?"

"Hold fast to this viewing, my friend. Bryndor's sacrifice will allow me to open the way for your return. When next you see me, commit to the emergence, and we will meet Tarkannen together."

Seldora looked at someone unseen over his shoulder. "Thank you for this chance, Somaya. I will not fail you."

The Ilovesh leaned back, took one breath, and dove into the pond. Lluthean watched his own reflection dissipate and half expected the man to crash directly through and into the Drift. But instead of emerging, Seldora simply disappeared. The pool on Lluthean's side of the vision sloshed as if a stone had been tossed in. When the ripples vanished, so too did any image of the Ilovesh.

SUBMERSION IN THE DEEPENING well defied all of Seldora's expectations. The water slicked against his frame, feeling less like water and more like waves of heat from a cooking stone. He inhaled, and zenith filled the spaces where his lungs should draw in air. A tingly sensation spread across his shoulders and arms as the manifestation of Bryndor's gift took residence in his form.

Instinctively, he welcomed particles of the blue energy and charged the runes on his shoulders. A steady gout of rune fire streamed from his upper back and propelled him through the current of the deepening well. He had no experience with submersion in water and found the passage bewildering.

He looked back expecting to spy some reflection from the luminous plants in the garden of the elders, but the short nimbus of light emitted by his borrowed runes failed to penetrate the darkness in the depths of the deepening well. He hovered a moment in indecision, turning his head in all directions but having no sense of up or down.

He stilled his mind and triggered the flow of zenith to activate the foreign runes on his forearms. Below him, appearing as a pinprick beacon in an ocean of darkness, a tiny particle of zenith glittered. Seldora cupped his hands and pulled, shifting his direction, then rekindled the borrowed runes and jetted forward under the force of more rune fire, toward the alternate entrance to the deepening well in Stone's Grasp.

Chapter Sixty-Seven: The Giver's Divine Touch or the Taker's Grip

Steam rose from Kaellor's plate. The herby aroma of fresh-baked bread, aged cheese, and smoked meat should have enticed him to eat, but he pushed the plate forward and drummed his fingers on the table. He tapped a finger on his shek, hoping to evoke a response as he directed another delicate flow of zenith into the device.

"Is this thing working?"

His voice echoed from Laryn's shek sitting not more than two feet away. She tore a piece of bread and applied crownberry preserves, then pushed his plate back under his chin, enticing him to eat. "He will answer when he answers, but starvation will not make him respond any sooner."

Kaellor pushed back in his chair, walked to the window, and rechecked the fading sun's position on the horizon. He returned to sit beside Laryn and stared at the food, finally nibbling on the portion of bread she had prepared. He tapped the shek on the table. "These things. I can't decide if they are the Giver's blessing or the Taker's curse."

Laryn sipped at a cup of wine and gave him a compassionate smile. "Why do you say that?"

"Because I can't get away from it. I wake up in the middle of the night and check the shek. If I have a random moment in the morning or at night, I check the shek. Just today in the privy, I checked the grinding shek. I've channeled more zenith in the last week checking the shek than I did in the entire past year!"

She pushed back her chair, stood behind him, and massaged his shoulders. "You could appoint a trusted staff member to mind the shek. Fagle employs his daughter since he is ungifted, and he never misses an update. That way you could rest easy until Bryndor or anyone in the closed council attempts to reach you."

Her touch eased his tension and he dropped his head forward. "I thought about it, but there's too much at stake. It's not just Bryn, tracking the war preparations, coordinating with everyone . . . I'm not ready to hand over those secrets to a random staff member."

Through the shek, one of the other council members cleared his voice, evident from a deep grunt. "Apologies, Your Highness, Overwarden Kaldera here. I don't want to insert myself into the conversation. Would you prefer a report now, or shall I postpone my report until morning?"

Kaellor huffed a laugh at his own folly. "Kal, I'm a monk twice over. I apologize that any of you had to listen to my grumbling. How many others are present this evening?"

"We're listening," said Therek. "Salveen is with me. We are actually on our way to your rooms now and should arrive shortly."

Fagle Hoff's voice chimed through the shek. "I'm listening, friends."

In unison, Hestian and Venlith chimed in, "Here."

"Please, Kal, tender your report; we've all waited long enough," said Kaellor.

"Your Highness, the combat engineers completed the fortifications. The palisade is now worthy of the title, Eldrek's Wall. Ballista and trebuchet teams have already deterred grondle from making an approach, but our greatest success has been the deployment of deadfalls and munitions beyond the wall. We are experimenting with adding munitions to the trebuchet teams, but, as you can imagine, great caution must be exercised to prevent friendly fire. Our scouts have identified the arrival of the first wave of Kreeg forces. They established the front line of their camp only a half mile south of the wall. The Outriders have skirmished with numerous forward elements, including Kreeg scouts, grondle, and grotvonen. Thus far, our efforts to apprehend a Kreeg scout for interrogation have not met with success."

"Have they sent any diplomats forward?" asked Therek.

"Not at this time, Your Grace. We did receive a few refugees from Norfold. They describe horrors that defy logic," said the overwarden.

"Can you explain further, Kal?" asked Kaellor.

"From what we can tell, the Kreeg army is frankly massive. Mobilizing and maintaining a force that large is a logistical dilemma that staggers the mind. As we predicted, they conquered Millstone and Norfold, absorbed their resources, and have likely enslaved the population. Norford in particular attempted diplomacy, but the refugees describe attacks that laid waste to everything: men and women, but also all manner of animals. The descriptions vary, but it's clear that whatever devastated Norfold employed attacks grounded in nadir. We presume Tarkannen has procured some new shock troops that will pose unique challenges."

"Our entire inventory of reagents for the manufacture of Eldrenol's solution should arrive tomorrow," said Fagle.

"And two days from now, another supply of brittle amber should arrive as well," said Venlith.

"Noted. I will have Outriders posted to escort the caravans," said Kaldera.

"Stellance has risen to the occasion and provides ample housing for the rotations of troops between the Pillars of Eldrek. Fresh soldiers should arrive tomorrow," said Hestian.

Laryn leaned forward to speak but kept working her thumbs into a spasm of muscle between Kaellor's shoulders. "What happened to the Outriders posted to Norfold and Millstone as advisers?"

Kaldera released an uncharacteristic sigh. "We know our emissaries arrived in Norfold; the refugees confirmed as much. It's almost certain they fell victim to the abrogator attacks. Beyond that, we lost contact with the group that reached Millstone. Given the density of the Kreeg forces, we recalled all Outrider forces from the Borderlands after that. They reinforce the troops at the wall and continue surveillance in the foothills of the Great Crown, thwarting the Kreeg scouts."

A disorienting knock echoed both at the door and through the shek, causing a strange ringing for several seconds. "Apologies everyone. Kae, that would be Salveen and me," said Therek.

Laryn opened the door to welcome the two members of the closed council into their royal suite. Therek's appearance was nothing notable, but Kaellor could count on one hand the number of times he sat in the same room with the leader of the Spicers. He stood and offered her a seat at the small table. A bright scarf designating her station among one of the Luna Rova clans pulled back dark curls of hair. The woman dipped her head and sat down.

"Anything else to report this evening? Anyone?" asked Kaellor. When no one answered, he continued, "Kal, any predictions regarding when the Kreeg forces might attack?"

"We expect at least another week before the entire host of the Kreeg army arrives. After that, given their blatant destruction of the border kingdoms, we anticipate the conflict to begin in earnest."

"Unless anyone has anything else, I suggest we adjourn for this evening. One of us will always be available by shek for any emergencies. Until tomorrow, eyes to the horizon."

Kaellor stood behind his chair and allowed his shek to fall dormant. He considered Therek's arrival with Salveen. The woman returned his gaze, polite but unwavering. Therek remained uncharacteristically reserved. Kaellor walked across the room and retrieved a bottle of resco and four glasses. He poured a finger in each, and Therek retrieved his glass, drank the entire portion in one gulp, then tapped the rim, indicating a desire for more.

Kaellor obliged and added a second finger to his own glass. "Is it that bad then?"

Therek swirled the amber liquor. "It's not bad exactly, but you are not going to like what we have to say."

"Which is why you came in person," said Kaellor.

Therek bobbed his head side to side, with unusual indecision, and Salveen broke the odd silence. "Your Highness, what we have to say should probably not be communicated through the shek. The fewer people who know, the better."

"Alright. You have my undivided attention," said Kaellor.

The regent took a smaller sip of resco, pursed his lips and blew out the fumes, then continued, "We know why Bryndor hasn't reached out through the shek. I just received word from the sender, Craxton. His brother, Dexxin, rides as part of Bryndor's escort. Apparently, Bryndor made some kind of arrangement with the Ilovesh."

Kaellor took a large gulp of his own resco, but held his tongue, waiting for his friend to continue.

"The details are not entirely clear, but in order to recruit the aid of the Ilovesh, and help Lluthean emerge from the constraints of the Revealing, Bryndor had to surrender his gift. He can no longer channel," said Therek.

The news washed over Kaellor, sobering and unwelcome. So many questions bubbled in his mind. "What about the others? Any of them could have used the shek to communicate with us."

"I inquired. Apparently, the ritual Bryndor endured ruined his shek. It's a dormant piece of jewelry now," said Therek.

"Is he otherwise well?" asked Laryn.

"They travel with a medic, Tovnik. He assessed Bryndor and found no injury or malady except that our heir is oddly severed from his gift. They are making a hasty return, skirting the north edge of the Stillness, and anticipate arriving near the Pillars in about one week."

"What boon did he secure from the Ilovesh for his sacrifice?" asked Kaellor.

Therek nodded, anticipating the question. "Apparently, we have misjudged the significance of the reflecting pool in the inner sanctum. It's somehow connected to a pool of similar consequence in the Ilovesh kingdom. They refer to it as a deepening well. One of them, the emissary they first met, an Ilovesh named Seldora, is, apparently, traveling here through the deepening well and is supposed to emerge from the pool within the week. When he arrives, he should be able to aid Lluthean's return."

Kaellor mulled over the revelations. "That's a lot of things that are supposed to coincide within a week: the Kreeg's attack, Bryn's return, and the arrival of this foreigner who has demonstrated dubious motives. I can't tell if that's by the Giver's divine touch or the Taker's grip."

"And, I'm sorry to say, my friend, that we are not done with this evening's revelations," said Therek. The regent looked sidelong at

Salveen, who had cupped her resco in two hands, inhaling the fumes but declining the drink.

"We each have our part to play if the kingdom is to survive the abrogator's assault on the kingdom. Yours, it seems, is not within the walls of Stone's Grasp, Your Highness." The woman spoke softly, with a reverence that underscored her apparent sincerity.

Therek adjusted himself in his seat and leaned forward, propping gangly forearms on the table. "Salveen is a prophet, Kae. Her gift of premonition is stronger than anything I've ever managed. We've relied on her insights to make any number of critical decisions in the past year. At her request, I've taken credit for many of those premonitions. We've been . . . comparing visions for confirmation. And I believe that she is correct."

"I get the feeling I'm not going to like this particular bit of prophecy," said Kaellor.

Therek and Salveen shared a look once again. The regent nodded, encouraging her to explain. "Your Highness, my visions have been clear. You need to meet Bryndor on the outskirts of the Great Crown, somewhere near the eastern of the Pillar of Eldrek. If you remain here, Bryndor doesn't survive the return trip and, worse, Aarindorn falls to shadow and ash."

The woman paused, lifting a gentle gaze to Laryn, then turned back to him. "You need to see him first, before kingdom and before politics or none of it will matter."

Hearing the echo of words he once uttered to Laryn in the privacy of their own suite was more than sobering. He sat back in his chair, unsure what to make of the revelations. "Would you mind if I seek confirmation myself?"

"You would not be the man I respect if you took such information on faith. Please, subject our premise to your gift," said Therek.

Kaellor channeled into his runes of balance and judgment, and focused on Therek's proposal with ferocious intensity. With eyes closed, he turned over the possible scenarios in his mind: remaining in Stone's Grasp to help coordinate the military response and preserving the wards that prevented abrogators from entering the city, or traveling to the edge of the kingdom. To his surprise, the path beyond Stone's Grasp felt right.

Giver, if you're listening, you know I would love nothing more than to be with him, but how can it be better for me to release the wards that protect Stone's Grasp?

He tried to imagine directing the Aarindorian forces from the safety of Stone's Grasp, and an oppressive shadow invaded his thoughts, leeching his breath and even pressing him down into the chair. With a gasp, he stifled his channeling, then opened his eyes to see his friend staring back with empathy.

His knuckles stroked against the grain of his beard. "Alright, I believe you. But what about the wards? Tarkannen already tried to breach them once. If I leave, we can't be certain they will hold."

Salveen rested both hands on the table and rolled her palms up. "Though the visions have been consistent, they're still only visions, possible futures. We can't be certain of anything, Your Highness. For as much as it gives us concern, fearing what might happen if the wards drop pales in comparison to the destruction visited upon me, on both of us, in our visions if you stay," she explained.

"When do you think we should leave?" asked Laryn.

Therek and Salveen shared a look of uncertainty, but Kaellor didn't need their advice. "Love, you can't go. One of us has to stay here. Someone from the royal line has to remain in Stone's Grasp in case—"

"In case you don't make it back?" she finished.

"Yes. But more than that, we don't have any idea what condition Llu will be in when he returns to us. You're the only healer with the experience to help him," said Kaellor.

She stared at him, and emotions colored her face. Stubborn, righteous anger tightened the muscles of her brow, but as she searched his eyes, her expression softened. The redness in her cheeks cooled, and at last she relaxed her shoulders, accepting the truth of his words. Finally, she shook her head from side to side. "You just want to be on the front lines swinging that guardian blade."

He grabbed her hand. "If any of the Kreeg or Tarkannen's minions cross my path, I might just have to do that. But if my leaving gives

Aarindorn a chance, and if my staying means Bryn dies, then there's no choice, love."

Therek finished his resco and tapped his glass on the table. "I hate to say it, but I agree. And to be frank, you should leave in the morning, Kae. As it stands, you'll be hard-pressed to get beyond Eldrek's Wall without the Kreeg scouts findings you. We can coordinate your departure with the overwarden, and you can continue to participate in the briefings through the shek. Nobody else need know that you are out of Stone's Grasp."

Another knock on the door interrupted further conversation. Kaellor stood and answered to find Karragin standing in the hallway, her riftwing perched on her shoulder. He signed, *"Please come in."*

Karragin dipped her chin. "I can hear you through Iska, but the signing is a kindness all the same, Your Highness."

Karragin entered but stopped short upon finding the others in the room. "Apologies, I should have asked about guests. I can return later."

"Nonsense," said Kaellor. "There are no secrets in this room. Please, tell us what brought you here."

Karragin tilted her head and rubbed her cheek against the bird's wing. "Iska visited Lluthean, in the Revealing, or the Drift, or wherever he is. I was able to communicate with Neska and overheard the strangest conversation."

Karragin rarely betrayed her emotions, but genuine concern flavored her expression. "Llu has not been idle. From what I can tell, he's been training with some sort of spirit, an Ilovesh if I understood correctly. She's been training him about his tether and ways to defend himself when he returns."

"Why does that give you pause?" asked Therek.

"Because, Father, I'm not so sure that what she has been teaching him is valuable. I can't explain it, really, but Neska seemed reserved, or nervous maybe? It felt like even she wasn't sure that what he was doing was safe. She said he was becoming what he needed to become, but it sounded like he was losing parts of himself to get there. Does that make any sense?"

Kaellor gripped his beard so hard that his chin stung. He turned to Laryn. "It's more confirmation that when I leave, you should remain."

"Did you learn anything else? Anything more specific about Neska's concern?" asked Laryn.

"This is going to sound really weird, but I think an Ilovesh is going to pay us a visit through the reflecting pool in the inner sanctum."

Chapter Sixty-Eight: A Girl Named Pash

Ranika's mind walked through the old, familiar nightmare. The inebriated Lord Drassle pursued her through the shadows along the Callishite harbor. He staggered closer, and Mogdure's breath, the man reeked of armpit sweat and ale. He brandished the bloodied tankard he had used to dash in her mother's skull. Normally, this was about the time the events caused her pulse to thrum, quickening her gift; like the first time she cloaked herself in shadows.

Instead of traveling through the turbulent imagery as a powerless passenger, she managed the dream, shaping it to her purpose. Her gift rose to her bidding, and she stepped from the shadows to face Lord Drassle. Tentacles of nadir sprang from her forearms, immobilizing the man, then she simply tore him limb from limb.

She felt no satisfaction in his precipitous end, so she replayed the scenario. In the second version of the events, she tossed him back over the edge of the cliffside and watched him dash against the rocky shore of the Callishite bay. There was a brief reward when he cried out, but nothing that mollified her anger.

More conflicts unfolded in her mind until at last, she held him firm, then struck him with a single reductive shard and dissolved pieces of him one by one: first his manhood, then his hands, and finally his eyes. That last one was . . . better. It left him alive and suffering, bereft of any means of inflicting harm on any other woman in Callish.

The echo of a voice shifted her attention. It was Bryndor. Without explanation, they were sitting under a canopy of pine while rain pattered down around them. Part of her clung to the prior scenario. There was something powerful about holding the image of Drassle in that vulnerable state; powerful but dark.

Bryndor spoke her name again, and she encouraged the dream sequence to embellish his surroundings. The smell of rain and pine gave her comfort. He sat not three feet away and offered her a cup of hot tea and spoke to her in a measured tone. "It's already too much. Look, I know what it is to wake up and the first thing you think about is how you're going to kill your enemy. I still wrestle with the grip of that anger, and the man who killed Rona has wandered the Drift for a year now. I've got to believe that's not the life Red would want for you."

A hazy shadow leaned over Bryndor's shoulder, and Reddevek's face resolved. He stared at her first with one eye, then shifted to the other, then at last crossed both and stuck out his tongue. The vacancy of a palpable ache settled in her chest, and she struggled even to draw the air to speak his name.

"He's right, little gnat. You were meant for better things. Drassle is in the past. Keep your eyes to the horizon. The world needs all of its gifted. That includes you," said Reddevek.

A strange scraping sound invaded the dream, and Reddevek began rummaging through her pack. His arms lifted and discarded her things with a dramatic flair, each movement causing a visible, rancid cloud of body odor to pollute the atmosphere. Something was wrong with him. His behavior felt contrived, incongruous with the joy she felt at their reunion. Her mind withdrew from the imagery, and she fluttered her eyes open.

She lay on her side on the cold mountain stone, and it felt as if her shoulder had pushed its way to the center of her chest. The sound of something or someone rustling through her things brought her orientation into focus. The hollow clank of her empty canteen rang out as it struck the ground. Then there was that smell, the unmistakable reek of a man who had spent too many days without bathing in the same set of clothes.

She moved a hand to her belt, searching for the ruby-hilted dagger. *That's right, I gave it to the Balladurens, along with Zippy, to show as proof of my death. It's gone, Zippy's gone, and I sent them on their way so I'd have a better chance of slipping past the Kreeg scouts. Foden's teeth, I should have at least asked them to stay until I could channel again.*

She reached out instinctively for the flows of nadir, but they flowed across her with no more substance than a faint breeze. A gurgling rumble traveled across her stomach, and she panted through a wave of nausea. The lingering effects of Eldrenol's solution still sapped her strength. With a pained grunt, stiff muscles resisting movement, she rolled to her hands and knees.

A man, rawboned and dressed in soiled leathers, squatted not more than two paces away. At least two weapons, a knife and short sword, hung off his hips. He glared at her once without menace, more an acknowledgment that he was well aware of her movement, then upended her small pack.

He set the moonstone to the side and combed through her other meager possessions. In the bright daylight, he failed to notice the pale blue glittering crystal of the moonstone. She watched him sort out her possessions: a simple comb, a pouch of tea, and another of salt for cooking were pushed to the side, along with a bound lock of Zippy's mane.

He popped open the tin of boot grease Reddevek had traded from the Luna Rova and sniffed at the contents, even dipping a finger into the grease and running it across his tongue. Finally, he held up the silver flask with copper filigree she had pilfered from the bakery in the Delve.

Without making eye contact, he spoke in the guttural Kreeg accent. "Girl. What is this?"

"Well, for starters, it's mine."

He pushed out his lower lip. "Not anymore. Come, tell me what's in this. Is it of any value?"

Ranika had been shaken down more times than she could count on the streets of Callish. She slumped her shoulders and made herself appear even more vulnerable, casting her eyes to the ground. "It's truffle oil, for food. You can dip bread in it, or use it to fry. I got it from a bakery, the Golden Crust. You can likely sell it, or trade it for something."

He nodded to himself and began to replace the items in her pack. "Why does a girl wander alone in the mountains?"

"I got lost and then I was robbed. Two men stole my horse and my only valuable possession. They didn't even leave me my knife."

The scout stepped forward and, without waiting for permission, gripped the muscles of her upper arm, then pulled down on the skin under her eye. He rubbed a thumb across her cheek, showing her the purple smear of Eldrenol's solution.

She sighed and wiped her face on her sleeve. "I think the men who robbed me used that to make me sleep. Did I get it all off?"

"Yes, better." He removed her scarf and pulled back in surprise, then patted the palm of his hand against an unruly sprig of her hair. He pulled on the curl several times and watched it spring back. "Teeth," he said.

Ranika wasn't sure she had heard him correctly. "What?"

"Show your teeth."

She slowly lowered her jaw, standing fish-mouthed for his inspection. He removed a palm-sized mirror and reflected sunlight into her face. "Good. You will come with me. Talk to captain. If you survive, maybe we keep you. Can you cook?"

She bobbed her head agreeably. "Yes. I'm a fair cook."

The scout shrugged. "Some truths are self-evident. It's not mean to treat the ant . . . like an ant. Now turn around."

He unshouldered his own pack and withdrew a coil of rope. "You don't have to tie me up. I have nowhere to go. In fact, I was hoping you might take me with you," she said.

In seconds, his nimble fingers wove a noose, which he placed around her neck. Next, he made her shoulder her own pack, then bound her wrists together. Blessedly, the cord felt smooth against her skin, and he didn't pull it tight, but cinched it around his waist. He replaced her scarf, pulling the edges tight and smashing the curls against her forehead, causing more discomfort than the rope.

"Come. We have lost time and I must meet the others tonight."

He set off walking northeast, but instead of descending to the Borderlands, they began a winding climb up into the Great Crown. In minutes, her breath came labored, and the muscles in her legs burned with fatigue. "Might I at least know your name? Mine is—"

"Yours is Pash. It means slave. You can call me Behklek."

She stumbled behind the man. If she walked too many paces behind him, the noose at her neck tightened. If she scurried too close, the man's body odor churned her stomach. She settled for the latter and tried to breathe through her mouth. "Behklek, that's a foreign name. I heard rumors of an army. Is that you?"

"Yes, Pash. I am one of many emissaries from the mighty kingdom of Kreeg. We need to find passage beyond these mountains. You will share what you know with my captain."

Ranika knew she should continue to foster the belief that she was insignificant, but fatigue sharpened her tongue. "So, why does a Kreeg scout rob a girl in the mountains? Doesn't your krug rai'al pay you well enough?"

Behklek turned with a slight grin. "If you know the name of our king, then you have met others like me before, yes? Besides, all this you see is soon to be Kreeg. And what is Kreeg is already mine, not yours. The sooner Pash learns this, the better."

Ranika's staggering feet matched her mental stumble, and she cursed inwardly. "I did meet one other like you. Coglek, if I got the name right."

Behklek drew up short, obviously recognizing the name, but spat to the side. "Pretty girl like you, alone? If you survived a night with Coglek, then either you did not see Coglek or something else happened. I think it is not the first thing. Where is Coglek now? He missed a meet two days ago."

"I was with friends before. They left now, fleeing the Kreeg army. They had words with Coglek, and he left. That's all I know."

He looked past her, his gaze searching the cliffs above. "Where are these friends now? Is there a way inside these mountains? The krug rai'al would reward you for such information."

"Not that I know of. My friends travel by caravan in the foothills. They planned to settle north of here for the season."

"Hmm. We know of this caravan, harmless rovers. But still, they left you behind? This makes no sense."

"I got lost. My horse spooked, and then I was robbed, and then you found me."

If Behklek believed her, he made no comment. As exhaustion overtook her, the effort of picking up her feet and pacing her breathing prevented her from initiating further conversation. Several hours later, he stopped at a stream long enough for her to drink her fill.

She reached out once again for nadir. Where before the sensation felt like a gust of wind through her fingers, now it seemed more palpable, like water. But she failed to bring the force to her bidding. Behklek gave her two sharp jerks of the rope, and they continued on in silence.

As the afternoon wore on, her breathing acclimated and her legs felt more vigorous. The sun dipped below the western edge of the Great Crown and the temperature plummeted just as they reached the top of a long and winding trail.

Spread across a plateau, a camp of more than thirty Kreeg scouts milled about. The entire lot, men and women, appeared cast from the same grizzled mold as Behklek. Far different from the chaotic sights and sounds of a Luna Rova camp, the Kreeg scouts carried on in professional silence. Each of the "emissaries" wore similar weapons and gear. Some sharpened their weapons, others sat around a fire applying salve to sore feet or rubbing oil into boots.

Behklek walked directly to the center of camp, nodding at his companions without speaking. They approached a Kreeg who stood beside a fire turning a crude spit. Behklek untied the rope from his waist and used the excess to bind her ankles. She had enough slack to take short steps and could use her arms, but the bindings were more than adequate to prevent escape.

He lifted his chin to his colleague. "Captain, this is Pash."

A salt and pepper beard framed the face of the captain. The veteran focused on the sizzling meat. "You are late. All because of a pash?" He eyed Ranika and spat into the flames. "She is not worth the food it will take to keep her alive. You chose poorly."

Behklek shrugged with indifference. "Maybe. But she met Coglek. She traveled with the rover caravan. She might know more about these mountains."

At the mention of Coglek, the captain whistled for another to turn the spit, then turned to inspect Ranika with renewed focus. "When did you see Coglek?"

Ranika didn't have to pretend to be fatigued, and allowed the weight of her bindings to exaggerate her distress. "Three, four days back maybe? I was with the Luna Rova. We were traveling by caravan on the southern edge of these mountains. He shared the fire and had words with the speaker."

The man considered her with a predatory gaze, but where Coglek voyeuristically undressed her, the captain seemed to be considering the veracity of her statement. "Did you meet Coglek?"

As Ranika spoke, she labored both to edit her words and yet sound credible. "No, sir. I did sit close enough to the fire to listen. We don't get strangers in the Luna Rova very often. I was curious. He asked the speaker about a way through the Great Crown. They shared words, a bit of food, and then I was asked to leave. I didn't get to hear what else they talked about. But everybody in camp knew we entertained a stranger. And by morning, he was gone."

"And what did your speaker say when he asked her about passage into the heart of Aarindorn?" pressed the captain.

"Everyone knows the only way in is through the Pillars, sir," said Ranika.

She should have expected the blow, but in her attempt to appear meek, she'd kept her gaze on the ground and didn't see the captain's backhand until it flared across her face. Pain blossomed across her cheek, and the salty, iron taste of blood painted the back of her tongue. Ranika released an involuntary grunt and fell to the ground only to be hoisted to her feet by Behklek.

"I don't think the captain believes you, Pash," hissed the scout.

Ranika glared at the captain. He gripped her jaw in one hand and turned her head back and forth as if he could see inside her. She considered spitting in his face, but swallowed a mouthful of blood-tinged spit and returned his glare without emotion. He lifted his hand to strike again and paused, a look of surprise dawning on his face.

"I can take her to task, Captain. Me and the boys could probably beat some sense into her. I bet we can get her to talk," said Behklek.

"She's not afraid, didn't even shed a tear," said the captain. He released her jaw and stepped back. "You see, Pash, we know the Luna Rova migrated out of the Great Crown, which means there must be a way into the Great Crown. I am going to grant you this one night of reprieve. Put her to work, Behklek. In the morning, if she can't see fit to share that knowledge with us, strip her down, have the men rape her, then kill her. And since you were the last to return to camp tonight, you're on perimeter patrol."

The captain strode off to another campfire and engaged other scouts in jovial conversation. Behklek leaned in. "Thanks for that, Pash. If you hadn't soured his mood, I wouldn't have to go hungry tonight. He's not joking. Whatever you know, tell him in the morning."

Ranika gave the man her best Karragin face, showing neither fear nor anger, and the scout shook his head in disbelief. "Have it your way."

He turned to the Kreeg man tending the fire. "You heard the captain. May as well make her turn the spit. And don't burn the meat, Pash."

Behklek stomped off into the darkness, and Ranika manned the spit. Her arms ached with fatigue, but at least, standing so close to the smoke, she lost track of the collective stink of the Kreeg scouts. A few hours later, with the rations parceled out, one of the scouts dropped three sets of boots, a wire brush, and boot polish at her feet.

She sat down by the embers and got to work, finishing the last pair by the pale light of the blue moon. When none of the others approached her with other tasks, Ranika slumped onto her back, utterly exhausted. Her dreams evolved beyond her awareness or control. She awoke to a panicked voice and Behklek shaking her to consciousness in the early morning hours. "Pash! Pash, what happened?"

Ranika blinked open her eyes and stifled a yawn. "I cleaned the boots. Nobody gave me anything else to do, so I slept. I'll meet the captain, I'll tell him everything. Just let me get some sleep."

Behklek stepped back and withdrew his short sword, holding it out, arm shaking. Something had the man riled up. "Get up. You did something. What did you do?"

Ranika rolled to her side and then pushed up to her knees and elbows. She gazed across the camp. To her relief, there was no wave of nausea or even the bone-aching fatigue she expected to feel. Countless forms lay slumbering on the ground. The only sign of life came from Behklek. "I don't know what you want me to see; everyone is still sleeping, which is what I should be doing."

"They are not sleeping, you damned Pash, they are dead! All of them, even the captain, dead! What did you do?" Behklek screamed, and spittle flew from his mouth.

Ranika reached up and scratched to relieve a particularly itchy strand of hair on the nape of her neck. Because of the ropes, she had to use both hands, which was a nuisance. "All of them? Moons. I thought the baker's poison might make some of you sick, but I guess a little bit goes a long way."

Behklek stammered, unable to respond for several seconds. A maniacal expression eventually settled across his face as her words penetrated his disbelief. He lifted his arm to chop at her with his blade, and Ranika surged her nadir. Without forethought, four onyx shards erupted from her palms. Two impaled his feet, searing through his boots and sizzling into the ground, leaving blackened holes. The other two plunged into each shoulder. The attack, initiated, sequenced, and deployed, concluded with the efficiency of an adder strike.

Next, she coiled a reductive tentacle around her body, and the ropes fell in tattered pieces to the ground. She rose to her feet, thinking about the moment she had felt her ability to channel return. It was last night, after she had finished with the boots but before she drifted off to sleep.

Behklek gasped in pain and staggered back to a seated position. His arms hung lifeless from odd, vacant cavitations where his shoulders used to be. Blackened bone and sinew stretched across the empty sockets and dark blood oozed from the wounds. "You are a child of Mogdurian. Why? Why would you do this?"

"Tell you what. I'm done answering your questions. You Kreeg think you're the boot and everyone else is an ant. I'm not an ant. I never was. None of the decent people who live in this part of the world are ants."

The man shook his torso in a comical attempt to get his arms to move. Several seconds later, he cursed and glared at her. "The Kreeg army will wash away all of you from these lands!"

Ranika leaned in and flicked him hard on the nose. "Do I have your attention?"

Behklek spat and cursed more, so Ranika drafted a tentacle of nadir and coiled the appendage around the scout's neck. She waited, feeling him wriggle under her power, and eventually tightened the coil. He panted but stopped his thrashing and looked at her.

She brushed a spiral of hair from her face. "How many Kreeg scouts are left in this part of the Great Crown?"

The man snarled a lip and hocked another glob of spit. Ranika drafted a second, smaller tentacle and slapped him in the berries. "Don't do that. I'm trying to have a conversation here, but if you anger me, I'll crush them one at a time and grind the rest into sausage. It's really no less than your captain threatened me with last night."

The man paled and swallowed, then visibly deflated. "There are two other companies, but they are farther south. Already they meet up with the main host."

"What about the grot? How many of them are left and who controls them?" she pressed.

"Those beasts? They have their own chain of command. Most raid in units with an elite. Some travel with grondle. They do not answer to my commanders. We leave them, and for the most part they leave us. As for their numbers, I cannot say, but they are held on the northwest flank. If you crossed them here, they are raiding on their own."

Ranika wondered what else she might get from the man, but then didn't really know what kind of questions she should be asking an enemy combatant. At any rate, he was in no condition to cause her harm. She leaned forward and unbuckled his belt to remove the dagger at his hip. Up close, the smell was as revolting as the bizarre cavities where her nadir shards had burned away his tissue. She glanced at one of the wounds, which glistened black with a bubbled edge of lung that billowed back and forth with his breath.

Mogdure's breath, she hadn't meant to do all that to the man.

She strapped on the dagger, situating it on her hip where the ruby-hilted blade used to sit. Some kind of leather gave the grip a nice feel, and the metal pommel curved back in a hawk's bill. She thumbed the curved edges, appreciating the scout's diligence in keeping the weapon clean and serviceable.

Next, she removed his pack and unceremoniously dumped the contents onto the ground. She knelt down and gathered a ball of waxed hemp, flint and steel, dried fruit and jerky rations, a coil of rope similar to what he had used on her, and finally an oiled skin. She placed these into her own pack along with her moonstone and the lock of Zippy's hair before releasing the coil of nadir wrapped around his neck.

The man stretched his neck and used his feet to wedge his back against a boulder. "We are not so different. I take from you, and you take from me. Not because it is right, but because you can. This is why the Kreeg come."

"There might be some truth in what you say. But does any part of you feel that what you tried to do to me was wrong?"

The scout shifted his weight and dropped his eyes, so she continued, "Because what you did, and what you tried to do, what the Kreeg are doing? It's all wrong. If you and I met in Kreeg, I would never stop to rob you or . . ." She stepped back and shook her head in disgust. "Or take you prisoner. You see the difference?"

He pursed his lips but couldn't meet her eyes. "It's not so different."

Ranika threw up her hands. "You're a monk. I'll leave you to your misery. Hopefully, one of your scout buddies will find you. It's more grace than you deserve."

She shaded her eyes and searched for the best way across the high places. She had to admit, without his guidance, she might never have found her way up this far. Not five steps away, the scout called out, his voice echoing across the mountains. "We will find you! You and your friends, your rovers—all of you will answer for this!"

Ranika stopped. She didn't really want to kill another person. Reddevek's words echoed in her thoughts. *You were meant for better things.*

Then she thought of Bryndor, and Ksenia, the Outriders, and even Neska. She thought of the way Dania made her feel wanted, and how Vekkuh made her feel significant. All these people gave her life meaning, made her laugh, made her feel safe, made her feel loved. They were her better things.

She manufactured a thin web of nadir and draped it from her head to her feet, removing all remnants of the Kreeg stink, the campfire, even the bruise on the side of her face. Without another thought, and without looking back, she surged more of her gift into a tight ball of spikes and shards, then detonated the globe immediately behind her. She didn't have to look back to confirm the outcome.

"You're right, Red. All I can do is try to do better."

Ranika Taim adjusted her pack, situated her new dagger on her hip, and searched the horizon of the Great Crown until she found a familiar landmark: the eastern Pillar of Eldrek. She thought back to the vision she had witnessed in the reading with Vekkuh, and without another thought of Behklek or any of the dead scouts, she set out.

Chapter Sixty-Nine: A Race Against the Sun

Nolan crept forward through the underbrush and checked the corpse of a grotvonen. He had remained perched high in the trees and tracked the roaming creature for two hours by the light of the moon of Baellen. It had finally caught his scent and approached close enough that he feared their camp would be discovered.

The bowshot would have been nothing remarkable by the light of day, but in the darkness, he had to rely on his gift for sighting and aiming. If he had missed the creature, it would have howled and alerted others in the area. The grotvonen's signature dwindled under his gift, a sure sign of the kill shot, but he had to be certain.

The creature reeked of oily musk. It was one of the smaller, swift ones that the grotvonen used as spies. Instead of running like a human, this one had calloused knuckles from running on all fours. The arrow had punctured through one shoulder and must have hit a lung, or maybe even its heart. It had dropped dead, thank the Giver.

He gripped the shaft, and with a sharp, jerking motion, withdrew the arrow. His gift cast all about; countless grotvonen trails flared in his augmented sight. Fortunately, no other beasts approached their location.

He looked back down the hill and swept his gaze back across the Vastlands. In the distance, the four druska lounged near the Aarindin. In the past week, Bryndor had pushed a brutal pace to return home, challenging even the Aarindin. Nolan had never thought any animals capable of matching the Aarindin's stamina, but the druska had disabused him of that sheltered notion. It made him wonder about how many other things he might unlearn if he traveled beyond the confines of Aarindorn.

The first part of their return journey had been uneventful. Ksenia managed the druska through her sympath gift. The rest of them took turns rotating guard duty at night. The Ilovesh's recommendations to avoid the Stillness had easily shaved two or three days from their journey.

Those easy days of travel across the Vastlands had lulled them into a false sense of security. The pace was brisk but uneventful, and the ample supply of hesk allowed them to eat without pausing to hunt. They enjoyed fair weather and restful sleep. They had shared stories, easy smiles, and comfortable nights around the campfire.

On their third night camping under the stars, all of that had changed. It was the wolvryn, Boru, who had tipped them off. Though severed from his gift, Bryndor could still embrace the wolvryn's augmented senses. Together, they identified small groups of grotvonen roaming the western edge of the Vastlands. The small grot packs acted more like wild animals. None of them carried weapons or wore armor. Nolan suspected they were deserters or undisciplined beasts who had migrated east in search of easy prey.

They had avoided the packs in the first few days but skirmished on two occasions in the last afternoon. Now, as the silhouette of the Great Crown loomed on the horizon, the Taker saw fit to complicate their return. As the moon of Baellen rose, so many campfires dotted the western horizon that their collective glow created an umber miasma under the night sky.

To make matters worse, the grotvonen packs thinned only to be replaced by crushes of grondle. Out on the plains, with little cover, they could likely manage a few of the muscled beasts, but not a crush. With that thought in mind, Nolan adjusted the filter of his gift and surveyed the area for umbral and then grondle.

Finding none of the invaders nearby, he retreated to their camp. Boru rose to his feet as Nolan approached. The wolvryn sniffed at the wind and tilted his head. Nolan signed, *"One grot, dead. All safe for now."*

"He appreciates that," said Bryndor.

Nolan turned to find his friend offering him a canteen of water. He upended the canteen, slaking his thirst. "When we came out of the ursulu forest, you didn't wait for Ksenia to use her gift. You told him everything in the hand language."

Bryndor nodded and gave him a soft smile. "Our time in the Revealing . . . let's just say it changed us. Anyway, he appreciates being treated like one of the team."

Nolan giggled. "One of the team? I think the rest of us are grateful he's here. I can't count how many times he's allowed us to avoid a confrontation, and it's no secret we lean on him to alert us while we sleep."

Bryndor stretched arms overhead and yawned. "That's the Giver's truth. You were gone longer than I expected. Find any trouble?"

"A lone grot scout, but the area between us and the foothills of the Great Crown is thick with grondle."

Bryndor chewed on his lower lip. "Is that woodsmoke on the air?"

"Yes, it's the Kreeg. See that faint red glow on the western horizon? That's them. I climbed a tree and . . . it's like nothing I've ever seen before."

"It sounds like you're saying we're too late. Can the mounts get us to the Pillars safely?"

Nolan considered the density of the enemy camped along the Borderlands. "I don't think so. We would never avoid detection, and even if we managed to stay ahead of any pursuers, you heard Dexxin's last report. The Outriders have the entire region trapped with deadfalls, pits, and munitions. We might escape the enemy and run headlong into friendly fire."

"How many hours of riding until we reach the foothills? Up there, we might stand a reasonable chance of defending ourselves. Out here, we're just waiting to be overrun by an enemy we can't hope to fight."

"Best guess? Three hours, maybe four."

"Well, that settles it. Wake the others. We need to skin out now. We'll have Boru lead us into the foothills. If we hurry, we should be able to find cover before sunrise."

Nolan dropped his chin and rolled his neck back and forth, stretching muscles that threatened to cramp. He loathed the idea of a brisk ride in the darkness. The druska had demonstrated themselves to be as sure-footed as any Aarindin, but even a first-week tender in the Outriders knew not to push a mount under such circumstances. The Aarindin had to manage every stride with balanced perfection every time. Gravity only had to win once.

He considered telling his friend as much, but Bryndor had already knelt down by Ksenia's bedroll. He ran the back of one finger against her cheek, coaxing her to wakefulness. Giver's last breath, the prince really loved the woman. Not that Ksenia was hard to love, but somehow in the last year, those two had become more than he would have imagined. He and Savnah exchanged passions, and he both respected and cared for the woman, but could he say he really loved her?

With Bryndor and Ksenia, there was no question. Their mutual love affected everything they did, every day, in hundreds of tiny ways. He cared for her concerns before ever addressing his own, and she acted much the same way. In idle conversations, they spoke of each other with not just adoration, but genuine respect. It was a relationship that felt more like two old souls rather than something only newly blossomed. It reminded Nolan of his parents. To see it up close, not just modeled but lived so naturally in a world of endless conflict . . . it felt like something rare.

He turned at the sound of Savnah's rhythmic, droning snore. The woman lay on her back, mouth agape, muscled arms twitching. One of her hands gripped the haft of a moonblade axe, but the weapon remained tethered to her belt. She was perfectly imperfect, and a smile crept across his face. He could love this woman, did love her already in some ways. The question, he supposed, was did she love him?

Savnah's voice echoed in his mind, and he laughed inwardly. *Not something you'll figure out this morning, scout boy.*

He didn't trust that Savnah's response to being awakened in the middle of a battle dream would be as welcoming as Ksenia was to Bryndor. So, he retrieved a canteen and slice of hesk, then tapped the toe of his boot on her foot. She snorted a breath in, sat upright, and rubbed

726

at eye grounds. "It's still dark and I'm not on watch this morning. What's wrong?"

"It's a three- to four-hour ride to the foothills of the Great Crown, but the area is riddled with grondle, and the Kreeg have already arrived. There is no way for us to cross through the Pillars."

He took a knee and offered her the water and rations. She accepted both in silence. To her credit, Savnah synthesized the information without complaint. That too was new. Last year she would have berated him first and asked questions later. "Thanks, Nolan. Help me up?"

Savnah held out a hand, and he pulled her to her feet. She chewed down the last bit of hesk and grimaced, pounded a fist to her chest, then swallowed more water. "We're later than we intended, and Bryn wants to push on under cover of night?"

"You sorted that out fast."

She shrugged. "I could smell the woodsmoke as I fell asleep and wondered as much. What's his plan then, cross the Great Crown?"

"We didn't get that far. For now, we're pretty exposed out here. It's the Giver's blessing that we've not run across a crush of grondle, but if we push close, in the daylight? I don't like our odds. We could backtrack to the east, but—"

"Then we run the risk of bumping into a larger grotvonen pack. Taker's grip. Alright, well, if nothing else, we can likely skirt the mountains and travel north, seclude ourselves well beyond the conflict, and maybe Dexxin can relay our position. From there, we could wait for reinforcements."

The familiar snuffle of a druska preceded the appearance of one of the mounts, and a black, fleshy snout emerged from the shadows to sniff at Savnah's ear. Bryndor had already packed up their meager possessions. Savnah stroked the long jaw of the creature. "Wake Dexxin, I'll grab Tovnik."

In minutes, they stood in a circle, reviewing Nolan's scouting report. Savnah hocked spit into the shadows. "If we're going to do this, the sooner the better. It's going to be a race against the sun as it is."

She looked to each of them for confirmation. Finding no resistance, she pressed on. "Alright, Kess, if you would, relay all of this to the anim—to our friends. Boru will take point and lead us away from any encounters. I'll be next, then Bryndor and Kess. Tov and Dexx next. Nolan, you have the rear guard. Any questions?"

They mounted up and began the final leg west toward the Great Crown. Boru loped ahead at surprising speed, and despite the druska's smooth gait, the inability to anticipate when the mount might drop into a depression or climb a hill threatened to topple him to the ground. Eventually, he shifted his hips forward and gripped the back of the broad set of antlers.

The beast fell into a steady canter with easy breathing. Grasses and shrubs whipped against his legs. Beyond that discomfort, they made swift progress over the next few hours. As the sun flared behind them on the eastern horizon, the shadow of the Great Crown rose as a craggy, unwelcoming barrier that blotted out the stars.

Gradually, twilight brought the terrain into focus. To Nolan's surprise, Boru had led them well into the foothills of the Great Crown. As they rode ever farther west, Nolan had to periodically prime his gift to track the path of the party along ravines, around rocky hills, or through stands of timber. The druska possessed intelligence rivaling the Aarindin, and always adjusted course at his prodding.

Nolan relaxed on the mount's back. They'd made it. They were nestled in the foothills of the Great Crown and should by all rights have a reasonable time finding a place to hide and wait for reinforcements. He chanced a glance over his shoulder and was relieved to see that his view remained obstructed by a rocky hillside, then barely managed to remain mounted as his druska grunted and turned to the north.

Once he recovered, Nolan deployed his arca prime. Savnah and the Aarindin had shifted course, veering to the north. He estimated he was only a few minutes behind the group, but this marked the first time that they had diverted with such a strong course correction.

The druska cantered along a relatively flat ravine. Nolan had to duck under the shelf of a rocky outcropping. He adjusted the filter of his gift, searching the area, and the corrupt taint of grondle assaulted his senses. Trails of the beasts crisscrossed all around them. The strongest emanations came from the ledge just overhead.

He reached into his pack and clutched a single brittle amber filled with embertang in one fist. His druska lurched into a gallop and separated from the shelf. The sound of clattering hooves and bestial snorts echoed from his left, and a grondle ran along the shelf, keeping pace.

One glance showed that the beast wore some kind of chest armor, and sunlight glinted off the broad blade of a massive axe. *Grind it, we ride all the way here and bump into an alpha of all things.*

Nolan settled into the rhythm of the druska and allowed his hips to scoot back. Hoping to deter or at least delay the grondle, he twisted his torso and tossed the brittle amber at the alpha with his offhand. The throw was clumsy and failed to strike the beast directly, but shattered on the ground. The grondle trumpeted out with three sharp, low-pitched snorts in disdain. It charged forward to match the druska's pace, pulling up even to them, then leaped into the ravine behind them.

He lost sight of the beast for the next few minutes, but the druska began to pant hard, grunting with fatigue. Another look over his shoulder showed the alpha making up the distance it had lost when it jumped down to the ravine.

Nolan leaned forward and yelled, "Come on, boy, give it all you got!"

The druska grunted, but instead of lurching ahead faster, the mount slowed as it followed a bend in the ravine. Behind him, the grondle snorted. *Taker's bite, was that excitement? It sounded excited.* The sound was certainly ominous.

He looked over his shoulder and the grondle, now only a few strides behind him, lifted its weapon. A wave of fear, exhilarating and nearly incapacitating, threatened to freeze him in place. He had never soiled himself while mounted, but Taker's grip, he surely could now.

He reached into his pack and was wrapping his fingers around another brittle amber when something familiar flashed to his side. Savnah stepped out from behind a tree trunk and slashed out with two hands wrapped around one of her moonblade axes. A loud crack, like a thick timber splitting, echoed across the ravine, and the front leg of the grondle sheared off at the knee. The beast bellowed and tumbled to the ground, rolling head over foot in a cloud of dust.

Nolan threw a leg over and dropped to the ground, turning in time to see the dust begin to settle. The alpha snorted and bellowed in a mixture of pain and rage. It flailed about with wild swings of its massive weapon, but Savnah danced back out of the way. With its attention focused on her, he jogged to the side then hurled his brittle amber. The egg smashed against the beast's chest piece, releasing embertang across the dark gill slits.

Seconds later, the alpha coughed, releasing pitiful, high-pitched squeals of pain. In the distance and from overhead, the rumble and clatter of hooves announced the approach of the rest of the crush. Savnah considered the alpha again, but whether it lived or died, the beast would pose no threat to them.

She placed thumb and finger between her lips and released a sharp whistle. Her druska and, thank the Giver, his walked forward. Both mounts panted. "Thanks for coming back," he said.

"Save it for later. We're not out of this yet. How many more brittle ambers have you got?"

"Two."

She nodded. "It's better than nothing but less than we need. For now, keep with me. The four of us are going to lead this crush back to the northeast. Maybe we can lose them. Who knows, without their alpha, they might even give up the chase. Don't push your mount into a gallop if you can help it. Ksenia says they can't maintain that pace, but they can canter for hours on end."

He mounted his druska and leaned forward, grabbing the back edge of the antlers once again. "Bryn and Kess?"

"If we do our job, they will be fine and we can find them after. Boru found a shallow cave under this ledge, but it's only big enough for the two of them and their Aarindin. Come on, scout boy, we need to give that crush something else to follow!"

She wheeled her druska about and they set off at a canter. Nolan primed his gift, and within five minutes they passed the cave where the wolvryn, Bryndor, and Ksenia took refuge. Savnah's druska veered to the right, taking a course to the northeast along the trail Tovnik and Dexxin took.

REVEALING THE ARCA PRIME

As they passed the cave entrance, Bryndor stepped out of the shadows and flashed a sword blade up in a grim salute. The silhouette of Boru's broad muzzle appeared just behind his shoulder. *I don't know who to pity more, those three or any unfortunate grondle who stumble across that cave.*

He turned his attention back to Savnah, the prime who wouldn't leave him behind, and their flight out of the Great Crown.

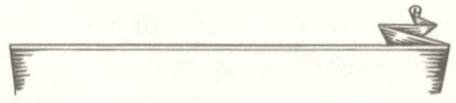

Chapter Seventy: Arrivals

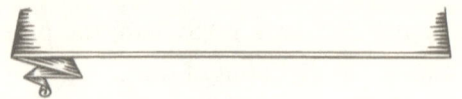

T he youth in the kingdom believe that Father's statue holds a dragon in one palm and a hawk in the other. I can't say that I understand why the prophets thought that such an important detail, but for accuracy, he holds a riftwing in one hand, and a symbol of his arca prime, the reaver, in the other. It's a metaphor really, for a creature that both siphons and magnifies zenith. Sadly, the last of its kind was found dead in the Great Crown several years ago.

—The Tome of Nivosh, 75 PC, translated by Veeble Hebben

LLUTHEAN KNELT BY THE side of the pond waiting for the surface to give him some indication of how or when he might return. Iska had returned to Karragin, leaving him alone with Neska. But when did she go? As he considered the riftwing's departure, he could not tell if she had only just left or if they had been sitting alone for an age. The pervasive inability to feel himself moving through time was maddening.

Neska must have sensed as much. She stepped close and bumped him with a shoulder, then sat down. *"Perhaps while we wait, you should check on our brothers."*

Without words, he nodded and passed a hand over the pool, willing the images to reveal Bryndor's current situation. As before, numerous images of his brother appeared, reflections of the young man's life: Bryndor working in the kitchen beside Aunt Rona, learning some of her cooking techniques, Bryndor practicing sword techniques in the predawn light of the Valley of the Cloud Walkers, Bryndor pulling a blanket around Ksenia's shoulders.

Lluthean sifted through the experiences, finding them static and well-defined. These he cast aside, understanding that they represented Bryndor's past. At last, he found a manifestation of Bryndor in which the leading edge remained poorly resolved, obscured by shadow and watery currents. He paused and settled his focus.

His brother stood at the mouth of a cave and held his sword up high in salute, or possibly a challenge. Something stirred in the shadows behind Bryndor, then Boru and Ksenia stepped to his side. "He's not alone, that's good, but what happened to him? Something's different."

Lluthean leaned in, magnified the image, and sucked in a breath when his brother cast one more look out of the cave. Intense grey eyes resolved in the image, and though Lluthean could see the outlines of Bryndor's runes, they lay dormant. "Oh, brother, what have I done to you?"

Lluthean sat back and coerced the images to give him a panorama view of the cave's surroundings. Savnah and Nolan rode the strangest mounts through rocky terrain, and behind them, a crush of grondle gave chase. He watched as the beasts pursued the Outriders onto a grassy plain, then pulled back to Bryndor.

Boru stalked out of the cave followed by his brother, Ksenia, and two Aarindin. They wound their way up a game trail, across steep inclines with loose scree, then switched back and climbed higher into the mountains. The viewing felt like it took minutes, but as Lluthean watched, willing his brother's steps forward, the sun set, rose, and set again.

A gentle flutter of wings announced Iska's return. "My Lluthean," said Neska. "Bring Karragin to your focus. She is in the inner sanctum. Something disturbs the water there."

Lluthean shifted the images, sifting through the events of Karragin's life until he found her current circumstance. She stood at the edge of the reflecting pool, saber drawn, staring at something in the depths.

Something in the woman's silent intensity lured him in, and he lost himself studying her poise, her posture. There was something vaguely familiar in the way she gripped her blade, how her simple presence in the room exuded fierce determination. It was utterly intoxicating and, again, familiar.

"You're losing the room, my Lluthean. Concentrate," said Neska.

He redirected his attention. Neska was right; he had focused so much on Karragin that the images of the inner sanctum had fallen into watery resolution. He pulled back, and the room coalesced. Benches lined the vast chamber, and the statue of Eldrek stood, arms forward, palms up, eyes to the horizon. But just as the appearance of his brother seemed oddly bereft of zenith, so too did the room appear muted.

Before he could give the matter further consideration, bubbles broke the surface of the reflecting pool and swirls of light glimmered from the depths.

"Neska, is Karragin . . . can she hear you through Iska? Send Iska back and tell Karra not to kill the bald Ilovesh!"

TRAVEL THROUGH THE deepening well should evoke a sense of reverence. Somaya and two other ancient Ilovesh had accomplished the task once, but the elders, choosing isolation, had forbade further use of the conduit to connect to the outside races. Despite the momentous endeavor, Seldora found the experience tedious, even mundane.

The fluid of the conduit sluiced across his body as he continued to propel himself in what could only be described as forward, toward his perception of light at the end of a long tunnel. Except it was not just a tunnel. The deepening well was expansive beyond his comprehension. On the few occasions that he chanced a glance over his shoulder, all he could sense were turbulent swirls of fluid disturbed in his wake. The region of the well expanded far beyond the faint radius of light cast by his borrowed runes.

He snapped his attention forward and realized, not for the first time, that he had lost his bearings. He shifted the flow of zenith once again into the runes on his forearms. He had come to understand that these imparted wisdom, insight, and even orientation. Perhaps clarity was a better explanation for the sensation he felt. Regardless, in moments, the beacon of light resolved in his vision, and he chided himself for losing his focus.

That is the challenge of this place: surviving the mundane and preserving one's focus.

A quick burst of rune fire sent him on his way. His thoughts wandered. Already he missed the way Sephora had visited him in her time of lingering. He wished even now that he could seek her counsel, exchange barbs, and determine if his path was indeed the one that would lead to their redemption. At least she'd found peace in the merging; for that small miracle, he was thankful.

He sighed, and the gesture caused particles of zenith to strafe through his lungs, at once tingly and slightly itchy of all things. By the moons, how long had he been in the well, and when would the journey end?

Just as those thoughts rose in his mind, the distant beacon of light expanded, dilating into a brilliant portal that assaulted his senses. He tried to restrict the flow of zenith, to give his eyes time to adjust to the harsh light, but something in the current of the deepening well propelled him forward.

His body broke the surface with all the sensation of falling from a great height, and he collapsed, gasping, on hard stone. Involuntary retching overtook him as the fluids of the deepening well fled his lungs, searing his airways and leaving him in spasms.

He pushed to a sitting position, feeling surprised by the weight of his body, and dangled his feet in the water. Now that he sat outside the well, the liquid felt cool and swirled against his skin without the saturation he had experienced only moments before. The journey had left him more fatigued than he anticipated, but that concern dissipated upon discovering the edge of a cold blade pressing down on his shoulder.

Seldora channeled zenith, but chose not to prime the borrowed runes. The sword hilt jarred against one of his kesaks, and a woman's voice spoke from behind him. "I can feel the currents of zenith responding to your need, so you're no abrogator. That will not save you if you speak lies. Tell me your name."

"I am Seldora of the Ilovesh. And I am no abrogator's friend. Do all guests receive such welcome?"

The woman removed the blade and sheathed the weapon. "Please forgive my caution. This chamber is sacred to my people, and no one has ever used it to gain entrance to Stone's Grasp."

Seldora struggled to his feet, his balance wavering. "No forgiveness is needed. If a manling used the deepening well to enter Vellendar, the elders would not treat them kindly."

He turned to consider the woman. Slate-grey hair framed a serious face, and she stood perhaps half his height and stared into the pool, tongue resting on a delicate scar furrowed in her upper lip. A riftwing of all things perched on her shoulder, and the creature preened a wing, then turned to consider him.

Seldora held out a finger, and the hawk hopped onto his hand. He ran a finger over its crest, watching the plumage flare in a line down its neck. The hawk sprang into the air, swooped around the chamber, and landed on the shoulder of an oversized statue. "Riftwings nest among the ursulu of the Ilovesh, but I've never known one to treat so casually with anyone."

The woman finally lifted her gaze from the pool to consider him. "My name is Karragin Lefledge. This is Iska. Ours is a . . . long story. Welcome to Stone's Grasp. Are you here to free Lluthean?"

"That and more. First, we will see to the prince's release if we can. Then, together, we shall seek Tarkannen's destruction."

The woman tilted her head. "Alright. How can we help?"

"What can you tell me of this place, and of the means by which the prince remains trapped in the Drift?"

Karragin inhaled once and closed her eyes in a slow blink.

"Have I given offense?" he asked.

"No, nothing like that. I'm just not sure where to begin. I'm not even sure any of us understand it all. Let's sit, and I'll tell you what I can."

She led him to one of the benches, and over the next few hours shared the explanation of what she knew of Lluthean's tether to Tarkannen. Their conversation ventured into tangents, but it was clear she had a limited understanding of the specifics of the Revealing, and even less knowledge of the deepening well.

"Tarkannen sought entrance to the deepening well in Vellendar but was rejected by the elders. How have you kept him from this place?" he asked.

"Prince Kaellor, Lluthean's uncle, was able to activate the castle defenses. As I understand it, the barrier prevents Tarkannen, or any abrogator for that matter, from gaining entrance to the city."

"You speak of this in the past tense. Is the well at risk?"

"Kaellor had to leave. He's riding to confront the abrogators and help Bryndor, Lluthean's brother. The barrier persisted for a few days after his departure." She stood and walked over to one of the stone walls, then tapped a finger on the silver veining. "But I don't think it stands any longer. Without Kaellor here, the defenses are dormant."

The revelation gave rise to a grave concern within Seldora, and he stood and studied the statue of Eldrek. A complex tapestry of runes wove up the legs of the statue, covered the torso, sprawled across the arms, and accentuated the jawline. In each palm rested delicate figurines. "Does anyone else possess the knowledge to activate the defenses?"

"I don't think so."

"What's the significance of the riftwing and the reaver?" he asked.

Karragin rose to stand beside him. "You mean the hawk and the dragon?"

Seldora's height gave him a clear view of the figurines, and he leaned in to recheck the accuracy of his statement. "The hawk is definitely a riftwing. The talons are clutched together like a basket. I don't know this word, dragon, but that's a reaver. The Ilovesh hunted them to extinction. I'm surprised to find its likeness here."

"Now I'm intrigued. Why did your people hunt them to extinction?" she asked.

"Who can know for sure? Ilovesh legends hold that the creatures consumed zenith, leeching it from all life and repurposing it. Some stories tell how the great winged serpents created paradise, while others only recount their destructive nature."

"I should let my superiors know that you have arrived. Would you like to see other parts of the castle?"

"It's a generous invitation, but I think I'll remain here and learn what I can. Besides, if your defenses are down, as you say, someone should stay here to bar the abrogator access to its secrets."

The woman took a step toward the door and then hesitated, the gesture completely incongruous with her nature. "I know from conversations with Lluthean that you are here to help, but I would ask that you wait for my superior before taking any action."

Seldora found the request more than reasonable and besides, he needed time to study the magical cocoon encasing the young man. "I can use the time to prepare."

"By chance are you hungry, or in need of sustenance?" she asked.

Now that he thought about it, some of the weakness he felt likely stemmed from a combination of thirst and hunger. "I could eat, though Ilovesh have unique diets. We do not consume our friends."

She regarded him coolly. "Well, that's a relief, neither do I."

"Meat, we do not eat meat," he clarified.

"Ahh, of course. I will return shortly," she said. The riftwing swooped down and landed on the woman's shoulder, and she left him alone in the chamber.

Seldora walked over to the cocoon and ran long fingers across the surface. Karragin had referred to it as a zentrist. Countless layers of zenith wove underneath his touch and emitted a static friction that tingled his fingertips. He considered stabbing into the barrier to peel it away, but set the notion aside as a last resort. Perhaps he could deploy rune fire and melt the structure.

Somaya and the elders had intimated that he would have to borrow the full measure of Bryndor's gift if he were to succeed. "Of course," he said to the empty room.

He siphoned zenith and channeled once again into the runes on his forearms, then returned his focus to the problem at hand, the Revealing, the tether, and the way the young man seemed stranded in the Drift. Time flowed beyond his awareness, but eventually the solution rose to his mind. He allowed the runes to fade to dormancy and left the meditative trance.

"That's oddly rather simple."

Without a second thought, he reached out, waving his arm back and forth around the cocoon, searching. At last, he found it. The remnant of the tether drifted across his wrist and settled between his fingers with no more substance than spider's silk.

A wave of revulsion passed through his core as the taint of abrogation bled from the filament. No wonder these people didn't recognize the tether. It barely resembled the uncorrupted bond shared between two Ilovesh. But it was there, and he had it firmly in his grasp.

Seldora took care to entangle his fingers through the tether, then knelt down and pried his hands under the cocoon. As he lifted, the entire structure wobbled and rocked, but the zentrist resisted his efforts, even pulsing out with painful discharges of zenith. He stood back, double-checked his hold on the tether, then quickstepped and slammed a shoulder into the cocoon.

He bounced back a few feet, but the zentristt tottered on the edge of the pool. He waited and slowly, but inexorably, the entire blue fibrous mass of zenith slid into the depths of the deepening well.

LLUTHEAN POURED ALL his focus into maintaining the scrying pool, keeping a clear view of the Ilovesh in the inner sanctum. When the last edge of the zentrist and all its contents slipped under the surface of the water, his control of the images vanished, and the pond took on a reflective, mirrorlike surface once again.

A distinct tugging sensation pulled him toward the reflection, but when he looked, it was not his face that stared back, but something altogether alien. Black sigils wriggled and shifted about the face and bald head of the man staring back, and he knew at once that he looked on the face of the abrogator, Tarkannen. In that moment of recognition, the abrogator seemed to stare back through the mirror.

A forearm encrusted with black sigils reached through the mirror and grabbed something unseen. A painful sensation tugged at his core, and he knew at once that the tether was drawing him in, threatening to pull him through the mirror.

Lluthean threw himself back, kicked to gain purchase, and flailed about, grasping for anything to resist the relentless pull, but the substance all around them began to fray. His hands grasped soil and grass only to feel it wither into nothingness. He began to panic, and then Neska was there, soft-mouthing his wrist, soothing his mind.

"Peace, my Lluthean. This is what must be. I know you are scared. Get on my back, and let's leave this place to the spirits."

Somehow, he rolled, and she managed to negotiate herself under him. He had just enough time to lean forward and wrap his arms and legs around her before she lurched ahead into the mirror. They fell into the inner sanctum, and Neska found her feet with agile grace.

Lluthean landed hard on his back and struggled to breathe. The muscles under his lungs seized up and his vision darkened to a tunnel, but at last his body acclimated, and he drew in a full breath. Neska walked over and licked him on the forehead. He sat up and signed, *"Thank you, my Neska. I already miss your voice."*

He became aware of the authentic weight of his body on the stone and the feel of humid air filling his nose, entering his lungs, and carrying with it the pine scent of survivor's essence. Neska's fur tickled the side of his cheek, but beyond this, he was aware of something else. Zenith tickled across the runes on his chest, tingling the edges of his arca prime.

Seldora's deep voice echoed from across the pool. "Welcome back, Prince Lluthean. Prepare yourself; Tarkannen will surely arrive soon."

TARKANNEN STOOD AT the back of the command tent and listened to Zsheck's generals bicker about the best way to engage the forces at the Pillars of Eldrek. Several counseled an attack this very night, stressing the tenuous resources left to the army. While the supply lines remained intact, neither Millstone nor Norfold had provided the windfall of resources they had anticipated.

Some of the generals blamed the otherworldly butchery and destruction on the umbral; others assumed that people had fled before the army and destroyed their city to prevent the conquering army from enjoying the spoils of war. Tarkannen recognized the situation as something else: creatures from the Drift had crossed over. He would have to hunt them down and deal with them once he had access to the deepening well. Once he was made whole.

"What does the child of Mogdurian have to say?" asked Zsheck.

"Begin the attack tonight. Time and resources are not on our side," said Tarkannen.

An elderly general with a white beard nodded agreement. "Your words are true, High Abrogator, but would you have us run afoul of their defenses at night?"

"Send the grondle. Sacrifice all of them if you have to. Their bloodlust is barely constrained by the umbral as it is. Turn them loose and begin the conquest."

Zsheck leaned forward. "Your grotvonen forces have superior capabilities at night. Why would you not summon them, deploy them first, then follow with the shock troops?"

Tarkannen shrugged indifference. "Upon the advice of this council, Volencia holds the grotvonen in reserve, guarding our northwest flank against the possibility of attack. We could likely have the grotvonen in position within a day, but to what end?"

Zsheck stared at him for a time, then chuckled and wrapped his onyx scepter on the table. "You don't want the grondle to survive this conflict, do you?"

"The question is, my krug rai'al, do you? Do any of us? The grondle are a necessary means to an end, but none of us should prefer to deal with them when the fighting is done. So, send them in. They will be the meat through the grinder."

Zsheck blinked in a rare moment of disbelief, then nodded. "Alright, recall the scouts. Signal the advance. We'll send the grondle in after the moon drops behind the mountains."

Tarkannen bowed his head. "By your leave, I will confer with the umbral."

He stepped out into the night and glanced at the moon of Baellen, once again pinching the blue orb between thumb and forefinger. *So close now.*

Through a filter of nadir he screeched out, summoning the closest umbral, a creature that lurched on one good leg and one withered one. He couldn't recall now which of his protégés he had enslaved to this form and ran a thumb around the sigils of enslavement marking the brim of the umbral's flat head. Nothing, no spark of recognition, rose to his awareness.

He issued the attack commands to the creature and bid the dissemination of orders to the others. The umbral lurched off into the night without comment. He was going to return to the command tent when a pleasurable wave of warmth blossomed through his core.

At first he mistook the feeling for an unseasonably warm wind, but in moments he recognized the sensation. It was the tether. His interlace remained intact and secure, but even so, the tether usually provoked an aching, drawing sensation. Just now though, there was the unmistakable sense that he could siphon from the connection. And that could mean only one thing. Lluthean Baellentrell had left the Drift and was alive.

More than that, he was close, close enough that Tarkannen could sense his location, feel his emotion. The prince was back inside Stone's Grasp, and he couldn't say how he knew, but he sensed that the barrier that had prevented him from entering the Aarindorian city all those months ago no longer separated him from the other end of the tether.

Sigils shifted across his entire body, caressing his flesh with pleasurable anticipation. Tarkannen grasped the remaining shaft of crystallized nadir and devoured the power, but resisted the initial impulse to travel directly to the inner sanctum.

The Giver's blessings are nothing more than the combination of preparation and opportunity. You have time to recruit muscle to your effort.

In the darkness of night, a black vacuum opened up just long enough for the abrogator to step through.

Chapter Seventy-One: Uninvited Guests

Seldora held out his hand and helped Lluthean to his feet. At the moment their grip locked, several revelations rose to his awareness. The first was the abrupt loss of his borrowed runes. The elders had made Bryndor donate his gift so Seldora could pass through the deepening well. Ilovesh had no cause to swim. Only through the use of the borrowed runes could he navigate and exit the sacred waters. The runic enhancements also enabled him to open a return portal for Lluthean. With those tasks complete, the runes, their raw power, and even the awareness they granted all dissipated.

Of equal if not greater concern, he also sensed the dark tether connecting the manling to the abrogator. It resonated through their touch like a shearing, scraping noise at the edge of his perception.

The young man staggered for a moment, appearing unsteady. Seldora pulled zenith into the fibers of his limbs, reinforcing their density and strength in preparation for the anticipated battle. Now would be the perfect time to destroy the tether. A quick thrust with one of his kesaks would incapacitate the man. Seldora could dispose of the body in the deepening well, permanently disrupting any connection that might sustain Tarkannen.

But his sister believed there was a different path. Indeed, she'd taken great pains to resist the merging, to imbue the manling with knowledge and the ability to fight back. He would not dishonor her sacrifice with such a rash action. Besides, Lluthean had a friend. The wolvryn creature standing beside him must have sensed his inner turmoil by the way she stood at attention.

Seldora considered the creature. Where the other surpassed her in pure size and strength, this one held cunning in the depths of her eyes, and he would not likely survive beyond a few seconds if he attacked the young prince.

"Well met, friend Lluthean. I am Seldora of the Ilovesh. Are you ready for the conflict?"

The manling stomped a foot on the ground and shook his hands violently. "I'm getting there, I think. Everything is tingly. I don't think we were meant to remain in the Revealing for so long."

He turned and wrapped his arms around the wolvryn's neck. "You're the Giver's real blessing, Neska. You did it again. You saved us."

He turned to face Seldora and considered the room. The inner sanctum spread out in an oval with the surface of the deepening well standing beside them and a massive statue at the far end of the room. "I knew your sister, Sephora. She taught me things, the secrets of the interlace."

"You knew a version of my sister. She lingered in the Drift waiting for you. It pained and reduced her more than you will ever know, but she is at last at peace in the merging. Let's hope her sacrifice imbued you with enough knowledge to thwart the abrogator."

"I'm sorry for your loss, truly. I'll try not to let you down. To that end." Zenith flickered across the runes visible on the young man's body, and Seldora felt the telltale shift in the ambient currents.

Lluthean reached out as if grabbing invisible strings, his hands pulling and weaving filaments into the interlace. Seldora watched him, intrigued by the gestures, which appeared clumsy at first, but as he continued to weave the cords into an impenetrable pattern, the precision and intricacy of his work spoke for itself. He expressed in gestures what the Ilovesh completed in their minds, and to see it artfully displayed was no small wonder.

The interlace became visible as a tangled knot of zenith hovering before Lluthean's chest, there one moment and gone the next. Seldora had to check his surprise and inwardly admonished the rigidity of his own preconceptions. "Again, I have misjudged you. I did not think you capable of such expertise. My sister taught you well. Not many Ilovesh can weave an interlace with fifteen nodes. I see that I . . . still have much to learn about manlings."

Lluthean began to walk around the outside of the deepening well. "Tell you what, let me see if I can raise the wards protecting Stone's Grasp, and then we can introduce you to an entire cast of people who might surprise you. Only, I might drop the manling reference. I don't mind, but some of the women I know might take offense."

Before he managed another step, a harsh, shearing vacuum erupted at the far end of the chamber. A black void ripped into the space directly before the statue, and two creatures of shadow spilled onto the floor. Their amorphous, smoky forms coalesced into humanoid figures encased in smoldering scales. They wore no clothes or armor. Instead, they appeared chiseled from a single piece of glowing rock, scalloped from head to toe with black scales.

The humanoid torsos sprouted muscular arms and legs. On their craggy, scaled heads, a cluster of horns twisted around in a basket encasing some kind of glowing ember. Only, instead of emitting heat, their horned crowns exuded pale blue light. The unmistakable reek of sulfurous fumes laced the air. Each figure crouched beside the portal, holding a single saber crafted from glowing embers.

Seldora cursed and labored to finish the reinforcements to his body, thickening his skin, hardening the tissues, and shaping his fingers and toes into cutting instruments. "He should not be able to summon such things, not without consequence. He gambles everything."

Lluthean gagged at the stench of the otherworldly sentinels. "What are those things?"

"Logrend slag knights, creatures from another land. Leave them to me. You find a way to activate the defenses," he said and withdrew his kesaks.

"We can help," said Lluthean.

"No, my friend, you cannot. Tarkannen brought these here because they are impervious to rune fire. I also don't think your wolvryn will be able to touch them without serious injury. Let's hope he did not prepare other surprises."

Without waiting for his response, Seldora sprinted along the opposite side of the reflecting pool. He made no yell or other gesture, but both slag knights turned to face him, then rushed forward, dividing to approach from both sides.

Seldora needed to get his back to a wall and leaped to the side, but one of the Logrend expected the move and surged to the side. He landed, ran two steps up the wall, then bounded over the head of the other slag knight and engaged the creature. Sparks showered the ground when his crossed kesaks collided with the Logrend emberblade.

Seldora twirled the kesaks high and low in a blinding flurry of attacks. The slag knight parried most and received blows when they came. The kesaks were made for thrusting and piercing, but could also be wielded as batons. Seldora brought his considerable augmented strength and speed to bear and caught the slag knight on the torso with the full might of a swing. Something cracked, and painful vibrations traveled through the kesak. At first, he feared that the heartwood shaft of his weapon had splintered, but the metal reinforcements had instead delivered a crushing blow. A fissure appeared on the Logrend's torso, and the creature folded sideways over the injury.

He stabbed in for a killing blow, but the other knight lurched forward and grasped Seldora's wrist, halting the attack. The two struggled against one another, neither able to dominate. While Seldora held his ground, searing, raging pain erupted from his forearm where the knight grabbed him. A sickening, acrid odor of burned flesh and hair rose to his awareness. To make matters worse, the first slag knight straightened, sealing up the crevice that had formed across its torso.

Seldora jerked his wrist back, but the second knight held on and swung wildly with its emberblade. It was all he could manage to keep his wits, try to dislodge himself from the searing grip, and deflect the knight's attacks. Showers of sparks spilled all around them as the knight struck over and over. The strangest sensation of panic crept into his mind as he imagined the Logrend's grip burning clean through to the bones of his wrist.

After all, Logrend were trophy collectors. Possessing neither innate stores of zenith nor nadir, instead they harvested foci from zeniphiles and abrogators alike. He wondered now if the bones of his hand might one day rest within the crown of this particular foe.

Ilovesh lived without fear or panic. In his hundreds of years of life, he had never had cause to experience the sensation, but recognized it at once for its debilitating effect on the mind. Seldora set the feeling to the side as he continued to deflect the endless attacks. In a moment of clarity, he shaped the end of his arm into a tapered point, dropped the kesak, and twirled in a tight circle.

The slag knight flew back, dashing against the wall with a cracking noise like a sledgehammer striking stone. Seldora reformed his fingers, retrieved the discarded kesak, and tested his grip on the weapon. Pain blossomed as a persistent bracelet of fire on his wounded forearm, but he had no more time to give it consideration as the first knight charged.

He maneuvered his back to the dark portal and engaged the first knight in measured strikes and counterstrikes, searching for a weakness in the creature's tactics. He noticed Lluthean stepping lightly around the far side of the chamber in an attempt to reach the statue. The young man pointed to his destination and Seldora tipped his chin, but the slag knight caught the gesture, parried, then backstepped.

The thing crouched and sprang, leaping across the breadth of the deepening well with unnatural alacrity. It landed practically on top of Lluthean, sweeping down with its emberblade in a killing arc. Time never slowed. The tempo of the battle raged forward, and the sweep of the ugly blade slashed directly into Lluthean's neck, cleaving into his torso. A killing blow if ever there was one.

But in the instant of the Logrend's attack, Lluthean simply dissipated, there one moment, but existing as a blue, misty outline the next. Seldora sensed the young man's surge of zenith and wondered how he had managed such a miracle. The slag knight set its feet and swung at the apparition of Lluthean, sweeping its blade back and forth, clearly confused by the utter lack of the manling's substance.

The distraction gave Seldora the opportunity he needed. He sprinted several paces, launched himself over the deepening well, and collided with the slag knight. The thing recoiled and staggered several steps back, tottering on the edge of the deepening well. Seldora heaved both kesaks overhead once, twice, and a third time, then kicked into the slag knight's torso.

A stab of pain flared in the sole of his foot upon contact, but the otherworldly foe toppled into the deepening well. Steam hissed, and the surface waters boiled. For the first time since entering the inner sanctum, the slag knight emitted a moan of pain as it shuddered and tried to reach the edge of the pool.

One clawed hand reached the edge, but its fingers curled into a useless fist. Seldora hit it with a single strike of his kesak, and the thing's entire arm fractured into rubble, then the rest of it sank beneath the surface.

He took a knee and submerged his wounded forearm into the pool. Pain caused his breaths to come short and labored, but he was Ilovesh and called on the well to respond. The soothing waters began to mend the singed tissues. He kept his eyes trained on the portal at the far side of the chamber, and Lluthean re-materialized beside him.

"Good trick," said Seldora.

Lluthean pounded a fist to his chest. "Thanks. Sometimes the Giver gives. Is the other one out of the fight?" asked Lluthean.

Before he could respond, the second slag knight rose and walked toward the deepening well, assessing the room. It swept the tip of its emberblade into the water, then recoiled as if in pain. With an uncanny human gesture, it tilted its head in recognition of the deadly obstacle.

"I assume you need to reach the statue?" Seldora asked.

"Yes. It's the only way to activate the castle wards. I can feel Tarkannen drawing close. It will be the edge we need."

Echoing from outside the chamber, a low-pitched droning howl rose through the castle.

"Where is your friend?" asked Seldora.

"Neska? I sent her out the doors to recruit help."

Seldora withdrew his arm and inspected the pink flesh. He rolled his wrist back and forth, finding the limb stiff but serviceable. When he tried to reinforce the tissues, zenith flowed down to his hand but failed to saturate the newly mended tendons.

"I'm no mean hand with a sword. Give me one of your weapons, and we can take that thing together?" asked Lluthean

"No, friend. I have the measure of this thing. Get to the statue, activate your wards. I will tend to our uninvited guest."

Seldora stood and pointed one kesak at the slag knight in challenge. The Logrend stepped back from the deepening well and swept its emberblade across the ground, scoring a burn into the stone. He clanged the kesaks together and walked around the far side of the well, turning the knight's back to the portal and the statue. As he reached the other side of the chamber, the slag knight struck.

It fought with feral intensity, slashing, stabbing, and swinging its emberblade in wide arcs. At the same time, it tried to dart a hand forward to grab Seldora's arm. He fell into a defensive posture, blocking, deflecting, and parrying the blows, even backstepping when necessary.

The contest continued with neither combatant gaining the upper hand. On several occasions, Seldora managed to land a blunt strike on an arm or shoulder. An opening finally appeared in which he might plunge forward with the point of his kesak, but he recoiled at the last second, recognizing the maneuver as a feint. The slag knight's clawed fingers seared a line of pain along his wrist but failed to gain purchase.

Seldora swore at his own impatience more than anything else. He had time. His stamina was not in jeopardy, and Lluthean would erect the castle wards any moment now. The exchange of blows continued until the tops of Seldora's feet burned from the countless showers of embers.

Whether it was motivated by the death of its partner, or had simply found some inner reserve, the Logrend fought with renewed purpose. Seldora caught two particularly savage blows on the kesaks and tried to ignore the burning pain that traveled through the weapons and into his forearms. But as the melee continued, realization dawned on him that the pain was not so much from absorbing vibrations as it was from heat.

The ends of his kesaks began to glow, and every time he deflected a strike from the emberblade, more heat transmitted into his weapon. So that was it. Somehow the slag knight, this creature of fire and brimstone, understood that if it could drag out the fight, he would eventually have to set down his weapons. To make matters worse, Lluthean had not managed to activate the defenses, and motion flickered in the mouth of the black portal as two more slag knights stepped into the chamber.

"Fth, fth, fth!" he swore with uncommon purpose.

Ilovesh had no cause to gamble; Seldora never understood the human convention. But as his mind searched for a means to bring the contest to an end, he committed to action that would conclude the fight once and for all.

He dropped one kesak and turned to deflect the attacks of the knight with his remaining weapon. Wincing with genuine pain, he reshaped his offhand, molding it to his purpose. He backtracked and staggered, narrowly avoiding the searing, grasping attack of the slag knight as it lunged forward.

Seldora stumbled back and held the lone kesak overhead, absorbing several repeated blows. His remaining weapon became superheated, and he finally had to release the hilt. The slag knight paused and stepped back in surprise, but scales quickly shifted in a ripple across the surface of its face into something resembling a smile, and the monster raised its weapon to strike.

Seldora cowered at the edge of the deepening well and dipped his offhand, now cupped into the shape of a massive, unwieldy spoon, into the pool. The slag knight began the terrible descent of its emberblade just as water sluiced up in a long streak, spraying its right leg, crotch, center torso, and even splashing a line across the slag knight's head.

From within the knight, a sharp rasp of pain escaped. Something inside the creature popped, and the emberblade clattered to the stones. Seldora stood with a second cupped handful of water. The knight tried to retreat, but its right leg fractured at the knee, and it toppled. He poured more of the deepening well onto the creature. Underneath the hissing of steam, a pitiful last moan escaped, and the Logrend broke apart into chunks of smoking rubble.

He looked up to see the two new slag knights charge. There was perhaps enough time to reach the distant kesak, but the weapon he had just discarded hissed when water touched the hilt. He rolled and came up with the cooled weapon in hand, but in his haste, he'd jostled most of the water from his offhand. With regret, he turned to face the oncoming attack.

KARRAGIN RACED UP THE stairs, weighed down by nervous trepidation. She'd known that an Ilovesh was going to arrive. Neska had communicated as much through Iska. But the memory of leaving the strange figure standing alone, unguarded, in the sacred space of the inner sanctum now made her question her decision to find Laryn.

What did she really know about the strange man with the shifting pigments under his purple, marbled skin? She had listened to enough of Sephora's conversations with Lluthean to understand that the Ilovesh considered other races beneath them. What if he intended to harm the prince or desecrate their sacred space?

Those fears spurred her on, and she set Iska to wing, then flooded her arca prime. She managed the entire circular stairwell in seconds, leaping from side to side. Once at the top, she sprinted through the upper levels to reach the royal suites. At the late hour, the halls remained empty. She pushed past the door guards, pounded a fist on Laryn's door and waited, breath barely labored.

Shadows shifted under the doorframe, and Laryn appeared. *"What's wrong, Karra?"* she signed.

Iska landed on her shoulder perch as she explained, "We have a visitor in the inner sanctum. The Ilovesh is here."

Laryn drew back her head. "Alright. Can you find the other Mirrare, then we can receive our guest. I need a moment to dress."

"Yes. We will return shortly."

She jogged back down the hallway, exited the royal suites, and woke Amniah and Baccal. Both women rose with professional efficiency without complaint. Once dressed in their Mirrare gear, the three of them returned to Laryn's door. Several minutes passed, and Karragin took the opportunity to explain what she knew about Seldora's arrival.

As Laryn opened the door, the unmistakable low-pitched rumble of a wolvryn echoed from the depths of the castle, rising as a sustained, penetrating ribbon of sound, beckoning, longing, and dominant. Baccal and even the stoic Amniah stood fish-mouthed. "What is that exactly?" asked the guster.

Karragin trapped her scarred lip between teeth and bit it in anger. "I shouldn't have left the Ilovesh alone. I believe that's the howl of a wolvryn."

Laryn nodded agreement. "Baccal, can you see into the inner sanctum?"

"Yes, but shapes only," signed Baccal.

Zenith ignited behind her eyes, illuminating the dark hallway as the Mirrare focused her gift and searched down through the layers of Stone's Grasp. "Something is wrong. I believe there is a wolvryn and four others in the sanctum, but two burn like bright torches."

"Are they human?" asked Karragin.

"At least two are not," said Baccal.

"Go. Safeguard the prince if he is there, and do not harm the Ilovesh," said Laryn.

Karragin turned to her Mirrare and issued commands, her voice unusually curt, "Amniah, wake the sentinels. Bring them all. Baccal, escort Her Radiance."

She vaulted out of the hallway with such speed that Iska took to wing. Karragin streaked back down dark corridors and reached the top of the stairs before the others. She again flared zenith into her arca prime and flooded her gift, reinforced her strength, then leaped out and dropped all the way down to the level of the inner sanctum. She landed in a crouch. The stitching on her boots ruptured and her socked feet splayed out to the sides, but she felt no pain.

Neska stood not more than two paces away. An uncharacteristic pensiveness affected her stance, and the wolvryn remained still with bated breath.

"I'm here. Lead on," signed Karragin

Neska turned and ran to the door of the inner sanctum. Karragin kicked off the remnants of her boots and sprinted down the last hallway, saber in one hand and dagger in the other. As she pushed past the wolvryn, smoke and something resembling rotten eggs assaulted her senses. To her right, a black vortex hovered in the air in front of the statue of Eldrek. Lluthean was running his fingers along the back leg of the statue, clearly searching for something.

To her left, the Ilovesh prepared to defend against the charge of two reptilian humanoids that glowed as if cast from molten steel or rock. She resisted her first impulse to charge the smoldering enemies, and instead jogged over to Lluthean.

He startled when she tapped him on the shoulder, even swearing something she couldn't hear. *"Do you know how Kae activated the castle defenses?"* he signed.

"No."

"Right. Are more people coming? I don't know how many things are coming out of that portal."

"Yes, Laryn and the Mirrare and sentinels. How can I help?"

He shook his head and pounded a fist on the marbled calf of the statue. *"Buy me time. Help him. They can't survive the pool, but their touch is fire."*

Karragin watched as the Ilovesh swept one hand out, spraying a fine mist of water against the approaching humanoid reptiles. He blocked and parried with a single weapon that looked more like a thick rod filed to a point. Seldora tried to circle, but the fiery duo recognized the danger the water posed and worked to prevent him from accessing the edge of the pool.

Karragin sent a fast message through her sympath rune. *"Neska. Protect Lluthean. This fight is not for you."*

Without waiting for a response, she rolled her shoulders and redirected the flow into her arca prime. She crouched low and circled wide around one of the knights, waiting for her opportunity. The Ilovesh gasped in pain as one of them scored a slash across his leg. The wound drew the invaders into a frenzy, and they began to attack in rapid succession.

The Ilovesh maintained his defenses, but she could tell he was tiring. She sprang forward, lowered a shoulder, and slammed into the closest combatant. Her blow caught the thing from the side. Karragin felt like she had run headlong into a flaming tree trunk. Pain seared her face and ear, but her impact sent the creature careening up and off its feet to land in the middle of the deepening well.

She rolled away and to her feet in time to parry an attack by the lone remaining enemy. It raked a hand forward with a surprising reach, but she stepped back, creating just enough space, blocked a swing from its emberblade, then riposted. The exchange gave her a sense of the thing's timing, and she held her ground.

The lone reptile waved its blade back and forth between Seldora on one side and Karragin on the other. The Ilovesh lunged, a clear feint, then committed to an attack by whipping his weapon in an arc aimed at the slag knight's legs.

It had no choice but to attempt to block the swing. Karragin cocked her arm and slashed, cleaving through the knight's upraised hand and chunking off the majority of its horned head. Flecks of hot scales seared onto her arms and face, but she kicked at the head, sending it rolling into the deepening well. The remaining portion of the thing fell smoldering to the ground.

She turned to acknowledge Seldora when the Ilovesh reached out a hand, beseeching her to action. He yelled something just before she felt the impact. It struck her hard, something biting and cold. There was a pinch just inside her shoulder blade, and it leeched all her strength as it blossomed into incapacitating pain. Her hands felt numb, and she lost the ability to hold her weapon.

Karragin then had the strangest sensation. When she drew breath, air simply failed to fill her lungs, leaving her panting and hungry for another empty breath. A tingly sensation prickled the skin of her face, and she broke out in a sweat.

Her knees collided with the ground, and she followed the utter look of horror on Seldora's face. He stared, eyes fixed on her breast. She looked down. Where she expected to find the flawless brown leather cuirass of the Mirrare, she discovered a perfectly round cavity with blackened edges.

She probed at the wound with two fingers, and they went in knuckle deep, without resistance, as if she were probing a hollow channel.

"Taker's grip. Nadir burn."

She tried to say more, but collapsed face-first.

SELDORA OF THE ILOVESH blinked, eyes burning with ash and the stink of Logrend slag knights. He had never seen the work of abrogation up close, and it utterly horrified him. The devastation was so absolutely wrong; the utter antithesis of creation. Those thoughts threatened to unravel him as a volley of onyx shards flew past, most scattering wide. But one found its mark and struck the woman in the back.

It was a coward's attack, one made without warning or preamble or negotiation. And Tarkannen had just employed it to snuff out the life of one of the most amazing humans he had ever encountered. Though he had only briefly met the young woman, the masterful way she utilized her gift to dispatch the slag knights left him both humbled and impressed. His gaze lingered on the blackened hole in the center of her chest with a profound sense of loss.

Movement caught his eye and he looked back across the chamber. The abrogator stepped with casual grace from the threshold of the black portal, and the strange portal winked out to reveal a clear impression of the statue behind him.

Seldora recognized the wave of fear he had felt when the slag knight gripped his wrist, threatening to burn off the appendage. That sensation fluttered in the back of his mind now, overshadowed by another strange emotion: righteous anger. Before him stood the man who'd stolen the secrets of the Ilovesh. The man who had led his sister to betray the covenants of her people. The man who would call himself the Eidolon.

Disdain sharpened Seldora's tongue. "I call you coward, abrogator! You defile and betray everything Sephora ever invested in you!"

Tarkannen spread his hands wide, and another volley of nadir sped forth. Seldora dove to the side, rolled, and came to his feet. He sensed that the attack was one of contempt.

"She spoke of you often, you know. She waited for you in the Drift. It pained her to linger without merging. But she did it for you. And you betrayed her!"

Tarkannen sauntered forward. "Ilovesh . . . none of this would have been necessary if your elders had granted me access to the deepening well. I could have become all. I could have saved your sister, you know. I would have had the strength to reclaim her in the immediacy of her death. But now things have changed. I have changed. And once I reclaim all, I will become the Eidolon. I will save this world and end the Ilovesh."

Clouds of nadir manifested around the abrogator, like hovering swarms of biting insects. Tarkannen released the attack, surging them forward. Seldora sprinted back and to the side, almost tripping over one of his discarded kesaks. He skidded to a stop and changed directions, zigzagging throughout the chamber. The first two volleys pelted the ground.

The third swarm pursued him around the far end of the chamber only to collide into the wall when he once again switched direction. "To think I would have called you brother. But now, you are exhausting," said Tarkannen.

The abrogator walked forward, extending multiple tentacles that were impossible to escape. Seldora swung at one of the appendages, but it dissipated only to reform, and his kesak passed through it, causing no harm. He dove over another and finally, the cold grip of a rope of abrogation wrapped around his waist, lifting him high above the deepening well.

Tarkannen shrouded himself in a globe of nadir and suspended Seldora as he approached the well. "Is it true that Ilovesh can't swim? Shall we put that to the test?"

Before Seldora could answer, zenith fled the room, as if something had gathered up any excess of the ambient currents. And then a low-pitched rumbling whoosh filled the chamber as a torrential, continuous beam of rune fire roared into the abrogator's back.

Chapter Seventy-Two: Isolation

Lluthean searched for any defect or blemish on the surface of the statue of Eldrek, trying to discover the mechanism by which he might activate the ward around Stone's Grasp. His fingers probed the striations of muscle carved into the polished stone. How had Kaellor done it? When they had first arrived, he was overwhelmed with the likeness of his parents frozen in time. The lifelike preservation of his mother in particular had grounded him in the room, and the entire world had been reduced to her focused intensity.

Lluthean knew he had lost parts of himself in the Drift, but he remembered that day. *So why can't I remember how Kae did it?*

As the battle between Seldora and the flaming creatures unfolded, he chanced a glance and was instantly mesmerized by the fluid grace and athleticism of the Ilovesh. Seldora moved with stunning alacrity and economy that would impress even Kaellor in full command of his gift.

Thoughts of his uncle caused him to return to the statue. He considered climbing up onto the outstretched hands but knew that Kaellor had never attempted such a task before. And then Karragin entered the melee, decimating the otherworldly knights with her skill.

Lluthean sensed Tarkannen's presence a moment before he stepped through the portal. In such proximity, the tether became a perceptible anchor, tugging at his core. The reinforced intimacy conveyed a sense of the man's mood. There was no fear within the abrogator. Rather, he harbored contempt, certainly, and there was rage . . . but there was also something else. Underneath it all, there was unrelenting hunger.

Was that the result of abrogation? Did abuse of the reductive force always leave you wanting more, or was the man just insatiably power hungry?

Karragin decapitated the last of the slag knights and saluted Seldora, and that's when it happened. A volley of onyx projectiles sped forth, and one of them seared a hole into her back. A glacier of ice slid into Lluthean's stomach, and he broke into a cold sweat. It challenged all his dexterity to climb down from the statue's pedestal and find his feet.

By the time he stepped out from the statue of Eldrek, Tarkannen had snared the Ilovesh with a dark tentacle and was threatening to drown him in the deepening well. If the abrogator could attack without warning, then so could he. He summoned all the zenith he could stand until it felt like he had inhaled all the air in the room, then primed the runes on his shoulders and unleashed the full might of his attack.

The beam that shot forth was constrained to his will. He focused the conflagration into a dense stream of burning white rune fire and poured everything he had into its construction and release.

Seconds bled into minutes as he gorged himself on zenith, the force visibly coursing through his runes, flooding the chamber with the cerulean light of his gift. A deafening roar, punctuated by concussive thunder, shook the foundations of the inner sanctum. His head swirled with a wave of dizziness, and he swallowed back the urge to retch. Through the corruption of the tether, he sensed Tarkannen's unwavering presence as a silent, bemused observer. Finally, Lluthean staggered a step and suspended the surge.

The air warped, and waves of red heat rippled across the surface of the stones under the path of his rage. But Tarkannen stood shrouded in a murky sphere of shadow. The man turned to face him, still suspending the Ilovesh from a tentacle that whipped back and forth behind him with the casual grace of a cat's tail.

Seldora grunted and slashed his hand into the dark lashing, but Tarkannen reinforced the appendage and dashed the Ilovesh against the back of the chamber. He whipped around like a rag doll, striking the stones once, twice, and a third time, when something cracked. The Ilovesh fell limp and was discarded to the floor of the inner sanctum.

Black tentacles retracted into the abrogator, who lifted his dark face to the ceiling and searched the room. "I used the last of my of my nadrean to get here, and now that I've arrived, it's not so grand as I remember."

Eventually, he turned to face Lluthean. "It's a strange thing to face the man who is trying to kill you, don't you think? Especially when we can sense each other's thoughts." He stepped away from the streak of hot stones and nudged a boot against Karragin's lifeless corpse. "Who was she to you? Wife? Lover?"

Tarkannen thinned the shifting layers of his nadir globe enough that Lluthean could see his face. Black sigils shifted across the man's cheeks and forehead, sometimes passing behind his eyes. Lluthean didn't know what he'd expected, but the way the shadows shifted as if of their own volition was unnerving. "You don't even know, do you? I lost things when I crossed back from the Drift. I can feel it inside you, the confusion. The sense that you've misplaced something vital. It's there, but just beyond your reach."

Lluthean's breath rasped as the first stages of the draft rose up in his chest. The cold fingers of dread gripped his core, distracting him from the conflict. Part of him stared in defeated disbelief that the abrogator had withstood his strongest manifestation of rune fire without so much as a singed hair, and part of him recoiled at the simple invasion of the man. A shiver of revulsion also prickled his skin at the abrogator's touch on his mind.

What made it worse, Tarkannen was right: he felt the vacancies in his memory. Sephora had trained him, shaping his mind for this very conflict, but parts of him felt displaced beyond his grasp. It was like startling to wakefulness from a nightmare and fumbling around in the dark for the security of a weapon, only to close your fist around empty shadows.

Karragin's death was tragic, but he had lost friends before. So why did her absence magnify the emptiness he felt, stretching it from a moment of sadness to a disorienting cavern of absolute grief?

He backstepped and began to doubt the integrity of his interlace. Numbly, he mentally probed the protective barrier. Once again, the abrogator broke into his thoughts. "Oh, it's quite intact, your interlace.

But so is our tether. How did you manage it? My own interlace is a decahedron, but yours is constructed with all the mastery of an Ilovesh."

Tarkannen turned and glanced at Seldora's limp form. "She taught you, didn't she?"

Lluthean didn't know how to answer. Beside the statue of Eldrek, Neska crouched in the shadows. He signed to her, *"Hold, Neska. Not your fight."*

But if the wolvryn saw his communication, she ignored him and prowled forward. Her muscled form crowded the doorway, and a throaty, ominous growl rumbled into the room. Something in her fierce presence allowed him to find his voice.

"Sephora did train me. It pained her, I think, but she judged the cost of stopping you worth the misery. She loved you once, but you've become everything she abhors."

Tarkannen leaned forward, his shadowy barrier swarming with agitated shadows. "Lies!" he hissed.

The revelation caused the abrogator's emotions to shift from uncertainty to anger and, underneath it all, there was a ripple of doubt. Lluthean fed on the realization, using it to bolster his confidence, and shrugged with indifference. "You can sense my thoughts through the tether, right? Look again and tell me if I'm lying."

"I've no need."

"You mean you've no courage!" Lluthean shouted. "Seldora was right. You're not the savior of the world. You're just a coward, cloaked in a blanket of your own lies. Well, look inside, parasite. See the truth!"

Where did that clever cut come from? Why couldn't Bryndor be here to hear that particular bit of rhetoric?

A cold, leeching sensation drew out from the tether as the abrogator searched for any signs of obfuscation. Where before, Lluthean had resisted the probing, now he welcomed it, hoping that the truth of Sephora's disappointment would cripple something inside the man.

Again, the tether betrayed Tarkannen's inner turmoil. At first, the revelation seemed to deflate the abrogator, but then he lifted his head. Lluthean felt the rising tide of the man's wrath. When he spoke, menacing conviction flavored his tone. "I'll just have to show you. All of you."

The nadir sphere dropped, and a volley of nadir shards streaked forward. Lluthean dove behind the statue of Eldrek. The missiles hissed into the surrounding walls. He ignited his gift, stepped to the side, and hurled hot marbles of rune fire. Tarkannen swept a hand, meeting the globes with individual lances of nadir. Where the two collided, they dissipated, bursting with nullifying bursts of power.

The abrogator whipped a hand, and another series of shards flew forward. Lluthean felt the man's intent and sent a barrage of more rune fire, his missiles deflecting the attack.

Again Tarkannen swept a hand, again Lluthean flared a barrage of incinerating globes forward, and again the two forces collided, the air smoking with tendrils of dissipated zenith and nadir. Tarkannen unleashed rolling volleys of the shards, and Lluthean barely managed to summon enough rune fire to defend himself. Three onyx shards slipped past his defenses.

Through the tether, Tarkannen shouted with rapture. And that was the last thing he felt before he slipped into the Drift. He became overwhelmed with the sensation of falling as a searing cold splashed against his back, enveloping him in the void and shifting him into the ethereal. Icy, prickly lances of pain needled his skull, his limbs, and even strafed into his eyes. The substance of the Drift infiltrated his mouth and nose, and when he inhaled, his lungs seized up as if filled with sand.

Then his arca prime pulsed again, and the pain simply vanished, along with all traces of the draft. He opened his eyes to see that he stood in the inner sanctum. "Taker's grip—that really grinding hurts."

The first time his arca prime activated, it had pulled him into the ethereal, and he'd remained there for several seconds before reconstituting. The pain of the initial transition had surprised him, and he'd released his hold on zenith. This time, he'd both dreaded and anticipated the transition, but made sure to continue the flow of zenith into his arca prime.

The entire inner sanctum appeared in shades of grey, as if cast from a charcoal drawing with smudged edges. Tarkannen too appeared with poorly refined edges and shifting shadows. The abrogator called out, but the man's speech was slow and bled into echoes. "I can see you . . . in the ethereal. Say hello to the dead for me."

Tarkannen turned to walk toward the deepening well, but his gestures seemed lethargic, as if he walked through sand. Somehow, in his transitioned state, Lluthean moved outside the flow of time, which meant he still had a chance.

He looked back to the statue of Eldrek. Lines of power streamed up through the complex runes, but he still didn't understand how Kaellor had activated the castle wards. "Grind it, Kae, how did you do it?"

"I believe the activation point is on the underside of the right hand," said Karragin.

Her voice startled him so much that he fumbled the flow of zenith and his arca prime sputtered. He turned to see Karragin standing beside him in stark clarity. Iska flapped her wings and perched on Karragin's shoulder. Their motions seemed natural, not suspended in molasses like Tarkannen's. She still wore her Mirrare armor, but without the garish nadir burn. That particular blemish marred her actual corpse, the shadowy outline of which lay several paces away on the floor of the sanctum.

"Giver's tears, can you hear me?"

She tilted her head, as if positioning her ear to better capture any distant sounds, and nodded.

"Moons, Karra, are you really—I mean, is that it then? Am I talking to your ghost?"

"Seems so," she said with as much nonchalance as a house cat.

The surreal experience displaced any concerns about Tarkannen, and then guilt climbed from his stomach into his throat and his voice cracked, heady and raspy. "I don't know how to express my regret. I am so sorry. I knew he was coming, but I didn't anticipate his attack. I should have done better."

True to form, Karragin remained silent, as much an observer to the weird events as he was. In fact, her attention seemed to wander. "Karra, why are you still here? Why haven't you merged on?"

762

"I'm not sure. It doesn't feel right yet. Iska is still here. Maybe I want to see you kill an abrogator." She turned toward Tarkannen, who made slow progress toward the deepening well. "You could retrieve one of those emberblades. If it's like a zeniscrawl, all you need to do is channel a bit of zenith into it."

"Maybe, but I think I'll take my chances with your saber if it's all the same."

"It's not doing me any good."

"If I do this again, use my arca prime, will I see you?"

"I don't know." Her eyes searched the ceiling, as if she could see well beyond the shadowy confines of the inner sanctum.

He held out a hand. "Are there any words you want me to share with your father or Nolan?"

She turned back to him. "Outriders never know when they might set out on their last ranging. In my suite at the bottom of a trunk are letters drafted to each of them. Those say it all."

She reached out and took his hand, but in the ethereal state her touch felt no more substantial than a breath of air. And yet, something in their connection startled Karragin. Raw emotion washed over her face. Surprise and utter astonishment colored the face of her apparition. She withdrew her hand as if touching a hot kettle. "Oh, Giver. And you don't remember any of it, do you? Nothing about our time in the Revealing. That's what Sephora meant. I can see it now."

He stared at his feet. "Apparently when you cross back from the Drift, you lose parts of yourself, or maybe you don't retain everything? I don't know. Right now, it's another thing on a long list of regrets. Whatever it is or was, whatever I forgot, again, I'm so sorry."

She shook her head. "Don't be, my stupid monk. Go, he's nearly reached the water's edge."

"Right. Eyes to the horizon?"

"Yes, my . . . yes, Lluthean, eyes to the horizon."

He turned away from her and found her corpse. His hand grasped at the sword hilt, but the weapon remained insubstantial. He could shift back from the ethereal, but wasn't sure he could reach Tarkannen in time from this distance. It took him several seconds of concentration, but slowly, he pulled the saber into the ethereal.

With relief, he sprinted to intercept Tarkannen. The abrogator continued the strange, slow progression and appeared oblivious to Lluthean's presence. The man had dismissed the surrounding shield of nadir, but a thin layer of shadows flowed over the surface of his body like a second skin.

Lluthean plunged the blade forward, bypassing the shadows and sliding through Tarkannen with no more substance than vapor. *Of course, it can't be that easy.*

He looked over Tarkannen's shoulder one last time at Karragin. The apparition lingered near her corpse and fanned her hand at him like a mother telling a child to get on with the daily chores.

Lluthean inhaled and redirected zenith from his arca prime. The return from the ethereal felt like synchronizing his senses to Neska. The sulfurous fumes from the Logrend slag knights lingered in the humid air, and Tarkannen screamed in rage and surprise. Unfortunately, Lluthean's body adjusted poorly to the transition, and he stumbled to a knee while lunging with the sword.

The tip of the blade slid forward, then met resistance as Tarkannen's shadow armor coalesced around the weapon. The abrogator slapped his hands together, trapping the sword, but Lluthean set both hands to the pommel and thrust. They remained locked in the struggle, neither able to advance.

From the corner of his eye, motion flashed, and he saw Neska charge the abrogator. Tarkannen must have sensed her approach, as tentacles of nadir sprouted from his torso. A single black appendage snaked around the sword, wrapping its way up to the hilt.

Neska bounded forward, but in the next breath, the sword wrenched from Lluthean's grip and two other tentacles hoisted the abrogator up and away to land safely at the opposite side of the chamber. Neska slid forward and toppled into the deepening well.

Lluthean sensed the abrogator's attack before he saw it. A thick cloud of swirling shadow erupted before the man, then shot forth as a continuous gout of nadir. He met the attack with an equal measure of rune fire, and the columns collided in the middle of the sanctum. At their center, the two forces detonated. The energies roiled against one another, emitting flickers of zenith and striations of nadir that dissipated into the air.

Tarkannen poured more strength into the deluge, and the vortex where the forces collided moved closer to Lluthean's position. A fetid, cold wind gusted out from the leading edge of Tarkannen's assault. Lluthean siphoned more zenith, flooding his runes, and pushed back. Tingly, prickly pain spread across his shoulders as the runes worked to shape and constrain the force to his will.

The draft should have claimed him by now, but something about the transition to the ethereal seemed to have reset his tolerance for channeling, and so he pressed on, heedless of the consequences. From the center of the vortex, an abrasive, shearing noise erupted, and a literal crack appeared in the air.

Lluthean recognized the tear at once as something unnatural. The unmistakable reek of decay leeched out from the wound, and thick, curled claws reached through the rent. Lluthean divided his rune fire, sending a pulse of small globes at the black cleft in space just as a black, reptilian head pushed through.

His attack caused the creature to retreat, screeching in pain, and the rift sealed closed. But Tarkannen used the opportunity to pour more power into his endless barrage, and the vortex where rune fire and nadir collided shifted alarmingly close to Lluthean. From the far side of the sanctum, Tarkannen shouted a taunt, "Impressive! I wonder how many more times we'll tear the veil before this is settled? I can keep this up forever, whereas you will eventually succumb to the draft."

As if on cue, the draining effects of the draft clawed at his stomach. His head swooned, and the room tilted. Tarkannen must have sensed his doubt, as he took several deliberate steps forward. Lluthean dropped to a knee, barely managing to maintain the flow of rune fire. In the same moment, Neska clambered out of the pool.

She charged directly at Tarkannen, and the abrogator diverted the strength of his attack, reforming nadir into a cohesive globe. Lluthean gasped and shifted back to the ethereal. The pain, even more intense than his last transition, seared his senses from the inside out. A mixture of pressure and heat erupted with bone-splitting agony, affecting everything all at once. He lost himself in the agony, only barely managing to maintain the flow into his arca prime.

Eventually, the pain stilled, and he looked around the ethereal rendering of the room, amazed again that the transition to the ethereal dissipated all traces of the draft. Tarkannen stood with casual arrogance in the inner sanctum. At the shadowy edge of the room, Seldora's broken form lay on the ground, still but for the frenzied flows of zenith that cascaded from within the Ilovesh.

The abrogator had drafted more of those infernal tentacles, and Lluthean watched in horror as Neska's struggling form was lifted into the air, suspended in Tarkannen's black grip. Before he could transition back, the writhing coils flexed. The wolvryn jerked unnaturally, then collapsed boneless to the ground.

For the first time since leaving the Revealing, the evolution of events utterly crystalized. Lluthean's mind fell into paralysis as an overwhelming sense of isolation and hopelessness displaced all other emotion. His will to endure in the fight waned, and he considered lingering in this space between spaces. Karragin was dead, Neska had now sacrificed herself, and the abrogator turned to approach the deepening well once again. What was it all for?

Tarkannen was not more than ten steps away from the well when a ragged voice rose in his mind. "You didn't survive this long to give up now, old man. Deal with regret later. Keep your eyes to the horizon."

He couldn't say where he had been hiding that sense of inner strength, but Lluthean knew at once that the voice was his. It felt familiar, internal. Something in the echo of his own voice was comforting, demanding, and full of perspective well beyond his years.

"I'll do it for you, Nes."

He walked over to the statue of Eldrek and stood directly under the hands. Movement from the main doorway caught his eye as sentinels crowded at the threshold. They were too late; Tarkannen was two steps away from the water's edge.

Lluthean set his intention and transitioned back. He touched a finger to the underside of the statue's outstretched hand and willed the castle defenses into place. Instantaneously, the ambient flows of zenith shifted, pulled into the foundations of Stone's Grasp. Blue lightning raced through the veining of the castle walls, igniting the castle wards.

Thick sheets of zenith slammed into place, creating barriers that prevented Tarkannen from accessing the pool and isolating the sentinels beyond the room in relative safety. Zenith raced along the surface of the castle wards, building in strength as chaotic striations of blue energy, but the abrogator stood fast. Unbidden, a resolute tone of confidence pulsed through the tether.

Before the castle wards had unleashed their power, thick sheets of nadir, like tainted black ice, rose alongside the zenith barriers. They sheared through the air, emitting corrupted vapors of putrescence. Lluthean felt the pulse and vibrations as the wards flared and detonated against the dense shadow barrier, and then he sensed something else: smugness.

Zenith flickered against the shadow barrier like distant lightning dancing across storm clouds, but the abrogator came to no harm. "Your parents nearly had me once, but I won't fall prey to that trick again, young Baellentrell."

"Still, now it's just you and me," Lluthean said, and unleashed rune fire.

This time he had no desire to test his stamina against the abrogator. Instead, he engaged the source with absolute commitment. A roiling thundercloud of rune fire manifested all about him, and Lluthean willed the entire mass to descend on the man.

Tarkannen matched the intensity with a swarm of shadows, the leading edge hissing like torn silk, and the two forces collided again in the center as warring storm fronts of power. The clash reverberated with a thunderous crack, the air thick with an acrid tang and the metallic bite of raw energy. Lluthean siphoned zenith with reckless abandon, his veins burning as if molten glass coursed through them, ignoring the stabbing ache that permeated his runes while deliberately sinking his body deeper into the draft's suffocating influence. In turn, Tarkannen magnified his assault, shadows writhing like serpents in a gale, and his laughter rang out maniacally, obviously sensing Lluthean's fatigue through the tether.

A tiny voice of intuition crept forward from the corner of his awareness, whispering like a chill draft against the back of his neck even as he poured every shred of focus into sustaining his attack. If they felt one another's emotions through the tether, then what else might bleed across its unseen strands? Lluthean's interlace shimmered with a strength and resonance superior to the abrogator's. In the frantic strain of the moment, he couldn't say how he knew, and maybe he didn't know, maybe he simply believed in the gamble, but a certainty throbbed in his bones. He understood something about the tether—something Tarkannen had dismissed.

His focus snapped back to their contest of wills as his siphoning faltered, zenith sputtering like a dying flame. The oppressive mass of nadir swelled, a suffocating tide that pressed against his senses with the weight of a collapsing sky, filling the arena of the inner sanctum with a choking heaviness. The air grew putrid and rank, as though the Drift itself had once again torn open, its cold breath seeping in to surround him. At the leading edge of the black wall, onyx shards churned and twisted as they prepared to rend his flesh on contact.

With one last desperate act, Lluthean committed to the gamble and unraveled his interlace, the protective threads snapping like a ruptured bow string, and at the same time, he pulsed a final burst of zenith into his rune fire. The blaze flared white-hot, searing his vision with a corona of light. He plunged his awareness into the tether, an unyielding cable of twisted silver light braided with shadow. Instead of siphoning from the ambient currents of zenith, he leeched directly through the binding, tasting its bitter essence as though drinking from a poisoned well.

At first, there was no response, and the dark mass of Tarkannen's will loomed ever closer, but then a surge of zenith left the abrogator, coursing through the tether and reinforcing Lluthean's rune fire. The man staggered back several steps, and the mass of nadir lost cohesion. Still, Lluthean pulled, summoning every last bit of zenith from the man, choking on the raw power steeped with the taint of nadir.

Tarkannen gasped, and panic thrummed through the tether like a struck iron wire vibrating between them. The abrogator's body withered, shoulders collapsing inward as he dropped to his knees, clutching at his chest with tremulous fingers. His other hand flailed outward, desperate, clawing at the air to sustain the walls of shadow that shivered around him.

The planes of black ice quaked, edges rippling like torn banners in a storm, while the castle's defenses pressed in with relentless force. Blue lightning speared through the seams of shadow, sizzling with a sharp tang, fracturing the abrogator's defenses in jagged bursts of brilliance. Lluthean felt the balance tilt inexorably in his favor, the tether humming with the resonance of Tarkannen's fear.

He consumed Tarkannen without remorse, overwhelming him in a furnace of rune fire that roared like a forge bellows. The heat blistered the air, and sterile, galvanic currents scoured the space between them, incinerating every trace of corrupted taint until the air itself seemed purified by violence. A deluge of flames surged outward, the tidal roar of incandescent wrath drowning Tarkannen's screams beneath the crackling thunder of rune fire.

He maintained the incineration until there simply was no more zenith to draw upon, and then, as if he were a marionette suspended by strings, the constraints of the tether snapped as the persistent, intrusive violation vanished. Lluthean fell forward, released his channeling, and caught himself on hands and knees. The world shifted as he succumbed to the draft.

He drooled and panted, swallowing back the acidic bile gathered at the back of his throat. Bone-deep fatigue accompanied waves of throbbing pain that rippled from his head, down his back, and into his limbs. He eased onto his side and lay there, panting, retching, existing in misery eased by one thought: if he was alive to experience the draft, then Tarkannen was dead. When at last he lifted his head, a smoldering ash pile was all that remained of the abrogator. Thin rivulets of nadir wriggled over the remnants for several seconds, and then the mass stilled.

Lluthean tried to rise but his head swam, and the room tilted like a shifting floor of ice. He contented himself with crawling to the statue of

Eldrek. From beyond the zenith barrier, cheers arose from the sentinels gathered outside the inner sanctum. He pushed to a standing position, touched the underside of Eldrek's hand, and released the wards before collapsing to the floor.

Chapter Seventy-Three: Unshackling the Arca Prime

B ryndor crouched in the shadows cast by a rocky overhang, his senses attuned to Boru's, searching the mountainside. Kreegorian scouts had passed below them searching for any passes through the Great Crown, and finding none, now made a return to the valley where the main host of the enemy gathered before the Pillars of Eldrek.

That the scouts found their way on the darkest of nights made him wonder if they possessed unnatural sight. Beneath a new moon's hidden face, the twinkling of stars above and campfires below blazed in stark contrast to the pervasive, chilling darkness. The red moon, still an afterthought most nights, twinkled only as a faint ember on the distant horizon.

He searched across the landscape with Boru's enhanced senses and watched as a trio of scouts climbed up the same path he and Ksenia had used less than an hour ago. She stood in silent communication with Tacit and Winter, keeping the Aarindin calm and utterly silent.

Despite their caution, the scouts continued to climb toward their ledge, unaware that they sat in waiting. He wondered if they could smell the Aarindin and cursed the Taker for their luck. It would be no difficult task to summon rune fire and obliterate the trio, if only he had not ceded his gift. If they could buy a little more time, he felt certain they could skirt around the eastern Pillar of Eldrek and drop into safety behind the forward staging area.

He signed to Boru, *"Wait until I say, then charge the one on the left."*

The wolvryn rose from sitting to all fours, but understood enough to stifle his growl. Acting as an ambush predator was more the style of a cat, but in the years they had spent together, Bryndor trusted that he understood the stakes involved.

The scouts crept closer, then drew to a stop, studying the ground and whispering to one another in thickly accented speech. "See, here, put your hand here. Hoof print. We must be close now, and I can smell horse flesh."

Bryndor retrieved the petrified wolvryn eye from a leather satchel at his waist, holding it behind his back to charge under the moonlight. After only a few seconds, he tossed it behind the trio, where it glowed like a pale ember, made all the more visible in the moonless night. As one, the scouts turned, and Bryndor whispered to Boru, "Now."

The wolvryn took a bounding leap, smashing into the scout on the left, and Bryndor charged, trusting the few seconds of afterimage before Boru's sight left him. He reached the first scout just as the images faded to dim outlines. The man's attention drew first to the stone, then the commotion between Boru and his fallen comrade. Bryndor gripped the hilt of his sword and hacked into the back of his neck, feeling the blade cleave through muscle and bone. The Kreegorian dropped with a grunt of surprise.

He sensed more than saw where the middle scout crouched. Before the man could cry out or attack, he lunged forward, extending everything into the attack. The familiar shearing sensation of metal parting flesh traveled through the blade, and Bryndor felt the weight of the man drop to the ground. He twisted the blade, withdrew, then scythed through the scout in a vicious arc, ensuring the man's death.

Boru growled once, the sound followed by a man's muffled cry of pain and thrashing noises as he dispatched the last scout. Bryndor retrieved the wolvryn eye. He passed the dim illumination over the corpses and, finding them lifeless, returned to Ksenia.

"That was well done. Are there any more?" she whispered.

"No. This last group caught our trail somehow, maybe from the smell of the Aarindin, I don't know, but all the scouting parties have returned to their camp." He held the wolvryn eye between them and smiled. "It's too dark for safe travel without the moon of Baellen."

She tilted her head. "Unless you're a wolvryn."

"Unless you're a wolvryn. I think it's safe to keep this out now," he said, brandishing the glowing orb. "If we climb this trail, it crosses back to the southwest. From there, I'm hoping to find a way down into Aarindorn."

"It's as good a plan as any," she said.

What he imagined would take a quarter hour became a winding saga of climbing, then dropping along broken switchbacks. Several times they followed promising trails only to backtrack when the path became too steep. He marveled at the way Ksenia kept the Aarindin calm. The task of turning in place on loose, rocky cliffsides in the dark would spook most mounts, but Tacit and Winter remained sure-footed.

After a few hours, Boru disappeared, running ahead. Bryndor began to doubt their chances of success and wondered if they should retreat down the eastern side of the Great Crown to safety. Perhaps they could find the Outriders and wait for rescue. He stopped on the trail and chewed on his bottom lip, but the warmth of her hand in his drew him from his brooding.

"We're getting nowhere. I'm a monk twice over. Why did I think we could find a way in when nobody else could?"

"I didn't exactly try to talk you out of it. Maybe if we try again, farther north and in daylight, we might be able to find a way in," she suggested.

He pulled her into an embrace, finding peace in her unconditional return of the contact. "Maybe we find a private valley on the eastern slopes, build a homestead, and wait for all this to blow over."

She took the wolvryn eye from his hands, holding the glowing orb up to better survey his face. "Don't make a girl false promises, my prince."

Before he could respond, Boru reappeared, tail swishing and head cocked. "Kess, he's found something. What is it?"

She turned to face the wolvryn. "He says the trail ahead leads to a precipice that overlooks the enemy. He thinks there might be a way down."

"Finally. The Taker never makes it easy. Let's have a look."

He followed Boru, pushing through a few low-hanging boughs of mountain pine to emerge onto a broad cliff that cantilevered out into space. An amber glow silhouetted the end of the outcropping. He replaced the wolvryn eye inside the leather pouch and waited for his eyes to adjust, then walked to the edge of the plateau.

Far below, the lights from an ocean of fires blazed in the valley before the Pillars of Eldrek. Despite their elevation, the acrid smell of smoke displaced even the scent of mountain pine. Ksenia left the Aarindin behind and walked out to join him.

The sheer scale of the Kreegorian forces left them speechless. Campfires from the endless ranks saturated the ground and stretched beyond the horizon. Even at the late hour, the murmur of thousands of soldiers milling about echoed up the mountain. The air, thick with the metallic tang of armor and weaponry, hung heavy with anticipation.

"It's like the forward base camp is a dam holding back a surging tide," said Ksenia.

"And the Taker saw fit to send a flood. There's no way we can defeat an army that size."

He withdrew from the edge of the cliff and walked its perimeter, hoping to find a pathway that dropped behind the palisade. But the only way on or off the plateau was the way they had arrived. On both sides, the cliff dropped away. Never mind the Aarindin; even if they had adequate rope and gear, he didn't think they could manage the descent.

He returned to join her still gazing down at the enemy camp. Directly below them, a small explosion flared, followed moments later by the vibration of a pressure wave. Eventually, the clamor of screams and shouts of alarm echoed through the valley. "Those must be the munitions traps."

"That ought to give them something to think about."

"It won't be enough. It will take a miracle of the Giver to—"

Before he could finish his thought, heat blossomed across his chest and seared as painful striations throughout the runes covering his body. He grunted in pain, but the agony vanished, replaced by the pleasurable warmth of zenith pulsing across his runes.

Unbidden, the flows coalesced over his chest and swept into his arca prime. Without guidance or direction, his sight shifted to something resembling Boru's enhanced perception of the world, except that everything revealed itself to him in currents of zenith.

He reached a hand forward, caressing the flows as palpable currents in the air. Life was all around them—not just Boru or Ksenia, but the trees, the rocks, even the Great Crown itself, resonated with flows of zenith. In the rocks, zenith eddied as sluggish midnight blue swirls. Ksenia and Boru shed bright, streaming halos of the essence.

"What is it?" she asked.

He swallowed, then tugged at the neckline of the sheff gifted to him by Seldora. Light played across the runes there, and Ksenia gasped as Bryndor said, "Moons, I can't believe it. Lluthean must have made it back, or completed the trial. I never thought I could channel again, but my gift has returned, and I . . . I can feel my arca prime."

Ksenia stepped forward and separated the folds of the thin material, inspecting the rune as it flared to life. "It's beautiful. Can you tell what it does?"

"I'm not sure. I can see zenith, but not just the ambient currents. It flows through everything. I can even sense it from the Kreeg."

At the thought, he turned his attention back to the enemy far below. Acting on instinct, he sought to siphon off the flows of zenith from the enemy. His intention was to sample the zenith permeating from the Kreeg to see if it revealed anything about their foe. But where he intended only a taste of the source, a deluge of power flooded his awareness and primed his lesser runes.

The surge was so abrupt that he felt compelled to divert the current into the runes on his shoulders. Heat burst forth, the intensity thrumming his core and threatening to overwhelm him. Before he could think of an alternate course, he unleashed a colossal blast of rune fire that carried out into the night sky.

Ksenia dropped to her knees and clasped hands to her ears a second before the rune fire detonated. Bryndor watched as the cerulean wave rippled across the southern horizon. Not once had he ever summoned so much of the force, and he waited, expecting something of the draft to leech his strength, but nothing happened. If anything, his arca prime beckoned him to siphon more.

He crouched near her. "Kess, I don't imagine the Kreeg will miss that little display. We should retreat before they send scouts up here."

She studied his face, then cocked her head. "That was absolutely the most amazing display of rune fire I've ever heard of. Did it tax you at all?"

He rolled his shoulders, expecting to feel some sense of fatigue. "No, actually. I feel fine."

Ksenia looked back down into the valley, where the Kreeg forces were beginning to stir. Shouts of alarm rang out across the camp, and torchlights flickered with chaotic motion. "I felt the vacuum of zenith when you channeled, Bryn. If you can do it again, only bigger, hotter, could you send the rune fire down on the Kreeg?"

Unbidden, his arca prime kindled awake, and without calculation or boasting, he knew that if he commanded enough zenith, he could deliver a terrible assault on the Kreeg. His head bobbed up and down. "Yes. I don't know how I know it, but yes, I think I can."

"Alright, give me a minute. I need to kindle my arca prime, but be ready."

"What are you going to do?" he asked.

"I'm going to magnify your gift. You should feel it, and when you do, use everything the Giver gave you and send as many of the Kreeg as you can to the Taker."

At first, he doubted the sanity of her plan. But then he realized, in all the time he had known her, even in the pseudo-reality of the Rite of Revealing, he had never witnessed her use her arca prime. They still had plenty of time to retreat. And yet, he had to admit, he was curious. What if her gift could somehow augment his? What if they could deliver a crippling blow to the Kreeg forces? Surely there was enough time to find out, but at what cost?

"Kess, if you do this, will it drop you into the draft? We could still slip down under cover of darkness before their scouts arrive."

She grabbed the front of his sheff and pulled him in for a kiss. "Let me worry about the draft. You worry about raining rune fire down on the Kreeg. Eyes to the horizon, yes?"

Her unbridled confidence displaced any lingering apprehensions. A hundred memories surfaced in his mind. Ksenia galloping bareback across open fields, her open hand encouraging him to step into Stone's Grasp for the first time, the two of them braving the worst parts of the Stillness. With this woman as his partner, what did he have to fear?

"Alright, I'll be ready."

He stood and turned to look down at the gathered forces. Torches streamed about the camp as the Kreeg military came to life. Ksenia situated herself in a sitting position and in the periphery of his awareness, he sensed her channeling. In tandem, he opened his arca prime to the flow of zenith.

He felt Ksenia place a hand on the back of his leg, her touch at once intimate and soft, but insistent. There was a lone pulse, as if something prodigious had collided with his awareness. Instead of physically staggering forward, his body became weightless, and his sense of self propelled out into the night.

He hovered outside his body, sensing the flows of zenith as pleasurable filaments of power that caressed, massaged, and demanded to permeate his gift. Repositories of zenith lay all about him, insisting to be siphoned and manipulated. He inhaled once, then beckoned the force in and was inundated with ecstasy as zenith, pure and limitless, suffused his awareness.

The torrential surge rushed through his runes with such force that they lifted from his skin, straining with achy pleasure to shape the zenith to his will. The runes on his forearms blazed with unbridled consensus, confirming the rightness of his actions.

He directed his attention to the canyon below and unleashed a flood of rune fire. The wave gathered at the far eastern end of the Kreeg forces, expanding south for hundreds of yards, then building in height. He pulled on more zenith, feeling the flows from the Kreeg, from the animals and trees, from the very mountain itself. He siphoned more and more, his thirst for the power unquenchable, his hunger and need ravenous.

Thunder and lightning sheared the night sky overhead, and an otherworldly glow bled through the heavens and bathed the valley in one last beacon of warning. At last, he unshackled the tsunami of rune fire and released it on the forces below.

Liquid death splashed down into the valley, gathering speed as it roared across the Kreeg army. Bryndor continued to siphon, shaping just enough countercurrent to prevent the flows from splashing against the Aarindorian palisade. Hot gouts of smoke and ash shot up from the canyon. The deafening roar of the flood of fire drowned out the screams of man and beast alike.

He stood immersed in the currents and lost track of time as he fueled the rune fire, shaping the surge into a river that pursued the Kreeg army down the valley and to the west. Eventually, the trailing edge of his rune fire thinned to reveal a blackened, smoldering, lifeless wasteland. He sensed the ambient currents of zenith wane and was reminded of the edge of the Stillness. With an effort, he clamped down his will in an attempt to prevent his arca prime from pulling on more of the power.

To his surprise, swirls of zenith continued to leech in and sustain the rune in a strange, sickening mixture of pleasure and power. But a wall of fear swelled in his mind as he realized that he had depleted the flows of zenith all about him, and only now was he beginning to understand the magnitude of his channeling.

With a sharp and furious effort of will, he closed himself to the flows of zenith and watched as the blazing light from his arca prime receded to a faint glow. He stood panting, staring at the wreckage of the valley below. Far to the west, the torrential surges of rune fire flowed, leaving behind a nimbus of light on the western horizon.

"Giver, Kess, I think that's done it."

He realized then that he couldn't feel her touch on the back of his leg. When had that stopped, exactly? He turned, expecting to see her in the throes of the draft, but she lay in the fetal position. He crouched down and placed a hand on her shoulder. Through the thin material of her sheff, her skin felt cold.

He swallowed back a wave of nausea and turned her onto her back. One arm flopped to the ground, the top of her hand smacking painfully on the rocks, and her head lolled to the side. He pulled her into his lap, waiting for some hint that she lived, his senses straining to feel the smallest flicker of zenith through her runes, any twitch of muscle, any shift of her chest as she drew breath. But she remained flaccid. And over the minutes, the horror of what he had done began to smother him.

He recalled drowning in the zenith he had siphoned and feeling the distinct and familiar ribbons of her zenith, zenith that he stole. He had thought it was part of her gift, the way she magnified his arca prime, but now he realized that her gift had pushed him over the edge and well beyond any control, beyond any awareness of his actions. He had lost himself in the absolute power over all the life around him. But now that he thought about it, he realized that her essence had been there, contributing to his unbridled consumption. The memory of it bubbled up to his awareness and suffocated him with the weight of his actions.

He shuddered and screamed out in rage. The sound echoed out across the canyon, wordless, yet carrying the unmistakable tone of primal, undiluted misery and loss. He cradled her lifeless form in his arms, rocking back and forth, unable to marshal any coherent thoughts as he waited for her to return. When the sun broke on the eastern horizon, Bryndor Baellentrell sat alone on the cliffside of the Great Crown, witness to the destruction he had wrought, while Ksenia Balladuren faded to the Drift.

His awareness of the world vanished. Nothing mattered but her face, the peaceful expression of her still sleeping eyes, the strange way he had to keep propping up her head when it lolled boneless to the side. She remained motionless in his arms but for the vibrations of his shuddering sobs.

He lingered there, holding her, his mind numb from everything that had transpired, from the horror of everything that he had become. Thoughts floated up to his awareness, but they were smothered as a moth beneath an avalanche under the monumental weight of abject self-loathing. The only thing his broken mind could manage was to remain with her, to exist in the misery of the moment.

In the periphery of his perception, the sound of racing footsteps approached, and someone dropped to their knees beside him. A deep, muffled voice spoke, then someone shook his shoulder, gently at first, then insistent. "Bryn, can you hear me? It's me, Kae!"

And at last, he looked into Kaellor's haunted eyes. His uncle's eyebrows lifted, lips parted as if to say something, but his voice caught, and Kaellor had to swallow before speaking. "Giver, Bryn, what happened?"

Chapter Seventy-Four: Falling Stars

Kaellor had raced out of Stone's Grasp with a trio of Aarindin. Through the shek, Overwarden Kaldera had directed him to Stellance, where a quad of Outriders with a sympath exchanged his mount and provided fresh provisions. After a single night of rest, the quad escorted him in relative secrecy into the high places above Stellance.

After two days of riding, the sympath coaxed an Aarindin to grip him, and he dismissed the Outriders, then followed trails used by goat herders toward the eastern Pillar of Eldrek. That was a day and a half ago, and since then, he had pushed his mount beyond exhaustion.

The dark pillar rose as a clear landmark but was still hours away as the sun set. The new moon of Baellen was dormant in the night sky, making travel treacherous. He considered stopping but knew he must be close. Taker's breath, he could smell the smoke from enemy campfires. And so he pushed on through the darkness, trusting the mount to pick its way in the night.

Hours later, the Aarindin walked along a cliffside, and a warm glow kindled on the southern horizon. Chaotic currents of zenith gathered overhead, reminding Kaellor of the wild discharges of energy over the Korjinth Mountains. Blue lightning skittered and flowed to a central location, silhouetting the eastern pillar in stark relief.

Kaellor sat erect to get a better view when the Aarindin lurched to the side, stumbled, and ungripped him. He staggered from fatigue as a torrential vacuum of zenith sucked across the mountains, draining toward the eastern pillar. The sensation reminded him of the pervasive feeling of emptiness and loss he had felt years ago when he and Laryn had committed to binding their gifts.

Moments later, thunderous vibrations reverberated across the mountainside, and the unmistakable flare of rune fire illuminated the horizon. The mount wheeled to turn back down the steep trail. He reached out and grabbed a stout branch as he slid off, barely landing on his feet, the pommel of the guardian sword scoring across the side of his ribs.

As the thunder of rune fire reverberated, another feeling assaulted his senses, and it felt as if a great hole had opened up in the center of the world, like a huge bellows was sucking everything into its center. The detonation that followed vibrated through his feet and belly all at once and left him staggering about to keep his footing.

Boulders from overhead clattered through the timber, and Kaellor responded to the urging of his guardian sword. The anemic flows of zenith were barely enough to support a small guardian shield. He knelt against the cliffside, struggling to maintain the protective shell as rubble bounced down around him, burying him in a mound of broken timber and mountain stone.

He couldn't say how long he remained there, holding the meager guardian ward in place. But eventually, the flows of zenith returned to normal, and he magnified the shield, then pulsed a force wave, sending the avalanche down the mountainside. He chanced a look to see where the debris field landed and was surprised to discover the first light of dawn.

That revelation ignited the fear that he would be too late, that something of Salveen's premonition would still ring true. He launched into a sprint, clambering up a steep and winding trail. At last, he reached a rocky precipice.

He wasn't sure what to expect, but drew up short, dumbfounded to find Ranika. The young woman stood beside Boru, her arm draped over the massive wolvryn's neck as he lay prone on the ground, muzzle resting on forepaws.

"Nika! Where is he? Am I too late?"

Ranika turned to face him, reddened, puffy eyes her only response. She held his gaze for a moment, then ever so subtly gestured, pointing her chin toward the edge of the cliffside. Some thirty steps ahead, a man sat alone with unnatural stillness, facing the southern horizon. Kaellor recognized Bryndor's broad shoulders but couldn't tell if his nephew drew breath.

A foreboding sense of dread gave rise to a sour taste, and he spat, then raced forward to collapse to his knees beside Bryndor. It took a moment for him to recognize what he was seeing. His nephew sat almost lifeless, eyes unfocused, staring unblinking, holding the limp body of Ksenia Balladuren in his arms.

Her limbs sprawled out, elbows and knees hyper-extended, her head listing to the side. "Bryn, son, look at me."

But Bryndor remained lost inside himself and made no response. Kaellor set a hand on his nephew's shoulder and spoke again, louder. "Bryndor, I'm so sorry. I should have been here with you. I should have been here all along. Bryn."

He waited, but the young man only stared ahead. Kaellor began to worry that perhaps his nephew had burned through his entire reserve of zenith, that maybe the figure sitting before him was just a husk, and that the essence of his nephew had somehow burned away. He shook harder, with more insistence. "Bryn, can you hear me? It's me, Kae."

At last, Bryndor turned to face him, but there was no recognition in his eyes. Delicate currents of zenith spiraled and flickered in the depths of his pupils, but instead of adding depth or a sense of vibrance, the effect made it seem like his nephew had retreated somewhere behind the miasma of his gift. It felt like looking at the lifeless statue of his brother in the inner sanctum.

He tried to speak, but phlegm gathered at the back of his throat, and he had to swallow. "Giver, Bryn, what happened?"

They stared at one another for long moments, and Kaellor reached out with his other hand to cup Bryndor's cheek. At last, the young man blinked, but when he spoke, his voice was hollow, devoid of emotion. "It was me, Kae. I killed them all. And I lost her. I lost her all over again."

Kaellor followed Bryndor's gaze and glanced down into the valley before the Pillars of Eldrek. Where he expected to see rows of enemy forces, instead, the entire region appeared as a hellish wasteland. Blackened slags of rock jutted up through an ocean of ash. Chaotic swirls of blue rune fire skittered around the bases of charred tree stumps. Beyond the remnant surges of rune fire, the valley floor was dormant. In only moments, Bryndor had quite literally reduced everything to a sea of ash.

"I've become everything the kingdom expected of me, and more. I'm a monster," he said.

Kaellor pulled his eyes back to meet Bryndor's and shook his head. "No, son, you're no monster. You're—"

He stopped speaking, overwhelmed by a vacant feeling as Bryndor siphoned all the ambient zenith around them—but it was more than that. He felt the vacant emptiness again as Bryndor drew out the zenith from inside Kaellor's core. A nimbus of rune fire flared across Bryndor's skin and he set Ksenia's head gently on the ground, then stood, his back to the edge of the cliff.

Kaellor rose to his feet, feeling like an invalid rising from a sickbed. Bryndor held his arms out to the side, the glow of rune fire casting dancing shadows on Ksenia's face. "I devoured everything. I will devour everything, Kae. How am I not a monster?"

"I don't have any answers that will make sense right now, Bryn. Son . . . please, just let it go for now. Release the zenith. Come back with me and we can sort it all out."

Rune fire roiled across Bryndor's arms and legs, streaming across his torso and face. Through it all, Kaellor could see streams of tears on the young man's face. More zenith fled from Kaellor's center, and the feeling caused him to drop to his hands to knees. Instinctively, he clutched the hilt of the guardian sword.

Bryndor's absolute command of zenith was staggering. He had never heard of anyone with that kind of control over the force. Kaellor's head swam, and he felt like he might vomit, and then the withering fatigue dissipated as Bryndor released his command of the currents.

"I can't be this, Kae. You have to stop me, stop . . . whatever this is."

Kaellor straightened to see Bryndor holding out one hand, shrouded in chaotic streams of rune fire. His nephew studied his own hand, examining the limb as if it belonged to someone else. "All you have to do is stop, Bryn. Stop channeling, and then we can go home."

Bryndor sucked at his teeth and frowned. "I'm trying. But I can't shut it off." He savagely tore apart his tunic to reveal a gleaming arca prime. Intricate runes sifted across his chest in a circular pattern. The runes formed the shape of a serpent, then transitioned into a set of glowing eyes, and finally shifted into a complex pattern that streamed around his chest, brilliant and alive with zenith. He pounded a fist at his chest, and sparks of zenith flared to the ground, spilling out of the arca prime like hot embers from a forge.

Bryndor grimaced in pain and arched his neck back. "I don't want to be this. You never should have brought us back here. Make it stop, Kae! I can't make it stop!"

More zenith flowed out of Kaellor, leaving him again on the verge of retching, when Ranika staggered forward. She lifted her hand, and he felt a gentle pop, then relief as she erected some kind of globe of nadir around them. The shadowy sphere seemed to prevent the leeching effects of Bryndor's arca prime, but also muted all sound and light.

Bryndor's muted cry still pierced her barrier. "Please Kae, you have to end it. Nika's shielding won't stop it!"

Zenith blazed across Bryndor's torso, gathering in intensity, roiling around his arca prime, difficult to look upon even through the gauzy haze of Ranika's nadir shielding. The ground started to vibrate and Bryndor clutched his arms across his chest. "It's happening! Grind it, Kae! Look out!"

Kaellor responded to the urging of his guardian sword and allowed instinct to trigger his gift. He summoned a guardian ward, reinforcing Ranika's nadir shielding. A concussive pulse erupted with blinding light as a deluge of rune fire detonated across the precipice. Kaellor squinted against the blinding light in time to see Bryndor jettison backward off the cliff and down toward the valley floor, trailed by streamers of zenith and rune fire.

He rushed to the edge of the cliff to watch as Bryndor streaked to the ground like some falling star from the heavens. Ash mushroomed up in a cloud where he landed, and when it settled, there was no sign of his nephew below.

Chapter Seventy-Five: Consent

L aryn stood with Therek in the anteroom outside the inner sanctum, waiting for Hestian to allow entrance inside. The field marshal barked orders to secure the floor and then the room. The seconds ticked by into momentous, painful minutes as sentinels poured into the chamber. At last, Hestian turned with a grim expression.

"What is it, Hestian?" she pressed. "Is the prince, is Lluthean dead?"

"The prince lives, but . . ." he said, turning to Therek. "I'm so sorry, my friend. We lost Karragin. She was killed in the fight. I can take you to her."

Therek stood blinking, mute but unwavering. He nodded with silent consent, and Hestian led him over to Karragin's body.

Laryn pushed into the room to find Lluthean sprawled on the floor underneath the statue of Eldrek. The murmur of her healer song filled the chamber even before she reached him. She inserted probing tendrils, searching for injuries, but a hand grabbed her wrist.

"I'm fine, Laryn. It's just the draft. I think I just need a rest," Lluthean croaked.

"I'll be the judge of that. Now, lie still." She completed a thorough survey and, sure enough, the young man was well steeped in the draft, but beyond that, he suffered no injury. Zenith flowed with a sluggish but otherwise smooth rhythm in his body, and she found no other concerns.

A voice from the far side of the room called out, "Got a strange one over here. I think he's alive!"

Lluthean's eyes fluttered open. "That would be Seldora, the Ilovesh. He's a friend. See to him if you can. And Nes, check on Neska."

He stopped speaking when his muscles clenched with dry heaves. Laryn sent soothing tendrils into his head and abdomen, relieving the nausea. She suspended her gift and turned to Baccal. "Find a healer or medic. On my authority, bring lammen berry and spiritwort tea for the prince."

Baccal looked to Amniah. They shared a look of understanding. "I won't leave her side," said the guster.

Laryn rose to her feet and searched the room for Neska, but her gaze first fell upon the Ilovesh lying against the back wall. Even on the ground, she could tell he rivaled Therek in height. Cold sweat covered pale, lavender skin. She crouched down and removed the thin material of a shirt covering his lean frame. After placing one hand on his head and another on his chest, she fell into her gift.

Her surveillance was immediately disorienting. Zenith flowed in dense currents through even the most delicate tissues. Where humans and other creatures possessed innate stores, this being seemed saturated with zenith. Wherever she searched, the essence of zenith blinded her probing. Even his fluids ran tingly and rich with the essence.

After several minutes of probing, she gave up and stifled her gift. She signaled two sentinels to roll him to the side and began a manual, tactile examination of the man. She ran her hands across his head and found swollen, bruised tissues behind one ear. His neck moved without crepitus, but when she palpated his ribs, it was clear that several were splintered, and she suspected by the sucking motion of his chest that the lung underneath had collapsed.

"Giver, guide me." She opened herself up to her gift, but instead of sending in the probing tendrils to survey and monitor the healing process, she worked blind. She had no knowledge of Ilovesh anatomy or physiology, but if the being lying before her had lungs—and by every observation there was reason to believe so—then there should be a tear she could mend.

She slid her gift around the sac lining the lung and, sure enough, directly underneath a cluster of broken ribs, she felt a rent in the lung tissue. Before she could doubt herself, she opened her eyes. "Amniah, give me a knife, quickly child."

The guster withdrew a blade, flipped it hilt first, and handed it over. Laryn pushed the blade over one of the broken ribs, and a loud whoosh of air escaped. She pulled the edges of the torn lung sac together, then waited. Beneath her gift, it felt like the lung inflated. She made quick work, coaxing the tissues back together, sealing the wound she had just made.

To her surprise, the work required very little expenditure on her part. Once begun, the tissues seemed to heal of their own accord.

She sifted filaments across his ribs, feeling more than viewing where the fracture lines occurred, and noted where a rib fragment had dropped into the man's thorax. One by one, she tried to shift the pieces back into place. They knit together almost as fast as she oriented the fragments.

Last, she cupped his skull, uncertain of how to proceed. She chanced sending probing filaments in once again, and once again the saturation of zenith in his tissues all but blinded her gift. There was no reliable way to tell if he suffered from internal hemorrhaging.

"Sometimes less is more," she mumbled and sat back, stifling her gift.

A secondary visual survey showed that Seldora breathed with what appeared to be normal mechanics. The sagging flail portion of his chest now moved in concert with the undamaged side, and his skin was taking on hues of a ruddy, purple color. She hoped that was normal; it certainly made him appear more hearty.

The sound of footsteps caused her to turn. Baccal leaned forward. "Prince Lluthean is demading to speak to you, Your Radiance."

"Did you get him the lammen berry and spiritwort?"

"Yes. I think that they are helping already. He's sitting upright. But he's not making sense," said the guster.

"Explain."

"He wants you to mend Karragin's nadir burn."

Laryn cursed under her breath. Neska's broken form lay in a lifeless heap against the wall just steps away. "I haven't had time to check on Neska. See if she yet lives. I'll be right there."

Laryn stood and walked across the inner sanctum. Her path took her close to Karragin's corpse. Therek had dropped to his knees beside the woman. But for the blackened hole in the right side of her chest, she appeared to be sleeping.

She found Lluthean sitting, back leaning against the base of the statue of Eldrek. She crouched down and activated her gift. Lluthean held up a hand when the murmur of her healer song began.

"Laryn, I can't explain this yet in ways that will make sense. But I think I have a way to get her back. Can you repair the damaged tissue?"

"If she had survived the initial wound, yes, but that kind of healing relies on the patient's internal stores of zenith. Once a person dies, the tissues don't respond to my ministrations."

"I understand. I only have enough for one person, one . . . patient. Is Seldora going to make it?"

"He's alive. I repaired what I could. I think his chances are—actually, I don't know what they are."

"What about Neska?"

Laryn felt a weight press down on her shoulders. She glanced back to where Baccal knelt beside Neska's still form. "Honestly, Llu, I don't know, not yet. She's next. But look, what is this really about?"

Lluthean's expression fell distant. She began to wonder if the draft had addled his mind and considered having him transported back to the royal suites. Before she could stand to garner Hestian's attention, he grabbed her wrist.

Sentinels had gathered around him, so he spoke to her in the hand language. *"I need you to trust me, and we have to do this before I change my mind. I have one spare dose of crystallized zenith. I think it can temporarily restore Karragin and allow you to mend her body."*

Laryn considered the proposition. *"Even if that's true, I can't anchor her soul, Llu. She already wanders the Drift."*

"No, she does not, and in this you have to trust me. Mend her body and leave the rest to me."

"If you are wrong, it will kill Therek."

"I'm not wrong. Bring us together, or get me to Neska. I'm not losing both of them today."

She stood up and cleared her throat. "Alright, Llu. Get him to his feet and bring him to Karragin's . . . to Karragin."

Other than two sentinels guarding the entry and a healer assigned to monitor the Ilovesh, everyone in the room gathered around, more than thirty people, as Lluthean staggered under the support of two sentinels. They lowered him to the ground beside the Mirrare.

Lluthean panted, swooned in place, and looked up to Therek, who knelt on the opposite side of his daughter. "Sir, I don't have time to explain why I know what I know. But we're going to try to get her back. Laryn, quick, we can't lose any more time."

Laryn knelt beside Therek and placed a hand on Karragin's brow and chest, activated her healer song, and identified the defect. The nadir burn had bored clean through the lung, missing her spine but nicking the major artery to the woman's right arm. With her gift primed, she nodded to Lluthean. He poured iridescent granules from the pouch into his palm, then sprinkled the crystals into Karragin's mouth, across her chest, and even into the wound.

Laryn gasped as the tissues responded, thrumming with zenith in much the same way as the Ilovesh. Already blood welled out from the gaping hole, and she scrambled to seal the rent in the damaged vessels, then guide the layers of tissue back together, from lung to muscle and bone and finally skin. The absolute rapidity with which the dead woman's body knit back together was nothing short of miraculous. As Laryn withdrew, Karragin's heart pulsed with weak and irregular flutters, and she drew independent breaths.

An anguished scream brought her out of her healer trance as Lluthean fell, writhing in pain. His back arched, hands clawed the air, and his eyes rolled about with wild abandon. Zenith flashed across his arca prime, and then he dissipated into barely visible blue mist.

LLUTHEAN TOOK A MOMENT to orient himself. The first transition hurt, the second was agonizing, but the third was beyond brutal and left him wondering if he would ever be able to call on that portion of his gift again. He flexed his limbs, surprised to feel that they moved without the mind-consuming pain.

In the ethereal version of the inner sanctum, countless ghostly figures pressed in around them. Therek and Laryn knelt beside Karragin's body, but beyond that the room faded into obscurity. He cupped his hands and called out, "Iska! If you can hear me, I need Karragin!"

The subtle flapping of wings preceded the riftwing, and Iska approached from behind him, landing on his shoulder. He spoke in soothing tones and signed, *"I think you're the reason she might come back. Find Karragin."*

The hawk lifted off and flew beyond his perception. Lluthean waited. What if Iska couldn't bring her back? How long should he wait? How long could they wait before Karragin's body deteriorated? He couldn't spare more crystallized zenith—the small portion that remained would be required to neutralize the remaining nadrean that Tarkannen had brought forth into the world of the living. He imagined how awful the mental anguish would be if Therek had to watch his daughter perish all over again.

Her voice, when she spoke, relieved him from dwelling on that misery. "You're not supposed to be here anymore."

He turned to see her standing in her Mirrare gear, Iska perched on her shoulder. "Karragin. Giver's good fortune. Good, so you haven't merged on?"

She shook her head. "No. I was going to say goodbye to Iska, and she was going to guide me. But she brought me here instead."

"Right, sorry, that's mostly my fault. Listen, this is going to sound strange, but would you come back with me? Leave this place and come back? Your father needs you. We all need you."

She studied his face. "You don't know what you are asking, from either of us."

"I know that your story isn't finished. The pages of your life, they weren't for Tarkannen to tear out and toss away. Those are for you. But that only happens if you take my hand and my gift, and come back."

She smiled and shook her head in amusement. "I know what you are suggesting, and it's too much. I can't take that from anyone, but especially not from you."

He puzzled over her words, trying not to feel wounded, but if he were honest, they stung. "Look, I'm not asking you to be mine or to owe me anything. If you come back, you can live your life and I'll live mine. Yes, we would be tethered, but it's not like the binding I had to Tarkannen. Ours would be one of mutual consent, mutual benefit. I get it. I'm just a dumb kid, but it's still a second chance."

"That's not what I meant, Llu. You don't remember, but I saw it, I experienced it, what happened to you in the Revealing."

"I can't change what Sephora did to me in the Revealing, and I only remember half of the things that happened there, but that shouldn't change—"

"It was before your time with Sephora, Lluthean. There was more than that, so much more." Karragin shook her head from side to side, appearing genuinely at a loss. He couldn't ever recall the woman demonstrating so much open emotion.

He sensed that he was losing the argument and couldn't find the words to explain why he knew that his was the right course of action. How could he get her to trust him when she still saw him as a spoiled prince?

"I don't know what to say. I don't remember it. If I hurt you or made mistakes, I don't know how to make amends, but I just know that you have to come back with me. Please, just come back."

"Why?"

The choice he had made rose full to his awareness, spreading at first as a vacancy of grief that hollowed out his chest, threatening, even in his ethereal state, to collapse everything into a bottomless pit of despair. He couldn't look her in the eye. "Because. I chose you, alright? I gave up the chance to revive Neska to try this, and I don't . . . I can't do it again. This is the one chance I have to salvage something from today's ashes."

LARYN CONTINUED BOTH to monitor Karragin's vital functions and watch as the faint blue apparition of Lluthean flickered in and out of focus. It appeared that he stood, but beyond that, his movements shifted beyond her perception and made his outline blur. It reminded her of trying to see the individual wingbeats of a hummingbird.

After more than an hour, the borrowed zenith that the crystals imparted began to fade, and Karragin's heartbeat slowed. Laryn began to doubt the young man and wondered if he had lost himself once again in the Drift. She reached out with her probing, trying to sense his status, and he materialized, standing upright, appearing rejuvenated and robust.

He knelt beside Karragin. "Lluthean, I was able to heal her, but she's slipping away. The zenith you gave her—it wasn't enough."

Lluthean pressed his lips to a thin line and shook Karragin's shoulders with anger. "You've got to be the most stubborn woman. Don't come back for me or Neska or any of that, come back because you want to. You hear me!"

Something shifted in Karragin's breathing. She inhaled a full breath and, to Laryn's surprise, vibrant currents of zenith suffused the woman's body, traveling through an invisible conduit from Lluthean to Karragin. *Oh, my stupid boy, what have you done?*

In answer to Laryn's question, Karragin's eyes fluttered open. Cheers and murmurs rose again, and Karragin stared around in confusion. When at last her eyes found Lluthean's, he signed, *"Took you long enough."*

Karragin lifted her hands, her gestures clumsy but understandable. *"My stupid monk. You don't know half as much as you think, and even less than you should. Turn around and be with the one who loves you the most."*

A look of exasperation deflated the prince, and tears of frustration brimmed in his eyes. He stood and signed with sharp gestures, *"I don't understand you . . . at all. Welcome back."*

Lluthean turned in anger, preparing to storm from the sanctum, and came nose to nose with Neska. The wolvryn had pushed forward through the crowd on three legs. Fur was matted to a wound on her hind flank and flecks of blood frothed with her wheezy breaths, but she stood on her own strength and licked him on the face. Lluthean gasped and pressed his face against wolvryn's, holding her there long moments.

Laryn's heart swelled, and she thanked the Giver for miracles big and small. She embraced her gift in preparation to heal Neska's injuries and wondered how she would explain any of this through the shek. Kaellor was never going to believe it.

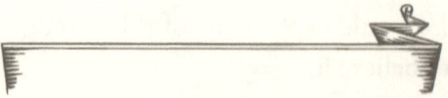

Chapter Seventy-Six: Dark Horizons

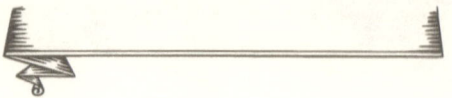

My old hands ache from writing, so this shall be the conclusion of my biography. If you have taken the time to read the ramblings of an old woman, then I say to you, I am grateful. Grateful that lessons learned over a lifetime are not lost on tomorrow's youth. If I could leave you with one more lesson, the words scrolled at the base of Eldrek's statue are the only truth you need remember: unconditional love wields the greatest power. Embody these words, inspire them in the people around you, and the world will be a better place as you lift your eyes to the horizon.

—The Tome of Nivosh, 75 PC, translated by Veeble Hebben

Translator's personal note: I lack the skill of Ksenia Balladuren, and all credit for deciphering this work should be given to her and her alone. But I am confident in the accuracy of the translation, for only with such conviction could my friend, Ms. Balladuren, have inspired Prince Bryndorllean Baellentrell to perform miracles on behalf of the kingdom and repel the Kreeg invasion. Balladur cor delledence indeed. Would that we all live up to Ms. Balladuren's example.

THE HALF-MOON OF BAELLEN cast pale light across the Borderlands as Ranika pushed through brambles to get a better view of her quarry. She stifled a curse when a thorn scraped across her neck. She had half a mind to erect a dense null field, but had already drafted enough nadir in the last few days to make her head feel buzzy. Boru must have sensed her angst and licked the spot where the thorn had scratched her.

She rewarded him with a massage under the chin, but set her focus on the enemy camp only twenty paces ahead. She enhanced her vision to survey a cluster of over ten tents, remnants from the Kreegorian army that had marched on Aarindorn only weeks before.

Outriders had skirmished with Kreegorian forces on several occasions, harrying the remnants of the enemy as they retreated to the west after the devastation of rune fire. Patrols of Aarindorian soldiers hunted the grotvonen and grondle with impunity. Ranika left the paramilitary groups to their tasks. Her interests lay in a different direction.

A throaty rumble gathered in Boru's throat. "Hush now, Boru. It's not safe yet, and there's too many of them for you and me."

The wolvryn huffed in frustration and settled down, belly to the ground, head resting on his paws. She adjusted a bundle of stolen clothing under one arm and rubbed at his ear.

A sentry called out from the camp, speaking in the Kindred tongue with their thick accent, as if the words rolled out from the back of his throat. "Stop and announce, who goes there?"

Ranika cast her vision across the camp and identified the sentry, a lone Kreegorian holding a spear and torch. He issued the challenge to another man, covered in ash and wearing the singed uniform of a Kreegorian soldier, who limped into view from the east.

Boru lifted his head, ears perked up. "Yup, that's our man. Let's wait this out and see if it goes any different."

The wounded soldier staggered ahead, heedless of the warning, head bowed low. The sentry dropped his spear and stepped forward to put an arm under his comrade, ushering him toward a campfire. "Commander Keel, another straggler from the war. This one's covered in ash and seems battle-shocked!"

The sentry led the weary survivor to the center of camp toward a small fire, even assisting him to a seated position on a log. A Kreegorian dressed in an officer's uniform exited a tent and stepped forward to inspect the wounded newcomer. Other members of the camp staggered out of their tents. Some men rubbed sleep from their eyes; others labored to find weapons or don armor. All in all, nearly thirty men gathered around the stranger.

For his part, the refugee took a seat and stared at the ground, matted locks of dark hair obscuring his face. If the trail dust was any indication, he had survived a lot. The man appeared exhausted.

Keel filled a wooden mug with water and held it out to the soldier. "Were you there when that valley roiled like an ocean set aflame?"

The man took the cup with a nod. He cleared gravel from his throat, spat at the ground, then looked up. "Yes, sir, I was. I thank you for the drink."

He drained the mug and held it out. "Might I trouble you for more?"

Keel considered the soldier for a moment. "Has he got any weapons?"

"No sir. Arrived as you see him," said the sentry.

The commander studied the newcomer a moment longer, hesitated, then motioned for one of his men to refill the newcomer's mug. "We lost a lot of good men, friends of mine. Who was your commanding officer? Guyver? Colley?"

The stranger drained the second mug and licked his lips before setting the mug on the ground. "Why did we come over here in the first place, all the way from Kreeg?"

"Soldier?" asked Keel.

"Commander Keel asked you a direct question. I suggest you answer him," said the sentry. He had retrieved his spear and held the weapon forward.

The newcomer raised his hands, palms open in surrender. "I meant no disrespect, sir. I can tell you my commanding officer's name if you can tell me why we came all the way over here. Lots of people died. I would like to know why. I'm just trying to make sense of the madness, sir."

The commander stared for long moments at the refugee and eventually sighed, then gestured a command that brought most of his men to attention. The Kreeg camp formed a defensive ring around Keel and turned grim faces toward the newcomer. "We marched because our orders said to march. But it's no secret why we came here. It wasn't because of the drought, or the witch-king of Aarindorn, or the sorcerers beyond the mountains. It was for the fight, for Kreegorian pride, and of course all the spoils of war. But none of that would make much sense to you, since you're not from Kreeg, are you son?"

The stranger dropped his head. "You know, no matter how many Kreeg I encounter, I just can't get my tongue to bend the sounds to your accent. I mean, it's like you all try to choke yourselves with the words. I appreciate the information, Commander Keel. It makes this easier."

Even from her distance, Ranika could feel the siphoning of zenith. Though she couldn't summon the force, it still resided inside her, as with all living things. She swallowed back a wave of nausea and flared nadir into a null field to prevent the leeching effect as the Aarindorian siphoned all the ambient zenith about them. Commander Keel raised an arm and shouted, "Kill him!"

But before one spear was jabbed, one sword drawn, before even a single crossbow bolt was fired, a roiling blue and white ball of rune fire manifested in the stranger's lap and detonated in a circle. She felt the vacuum of force before the wave of light and heat washed over her vantage point. The vacuum was followed by the rumble of thunder, and then the predictable rain-patter-staccato of weapons and body parts falling to the ground all about her.

She released her null field, and the nauseating taint of sterile galvanic vapors, burned flesh, and boiled blood assaulted her senses. When the dust quite literally cleared, she stood and assessed the remnants of the camp. None of the Kreeg had survived the blast. She released her hold of nadir and signaled Boru. They sauntered forward to inspect the zeniphile. Bryndor Baellentrell lay on his back in a tattered Kreegorian uniform that only just managed to cover his small bits.

She dropped the bundle she had tucked under her arm, letting the clothes drop onto his chest. Boru crept forward, sniffed at the man from top to bottom, then began licking the ash from his face. He fluttered his eyes open. "You know, Bryn. If you're going to keep wiping out the leftovers, you could at least save a tent or two. A girl's gotta get her beauty sleep."

Bryndor coughed ash, then lifted one shaky hand to pat Boru on the side of the jaw. "You should take Boru back to Karragin. She and Neska can keep him from going feral. You two . . . you need to get away from me, Nika."

She removed her indigo Moonie scarf, allowing her spirals of hair to catch the breeze, scrubbed at her scalp, then replaced the garment to tame the offending strands. "You know I will not do that, Bryn. There's nothing you can say or do to make us leave your side. You think you're broken, and maybe you are. I was broken once, and you helped put me back together. The way I see it, ol' Boru and I are with you until the end, even if you do make a messy travel companion." She patted at her tunic, displacing dust and ash to emphasize her point.

Bryndor sat forward and blew more ash from his nose, then wrapped hands around his knees and dipped his head. "I can't. I don't want to hurt you, Nika."

"Well, that's a relief, because I don't want to get hurt," she quipped. She crouched down in front of him, waiting.

He huffed once, then looked up at her. The initial expression of mirth wilted as utter grief stole across his face. Tears welled and fell freely down his soot-stained cheeks. "I'm so angry . . . all the time. And I can't shut it out. Grind me, I don't know if I want to. I'm barely keeping this thing from leeching all the zenith from the air right now." He pounded at his chest, still iridescent with the runes of his arca prime.

She watched him wrestle with self-loathing, uncertain how much space to give the man. But eventually her calves started to cramp, so she shifted to a sitting position. "Look, I've been right where you are. Well, maybe not right where you are, but pretty grinding close. I'm not going to tell you how to get better, and I won't promise you that you will. But whatever happens, we'll face it together. Like Red always said, eyes to the horizon."

He rubbed at his eyes, sniffed back tears, and nodded. "Thanks for the change of clothes."

She shrugged indifference. "They weren't my clothes, and it's better than looking at your moon-kissed bare ass for the rest of the journey."

"Fair enough," he said and threaded one arm through the fresh shirtsleeve. A dark scab marred the back of his shoulder, a remnant of his descent from the cliff near the pillar. She resisted the urge to pepper him with questions about how he had survived the drop. They had time, and she sensed that any revelations he cared to share about his newfound gifts would need to be unveiled only when he was ready.

"How did you even know to come find me?" he asked.

She recalled standing with Kaellor on the Pillars of Eldrek, completely out of her element as he broke down into uncontrollable sobs. The two of them had stared, transfixed, at the spot where he had landed. She didn't trust her eyes when Bryndor shifted his position on the ground, not until Boru huffed and started retreating down the mountainside.

In that singular moment, Kaellor's weeping had shifted from utter agony to joy. "Kae sent me after you. We saw you land and honestly thought you were dead. But then you sat up, and Boru took off. Your uncle was incapable of saying much. But he made me promise to find you, to look after you if I could. He said he knew you wouldn't come back. He sensed it, with his gift, I think. Anyway, he wanted me to tell you it was alright. That you didn't have to return to Stone's Grasp unless you wanted to."

She reached into a pocket and retrieved the small bauble Kaellor had thrust into her hands. "He said to give you this, his shek. One of them will listen every night at sundown, in case you need to reach out." A frown stole across her brow. "But then he also said he didn't expect that you would want to use it for a long time."

She placed the shek in his hand. Bryndor ran a finger across the white stone and pocketed the pin.

"Did he say anything else?"

"No. But we were interrupted," said Ranika.

Bryndor turned his back, removed the tattered remnants of his pants, and pulled on the clean leggings. "What do you mean?"

"When we were standing there, I felt it. Something shifted in the currents of nadir. Lluthean did something and . . . I think Tarkannen is gone. Overwarden Kaldera surmised as much in his report to your uncle. All the umbral fell lifeless. I passed a few on the way to find you. They looked like the empty husks left when an insect sheds its skin. Anyway, without the flatheads, the grot and grondle began attacking one another, and even some of the Kreeg. Our allies from Faltusch swept down from the north, routing what was left of the beasts and had an easy time of it."

Ranika shook her head from side to side and tucked a sprig of hair under her indigo scarf. "That wave of rune fire you unleashed all but wiped out the Kreeg. The debris field I crossed was more than a mile wide in front of the Pillars, and I couldn't see the end of it to the west. Anyway, after that, the regent and your aunt chimed in. Lluthean escaped the Drift. I couldn't make sense of what Laryn said, but some crazy stuff happened back in Stone's Grasp. If I have the right of things, your brother killed Tarkannen. Karra was dead, then wasn't dead. Foreigners, an Ilovesh and some Logrend if that makes sense, fought in the inner sanctum? Neska was wounded and then healed. Anyway, after hearing all of that, Kaellor sent me to find you and told Laryn he was going to assist the overwarden."

She expected her report to evoke a response, but Bryndor stared at the southern horizon. He'd released a single grunt, almost a laugh, when she said that Lluthean had escaped the Drift, but beyond that, he seemed like a man separated from himself. None of her attempts at lighthearted banter caused him to smile. Something inside of him was wounded. She knew the feeling well. She still felt it when she thought too long about Reddevek.

At the thought, she turned to the north, where stars twinkled in the night sky. "Where are we going, Bryn?"

"I have to get inside the Korjinth, to the Valley of the Cloud Walkers."

"Sounds fun."

He shook his head. "It isn't. The trip across could kill us. Moons, it might make Boru grow even bigger, I don't know. There are predators in the mountains and random strikes of zenith and nadir. They hit the ground like wild lightning. I won't say my chances won't be better with you along."

"Are there Kreeg up in the Korjinth?"

"No, I don't imagine so."

He looked down and wriggled bare toes through the ash. "I don't suppose you found boots or socks?"

She walked back to her surveillance point, retrieved a pair of wool socks and boots, and then returned. Instead of handing over the footwear, she stood several steps back, arms folded, waiting.

He chewed on his lip, studying her resolute pose for a moment, then nodded with understanding. "The Damadibo, they might be the only people who can let me talk to her again. I have to talk to her, Nika. I can't move past this, or sort this out"—again, he thumped a fist at his chest—"until I talk to her."

She considered his words, then handed him the socks and boots. He sat down, then stood back up to stomp his feet into the boots. A puzzled expression crossed his face. "How did you know my size?"

"You aren't as mysterious as you think."

Finally, a soft smile pierced his exhaustion. "I meant everything I said before. You and Boru really should turn back."

"After what you just said, you think I'm going to turn back? Bryn, if you can reach someone in the Drift, then maybe I can too."

Her words sobered his expression, and he dropped his head, strands of matted dark hair falling across his face. He inhaled and finger-combed the strands back, then lifted his eyes to meet hers. "Giver take me for a monk. I'm sorry. I didn't think of that. You've lost as much as anyone. I won't ask you to leave again, Nika. And I'll be happy for your company."

He shook his fingers through his hair, displacing ash, then pulled the untamed strands into a topknot. He signed to Boru, *"You know what awaits us if when we cross again. It would be safer for you to stay with Neska, but I hope you'll come with me."*

The wolvryn dipped his head and stretched his hips back, front legs extended, his casual gesture a mockery of Bryndor's suggestion. "Alright. Have it your way."

Boru rose to his full height and stepped forward, resting his wide jaw on Bryndor's shoulder. He searched the night sky, and she stepped beside him, grabbing his hand. "So then, eyes to the horizon?" she asked.

He exhaled through his nose. "Alright, together then. Eyes to the horizon."

Ranika studied the southern skyline, where the rise of the Korjinth blotted out the stars on a very distant and very dark horizon.

Epilogue: Assimilation

Beyond the familiar compass of constellations and the tether of time, Tarkannen existed in the black immensity of the Drift. The velvety, smothering silence pressed in, a hollow thunder without source. Memory flickered as a fragile flame against the ocean of shadow. He had expected the endless searing, the leeching torment that had marked his banishment, yet instead there was a strange freedom—neither joy nor pain, only the hollow equilibrium of being without loss or gain, without passion or obligation.

Ethereal currents brushed against him, like flows of ash, the subtle frictions guiding him forward and whispering of transition. The pale glimmer of other souls surged past, eager to merge, embracing the promised sense of belonging. Detached, he lingered, sensing their resonance of joy with a numb incomprehension. Why did the currents not usher him forth with that kind of longing? A faint ember of regret kindled, then dwindled in the Drift's indifferent tide.

Then, the void itself shifted. An entity came, neither walking nor flying, but arriving as inevitability itself. A formless pressure displaced him from the currents, isolating him from other souls. Its biting wind slashed through him, cold and searing. Utter agony became his only awareness.

A chorus of voices erupted—harsh, rasping, overlapping vibrations that violated his essence. They tasted of iron, ash, and smoke, bitter on the soul's tongue. "This one might do, but he is broken. Yet there is opportunity."

He forced words out, breaking through the all-encompassing pain, each syllable released as a shard of broken glass. "Who are you? What do you want?"

"We are many things and have many names. You of all the man-things should know us, Tarkannen."

"You're the Taker." He spoke the words as he resigned himself to the pervasive torment of the entity's intrusive touch. Yet with his declaration, the agony ceased abruptly, replaced by a blissful cessation of the defilement.

Formless flows gathered around him as slicks of shadow, mercurial and shifting. "We know this name. Yes, in your world . . . we . . . are . . . the Taker."

Tarkannen's essence flickered as a guttering lantern flame against the Taker's boundless dominance. The revelation, accompanied by the ease with which the Taker had violated his soul, gave rise to a panicked wave of revulsion. Against the surging fear, he struggled to bring his thoughts into focus.

The entity intruded his mind again, but flowed now as a warm caress of refined powder: silky, smooth, and alluring. "Your world is out of balance. She allowed one to return, your . . . Giver. We could send you back. Would you like that? Would you like to return? Be our dark scion?"

Souls skirted past, oblivious to the conversation, continuing their merging, while the Taker's words anchored him like iron chains. The aching cold of longing penetrated his marrow, though he lacked the flesh to feel it. A faint desire to join the others in the merging sparked to life, then dissipated like smoke in the windless dark.

"That is not for you, man-thing. You can wander the Drift as a wraith, but you are too broken to join that merging."

He could not say how long the statement hung between them, but at last, a curious thought rose. "If not that merging, then what?"

"He begins to see. Yours could be a different kind of assimilation. There are any number of creatures we could bend to our purpose. Choose, man-thing. You must choose."

EXEMPLAR GRE'KANTH, Supreme Leader of the Immaculine, stood on his private balcony set on the highest suite of the south tower of the church of Gaskayah. He stared at Voshna, the blue moon shining on the Sea of Valgareth, and reached a hand forward as if to claw the moon from the sky, but settled for pinching it between his thumb and forefinger.

Even if such a miracle were his to command, what of the red moon? And why did none of them yet recognize the void moon responsible for nadir? The skin, bones, and muscles about his eyes, indeed even the very eyes themselves, were all quite malleable, and he reshaped the orbs, dilating the structures to allow him to view in the night sky what no others could. Low on the southern horizon, a distinct black moon hovered.

He understood why they might miss the object when it waned, but tonight the moon stood full and blotted out the last two stars on the tail of Epachna, the monkey constellation. Perhaps it had more to do with the black moon's strange orbit. Since usurping this form, Gre'Kanth had never seen the moon leave the southern horizon. But in the last week, the void moon had lifted slowly across the sky, tracking north.

A knock at the door pulled him from his thoughts, and he reshaped his face to the Exemplar Gre'Kanth everyone knew and adored. Short-cropped salt and pepper hair topped an oval-shaped head with a chiseled jaw and angular cheekbones. He swept back into the room, flowing white robes trailing out behind him.

"Enter!"

Archon Bulben backed into the room holding an open crate. He stopped two steps in and bowed, setting the crate on the floor and retrieving a white silk to blot his sweaty brow. The poor man weathered the boxy white uniform of the Immaculine without complaint, though the stains under his armpits and down his back spoke volumes of his intolerance of the tropical heat. It was a shame he took his responsibilities so fervently. He could have sent any number of younger porters to deliver the crate, though climbing the stairs would likely benefit the man's pudgy midsection.

"Honor to serve you, Exemplar Gre'Kanth. May your light shine ever brighter that we might recognize the shadows of thralls and reachers alike."

"Archon Bulben, to what do I owe the pleasure?"

"I brought another batch of tongs for your inspection. We've infused the gold ones with the blood of zeniphiles. As such, they will resonate if a thrall is within a quarter mile. The silver ones still only detect an abrogator by direct touch, but then we've never encountered an abrogator, so it kind of makes you wonder if they ever existed at all."

Gre'Kanth studied the clutch. Gold and silver bracelets of various sizes clattered in the box. He retrieved one of the gold baubles, careful not to touch any of the silver. He held the tong up to his eye and spied the moon of Baellen out the window. *Voshna, Baellen, it matters not as long as those who draft from its essence are sent to the Drift.*

"Do we have enough to outfit the church at Kordon's Landing?"

"Yes, sir. The high archon informed me that we can pull men from Grenn and move on Hammond within the month," said Bulben.

"Bring any thralls or reachers to me, especially if they have ties with the Braveska royal line. King Vendal was loath to allow us to establish a church within his kingdom. I would hate to see any diplomatic misunderstandings undermine our footholds in Hammond or Malvress."

"I shall personally dispatch messages to the high archon in Hammond myself, Your Holiness."

"What news from our expansion efforts in the north? I should like to see our light shine beyond the Korjinth Mountains."

Bulben removed spectacles and rubbed them with the same sweaty silk. "Archon Gavid Strictor leads our efforts there. By his reports, we've had no difficulty converting the great majority of the villages scattered along the western coast. There is a Margrave Rolsh in Riverton who is favorable to our cause and guarantees assimilation under the light."

"What monarch rules Riverton?"

"King Borsec claimed that right, and as long as he remained secluded in his castle on the eastern shores of Lake Avonell, none chose to contest his rule," said Bulben.

"You speak in the past tense?"

"Just so, Your Holiness. The king faded to the Drift this past week. The margrave was the king's man, but in recent years has developed a bit of a taste for making autonomous decisions. Archon Strictor reports that he has supported the margrave in these designs and in so doing cultivated a loyal ally."

"What of the port city, Callish?"

"We have agents in Callish, of course, Your Holiness, but the city is governed by a Triumvirate. The callishian is their general. He controls their military and naval operations, coordinating with sea trade and the like. The patrician represents the merchants and affluent families, while the orator is a demagogue of sorts and speaks for the common people."

"Let me guess, our only successful inroads have been with the orator's people, and he or she doesn't hold any of the true power in Callish."

"Yes, Your Holiness, astute as ever."

Gre'Kanth walked back out onto his balcony. He didn't mind the humid sea air; some property of the water and salt facilitated the malleability of his sinewy tissues. He reached his arms overhead and inhaled the briny tang. A sudden gust buffeted the loose fabric of his white robes, snapping the material. "Moons and stars, but I do love the sea air. How about you, Bulben?"

"Me sir? I've never given it much thought. My place is by your side; standing in your holy light is all the reward I require."

He turned to consider the man. Did he sweat from the heat, or did obsequiousness simply leak out of his pores? "Tell you what, Bulben. I think we are overdue for a visit to the north. We've been talking about the Crusade of Light for over a year now, right?"

"Well, yes, that's correct, Your Holiness."

"I should like to see in person the progress our Archon Strictor has made, and then I think we will personally pay a visit to Callish. If our agents have not been able to impress this callishian or the patrician by the time we arrive, then perhaps a personal visit from the leader of the Gaskayan Church will open doors otherwise barred to our progress."

Bulben dipped his head for several seconds. "I would be honored to see to your travel accommodations. When would you like to depart, Your Holiness?"

"As soon as you can manage it, Bulben. If the weather holds, we could make the journey before winter sets in."

"A wise and tactical decision, Your Holiness. I shall see to it at once. Would you like me to leave the tongs here for your personal inspection?"

He considered dismissing the man and his box of bangles, but knew he should likely feign interest. "Yes, I want to personally assess their quality and make. I'll have a porter return them in the morning. I do agree with your assessment. We've not come across an abrogator ever. It almost seems a waste of resources to continue making the silver tongs. Let me think on it a bit longer, though."

Bulben dipped his head. "Will there be anything else this evening, Your Holiness?"

"Walk in the light, Brother Bulben. We can speak in the morning."

"By your light, Your Holiness." The man bowed and departed.

Gre'Kanth waited a moment before locking the door. He walked over to the box and plunged an arm into the tongs. The silver bracelets began to vibrate and rattle. He removed his arm, and the jewelry settled.

He turned to stare at his reflection in the mirror. Eventually, he would have to settle into this shape and release his use of nadir. That might be the only realistic way to avoid detection. A sigil-laden visage stared back as a flickering memory, there one moment and gone the next. The voice of his other hissed in the back of his mind. *You would surrender the very power that allowed us to return?*

Gre'Kanth stared deep into the eyes of his reflection. He pursed his lips and pressed his tongue to the roof of his mouth. "Not surrender, not exactly. There may be times when we need to suspend channeling altogether, especially if the silver tongs are not discarded. Restraint is the rune that unlocks abundance."

You sound like a zeniphile. Abrogation, dark sigils—those are the foundation of our strength.

"True enough, but in the days ahead, a check on our desires will safeguard our long-term plans."

Gre'Kanth felt the inner voice brood a moment, before withdrawing to the corner of his mind. He stepped out of his white robes and stood naked. A sneer of disdain curled his upper lip as he considered the human form. Gre'Kanth was no slouch; broad shoulders and a lean physique accentuated his gravitas. But every day, he resented the labor required to restrict himself to this skin bag with its limited abilities.

But such restrictions were for tomorrow. *Tonight, Gre'Kanth, you will hunt.* He noted that he'd unconsciously used the name to reference himself, and why not? He had, after all, become the embodiment of the man.

He sighed, and the form melted into something waxy and amorphous. Moments later, a cacophony of pops and cracks filled the air as his native shape reformed. Skin creaked, stretching tight over newly formed ridges. Wings unfurled, the leathery membranes rustling. A crown of eyes erupted, each one reflecting the dim light. Exemplar Gre'Kanth turned in a circle, admiring his true form.

He approached the balcony and allowed the ocean breeze to caress his wings. Oh, how easy this world was to dominate. He was beginning to like it here. What would happen to his influence if others of his ilk broke through the veil as he did? If he facilitated the breach at a time of his choosing, he could position himself as their alphreyn, their king. None of them would be a match for him in this assimilated state. The Taker had facilitated his entrance into this world, and none would swim against the inevitability of that current. Such concerns were for another day, though. The greater feign, with its fused consciousness, hopped once, cleared the balustrade, and took to wing in search of new prey to assimilate.

Glossary of Names and Places

Aarin (AIR-in)—the name given to any unnamed patient at the Sanitorium in Aarindorn.

Aarindorn (AIR-in-dorn)—a kingdom in the Northlands, surrounded by the Great Crown Mountains.

Abrogator (AB-roh-gate-or)—a term used to describe one who wields the reductive force of nadir.

Ahben (AH-ben)—a Cloud Walker herb gatherer.

Alphreyn—term used to designate the sovereign over all the greater feigns.

Amniah (am-NIGH-yuh)—a young female Outrider gifted with the ability to gust (shape wind) who hails from Stellance. An original member Karragin's quad.

Arca prime—the central rune of a zeniphile located on the center of the chest and determining the zeniphiles strongest affinity or ability.

Baellentrell (BAE-len-trell)—the last name of the current ruling family in Aarindorn.

- Bierden (BEER-den)—Kaellor's grandfather, capable of summoning rune fire.
- Brekka—queen during the time of Nivosh.
- Bryndor (BRIN-dur)—oldest of two nephews to Kaellor. Older brother to Lluthean.
- Eldrek (EL-drek)—founder of the Baellentrell line and first king of Aarindorn.
- Japheth (JAY-feth)—king of Aarindorn during the Abrogator's War. Father to Bryndor and Lluthean, brother to Kaellor.
- Kaellex (KAY-lex)—father to Kaellor and Japheth, grandfather to Bryndor and Lluthean.
- Kaellor (KAY-lore)—uncle to Bryndor and Lluthean.
- Lluthean (LOO-thee-in)—youngest of two nephews to Kaellor. Younger brother to Bryndor.
- Naldrek—brother to Nivosh.
- Nebrine (neh-BREEN)—mother to Bryndor and Lluthean, wife to Japheth.

- Nivosh—youngest daughter of Eldrek and author of an ancient history translated by Ksenia.
- Phethnem (FETH-nem)—mother to Kaellor and Japheth, wife to Kaellex.

Balladuren (bal-uh-DOO-ren)—family in Aarindorn famed for breeding Aarindin.

- Elbend (EL-bend)—father of the family, spouse to Madola. A gifted sympath.
- Madola (muh-DOLE-uh)—mother of the family, spouse to Elbend. A gifted sympath.
- Kervin (KURV-in)—fourth brother, senior only to Ksenia. As a sympath, he can communicate with animals.
- Kovle—Ksenia's great-uncle, a man whose arca prime was linguistics.
- Ksenia (keh-SEN-yuh)—youngest child of five and only daughter. Her runes enable her to channel zenith to empathically communicate with animals and decipher languages, among other talents.
- Rugen (ROO-gen)—oldest brother. Member of the city watch in Stone's Grasp.

Barl Fodensk (Barl FOE-densk)—this zeniphile led his forces from the deep south by ship to fight against the abrogators in the Great War. His forces were gifted in controlling the wind and water. Southlanders adopted him as the god of the seas.

Barton Sparks—skilled armorer and weaponsmith in Stone's Grasp.

Bashing Ram—a tavern and inn at Journey's Bend.

Beclure (beh-KLURE)—a duchy in west Aarindorn.

Benyon Garr (BEN-yun)—a wizened trainer of the gifted in Aarindorn, member of the Aarindorian military, and adviser to the Outriders.

Berwek (BURR-wek)—a prime in the Outriders.

Besken (BES-kin)—a kingdom in the western Northlands of Karsk.

Bekson's Fine Restoratives—a tavern and eatery in the Delve in Stone's Grasp.

Binta (BIN-tuh)—a serving maid at the Wolf's Maw in Midrock.

Boffle (BOFF-ul)—a minor lord from Dernegia taking residence in Sifter's Valley during the Winnowing of the Shades.

Borsec (BORE-sek)—ruling monarch over the northwest region of the Southlands, including Riverton and Journey's Bend.

Braveska (bra-VES-kuh)—the royal family in Hammond and Malvress in the Southlands.

- Leland (LEE-land)—the duke in Malvress and youngest brother to Vendal.
- Lesand (leh-SAND)—niece to the king of Hammond and daughter to Duke Leland in Malvress.
- Shelland (SHELL-and)—queen in Hammond.
- Vendal (VEN-dull)—king in Hammond.

Cabe—owner of the King's Respite, a tavern in Sifter's Valley in the Torgrend Range northeast of Dernegia.

Callinora (cal-in-NORE-uh)—a city in northwest Aarindorn composed of erudites, scholars, and healers. The formal educational training of medics, healers, alchemists, and related fields takes place here. The city is a protectorate of Stone's Grasp with no specific familial loyalties but rather loyal to the welfare of Aarindorn. The kingdom's Sanitorium is located here.

Callish (CAL-ish)—port city along the northeast coast of the Southlands.

Cataclysm—the Great War in which the forces of abrogation caused a rent in the barrier between the world of the living and the Drift. The death toll was estimated at well over thirty thousand and led to the separation of Karsk into the Northlands and the Southlands. The timing of this event is used as the source of the dating system on Karsk, with dates being either before Cataclysm (BC) or post Cataclysm (PC).

Cloud Walkers—a tribe native to the valley deep in the center of the Korjinth Mountains. Formally called the Damadibo.

Consort—the Consort are the group of umbral pulled from the Drift and acting on Tarkannen's direction.

Crush—a herd of six to ten grondle.

Damadibo (dahm-uh-DEE-boe)—the Cloud Walkers; the term means "the people."

Deadener—a zeniphile skill allowing one to ignore all pain.

DeChance

- Silvy—mother to Ranika.
- Ranika (RAN-ih-kuh)—found as a street urchin in Callish where she spent her childhood. One of the first innately gifted abrogators to walk Karsk since the Cataclysm.

Dedicant—the Dedicant is the title given to the leader of the ungifted, or the runeless, in Aarindorn.

Della—the proprietor at the Bashing Ram of Journey's Bend. She manages and owns the tavern with her brother Ingram.

Delve, the—a district in Stone's Grasp housing affluent merchant stores, shops, and wares.

Derrigand (DARE-ih-gand)

- Burl—owner of the Wolf's Maw, Savnah's father. A member of the Lacuna's inner circle.
- Kovesk (KOH-vesk)—brother to Savnah, a zeniphile gifted with forecasting the future when he dreams.
- Savnah(SAWV-nuh)—a prime in the Outriders, known for her battle prowess with twin moonblade axes. A skilled deadener and minor nascent.

Drassle (DRASS-ul)—Lord Drassle was a customer at Felpinge House, where Silvy DeChance worked.

Dressla Rudang (DRESS-luh roo-DANG)—the queen of Voruden.

Drexn (DREK-sen)—the name for the sun god in the Southlands.

Dulesque (doo-LESK)—a duchy in west Aarindorn.

Eguma (eh-GOO-muh)—a lithe and small grotvonen possessing more-than-usual intelligence and the capacity for human speech.

Eidolon—prophesized in The Book of Seven Prophets as a person capable of wielding both zenith and nadir, and someone required to save the world.

Elcid—a bandit in Hammond.

Ellisina (el-eh-SEE-nuh)—a Cloud Walker child.

Elgruh—an adult female of the Cloud Walkers.

Endule (en-DUEL)—a family of nobles in Aarindorn related to and branching from the Lellendules. Currently ruling the duchies of Dulesque and Beclure in Aarindorn.

- Alvric (ALV-rick)—former Outrider recruited into the city watch in Stone's Grasp.
- Aldem—a zeniphile known as the Leech, a man who can siphon zenith and vitality from other living creatures. An assassin employed by the Lacuna.
- Berling (BURR-ling)—a young man gifted in the healing arts and a medic in the Outriders.
- Bextle (BEX-tul)—a member of the guard in Stone's Grasp, older brother to Craxton.
- Bexter (BEX-turr)—husband to Phelond, the matriarch of the family; he married into the family and assumed the Endule name.
- Craxton (CRAX-ton)—younger brother to Bextle and representative speaker for several guilds in Stone's Grasp. A sender who is a triplet.
- Dexxin (DEX-in)—an Outrider, sender, healer, and triplet to Craxton and Mullayne.
- Endera (en-DEER-uh)—the duchess of Beclure, mother to Velda.
- Edlemund—son to Endera, assumed the position as the prima dicta representing the interests of several high houses in Stone's Grasp.
- Kevka (KEV-kuh)—Endera's half brother. Wounded by rune

fire.

- Mullayne (mull-AIN)—a member of the city watch in Aarindorn and sender triplet to Dexxin and Craxton.
- Phelond (feh-LOND)—the duchess of Dulesque, married to Bexter, mother to Berling.
- Velda (VEL-duh)—an Outrider skilled in archery. Daughter to Endera, from Beclure.
- Zachus—a young gifted who perished in the Rite of Revealing.

Exemplar Gre'Kanth (greh-KANTH)—the holy leader of the Immaculine, a sect founded in Gaskayah in the deep south of the Southlands.

Faltusch—a kingdom adjacent Aarindorn on the Rodendian Sea.

- Fenna—the fifth queen consort to King Yugan.
- Yugan—the Sea King in Faltusch.

Festian Planes (FES-tee-un)—prairies and plains south of Callish in the Southlands.

Feth—a stableboy who works with his father, Steckle, at the Bashing Ram.

Firth—a name utilized by Lluthean while traveling anonymously.

fo'Vaeda (VAY-duh) and fo'Voshna(VOSH-nuh)—zeniphile sisters gifted in prophecy and prediction, both involved in a tangled relationship with Eldrek in the time of the Cataclysm.

Foden (FOE-den)—Southlander name for the god of the seas and wind.

Gauvin (go-VON)—a bard playing in the King's Respite.

Gavid Strictor (GAV-id STRIK-turr)—an official of the Immaculine.

Geddins (GEDD-ins)—a noble family in Aarindorn.

- Ashrof (ASH-rof)—the oldest son gifted with the ability to survey and measure distances.
- Marsona (mar-SAW-nuh)—younger sister to Ashrof.

Grasdok (GRAZ-dock)—the chieftan of the Brognaus, a clan of grotvonen in the Torgrend Range.

Griggs—a guard at the southern gate to Aarindorn. He is a sifter.

Grotvonen (GROT-voh-nen)—the "grot" are humanoid creatures who live in clans underground. Their senses evolved to survive in that environment. They possess only vestigial lips and utilize a language of nasal snorts, clicks, and a guttural speech pattern.

Guster—a zeniphile who controls and manipulates winds or air.

Gwillion (GWILL-ee-un)—the former alchemy master in Aarindorn, disgraced by his addiction to vivith.

Havish—a healer stationed at a House of the Moons in the Great Crown.

Hawklin (HAWK-lin)—a family in Journey's Bend.

- Bruug (Broog)—the oldest brother.
- Heff—the middle brother.
- Rusn—the youngest brother.
- Gruus (Groos)—the father of the Hawklin family.

Hillen—a deceased Cloud Walker. When he died, a pregnant wolvryn bonded to him (Vencha), became feral and slipped from the misted valley, later to become the mother to Boru and Neska.

Hoff—a mixed family of gifted and ungifted living in Stone's Grasp.

- Fagle Hoff (FAY-gull)—the royal gardener in Stone's Grasp.
- Heathering—daughter to Fagle, a respected rector in the Church of the Giver.

Homnibus (HOM-ni-bus)—the lead rector or abbot in service at the Abbey on the Mount in the Southlands.

Immaculine, the (im-MAC-u-you-leen)—a religious sect from Gaskayah. They hunt and kill abrogators and zeniphiles alike.

Inasia Kell (in-AY-shuh)—a member of the inner circle of the Lacuna, planted in Callinora.

Ingram (ING-ram)—the proprietor and co-owner with sister Della of the Bashing Ram of Journey's Bend.

Ilovesh—an ancient people, "tree singer" in High Aarindorian. They live in tree cities in the far east of Karsk.

- Leandur and Vellendar—Ilovesh cities in the ursulu forest.
- Seldora (sell-DOOR-uh)—last surviving brother of a family disgraced and ostracized in Ilovesh society.
- Sephora (SEPH-or-uh)—deceased sister to Seldora, considered the betrtayer for revealing the secrets of the tether to Tarkannen.
- Somaya (soe-MIGH-uh)—elder prophet among the Ilovesh.

Jaspen Holling (JAS-pen HOLL-ing)—an entrepreneur and vineyard owner in Stellance.

Journey's Bend—a rural Southland town not far from Riverton, childhood home to the "Scrivson boys," Bryndor and Lluthean.

Jorund (YOUR-und)—a henchman working for Mallic and Volencia in Callish.

Kade—a sentinel in Stone's Grasp gifted with unnatural hearing.

Kal'malldra—a zeniphile who rose in power and assumed the title of the Eidolon in the time before the Cataclysm.

Kaldera (kal-DEER-uh)—Overwarden in the Outriders, he serves at the pleasure of the regent and sets strategy for the group. Brother to Reddevek Taim, he grew up as a Luna Rova in the Dev'advari clan.

Karsk—the continent of the Northlands and Southlands, used interchangeably by the people there to describe the world.

Kemp—an alias name used by Bryndor during anonymous travel.

Keska—chambermaid in Stone's Grasp.

Kevold—alias used by Kaellor in the Southlands.

Kindred—the term used to describe the common speech known by most humans on Karsk.

Korjinth Mountains (CORE-jinth)—the mountainous peaks of this range erupted, and the central valley was formed, after the Great War when Eldrek Baellentrell marshaled the zeniphiles to wield their collective zenith in tandem with Mogdurian's abrogators. The colossal release of force, poorly synthesized, resulted in the formation of this range on the Plains of Jintha, and divided all of Karsk. Currently, warring currents of zenith and nadir make crossing the summit nearly impossible.

Kreeg—a military kingdom in northwest Karsk.

- Behklek—Kreegorian scout.
- Coglek—Kreegorian scout.
- Colley—Kreegorian captain.
- Guyver—Kreegorian captain.
- Dalkreeg—the coliseum in Kreeg.
- Havka—a general serving under Zsheck.
- Kilken—a general advising Zsheck.
- Krug rai'al—the king of the Kreeg, currently Zsheck.
- Kruga—Kreegorian war horse.
- Reinner B'vakla—a Kreegorian soldier encountered by Tarkannen.
- Szikes—a warrior in the Trial of Nines.
- Thuum—a general serving under Zsheck.
- Zsheck—king of Kreeg, a.k.a. the krug rai'al.

Krestus (CREST-us)—a fallen knight from Malvress.

Kunzie (KOON-see)—a member of the inner circle of the Lacuna.

Kyvon Murk (KAI-von)—nephew to Valdesta.

Lacuna (luh-COO-nuh)—a secret sect in Aarindorn seeking to replace the monarchy with a democracy. They seek to break the circle of recurrent or inherited familial leaders. Also known as the breakers.

- Choff—a merchant lord in Stone's Grasp.
- Mikkum—a chiller.
- Rounders—sub-bosses in the Lacuna.
- Tixon B'gin—Valdesta's assumed name as leader of the Lacuna.
- Woodruk—an enforcer.

Lawn Whirik (WHEER-ik)—constable in Journey's Bend.

Lefledge (leh-FLEJ)—a noble family in Aarindorn.

- Karragin (CARE-uh-gin)—an Outrider, gifted with unnatural physical strength and sympath abilities, sister to Nolan, daughter to Therek.
- Nolan (NO-lun)—an Outrider, gifted as a scout, son to Therek, brother to Karragin.
- Therek (THARE-ik)—the regent in Aarindorn, gifted with abilities in premonition and able to discern truth from lie.

Lellendule (lell-en-DOOL)—a noble family in Aarindorn.

- Aldrik—oldest brother of Volencia.
- Chancle (CHANS-ul)—the vice regent in Aarindorn, brother to Hestian, cousin to Laryn. He is a trusted friend to the regent and helped stabilize Aarindorn after the Abrogator's War.
- Charlest (char-LEST)—the last ruling Lellendule queen in Aarindorn and mother to Tarkannen.
- Eidan—Chancle's dead son.
- Elbare—Volencia's father, a disgraced drunkard.
- Evonda—Hestian's wife.
- Hestian (HES-tee-en)—older brother to Chancle. He is a trusted friend to the regent.
- Kelledar (KELL-eh-dahr)—one of the first Lellendules, loyal friend to Eldrek Baellentrell.
- Larik (LARE-ik)—Hestian's son, a prime in the Outriders.
- Laryn (LARE-in)—a healer trained in Callinora; she married Kaellor in a secret ceremony and returns to Aarindorn as his wife and a prominent member of the Lellendule family.
- Maelos (MAY-lohs)—the last king in the Lellendule line, father to Tarkannen.
- Phesteq (FEZ-tek)—a young man who attempted the Rite of Revealing only to perish in the trial.
- Shalla (SHAHL-uh)—mother to Volencia.
- Tarkannen—the Usurper who reintroduced the utilization of

nadir over zenith and resurrected the abrogators. In real life, the author's daughters argue about the best pronunciation. Some prefer "TARK-anon," others "tar-CANN-on." The author is perfectly content to let the reader decide which pronunciation suits their worldview for Karsk.

- Veldrek—Volencia's middle brother.
- Volencia—born gifted with affinities in water manipulation, she never sat for the trial to unlock her arca prime and instead embraced the path of the abrogator.

Lemm Sogle—a drunkard from Journey's Bend.

Lentrell (LEN-trell)—minor nobles in Aarindorn related by blood to the Baellentrells.

- Elbiona (el-bee-YOH-nuh)—an Outrider warden in Aarindorn. She is rumored to be exceptional with a bow.
- Venlith (VEN-lith)—a healer of the fourth circle (the highest rank) and referred to as docent. She is the leader overseeing the Sanitoruim in Callinora. A known master of the healing arts.
- Drevan and Bartoll—brothers who knew Volencia as a child.

Leveck (leh-VEK)—an officer of the court in Beclure in the employment of house Endule.

Luna Rova—see Moonies.

Lutn Egaine (lutn eh-GAIN)—an abrogator and famed mathematician and tactician who sought a neutral relationship between zeniphiles and abrogators. Because he was seen by some as playing both sides, he was later remembered as the trickster and in the Southlands incorporated into the pantheon.

Lutney (LUT-nee)—Southland god of luck, tricks, and the unseen.

Maedra (MAY-druh)—Southland god of nature and healing.

Maedraness (may-druh-NESS)—in the time of the Cataclysm, this zeniphile, known as the Shaman Queen, joined Eldrek and the other zeniphiles. Their natural talents lay in the healing arts and communicating and controlling plants and animals.

Mahkeel (mah-KEEL)—the wolvryn handler of the Cloud Walker tribe.

Malldra (MAHL-druh)—Southland term for the mother of the pantheon of gods, thought to have died birthing the other gods.

Margrave Rolsh—the ruler in Riverton and by default the territories in Journey's Bend, loyal to King Borsec.

Mawg—a Brognaus grotvonen.

Miljin (MILL-jin)—an elder shaman among the Cloud Walkers.

Mirrare (mere-ARE-ay)—Laryn's personal, elite, royal guards.

Mogdure (mog-DURE)—the Southland god of death, darkness, and illness.

Mogdurian (mog-DURE-ee-en)—in the time of the Great War, he led all the abrogators in his quest to bring order to Karsk.

Monk—affectionately, a Man of No Knowledge.

Moonies—nomadic clans who travel the Northlands following the moons. They refer to themselves as the Luna Rova.

- Dev'advari clan—the clan that Reddevek grew up in. As highlanders, they hold to the mountains.
- Dania—love interest to Ranika, member of the Dev'advari.
- Dergan—a young Dev'advari man injured after a reading with Vekkuh.
- Do'—proper title for a man.
- Movshka—speaker of the Rovinary clan.
- Rovinary clan (roe-vin-ARR-ee)—encountered in Aarindorn in book three. This clan roams the low country.
- Sintra—proper title for a woman.
- Vekkuh (VEHK-uh)—speaker of the Dev'advari clan, Reddevek's aunt.

Moorlok (MORE-lock)—a vast and ancient tract of timber in the Southlands bordering Journey's Bend.

Munts—stableman in the royal stables at Stone's Grasp in Aarindorn.

Nascent—a zeniphile skilled in projecting an image of him/herself.

Oren (ORE-en)—the captain of the city watch in Stone's Grasp.

Outriders—an elite paramilitary group excelling in spycraft, martial arts, woodcraft, and ranging.

- Argul—a munitions expert killed fighting an umbral.
- Amniah—a guster and former Outrider wounded in the line of duty, she transitions to the Mirrare.
- Boljer—a prime wounded trying to capture a grondle.
- Bacall—a prime in the Outriders gifted with unnatural sight. She becomes part of the Mirrare.
- Feille—a medic.
- Kap—a munitions expert.

Ozhen (Oh-zhen)—a thug in the company of the Hawklin brothers in the Southlands.

Reacher—a term used by the Immaculine to describe anyone who "reaches into the Drift" to summon power, whether it be zenith or nadir (they make no exception in using the terminology). Also called a thrall, with the implication that anyone using the power is enthralled or enslaved by a lust for power.

Reddevek (RED-eh-vek)—a warden in the Outriders. One of the few gifted with tracking. He rarely uses his last name, Taim. Grew up in the Dev'advari clan of the Luna Rova.

Retta—Cabe's daughter.

Riverton—a city adjacent to Journey's Bend in the Southlands.

Rolsh—the margrave in Riverton.

Rona (ROE-nuh) Scrivson—the aunt to Bryndor and Lluthean in the Southlands.

Runefather/mother—an adult zeniphile in Aarindorn who assumes a semi-formal relationship with a gifted child to uphold the cultural norms of society. This person is often involved in training and the rituals such as the Rite of Revealing.

Runeling—the gifted child who is the recipient of the mentoring relationship with a runefather/mother.

Runta—a mediocre healer among the Outriders in Savnah's quad.

Salveen (sal-VEEN)—the female leader of the Spicers, a gang that runs the vivith trade, gaming rackets, and brothels in the quarter known as the Sprawl in Aarindorn. She is revealed to be descendant "of the 'fo" and so gifted with prophecy. Her last name is fo'Veskari.

Sadeen Tunkle (suh-DEEN TUN-kull)—a townswoman in Journey's Bend.

Senda—a Cloud Walker herb gatherer.

Sender—a zeniphile who can telepathically communicate with another sender. In the entire history of Aarindorn, senders have always been born as twins, triplets, etc. As such they are rare.

Shass—the former servant to Volencia and Mallic at their estate in Callish.

Shaveen (shah-VEEN)—one of a set of five albino quintuplet zeniphile senders who lived in the time of the Cataclysm. Their arca prime gifted them with the ability to telepathically communicate with each other over any distance.

Shek—unique pendants, which, like zeniscrawls, can be triggered with zenith and allow two-way voice communication.

Sheklith (SHEK-lith)—an artificer in Callinora, brother to Venlith, able to imbue inanimate objects.

Shelwyn River (SHELL-win)—a river in the Southlands.

Sheshla (SHESH-luh)—a butterfly named in the Valley of the Cloud Walkers.

Sifter—a zeniphile who can recall people or events with an eidetic memory.

Skellig—a drug courier in the Sprawl.

Skoon Fepl—the resource administrator in Stellance.

Sprawl, the—the poor part of Aarindorn where houses are crammed into winding neighborhoods, overcrowded slums, and poorly maintained streets. The brothels, gaming houses, and taverns outnumber more reputable businesses.

Steckle (STEK-ul)—hired hand and handyman at the Bashing Ram in Journey's Bend.

Stone's Grasp—the castle and capital city of Aarindorn.

Suvi (SOO-vee)—an ungifted woman who manages several orphanages in the Sprawl.

Tellend (TELL-end)—a family of farmers in Journey's Bend.

- Emile (eh-MEEL)—wise matron of the family.
- Harland—son to Emile and Markum.
- Markum—Emile's husband.

Timson (TIM-son)—a stable boy at the Abbey on the Mount.

Tomlek (TOM-lek)—a rector in Journey's Bend.

Tovnik (TAHV-nik)—a medic among the Outriders.

Torgrend Range (TORE-gend)—a range of mountains in the far northwest finger of Karsk.

Umbral—a.k.a. shadowmen, creatures wandering the Drift and wielders of nadir ruled by the forces there. Their origins are poorly understood, but they are likely abrogators who died while steeped in the frenze and are now enslaved by forces in the Drift.

Vaeda (VAY-duh)—Southland name for the goddess embodied as the red moon.

Valdesta (val-DEST-uh)—a member of the inner council of the Lacuna. Proprietor of gaming houses, brothels and other unsavory enterprises. Also known as Tixon B'gin.

Vardell Becks—an assassin hired by the Lacuna from Aarindorn. He is gifted with gusting.

Vatha—a sentinel in Stone's Grasp gifted in knifework.

Veeble Hebben (VEE-bull HEH-ben)—an autistic savant who works in the archives of Stone's Grasp.

Vesta—servant to Mallic and Volencia in their estate in Callish.

Vinnedesta—a scribe in service to the regent in Aarindorn. Valdesta's daughter.

Voruden (voe-ROO-den)—a queendom in the Northlands on the north face of the Korjinth Mountains, ruled by Queen Dressla Rudang.

Voshna (VOSH-nuh)—Southland name of the goddess embodied as the blue moon.

Weckles—the deceased former steward of the archives and master linguist in Aarindorn.

The Creatures, Elements, Items and Plants of Karsk

Aarindin (AIR-in-din)—a prized stock of horses bred for their combination of stamina, speed, and intelligence and preserved for use by the Outriders, a branch of the Aarindorian military and elite classes. The breed standard are a jet black or ebony color. They can use zenith to grip a chosen or preferred rider and are most often ridden bareback for this reason.

- Tacit—mount trained by Ksenia Balladuren with above-average intelligence for the breed.
- Trini—a spirited and loquacious young Aarindin ridden by Karragin.
- Winter—Ksenia's personal friend, an albino.
- Zippy—Reddevek's loyal steed.

Acoustics—names given to the rumbler beasts from the Drift that employ rattling sonic attacks.

Annan—a common horse in the royal stables in Stone's grasp.

Baellen's eclipse—a water flower that grows a dense purple-blue bloom that opens to reveal a tiny orange center.

Bandle root (BAND-ul)—a.k.a. stilben root in the Southlands or dreamsong among the Cloud Walkers. The herb can be steeped into tea or ingested raw. Low doses cause sedation, while concentrated dosing leads to dissociation or temporary paralysis and numbness. The herb smells and tastes like anise or black licorice.

Bartusk—a herd animal led by a matriarch, vaguely resembling the wild boar but with multiple sets of tusks and rivaling the size of a draft horse.

Bear-claw leaf—used to treat minor pain and fever.

Billow tree—a common tree along riverbanks in the Southlands. The tree produces seed pods with a woody outer husk of smooth, marbled brown. After a time, once exposed to water, the husk splits to release wispy seeds of white fluff, which billow into the air.

Blue trumpet—a vine that grows in the Borderlands and can be used to aid breathing/wheezing.

Bosulk (BO-sulk)—a.k.a. a greater driftian, a massive creature from the Drift.

Broga's beard—a flowering plant that lives on its ability to absorb concentrated strands of zenith. Broga was a fabled mountain god from the Cloud Walkers, the native region of this plant.

Caligot—a beast from the Drift trapped in the Kreeg arena.

Cave lark—a large cave-dwelling herbivore cat that uses its underbite to chisel away plants and lichen from rocks.

Crag-horned ram—a rare white ram native to the Torgrend Range in northwest Karsk. Believed by the locals to serve as vessels to house the spirits of the dead.

Darksun—a flowering plant that grows wild in the Borderlands and can treat the flux.

Eldrenol's solution—an oil that prevents abrogators from channeling nadir when ingested or inhaled.

Embertang—referred to as embertang in the Northlands and devil's tail in the Southlands, an antiseptic, hemostatic oil that, especially if undiluted, causes severe caustic pain even to casual skin contact. The less potent devil's tail is found as more of an oily resin. Both are harvested from varieties of redleaf.

Feign—a shapeshifting creature from the Drift. A greater feign is rumored to possess superior intelligence and cunning.

Gellseed root—given with blackberry tincture to treat diarrhea.

Gelspar—a rare antlered mountain beast native to the Great Crown. Its sheds are rumored to possess magical healing properties. It can cast off a temporary clone of itself called a quickling.

Gendek—mountain relative to vestek, an elusive herd animal found only in the Valley of the Cloud Walkers.

Heh-gava—a powder used to treat a cough or wheezing.

Hesk—a dense food material of tubers, mushroom, ursulu leaf and nuts. Food staple of the Ilovesh.

Kaliphora—antiemetic.

Kevash—a juicy, tangy fruit that grows all year in the Valley of the Cloud Walkers.

Lammen—a bush that drops tart red berries in early winter, found in the Great Crown. The berries are restorative.

Maedra's pitchers—a plant that blooms south of the Korjinth Mountains and can be steeped into a tea that dulls pain and improves healing. Scholars suspect that the tea somehow enhances a body's ability to absorb zenith.

Moonstone—a drab round rock which, when fractured open, reveals a set of gemstones that collect, store, and emit the moon's light.

Moonwing—see riftwing.

Mursk—a formless shapeshifter from the Drift capable of excellent physical mimicry but possessed of low intelligence and even less agency.

Nadrean—solid rods of refined nadir.

Nettle tea—a diuretic.

Pepperbark—found in the highlands of the Great Crown, the berries relieve minor muscle aches and pains.

Redleaf—a plant cultivated to create embertang.

Resco—a distillate of wine akin to whiskey.

Riftwing—a nocturnal hawk that flies with its talons clutched together in the shape of a basket. Not much is actually known of the elusive creatures, but they have the capacity to fade into pure zenith. Folklore in Aarindorn indicates that the creatures ferry the spirits of the dead to the Drift.

Rumbler—see acoustics.

Spiritwort—a tea that lessens pain without causing drowsiness.

Ursulu—an ancient tree revered by the Ilovesh

Veramanth's decoction (VARE-uh-manth)—a.k.a. stillers powder or severance, mixed as a tea that prevents zeniphiles from channeling zenith for two to three days. When 'ranthed, a zeniphile cannot channel zenith. When ingested as a raw plant, the effect is more potent.

Vellevlin—a volatile spritz marketed as perfume to disguise its true purpose as an aerosolized version of Eldrenol's solution. It is remarkable for a musty, unpleasant odor.

Vestek—agile plains herd animal in the Northlands.

Vivith—an illegal stimulant. Brewed as a tea or smoked, it is highly addictive and often leads to paranoia. The smoke smells like pine resin.

Weeping bark—used to treat minor pain and fever.

Widow's tears—a potent but tasteless and odorless poison that must be ingested.

Winter night's asylum—a green leafy plant that has the unusual feature of dropping white flowers to the ground midwinter. Botanists believe the plant stores zenith and uses it to create an exothermic reaction that releases heat, thereby thawing the ground and allowing the plant to spread uncontested by other foliage. The petals are quite fragrant and can be refined into an exotic perfume with sultry, sweet, and even musky qualities.

Wolvryn—creatures related to wolves but much larger, far more intelligent, and gifted with unique abilities to see and smell through a spectrum of zenith.

- Boru (bo-ROO)—male companion to Bryndor.
- Ghetti—matriarch of the pack in the Valley of the Cloud Walkers.
- Neska (NES-kuh)—crafty female companion to Lluthean.
- Vencha—mother to Boru and Neska.
- Voozsh—Reddevek's wolvryn as a young man.

Zendil—zenith-powered heating element.

Zentrist—zenith-powered magical cocoon that encases a petitioner sitting through their Rite of Revealing.

Zeniscrawl—zenith-powered writing tool.

Book 4 of The Rune Fire Cycle

Don't miss out!

Visit the website below and you can sign up to receive emails whenever Lance VanGundy publishes a new book. There's no charge and no obligation.

https://books2read.com/r/B-A-LQHL-UUFWI

BOOKS 2 READ

Connecting independent readers to independent writers.

Also by Lance VanGundy

The Rune Fire Cycle
Awakened Runes
Awakened Runes
Runes of the Prime
Rise of the Abrogators
Revealing the Arca Prime

Watch for more at https://www.lancevangundy.com/.

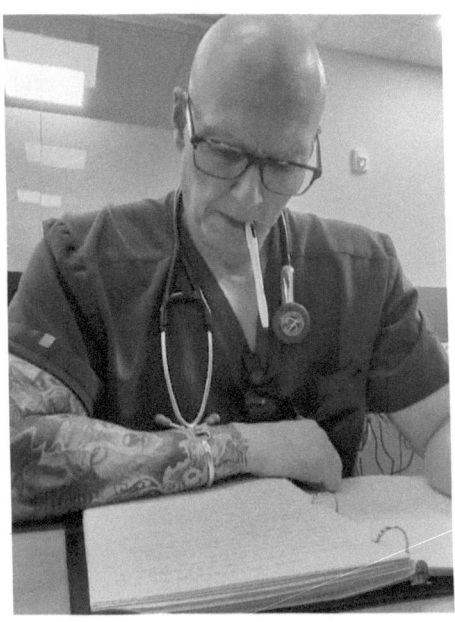

About the Author

Lance came of age in rural central Iowa, the product of public education and good parents. He studied anthropology and biology, earning a bachelor's degree from Cornell College in Mount Vernon, Iowa. He then attended medical school at the University of Iowa. He and his wife, Kristin, have been married for over thirty years and raised three daughters. He continues to practice emergency medicine in central Iowa but escapes to all things fantasy in nature for as much as his wife can tolerate. That is no small amount, for he is, after all, a very lucky man. His prior books published in the Rune Fire Cycle include *Awakened Runes* and *The Runes of the Prime* and *Rise of the Abrogators*.

Read more at www.lancevangundy.com.